China Dawn

China
Dawn

ROBERT L. DUNCAN

DELACORTE PRESS • NEW YORK

Published by
Delacorte Press
The Bantam Doubleday Dell Publishing Group, Inc.
1 Dag Hammarskjold Plaza
New York, New York 10017

Manufactured in the United States of America

First printing

Designed by Judith Neuman-Cantor

LIBRARY OF CONGRESS CATALOGING IN PUBLICATION DATA

Duncan, Robert Lipscomb, 1927–
    China dawn: a novel/by Robert L. Duncan.
        p. cm.
    ISBN 0-385-29620-7
    I. Title.
PS3554.U465C47 1988   87–16839
813′.54—dc19   CIP

China Dawn

Paris . . .
October 1981

JACQUES VERDUN HAD learned quite early in his career as a Parisian real estate agent to be circumspect. He neither gossiped about his clients (even with his curious wife) or questioned the purpose of any instruction except to clarify.

He had never handled a transaction for the Count Emile Riboud before, but he knew of this man who now lived on his ancestral estate outside of Paris, retired from business after the sale of his newspapers and the last of his fashion interests last year. When Count Emile had authorized him to find and rent a house in Montmartre, the leading stipulation other than luxury was absolute privacy. Verdun had located just the right place almost immediately, a house built at the time of Louis XIV and completely restored. The Count had specified tall windows for one room, which would be used as a studio, and that the house should have a light and airy feel to it, which it certainly did, with twelve bedrooms, a drawing room, three sitting rooms, besides a glass-enclosed atrium and kitchen facilities sufficient to service the larger and smaller dining rooms.

But most peculiar was the arrangement for taking possession of the house. It was prepared for occupancy by a staff of servants in early October, then the servants were paid and discharged in favor of the staff being brought in by the new tenant, the formal possession to take place at midnight on the morning of the tenth. At the appointed hour Verdun found himself unlocking the massive door with an oversized cast-iron key to admit two Japanese ladies, one wrapped against the chill in sable, the other in chinchilla. They were obviously mother and daughter, the older of the two in her sixties, the daughter a beauty in her forties. The daughter was Eurasian, Verdun decided, a mixture of Oriental and European perhaps, exotically regal, and it occurred to him that she was the Count's mistress (if the rumors going around were true) and that the Count had extraordinarily good taste.

Verdun had been told the occupants were the Mesdames Osano, coming to Paris on vacation with a retinue of servants. He was certain the name was as bogus as the reason for the visit, but he did not question, conducting them through the house, which blazed with light.

After the tour he led the way into the smaller drawing room, where tea, with small sandwiches, had been prepared. "The Count directed me to procure a limousine and a driver at your discretion. There's a garage, of course, and living quarters for a chauffeur."

"A black Rolls will do," the younger woman said. "And a driver who will be discreet. You may inform him that we will want him for a month at least. He will need to be on call twenty-four hours a day. If he proves reliable, I'll give him a handsome bonus."

"That's most generous of you, madame."

"We also want to engage a security service."

"The Count informed me, madame. It will commence tomorrow."

Once the agent was gone, Yuki wandered into a book-lined study, looking at the rich leather bindings with unseeing eyes, trying to decide how much she would tell her daughter, Dawn, and her accountant, Segawa. There was work to be done despite the lateness of the hour and the jet lag, which confused her biological clock. Sooner or later they would have to be prepared for trouble from an unexpected quarter.

As yet she had no real proof, only a warning from the Tokyo banker with whom she had done business for years. She heard the cars outside, the opening and closing of doors. Segawa and the staff had arrived. She rejoined her daughter, who sat at a table studying a schedule. Dawn looked up at her. "Why don't you go to bed, Mother?" Dawn said. "I'll take care of everything."

"Soon," Yuki said. "Arrange for the staff first."

Dawn called for the cook only to find he had already scouted the massive kitchens, and she asked the members of the workroom staff, the *directrice,* the *midinettes,* the seamstresses who had spent so many years in her mother's service, to gather in the drawing room, where Yuki was waiting for them.

"I appreciate your patience and your devotion," Yuki said in Japanese. "Unfortunately, we are behind schedule so we begin tomorrow, after you've had time to rest. Now there's tea in the dining room and the *directrice* will let you know about the room arrangements."

She would give them all a vacation when the work was finished, but for the next few weeks they would be working twenty-four hours a day. The designs were complete, but now the garments had to be adapted for the mannequins who would wear them on the runway while the sets were being built at the Opera House and the Japanese orchestra rehearsed, everything to be done within a strict budget of time and money.

"We're blessed to have such a staff," Yuki said, looking after them as they went into the dining room. She led the way into a large room with massive windows and a skylight, where a drafting table was already in place. Yuki was pleased at the Count's thoughtfulness. He had duplicated all the ink blocks and brushes that Dawn used in Tokyo. And the room was filled with flowers, welcoming them to Paris after the fatigue of coming halfway around the world.

"The Count is a thoughtful man," Yuki said. She looked at Segawa, who had just stuck his head in the door. "What time is it in Hong Kong?"

"Business hours," he said.

She joined him in the next suite, which had been set up as an office. She picked up the telephone and began the laborious process of calling the factory in Hong Kong while she watched Segawa, an earnest young Tokyo University graduate, unpack his computer and plug it into an outlet.

Yuki heard the Chinese voices on the line and the chatter of sewing machines in the background as Mr. Liu came onto the telephone. She spoke to him in Mandarin, aware that Dawn was not listening and that Segawa could not speak Chinese.

"We're in Paris," she said. "Is everything on schedule?"

"We are ready to begin the moment the fabrics arrive," he said.

"Then you have received none of them yet?" she said, feeling an alarm that she took care to conceal.

"Yes," he said. "None."

"I apologize for the delay," she said. "You'll have them soon."

She severed the connection and accepted the tea Dawn handed her, sipped it while Segawa muttered at his computer printouts, an exasperated expression on his face. He was engaged in an eternal battle with rising costs, which he approached as a personal war.

"How are things in Hong Kong?" Dawn said.

"Mr. Liu has received none of the fabrics," Yuki said.

"I'll track them in the morning," Segawa said.

"No need," Dawn said. "I'll call Armand. That's his responsibility."

"It shouldn't be our responsibility to remind him," Segawa said. "But there's something I must tell you."

Yuki sipped the green tea and studied her daughter's face, the way she sat with her fingers laced together, the nails painted golden, reflecting the light. There was a worry line in her forehead, and Yuki could read her daughter's feelings, the doubts that came along with the fatigue.

"I'd like to put off this discussion until tomorrow," Dawn said.

"I think we have to talk about it now," Yuki said, knowing that the right time had come to tell them, but willing to wait until Segawa had his say.

"I've been keeping an unofficial total," Segawa said earnestly, "and the expenses are running much higher than we anticipated." He looked around at the high ceilings and the shelves of morocco-bound volumes, the priceless antique furniture. "Unless the Count is donating the use of this house, I'd say that this is going to cost at least twenty thousand dollars more than we budgeted."

"The Count is furnishing nothing," Dawn said. "I gave him a description of what we needed and he found it for us."

"I'll contact the agent in the morning and get the exact costs," Segawa said. His forehead furrowed as he examined the printout again. "I had a last-minute call from the agent who's handling the rental of the Opera House. He forgot to include the price of the union stagehands we're going to pay whether we need them or not. And we didn't figure in the cost of our own security, since we're not showing in the pavilions."

"Then where do we stand?" Dawn said.

"I think it advisable to cut back on certain things," Segawa said.

"How much?" she said.

"The rapidly inflating costs leave us about a half million dollars short." He fished a cigarette out of his pocket, lit it. "I'll set up a ninety-day loan tomorrow. I might be able to get a break on the interest rates by going through Tokyo."

Now was the time, Yuki realized, and she could put it off no longer. "Unfortunately, you will have no success there," she said. "I talked with Mori-san in Tokyo two days ago and he advised me that we have reached the limit of our credit."

"It would have been better had I been informed," Segawa said politely.

"I saw no need," Yuki said. "I didn't expect a shortfall."

"That's not all, is it, Mother?" Dawn said, reading the troubled expression on her mother's face.

Yuki sipped her tea. "I've known Mori-san for many years and I trust him. He told me that the bank had received an offer to buy our notes at a considerably higher price than the bank will realize by holding them to maturity. Mori-san refused, of course."

"Who made the offer?" Segawa said.

"I don't know. It would have been improper to ask because Mori-san could not have told me."

Dawn lit a cigarette. "It has to be Ito Kanao."

"Ah, Kanao," Yuki said. "I had thought of him, of course." And for a moment she thought of his father, General Ito, and it pained her to realize that such love in one generation could become such bitterness in the next.

"Why Kanao?" Segawa said.

"Past bitternesses," Yuki said. "Much too long to explain."

"I don't see any point in not knowing for sure," Dawn said. "I'll confront him with it."

"It's better to leave things where they are for the moment," Yuki said. "If it is Kanao, it's better that he thinks we don't know it. He will be considerably less cautious. I believe that we should all be on guard, but I don't believe in borrowing trouble. Right now I intend to go to bed and I would suggest that you do the same. A fresh mind makes fewer mistakes. Good night." And she followed a maid who had been waiting in the corridor to conduct O-Nakamura-sama to her bedroom whenever she was ready.

Once Yuki was gone, Segawa leaned back in his chair, eyes still bright, very much awake, alert. Dawn envied his extreme youth, the confidence of the new generation in Japan. It was obvious he would not contradict her mother, but it was also obvious he did not agree with her. He sucked the cigarette smoke into his lungs, blew it toward the ceiling. "I'm not an artist," he said. "I would like to have gone into design but I never had the gift for it. I've always been good with figures and computers. I trust the numbers. If you listen to them, they'll give you a good sense of direction that you can't get anywhere else."

Dawn smiled tolerantly. "And where do the figures lead us, Ken?"

"You won't like what I have to say," he said.

"That hasn't stopped you before."

"The only way we defeat any enemy, including Kanao, if he's the one, is to succeed," he said. "And that means making a profit." He was about to launch into his favorite subject again. "I would be less than honest if I didn't give you my best professional advice."

"All right," she said. "I'll listen."

"I want you to consider using a middleman, a factor," he said. "It's common business practice and I can arrange for one within a couple of days. He'll pay all the costs in Hong Kong and get his money back when the garments have been shipped."

"At a high fee," Dawn said. "This is our first time out."

"It's a way of maintaining a reserve fund," Segawa said. "I want to talk about licensing too. We're establishing the House of Dawn name. I can find manufacturers willing to pay a lot of money to merchandise what you've created. I can license out perfume, lingerie, sheets, dozens of items tomorrow, just on the strength of the advertising campaign."

"My mother wants to retain total control. I agree with her. That means no licensing yet, no factor."

"Total control means total risk," he said.

"And all the profits."

"If," Segawa said. "If everything works. If everything comes together. We're overextended. We're using unorthodox methods and we apparently have an enemy. If we win, we can buy our own bank to store the money. But if we lose, it's everything."

Dawn poured a fresh cup of tea. She was fighting fatigue, knowing how much there was to do before she could sleep. "Let me tell you something about my mother," she said. "She started with nothing except a bright mind, a belief in the Lord Jesus and the Lord Buddha, and a radiant beauty, which was often more of a curse than a blessing. Whatever she has now came from her refusal to quit and a lifetime of struggle and hard work. This business is her life and it's unthinkable she would ever sell pieces of that life to strangers."

She was tired of the questioning and the pushing and she felt vaguely disturbed. She did not fully agree with her mother, but she would never let Segawa know that. She put the thought out of her mind. "The musical director, the Japanese choreographer, and the cast are coming in from Tokyo on Friday. I suppose those costs are going to run higher too."

"Yes," he said. "I don't know how much. If you approve, I think I can get the French banks to give us a line of credit. We'll only pay on what we use."

"Fine," she said. "I don't want you to think that I'm ignoring what you advise," she said. "But for the moment, we do things just like we have them planned."

"Of course," he said. "But if you decide on any alternatives, give me a little lead time. Once the showings start, everything will take twice as long to do."

"I will," she said.

Once Dawn was alone, she drank her tea and tried to concentrate on business. But the ache of loneliness set in, the realization of those things she had sacrificed for those things she had attained.

She put her hand on the telephone, had to force herself to resist picking it up. She could call and Emile would be here within the hour and they could make love in any of a dozen rooms in the house, blotting out all the worries about business and enemies and shortfalls. Then, afterward, she would lie with her head in the crook of his arm and tell him what she wanted, anything, and he would make it possible. He would marry her tomorrow. Or, with his skill in the fashion business and his vast fortune, he could wipe away any financial problems, and if an enemy truly existed, Kanao or anybody else, he would take care of it.

She did not call. The immediate future belonged to her mother until she had accomplished what she had set out to do, until the family name was redeemed and established. There was so much to be done and a short time to accomplish it.

She began to unpack those things that were most important to her. She took out the small wooden block, worn smooth from her touch. She had used it in many dark moments when she needed to remember a time when there had been no hope. She turned it over in her hands. The four small crescent impressions were still there, where her fingernails had dug into the wood with such desperate force.

All a part of the past. She had endured. She would continue to endure. Dawn placed the piece of wood at the top of the drafting table as a talisman, then sat in an overstuffed chair and, without willing it, fell asleep.

She was awakened by cold sunlight streaming through the windows. Her personal maid, Ryoko, was standing in the doorway, waiting for her to come awake. "Good morning, Nakamura-san," Ryoko said. "Would you care for tea?"

"Please. No, make that coffee instead. And what time is it?"

"Half past nine."

Her mind was fuzzy. She looked up Armand Meyer's number in her address book, then waited until she had finished a cup of coffee and was fully alert before she dialed the number. In a moment he came on the line, speaking in English. "You marvelous woman. How delightful to hear from you. I knew you were coming to Paris. One could hardly be ignorant of that fact. Your publicity has been breathtaking to say the least." He was never so cheerful unless he was covering something.

"Do we have problems, Armand?" Dawn said.

"It's possible, unfortunately. But undoubtedly you can find a bright side," he said. "If you don't mind, I'll send my car for you. We need to discuss this face-to-face."

"Do I need my accountant or my lawyer?" she said.

His laugh was hollow. "Neither. We'll talk about it. There's a solution to every problem. My car will be there shortly unless you're too fatigued."

"Give me an hour." She gave him her address, then put down the telephone. She leaned back in the chair and closed her eyes.

"What kind of problems do we have?" Yuki said from the doorway.

"You didn't sleep long," Dawn said.

"I slept enough. What's gone wrong?"

Dawn told her of the conversation. Yuki nodded. "Do you remember all the warlords in China, roaming the countryside, leaving nothing but scorched earth behind them?"

"How could I forget them?"

"I thought we left them in the past," Yuki said. "But they just changed form and moved to other countries. Armand has never worn a sword, but he's a bandit just the same. I think he's going to try to raise his price. In China it was more direct. A sword at the throat. Here it's a grave and sorrowful look. But in the end they take the money if they can."

"He can't take it this time," Dawn said. "We have a contract with his mill. I intend to see he honors it."

Armand Meyer lived well in his semiretirement in *le seizième arrondissement,* one of the most elegant parts of Paris, a stone house tucked away in the trees, so surrounded by grounds it seemed to exist in its own park.

The large stone house was ornate, two centuries old. The servant ushered Dawn into a marbled foyer and then up a flight of stairs to the library, with a bay window comprised of hundreds of small diamond-shaped panes, the smell of rich leather and fine woods, and above all the grace and patina of age, of which Armand Meyer was the finest example. He was in his mid-sixties now, with a mane of white hair and a slight paunch beneath the vest of his expensive three-piece suit. He took her hand and kissed it and conducted her to a soft chair near the window.

"You have no idea how good it is to see you," he said. "How long has it been? Three years at least, when Itsugi-san brought you here last. You're as beautiful as ever."

"And you're every bit as gracious," she said.

"How is your lovely mother?"

"Quite well."

"Thank God for good health. That's all that's really important. Money comes and goes and fortunes can be recouped, but health once gone can never be regained."

An elderly maid in a starched white cap and apron over her black dress brought demitasses of strong coffee. Armand sat down opposite Dawn and raised the exquisite porcelain in a nodding toast before he sipped it. "I have this coffee specially imported for me from Indonesia, a new mocha. But I didn't ask you here just to sample the best coffee in all the world. I'm faced with a problem that has negative consequences and I feel we should discuss it face-to-face, as friends."

"What's the problem, Armand?"

He rubbed his stomach as if soothing himself. "Sometimes I think that I'm just like my father, may God rest his soul, because he lived above his store, every part of his life contained in one place. Now, in a sense, I do the same thing. Only he dealt in provisions of a different sort, in groceries, where I deal with money and real estate. But I have one thing in common with my father, and that is an absolute devotion to family. He always called himself a conservator for his children and I feel the same way. I'm almost seventy years old and so nothing I do now is for my benefit, or for my wife's. It's all for my children, my grandchildren, and, now, a new generation. I'm grateful to God to have lived so long." There was a screech from the lawn. He looked outside and smiled. "Peacocks are the essence of vanity."

She began to feel uncomfortable. He was rambling, wandering around in the present and the past. He had never done this with Itsugi unless bad news was to follow.

"I don't mean to press you, Armand," she said. "But I'm still suffering from jet lag and I have a lot to take care of."

"Precisely," he said, as if she had made his point for him. "And you, thank God, have the energy for it. But do you know what a headache the mill has been to me? All of my equipment is so old and my young textile designers are so impatient. They all want to go to work for a top designer by tomorrow at six o'clock." He sipped his coffee, his eyes watching her, cold remote eyes that did not go with the emotions he expressed. "So I thought to myself, why should I have to deal with this at my age, when the doctor tells me that my heart isn't so reliable anymore and I don't need the stress?"

She felt a chill now. She knew what was coming and was praying that she was wrong. "Tell me about the mill, Armand," she said.

"What is there to say?" he said with a shrug. "I sold it."

So now the worst was right there before her. Quite without thought, a memory from the old days in China intruded. The garden of the house in Shanghai had been shelled by artillery, and later she had come out and begun to poke through the rubble to see what she could find that was still intact. And now she was faced with another kind of rubble. "But my fabric is still in production," she said firmly. "My order will be filled."

He shrugged again. "Your initial order is already in hand. Beautiful material, absolutely gorgeous." He averted his eyes, looked out the window.

"That's only enough for the samples. What about the rest of it?"

"I don't know. I no longer have the final say."

"Who are the new owners?"

"I'm not at liberty to say as yet," he said. "They seem to be most cooperative but I can't speak for them."

"Do you know what you're doing to me?" she said quietly. "Two thousand yards of the brocade should have already been delivered to Hong Kong and the watered silk should be there by tomorrow. Without the fabrics, I'm out of business. In effect, I'm ruined before I even get started."

"Perhaps they will honor the contract. But even if worst comes to worst, there are other mills."

"You know better than that. They can't set up in time and they're already so overbooked my run would be back-ordered for months."

"It's out of my hands." He looked mournful. "What is an old man to do?" he said.

"Honor your commitments, for one thing."

"Your order is the mill's business, not mine. My commitments are to my family."

"You'll see that my contract is honored or I'll sue you for damages."

From the comfortable expression on his face, she could see that she had now moved into territory that was immensely familiar to him. There was not the slightest sign of distress on his face. "Our French courts are so terribly slow. And even so, I have the law on my side. With the sale of the property and the contracts, I am not legally liable."

She shook her head. True. There was no place for her anger to go. "Will you put a proposition to the new owner for me?"

"Certainly," he said.

"My contract has to be honored. Will you communicate that urgency for me? If it's a matter of money, then we'll renegotiate. But it has to be done."

"Of course I will," he said. "I'll do my utmost to see that everything turns out well for you, especially since I have inadvertently caused you distress." He rolled his arm, checked his watch. "And now I'm sure that you will be wanting to take care of other matters. My driver is at your disposal."

As she left the grounds she saw a peacock spread his magnificent tail, for no apparent reason. *Born with the vanity of self-satisfied power,* she thought.

And not the only creature on the grounds with that shortcoming.

He waited until he saw the car drive off through the trees toward the gate before he picked up the telephone and dialed the number. When the call was answered he attempted to remedy the situation. "It makes it highly awkward for her," he said. And then, after listening: "Certainly, I understand your position. You have to do what you have to do."

He put the telephone back on the cradle. He resolved not to feel the slightest shred of guilt. After all, he had done his best. He could not control other people, neither their motives nor their actions.

Trish Devane stretched languorously on the bed. She had slept late after her party for fashion writers and she came awake slowly, admiring Claude in his maleness as he left her and stood naked to answer the telephone. He was muscular, well toned, firm skin with the right amount of sun. He jotted down something on a notepad and put the telephone back on the cradle before he sat down on the bed again.

She patted his leg. "Who was it?"

"André."

"What did he want?"

"Just to pass along a message. The House of Dawn has requested arbitration of a dispute."

Trish sat up on the bed. "What kind of dispute?"

"It seems that the mill in Lyon that was weaving her fabrics has been sold. There's a question as to whether she can force the new owners, as yet unnamed, to honor her contract."

"Will the *chambre* mediate?"

"Your friend thinks so. After all, the *syndicale* is dedicated to protecting the designers."

"It may turn into a marvelous scandal," she said.

"Yes."

Fascinating. As Trish felt Claude's hands move over her again and the warmth of his body pressing against her, she thought of the House of Dawn. The business of the mill was an obvious double cross of no small proportions, for to abandon a large order would cost the new owners lots and lots of money.

She loved it. What was happening now meant that the House of Dawn had an enemy, and enemies in this business always made absolutely riveting copy. On that thought, she put her arms around Claude and surrendered to the rising feelings.

As Yuki stood at the window of the Montmartre sitting room and looked out through the trees to the city below, she could feel the hum of activity in the house, which had been turned into an atelier, sewing machines clicking, the babble of voices, the incessant jangling of the telephones, and as a background noise the high-pitched whine of Segawa's computer printer.

She saw the Count's Daimler pull into the circular driveway, the uniformed driver opening the door for the distinguished-looking man who stepped out onto the curb in the cool fall air. Count Emile Riboud was in his forties, an athletic man with an angular face and hair prematurely streaked with gray. She had known him for fifteen years, but only as her daughter's friend and lover, and now as an adviser on the advertising campaign. He had the reputation of being as fierce on the handball court as he had been in quadrupling his family fortune. In the past year he had divested himself of everything except the ancestral estate outside of Paris and the family portfolio.

He had been married to a graceful young woman whose photograph Yuki had later seen in the tabloids mounted on the Arabian stallion that had thrown her and caused her death. Twenty years had passed since then and he had never remarried.

Yuki could see what Dawn found attractive in him, because he exuded virility and wore his power as becomingly as his blue pinstriped suit.

She had left instructions to have him brought up to the sitting room and she could hear Segawa talking with him as the two men climbed the stairs. There was a light rap on her door and Emile smiled as he came into the room and kissed her hand. "Less than two days in Paris," he said, "and you have the whole city in an uproar."

"A little more than I wanted," she said, returning his smile, genuinely fond of him. "How are you, Emile?"

"I can't complain."

"Dawn's at the Opera House."

"So I hear," Emile said.

"I've taken the liberty of consulting the Count on the French money market," Segawa said. "He can get us a rate of thirteen percent on what we need."

"I'm sure that's very kind of him, but we'll discuss it later," Yuki said. "When you get downstairs would you have fresh tea brought up for me and Turkish coffee for our guest?"

"Certainly," Segawa said.

"He's a very bright young man," Emile said after Segawa had departed. He sat down in a velvet armchair opposite her.

"And enthusiastic, too much so I'm afraid. I apologize to you for his forwardness."

"I find it refreshing."

"You've seen Dawn, of course?"

"Yesterday."

At a hotel, no doubt, she thought, or did Emile have a town house in the city? "So she's brought you up to date," she said.

"Yes," he said. "I have a number of things to go over with you. First, my agent has found an office and it's being set up. Next, I had a firm run a name-recognition survey, and the advertising campaign has been very successful."

"Which means nothing unless we can manufacture and distribute."

"True. I took the liberty of contacting friends at the *chambre* on your behalf."

The maid came in with the tea cart and Yuki studied the Count as the black and bitter coffee was poured for him. A kind man, she thought, truly without malice. She waited until the maid was gone. "I'm grateful for your help."

"I'm glad to do it," he said. "The *chambre* sides with you but the situation is complicated. It seems that the sale may have been made to a foreign holding company with offices outside France. The *chambre* has yet to locate the principals to begin an action."

"I see," Yuki said. "I am not surprised. I didn't expect an easy solution."

"We'll have to wait and see," he said. "But we have something more immediate to take care of. I have received a telephone call from a journalist named Trish Devane who has heard of the mill sale

and is prepared to publish a long article in her syndicated newspapers about the vicious infighting in the world of fashion, using this incident as a pivotal point of her story. If she even hints that you can't produce, it's all over. The buyers will fight for invitations to your collection, because they're all very curious, but they won't give you any orders because they won't believe you can fill them."

"What do you suggest?"

"Trish wants an interview and she's agreed to publish nothing until she has the full story. I suggest we cooperate with her. And if rumors pop up elsewhere, we deny them. The House of Dawn is in no trouble at all."

Yuki looked out the window at the bare branches of the trees. "Very well," she said. "Dawn will meet her."

"I'll arrange it then," he said. "Now, at the risk of offending you, I want to offer you a line of credit for as much as you need."

"I appreciate your offer, but I can't take it," she said. "I will not use my daughter's lover for my financial advantage."

"It's not like that at all. Think of it for what it is, strictly business."

"Nevertheless, I can't do it," Yuki said. She choked off a memory of her father's voice that threatened to push into the present, a tone of desperation and shame barely suppressed. *My daughter, my beautiful daughter,* he was saying in a thick, slurred voice. *How I regret your going.* "I thank you for your kindness, and I will pray to the Lord Buddha and the Lord Jesus to give me strength. Because I do not intend to be defeated."

"I believe you, madame," the Count said.

Once he was in the car, he told his driver to take him to the Opera House. He opened *Le Figaro.* He was delighted with the coverage of the approaching shows, all of the gossip about the designers, and the speculation about the lines from people in the industry who claimed that this year's collections would make women essentially feminine once again while Saint Laurent was predicting that women would choose to be more subdued this year, more elegantly tailored.

As he lit a cigarette his eyes fell on an article by Trish Devane, a piece ostensibly dedicated to the finances of the fashion industry, concentrating on the fact that it cost any of the designers showing in Paris at least two million dollars to mount their *prêt* collections, sometimes resorting either to outrageous designs or heavy money in advertising just to provoke interest and create a salable image. But sometimes the attention-seeking behavior backfired.

She included a quote from a designer who had obviously been in his cups at a party when he had talked of his clients as "sheep waiting to be shorn" and limiting the women with true fashion sense to perhaps half a dozen. All the rest were "mindless camp followers" who would wear whatever they were told was fashionable whether they looked like "sluts or machinists or little bitches dressing up in daddy's old suits."

He sighed. Trish could do a great deal of damage.

He folded the newspaper in disgust, put out the cigarette, turned his attention to his appointment calendar that involved his family's business.

It was ironic, he thought, that in freeing himself to follow his own interests, he had become, in effect, a superintendent of family investments, in gold and foreign currencies, in stocks and bonds of a conservative nature. More than one investment firm had tried to recruit him as a partner to administer commercial or charitable estates, but he always declined. The world of finance was becoming increasingly abstract and he was bored with graphs and charts and computer projections.

He felt a keen sense of anticipation as his car threaded through impossible traffic and delivered him to the Opera House's baroque lobby, where he cleared security. He went into the dark auditorium, where two choreographers were working on the vast stage. An older Japanese was quietly directing the movements of the dancers, while a vociferous young Englishman was working with a handful of bewildered Japanese mannequins who did not understand English and waited until each of his remarks was translated before they followed through.

At the moment they were trying to time their movements to the recorded strains of a Japanese samisen and flute orchestra, until the Englishman interrupted them. "No, no, no, that won't do at all. Girls, listen up. Listen carefully to me now." And all the time he spoke a small Japanese woman interpreted simultaneously, a running commentary that divided the attention of the girls, who looked from him to her and then back again.

"You have to *adapt*, for Christ's sake. You can't use the traditional model's turn. Now, Sumiko, your name is Sumiko, isn't it? You come out of the door and then you pause and look down the street as if you're looking for a lover and then you make a *slow* half-turn, that's *slow*, do you have that, darling?" And then to the old woman: "Does she have that? All right, now we'll take it again from the top. Roll the music."

The girls started moving again while the young English choreographer shook his head with bewilderment.

The Count found Dawn halfway back in the orchestra section, sitting in the darkness. She lifted her face to be kissed as he slipped into the seat beside her. "How's it going?" he said.

"I don't know what ever led me to believe that I could bring this off," she said. "The French stagehands don't speak Japanese and refuse to speak English. My Japanese choreographer doesn't speak anything but Japanese. My English choreographer hates the French stagehands and can't communicate with his Japanese colleague or the girls. And the little woman who's doing the translating is so polite that it takes her forever to turn a direct order into a polite request." She let out a short and nervous laugh. "Pandemonium."

"It always is. Let's go have a drink."

"God knows I could use one."

Outside, she blinked against the sunlight and he saw how pale she was, tired, overworked. She took his arm and he led her down the street to a mezzanine cafe that overlooked the street. "How long has it been since you've eaten?"

"I have no appetite," she said. She ordered a white wine. He waited until the bottle had been served and then raised his glass to her. "To my understanding nature," he said.

She smiled. "I'll drink to that."

"I've wanted you to marry me and I've wanted to take care of you for more years than I find it comfortable to count."

"I love you," she said. "You know that."

"Not enough. I want more. Living in the same house, sleeping in the same bed on a regular basis."

"Oh how tempting you are," she said.

"Then give in."

"Not yet. When my mother and I discovered I had a talent for designing, we made an agreement." She sipped the wine, looked down at the crowds on the street. "I would take care of the fashion end. She would manage the money."

"I understand that," he said with some frustration. "But why won't she accept the help I'm offering?"

"There is a reason, a very deep-seated one, but I'm not going to tell you about it," she said. "If it were my decision, I'd borrow the money from you in a minute, but that's because I'm half *gaijin,* half Japanese and one hundred percent opportunist."

"Then we won't argue money," he said. "But there's something I want you to do for your own good. I want you to meet Trish Devane."

"I don't like the kind of things she writes."

"All the more reason to talk with her," the Count said. "Leave it to me. I'll arrange everything."

Dawn had difficulty distinguishing between night and day. When she was not at the house in Montmartre, working with a fitting model and being besieged by the needs of Segawa, her workroom ladies, hems that would not hang right, or the seemingly hundreds of accessories needed for these garments—the tortoise-shell combs, the Manchurian beads, the Chinese shoes with the elaborate brocades—none of which seemed to be where they were supposed to be and all of which required her attention, she was at the Opera House inspecting the flats that were being painted in the construction rooms, approving the colors of stone walls, and enduring the complaints of her English choreographer, who had accomplished a miracle and brought all the girls into reasonable shape. But now, leaning against a false stone wall that would eventually represent a garden in Shanghai, he smoked a cigarette and issued his form of ultimatum.

"It's costing you a bloody fortune, you know," he said. "And we can't really finalize the routines until our star is here. Our bloody lead model, the overpaid darling of the catwalks, was due two days ago from London, am I correct? London, right across the English Channel and a bit of landscape on either end, but not the moon, for Christ's sake. She could have walked it by now, couldn't she?"

"She'll be here," Dawn said.

"I have a dozen mannequins better than Sakura. Why not give her the sack? We can give any girl a Japanese look."

"She's what I want," Dawn said with finality.

"She's wild as a March hare, and that means she can raise bloody hell with schedules. The other girls are pretty damn sharp at the moment, but if she takes much longer getting here, then we lose the keen performing edge."

"This is not my first show, Mr. Keating," Dawn said. "I appreciate what you're doing, but I don't happen to need any more prima donnas at the moment."

"If that's the way you want it," he said. He ground the cigarette beneath his heel as he went back to the stage.

She stood in place a long moment, aware that she was past the point of being able to soothe the multiple egos of all the people who worked for her. She was close to being overwhelmed, but she could not afford to show it. She went into the office and found her mother on the telephone, as usual, and waited for her to finish.

"I'm going to disappear for an hour or two," she said. "I need to walk and think."

She did not make it out of the Opera House before a clerk flagged her down and told her she had a call waiting. She picked up the nearest extension.

"This is Dawn," she said.

"I'm delighted to be talking to you," came the woman's voice on the line. "This is Trish Devane. Do you know of my column?"

"Yes," Dawn said. "What can I do for you?"

"I've been talking with your Count Emile. Is it possible you might be free to have a drink?"

"Now?"

"I realize this is terribly spontaneous."

"All right," Dawn said. "Where?"

"There's a delightful little place not far from you, I believe, called Le Petit Chien. Shall we say fifteen minutes?"

"I'll be there," Dawn said.

Trish purposely reached Le Petit Chien early and took a sidewalk table. She was curious to see how this Madame Dawn would arrive, in a limousine perhaps, or a sports car. To her surprise, she saw an elegant oriental woman coming up the hill on foot, dressed in layers of soft peach silk topped by a deeper peach and white floral adaptation of a kimono that served as a smashing top coat for the cool afternoon. Her hair was covered by a soft silk scarf.

Dawn approached the table to accept the outstretched hand and then sat down. She ordered black coffee while Trish permitted herself the indulgence of a half carafe of wine.

"I'm really delighted you accepted my invitation," Trish said.

"Only to get acquainted," Dawn said. "I'm not ready to make any official statements to the press. When I am I'll issue a release."

"I'm not interested in a release," Trish said. "I'd like an interview, and if I decide to write a story, I'll feel free to quote whatever you say unless you specifically request that something be held in confidence."

"Did the English designer agree to an interview?" Dawn said evenly.

"He was drunk and he made his remark about women and sheep in a public place. There was no confidentiality."

"I see," Dawn said. "How did you come to know Emile?"

The coffee and wine were served. Trish lit a cigarette. "From the days when he was in the business. We're uneasy friends, your Emile and I," she said. "But we have a certain mutual respect."

"What do you want to know?" Dawn said.

"What work have you done that qualifies you to hit the world market?" Trish said.

"My designs will speak for themselves."

"But you must have had some experience before you came here."

"I won't answer questions in that area."

"Is it true that your lover is financing your collection as a whim?"

"If you're talking about Emile, he's provided expertise and advice. No more than that. My mother and I have put up the money."

"How fortunate to be rich," Trish said. Her vague smile telegraphed the trap inherent in her next question. "What is your relationship with Itsugi?"

"I don't want to talk about that."

"Then I'll talk about it and you can either confirm or deny," Trish said. "Frankly, my dear, it's common knowledge that Itsugi's collection this year is terrible. His models are so worried about him that they're trying to persuade him to change his line, even at this late date. But he's completely abandoned what I've always called his 'spare elegant' look. So I inquired around and I found that the only difference between this year and previous years is that his chief assistant designer left him to go on her own."

Dawn said nothing.

Trish sipped her wine. "Are you that designer? Are you responsible for his years of elegance?"

"I worked for the House of Itsugi," Dawn said.

"And created those splendid collections."

"I was an employee. He made the decisions."

"Fascinating," Trish said. "You're one in a million, my dear.

There's not another assistant in the business who wouldn't have taken the credit if they were in your place." She made a sudden switch. "Who doesn't like you?"

Dawn did not blink. "I don't know what you mean."

Trish looked at her quizzically. "Do you think it's a coincidence that somebody bought the Guillam mill in Lyon from Armand Meyer?"

"Businesses are bought and sold every day."

"Did you know that yours is the only order they've canceled?"

Dawn did not allow her expression to change. "We have a contract. I assume the new owners will honor it."

"And you're not worried?"

"No more than is normal at this stage in a collection."

Trish finished the glass, poured another. "You're formidable," Trish said with admiration. "I think you have a very powerful enemy, and I believe you know it too. Not just some seamstress with a grudge. No, somebody very rich and sophisticated with enough money and knowledge to know *how* to block you, somebody who knows your financial situation well enough to realize that if you lose this season, you don't have enough money to start over."

Dawn studied her for a long time. "Everything you say is hypothetical."

"I'm willing to deal with it at that level," Trish said. "Are you willing to talk about hypothetical enemies?"

"Not now," Dawn said. "Right now I have my hands full with reality." She looked at her watch. "I have to run."

"I'd like to talk with you again," Trish said. "When you have more time."

"We'll see," Dawn said.

Yuki sat by the window in Dawn's studio and watched her daughter making adjustments in the muslin on a dressmaker's form while Dawn repeated her conversation with Trish.

"She said that the mill has canceled our run."

"Do you believe she's telling the truth?"

"Yes." Dawn jabbed a pin into the material, obviously distraught.

"Then we have to consider the possibility of substituting fabrics," Yuki said. "Can you adapt to Kyoto silk? I can start calling to see what kind of overruns we can pick up in Asia."

"There isn't time to adapt," Dawn said. "I know you won't like it, but I want you to consider something, Mother."

"No," Yuki said, interrupting, knowing what her daughter was going to say. "Absolutely not."

"You have to hear me out," Dawn said. "We don't have any options. I want us to consider canceling everything. I'm sure we can salvage enough to go back to Blossoms and the way things were. We'll be short of money, but we can make it up over a period of time."

"Severance pay and transportation back to Japan for everyone we brought here," Yuki said. "Is that what you're thinking?"

"Yes."

"Some of these people have been with us for twenty years. When I employed them I agreed to look after their welfare. I don't take that responsibility lightly."

"I don't think we have any choice."

"There's always a choice," Yuki said. "And I am still the head of the house. You will go on with the collection and you will leave the business to me."

Dawn sighed her acceptance and her hopelessness. "I'd like you to see a run-through of the first section," she said. "The new model has arrived. Her name is Sakura and she's expensive."

"Is she what you thought she would be?"

"Perfect. High-spirited, arrogant. She has great stage presence."

"I'll come down and see her," Yuki said. She stood up, kissed her daughter on the cheek. "Now I want you to rest awhile."

"Not a chance. We're translating the Manchu *toiles* into brocade."

"Nobody will miss you. I'll wake you in half an hour."

When Yuki was alone she sat down at a carved teak desk with the form of a dragon imprisoned beneath a sheet of glass, and it seemed to her that one of her Lords was reminding her that only a thin and transparent shield of faith protected her from the evils of this world.

She remembered a time in Shanghai when she stood in the shadows while a wretchedly poor Chinese woman, thin beyond belief, standing on the muddy bank of the Whangpoo, placed the body of the infant she had just smothered into a wooden box decorated with paper flowers and slid it into the river, and then watched it catch in the current and swirl away in the yellow waters. And Yuki had understood the woman's feelings, for she, too, would have welcomed a peaceful surrender to the oblivion of the muddy river. But the Lord Jesus and the Lord Buddha would not allow her to do that. She had been put upon this earth to struggle and survive, any way she could.

Now she pulled a piece of paper in front of her and decided to make a list of possible enemies, all people with vast personal fortunes who could have bought the mill.

1. Ito Kanao.

In the times she had met Ito's son, she had seen many of his father's features in his face: the piercing, quick comprehension of the brown eyes, the set of the jaw, the texture of the skin, and even little mannerisms of the General. But she had never seen any of Ito's warmth in the son, only a guarded dislike that could easily approach hatred. She did not know whether he was capable of this final revenge, but she had to put him first on the list.

2. Itsugi.

She sat back, studied the name, and considered the man, a giant in the fashion world, with whimsical moods that could turn malevolent in an instant for no apparent reason. *Mercurial,* yes, that was the word, a tyrant capable of great generosity and immense cruelties as well. He felt betrayed by Dawn, wounded, and he could be seeking revenge.

3. Armand.

He was capable of great duplicity and he could have pretended to sell the mill as his way of forcing her out of business.

Her pen paused in the air. A list was useless. There were too many possibilities, not just current enemies but those of the past.

"Never forget the past," her mother had told her as a child. "For that is where you learned all that you know. But remember that the past can be a friend or an enemy. So you must be ever watchful. Remember, ever watchful."

Ever watchful, Yuki thought. *You were right, Honorable Mother, but perhaps I wasn't watching closely enough. Perhaps the past has brought us an enemy this time. And we may not survive.*

The Japanese
Village . . .
June 1931

THE THATCHED ROOF of the old house seemed to the child to
sweep toward the ground like a gray bird's wing, and in that terrible
summer to be the only place of refuge. For the *kami,* the spirits that
Yuki's father said inhabited every living thing, had found him and his
family in disfavor. For three years the spirits of the ground had
yielded very little. One summer there had been no rain and not
enough water for the paddies, and the next summer there had been
only enough rice for seed and just a meager ration for the family.
This year there was something wrong with the seedlings. The green
shoots to be planted in the mud were a mottled yellow, and a bind
weed had taken over the terraced fields.

From the first light of morning until the last glimmer of sunset the
family worked in the terraced paddies, her two brothers delicately
pulling the weeds away from the shoots, her father guiding the plow
with the cultivator blades between the rows while her mother led
the ox by a rope attached to a brass ring set in its flaring black
nostrils.

Her father was the last survivor of his family, a branch of one of the important *miyaza* families, centuries old, who had fallen onto hard times, the land holdings diminished by a world depression that had rippled across the oceans.

Her father had inherited sheds of silkworms when he first took over the family farm in Japan, and the delicate cocoons had sold to the factories and the mills at a premium price, but then, seemingly overnight, the bottom had dropped out of the market and the people of the United States could no longer afford to buy silk, and so could no longer buy his cocoons, and her father could not afford the cost of the mulberry leaves. Eventually the silkworms died. Her father sold the lumber from the sheds and converted the area to a small paddock for the ox and a place for his wife to keep her few chickens.

Yuki's mother had been born of the Kawaguchi family, merchants who had disinherited her when she had gone against their wishes and married a man of her own choosing. She was small-boned, with a thin face and large brown eyes that reflected sorrow or pleasure, and hands that were shaped to do flower arrangements or the formal tea ceremony, but not to blister against the rough ox's rope or pucker like prunes in the brown water of the rice paddies or turn blue with chilblains in the freezing cold of winter.

Yuki felt shame because she had never had to work with her family in the fields. She had been set apart because her parents wanted more for her. A missionary truck had come to their village and her family had gone to hear the two officers from the Salvation Army, Captain Ernest Thompson and his wife, Elsa.

They had a small brass band that had sent rousing hymns ringing across the countryside, "the voice of God" as the Captain called it, and curiosity-seekers gathered in the square for a sermon, preached by the Captain in a stern, brusque Japanese. He was a tall middle-aged man with sandy hair and splotchy skin who looked as if he had been in the sun too long. Only after the call to repentance were English lessons offered to children whose parents would allow it. Yuki's parents asked them to teach her. At first she took lessons only when they came to the village. Then the Thompsons had said she was naturally adept at English and had persuaded her father to permit Yuki to live in the Salvation Army compound and attend their school at the Tokyo suburb of Ueno. Not only would her absence give the family more food, but the Thompsons felt that Yuki would become proficient as an English translator and thereby earn money.

There were always at least a dozen girls at the compound in Ueno, but from the beginning Yuki felt set apart, overprotected by the Thompsons, as if she needed constant guarding. Yet why it was so was never explained to her. She sat at her desk, learning to type under Elsa's patient tutelage, studying arithmetic without the aid of an abacus, "doing things the American way," Elsa explained. And each morning, during prayer service, Captain Thompson would admonish the girls to keep their hearts pure from the sins of false pride, vanity, and covetousness.

One day Yuki was seated at her desk translating a practice business document from Japanese into English. She chanced to look out the window just as a *gaijin* woman in a Western dress went by on the street, her full skirt swirling about her ankles, her feet foreshortened by high heels, her blouse sheer and gauzy, her blond American hair bound by a brilliant red scarf. Yuki was entranced by the dress and made a quick sketch of it.

Elsa had gathered up the papers to be corrected, glancing at the drawing without comment. That evening, after the band had played on the street and vespers had been said for the girls in the school, Yuki was summoned to Captain Thompson's office. He held the paper on which she had made the drawing.

"How old are you now, Yuki?" he began.

"Sixteen, if you count the years the Japanese way," she said.

"Almost a woman but not quite," he said. He handed her the paper. "What does this drawing mean to you?"

"I saw an American woman go by the window. I liked her dress. If I had the money for cloth, I would make one like it for myself."

He sat down, facing her. "What did you like about the dress?"

"She could take long steps. In a kimono, one has to walk slowly, with short steps. I like the feel of fine fabric, sir. I'm very good with my hands. If I were rich, I would make many fine dresses."

"You're not rich," he said. "But if you were, I would hope you would give your money to the poor, considering the fact that these are hard days for everyone and you are a very lucky girl to have food to eat." He looked at her sternly. "Fine clothing is always a sign of vanity. It enhances the flesh and impoverishes the spirit. So I want you to tear the drawing in two and drop the pieces in the wastebasket."

She looked at the drawing and then at his stern face. Very slowly she tore the paper and then dropped the pieces in the wastebasket.

"That's the first step," he said.

He dismissed her. She was puzzled. She saw no danger in thoughts of becoming wealthy or in her admiration of fine clothes. And to her surprise she found that she did not need the drawing to remember the dress. She had but to close her eyes to be able to see every detail of it.

Two nights later she was polishing the brass cornets in the music room, enjoying the gleam of the rich metal, and through the window that opened into the courtyard she heard the Captain talking to his wife.

"I don't think the drawing means anything," Elsa said. "After all, she hasn't seen many Americans, particularly well-dressed ones."

"As beautiful as she is, she needs protection from such people. She's growing up too fast and she's had little experience in this world."

"I think you're worrying needlessly. I had a call today, an English firm looking for a translator."

"Let's send her home," Ernest said. "I think she needs to be with her family for a while and do some real growing up."

Yuki slipped from the music room and climbed the stairs on the west side of the compound to the full-length mirror that was fastened to the door outside the room where the female students slept. There was little light in the hallway. A sign above the mirror read DO YOU LOOK LIKE THE CHRISTIAN WOMAN YOU ARE?

She examined herself in the mirror, running her hands over the smooth skin of her face, the high cheekbones, the full mouth, looking for this illusive thing called "beauty." She could not see it. Beauty in her village was a round moon face, and hers was narrow. But she did look quite grown-up and would like to have had the job with the English firm.

On the day she arrived home with her possessions, and a double ration of rice tied in a cloth, she heard a cry from the nearby field where her family was working.

She saw her father standing behind the ox and yelling at it to move, slapping the reins against the massive rump, while her mother put all her weight against the rope, but the great beast just stood mired in the mud, making no attempt to move. It stretched its neck and gave out a long low throaty moan before it collapsed and fell into the mud.

Her brothers helped her father remove the yoke. They left the animal there and returned to the house. Her brothers nodded to her, but her father was so caught up in his own misery, he did not seem to notice her. He went down the road toward the village with the boys while Yuki stood with her mother, who looked after them with great pain on her face.

"He's going for a priest," she said.

"Then the ox is dead."

Yuki understood her mother's despair. She knew of other farms where the animals had died and the butchers had been called to salvage what they could. And even in the face of disaster, there had been meat for the family.

But not so with them, because her father was a religious man and the purification ceremony prohibited the use of the meat.

She and her mother stood silently waiting and after a time the father and sons returned. Along with the priest they brought four heavy men, all of the *eta* class, the untouchables, dirty men dressed in rags. Her mother bowed to the Shinto priest in his blood-red robes and ornate black hat. He was a thin old man who was already chanting as the untouchables, purveyors of dead animals and all things unclean, waded out into the field and, attaching ropes to the forequarters of the ox, proceeded to drag him through the mud with great effort, a centimeter at a time, the giant carcass sweeping the ground clean of plants, wiping out a whole area of rice shoots.

It was late afternoon and the shadows had become long when her father poled the priest in the boat out to where the ox had died, her father desperately hoping that by undoing the terrible contamination that his fields had suffered, the course of his misfortune might be changed.

The boys watched the boat go through the shallow connecting canals and the *eta* loading the ox onto a wagon in the road. And at the side of the house where there was some privacy, Yuki helped her mother remove her muddy trousers and working blouse and brought water in a bucket to help wash her mother's naked body, stringy from years of hard work and so little food.

"I didn't expect you home so soon," her mother said. "Are your studies finished?"

"Soon, Honorable Mother," Yuki said. "What happened to the ox?"

"He died of starvation," her mother said. "But your father thinks the *kami* killed it to punish him."

Once clean, her mother dressed in a summer kimono and they went into the house. An east wind was blowing across the ridge that separated the fields from the ocean, and as the sun retreated the late afternoon began to cool. In the kitchen, Yuki gave her mother the double ration of rice and her mother measured out half of it, preparing a parcel that would be payment for the priest, including one of the precious eggs that she hoarded to use for trading in the village.

At dusk her father and the priest returned from the field and her mother handed the parcel to her father, who put it in the priest's hands with a formal bow and then watched as the priest walked down the narrow road toward the town.

Her mother served a bowl of weak tea to her husband in the *ima* while Yuki put rice on to steam in the small kitchen, trying to keep her growing sense of despair bottled up within her. It was obvious that there was little food left in the house now, not enough for more than a day or two at the outside. And her mother would eat even less as the food diminished, passing rice from her bowl to her sons, drinking hot water and giving the tea to her husband, saving the eggs, which could be traded in town for salt. The anger mounted within her that she had been returned to burden her parents for no good reason while the translator's position that could have been hers had gone to another girl.

Above the bubbling of the water Yuki could hear the voices of her parents from the other room, and although she could not make out all the words, she could hear enough to understand the general drift of the conversation. It seemed that her father had exhausted all the possibilities he could think of, all except one, and the land was not purified and the priest could not tell him when the spell of misfortune would be lifted.

"Then it has to be done?"

"It's for the best."

"Can it wait until tomorrow?"

"No. I'll walk into the village and make arrangements for tonight."

"The boys shouldn't be here."

"They will stay at the temple."

"Hai."

Dinner was eaten in silence. When the father was finished he washed and changed into his best kimono.

Yuki stayed with her mother in the kitchen to clean the bowls as her father departed, a lantern in his hand. It would not be lighted until it was absolutely necessary in order to conserve the oil. The only light in the kitchen came from a window opened to the west from which a final pinkish cast to the sky reflected into the room.

Her mother set the teapot on the last of the charcoal to heat. When it steamed she poured some into a cup for Yuki and then one for herself.

"I am afraid, Honorable Mother," Yuki said abruptly.

"We will not talk of fear."

Yuki's throat was dry. She sipped the hot tea. "The ox died and we don't have any food left. Yet Honorable Father dresses in his best kimono and my brothers have been sent away." The words caught in her throat.

"I had wanted you to finish your English studies with the missionaries and then find a job in the city. But it is not to be so. I will tell the Thompsons you are not returning." She stood up, took a box from a shelf. "I hoped that this time would not come, but I prepared for it." She unfolded a summer kimono, a *yukata*, which Yuki had not seen before. The cloth was covered with pale flowers, beautiful in the fading light. "I want you to put this on," her mother said.

"Where did you get it?" Yuki said, enchanted. "It's beautiful."

"I bought it for myself in Shanghai a long time ago. And then, when we moved here and things went bad, I put it away to save for you."

The kimono was silk, the feel of it luxurious against her body as she dressed herself. "Why am I to have it now?" she said.

Her mother sipped the hot water. "Your father borrowed money from a man named Suzuki-san. He lives in Tokyo but he owns much land here. Do you remember my pointing him out to you in the village this last spring?"

"Yes."

"He is a very important man because he has rich friends. He has made a proposition to your father every spring for the last three years and your father has always refused it. Now that the ox is dead, we must accept it."

"What proposition did he make?"

"There is a very rich *gaijin* who lives in Tokyo," her mother said. "He has a large house and a wife who came from an important family. But she has never pleased him and he wants a younger woman of beauty to come into his house, not as a servant, but as a concubine. Do you know what a concubine is?"

"No, Honorable Mother."

"An extra woman, *ne?* To sleep with him like his wife, and perhaps to please him in ways that the wife does not."

"And I am to be that woman?"

"Hai."

She wrapped the obi around herself. "How did he pick me?"

"Suzuki-san is aware that you are a great beauty. The man will be pleased."

"But I'm needed here," Yuki said.

"Suzuki-san will be paid by the rich man in Tokyo for finding you," her mother said with great patience. "And in turn he will give your father enough money to buy a new animal, to buy rice to eat and rice to plant."

And now, for the first time, Yuki began to understand something of what the Thompsons had meant, for the rich man would not have wanted her unless he considered her beautiful. She was grateful that she could save her family from starvation and provide many advantages.

If the man was very rich, then he would live in a large house where the bath would be heated all the time. And she would persuade him to allow her family to come to Tokyo and visit as often as they liked. And he would send his workman to rethatch her father's roof. She would persuade him to allow her all of the fine cloths she wanted to be made into dresses for her mother and herself.

Her mother prepared the lamps, the wicks that floated in their shallow dishes of oil, a sure sign that this was a special night. The oil was expensive and never was there a light in the house once the sun had disappeared unless one of them was sick. She put a straw in the residue of the coals in the hibachi until the end of it burst into flame and then she lit the wicks, which sputtered before they began to burn. Her mother was beautiful in the dim light of the lamps, which smoothed the lines in her face. She reached out, took Yuki's hands in her own.

"I want you to listen to me, daughter. When Suzuki-san comes tonight, you must show him the greatest respect," her mother said.

"When he engages you in conversation you will sit on your feet. I want you to guess in your mind what he wants you to say and only then do you speak. And if you can't guess, then you remain silent and keep your eyes downcast. He is bringing honor to you and our family. If he asks you any question, you agree with him and you show gratitude that he should ask. Use your most polite language. Do you understand? A rich man will want a woman with manners. Whether your father regains his pride depends on you."

"It's enough that you ask it, Honorable Mother," Yuki said.

It was late and very dark outside when she heard the sound of a motor and saw two very large round beams of light that looked like the eyes of some magnificent night creature reflecting in the water of the paddies. A motorcar had never come to the farm before, only an occasional truck.

Her mother urged her inside, put her in the room where she slept, and then made one last-minute inspection of the room where the visitor would be received, adjusting the lamps, inspecting herself in a mirror, and then, as the car stopped outside, walking in tiny steps to the *engawa* to welcome the visitor in a soft and formal voice while Yuki sat in the semidarkness, the shoji closed so that she could hear but not be seen.

She heard her father's words, subdued, and Suzuki-san's deep-throated voice, which was almost a growl. He had brought presents, and Yuki could tell from her mother's voice that she was most grateful, for the gifts included rice cakes and sake and other foods that the family had not had in a long time. Her mother went to the kitchen to warm the sake. Yuki sat very quietly, listening to the conversation between the two men, a ritual that ended in the serving of the sake and the first toasts, the *compais.*

"I am most lucky to be in Towa today," Suzuki-san said. "My astrologer told me that this would be a time of very good fortune for me." They began to talk about the crops and the bad times and after a long wait the door slid open. Her mother's face was pale, strained. She nodded to Yuki, who rose effortlessly and padded into the other room and then sank to her knees. Laying her hands palm-down on the floor in front of her, she bent forward and touched her forehead to them. But she had glimpsed the man, short, squat, heavy-jowled, thick spectacles sitting on the wide bridge of his nose. He wore a gray kimono of very rich material. He raised the shallow sake bowl in his big fingers, drank.

"Please sit up so I may look at you," he said with a smile.

Yuki raised up. Her father's face was flushed red from the sake. *"Konbanwa,* O-Suzuki-sama," she said in a soft voice.

"A voice like the singing of birds," Suzuki-san said, smiling, nodding to Yuki's father. "You're to be congratulated for having such beauty in your house." Now he picked up a presentation box of sushi, each piece in its own paper wrapper. He extended it to Yuki, spoke in English. "Please," he said.

She picked one from the wooden box, aware that her mother would not approve. Her hunger had overcome her manners.

"Arigato gozaimashita," she said. She bit into it daintily.

"Please to speak English with me," Suzuki-san said.

"What would you like me to say, sir?"

"The gentleman to whose house you shall be going enjoys the speaking of English. So I engage you in this conversation."

She could not resist, knowing that neither her mother nor her father could understand what was being said. "If you could, please, sir, I would like to know more about this gentleman."

"Of course," Suzuki-san said. The light from the lamps winked on a gold tooth as he smiled. "He owns grand house, rooms with many mats, many motorcars, a country house at Izu and snow house for wintering sports in the mountains."

"I will be pleased to go to his house," she said, bowing again.

Suzuki-san smiled, nodded to Yuki's father and then to her mother at the far side of the room. He switched back to Japanese again. "I am honored to be the go-between in this matter," he said.

Shortly, Yuki received a sign from her mother that it was time for the women to retire. She followed her mother into the *ima.* There was another lacquered box full of sushi and a tin of tea, a *tin,* not the coarse cloth sack that contained the cheaper kind, and a sack of rice, and another package of dried fish. "You may eat as much as you like," her mother said, opening the box of sushi.

"I will have plenty to eat at my new house," Yuki said. "So save these for my brothers."

"There will be more for them as well," her mother said.

"Only if you join me," Yuki said.

"The *kami* have sent us a gift," her mother said. "We would be impolite to refuse it."

They ate, listening to the voices from the other room, the end of the bargaining between the two men. Suzuki-san would give her father another ox and sufficient money to plant the crop and buy food until the new crop came. Too, he would not be pressured for any past debts.

There was a rustle of clothing now as Suzuki-san raised himself to his feet and her father struggled to join him. "I will send a car for your daughter in the morning."

Yuki followed her mother out of the *ima* in time to see Suzuki-san, in the *engawa*, putting on patent-leather Western shoes, which seemed incongruous with his kimono.

All the proper form of parting, and then the three of them were alone in the room, and Yuki was aware of the envelope on the mat, unopened, the red ribbon still tied around it. Her father sank down, poured himself a bowl of sake, picked up the envelope without opening it.

"My daughter, my beautiful daughter, how I regret your going," he said, his voice breaking with shame, tears beginning to stream down his face. "I hope you will have a better life." He downed the sake and, rising, stumbled from the room.

Her mother knelt beside her. "It is only the sake that allows him to show you his true feelings. Never forget how hard this moment has been for him. He would have preferred that you marry and to a man of your own choosing, but it was not to be," she said, sighing. "Now we must talk, and it is my duty to tell you what men and women do together."

"I've heard the girls talking."

"They had no business talking of things they know nothing about." She removed a cloth that was wrapped around a book and opened it. In the flickering light Yuki saw the woodcut engraving of a man and a woman in the clothing of the Tokugawa period. The man and woman were lying together and the man's organ protruded from the clothing and entered the cleft of the woman. There was a scowl on the face of the man and a passive expression on the woman's whitened face, as if she were unaware of what was happening. The man was above the woman.

Yuki's mother turned a page. In the next picture the man rested on his back with the same scowl and the woman was above him, her legs spread, the same stylized penis rising from the man to penetrate the woman between the legs.

"I never thought it would be so ugly," Yuki said. "Does it hurt?"

"Only the first time." Her mother turned another page. "Since your new lord has a wife who does not please him," she said, "then you must learn from this book the ways that will. And, daughter, a woman may take pleasure also. Do you understand?"

"I don't know, Honorable Mother. But I'll do my best."

Her mother closed the book, bound it in the cloth. She leaned over to blow out the light, to conserve the oil. In that moment Yuki saw the great pain in her face, which she was trying to hide. Yuki put her arms around her. "We'll only be separated for a little while," she said. "And I will make you proud of me."

"I'm sure you will."

"Did Honorable Father get a good price?"

"*Shirinai,*" her mother said. "I don't know."

Yuki thought for a moment. "Do you believe in God?" she said.

"Which God?"

"The Lord Jesus."

"No," her mother said with a sigh. "Sometimes I express belief in the *kami* to please your father. But I'm afraid I don't believe in anything." She gave her daughter a final hug, then rose to her feet in the darkness. She reached down, ran her hand over her daughter's hair, as if allowing herself a luxury. "The car will come early for you, before I go to the fields."

"Yes."

As the shoji closed behind her mother Yuki felt a great sadness in the parting. It had to be. She removed the kimono, folding it neatly. She opened the screens to the outside, and her room was flooded with the warm smells of the summer night, which she would never experience again quite like this. She heard the far-off lowing of a cow. A crescent moon was rising in the east, above the rocky ridge of hills that flanked the sea.

She unrolled the futon and lay down. When she closed her eyes she was back in the gardens outside the American Consulate in Shanghai, where her father was in charge of the grounds, and she and her mother were gathering flowers for the table of the consul's wife, who was having a dinner party. The terraces of summer blooms took shape, the boxed hedges, the lawn, the red brick walls of the mansion. And slowly the colors filled in, the greens in the massive trees, the banks of peonies, shading from white to soft pink to fuchsia. She could see her father as a young man working up the slope, and her mother's face glowing with happiness. A cool breeze had been blowing off the river, and the rich and heavy air drifted down from the massive trees that buffered the estate from the city beyond the walls, and her mother was laughing, that shy laugh that was so becoming to her, which welled up out of her when she was happy.

"You must remember this day," her mother had told her on that perfect afternoon. "And whenever you are troubled and need someplace to go, then you can come here again. You understand me, *chi chai, ne?*"

Those times will come again, Honorable Mother, she thought.

She would find a way to bring her mother to the house in Tokyo and dress her in a kimono made of the finest brocade and seat her at a table where the supply of food would be endless.

She stretched out on the futon, the screens still open to the night. And knowing she was so excited she could never sleep, she promptly slept.

When she awakened the next morning her father was already in the field and her mother was in the small kitchen preparing the rice for the day, using fresh charcoal, a sign of the new prosperity. Yuki was suddenly apprehensive. She would be leaving today, and nothing would ever be the same again. She was already homesick for this world that she was losing.

When the rice was done Yuki prepared a small plate with a pinch of rice and placed it on the godshelf in the main room. The Thompsons had told her that the spirits no longer came to the house shrines, that it was just pagan superstition, but there was no way of knowing. In any event, she would have her own small shrine from now on, hanging on the wall of her room in the new house, as if she were carrying her family with her.

She heard her father's voice calling out *"Tadaima"* as he came into the house: "I'm back."

But there was little time for the breakfast of rice and real tea before she heard the distant horn sounding, the driver honking against a flock of geese on the narrow road.

She went to her room and packed all of the things that were precious to her in a small bag, the comb made of ivory her mother had given her in Shanghai, the single picture she had of her father and mother when they were young, the worn Bible from Mrs.

Thompson, a small china doll with arms and legs that could be moved into different positions, and finally the pillow book.

Her mother came into the room and opened the closet. "You must take the kimono with you. It contains the flower crest of my family as well as other flowers. The silk came from Kyoto and the kimono was made in Shanghai." She brought it out, and Yuki took it from her mother and held it with a feeling approaching reverence.

"It is the most beautiful thing in the world."

"Then it is entirely fitting that my beautiful daughter should have it."

"Oh, how I shall miss you," Yuki said, flinging herself into the arms of her mother, who held her close and stroked her hair.

"And I you," her mother said. "You have always been a joy and a comfort to me." She heard the car stop outside and gave her daughter a last embrace.

Yuki wrapped the new kimono with her possessions and paused at the *engawa* to trade her slippers for the wooden *geta,* and for the last time said the ritual words of leaving the house: *"Itte mairimasu.* I am going."

Outside, her mother stared off into the morning haze toward the southwest. It was a mystic belief that on days when the top of the sacred mountain appeared in the sky, good fortune would invariably follow, but Fujiyama did not show herself this morning.

Yuki bowed to her mother and then to her father and turned away quickly lest she cry again. She was so frightened that she was trembling as she got into the car, and all her brave resolutions fled. She did not want to leave. The driver closed the door and then started the engine and pulled down the winding track. Only once, when the car was far from the house, ready to enter the main road toward the village, did Yuki look back.

She soon discovered that she was not to be the only passenger. The driver, a young man with a poor complexion and ill-kempt hair, pulled to a stop at a train station in a small town. The train came into the station like a dragon and a man got off, herding two girls smaller and younger than Yuki. He approached the driver and handed him a paper on which the driver scribbled his chop mark before handing it back.

The train made so much noise that Yuki had trouble hearing the conversation between the two men, but it had to do with the famine in the Tohuku Prefecture, much worse than anything around here, and the great fire at Hakodate, with thousands of deaths. And the train man spoke of the little birds of the north, now plentiful. The driver made a perfunctory bow, opened the back door, and admitted the little girls. They were dressed in ragged kimonos. Both smelled of cinders.

One of the girls, no older than twelve, began to cry inconsolably as the car moved off. The other girl was smaller, eight or nine, with a round moon face, her body no more than bones covered with skin. Yuki tried to talk with the younger one, but the girl was so frightened she could answer only in short bursts of speech. Her father was dead. Her mother too. She did not know where she was going. She did not know the other girl. Yuki put an arm around her to quiet her shivering. Eventually she fell asleep.

"Where did these little girls come from?" Yuki asked the driver. The man shrugged, said nothing. "Where are they going?"

When he didn't answer she sat back and held the girl to her. As the day passed she grew hungry and thirsty and the driver made no provisions for stopping, even to allow the girls to go to the toilet.

In the late afternoon she dozed off, and when she awakened they were in the outskirts of the city, darkness just beginning to set in. The car turned into a maze of narrow streets, the driver constantly honking his horn to force the people on foot to give way. They came to a section of small teahouses among the cherry trees fronting a canal, with Gifu lanterns hanging in colorful strings across the narrow passageways. The lanes were full of men. The driver looked back over his shoulder. "Say *konbanwa* to your new home, little birds," he said.

"There's been a mistake," Yuki said. "I am joining a household."

"That's none of my business," the driver said. "I was paid to deliver you to the Yoshiwara."

"What's the Yoshiwara?" Yuki said.

The driver said nothing more. He leaned on the horn and almost ran down two British sailors before he turned into a lane bounded by heavy walls and finally into a courtyard where there were at least twenty girls standing on the cobblestones, many of them in rags, facing a table where an old man sat with a brush and paper, occasionally clicking the beads of an abacus.

"You will get out here," the driver said, stopping the car.

"What will we do here?" Yuki said, alarmed.

"Keep your silence," the driver said. He reached back and slapped the older girl, who had begun to cry again. The blow was enough to quiet her. She opened the door and climbed out. Yuki kept a grip on her cloth-wrapped parcel, her other hand clutching the bony arm of the little girl. The courtyard was lit by a string of bulbs on an electric cord strung overhead, the light harsh, and Yuki could hear the cries of men from behind another wall.

A woman emerged from the house behind the old man, a woman of indeterminate age whose face had been disfigured in a fire. She carried a willow switch in her left hand, waving it back and forth in front of her.

"Form a line in front of the table," she said to the girls. As if to give emphasis to her command, the switch whistled and stung the leg of the girl closest to her, who moved very quickly to begin a line, the rest of the girls following. "Very good," the woman said with a smile. "You prove that little girls can hop. You also prove that little girls can obey. Now, when you are asked a question, answer very quickly and pleasantly so I will not know how ignorant you really are."

Yuki placed the shivering little girl in front of her. "There's been a terrible mistake," she whispered. "I'll take care of you. Just remember that you're my sister now."

The line moved swiftly. The girls stood before the old man, who gave them a glance, clicked the beads on the abacus, painted numbers and ideograms on the paper below his hand.

He looked at the girl in front of Yuki. "Name," he said flatly.

"There has been a mistake," Yuki interceded. "We are not supposed to be here. This is my little sister, Nakamura Juniko."

She felt a sudden fire across her shoulders as the woman hit her with the willow switch, still smiling. "That was because you did not tell the truth. When the Cricket demands the truth, then you must provide it." She nodded to the shivering girl. "So we shall begin again."

"Your name?" the old man said. The shivering girl spoke in a voice so low that Yuki could not hear. The brush moved deftly. The name was reduced to ink on paper. "Your village?" Again the brush moved. And the old man looked at the Cricket, who peered through slitted, appraising eyes at the girl and then gestured toward a small group at the side of the courtyard.

"Over there," the Cricket said.

Yuki faced the old man, her back still smarting. "There has been a mistake," Yuki said again. "I am to join the household of an important man. He will not like the way I am being mistreated."

"Your name?" the old man said.

"Nakamura Yuki."

"Your village?"

"O-Suzuki-sama made the arrangements. He is a man of influence."

"Your village."

"Towa."

The Cricket glanced at her and then spoke to the old man. "O-Suzuki-sama did buy this one himself. So you will put no price or destination down on the sheet." She motioned with the willow to Yuki. "Follow me and keep up," she said. She led her into an entryway, gave her time to remove her shoes before she proceeded down a corridor into a spacious *ju-jo*, a ten-mat room with clothing on racks, brightly hued kimonos, Western-style clothes, traditional wigs, which looked like raven-winged birds perched on wooden heads. "So," the Cricket said in English, "O-Suzuki-sama says you are worth a lot of money. Are you worth a lot of money?"

"No, Honorable Cricket. I am worthless."

The tip of the willow stung her arm. "O-Suzuki-sama says you are worth a lot of money. Are you worth a lot of money?"

Yuki kept her eyes downcast. "Whatever O-Suzuki-sama says is true."

"*Ii desu,*" the Cricket said. "Very good. Now, take off your clothing."

Yuki did as she was told. She stood naked in the middle of the room.

"There is a mirror on the wall," Cricket said. "Look into the mirror and tell me what you see."

Yuki looked at herself in the mirror. "I see whatever O-Suzuki-sama wishes me to be."

"You learn quickly," Cricket said. She walked around Yuki, examining her, Yuki watching in the mirror. The old woman looked at her breasts. "Large enough. The *gaijin* like larger breasts." The willow touched her buttocks. "Small, tight. Good." It moved down her legs. "Straight legs, well proportioned. Now, lie down."

Yuki did not move quickly enough. The willow stung her. She lay down on the tatami.

"Now, spread your legs."

She spread her legs. The Cricket leaned over and with two fingers spread the folds of flesh. She barked a little laugh. "True, then," she said, straightening up. "You have no idea how many of the fathers lie, just for an extra yen or two. But you are still a virgin. Now, onto your feet again and get dressed," the Cricket said.

Yuki did as she was told and the Cricket wrapped the obi. "You are now a girl from the floating world," she said, "and your kimono opens from the front."

"May I make a request of you, Honorable Cricket? I have not eaten all day."

"And I suppose you will make that complaint to O-Suzuki-sama?"

"I am hungry. I would simply like a bowl of rice."

The Cricket came very close to her now, looking her in the face. "If I wished, I could beat you to death and be thanked for sparing the world a person like you. Do you believe me?"

Yuki kept her eyes downcast, respectful. *"Hai,* Honorable Cricket."

"But you will be useless without food. No man likes a whining woman. Come with me."

With her cloth bundle firmly in hand, Yuki followed the Cricket out of the building and down a narrow lane, her way lit by strings of glowing paper lanterns in bright colors. Against the walls were glass display cases full of pictures of girls, most of them in kimonos, and the Japanese calligraphy for names that were not names, "Thousand Delights," "Spring Moon," the English immediately below the Japanese, and occasionally the photograph of a girl in Western clothing seated on a chair, one leg pulled up so that the flesh showed. The lane was crowded with men, foreign sailors in uniform and Japanese men in business suits and kimonos who studied the pictures, leaned against the walls, smoked cigarettes. Overhead, Yuki saw a narrow strip of black sky. She was very frightened.

They went up a narrow staircase and into a room where experienced girls sat waiting, some of them younger than Yuki, dressed in Japanese wigs, faces powdered chalk white, mouths painted in small bows, kimonos brightly colored, the obi sashes fastened at the front to be easily undone, a mark of their profession. They ignored Yuki as she followed the Cricket down a hallway to a room where the Cricket slid back the door and allowed Yuki to enter.

A Shinto wall shrine was hanging in one corner of the small room, a dressing table below it. "This is my room," the Cricket said. She clapped her hands and a servant came running. The Cricket told her what to do and then sent her on her way with a flick of the willow switch. The Cricket slid open the outside shoji to reveal a miniature Japanese garden with a bridge over a tiny pond, a garden bounded by a high wall. "The wall is to protect the girls as well as keep them in," the Cricket said. "But in these times a girl should have no reason to want to leave. Better that a girl child should be here than drowned, ne? I entertained men myself in the days before the earthquake and the great fire eight years ago. I was hurt by the fire, and I am grateful to O-Suzuki-sama because he gave me a high position here."

The servant returned with a tray on which there was a single bowl of rice with a slice of *daikon* pickle atop it and a pot of tea. Yuki waited until the Cricket had given her permission, and then, protecting the kimono with a bosom cloth, she ate ravenously while the Cricket continued to talk.

"The Yoshiwara has changed," Cricket said. "At one time a girl would come here as a baby, no more than seven years old, and she was properly instructed, not only in the arts of love, but singing, dancing, and the writing of poetry. And perhaps in twelve years she might become an *oiran*, a true courtesan. But look at you." Her face reflected scorn. "You've had no training at all. How are you to pleasure a man?"

"I don't know, Honorable Cricket," Yuki said.

"It is very easy for a girl to make mistakes," the Cricket said. "She becomes the concubine of a man and then she doesn't know what to do to please him. He is a man who has had a thousand women and she has never had a single man. If the girl pleases him, then she has more luxury than she can ever imagine. But if she doesn't, then there are countless other girls and he simply sends the one who has displeased him back to the Yoshiwara. A young woman in your position needs an instructress, a companion, a friend who can tell you what to do."

Yuki finished the rice and the Cricket poured the tea into the rice bowl.

"The only charm you will have to offer is the fact that you have been untouched. When you are first entered it will hurt. You can expect that. You are free to moan if you like, perhaps to cry if it suits you. But you must also pretend that you are feeling exquisite joy, that he is giving you great pleasure. Caress him. Call him 'lord.'

Pretend that you are so enslaved to what pleasure he has given you that you want even more of it." She laughed, a muted cackle. "He will not be able to do it more than once. But if you are skillful enough in your acting, he will be fooled because he wants to believe. Would you like more rice, more tea?"

Yuki laid the chopsticks in the proper position within the tray to show that she wanted no more. *"Gochiso-sama de gozaimashita,"* she said. The Cricket stood up, holding the willow switch beneath her arm. It was obvious she would no longer need it here.

"I should like one favor, Honorable Cricket, should all this fortune come to an unworthy person like myself. The girl who was with me in the courtyard, the one I claimed as my sister, I should like to have her as a servant."

The Cricket grimaced. "She is meat for the dogs."

"What happened to her?"

"She works downstairs. She was considered unworthy of training. You would have to buy her from the man who bought her. Perhaps I can do that for you."

"I am most grateful," Yuki said.

And now, for the first time, the Cricket made a light bow to her. "You should rest. I will come for you directly so that you may have a bath and then I will dress you."

With that she hobbled out of the room and slid the door closed, leaving behind a tired and very frightened girl.

At eight o'clock Yuki followed Cricket down the twisting back lanes of the Yoshiwara to Suzuki-san's house. She went through the servants' entrance and up a long flight of stairs to the bedroom with the Cricket beside her, hopping along, humming to herself.

Yuki was in awe at the bedroom. Twenty mats in size at the least, and there was a carpet on the floor, with intricate weavings of flowers. The bed stood on stilted legs, with a mattress at least the thickness of two hands with fingers spread, a brocaded silk canopy over the top. One wall was mirrored. She sat on the bed and stared at her reflection.

She had never seen a room of such luxury, with a sliding door that opened onto a terrace with potted plants in such profusion, she felt she was in a forest. Beyond them she saw the river and heard the calls of the boatmen echoing through the darkness, the rumble of thunder across the sky.

The Cricket stood near the door, watching her with great interest. "A beautiful room, *ne?*" she said.

Yuki put her wrapped bundle out of sight beneath the bed, only half listening, for she had discovered a door that led to a toilet with a seat instead of the customary foot tiles on either side of a slot. She came back into the bedroom while the Cricket stood at the open wall, looking at her.

"When you are taken by the *gaijin* you remember to tell him that you have a servant retainer you must have if you are to become a part of his house. He will agree. It's done all the time. It will cost him nothing in wages because I will do the shopping and keep back part of the money. That's only proper. And you may have the shivering girl as well."

"Certainly, Honorable Cricket. I am sure I will need your help."

"Of course you will. I never doubted it," the Cricket said. She looked over the room, then at the floral carpet with a crest in the center of it. "Come here, my little bird." And she placed Yuki in the center of the carpet and had her kneel, then arranged the folds of the soft peach silk kimono to spread around her like the petals of a flower. "How perfect and rare you are. But you will have your beauty for only a brief time and then the gods, whichever ones you believe in, will take it all away. Now, do you remember everything I've told you?"

"You're not leaving now?"

"Of course." The Cricket smiled. "I've done my work and soon you must do yours. Remember that a proper moan at the right time will do no harm."

"*Hai,* Honorable Cricket."

Then she was alone in the room and the rain began, pelting down hard on the slate roof.

When the men entered the room she prostrated herself, terrified, touching her forehead to her hands, flat on the floor. She heard Suzuki-san's voice as he stood near the door. "Judge her for yourself, Kingsley-san, worthless creature that she is." The *gaijin* walked without making any noise at all. She could see nothing more than his feet clad in silk socks, the cuffs of his white trousers. Her breath was half suspended in her throat as he approached, leaned over her, and with one gentle hand touched her hair.

"Look up at me, please," he said in English. She raised her face.

He was a tall, lean man in his fifties and his eyes seemed to be full of a great sadness. "What is your name, child?"

"Yuki, my lord."

He looked at her face, the absolute clarity of her skin, the aristocratic bone structure and the clear dark eyes, the hair blue-black, like a raven's wing, and he thought her the most exquisite girl he had ever seen. He ran his hand beneath the hair at the nape of her neck. "Has anyone ever told you how beautiful you are?"

"I am your unworthy servant, my lord."

He removed his hand and stood looking at her for a long time, then nodded as if he had come to a conclusion. He rejoined Suzuki at the door and he led Kingsley to the dining room, furnished Western style, chosen because Kingsley liked to sit while he ate.

"How much?" Kingsley said quietly.

"Let me consider awhile," Suzuki said. "And if it pleases you, I will have the dinner served." The servant women moved in silently to arrange the table, and from another room, screened from sight, came the harplike music of a *koto*, almost lost in the drumming of the rain.

After dinner they sat in a darkness broken only by candles and the lightning, which was almost continual now. The koto had long since stopped playing. Suzuki-san knew that even through all the conversation and the food, the girl had never left Kingsley's mind. But Suzuki-san did not mention her himself. He simply outwaited the *gaijin*, who, with a glass of plum brandy in his hand, came back to the point.

"I will give you three hundred dollars for the girl in the room."

"Her price is one thousand dollars, a cheap price as you know, having seen her. But only if you take twenty-five of the girls from the Tohuku District at thirty dollars apiece."

Kingsley sat in darkness, smoked a cigarette, thinking. "I don't need more than ten girls for the Kobe brothel," he said. "And even twenty-five dollars apiece is much too high." He exhaled the smoke. "I don't want to connect one transaction with another. I'll pay you a thousand for the girl in the room. And I'll consider the girls from Tohuku."

"I don't want to sell the special girl alone," Suzuki-san said, his irritation leaking through.

Kingsley ground out his cigarette. "A thousand dollars is a lot of money."

Suzuki-san said nothing, waiting.

Finally, Kingsley spoke again. "I'll be in touch with you tomorrow," he said. "Thank you so much for the evening. It's been a pleasure."

The evening was now over, Suzuki thought, and no deal had been concluded. He saw Kingsley to the entrance to the house, where a servant helped him with his shoes and another held an umbrella over his head until he reached his car. Suzuki watched the red taillights diminish in the rain and, fuming with anger, went into his drawing room. The *gaijin* had bested him, knowing very well that money was indeed tight and that Suzuki would not be able to turn down a thousand dollars for a single girl, no matter how beautiful she was. And Kingsley would try to cheat him on the girls from Tohuku. Suzuki drank sake for the next half hour, his anger increasing with each cup. And when he was drunk enough, he stood up unsteadily and made his way into the hall.

Yuki was standing at the window when Suzuki came back into the room. She sank to her knees, confused by his presence and by the car she had just seen driving away. The *gaijin* lord had left without her. Here in his place was Suzuki-san, his face flushed red from too much wine, muttering to himself. He sat down in a soft chair near the door, clapped his hands, and when his servant appeared ordered another bottle of sake.

She did not move, afraid he would strike her.

The bottle was brought to him on a tray. He poured a drink while she remained frozen, knowing he was looking at her. He drank.

"The *gaijin* always tries to take advantage of me," he said in a slurred voice, as if he were talking to himself. "I can't afford not to sell and he knows it, but you are still my property now." He poured more wine into the cup. "And I didn't promise him a virgin."

She said nothing.

"Raise your head when I speak to you."

She looked at him. In the light of the candles, his skin was flushed a deep red. She was now paralyzed with fear.

"Go to the bed," Suzuki-san said.

She raised to her feet, wanting nothing more than to escape from him, but he staggered toward her, hit her with the back of his hand, and sent her sprawling onto the bed.

Stunned, she looked up. He was standing there, parting his kimono, and his male organ leapt out, erect, more fiery than his face. His hands grabbed at her shoulder with such force that she screamed. The sounds she made were lost in the thunder and the incessant drumming of the rain. He ripped at her kimono and with his other hand forced her legs open, thrusting his penis at her. In absolute panic, she rolled away from him. He scrambled after her, yelling at her to stop where she was or he would kill her.

Her hand closed around the brass incense burner, the joss stick falling to the floor. She swung at his face just as he was in the act of turning and caught him on the side of the head. His spectacles flew off his face and his eyes rolled upward. He sagged unconscious on the side of the bed and then rolled heavily to the floor while she stood in hysterical shock, the terror of being attacked giving way to the terror of having killed this man. She hid her face in her hands, and then, abruptly, she pushed the panic away from her. She would have to save herself. She heard Suzuki groan. Not dead. Quickly she retrieved her bundle from underneath the bed. She took off the torn kimono, put on her old clothing.

The police will kill me. They will cut off my head.

She stood up, listening to the thunder. She had to think clearly. Very shortly one of the servants would come to this room and discover the man lying unconscious on the floor and they would put out the alarm for her. She would have to leave here, but where would she go?

Home was impossible, the first place they would look for her.

The missionaries, the Thompsons. She would go to the compound in Ueno.

She opened the door cautiously, peered out into the darkened hallway, realized that with the storm the electricity had disappeared. A lantern gave off a faint glow near the front stairs. She went in the opposite direction, staying close to the wall, looked around a corner before she proceeded down the back stairs, paused near the entrance to the kitchen, where the cook was eating with his staff. The back door. Out into the rain. The water soaked her through, took her breath away. She followed the narrow lanes until she reached the wall that separated the Yoshiwara from the city.

The only lights were from occasional oil lamps at the back entrances to the buildings, faint lights through the screen of rain. And then she saw a lantern at a gate in the wall and the shape of a man in the window of the small gate house. He was eating rice from a tin *bento* with his chopsticks. She shivered, knowing she would have to take the chance. She could not see it clearly, but the bottom of the wooden gate seemed to clear the ground by at least eight inches. She lowered herself to the ground, crawled along the wall, pausing every few seconds to make sure the man was inside the gate house.

When she reached the gate she lay on her back and inched her way beneath it, a little at a time. Then she froze. The cloth of her kimono had caught on the wood at the bottom of the gate and would not come loose. She forced her hand to stop trembling, then ran her fingers along the wood in the darkness until she found the snag, and praying silently to the Lord Jesus and the Lord Buddha, she worked the cloth free and then pushed on until she was clear of the gate.

Outside. Free.

She crawled into the dark street beyond. Only when she was beyond the sight of the guard did she begin to run.

A nightmare, wandering through unfamiliar streets in the rain, none of them named, knowing only that Ueno had a large railway station somewhere to the south of the Yoshiwara, with the mission compound close enough that she had been able to hear the trains in the night.

So she followed a railroad track and stumbled upon the compound shortly before dawn. She pulled the rope and rang the bell. The heavy wooden door swung open and a Japanese man let her in. The courtyard was crowded with families huddled in every open space, oilcloth raised on sticks for shelter against the rain. She rang the bell at the door of the north building and shortly a light went on and Elsa came to the door, a robe over her nightgown. Yuki burst into tears and threw herself into the comforting arms of the woman, who took her into a warm room where she dried her off and gave her warm clothing and then listened as Yuki blurted out her story.

"You're safe now, child," Elsa said in her soothing voice. "Nobody can touch you here. You'll have a bowl of soup and then sleep."

Yuki slept until midafternoon, awakened by the sound of the Salvation Army brass band playing on the street in front of the mission and Captain Thompson's booming voice exhorting his listeners to repent and seek the kingdom of God. She found Elsa in the massive kitchen where the rice pots were steaming and a dozen volunteer Japanese women were preparing fish for the evening meal. There would be at least two hundred people to feed tonight, and the lines were already forming outside the compound gates. When she saw Yuki, Elsa dried her hands on her ample apron and spirited her into a makeshift parlor furnished with odds and ends of chairs and tables and a bookcase.

"I think it wise for you to stay out of sight," Elsa said.

The street service was over and Captain Thompson came into the parlor. He greeted Yuki and then wiped his gleaming trumpet with a cloth and laid it to rest in a velvet-lined case. He studied Yuki sorrowfully over his half-moon glasses. "I would not have sent you home had I known this would happen, and I am glad you came back to us, child. We will keep you safe. I promise you that," he said. "Now sit down, for there are things we must talk about."

"Yes, sir," she said. She sat on an old horsehair divan.

Elsa came in, bringing a tea tray.

"I don't want to get you into trouble, sir," Yuki said. "I came here because there was no place else to go."

Thompson accepted a cup of tea from his wife, stirred it absently, giving himself time to think. "I went out to Towa this morning and I saw a lot of cars at your house," he said, sipping his tea. "I was questioned by the police because they knew you came to the mission truck for English lessons. I could tell them without lying that I had not seen you. I was also questioned by some gangsters who said you had been sold to a man named Suzuki and that you had run away." He looked directly into her eyes. "Did your father sell you?"

"No, you do not understand. Suzuki was a go-between," Yuki said. She told him of the gifts. "I was supposed to join the household of a very wealthy man."

Thompson sipped his tea thoughtfully. "Suzuki may have bought you to sell to another man. But you would have become a harlot."

"I believe Suzuki deceived my father. He is an evil man," Yuki said.

"Did you strike Suzuki?"

"Yes." She felt very ashamed. "He hit me and tore my kimono and pushed his thing at me."

"Suzuki considers you to be his property," Thompson said. "He's lost face. So he will have to punish you, if he can. Do you have any relatives elsewhere in Japan?"

"No."

"It's apparent that you won't be able to stay here. Would you be too frightened to go out of the country by yourself?"

"To where?"

"Back to Shanghai, I think, where you were born. You might feel at home there. I believe I can get you on as a clerk in the American Legation. The American chaplain there is a good friend of mine."

"I was born in the servants' quarters of the old consulate. It was my home."

"I'll send a wire this afternoon," he said. "We should have an answer by tomorrow morning. Now, bow your head." He propped his elbows on the low table, clasped his hands together and placed them against his forehead. "Oh, Lord Jesus," he said, "we ask Thy protection for your servants in this far and heathen land. We ask your compassionate safety for this new child of yours. Protect and guide her on the right path." He unfolded his hands and looked at Yuki, his face worried. "We'll work it out, with God's help," he said. "But until we do, it's better if you stay out of sight."

"Yes, sir," Yuki said. "I understand."

Suzuki's men came in the middle of the night. They seemed to materialize in the street outside the compound, a dozen of them. They poured through the door and swarmed into the courtyard with torches and lanterns, ripping away the makeshift lean-tos to examine the people, who stared up at them with expressionless faces.

They broke into the dispensary, which served as a makeshift hospital, moved from bed to bed, looking at the patients. It was there that Thompson intercepted them, just as they were about to open a closet where Yuki had taken refuge when she first heard the furor in the streets.

"Who are you?" Thompson said firmly in Japanese. "What do you want?"

"We come from O-Suzuki-sama," one of the men said. "He only wants what is his."

"And destroys what is mine," Thompson said. "Tell O-Suzuki-sama that I will meet with him tomorrow night to discuss this problem."

"You have one of his girls."

"I am a captain in God's army and I will discuss nothing with men who break into the house of God," Thompson said. He looked imperious in his uniform. "Tell Suzuki I will be at his house in the Yoshiwara tomorrow night at nine o'clock. And now you will leave this place. You have no further business here."

"We can tear your buildings down," the leader said. "We can burn everything that's left."

"Yes," Thompson said. "And I am an American citizen and my government will speak to your government on my behalf and you will have brought shame to Suzuki-sama. You have at least a hundred witnesses to what is being said here. If you wish to bring shame to him, then do it. If not, then I ask you to leave and let me settle this with your master."

The leader hesitated. He barked out orders to his men, who moved out of the compound and back into the street.

Only when they were gone did Thompson open the closet to free Yuki. His face was drawn, pale. "You're safe for now," he said. "But we have to get you out of here."

At noon the next day the telegram came from Shanghai, from a Reverend Litton:

YOUR REQUEST GRANTED. BLESSED BE THE NAME OF THE LORD. ADVISE ARRIVAL TIME. LITTON.

Elsa went to her husband, who sat in the living room, the cash box open, looking very worried. "We have enough to send her steerage," he said. "And I have enough left over to try to make reparations to Suzuki. But he'll have his people watching the compound. How will we get her to Yokohama and the ship?"

"The Lord will provide," Elsa said.

At noon the truck came into the compound carrying the bulging bags of rice. When it left, full of empty sacks, Yuki was beneath them, in the back. The man watching the compound for Suzuki was smoking a cigarette as the truck went past him. He did not bother to inspect it.

The long day finally passed and the time came for Ernest to leave for the meeting with Suzuki. Elsa kissed him, held him close to her for a moment, then sent him on his way. She sat down at her desk to wait, unable to work.

The minutes became hours. All at once she came awake with a start. One of the Japanese women cooks had touched her shoulder. The woman looked positively bereft.

"Nan desuka?" Elsa said. "What's wrong?"

"You must come, please," the woman said, beginning to cry. "It is terrible."

Alarmed, Elsa pushed past her, rushing out into the courtyard where two men were carrying someone through the gate. He was covered with blood, moaning. She went cold, rushed to him. "Ernest," she said with a cry and told the men to put him down. Both of his legs were canted at an obscene angle below the knee, where the bones had been broken. The blue uniform was stained with blood. She stifled the scream that was about to escape her. In a cool, clear voice she told one of the men to go down the street and bring the doctor.

She knelt beside her husband, who was trying to talk through a swollen mouth. She put her fingers between his lips and pulled out the wad of bank notes that had been stuffed there. They were covered with blood. "You be quiet," she said to him. "I've called for the doctor, dear. I intend to call for the police."

"No," he said, close to exhaustion, in shock. "The police will already know. They won't do anything."

"They can't be allowed to—"

"We saved a girl today. That's worth . . . everything." He passed out.

New York City . . .
June 1931

SAM CUMMINGS STOOD in the drenching rain of the June thunderstorm, soaked through, watching the sling at the end of the crane lowering his father's coffin in a slow arc from the ship to the New York dock. A representative from the American Consulate in Shanghai stood beneath an umbrella and signed the necessary documents. Phillip Halston was doing the family a kindness by accompanying the body back to New York on his way to retirement after a lifetime in the foreign service. He inspected the teak bracing in which the metal coffin had been packed and the unbroken Chinese seals in the company of a custom's inspector and Sam's Uncle Roger.

Sam watched the black hearse pulling into place, the four men sliding the packed coffin in the back. The vehicle pulled away slowly in the rain.

"I suggest that we buy Mr. Halston a drink," Roger said. His voice gave Sam goose bumps because the timbre was so like his father's. "Of course, that's up to you," Roger said. "This must be quite a shock to you, my boy."

No shock because it's all a monstrous mistake and it's not the body of my father in that coffin. My father is still in Shanghai, very much alive, noisy, perhaps a little drunk, but living every moment of his life, loving it.

"I'd like to talk to Mr. Halston," Sam said. "I have some questions to ask him."

"Of course." Uncle Roger led the way to his car, holding the door for Halston. Roger instructed the driver to take them to a brownstone on the East Side.

They were admitted to an elegant foyer where a maître d' smiled recognition upon Uncle Roger. An ornately carved door was buzzed open to admit them to a bar and restaurant. They sat at a table against a wall of the windowless room. When the drinks were served Sam downed his immediately, impatient at the small talk. Since Uncle Roger was with State, the two men had a great deal in common, and they chatted about Halston's retirement in Virginia and what he intended to do with his time now that it belonged to him. Reading, yes. Piles of books waiting on shelves. Fish waiting in sun-dappled streams for Halston's feathered lure. A kennel waiting to be populated with golden retrievers.

My father's dead. He's not retiring. Nothing but the cold ground for him.

He shivered slightly and thought he might never be warm again. "Mr. Halston, your letter said that my father killed himself."

"Yes."

"Exactly how did he do it?"

"The Settlement Police in Shanghai conducted an investigation," Halston said. He cleared his throat and obviously had a hard time summoning the next words. "There was a gun lying on the floor. Apparently, he shot himself. He felt no pain, as far as we know."

Sam felt the alcohol singing through his veins. "Why in the hell did he do that?" he said. "Why would he kill himself?"

"I have no real idea," Halston said.

"You can guess," Sam said. "My father was a very colorful man. I lived over there long enough to know that there must have been talk around the consulate."

"All I have is gossip."

"Such as?"

"He had a ruinous financial run," Halston said, with some hesitation. "He had spent a lot of money. No one seems to know where it went, but it must have been a series of bad investments." Sam had a feeling that Halston was holding something back. "I thank God for a prudent wife who invested our savings in a small farm near Richmond."

"My father had nothing left?"

Halston was momentarily embarrassed. "The Consulate General used discretionary funds to ship the body home."

"He was totally broke, then."

"Unfortunately."

"But he was worth millions of dollars at one time. . . ."

"I used to envy that about Arnold," Roger said. "He gambled in business on an extraordinary scale. I remember one year when he was up two million dollars American on a deal that took two weeks." He studied the blue smoke rising from the end of his cigar. "I think he relied on luck too much and one day his luck ran out."

"Are there any other questions I can answer for you?" Halston said. "I'll have to be thinking about catching my train shortly."

Yes, what is it you're not telling me? Sam thought. *My father lost his money but he wasn't a man to give up. He would've just picked himself up and started again. He wouldn't have taken the coward's way out.*

"No," Sam said. "Thank you."

"Your uncle tells me that you just graduated from Harvard and intend to assume a post in Shanghai shortly."

"Yes."

"How many years did you spend in China with your father?"

"My mother brought me home when I was twelve. I was back for one more summer when I was seventeen."

Halston's face reflected an obvious distaste. "It's changed. What was once enchanting is odious now. The Chinese are dying like flies from disease and starvation. There's no way to get rid of the stink of constant decay. I was told that one gets used to it after a while but I never did. It remains in my nostrils. I'm hoping the good Virginia air will clear it out. And I would advise you, young man, to take an assignment in Europe instead, someplace more civilized. China is nothing more than a dead end for any career."

"I'm afraid what he's saying is quite true, Samuel," Roger said.

"I appreciate your advice," Sam said.

But I won't take it. I've spent all my life preparing for a life in that country and I have even more reason to go now.

Shortly, Halston left to catch his train. "Good man, that Halston,"

Roger said, dismissing him. "I'm sorry your mother wasn't well enough to come down here today. I hope it's nothing serious."

"She has a cold," Sam said, lying, knowing that his uncle realized it as well. "She wants to be in shape for the funeral."

Not true, of course, because his mother was quite outspoken about her reasons for not coming to the dock. "I'm sure your father would never have wanted to be dragged home for burial," she had said to him only that morning. "He chose China over both of us a long time ago. I'll go to the funeral because it's the right thing to do, but you and your uncle will have to take care of things at the dock."

Sam signaled the waiter for another drink.

They drove back to the penthouse after the funeral. Noble Rawlings and his daughter, Charlotte, shared the limousine with Sam, his mother, and Uncle Roger. Sam's mother did not speak in the limousine. She turned her face to the window so Sam could see her only in a black-veiled profile. His father's voice whispered in his memory, full of pride: *She's like a rare Chinese porcelain, son, delicate and impractical, as helpless in her beauty as an empress with bound feet.*

Not true, Father, Sam answered without speaking. For his mother had gone through the ceremony without one tear, her gloved hands folded demurely in her lap or fondling the string of pearls that lay against the bodice of her black dress. No, the appearance was deceiving, that illusion of fragility which his mother projected. She had been strong enough to pull away from China and take Sam with her to be educated in the United States, all alone, with no help other than money from a husband who was far more interested in adventure and oriental fortunes than he was in the sedate life of the New York banker he would have become.

The Orient gets in your blood, his father used to say, both sober and in his cups, as if the one cliché excused all sins of omission and commission.

During the ride Noble sat in the front seat with the chauffeur so that he could smoke a cigar with the wing window opened a crack to suck the smoke out. A handsome, dignified man, Sam thought, with a Brahmin face that showed breeding and the vast resources at his disposal. It was no wonder that he and Sam's mother had been attracted to each other. Sam thought of the day six months ago when he had come home unannounced on holiday from Harvard, walked into the library, and found his mother and Noble in an embrace, kissing, and he had ducked away, burning with anger that his father was being betrayed. He had confronted neither of them because he did not want to be lied to. And he had not known what to write to his father about it. So he had written nothing. It was just as well now. His father would have suffered needless pain.

The penthouse was on Eighty-sixth Street, overlooking the park to the west, a spacious residence purchased many years ago during a time when Arnold was making millions and his wife had decided to come home from Shanghai and needed a residence. When they reached it Adele excused herself to change her clothes.

Sam wandered into the library, where Charlotte was serving Noble a drink. "Would you like a plate of something light, Father?" she asked.

"Not at the moment, my dear. Thank you."

"How about you, Sam?"

"A beer," he said. "But I can get it myself."

"I'll get it for you," she said.

He had met her the day he came home from China at the age of twelve. She and her father had been at the boat. She was a shy, awkward little girl then. He had seen her often over the years, and liked her well enough, but did not feel that he had ever come to know her. She brought him a beer. "I think I'll see if your mother needs anything," she said.

And she was gone. "Condolences," Noble said, raising his glass slightly.

Sam nodded. He tasted his beer and looked around him. Of all the rooms in any house, the library had always been his father's choice. He had sent his favorite books back here, to be shelved and catalogued, as if one day in his old age he would move back to the States and sit in the rich leather of the wing-back chair near the window and systematically go through his precious collection. But of course he would not, and Sam was not sure he ever really intended to come home.

Sam stood by the window, watched Noble as he sat down in that leather wing-back chair, adjusted the crease in the black trousers before he crossed his legs. "Would you like a cigar?" Noble said.

"No thank you," Sam said. "But I do have some questions about my father's business."

"Certainly, son," Noble said.

"I just don't understand how this could have happened."

Noble cut the end of the cigar with a gold clipper. He lit it, lean cheeks sucking in. "What, exactly?"

"You were in the same businesses together. You had a corporation together. Yet you're rich and he went broke."

"We *were* in a corporation together at one time. But Arnold dissolved it to go his own way."

"I'd like to see the records of the corporation."

"Your mother has the papers, such as they are," Noble said. "They're limited to the time of dissolution, of course." The blue smoke hung over him like a cloud. "Your father was my dear friend as well as my partner for many years. You know that."

"Do you know specifically how my father lost his fortune?"

"Does it really matter?" Noble asked.

"Yes, it does."

"So you're now officially Harvard, Class of '31. That's quite an accomplishment for a young man who's just come of age. And I understand you did very well academically."

"What does any of that have to do with this?"

"You learned the economics of the China trade, I'm sure," Noble said. "And with your degree, I'm sure your uncle would have no trouble getting you assigned to Shanghai. If you're curious, you can track the dissipation of your father's money in a year or two, but I hate to see you waste the time. You're a man now, old enough to accept the facts of life. What happened was unfortunate, even tragic, but it can't be changed." He took another pull on the cigar. "I've known you all your life, so I hope you won't take it amiss if I make a suggestion to you."

"What kind of suggestion?" Sam said.

"I've always looked on myself as a member of the family. I'd be delighted to have you in my company here, a comfortable salary, just to let you get the feel of the business world and see if you like it. Then, in a year or two, you can make a more objective decision about China."

"I appreciate the offer," Sam said. "But I was trained for China. I belong there. And I really want to know everything that happened to my father."

Noble nodded, accepting. "I understand. If there's anything I can do to help you, please let me know."

The conservatory's multipaned windows opened on the park to the west. It was a combination greenhouse and music room, with a grand piano that had been manufactured in Europe and then decorated by Chinese artisans in Shanghai, delivered to his mother one Christmas as a surprise present. It was an immense piano that had cost his father a fortune to have built and decorated and shipped, and when it arrived there was no way of getting it to the penthouse except through the costly removal of a terrace door and part of an exterior wall, followed by the hiring of a crane to lift it.

Nobody ever played it, and it seemed strange now to Sam to see Charlotte sitting on the ornate bench, brushing her hair back with the long fingers of her right hand while the left rested on the ivory keys. Twilight was approaching, the sun rapidly fading over the trees to the west. He did not want to be here making conversation with Charlotte when he longed for the comfort of Diane in Cambridge.

Charlotte pulled her sandy hair to the side, a gesture that gave her narrow face and long neck a kind of elegance in repose. Her black mourning dress draped gracefully over her slim body and made the pale flesh of her arms seem very white by contrast.

"I wish I'd had the chance to really know your father," she said. "You must miss him terribly."

"It's the suddenness of it," he said. "I always assumed I'd get together with him again in China this fall."

She looked out the window, her eyes sad. "What will you do now?"

"Probably go to China anyway."

"Father said he was going to talk to you about staying here and joining the firm."

"He did. Yes."

"That must seem terribly dull to you after growing up in China. But we would enjoy having you here if you decide to stay. I haven't really seen much of you since you've been at Harvard."

"It was a pretty demanding schedule. But enough of me. Would you play something on the piano?"

"I'm not very good, but I'll try."

She adjusted her skirt over her legs, reached out to touch the pedals with her feet.

She began to play a Johann Strauss waltz. It took him a moment to realize that Charlotte's personality matched the way she played the piano. All the notes were there and in the right order, but there was no feeling in them. She was so intent on getting them perfect that the notes just hung separately in the air and there was no melody.

Poor Charlotte, he thought, deciding that before the night was out he would get drunk. *You're never going to get married, because any man could listen to you play the piano and have a sure and certain knowledge of what married life with you would be like.* He ached for Diane.

By nine o'clock they were all gone. Sam was left alone with his mother and all of the food Noble had ordered in, plates of cold cuts and cheeses and liquor bottles that had not been opened. He checked on his mother, found the door to her bedroom still closed.

He was restless and went for a walk in the warm night air, south along the edge of the park, the dark sky threatening rain. By the time he arrived back at the penthouse, his mother was in the library, dressed in her at-home clothes, her reading glasses on her nose, going over some official-looking papers in front of her, a bottle of brandy on the desk.

"Noble said you wanted to see these," she said, handing him the papers. "You won't find anything there except the beginning of your father's financial disaster."

He glanced through the sheets, the accountant's reports, all of the legal documents stamped and embossed with a notary's seal, everything seemingly in order, the partnership between Arnold and Noble Rawlings dissolved.

"Your father was very good at finding opportunities in that partnership, but Noble was the stable businessman. Once the corporation was dissolved, it was just a matter of time until your father went under." She pulled another paper from the stack. "Do you know anything about insurance?"

"Some," he said. "Is that the policy Uncle Roger was holding?"

She pushed her glasses up on her forehead and handed the papers across to him. "Read the clause I've circled in pencil."

He scanned through it, shook his head. "A suicide clause?"

"Yes."

"Jesus," he said. "You don't think he killed himself just to provide you with a hundred thousand dollars in insurance money."

"Yes, I do," she said, her voice cold. "Do you have a cigarette?"

"You don't smoke, Mother."

"I do now. Do you have a cigarette?"

He shook one out of a pack and lit it for her.

She sucked the smoke into her lungs. "Even so, he had been away too long to have any sense of proportion. I've been going over the expenses on this apartment. The maintenance fees and the servants alone cost about two thousand dollars a month. And Roger was holding a mortgage your father took against it sometime ago so there are payments of a thousand dollars a month there. If I sell it in the present market, I'll be lucky to break even and I'll find myself on the street in the process."

"You won't end up on the street."

"Oh? And who's to prevent it?"

"I know about you and Noble. I've known a long time."

She looked at him icily. "And what is it you think you know?"

"Christ, you can't very well deny it. I don't blame father for not coming home."

"You don't know what you're talking about," she said, flaring.

"I'm talking about your rich lover, Mother. And you can tell him for me that he can take his goddamned offer and shove it up his ass."

In a single move she stood up and slapped him across the face with such force that his ears rang. "You will not talk to me that way. How dare you"—she was breathing hard—"how dare you take your father's side in anything," she said. "I didn't desert your father. He deserted *us*, you as well as me. He never intended to come back to us and I had to have someone." She snatched up the insurance paper, held it in front of her like a sword. "This was typical of him, an empty gesture poorly planned." She sank back into the chair, drained. She dropped the insurance papers onto the desk, picked up the brandy glass. "That's the way things are. You'll have to learn to live with them just as I will."

"I apologize," he said after a while. He had a headache. "What you do is none of my business." He picked up the brandy, drank from the bottle, looked around the room. "There's no way you can maintain this standard of living. But I can help support you."

"Doing what?" she asked with no irony in her voice. "As I understand it, you have a degree in international affairs and you're fluent in Chinese. There's not much demand for experts in international affairs during a worldwide Depression, and if any business wants somebody who speaks Chinese and English, they can find a thousand qualified people in Chinatown who'll work for fifteen cents an hour. Are you willing to work for Noble?"

"I'm trained for the Foreign Service. I can make money in China on the side. You don't need to worry."

"You'll have a hard time living on your beginning salary, and China will ruin you just like it ruined your father. I'll take care of myself, but it will require a sacrifice from you. You owe me that."

"What kind of sacrifice?"

"We won't talk about it now. But when the time comes, I expect you to make it willingly."

When he went to bed he took a bottle of scotch with him, and once he was in his pajamas, he began to drink it, a shot at a time. He could not get the expression on his mother's face out of his mind.

Goddamn it, Pop, I loved you. You did not go out of this world unloved.

And only then did he weep, heartbroken, until at last the cumulative effect of the whiskey hit him and he passed out.

Three days later he went over to the Harvard Club to have lunch with his Uncle Roger. They were seated at a table next to a window. A white-jacketed waiter approached with menus, which Uncle Roger declined. "We won't need those, Woodrow. What do you recommend?"

"The filet of sole is excellent today, Mr. Cummings, sir."

"Then that's what it will be."

"Would you care for wine, sir?"

"No. One needs a clear mind in these times."

"I don't care if mine's a little cloudy," Sam said. "Bring me a bourbon and water, Woodrow."

"Yes, sir."

"Well," Uncle Roger said, once the waiter had departed, "how are you feeling, my boy?"

"Better," Sam said. "But I would like to talk to you."

"Concerning what?"

"My father's business and how he could have lost so much money."

"Your father never talked to me about his business affairs, but sometime after he dissolved his business with Noble, he contacted me, wanted to borrow a large amount of money."

"Did you lend it to him?"

Roger smiled. "A deputy for the Far East doesn't make that kind of money."

"It's all so damned frustrating," Sam said. "I can't seem to get any facts."

"We all have to accept what life brings us, in the end." The salad was served and Uncle Roger set about decimating the lettuce while Sam nursed the bourbon and water. "I've secured an appointment in Shanghai for you if you want it. Halston's departure left an opening. This is highly confidential, my boy, but you would be collecting information for us out there, sending back regular reports."

"Are you saying I'm to be a spy?" Sam said, amused.

"That's not the language I would use, exactly. But it's a highly volatile part of the world and we have to know what's going on. Ostensibly, you'd be assigned as an aide to the consul but he would also be aware of your real mission. Very little money but a good opportunity. Do you have your sheepskin firmly in hand?"

"Yes."

"Then take a little time to consider it."

"I don't need to think it over. I want the job."

The main course was served. "Isn't this a splendid piece of sole?" Uncle Roger said before he began to pick it apart with his fork. "The food is always excellent here." He talked very little during his lunch. Once it was finished he ordered lime sherbet and coffee and then got down to what he had been avoiding during the meal.

"Now, we have some other matters to discuss, Sam, since we're the sole remaining males in this branch of the Cummings family." He removed a paper from his inside jacket pocket. "I've made an assessment of your father's remaining assets. Aside from the insurance, there's an equity remaining in the penthouse, a couple of automobiles, considerable amounts of stock, which frankly aren't worth much, a few first-edition books, your mother's jewelry, which is not to be considered, and nothing else. It comes to a total of, let me see here, yes, one hundred twenty-seven thousand four hundred and thirteen dollars and twenty-six cents."

"Not very much," Sam said.

"No, not very much." Roger was slightly uncomfortable. "Do you have a regular girl, Sam?"

Sam smiled. "All of my girls are slightly irregular. But if you mean am I seeing a girl regularly, the answer's yes. Her name is Diane and she will be finishing at Radcliff next spring."

"Is it serious?"

"I'm very fond of her, but I'm not ready to get married. Especially now."

"It's generally a wise move to be married when you take your first post abroad," Uncle Roger said. "The department seems to advance married officers much more quickly than the single ones. It's considered a sign of maturity."

"Are you suggesting I pop the question to Diane?"

Now his uncle's face was very serious. "Do you love her?"

"We have some good times together."

"In diplomatic language, that would mean uncertainty." His uncle did not look at him directly. "How do you feel about Charlotte Rawlings?"

Sam felt the dread settling over him. The real subject of the discussion had now surfaced. "She's all right, I guess."

"What does 'all right' mean exactly?"

"It means I have nothing against her but I don't have anything for her either. We've grown up together, and I'd say, just offhand, that she's the blandest girl I've ever met. Besides, I don't like her father. He ended up rich and my father ended up dead. Do you need any more reasons?"

"Noble's not such a bad person once you get to know him. As a matter of fact, he feels a great sense of responsibility both to you and his daughter. He's very concerned about Charlotte's dependency on him ever since his wife died."

"What does that have to do with me?" Sam asked, his stomach tightening.

"I told Noble that I would feel you out concerning a possible marriage between you and Charlotte."

"No."

"Just hear me out before you make a decision."

"It's already made. Charlotte's not the right girl for me."

"Perhaps not in a romantic way," Uncle Roger said relentlessly. "But this is something far more important than a simple marriage. Your mother is a fine businesswoman, but it's impossible to make something from nothing. Can you imagine her existing in any place other than the penthouse? Living without servants?"

"No," Sam said, wishing the bourbon would take hold, make the moment easier. "I can't imagine it."

"Noble's a very wealthy man and a generous one. He has fixed a dowry of two million dollars on his daughter. In addition, he is willing to give her a generous monthly allowance, which will make your life in the foreign service a good bit easier. The officer with private means always gets the best posts because the others can't afford them."

"Have you talked to my mother about this?"

"Obliquely."

Was this what his mother had in mind when she said that he would be required to make a sacrifice somewhere down the line? "The two million would go to Mother, I would think."

Uncle Roger abandoned his sherbet, took up his coffee cup. "That would be up to you, of course. But I rather imagine that's what Noble had in mind. Eventually he would like for you to join his company, at a salary, I must say, that's five times as much as you would make in China."

"Enough money and Noble damn well has the world to his liking. Is the job with the company a precondition?"

"Of course not," Uncle Roger said. "I just mentioned it."

"So Noble frees himself from a dependent daughter, Mother has working capital, and Charlotte has a husband. And I get an allowance as long as I keep her happy."

Uncle Roger sipped his coffee. "If you were to agree, the wedding would have to take place very quickly so you could assume the Shanghai post by the end of July," he said. "The arrangement would certainly solve a multitude of problems."

"And introduce a multitude for me." Sam held his glass overhead like a banner for Woodrow to see. He ordered a second drink. "Doesn't it make a damn bit of difference that I would end up with somebody I don't love? Everybody wins except me."

"It doesn't have to be a permanent arrangement," Uncle Roger said. "A year or two down the road, I'm sure that nobody would be unhappy if you considered a divorce. I'd like you to see this as doing something to settle your father's affairs."

The two men sat in silence while Sam thought. He had to go to China. That was the important thing. "All right," he said. "Sold."

"Beg your pardon?"

"I accept the deal, but with conditions. The two million goes to Mama, of course. It's none of my business what she does with Noble from now on. And if Noble wants to give his daughter an allowance, she can keep it in the bank or give it away, but it has nothing to do with me. I'm going to China. I'll marry her and take her with me, but

I won't be controlled by her money or her father. I want to make that clear."

"I'm sure those conditions will be more than acceptable," Uncle Roger said, relieved. "You've made the right decision, my boy. I'll talk to Noble and get back to you."

By the afternoon of the official engagement party at Noble's town house overlooking the East River, Sam had decided that he could not go through with it, that under no circumstances could he marry Charlotte and take her to Shanghai with him.

So, surrounded by the cream of New York society, judges, attorneys, businessmen who had escaped the Crash, and the bevy of expensively dressed wives, all of them congratulating him on his impending marriage, he realized that he would have to move quickly, before Noble made the official toast to the new couple.

He made his way through the drawing room furnished with English antique furniture of massive oak and decorated with Turners and Constables to where Charlotte stood talking to a bevy of girls.

She did not look half bad, he decided, and she would make a fine wife. For somebody else. Her sandy-colored hair had recently been cut in a bob around the ears. She wore a pink organza gown for this occasion and a softer pink gossamer hat that dipped down over her face. She was a tall, slim, small-boned fashionable girl, quite good-looking, really.

As soon as he could he managed to get her out on the terrace alone with a bottle of champagne and two glasses.

"Do you think we need a whole bottle?" she asked with a smile. "I'm having a wonderful time. How about you?"

"Everything's fine," he said lamely. He poured the champagne, handed her a glass. "I think we need to talk."

"We'll have years to talk," she said, and he realized she was slightly tipsy. "But I love it when you're serious. It makes you look so distinguished."

He rested his elbows on the parapet, looked out over the river, wondering how to start.

"Do you remember the first time we saw each other?" she said.

"Yes. The day my mother brought me home from China."

"No," she said with a sweet smile. "Long before that. Your father had a meeting with mine in San Francisco and you and your mother came along. My mother had just passed away so I was there too. And when they served dinner in the suite at the Mark Hopkins, they put both of us at a small children's table. It was the first time I ever tasted bananas. You were dressed in a blue sailor suit with a silver whistle on a cord around your neck, just long enough to reach your shirt pocket. I always wondered what the silver whistle was for."

"I don't remember any of that," he said, a slow sinking feeling beginning to reach his stomach. "And how long we've known each other really isn't important. What is important is that we don't know each other nearly well enough to establish a lifetime relationship. It's obvious you don't know how this engagement came about. I think you should have all the facts. You deserve them."

"I know about the arrangement between my father and your mother."

"And that doesn't bother you?"

"No."

He had to start over again. "You're a lovely woman, Charlotte . . ."

"Thank you."

". . . but I don't love you. And so I don't think it's fair of me to marry you. Besides, I'm going to China, and that's a hell of a place to take a new bride or even to think about raising a family. It isn't safe for women and children. All those germs and diseases." He studied her face. He could see no change in her expression. "So if you want to back out, I'll understand completely."

"May I have a cigarette?" she asked.

"Surely." He lit it for her and she looked at him, her gray eyes probing his. "This is hard for you, isn't it, dear?" She looked out over the river. "I know everything and what you're doing to help your mother and that you've refused to touch a penny of the allowance Daddy is giving me. I admire that. It shows an independent spirit. And I'm prepared to put up with China or anyplace you choose to live."

"And none of this bothers you?"

"I've read a lot about arranged marriages. They usually work out better than most people expect." She put her hand over his. "I've had a crush on you for most of my life," she said.

"A crush," he echoed, all hope gone now.

"It's very close to love, I think," she said. "It can turn into love, I know that. But if *you* want to back out, I'll understand."

He watched a sea gull flying overhead, as free as the current of air that carried it. There was no way he could back out now and he knew it. "No," he said, his decision final. "I'll go through with it."

"We'll have a good life, you'll see," she said. She glanced through the French doors into the drawing room. "I think Daddy's about ready to make the announcement. Shall we join him?"

He was surprised to find that by their wedding day on the twenty-first of June, he had become resigned to the marriage and determined to make the best of it. He was somewhat dazzled by the spectacle Noble had arranged. He had never seen so much white silk or so many lighted candles in a single church. He stood with a friend from college by his side as best man and watched Charlotte come down the aisle on her father's arm, her face radiant behind the mist of her veil, twin five-year-old girls carrying her silk train. She appeared to be ecstatic. Her eyes never left his face during the ceremony and she responded to the traditional kiss with fervor.

They spent their wedding night in a bridal suite at the Waldorf. The sitting room of the suite was full of white gladiolas. He looked at the card on the bottle of champagne in a silver cooler, and another card propped on the silver bowl containing fruit. Her father had thought of everything. His name was on the champagne and the fruit carried a card from Sam's mother, in his handwriting.

"It was all so beautiful, wasn't it?" Charlotte said.

"Yes, it was. Would you like some champagne?"

"Yes, I would. Very much. You can pour it while I go and change."

She disappeared into the bedroom. He poured a glass of champagne, drank it, then undressed and put on blue silk pajamas. When she finally called to him, he poured two glasses of champagne and carried them into the bedroom. He found her sitting up in bed, wearing a white satin gown and a nervous smile. "I guess I need that champagne," she said. "I'm a little nervous."

He was touched by her vulnerability and he raised his glass to her. "There's nothing to be nervous about," he said. "It's been going on since Adam and Eve."

"Maybe Eve felt this way her first time," she said. She drank, then set the glass down on the polished wood of the nightstand. She lay back on the bed and looked at him. "I don't want you to be disappointed in me."

He sat on the edge of the bed, looking at her, and found himself excited by the way she looked, so vulnerable, so eager to please, her face expectant. Gently he leaned over and slowly kissed her eyes, her nose, her mouth, and then slid a strap of her gown from her shoulder and felt of a small and perfectly shaped breast. She shivered and the excitement rose within him. He ran his hand along her leg, beneath the fabric of her gown, the flesh of her thigh warm beneath his fingers, and she put her hand over his and guided it upward while her mouth became feverish against his and she moaned slightly.

The lovemaking began with a fervor he had not expected of her, and when he entered her as gently as he could, she wrapped herself tightly around him, her mouth even more responsive, and her fingers dug into his back to draw him closer. But when the lovemaking was ended and he lay beside her, she looked at him with anxiety in her eyes. "Did I disappoint you?" she said.

"Of course not."

She gave him a kiss on the cheek, snuggled up against him, and fell asleep almost immediately while he remained wide awake, listening to the soft rhythmic sound of her breathing and wondering whether he would ever love her.

He doubled the pillow beneath his head and thought a long time about the future before he finally drifted off to sleep.

Tokyo . . . 1931

COLONEL ITO WAS pleased that his father's limousine was waiting for him at Tokyo Station. The uniformed chauffeur stowed the luggage in the trunk, held the door open for him. Ito relaxed as the limousine passed the Diet Building, where the Parliament met, and made its way into the estate section of the city, finally turning into a driveway off the avenue. In front of the grand villa the servants were in the circular drive to meet him, smiling and bowing.

In the master entrance, his mother, the Lady Ito, was waiting for him, a fragile and beautiful woman who bowed to him in greeting, an expression of vast pleasure on her face. She directed the maid to take his shoes and provide him with slippers, then bowed again. "Please come into the drawing room, my lord," she said.

The house was a combination of Western mansion and Japanese villa, a reflection of the great fortune left by his grandfather, a manufacturing innovator who had been one of the first to introduce the *gaijin* concept of the assembly line into Japan. The fortune had been enhanced by Ito's father, who had manufactured weapons for the military.

As Ito sat in the drawing room, taking tea with his mother, he realized how much he had changed in the past two years. The time he had spent in Shanghai in the company of the British, Americans, and even the Chinese had made him no longer bound by the formalities with which he had been raised. Yet here he must honor them. After a proper interval, he asked about his father.

"Your honorable father is in the garden house," she said. "He wishes for his son to visit him there."

Colonel Ito left his mother and went down the covered path around the sand garden and the open pavilion. He saw his father sitting in the classical position for writing, kneeling on the tatami, the bamboo staff of his brush held upright while he concentrated on his calligraphy. He added the last stroke and put the brush back in the holder before he raised his eyes to his bowing son.

"Many greetings," the Baron Ito said. "The house is now complete, with the return of my son."

"How are you, Father?"

"I cannot complain or the *kami* would hear me," the Baron said. "Come and see what I am doing."

His father was composing a poem of subtle grace.

> *"The stream becomes the river which becomes the sea,*
> *And so we follow the same way."*

"It is a poem of great grace and beauty, Father."

"I am very poor at it," his father said. He rose to his feet, smoothed the front of his gray kimono. "The subject for this year was *Shato no Yuki*, 'Snow at the Shrine Gate.' There were more entries than usual, thirty thousand, I believe. The one I wrote did not win, but it was one of the poems read aloud by our beloved Emperor. You did know the Empress had another daughter?"

"Yes."

"I am glad you could take some leave time."

"I came home at your request, Father."

His father looked up at the cloud-covered sky. The day was steamy. "Is it afternoon?"

"Yes, sir. Late afternoon."

"Are you tired?"

"No, sir."

"Then we will go down to the river."

The geisha house received most of its support from the Baron. The chief geisha, Moon Flower, was a graceful woman in her late thirties who had been his father's mistress for many years. The Baron was now in his late fifties, a tall, lean man who worked long hours in business but always reserved time for his poetry and relaxation.

The Colonel was assigned a young geisha named Plum Blossom for the evening. During dinner she catered to him and made witty conversation and then played the samisen as he had never heard it before, singing in a light, pure voice that sounded like the instrument itself, a traditional song about spring and the cherry blossoms blooming along the river. The Baron had drunk enough sake that he wept unabashedly, the tears streaming down his cheeks.

The Colonel drank very little. He had moved away from the habit after being stationed in Shanghai. In that city a man needed his wits about him every second. The Chinese were absolute masters of the nuance, and very often the implications in a conversation would be the substance of an agreement.

After the singing the Baron dismissed the geishas. He wiped his eyes with a bosom cloth. "She has an exquisite voice, does she not?"

"Yes, that is so," the Colonel said.

"I will make you a present of her if you like," the Baron said.

"That is a most gracious offer," the Colonel said. "If I were to live in Tokyo, I would certainly accept. But it would be a great waste for me to be a world away from here and for other men to be deprived of her singing."

"A charmer, yes," the Baron said. "How long can you stay?"

"Two days at the most."

"Conditions in China are that critical?"

"Yes, sir."

"Then we will have to make haste. I want a marriage arranged between you and the young Watanabe daughter. The Watanabes are noted for a fortune built on brokering, and the two families will merge to a mutual benefit. Do you agree?"

"If that is your wish, I certainly approve," the Colonel said.

A formal dinner was held for Lord and Lady Watanabe and their daughter. During the dinner the Colonel glanced at his bride-to-be. She was very young, he knew, having just come of the proper age to be betrothed. She was not beautiful, but she was graceful and she had a lively look about her. The astrologers had not yet come up with a suitable date for the wedding, but the Colonel was sure it would coincide with his next trip home from China.

It was his mother who expressed the most joy at the dinner, because she was sure the girl would make the perfect wife for her son, the ideal mother for his eventual children, and a good companion in the house for her old age.

The next day the Colonel shipped out for Shanghai again and found that once he was on the boat train bound for Yokohama, an enormous weight was being lifted from his shoulders.

Shanghai . . .
August 1, 1931

CHARLOTTE CUMMINGS WANTED to die, longed for death. Outside, the ship's bell was clanging on the deck as the steamer moved slowly up the estuary of the Yangtze River, and she alternated between feeling ill in the water closet and trying to rest in the suite.

Sam stuck his head in the door. "We're entering the Whangpoo River," he said enthusiastically. "Don't you want to come on deck to see Shanghai? It's fantastic."

"In a little while," she said. Once he was gone, she lay down on the narrow bed once again and wept until she had no more tears. She longed to be home, back in the States. Then she realized the ship had stopped moving. The pitching and yawing that had been constant for six weeks now existed only in her mind. She managed to get to her feet and examine her face in the mirror, running cold water in the basin to rinse her face.

She went through the top of her steamer trunk and found a light summer hat with a wisp of veil that trailed down over her eyes. It would have to do. She managed to make her way out on deck where the smells assailed her sense of balance once again. Their offensiveness was matched only by the ugliness of the river, which seemed to be a mixture of yellow mud and oil, with every conceivable kind of floating monstrosity sailing it, from small tankers and lighters, eaten by rust, to decrepit sampans and barges in the smoky twilight. On the fantail of an unpainted sailboat, in plain sight, a Chinaman was calmly urinating into the muddy waters.

The flatness of the landscape appalled her and the sight of the city revolted her, the long curve of the boulevard beyond the docks, the ugly buildings rising above a bank of trees in the terrible heat of midsummer.

She felt a hand on her elbow. Sam stood there beside her, an entranced expression on his face. "It's incredible, isn't it?" he said.

"Yes," she said, a hollow echo in which the irony was lost. "It is incredible."

The ship was easing into the dock, the steam horn blasting a warning to a small Chinese scow. The gangplank was lowered into the mob of people on the pier, and Sam scanned the crowd anxiously until he saw a sign that had his name on it. The sign was working its way closer to the gangplank, and now Sam could see the man who carried it, Caucasian, in his early forties, looking like a matinee idol in his white linen suit. But the crowd was almost impenetrable below, the Chinese steerage passengers streaming off the ship in a stinking unruly mob despite the efforts of the stewards to hold them back until the first-class passengers had disembarked.

"If you like, you can wait in the cabin until some of the crowd clears," he said to Charlotte, raising his voice to make himself heard.

"I would rather die than go back into that room," she said.

"Then let's make the gangplank."

In ten minutes they were on the solid concrete of the pier, and the man who had come to meet them abandoned the sign and shifted his leather dispatch bag to his left hand. He smiled and reached out to shake Sam's hand. "Mr. and Mrs. Samuel Cummings?" he said.

"None other," Sam said.

"My name is Harry Connaught," he said. "Are you all right, Mrs. Cummings?"

"I've been better," Charlotte said.

"We'll have you out of here in no time," Connaught said. "The car's over this way."

"I'll just see to my luggage," Sam said.

"That's all taken care of."

They bypassed customs, with Connaught showing an identification card, and then they were at the car, a black Pierce Arrow with burled-walnut inlays front and rear and a Chinese chauffeur in livery who mounted two small American flags on either front fender and hurried to open the door for them.

Seated, Connaught leaned forward and opened a small cabinet. "From the look of you, Mrs. Cummings, I'd say you have been a victim of *mal de mer.*"

"I still feel as if the world is rocking beneath me."

He took a bottle from the cabinet, poured a small amount of the liquid into a crystal glass. "This is the best cure I know," he said. "It's a Chinese brandy, normally unfit for human consumption, but it will cure what ails you."

"I won't be able to keep it down."

He extended the glass to her. "Trust me," he said gently. "I've handled at least a hundred cases of this particular kind of seasickness in the past two years."

She took the glass. Making a face, she drank the contents and then returned the glass to him. He watched her face. "Well?" he said.

"I do think it helps," she said.

"Connaught triumphs again," he said with a smile. "Actually, one of the things it does is to kill the sense of smell, which is the leading contributor to prolonged seasickness. In my spare time I've catalogued over three hundred separate foul odors in this city. Now how about you, Mr. Cummings? Care for a shot?"

"No, thanks," Sam said. "And just call me Sam."

"Very good, Sam. Most of my friends call me Harry."

"You sound English."

"Correct."

"With the American Consulate?"

"Righto. I've been out here most of my life. If there's a Chinese dialect I can't speak, I can certainly make a shrewd guess at it. In general, I know as much about Shanghai and environs as anybody else. My own consulate is far too stuffy to hire me, so I am an honorary American. I'm a born optimist, generally good-humored, and if there's anything you want, I can get it for you in an hour or less at the lowest possible price."

"You sound indispensable," Sam said.

"I try to be. That's the best job insurance there is."

There was a traffic jam in the street ahead where the police had barricaded the main boulevard and Connaught leaned forward to confer with the driver. The limousine swerved up a side street and across a canal. "Sorry to have to take you the scenic route," he said. "But Bubbling Well Road is closed and we'll make better time by going through Chapei, the old Chinese quarter."

The car was temporarily slowed by a truck ahead of them, and Sam recognized it as a dead wagon. A family on the street lifted the bony corpse of an old man to the workers atop the pile of bodies neatly stacked on the truck bed.

Charlotte squinted through the window toward the truck. "What's going on?" she said. "What's that terrible odor?"

With a glance of apology at Sam, Connaught answered, "The millions of unwashed, I'd have to say." But quickly he hoisted the dispatch bag to his lap, opened the clasp. "You must be anxious for your mail." He handed Charlotte a thick cable, clicked on a rear-seat light against the gathering darkness. From her happy expression, Sam knew the cable was from her father.

Connaught leaned forward to speak to the driver again, directing him in Chinese to get back to the International Settlement by the nearest possible bridge, and, momentarily, the car changed course and shortly was crossing Soochow Creek.

"How are things at home?" Sam said.

"My father has influenza," she said. "He misses me. I wish . . ."

Connaught gave Sam a look, as if to reassure him that everything would be all right, that Connaught knew exactly how to handle the situation. "It takes time," he said to Charlotte. "But you'll come to enjoy it here. You'll see. The French Legation has regular dances. Do you play bridge, croquet?"

"A little bridge."

"You might want to sit in at the British Legation. They're always short-handed there, always looking for a fourth." The man was a born charmer, Sam decided, with the skill of an emotional engineer. "The moment we arrive at your house, we'll send a cable off to your father. We're on the same planet, you know." Connaught turned his attention to Sam. "You spent your childhood here, I understand?"

"Part of it. My parents were in Peking and Canton as well."

"Things are a bit more precarious now than they used to be," Connaught said. "The International Settlement is like an island surrounded by a not-so-friendly sea. We're in the Volunteer Corps Sector now, manned by troops from your country and mine, at least on paper."

The lighted street was swarming with Chinese, some of them in Western clothes and others in Mandarin robes, a sprinkling of massive-shouldered coolies carrying impossible weights of goods at either end of balanced poles. The traffic was heavy with motorcars of every description, three-wheeled pedicabs, bicycles, and a flock of rickshas and their pullers, most of whom were very thin Chinese with wiry legs and an ability to pull their clients through the thickest of traffic without being hit.

Traffic lights blinked at the intersections, ignored by Sikh policemen standing on pedestals in the center of the crossings, fierce-looking men in their turbans and beards, blowing whistles to move the traffic as they wanted it to go.

While the limousine was stopped Sam looked down a side street, saw a group of men in ragtag uniforms drilling under the direction of an English army officer. "What kind of group is that?" he said.

Connaught laughed gently. "You're looking at our ace in the hole," he said. "That's our mercenary army, something fairly recent."

"What nationality are they?"

Connaught smiled again. "Mostly White Russians. They all fought for the warlords at one time or another. Then one warlord would kill another and the Russian mercenaries who found themselves on the wrong side didn't want their heads chopped off, too, so they came into the International Settlement where some humane officer, probably British, molded them into an army. They're window dressing and they make our ladies and our houseboys feel safe, but it's my feeling that they'd scatter at the first sign of battle."

The car turned off Bubbling Well Road and Connaught peered out the window at the houses recessed in the trees. "There it is," he said. He spoke in Chinese to the driver, who made a sharp turn into a winding driveway as a cast-iron gate was opened by Chinese servants and then closed behind them. The effect was overwhelming, Sam thought, the heavy bank of trees, which served almost as a curtain, preventing the view until the car swept past them and revealed the grand mansion, four stories high, stone and teak woods, with a sweep of perfect lawn in front rising to a flower garden that flanked the circular driveway with bursts of color.

"My God," Sam said.

"Is that our house?" Charlotte said, as if she could not quite believe it.

Connaught sighed a mock sigh. "It's something one has to get used to, I suppose. But such luxury is commonplace for the very rich over here." He took a paper out of his pocket and handed it to her. She looked puzzled until she saw the rows of servants waiting in line in front of the house to welcome the new masters.

"What's this 'one, two, three' business?" she said.

"That's what you are to call your servants," Connaught said. "You could never pronounce their Chinese names and you shouldn't have to. I've been over it with them myself and they should have it down. Number One is your majordomo, in charge of the rest of the servants. As a matter of fact, he likes to be called 'Majordomo.' If he's around, you just speak up. 'Majordomo, missee have dinner big-time this night. Many-person dinner.' And he will call the cook, Number Three on your list, and you instruct him what you want prepared. Your personal maid is Number Four, gardener Number Five, and so on. They're all on that list. An even dozen. The twelve disciples, I call them."

"Isn't that rather impolite?" Charlotte said. "This business of calling them by number instead of name?"

"They do the same in their own families. Number One son. First daughter, second daughter."

"It's gorgeous," she said with open pleasure, looking at Sam. "Isn't it absolutely superb?"

"Indeed, it is," Sam said.

The car drew to a stop and the door was opened instantly, and Charlotte smiled as all the servants bowed to her. An old man dressed in a blue silk brocade jacket greeted her. "Good day, missus," he said. "Welcome big city Shanghai. You wishee, I command."

"Thank you, Majordomo," she said, delighted, and she proceeded down the line to her personal maids while Sam looked at Connaught gratefully.

"You've worked a minor miracle," he said. "I owe you one, Connaught."

"My pleasure," Connaught said. "Now, I hate to ask you, but the

Consul told me to bring you to see him just as soon as possible. Do you feel up to an assignment tonight?"

"Certainly."

"I almost forgot. You have a couple of dispatches." Connaught handed him two cables, one from State and the other from his mother.

"I'll be ready in fifteen minutes," Sam said.

He toured the downstairs with Charlotte, following the major-domo, who walked proudly, surrounded by the house girls, who flitted like birds to open doors and make sure everything was perfect. Sam had never seen a finer house or a larger one. There were drawing rooms and parlors, a billiard room, and a library with such high ceilings that a rolling ladder was necessary to reach the upper shelves. The dining room sustained a table that could seat twenty-four at least, and beyond it was a terrace and a perfectly rolled grass croquet court, the wickets and posts already in place.

Charlotte climbed the stairs eagerly while Sam followed. The master bedroom was a suite of rooms decorated with priceless Chinese screens and a huge carved teak bed.

"It's absolutely gorgeous," Charlotte said again. "Don't you think so?"

"Magnificent," Sam said.

"I do think I'll arrange the furniture a little differently," she said. "And I would like fresh flowers by the bed every morning."

"They have gone to a great deal of trouble, haven't they?"

"Yes, and I do appreciate it."

"Do you think you can get along without me for a while?" Sam said. "The Consul wants to see me. I shouldn't be gone long."

"Surely," she said. "I want to send a cable to Father. I promised to let him know the moment we were safely here."

"A fine idea," he said.

He took the time to read his cables. The first was from his mother and it was full of her latest business ventures. Two million dollars in Depression dollars were worth ten million pre-Depression dollars, and she had bought up patents for metal-crushing machines for a song and was carefully putting together deals designed to triple her money. It was a long cable, but she did not mention his father once.

The cable from his Uncle Roger, however, was full of references to his father, most of them buttressing Roger's own opinions. "I'm sure your father would be proud of the course you have taken were he here. And I am sure that as time passes you will realize you made the right decision in marrying Charlotte and will not regret it.

"I have been in touch by cable with your Consul there as a way of introducing you, telling him of your training."

It was only when he was in the car with Connaught and pulling back into the traffic that Sam brought up the subject that concerned him most. "You don't know how grateful I am to you for all you've done," he began. "But we must discuss the matter of money."

"How so?"

"I'm a new member on the team. There's no way I can afford a house fit for a maharaja."

"Ah, dear chap," Connaught said with great tolerance. "You must leave these things to me. The house belongs to a very rich Chinese merchant, and when I say rich, I'm talking of so much money that he never has to think about it. The cost of minor things like grand houses never crosses his mind. Do you follow me?"

"Yes."

"This Chinese merchant has gone to Europe for three years. I just happen to know one of his business agents, who asked me if anyone connected with the American government would care to occupy it. No mention of money, of course. The servants are lifetime employees anyway."

"Why American?"

"The business agent is responsible for the property," Connaught said with a shrewd smile. "Your presence in the house will automatically protect it. No one wants to cross the Americans."

"I see," Sam said.

A uniformed American Marine stood guard beneath the green oval canopy that sheltered the front entrance of the consulate. Inside, the waiting room was dark and deserted.

The Consul himself occupied a suite of offices on the fourth floor, an aerie gained by ascending in a lattice-work cage of an elevator that jerked, moaned, and occasionally emitted a subdued screech as it bore them upward.

"You'll like Alcott," Connaught said. "He not only works here but quarters here since his wife died. He's a bit too fond of port, and he occasionally dozes off at official functions, but he knows the Chinese mind as well as any man alive."

At the landing on the fourth floor they were greeted by Mrs.

Worthington, Alcott's white-haired personal secretary, who led them into the office. The Consul looked to Sam like a Victorian gentleman who was down on his luck. The vest he wore over his ample chest and stomach was too small and held together by a single button. His suit was rumpled. His sparse gray hair needed trimming. He squinted through spectacles with round wire frames that obviously should have been refitted years ago. But he spoke with a friendly rumble as he shook Sam's hand and welcomed him to Shanghai. As if on cue, Connaught excused himself and departed, and Alcott asked Sam to have a seat, then went to a carved Chinese cabinet and, removing a bottle, poured brandy into two crystal glasses.

Sam looked around the office. A bay window offered a breeze against the summer heat and a magnificent view to the north and east. An old brass telescope set upon a tripod angled out the window. One wall was covered with a large map of China, colored flags on pins to mark the location of various military forces.

Alcott brought the glasses, stood in front of the map, and handed him one. "A proper toast, young Cummings. Here's to China, and may neither of us do anything to harm her."

"To China," Sam said.

Alcott put his glass down and picked up a pointer. "Now for a short lesson in current politics, in case your professors have been delinquent." The tip of his pointer rested on the strip of land separated from Japan by the Bay of Honshu. "The Japanese have total control of this territory both economically and militarily. From Korea, which they call Chosen up through the sparsely populated province of Manchuria to the north and down to Mukden. They own the railroads and have military rights to a strip of land along all the tracks. What of the Chinese, you might ask? What of the young Marshall Chang Hsueh-liang, the Commander in Chief for Peace Preservation in Manchuria, and his four hundred thousand crack troops? He is no threat to the Japanese, young Mr. Cummings, because he has moved the bulk of his troops here." The pointer moved south of the Great Wall. "He holds the balance of power in North China while Chiang Kai-shek, the great number one himself, is busy fighting off challenges from rebellious generals and warlords who would have his head and Communists who would like to undermine them all. So where does that leave Manchuria, sir?"

"Ready to be taken," Sam said.

"Quite so. No better time. Defenseless." He put down the pointer. "But how will that affect us here in Shanghai, that's the question." He picked up his glass. "Out the north window is Chapei, the main Chinese Settlement. You can see the top of North Station, where the Shanghai-Nanking railroad comes in from the northwest. And due east and a bit south is the Japanese Sector, fronting the river. Take a look through the telescope at the fires out there and tell me what you see."

"House fires, it appears," Sam said, squinting. "And a burning commercial building near the railroad station."

"The Japanese and Chinese have begun their little fights again. The Chinese are boycotting Japanese goods and occasionally the Japanese will sneak into the Chinese quarter and set fires. If they set too many at one time, the Chinese retaliate and infiltrate the Japanese Sector and set some fires of their own. So tonight we're lucky. A couple or so minor conflagrations and that means relative peace for a while." He sipped his brandy, then lowered himself into an armchair near Sam.

"I'm close to seventy years old," he said. "I am in a position to help prevent bloodshed. And at the same time I don't have the energy for it." He sipped his brandy again, looked directly at Sam. "What's the policy in Washington, the real position?"

"You'd know that better than I, sir."

"Not necessarily," Alcott said. "I sit here on the powder keg and exchange cables with the powers that be, and I get back the official line, that we Americans are to remain neutral, which means, of course, that American business is free to sell goods to either belligerent party."

"The State Department would like to ignore the whole situation in the hope that it will go away," Sam said. "They're short of money and they don't want to have to deal with the Far East. The professionals really don't give a damn. The American public is mildly anti-Japanese because they appear to be the aggressors, and mildly for the Chinese because they seem to be the underdogs, and besides that, General Chiang Kai-Shek has a Methodist wife."

"I'm afraid you're right, Cummings," Alcott said with a sigh. "Pour us some more brandy, if you please. I get cables from nincompoops all the time asking questions about what we should do with China. And I always cable back, 'There isn't any China.' Because there's not. As I said in my geography lesson, there is a collection of generals and warlords trying to kill each other while the Nationalists and the Communists try to recruit them all. And China will be lost in a battle between the Nationalists and the Communists if Japan doesn't destroy her first.

"And there are two Japans, the radicals, who would like to go to war and take over China, and the conservatives, who want peaceful trade between the two countries and a resolution by nonviolence." He sipped the brandy. "May the worms of the earth consume the flesh of your grandfather and his bones become powder and blow into hell," he said in Chinese, in the Shanghainese dialect.

"And may you join them, unworthy bastard," Sam answered.

Alcott smiled. "You didn't learn that at Harvard."

"I learned that on the streets of Shanghai when I was ten."

"Then Harvard taught you Mandarin, what I call court Chinese, I trust."

"Yes." Sam paused a moment. "There's something I'd like to discuss with you."

"Your father."

"Yes."

"A tragic affair. I didn't know him well. I've had the official papers concerning his death put together. You'll have them tomorrow."

"Thank you."

There was a rapping on the door and Mrs. Worthington poked her head into the room. "Colonel Ito is here, sir."

"Would you ask him if he would be so kind as to wait a short moment?"

"Certainly, sir."

She closed the door. "Drink up," Alcott said. "I always keep the oriental military waiting. It teaches them to listen, puts them in their proper place, although God knows nothing will keep them there for long. But to get to the point, would you be willing to take my place and accompany Colonel Ito to a meeting with a Chinese general? The Chinese general is an odious son of a bitch, but we need to know more about him. I won't ask you to do this if you're too tired."

"Not at all, sir," Sam said. "And what's my role?"

"Peacekeeper. If an American official is along, they can't very well kill each other. You simply listen, respond to questions, write a report for me on conclusions reached, if any. You'll like Ito. He's the best of the Japanese crop. He comes from Japanese aristocracy and is being groomed, so to speak. Shall we ask the good Japanese colonel to come in?"

"Absolutely, sir," Sam said.

Colonel Ito turned out to be a tall man with a close-cropped black bristle, a few years older than Cummings. He spoke excellent colloquial English.

They took off in a Japanese staff car with a rising-sun banner and one white flag in the fender holders, a signal that the car was on a peaceful mission.

"You are not what I expected," Ito said, lighting a cigarette and offering one to Sam. "You are a lot younger."

"You're a surprise to me as well."

"How?"

"I've been led to believe that Japanese officers are completely and uncomfortably reserved."

"Most of them are," Ito said. "I have been spoiled by the informal life here in Shanghai. When I am at home with my father I undergo a complete change of personality."

The car approached one of the north gates through a wall into the Chapei Settlement. "Maybe you'd better brief me on what we're doing," Sam said. "Who's the Chinese general?"

"Wang. Have you heard of him?"

Sam remembered the briefing papers. "A warlord, anti-Communist, thinks he can control the Chinese Nationalists."

"A bandit," Ito said candidly. "He has come to full power here in the past week. He controls Chinese Shanghai and he makes approximately half a million American dollars a month from his concessions. He runs the docks, the whores, a makeshift army. He is a coolie warlord. He came up from the docks himself and he has no manners and no regard for life."

"Who requested the meeting?"

"He did."

"Is there an agenda?"

"It is all a matter of show. He says he wants to discuss the difficulties between the Japanese merchants and the Chinese, but that is not really what he is about. He is really afraid of the Communists, who are becoming stronger by the day. He will bluster, hope to make both of us, as Japanese and American representatives, lose face, and then he'll boast to his followers about how powerful he is and exhort them to kill as many of the Communists as they can root out. That will intimidate the peasants, keep them under control."

They were in Chapei now, and the car threaded through dark narrow lanes, the maze of a rabbit warren. Overhead the wires strung between buildings held laundry and banners. The car passed an armed guard at the end of a lane that had been cleared of people. Parked in front of a courtyard restaurant was a long black car, two strangely colored flags in the bumper holders.

"I don't recognize the banners," Sam said.

"The General designed them. He also prints his own bank notes to pay his debts. They are worthless, but nobody dares refuse him."

The door was opened by two Chinese soldiers in brown uniforms, wearing white sashes to hold their short swords in place. Ito ignored the soldiers as if they did not exist.

They were led into a dimly lit restaurant furnished with bamboo tables and wicker chairs, separated from an open courtyard by a wooden lattice, and confronted by the General, an immense man for a Chinese, over six feet tall, with a broad Mongol face that displayed a scar along the left cheekbone and another just above his left eye. He wore a mufti uniform with red and white piping on the seams of the tight coat, riding trousers that were flared at the knee and tucked into tall brown boots, polished to a mirror sheen. The breast of his jacket was decorated with an array of medals, everything from the Croix de Guerre to the Iron Cross. There was a Chinese short sword in his leather belt on his right side and a holstered pistol on his left.

He bowed as Ito and Sam came into the room. "This unworthy person is grateful that you choose to honor my table," he said in a coarse Shanghainese dialect. "That powerful Nippon should sit down with humble China overwhelms me as usual." He looked at Sam. "And another representative of the exalted American government honors me with his presence. Is the old one indisposed, may the gods forbid?"

"Not at all," Sam said. "My name is Samuel Cummings. I am honored to represent the Consul General here."

General Wang asked them to be seated. Sam faced the latticework and the open courtyard beyond, where torches were set into the stone walls. He found himself looking directly at a soldier with a bandolier of ammunition looped around his chest. The General nodded and the waiters began to carry in platters of foul-smelling thousand-year-old eggs, white cut pork and three-layer shreds of beef while a group of singsong girls with brightly painted cheeks played their Chinese instruments and sang in thin reedy voices.

The General drank more than he ate, and Colonel Ito grew quieter and more disciplined, eating only small portions of the multiple courses. Sam ate enough to be polite.

The more the General drank, the surlier he got. Finally he glared at Ito. "You will stop the burning," he said. "I didn't care when your people burnt many businesses in Chapei because it scared the merchants and I gained even more support. But now your people have burnt too many, and I will have to take action."

"When the Honorable General says 'my people,' does he refer to the Japanese civilians or the military forces?" Ito said.

"There is no difference between the two," the General said.

Now Ito turned to Sam, almost casually, and spoke softly in English despite the General's quizzical frown. "No matter what happens, do not show any reaction."

Sam nodded, took a helping of the shreds of meat. He glanced at the General. "If your whole army eats this well, they must be very content."

"My soldiers would eat rocks, if necessary," the General said. "No enemy can stand against them."

The conversation continued over the high-pitched squeal of music while, behind the latticework, two soldiers were dragging a Chinese man into the courtyard, a man whose face had been reduced to a bloody pulp.

They pulled him through the dirt and then let him sag to the ground, where one of them kicked him with a boot, then reached down and grabbed him by the hair and pulled him into a kneeling position. Sam was transfixed, his mouth suddenly dry. The music wailed even louder, as if to drown out any sound from the courtyard.

One of the soldiers swept a short sword from his belt. The blade flashed through the torchlight, the head flew from the body as blood sprayed the feet of the soldiers. The body jerked and collapsed, twitching in the dirt while one soldier grabbed the head, the dead mouth contorted and gaping. He stuck a sharp pike up the neck and raised it aloft.

Sam did his best to hide his horror. Ito continued to eat as if nothing had happened, and the General studied them both with curious eyes.

You son of a bitch, Sam thought. He gulped the wine without tasting it.

The head was planted at the wall so the lifeless eyes gazed out on the street beyond the restaurant, blood still running from the neck down the wood of the shaft.

Common practice, came the voice of Sam's history professor. *Chang Kai-shek put the heads of his enemies in baskets and hung them from lampposts in the streets.*

The worst way to die.

No way to enter paradise with the head separated from the body.

"Would you care for American whiskey?" the General said. "Any kind?"

"No, thank you."

Soon the conference was finished and Sam went through the obligatory polite ritual of departure. Only when he reached the privacy of the car did he realize his hands were icy.

"He's a bloody son of a bitch," Sam said. He offered Ito a cigarette and then lit one for himself to counteract the stench of the evening.

"He revels in blood," Ito said. "He has managed to disgust the British and the French so much, they will not meet with him at all. But he plays these dramas especially for my benefit," Ito said. "The killing tonight was a warning. From now on, if there are fires in Chapei that can be connected with Japanese, then Japanese individuals caught in Chapei, either on business or otherwise, will be executed."

"I'll write a report," Sam said. "My government won't tolerate this kind of cruelty."

Ito smiled. "I wrote such a report after my first meeting with the General. The General undoubtedly executed a soldier under his command who disobeyed orders, my superior suggested. The reality is that as long as he confines himself to the Chinese districts and his own people, we cannot touch him. But someday he will go too far."

As they reached the American Consulate, Colonel Ito removed a sheaf of papers, written in Japanese, from an attaché case. "These are notes of some of the past meetings. Do you have a Japanese translator?"

"I'm sure we must."

He checked his watch. It was nine o'clock, and his chances of finding a translator tonight would be very small, but he went into the communications section, where Evans, the night duty officer, was coding the outgoing night cables. "Do we have a Japanese translator on staff?" Sam asked him.

"Yes, sir," Evans said. "We have a man on call, but if you need something in a hurry, check with the Visa Section. They generally have a girl who works a late shift."

"Where would I find her?"

"Two-twelve. Second floor at the back."

Sam went upstairs, and when he opened the door to 212 he saw a young Japanese woman working her way through a tall stack of official forms, filing them in drawers. She looked up at him in momentary alarm. "I didn't mean to startle you," he said in English. "Are you a translator?"

"Yes, sir," the girl said.

"Evans told me where to find you. I need you to do a job for me. Don't worry. I'll take full responsibility with the Visa Section."

She was a pretty girl, but she looked incredibly young to him. "Do you work late shift by yourself?" he said.

"Sometimes," she said. "I finished the translations early, so I decided to catch up with the filing."

They took the elevator to the third floor and at 301 found a Chinese workman patiently painting the name Cummings on the frosted glass of the door. Inside, Sam found a desk and a cabinet full of writing supplies and then handed her the papers Colonel Ito had given him. "I just need the most recent one translated tonight," he said. "Perhaps you could read it to me."

She examined it. "I can give you a more precise translation in writing, sir."

"Have at it, then," he said. "And what's your name?"

"Yuki Nakamura, sir."

"I'm Vice-Consul Cummings. Just do the first one and leave it on the desk. I'll read it in the morning. I'll have one of the regular translators do the rest."

"Yes, sir."

He looked at her closely. She had a quality of innocent beauty about her, flawless golden skin, black hair, and seemed just across the line that separated woman from girl.

When he arrived at his office the next morning, there was a pile of papers stacked neatly in the center of his new desk, and as he thumbed through them he saw that Yuki Nakamura had translated all the papers that Colonel Ito had left for him into clear, concise English, her handwriting Spencerian. He decided that she must have spent the night translating.

He packaged Colonel Ito's originals and sent them to the Japanese Consulate by special messenger.

Then he wrote a memo to Personnel asking that Miss Yuki Nakamura be transferred to his service from the Visa Section, full-time, as the beginning of his personal staff.

As he came through the front door Majordomo was waiting with the silver tray and the telephone messages neatly listed in Chinese on a piece of paper. Sam scanned the paper as he went into the drawing room, where Charlotte sat at the Louis XIV desk dressed in a long blue dinner gown. She smiled up at him from the list in front of her.

"What do you think of the Wilcoxes?" she said.

"In what sense?" he said, accepting the bourbon and water from Majordomo while he dialed the telephone.

"The dinner party Saturday night," she said. "Janet Wilcox is supposed to be very entertaining."

"There could be a full-scale war by Saturday," he said, his irritation with her showing.

"If our social life depended on a break in your perpetual crises, we wouldn't have any at all," she said.

Evans came on the line from the communications center. "You have three cables from State. They're very long. If you like, I'll send them out by messenger."

"Give me the gist of them," Sam said.

"All right. There's one from the Secretary to all consulates in East Asia. He advises that every consulate will remain strictly neutral in any local conflict so the United States cannot be accused of factionalism."

"Are the other two cables along that line?"

"One is from the Far East Desk. It specifies that no consulate official is to act in an advisory capacity to either the Nationalists or the Communists."

"Does the cable mention Japan?"

"No."

A loophole, Sam thought. He could still work with Ito in dealing with the Chinese unless the third cable ruled against it.

"The last cable?"

"Housekeeping," Evans said. "A request for an expense break-down for all consulate personnel for last month."

"That can't be addressed to me," he said. "Bookkeeping is not on my watch."

"Consul Alcott requested that it be relayed to you."

"I'll take care of it in the morning. I'd like you to stand by until midnight. I'm going to be sending a rather long cable and it will need coding."

"Yes, sir."

Sam put the receiver on the hook, sat down in a leather chair to have his drink, aware of the work awaiting him. He realized that Charlotte was looking at him. "Well?" she said.

"Well, what?"

"We owe the Sloans and the McGrews. They've already accepted. Do you want me to add the Wilcoxes or not?"

"We've been here less than a month and, with a nation of starving people and a threatened war, you've managed to become a social butterfly."

"I don't intend to quarrel with you just because you've had a bad day at the office," she said. "Yes or no on the Wilcoxes?"

Majordomo appeared at the doorway to announce dinner and Sam seated Charlotte at one end of the long table and then took his place at the other. "In the absence of a decision," she said, "I'm going to include the Wilcoxes. And I would appreciate it if you can arrange to be home by seven on Saturday."

"I can't guarantee anything," he said. "If you knew the kind of pressure I'm under—"

"You've made me very aware of the pressure," she said. The waiters were serving the soup course. "That's all you ever talk about, your wonderful and hardworking new translator, or how the political situation is going to hell in a hand basket or trouble upriver. I really don't care what's happening at the consulate anymore." She looked at him directly. "When you're home I want you to be with me. I want you to be aware of me."

He realized he had been eating without tasting the food. "You're right," he said. "I've been damned poor company lately. I apologize."

"Accepted," she said. "Did I hear you say you're going to work tonight?"

"I have to draft a cable," he said. "But what the hell. The world won't fall apart if I wait until morning. I'll call Evans and tell him not to stand by." He tasted the soup. "It's very good," he said, and then: "Truce?"

She smiled. "Truce," she said. "Now, give me your frank opinion of Harvey Wilcox."

"We'd better invite him," Sam said. "Washington considers his steamships important in the upriver trade."

When he made love to her that night he was aware of the unseen barriers that grew higher between them day by day, and he could not honestly say whether the fault was hers or his. For while he caressed her breasts, kissed her with a calculated fervor, his mind was never free of the work awaiting him, and he felt, even as her sharp cry signaled the peak of her feelings, that she was not entirely with him. Perhaps, he thought, this was the ultimate mutual deception, that as he lay beside her, her head on his arm, neither of them would admit how mechanical their lovemaking had become and the growing distance between them.

For him the solution was to spend as much time as possible at the consulate, where Yuki was at least very much aware of the world around them. He occupied himself in other directions, working with Colonel Ito on a temporary plan to preserve the peace between the Japanese merchants and General Wang.

As soon as he could, Sam prowled the city following the lead provided by Alcott's report on his father's death. The principal document had been his father's death certificate, listing the cause of death as suicide by gunshot.

Sam read the report while sitting in a noodle stall frequented by Chinese laborers along Soochow Creek. His father had occupied a flat in the International Settlement bordering Soochow Creek, and an inventory of the furnishings was listed in the report. His personal possessions were minimal, and of such slight cash value, it was recommended that they be given to his secretary, a woman named Bright Moon, in lieu of unpaid wages, as was the local custom in such cases.

Sam examined the sites mentioned in the investigative report. He peered through the boarded windows of an office building in Pootung, where his father's headquarters had been located, prowled near the charred ruins of a godown on the north bank of the

Whangpoo, which only now, months after the fire that had left it in rubble, was being cleared away by hundreds of coolie laborers who swarmed the ruins like ants, cheaper by far to rent en masse for a week than to hire a bulldozer for an hour.

He found the apartment house where his father had lived, prosperous in the Chinese fashion, but far removed from the elegance of the houses off Bubbling Well Road. He stood across the street, studied the round-moon gate through which his father must have passed countless times. Somewhere in that three-story building was the room where his father had ended his own life.

Late in the day he walked through the open streets near the mills when the flocks of small girls changed shifts. They were pale, wan children, no older than ten or twelve, who worked for pennies a day and still giggled and sang and chattered like a thousand birds as they made their way homeward.

He watched a ricksha puller whose small boy ran behind him between the shafts of a ricksha, learning the streets of the city. The boy was nine or ten, his legs already made of steel, and Sam knew that when the father thought him old enough, the boy would pull a ricksha of his own. A whole life running, unless tuberculosis or the thousand and one diseases that plagued the poor crippled him first.

With each hour Sam spent in Chapei or Pootung, he was aware of General Wang, for Wang's men were everywhere, collecting tribute from any Chinese merchant, even from those in makeshift food stalls. Sometimes they knocked down the crude shelters with their rifle butts and dumped the kettles of noodles into the streets, where children fell on them like hungry animals, eating the dirt with the food.

Frequently, Sam saw the General's bulletproof limousine cruising through the streets, soldiers perched on the front fenders, machine guns at the ready. Wang also had an armored railroad car that resembled a tank on wheels, sheets of gleaming metal with gun ports and an observation post atop it. Sam would see it one day on the Shanghai-Nanking line only to find it west of the city on the Shanghai-Hanchow line the next, a visible symbol of the General's power.

He came to hate the General to the same degree that he identified with the Chinese, who had begun to call Wang "the Wolf of Shanghai," preying on defenseless people, as so many ruthless men had done before him.

In the mid-twenties Shanghai had been dominated by Marshal

Sun Chuan-fang, a warlord who collected tribute from five provinces. He had given way to the controversial Pockmarked Hwang, who headed the Green Gang, and they cooperated with Marshall Chiang Kai-shek, who drove out a Manchurian warlord who terrorized the International Settlement as well as the Chinese districts for a month. Then Chiang Kai-shek collected forty million dollars for his efforts, moved on to form a government in Nanking, and left Shanghai open to exploitation once again.

No way to touch the Wolf of Shanghai except to see him replaced by another warlord.

On the first Monday morning in September he was in the middle of writing a report to Washington on Chinese tariffs imposed on the river trade when the telephone rang.

"Consul Alcott would like to see you in fifteen minutes," Mrs. Worthington said.

"I'll be there," he said. He had just placed the draft of the cable in a locked drawer when Owens approached his desk. Owens was the legation comptroller, a former banker who watched all consulate expenditures as if they came from his personal account.

"A word with you, Mr. Cummings, if you have a moment," he said, laying a stack of invoices on the desk in front of Sam. "I was wondering how you want to handle these."

"What are they?" Sam said.

Owens pulled a paper from the stack. "This is a summary of all the dates the cables were sent from your residence to various destinations in the States. They were charged to the consulate."

"There must be some mistake," Sam said. "The only cables I've sent have been on official business, through Communications." He took the paper from Owens and glanced at the total charges. "Two hundred and twelve dollars?" he said. "Impossible." And then he saw the addresses to whom the cables had been sent.

Christ, he thought. *She's talking with her father and her friends in New York as if she were calling them across the street.*

"Put these on a personal invoice, billed to me," he said. "They shouldn't have been billed to the consulate in the first place."

He was steaming as he went up to the fourth floor, where a rather sour Alcott handed Sam a photograph of himself at the rail yards in Chapei with an armored train car in the background. Sam was standing at an intersection, waiting for a truck to pass before he crossed the street.

"Does this picture strike a chord in your memory, young Mr. Cummings?" Alcott asked.

"Who took the picture?"

"A photographer for a Chinese paper. That is General Wang's armored railroad car. In the General's camp this is prima facie evidence of spying, and the General sets the rules for the Chinese court. In other words, with his picture as evidence, the General can have you picked up the moment you set foot outside these walls and have you shot before our attorneys draw up a letter asking your whereabouts."

"All I was doing was tracking down the details of my father's death."

"I thought as much," Alcott said patiently. "So perhaps we had better resolve that problem here once and for all. I want you to accept your father's death as suicide and put it out of your mind. There's nothing to be gained from further questioning. I'm telling you to give it up. And for your own good, confine yourself within the borders of the International Settlement and Concessions."

"Obviously the picture was taken a couple of days ago. I haven't been stopped."

"Only because the photographer chose to sell it to me," Alcott said. "From this moment on you will limit your expeditions outside the boundaries to those times when you are on official business. No other reason is acceptable."

"Then you're allowing General Wang to dictate the rules by which an American citizen has the freedom to move around in this city," Sam said with irritation.

"Indeed, I am," Alcott said. "Our presence here is pretty damned small when it comes down to it. A handful of Marines, brave to be sure, but far too few in number to come fetch you out of a situation that can easily be avoided."

"And what of any further meetings with Colonel Ito and the General?"

"You may continue those when the time is right."

He turned to go, but Alcott stopped him. "I understand how heavy-handed I'm being," he said. "I was young and adventurous once myself, and your reports on the political situation do get to the heart of things. To be curbed is not pleasant, but I trust you will abide by my rules."

"Yes, sir. I will."

"There is one assignment you may carry out in the next few days. Washington has asked for an approximation of the amount of foreign arms being carried upriver. Can you handle a boat?"

"Yes, sir."

"No great hurry. Do it at your convenience. Your right of movement can be expanded to include the river as long as you don't put ashore outside the settlement."

He went home early. Charlotte was not at the door to meet him. Instead, Majordomo offered to serve him a drink on the terrace.

"Where's missee?" Sam said, not in a good mood.

"Allee upstairs, thinkee," Majordomo said.

Sam mounted the stairs, two at a time, determined not to let his anger get out of hand, for she was responsible for only part of his irritation.

She was not in the bedroom but he went up to the third floor, attracted by the sound of Charlotte's humming. She was sitting in the sunroom, surrounded by swatches of expensive hand-woven fabrics. "You're just in time," she said. "I can't make up my mind which of the blues to use in redecorating the sunroom."

"I see." He picked up one of the swatches. "And how much is this one?" he asked.

"I don't know," she said. "It's gorgeous, isn't it?"

"You don't know?" he said. "You didn't ask? You must have some idea. Fifty dollars a square meter? A hundred? You can get some real goddamned bargains in Shanghai if you look around."

"You don't have to curse."

"Don't I? It does get your attention." He took the bills for the cables out of his pocket, handed them at her. "How do you explain these?"

She frowned as she looked at the bills, a baffled expression on her face. "I don't have to," she said. "Is all of this over a couple of hundred dollars' worth of cables?"

"Which you charged to the consulate."

"Of course I did," she said. "I deserve that much for living in this wretched part of the world."

"Wretched? My God, look around you. A staff of twelve servants in a house so large you can't even make use of all the rooms and you're complaining?" He shook his head. "Parties at least four nights a week, bridge in the afternoon, every conceivable luxury."

"And what am I supposed to be doing with my time while you're playing diplomat?" she asked. She picked up a piece of silk. "I don't know what all the fuss is about anyway. I can pay for all the cables, for anything I want, out of my allowance."

"No," he said, voice icy.

"No what?"

"I'm your husband and head of this house. You will send all these fabrics back. You may write as many letters as you want to your father and your friends. They can cable you as often as they wish. But you won't send any cables except in the case of an emergency and with my approval."

"I'll do as I please," she said.

"I mean exactly what I say. I won't tolerate this."

She looked at him defiantly, then carefully ripped the bills in two and dropped the scraps of paper on the table. "I'm going downstairs to see to dinner," she said.

"Not until I have your promise."

She looked at him coldly. "Never." She brushed past him and he heard her going down the stairs. Watching her go, he realized that he was married to a stranger.

Mrs. Liu looked first at the picture cut from a magazine and then at Yuki, as if measuring her for the dress in the illustration. "This poor excuse for a seamstress can certainly make the dress for you, but the material you bought is too conservative, more for the older woman than the girl you are."

Yuki picked up the dark blue material she had bought at a street stall. "I have a new job where it is necessary for me to look older," she said.

Mrs. Liu looked dubious. "It is a mistake to try to push time," she said. "You will be older soon enough. But if you want the dress from this material, then you'll have it."

"How soon?"

"Two days?"

"That would please me very much. And I need to ask the price."

"Two yuan," Mrs. Liu said.

"You are very kind," Yuki said.

When the dress was finished and she had paid Mrs. Liu, she went back to her tiny box room in the ancient walled Chinese city in the Mouth of the Rainbow District. She lifted the loose board in the floor and took out the painted tin box where she kept her savings. In the box were ten five-dollar bills, American, and another seven dollars in ones for a total of fifty-seven dollars.

Since Cummings-san had raised her wages to twelve and a half dollars a week, she no longer needed to keep so much money in reserve, so even as she replaced the tin she decided to find a way to send the cash to her mother in Japan.

The next morning she was up at dawn, knowing that it would take at least an hour to go to the public bath, have a quick cup of tea for breakfast, change into the blue dress, and join the queue waiting for the tram and the long ride to get to the consulate. By the time she was on the tram that morning, she was running ten minutes late and the crowd of commuters was so heavy, she was afraid a laborer covered with the gray clay of the countryside would brush against her. By the time she got off at her stop, she had made up her mind to move and find a place closer to the American Consulate. It would not only be more convenient but safer as well, for some nights when she worked very late she was filled with dread at the walk from the tram stop through the dark and dangerous streets of the poor district.

On this morning she reached the building before Cummings-san and was delighted to find that he had been moved to a new office with a separate anteroom for her, a desk of her own, and a chair where she would sit to answer the telephone. There was a hot plate on a table and so she went down to the kitchen, where she asked for a kettle and cups and a tin of Cummings-san's favorite oolong tea. By the time he came in at ten o'clock, long-faced and tired, she was able to take him a cup of tea in his private office.

"Thank you," he said. He looked at her dress. "A new dress, isn't it? It's very pretty, Nakamura-san," he said.

"Thank you. May I ask you a question?"

"Certainly."

"This is presumptuous of me to say, but it is very important for me to be properly dressed for the position you have given me. I wish to look appropriate. I will not be offended if you make suggestions to me."

He smiled. "You look just right."

"Thank you, sir." She went back into the anteroom and sat down at the desk, where a pile of papers awaited her translation, but her mind was not on her work. She wondered how old Cummings-san was. He could not be more than twenty-three or twenty-four in the Western way of counting, and yet he acted older than that, perhaps because the rest of the men in the consulate were so much older than he was.

She was about to go back to work when she was interrupted by a messenger from the Japanese Consulate with a dispatch from Colonel Ito's superior, written in Japanese. She went into Cummings-san's office.

"I am sorry to interrupt you, Cummings-san, but the Japanese Consulate has just sent an urgent dispatch."

"Read it to me, please," he said, looking up from the paperwork at his desk.

She studied the honorific language that always characterized a formal Japanese dispatch. "General Wang has just formed a secret alliance with the Nationalists, who have given him control of the Nineteenth Route Army."

"Give Colonel Ito's office a ring for me and ask if he can meet me here at four o'clock."

"Yes, sir." Back in the anteroom, she called the Colonel's office and spoke to an aide who verified the appointment.

On impulse, she used her lunch hour to take a taxi back to her room, telling the driver to wait. She went upstairs and removed the money from the painted tin. She was nervous on the long ride back to the consulate, for she carried a fortune in her bag. She did not like spending money for a taxi, but she had decided that the cash must be delivered to her mother before hostilities broke out. She knew that Sam would cooperate in any way he could, but he might not know how to get the money to Japan safely, while the Colonel certainly would.

Now the question was, how should she go about asking an aristocrat for such a favor? She was still wondering when the Colonel arrived for his appointment, sat in a chair in the anteroom, waiting for Sam to come down from a hurried conference with Consul Alcott. She had already put the cash in an envelope and sealed the flap, and now she carefully wrote her mother's name and address in Japanese on the front. She studied Colonel Ito, who sat ramrod straight in a chair, his profile silhouetted against the bright light from a window. She stood up, almost lost her nerve, and sat down again, but she forced herself to do it.

"Gomenasai," she said, making a formal bow despite her Western clothing, saying "Excuse me" to get his attention. The Colonel turned his head just enough to look at her.

"Yes?" he said in English.

She held the envelope where it could be seen, blurting out her whole story at once, how she wanted the money delivered to her mother. And midway in her recital it occurred to her how inappropriate this was that she should make a request of such a distinguished man, and she bowed again and immediately began to apologize in Japanese for her impertinence, begging his forgiveness.

He stopped her. "Please do not apologize," he said in English. "If you have the money in that envelope, please give it to me. I will see that your mother gets it."

He held out his hand, palm upward, a pleasant expression on his face. She handed him the envelope and then thanked him again and bowed once more before she returned to her desk.

Sam was back in five minutes and he swept the Colonel into his office to begin the meeting, but not before Ito had the opportunity to realize how especially lovely this secretary was in her confusion. He wondered if Cummings-san realized what a prize he had so close to him.

The day they argued over the cables Sam called and said he would not be home for dinner. And when Charlotte heard him coming in late, greeted by Majordomo, she did not stir herself from the bedroom to greet him. She heard his footsteps in the hallway and expected the door to open momentarily as he came in to attempt a reconciliation, but he went on down the corridor and moved into one of the guest bedrooms for the night. The next day she knew his move was permanent when he had a desk brought into it and a telephone installed.

A week after the beginning of their undeclared war, Charlotte was brushing her hair in her dressing room when she realized that the differences between them would probably never be resolved.

What am I to do, Father? Why did I ever agree to come to this godforsaken place with this man?

Her reverie was interrupted by excited Number Six, her personal maid, who burst into the room wide-eyed. "Missie," she said. "Oh, missie, big-time mister he downstairs."

"Big-time mister?" she said curiously, trying to sort out the pidgin.

"He say Number Six fetchee missee chop chop."

"Does this big-time mister have a name?" she said, standing up, but Number Six had already darted from the room. Charlotte examined herself in the mirror. She was wearing a light brown summer dress with a white collar, one that she had always liked.

When she went downstairs Connaught stood up. "Well, Mrs. Cummings, if you will excuse the impertinence, I must say you are the most refreshing sight I have seen all day."

"That's gracious of you," she said. "I'm afraid my husband isn't at home, Mr. Connaught."

"I know he's not," Connaught said. "He's slaving away at the consulate for the good of the American Republic. But I'm here to take you to the afternoon opening of the new Mexican gambling casino on Bubbling Well Road."

"I'm afraid that's out of the question," she said. "I couldn't—"

"Then you want to see me fired," he said with mock gravity. "You want to see poor Connaught thrown out for failure to do his job. You see, I'm required to give the wives of new personnel an orientation tour of Shanghai. The fact that you happen to be a beautiful woman whose company I would enjoy for the day is totally beside the point."

"All right," she said. "I wouldn't want to see you fired." She laughed and felt guilty because she found his vaguely dissolute air attractive. She wondered what her father would think of this situation and knew he would not approve. She could almost hear his voice! *You're much too young and inexperienced to be behaving in this way.*

They went to the gambling casino, full of internationals in formal dress, the Chinese conspicuously absent, the wheels run by French croupiers. She reached for her purse only to have him hold up his hand in caution. "No, entirely on me," he said, and he bought her stacks of chips and so overfilled her hands that the chips fell clattering to the floor.

He eyed the spinning roulette wheel. "Give me a number," he said. "The first one that pops into your mind."

"Seventy-two," she said.

"There are only thirty-six numbers on the wheel."

"Twenty-seven then."

"A certain ring to that," he said. "Excuse me," he murmured to a Frenchman as he pushed a large stack of chips out to the square marked 27.

"How much am I betting?" she said.

"I didn't count," he said, putting his hand absently on her arm as he watched the croupier, who had just flipped the ball into the wheel in a direction opposite to the spin. But she was aware of the touch of his fingers, warm, intimate, as the ball fell into a number and the bored croupier sang it out in French. She squealed with delight as she realized that she had won, that the stick was shoving stacks of chips out to join her bet.

"My God," she said, pulling all the chips to the side of the table. "What were the odds?"

"Thirty-six to one," he said.

"And how much did I bet?"

"Let me see. I would think about two hundred dollars American."

"You're saying we won seventy-two hundred dollars?"

"Not us. You."

"It was your money."

"Not at all. I *gave* it to you. A gift."

"Then I'll pay you back."

"You don't pay back gifts."

"I can't accept it."

"Of course you can. Unless you want me to take all these chips and throw them into the street. I'm afraid that would cause something of a riot, but it might be interesting. Now, do you want to bet again?"

"I couldn't stand that," she said, laughing.

"Then I'll cash in your chips and we'll go shopping."

In a double ricksha, he showed her the exclusive shops in the French Sector, accompanying her into the showrooms, and when she tried on a soft beige dress that she thought was rather nice, he shook his head, a sober expression on his face. "Won't do." He spoke to the saleslady. "We would like to see this in red," he said.

"Certainly, sir."

"I look positively horrible in red," Charlotte protested.

"How do you know?" he said. "I'm willing to bet you high tea that you've never had a red dress."

"You lose," she said.

"I think you're cheating. How old were you?"

"Three. You didn't say anything about age." *When I was three you were already a grown man,* she thought.

"You win tea. But I don't concede. Try on the red."

When she appeared in it he did not even consult her. "It's perfect," he said. "Madame will take it."

"But you didn't even ask the price," Charlotte said.

Connaught looked at the saleslady. "Madame will wear the dress. So box the brown one and I'll give you the address where to send it."

The red dress exhilarated her and her excitement was compounded by being drawn through the streets of Shanghai in a ricksha, sitting next to a man who kept one hand resting on her arm while with the other he pointed out the sights, the great villa of Sir Victor Sassoon, the manor houses owned by some of the wealthiest men in the world, and finally the shopping districts where each street was devoted to a separate item.

"You won't have to come down here again unless you wish," Connaught said. "You simply send a servant to the Street of the Stockings and a merchant will come to your house to spread his wares in front of you. Anything you want, you can have."

By late afternoon she was close to exhaustion, but he insisted that she must have a hat to go with the red dress. He told her to hold still while he adjusted a slight projection of red veil that came down over the eyes and gave her a certain air of mystery. Then he stood back to examine her. "Really quite elegant, if I say so myself," he said. "But not quite right," he said.

So into other millinery shops they went, until at last, from among the dozens of hats of every shape and description, he spotted the one he wanted for her, and he sat directing the French-Chinese saleslady as to how it should be placed on her head and then adjusted the veil himself while she sat with her eyes closed, feeling that she was in the company of a man devoted to what was best for her.

After the hat came a small cafe on one of the canals in the city, sufficiently removed from the business district that there was a small and perfectly kept green lawn extending to the ancient stones that lined the bank of the canal and a single weeping willow tree in full summer foliage. Connaught ignored the tables on the terrace. He talked to the Chinese proprietor, explaining precisely what he wanted, and shortly he led Charlotte down a path around the willow, and there the waiters set up a table for two overlooking a small clear pool with golden carp lazing in the water.

The waiter brought a chilled bottle of wine, which Connaught tasted and then poured himself. "You're going to like this," he said. "Nectar of the Chinese gods. In other words, damn good."

She laughed, tasted the wine, found it sweet.

"Who could ask for any more than this," he said. "A drink by the water with a beautiful lady who has luck on her side and looks perfect in red." He raised his glass. "Cheers," he said with a warm smile.

"Cheers."

She looked at the still waters of the pool, mirroring the summer clouds, and wondered who this man really was who sat refilling the wineglasses in the sunlight and why he was being so really nice to her. He was so much older than she, already accustomed to a kind of life totally different from hers.

"Penny," he said.

"Pardon?"

"For your thoughts. You seem a thousand miles away."

"Nothing important," she said.

Connaught emptied his glass. "I promised you high tea."

"I couldn't," she said. "As much as I've enjoyed the day, I need to be getting home soon."

"On one condition," he said. "You have lunch with me tomorrow."

"I don't know," she said.

"You're in no position to turn me down," he said.

"How so?"

"Nobody here speaks English. You'd have a very hard time instructing a ricksha driver how to take you home. And the telephone system is a confused mess."

"All right, then," she said. "Since I have no choice. But please, I must go home now."

In the ricksha, he took her hand in his. "This has been a very special day for me," he said seriously.

"I've enjoyed it enormously," she said. For a moment she was afraid he was going to kiss her. But when the ricksha puller went up the circular drive, Connaught merely lifted her hand to his lips, then escorted her to the door and told her he would pick her up at noon tomorrow.

She went immediately to her bedroom and found a cable from her father on the writing table. She picked it up.

MY DEAR DAUGHTER. I HAVE BEEN IN TOUCH WITH
HEALTH AUTHORITIES AND I HAVE BEEN ADVISED THAT
THERE IS A MINOR OUTBREAK OF CHOLERA UPRIVER FROM
YOU, SO I ADVISE . . .

She stopped reading and walked around the room, stopping in
front of the full-length mirror. She was startled. The girl staring back
at her was really stunning, a well-proportioned face with wide gray
eyes, a finely shaped nose, full lips. She turned to the side. The red
was such a bold color. She liked it.

She took off the hat, examined her hair, and decided that it would
look considerably better shortened. And maybe a shade lighter to
bring out the highlights. Perhaps she should wear a bit more
makeup.

Lunch tomorrow. Certainly Sam could have no objections, for this
was Harry's job after all. If an older man found her attractive, there
was no harm in that. And besides, it was time for her to make up her
own mind about what pleased her and what did not. If she wanted to
shower her friends and her father with cables, it was none of Sam's
business. She would use the account her father had opened for her to
use whenever and however she wanted. She was tired of orders from
Sam. After all, he wasn't supporting her. So why couldn't she do
what she pleased with her life?

"There is really no need for you to help me move, Cummings-
san," Yuki said, making her way up the narrow flight of stairs to the
tiny box room.

"I don't mind at all," he said. "I have a free Saturday and I'm sure
it will go a lot faster with the two of us."

He reached her box room and was appalled that she had been
living in such a small cubicle with only candles for light. All of her
possessions were contained in a single box and a bulky bundle
wrapped in a blanket with the four corners tied. He picked up the
box and retraced his way down the stairs with Yuki following close
behind him, carrying the bundle.

On the street it was quite obvious that the double ricksha he had
hired would not carry both of them and the box and the bundle, so
he signaled another ricksha to carry the box and bundle, directed
the puller to follow close behind, and then helped Yuki into the first
one.

"Where shall I tell the puller to go?" he said. "I don't know the address."

"I have to stop for one or two things first," she said. "You have been most kind to help, but I can manage from here."

"I wouldn't think of it," he said.

"If you're sure."

"Very sure."

She directed the puller to go straight ahead and then into a maze of narrow lanes that culminated in a square bounded by makeshift stalls on all sides. Yuki took time to check the money in her purse, and he could not help but notice that she had less than ten dollars American and a handful of Chinese brass coins. "If you need an advance on your wages . . ."

"I shan't be spending much money and I have plenty," she said. "But your offer is a most generous one."

He took a closer look at the merchandise laid out on the ground in front of the squatting merchants. He could see absolutely nothing that she would want. On display was everything from broken crockery to small pieces of wallpaper, Chinese tools, a saw with teeth worn smooth, a hammer head. But she moved from stall to stall, haggling over a small rolled-up dirty-looking carpet, a mutilated table with only three legs, a cracked mirror, dispensing coins grudgingly, having her purchases piled on the ricksha until it was full, and then into the double ricksha that had carried them.

He raised his hand and summoned a third ricksha and then a fourth, astounded at what she was collecting. She bought pieces of wood, a torn shade from a Gifu lamp crusted with dirt, a sack full of tile, so many things in such bulk that finally he had to summon a fifth ricksha, the first four overloaded.

And as they pulled out of the street market, a miniature caravan by now, she appeared to be quite pleased with herself. "You won't believe this, Cummings-san," she said. "But I managed to buy everything I need for less than a dollar and fifty cents, American."

He could believe it. They should have paid her more than that to haul it away. "I don't mean to be a spoilsport," he said, "but it appears to me that you have a number of rickshas following filled with worthless junk. What on earth will you use all of these things for?"

"I'm not sure yet," she said happily. "But one has to make do."

They came to an intersection marked by an ancestor stone protruding from the center of the street, and she instructed the puller, who then turned down a side lane without breaking stride and finally came to a stop in front of an apartment building that on first glance appeared to be slightly run down and on closer inspection proved to be a disaster. The private courtyard was full of trash and weeds that had grown waist high. The door was ajar to the first of two small rooms that smelled as rank as they looked, with soot and dirt covering the walls, a decrepit toilet, and a kitchen the size of a closet. He stood by and watched the pullers unloading the rickshas under her direction and decided she had taken leave of her senses.

He went down the line of pullers and paid them all except for the one he told to stay behind and wait for him. He felt very bad for Yuki, certain that she would recognize the mistake at any moment and come out into the sunlight with dismay on her face and the realization that she had worsened her condition by the move.

But when she came out to the moon gate he saw nothing awry in her expression. "I wish to express thanks to you, Cummings-san," she said. "For helping me."

"You're entirely welcome," he said.

Women, he thought, as the ricksha carried him toward his house. Charlotte had so many rooms she couldn't count them, filled with priceless Chinese antiques, waited on hand and foot by a full staff of devoted servants, and yet she was continually shifting things around. And Yuki was delighted with absolutely terrible accommodations and piles of refuse that needed to be hauled away to a garbage dump.

Women, he thought again. *I'll never understand either of them.*

At times it seemed to Sam that all of Shanghai was a rumor mill, with the American Consulate at the center. The main concern at the moment was what the Japanese were going to do in Manchuria and what the Chinese response would be. The American Embassy in Tokyo was filing its usual reports in Washington, known in the Foreign Service as OTOH's, "On the Other Hands."

Experts in Tokyo were certain the Japanese government would instigate a battle in Manchuria, but on the other hand a different set of experts noted a strong split between the civilian and military factions in Tokyo and had an increasing belief that the civilian faction would control the military and there would be no further trouble in Manchuria.

The one bright spot in Shanghai that Cummings could report to Washington was that General Wang seemed to be losing his stranglehold on the local Chinese community. As a matter of fact, Wang had ordered a camp built midway between Shanghai and Nanking, as if preparing to open new territory for himself.

Late on a Wednesday afternoon Sam received an envelope from the Japanese Consulate with Colonel Ito's chop mark on the front. He asked Yuki for an immediate translation of the contents. "I'm sorry to keep you so late," he said. "But this is from Tokyo, a written account of the debate on Manchurian expansionism. I'm having dinner with Colonel Ito and a Japanese admiral at a restaurant in the Japanese Sector, on Ward Road. I need to know what the Japanese government officials are thinking. I'll have an embassy driver bring you to the restaurant when you're through with it."

"Do you want a full translation?"

"No, there isn't time for that. Just read the debate and then give me a summary opinion."

"You do me honor, but I don't know that much about politics."

"The members of the Diet aren't all that sophisticated. If it seems to you that there's a popular support among them for a war in Manchuria, then I want to know it. If the majority opinion is against, I want to know that."

"I think that Colonel Ito would have a better opinion than I would."

"Colonel Ito has his limits as I have mine," he said. "He's not going to interpret what has not yet become the official policy of his government. So just write me your opinion."

"Yes, sir," she said.

"I'll give the address of the restaurant to the driver when I make arrangements for the car. I'm sorry you'll have to work overtime."

"I am honored to be able to serve you, sir."

At the restaurant Sam changed into slippers and followed the hostess down the hallway to a private room with cushions next to a low table on the tatami. Colonel Ito and Admiral Ugaki were already present. The Admiral was a short round man in full uniform, with a thin-line mustache on his upper lip. His face was flushed beet red. He had already had his fill of sake.

Colonel Ito poured wine for Sam. "How good is your command of Japanese by now?" he said.

"Still very thin."

"Fine," Ito said with pleasant candor. "Then leave all the Japanese to me. The Admiral's feathers are easily ruffled." The Admiral grunted something in Japanese, looked directly at Ito. "You see?" Ito said. "He insists that every word in English be translated for him." He spoke to the Admiral with a deferentially polite attitude.

"What did you tell him?"

"I said you were extending a welcome to him in the hope that he would enjoy his stay in Shanghai."

"What's he really here for?"

"The Admiral has come to Shanghai on a special mission," Ito said. "I have not been given any reason. He has a small fleet anchored in the estuary."

"A social visit, I trust," Sam said, smiling, raising his cup to the Admiral with a smile. *"Compai."*

"Compai," the Admiral said. He drained his cup, spoke in a high-pitched Japanese to Ito, who heard him out before he began a translation.

"The Admiral conveys his official greetings to you and the American government that you represent," he said. "As that representative, he would like your assessment of the current situation with General Wang."

Sam concealed his surprise, maintained his smile. "Tell him that I bow to him in his knowledge of military matters."

"Well put," Ito said. The message was duly conveyed and the dinner was served. The Admiral kept up a running dialogue about the bravery of the Japanese Navy and Marines. The navy was far more important than a land-based army in China because there were so many navigable rivers, and the Admiral could put a thousand men ashore from a river in a matter of minutes under the withering cover fire of the naval guns.

Sam ate sparingly, drank little, aware that the real reason for the meeting had not yet emerged. And then, as the final course was being served and the Admiral was washing down his rice with a mouthful of tea, he murmured a remark that was almost parenthetical.

"The Admiral has heard the rumor that the number of American Marines in Shanghai is being increased," he said. "He wonders if they are to protect the Americans here from General Wang and a Chinese attack."

Sam rubbed his chin thoughtfully. *Always address yourself to the real question beneath the verbal one,* his professors had told him. "You may not be able to answer this," he said to Ito. "But he's not really concerned about General Wang, is he?"

"I believe that is a fair way of putting it," Ito said.

Sam was very much aware of the ridiculous situation in which he had been placed, a young man just out of school, on his first post, being asked by a drunken Japanese admiral to interpret American intentions. "Please tell the Admiral that I am not connected with military affairs and therefore cannot comment on the reason for any troop movements," he said.

Ito translated. The Admiral took a sip of wine. Undeterred, he simply approached from a different direction, murmured again.

"The Admiral thinks that even with heavy reinforcement, your troops currently stationed in the International Settlement would be insufficient to protect foreign interests against a Chinese assault. So it is his opinion that America would welcome anything that might keep that Chinese assault from taking place."

Ah, Sam thought. The real question was now apparent. *Would the United States intervene if the Japanese took over Manchuria or would the United States feel a sense of relief that any Chinese hostilities might be diverted elsewhere?* "That's an interesting observation," Sam said.

"The Admiral wishes to know if you agree."

Sam was tempted to meet him head on, but it was not his place to engage a Japanese admiral in debate. "Unfortunately, any opinion I might have would be worthless," he said pleasantly.

The Admiral stared at him with visible frustration.

"The Admiral's getting very impatient," Ito said. "He says that surely you have an opinion or have heard an opinion expressed."

"Tell him that Consul General Alcott would be glad to give him any policy interpretations he might want. You can also tell him that, personally, I feel quite secure in Shanghai."

There was a light knock on the wooden jamb of the door. Ito was about to answer when Sam interrupted. "That will be my secretary," he said. "She's bringing a message to me here."

Yuki entered, looking tired. She bowed to Ito and the Admiral before she handed Cummings an envelope. "Shall I wait, sir?" she said.

"No, thank you, Miss Nakamura. You've worked quite enough for one day. I'll see you tomorrow."

"Yes, sir."

She left the room, the Admiral's eyes following her. "If you gentlemen will excuse me a moment," Sam said. He opened the envelope, briefly examined Yuki's script. The message was concise and to the point.

"I believe, sir, that there is much political pressure in Japan against any war in Manchuria. But the members of the Diet *think* that the troops in Chosen and Manchuria will make their own decisions, despite any instructions from Tokyo, and that therefore the civilian government is powerless. The military will decide whether to fight or not."

He folded the paper, put it into his pocket. Now it was his turn to fish for information. "I hope the Admiral is enjoying his stay in Shanghai. Where will he be going next?"

The Admiral answered with a smile, spoke in a low voice, which the Colonel translated reluctantly. "The Admiral says that his stay in Shanghai is not yet complete or his enjoyment a full one yet. Since the girl is obviously your servant, he would like to have her."

"What?" Sam said.

"He wants your secretary for tonight. Do not frown. He is being blunt, but that is his manner. He does not mean it as an insult."

Sam felt the adrenaline pump through him. "He can go to hell," Sam said coldly. "Tell the Admiral that I am a Vice-Consul of the United States of America and the lady in question is my assistant, an employee of the United States government, and she's sure as hell not going to bed with him."

Colonel Ito said something to the Admiral, and after a moment the Admiral laughed and filled his glass and lifted it in a toast to Sam.

"What did you tell him?" Sam was astonished at the Admiral's reaction.

"I told him that you said he should find his own woman," Ito said. "But that this one belongs to you."

Outside the restaurant, after the Admiral had been picked up by an official car to go back to his ship, Ito lingered while Sam waited for his driver.

"You did very well, I think," Ito said. "You dodged his questions like a veteran." He adjusted his white gloves. "I wanted to tell you that I will not be around for a while. I will be out of the city for a week or two."

"Where are you off to?"

"Manchuria."

"From the tone of the arguments in the Diet, there seems to be a good chance of war there."

"I don't know what's going to happen in Manchuria any more than you do," Ito said. "I'm not going up on any military mission. My father is going to establish a factory in Mukden and he wants my advice. My government gives concessions to businessmen willing to take a chance in Manchuria."

Sam lit a cigarette, blew the smoke into the warm night air. "Anyway, the Wang business seems to be finished for the time being," he said. "It's my guess that the next time we see the General, he'll be at the head of a major Chinese army."

"But not for a while," Ito said. "And I'll be back from Manchuria by then."

"Have a good trip."

On his ride home Sam realized how much he would miss Ito. He had come to trust the Colonel implicitly. When they were together there was none of the verbal sparring he encountered with some of the other entry-level officials, as if they were all practicing for the time when they would be arguing government policy on a high level. He had no doubt that in any hard differences between the United States and Japan, Ito would follow his country's policy without hesitation, knowing that Sam would do the same. But Sam could see no present likelihood of that.

It was late by the time the car pulled into the circular drive and Majordomo admitted him to the house. The light under Charlotte's door was already out. He found the coverlets turned back on his bed in the guest room, but there was a full moon out and it cast an unsettling light into the room, despite the drawn drapes. He mixed himself a bourbon and water, sat thoughtfully while he drank it, and then went to bed. Yuki's image formed in his mind and he could not dispel it. He had been startled by the real anger that had flared within him at the Admiral's request. He hadn't realized how protective he felt about her.

He was too tired to figure it out tonight and he had arranged a busy day for tomorrow on the river. Finally, from simple exhaustion, he fell asleep.

It took them over an hour to find the rental dock on the west side of the river, a collection of boats contained in a fenced pen with coils of razor-sharp barbed wire on the top. The dock was run by an Englishman who took the consulate authorization paper from Sam, examined it, and then with a shrug directed the Chinese workers to put the boat Sam chose into the water and lower the keel.

"The outboard is sometimes fitful to start, but once it kicks in, it's reliable. I would advise your making way upriver a few miles beyond the bend for your best sailing, sir," he said. "You can see the down-stream bedlam for yourself with all the commercial and military traffic." He looked out across the yellow waters under a bright sun. "I would also advise you to steer clear of the Chinese junks. There's no efficient patrol on the river and they'll nick you in broad daylight if they can."

Sam thanked him, and helping Yuki aboard, handed her the bas-ket, and then took his place at the tiller and pulled the rope to start the outboard, which sputtered and came alive on the first yank of the cord. "We'll wait until we clear the heavy traffic before we raise the sail," he said.

"Are you sure you have done this before?" Yuki said nervously as the boat slipped between a tug and a scow, perilously close to both.

"Yes," he said. "I spent time on this river as a child, and when I was going to school in the States and had a rough exam coming up, I'd take my sailboat out onto the bay." They had emerged from the shadow of a tanker in the channel and now he brought the boat around and headed down channel, immensely pleased to be on the water with a beautiful girl and a sparkling afternoon. "Let's break out the sandwiches and the bottle of wine," he said.

She opened the basket and handed him a ham sandwich, then uncorked the wine. "Can you tell me, Cummings-san, what we are looking for?"

"Sampans carrying military supplies upriver," he said.

"But how can we possibly tell?"

"They operate with impunity," Sam said. "If they wanted to hide cargo, they'd simply put it below deck, but they'd lose too much space. So they'll carry crates on deck with either Japanese or English markings, an occasional German shipment thrown in for good mea-sure. When we get below Hongkew we'll raise sail and tack back up this direction. And you'll use your binoculars and write down the crate markings and the kind of craft carrying them."

"All right," she said, and now, with a chicken-salad sandwich in one hand and a wineglass in the other, dressed in American-style clothes, with a red blouse and a blue skirt, she was obviously quite at home with the afternoon assignment.

They came abreast of a Japanese passenger ship moving into dock and the passengers at the rail began to wave at them. "Look, we're part of the local color," Sam said, waving back.

"May I ask you a question?" she said.

"Sure."

"How will you know from counting boats this afternoon how many arms are being shipped upriver?" she asked. "There may be a hundred more boats tomorrow than there are today. Or a hundred less."

He nodded toward a British gunboat chugging upstream past a pair of anchored Japanese destroyers. "Do you know what that particular gunboat is doing at the moment?"

"I have no idea."

"Counting the cannons and deck guns on the destroyers. And there will be Japanese teams out counting American guns and Chinese counting the British. It makes no difference that the naval ships move in and out of the area all the time. Everybody is reassured by numbers. So I'll supply numbers to make Washington more secure, and in return we are allowed a fine afternoon on the river."

"I see." She looked at him curiously. "Tell me, was your wife a *koibito* since childhood?" she said.

"I haven't got the slightest idea," he said with a smile. "What's a *koibito*?"

"How shall I say?" she said, perplexed. "That's one word the missionaries never taught me. It means a girl, not just a girl but one you like very much."

"A girlfriend," he said. "A sweetheart."

"Yes."

"What was the word again. *Koibito?* You'll have to write it down for me."

"Are you learning Japanese?"

"Yes, from a consulate tutor, but I find it rough going, especially when I'm with Ito."

"That's because his language is very special," she said.

"Oh?"

"Since he will be a baron, he knows the formal language very well, and many of the naval officers like to speak the same way. Now, back to the *koibito*," she said. "If it's not too personal."

"No," he said, relaxing. "She wasn't a childhood sweetheart. How about you? Have you had boyfriends?"

"No," she said.

"I don't understand that," he said. "You're such a pretty girl."

"Is that what you would say to girls back in the States?"

"Only if it were true," he said. "Which in your case, it is. Can you manage another glass of wine for me?"

She refilled his glass. "Another sandwich?"

"No, thanks." The thought hit him that he had never been sailing with a prettier girl. He forced himself to move his eyes past her. Off to port were the Japanese docks, the buildings flanking the river avenue. "We'll go as far as the bend," he said. "You might as well break out the binoculars."

She took them from the basket, scanned a junk on the far side of the channel. "They're carrying mortars from Yokohama," she said. "At least that's what the crates say."

"Count the crates and write down the exact markings if you will," he said. "And the ship's identification."

She wrote the information in a notebook, then lifted the binoculars again. "There's a Chinese scow with crates marked 'Machinery' in English. Shall I put that down?"

He took the glasses from her, brought the scow into focus. There was a single crate on deck, so heavy it weighed down the stern. "Probably a spare engine for heavy machinery," he said. "They don't take the trouble to disguise military equipment."

He had reached the bend in the river and now he brought the boat around and hoisted the sail. "We'll have a following sea on the west leg," he said. "Now, take a look at those six sampans along the south side of the channel. If they're carrying similar cargo, they're probably running a convoy against the attack of upriver bandits."

He lit a cigarette and began to hum to himself, the breeze bellying out the sail, his hand resting lightly on the tiller, and it occurred to him that Charlotte would never come sailing with him. Even as a girl she had complained of motion sickness, and the trip across the Pacific had only confirmed her dislike of being on any body of water.

At three o'clock the wind fell off and then shifted, and he had to tack a diagonal course across the river, watching the sampans switching their cumbersome sails to catch the freshening breeze, and now he became aware that he did not have the clear waters around him he had enjoyed before. As he neared the far leg of his port tack, he was in the traffic lane of the motorized sampans in convoy and close enough to see the scowling faces of the crews that watched Yuki making her notes.

"I think we had better put a temporary end to our survey," he said. "We seem to be drawing more attention than I find comfortable."

She put the binoculars down, closed the notebook, and put the pen back in her purse. "I counted twenty-six separate vessels carrying boxes that were clearly labeled as containing arms," she said.

"On whose boats?"

"All Chinese."

"That's to be expected," he said, trying to keep his voice even, all the while watching a makeshift junk running on an inboard diesel, which poured black smoke into the air. The junk was approaching quite slowly on the starboard side, its coolie crew all gathered on the deck. Sam asked Yuki to help him lower the sail, and when she was occupied with the lines he began to yank the cord to start the outboard, but the motor coughed and died, again and again, until his arm was aching and the junk was no more than ten yards away from them.

"Stop!" one of the coolies yelled from the junk. "Stand still!"

He could hear the men talking in Chinese, already dividing the spoils, with one man to take the binoculars, another any money the two might have, a third making a claim for Sam's Wellington boots.

"Ignore them," Sam said to Yuki in a conversational tone of voice. He gave the rope another yank. This time the motor sputtered and caught, but the lead coolie did not think it significant.

"Ten dollar," he called out to Sam. "You pay ten dollar and use our river."

"They won't settle for ten dollars when they can take everything, including the boat," he said. He looked around for anything to use as a weapon, decided on a grappling hook on an eight-foot pole lying on the deck. At the same time he eyed the narrow distance between one of the sampans and a tug maneuvering a larger ship toward a docking position. The timing would have to be right or he would run his boat into the side of the tug.

"When I yell you hit the deck," he said. "They may have firearms." She nodded gravely and he held his breath, watching the narrowing gap between the tug and the sampan, waiting until the junk had edged within six feet, coming bow on, the lead coolie on the fore deck, line in hand, ready to jump onto the boat and take it over.

"Now," Sam yelled, and Yuki flattened herself against the deck while Sam snatched up the grappling hook and with a sweep knocked the coolie into the water, at the same time revving up the motor and pulling the tiller sharply to the side. The momentum of the Chinese junk carried it forward and past the sailboat, but the coolie in the water had grabbed the fender line on the starboard side of the sailboat and was trying to pull himself aboard. And before Sam had time to move, he saw Yuki swing the binoculars by the leather cord, hitting the coolie in the side of the head. He yowled and dropped away, splashing after the junk as Sam edged through the opening between the tug and the sampan and cut around the side of the freighter, breathing a sigh of relief.

"My God," he said with admiration. "You're something else."

Yuki turned and made sure the coolie had reached his junk safely, then looked at the binoculars. "I am afraid that I have dented them," she said ruefully.

He was laughing as he entered the heavy traffic approaching the rental quay and bumped through the confusion of smaller boats, the naked swimming boys yelling at any vessel carrying Westerners, begging for coins. As he entered the fenced boat yard he killed the motor and slipped the boat alongside the dock.

As the Chinese workers held the boat steady he helped Yuki onto the wooden dock. The owner came walking up. "I hope you had a pleasant sail," he said dryly.

"Let's put it this way," Sam said. "I owe you for a grappling hook."

"And the line and rubber fenders on the port side," the Englishman said. Sam had a look and saw where the lines had been cut through with a knife and the fenders removed. "I'll be damned," Sam said. "The swimming boys."

"I'll add it to the rental bill to the consulate, shall I?"

"Yes," Sam said. "Do that."

In the taxi, on the way back to the consulate, Sam was aware that Yuki was in no distress at all. On the contrary, she seemed exhilarated.

"I had a marvelous afternoon," she said. "Quite exciting, *ne?*"

"Very," he said. "Weren't you the least bit afraid when the coolie tried to climb aboard?"

"Only after I had knocked him into the water," she said.

"We'll have to have another sail under different conditions," he said. "We'll try a less congested part of the river."

"Anytime," she said with a smile.

"It's marvelous," Connaught was saying as he examined her hair in the sunlight before they entered the car. "Turn around and let me look at it." She turned slowly. "Whoever did you get?"

"I think her name was Madame Francine. One of my servants called her in from the French Concession. She has a salon on the Avenue Joffre."

"What did your husband say about your new look?"

"He hasn't seen it yet."

"Then that's his loss." He held the door for her. "I'm driving today, no chauffeur, just the two of us. I'm known as something of a daredevil on the streets of Shanghai, but I can swear to you I've never had an accident."

"I trust you. Where are we having lunch?"

"The roof garden of the new Cathay Hotel," he said. "They have a White Russian chef who supposedly worked in the kitchens of Nicholas and Alexandra in his youth."

He accelerated the car and it leapt forward in the drive. She was impressed by his complete confidence behind the wheel, the way he whipped the car into the narrowest possible space, barely missing the ricksha pullers who competed with the trucks for space. He peered ahead, saw an ornate vehicle painted in gaudy colors and preceded by robed men on foot banging gongs.

"Damn," he said. "We certainly don't want any of that." And he whipped the car up a side street.

"What was it?" she said, intrigued.

"A big-time Chinese funeral procession," he said. "Very rare for the International Settlement. Undoubtedly a high functionary who's going to be buried near one of the temples in the center of the city. Most of the poor Chinese in Pootung or Chapei simply slip the bodies into the river or have them hauled away."

"I don't like to think about such things," she said.

"Then we won't," he said with an immediate smile. "How's your father?"

"Fine," she said. "Why do you ask?"

"You were very concerned about him the night you arrived."

"I love him very much. Tell me about your father, Harry."

"My father was a greengrocer in Leeds and my mother helped him. They were up at the crack of dawn and they worked hard and never owed a penny to a soul and both died of influenza during the World War."

"How sad."

"The living as well as the dying," he said. "It was a paradox, you see," he said. "They worked hard at something they didn't really enjoy because they were afraid of having nothing for their old age. Even when I was quite small I used to see them counting coppers and thought it must be a game adults play. So they conserved all right, and then there wasn't any old age. That seemed to me a joke of the gods. So I've chosen the opposite course. Give me a fine day today and the devil take tomorrow. I joined the navy early, was sent here where I mustered out, and saw no reason to go home."

"Then you weren't with them when they died."

"I was at sea, as a matter of fact. By the time I had the news, they had been buried for a full month."

"Have you ever been married?" she said.

He laughed aloud. "I never found a woman who would have me." He peered through the windshield. "Ah, here we are," he said, driving beneath the porte cochere of the Cathay Hotel, turning the car over to a White Russian valet.

At the roof garden the ease he demonstrated in dealing with the maître d' was not lost on her, nor the prearrangement of a window table overlooking the bend of the Whangpoo. The yellow water was covered with boats, sampans, junks, scows, barges, and an ocean liner was making its way through the heavy traffic under the guidance of a pair of tug boats.

A waiter came to take their order. "Good afternoon, Boris," Connaught said. "This is a special day, so I shall leave it to you to bring us the very best that your chef has to offer. We'll begin with champagne for the beautiful lady and my usual for me."

"Yes, sir."

She accepted the champagne and was curious about the drink brought to him in an opaque glass. "What are you drinking?" she said.

"A special concoction," he said. "A sailor's delight." He raised his glass to her. "Here's to this special day and our time together, my dear Charlotte."

"It's special for me too," she said, and then she blushed at what she had said. But he was so handsome and he treated her like a woman— a beautiful one.

Toward the end of the meal, when her champagne was almost gone and he was on his third drink, he looked at her with sad and penetrating eyes and asked, "You're not happy with him, are you?"

She knew she should deny it, but she found herself shaking her head. "No."

"I don't want to complicate things for you in any way, my darling Charlotte," he said. "All you have to do is to stop me now, tell me that you don't want me to pursue this any further."

She had difficulty breathing, but she looked directly into his eyes. "How old are you, Harry?" she asked.

"Does it make a difference? Forty," he said.

"I'm twenty-three."

"So?"

"You know so much more of the world than I do," she said.

"I've lived long enough to know what things in this life are important to me and to realize what I want," he said, putting his hand on hers. "You have no reason to be afraid of me."

"I should explain about Sam."

"You don't have to."

"I want you to know. It was a marriage of convenience, Harry, arranged by our families."

"Then it's no real marriage at all, is it?"

"Not in that sense, no. But I don't take my vows lightly."

"It's time for you to make a decision," he said. "If you want me to take you home, say so, dear Charlotte."

She was silent.

She watched him cross the room to the maître d', make a request, sign his name on a chit. The maître d' picked up the telephone, made an inquiry, then nodded to Harry. Connaught came back to the table. "Come with me," he said.

"Where are we going?"

He did not answer. They left the roof garden and took the stairs down one flight to where a Chinese bellboy was unlocking a door. Connaught tipped him, ushered her into one of the most elegant suites she had ever seen, a room of low tables and velvet divans with a wide window framing a view of the distant countryside.

"I can't do this, Harry," she said in a weak voice.

"Can you give me any reason why we shouldn't be together?"

"I don't know."

He took her in his arms. "You don't have to say anything, my darling. Just trust me." When he kissed her she lost her breath and began to tremble. He lifted her from her feet and carried her into the bedroom, where he undressed her with such swift skill that she knew nothing except that the barriers between them had disappeared. She wanted no part of her body to be concealed or withheld from him, and when he made love to her all of her feelings were shattered into glittering fragments, and she gave herself to him freely and without reservation.

Finally he lay beside her, his hand still holding hers. She was at peace, truly so for the first time in her married life.

Alcott called a meeting of his three vice-consuls on a Monday morning: Dawes, a workhorse of a man nearing retirement who handled Commercial; Miller, a rather sedentary lawyer in his fifties who saw to the legal rights of Americans enmeshed in the complicated court systems of Shanghai, and Sam as Liaison Vice-Consul to the other legations. They sat around a conference table examining the mimeographed sheets Alcott had handed out.

"If you will be kind enough to do the briefing on the first item, young Mr. Cummings, since you did the survey, I will be most appreciative," Alcott said.

Sam nodded. "The Japanese government is going to give their gunboats permanent moorage on the Whangpoo. Sooner or later they will try to interfere with vessels bound upriver. And there's a strong possibility that Chinese gunboats will blockade traffic on the Yangtze between the estuary and Nanking."

Dawes whistled slightly. "What are the odds the Japanese will really follow through?"

"I'd say it's certain," Sam said. "Just a matter of time."

"I'll pass the word to all American river traffic," Dawes said. "We don't want an incident."

"With all due respect," Sam said, "I think we should continue business as usual on the river. I have no hard information on the Chinese response, but I think the Japanese placement of their warships in the Whangpoo is a test of our will. If we cut off all our upriver trade because we're afraid of an incident, they will see us as dragons with no teeth and decide they can go right ahead in Manchuria."

"And suppose that the boat of one of my cotton dealers runs afoul of the Japanese and we lose it?" Dawes said. "What teeth do we have to use then?"

Alcott ignored him, studied Sam thoughtfully. "So the test concerns Manchuria," he said.

"Yes, sir."

"Once they have gunboats on the Whangpoo, what's their next step?"

"It's my guess they'll stop all incoming traffic and demand to see the manifest on the pretext of looking for arms being smuggled to the Chinese. They'll use that method to control all traffic on the river."

"How would you handle it?" Alcott said.

"I'd allow them to see the manifests, then take them to the Settlement courts for attempted restraint of trade. They'll back down. And it may save trouble in Manchuria if they suspect we'll take action."

"Very admirable, I'm sure," Alcott said without conviction. He lit his pipe. "We will make that ruling then. We will not cut down any of our traffic on the Whangpoo, Mr. Dawes, not on the strength of a rumor. Mr. Miller, I will expect you to lay the legal groundwork for a court protest should young Mr. Cummings be correct."

"Certainly," Miller said.

"Are you going to take the same attitude toward the Chinese gunboats?" Dawes said.

"No," Alcott answered. "They don't really give a damn about international law. They may very well decide to strip all boats going upstream or down for the booty. So we suspend traffic on the Yangtze for the time being, except for authorized gunboats, which are not under our jurisdiction anyway." He looked over his glasses again. "That takes care of item one. I shall make item two short and sweet. The Great Depression has now squeezed us and we have a directive from State. It may be that we will have to give up this building and take quarters in a hotel when our lease here has expired. We'll have a few months grace, but I want each of you to come up with halved budgets in your departments. That's all, gentlemen. I would like you to stay behind a moment if you will, young Mr. Cummings."

"I would appreciate it, Mr. Alcott," Sam said when the others were gone, "if you could bring yourself to drop the 'young Mr. Cummings' business."

"You find that objectionable, do you?"

"Yes, sir. I do."

Alcott turned to look out the window. "You may find the next subject equally objectionable."

"Why don't you try me and see?"

"Very well," Alcott said. "Where were you Saturday before last?"

"Helping my assistant move."

"From where to where?"

"A tenement in the Mouth of the Rainbow District to a small flat off Avenue Road."

"A Miss Nakamura."

"Yes."

"Who is Japanese."

"Yes, she's Japanese," Sam said. "She was working here before I arrived."

"And she has accomplished a miraculous elevation," Alcott said. "A veritable Cinderella story. Oriental style. A poor country girl, destined to spend the rest of her life translating routine visa papers, is lo and behold rescued by an American prince who, recognizing her great beauty—and I grant you that, Cummings, she is a beauty— raises her to a far higher station as a translator and then as a secretary. And since a princess should not be living in a box room with no windows in a tenement which is also a fire trap, she is removed to a quote small unquote garden flat off Avenue Road. Have I made any mistakes so far, Mr. Cummings, or strayed from the truth?"

"Have I broken any of the rules, sir?"

"It's not what you've done but what you might do," Alcott said. "You're young and you show great promise in diplomacy if you don't ruin your chances early on." He turned his eyes toward the window again. "Oriental girls are almost irresistible. They're very compliant, anxious to please, not at all like the wives we bring along."

"I am not having an affair with her."

Alcott looked at him with quizzical disbelief. "Aside from your personal involvement, I have other reservations. Since Miss Nakamura is your personal employee, you may direct her to type or take dictation and translate documents of a certain nonsensitive nature. But I must require that any documents reflecting on our

· 123 ·

official positions will be forwarded to my office and sent through channels to translators cleared for such assignments."

But Sam did not hear the end of Alcott's remarks, for he was stopped by one of the phrases. "What do you mean, my 'personal employee,' Mr. Alcott? She works for the consulate."

"Her paycheck is issued through the consulate, yes."

"Are you saying she isn't a regular employee?"

"That's correct, Mr. Cummings."

Suddenly there was a sharp suspicion in Sam's mind. "The consulate is down to counting paper clips because of an acute financial shortage and yet I live in a mansion with a staff of servants large enough to make a football team. I was told a wealthy Chinese merchant had donated the house while he traveled abroad. That's not true, is it?"

"Of course not," Alcott said. "Practically no one in this consulate subsists on the pittances we are paid. Mr. Miller, for instance, has a private income from industries in Florida, I believe. Mr. Dawes, in his department, is also quite wealthy."

"And what kind of arrangement do I have?" Sam said.

"You really don't know?"

"No. I really don't know."

"It is my understanding that your father-in-law made the financial arrangements through the consulate so you would not be troubled. He set up a fund that our comptroller has administered—that's the usual way of handling these things, by the way—and Mr. Connaught found the house and the servants."

"I see. I want these arrangements to stop immediately. This is a personal matter between my wife's father and me."

"That's your prerogative," Alcott said. "But it can't be immediate. I believe the house is paid for until the first of the year, and I also think there are agreements with the absentee Chinese landlord that require the retention of the servants. Personally, I see nothing wrong with the use of private funds in government service. And if I'm wrong about Miss Nakamura—"

"Where is her paycheck coming from?"

"Out of your household moneys, I believe."

"And it's impossible for me to have her as a secretary on a regular government employment basis?"

"We could pay a token portion of it, I suppose," Alcott said. "But she will not be listed on the roster of the consulate as an official employee. There's no way she can be included on our register. Even if it weren't for the money involved, it would not be proper to have a foreign national in a position that might appear to be a sensitive one."

"Connaught has no listed position and yet you keep him on full salary," Sam said. "How can you support him and refuse to pay a woman who does valuable work here?"

"Mr. Connaught is indispensable to the physical operation of the consulate. He saves us far more in expenses every year than we pay him. You do understand me, Mr. Cummings?"

"I understand you all right, Mr. Alcott. I just don't happen to agree with you."

"I don't require that members of my staff agree with me," Alcott said finally. "But since I am ultimately responsible here, I make the decisions and I expect them to be followed."

"Yes, sir," Sam said.

He walked for hours after the conversation with Alcott, stewing in his anger at Noble, who had set this up without his knowledge, and at his mother and his uncle, who must have known about it. He felt betrayed, not only by circumstances but by his own inexperience and naiveté, which had led him to believe Connaught's impossible story about the Chinese merchant and the rent-free house.

He called Connaught from a confectioner's shop on the Bund, only to learn that he was at his usual late-afternoon watering hole, the Shanghai Club on the Bund, a club that claimed the longest bar in the world and a policy that excluded Chinese but welcomed Americans.

He found Connaught by himself at the end of the bar, a drink clutched in his hand, and Sam wondered if war came and Connaught found himself bracketed by exploding shells that brought the building down around him whether he would not continue to smile as long as he had that glass in his hand.

"Why in the hell didn't you tell me how the house was being paid for?" Sam asked as he sat down.

Connaught was startled. "I'm afraid you've lost me somewhere. What house?"

"The house I live in that some altruistic Chinese merchant provided for me at no cost."

"Oh, that," Connaught said with seeming relief. "I'm sorry to have distressed you. I thought you knew. You see, pretense is the lingua franca here. I never meant to offend you, old chap."

"Do you know where my stipend comes from?"

"Not at all. It's not my business after all, is it? The money comes through the consulate and I make the arrangements."

"Did my wife know about this?"

"I'd say not," Connaught said. "We've never discussed it, but I don't think so."

"I see," Sam said. "You make arrangements of all kinds for the staff, correct?"

"Righto."

"So if I told you that I was going to have to get along on a salary of twenty-seven hundred dollars a year, plus the living abroad bonus of another five hundred or so, what kind of living accommodations could you find for me?"

"A hovel in which you and your lovely bride would be miserable," Connaught said. "You see, there isn't much of a middle class in this city. You're either frightfully poor or you're on your way to becoming rich. But if you're white and connected with a consulate, you can live on the chit system. The common belief is that only a fool can stay in this city without accumulating a fortune. Now, if you would care for tutelage in the fine art of accumulating funds—"

"I have a job here. I may want you to find such an apartment for me."

Connaught drained his glass. "I must tell you that when you move into a smaller residence, your position will be perceived to have shrunk. Right now, living as you are in the mansion, you are considered to be a person of considerable importance, even by the staff of the consulate who know your rank. And if you take a small apartment, your prestige diminishes accordingly." He waved his hand, ordered two drinks, signed the chit for them. "If I were you, I'd relax and accept what the Chinese call the gifts of the gods and let things be."

Sam finished his drink and went out on the street in the dying light to summon a ricksha.

As the ricksha made its way through the narrow streets toward Yuki's apartment, Sam was filled with sadness, for if he told her what he had come to say, he would not see her again. She would have to find another job.

The puller had slowed at an intersection, waiting for directions, and Sam looked around to get his bearings. He saw a generation monument in the center of the street, a carved stone containing the records of a family, people dead for centuries, and it reminded him of the lack of continuity in his own family. He told the puller to go left until he saw the round moon gate made of red bricks.

When he had helped her move into the apartment, the minuscule garden outside her two small rooms was overrun with weeds and cluttered with trash, but now, as he pulled the leather thong to ring the bell, he saw green plants and banks of golden chrysanthemums around tiles and polished cobblestones. She opened the door, obviously happy to see him.

"Please come in, Cummings-san," she said. "I want to show you what I've done with the apartment."

She had created a charming home, using the bits of nothing she had collected from the stalls. A small glass vase contained two orange wild flowers that matched a now lovely, old flowered carpet. She had cleaned and painted the walls, and he realized that what he had seen as small wood items turned out to be Japanese floor furniture, repaired and shining from polishing. The Gifu shade had been cleaned to become a splash of red against a mosaic of blue wallpaper and a silk ribbon covered the crack in the otherwise lovely mirror. He was amazed. But even more surprising was Yuki's personal transformation. She was dressed in a summer kimono covered with multicolored flowers, her hair loose, falling about her shoulders, her personality freed of the strictures of the office, which compelled her to behave as if she were older than she was.

"Now," she said, waiting for his judgment. "What do you think?"

"Miraculous," he said. "You've done a fine job."

"But . . ." she said. "Something's wrong."

He tended to forget how perceptive she was, how she could read his moods. "There's nothing wrong with the apartment," he said. "I'm truly impressed."

"Then there's trouble at the office."

"There's always trouble at the office."

"Please sit down. I will bring sake," she said.

He sat on a floor cushion while she went to the kitchen. He looked at the spirit shrine on her wall, a tiny pinch of rice to serve as an offering to the *kami,* the hanging scroll of her own calligraphy, her small Bible, the pictures of her parents. He had never thought of her having a family and he felt a slight pang of envy at her devotion to her mother and father, which had prompted the shrine. He could not imagine paying such homage to Adele, and he wondered where the picture of Noble would be placed in such an arrangement.

She was back. She sank to her knees and placed a black lacquer tray on the low table, poured two shallow cups of sake, and waited until he picked his up before she touched hers. *"Compai,* Cummings-san," she said.

"Compai." He drank, the rice wine vaporous, heady. He could not get the generation monument out of his mind. "Have you ever looked at the ancestor monument at the corner?" he asked.

"Only briefly."

"How far back do you know your ancestors?"

"Ten generations are interred in a cemetery near my father's farm."

"And you have brothers and sisters?"

"Brothers only. Two of them. Do you have brothers and sisters?"

He shook his head, no. "I'm an only child," he said. "And the whole future of my family rests on me." He looked at her bright face across the table. *Come on,* he said to himself. *Stop putting it off. Tell her.* "Do you ever think about the future?" he said. "What you want to do with your life?"

"I have this night," she said. "The Lord Jesus and the Lord Buddha will take care of tomorrow. Would you honor me by staying for dinner? It's simple, rice and fish, but I have plenty. I want you to be my guest."

"I'd enjoy that," he said. "Charlotte's gone to a reception tonight and she's not expecting me."

"It will take only a few minutes to prepare. You might be more comfortable if you take off your shoes." She poured another cup of sake for him and then disappeared into the small kitchen. She could not be seen but she was close enough to carry on a conversation. "Are your parents in the States?" she asked.

"Only my mother."

"And your father?"

"Dead," he said.

"I'm sorry."

She served the fish and rice and he ate heartily while darkness gathered in the room, and he realized he was not going to be able to tell her the truth, not now. He could not bring himself to spoil this evening. He would inquire in the British and American business communities until he found a spot for her that would pay enough money for her to stay here, because he had never seen her happier.

"I want to show you something," she said. She stood up and reached for a cord hanging from the miudle of a paper lantern. A light came on, showering the room with radiant colors.

"Beautiful," he said, momentarily taken aback by the soft light on her face, the beauty of the awkward innocence of this child-woman, the delight over an electric bulb and a paper lantern. He could not keep a comparison with Charlotte out of his thoughts, the woman who had always been given everything.

"You're easily pleased by life," he said.

"I have much to be grateful for." She served him more rice. "Could I ask you about something?"

"Certainly," he said.

"Am I making a proper conversation?"

He smiled. "Very proper. You're a fascinating combination, Yuki Nakamura. In the office your translations are subtle and sophisticated. And yet you can be fascinated by electricity and concerned about etiquette."

"I just want to be appropriate," she said. "I'm interested in your life and I want to ask more questions of you, but only if it's proper."

"Quite proper," he said with a smile, warmed by the sake, relaxed, more than comfortable in her presence. "Fire away."

"You said your father was dead. Was he ill before he died?"

"No, not really." He paused, taking a deep breath, finding it still painful. "He died here in Shanghai. You see, he had lived here many years and he loved China. It was home to him, but he lost all his money, and for reasons that I don't understand, he killed himself. Then I was forced into a marriage with the daughter of an old family friend who settled money on my mother. And that's the end of my sad little story."

"In my country sometimes a man preserves his honor by killing himself," she said. "And practically all marriages are arranged. It is the accepted thing." She lit two candles and then turned off the electricity.

"Are you happy?" he asked.

"From the night you came into the visa office and asked me to translate, I have been very happy," she said.

"I'm glad," he said.

She reached across him to fill his cup and he was aware of the perfume of her hair and the warmth of the candlelight on her golden face, and deliberately, as if he had known it was going to happen from the moment he entered the room, he took the sake bottle from her hand, set it on the table, and then cradled her head in his hands, searching her eyes until he found assent before he kissed her, softly at first, tentatively, before her lips responded with a fervor that surprised him.

He lifted her to her feet, caught her up in his arms, and carried her to the bedroom, placing her upon the futon, loosening the kimono, caressing her, kissing her until she trembled, and he was powerless to stop, beyond thinking.

Afterward, they lay together, her fingertips touching the slight stubble of beard on his face, quiet, content. "I didn't know this was going to happen," he said. "But I'm glad it did. I think I've loved you for a long time and there are things I must do."

She put her fingers on his lips. "Listen to me," she said. "There is nothing you have to do because of me."

"Oh, but there is," he said. "I have a wife, responsibilities I have to clear away."

"My love makes no demands," she said.

"Mine does," he said.

By the time Sam arrived home it was after one o'clock and Charlotte was asleep. He sat down at the table in his guest room and clicked on the light, intending to explain in a letter to Charlotte why he was going to divorce her. He had fallen in love with another woman and wanted to marry her, giving Charlotte the same freedom to find a happiness she would never have with him.

He uncapped his fountain pen and, sitting down at the desk, thought through a schedule. They would remain married until the first of the year because the rent had been paid on the mansion, and then he would leave it up to her whether she wished to be divorced in the American court here in Shanghai or return to the States for the dissolution of their marriage. He would pay her father whatever he owed him, and his mother would simply pay back the settlement Noble had given her out of her profits.

He started to write, and only then did he see the letter from his mother. Carefully he slit open the envelope.

My dear son,

This will not be a long letter because I have so very much to do, but I could not let another day pass without letting you know how very much your sacrifice has meant to me. Unfortunately, the profits I anticipated didn't materialize, but I still have over a million of my original principal and I have made some new contacts due to the fact that you are serving in Shanghai. I have every confidence that this will give me some influence with certain oriental governments. I will keep you informed.

Would you look around Shanghai for another generation vase in the same basic celadon as the one I have now? We should be able to pick up one for a thousand or so in these depressed times. I plan to come to Shanghai in the near future and we can go shopping together. Just like old times.

Love,
Mother

The letter made all of his plans impossible now. He could not divorce Charlotte, for his mother's world would come tumbling down. Noble was a man of his word and a deal was a deal. He did not know what he would do about Yuki, the house, the allowance, the consulate. It was all too much to consider at one sitting.

He capped his pen and went to bed.

Mukden,
Manchuria . . .
September 1931

THE BULLET RIPPED cleanly through the fleshy part of Colonel Ito's thigh, the blood staining the cloth of his uniform. Little pain, no time for it, only the pumping of adrenaline through his body as he faced the enemy, the five Chinese soldiers holed up in the old factory. His handful of green troops were gathered behind him, their young and watchful faces expectant, breath steaming in the cold morning air, as if he could see their souls.

He drew his sword and with a battle cry charged across the space between the abandoned railroad car and a deserted loading dock while bullets buzzed down from the upper story of the warehouse. He led the charge, his men firing their rifles up the staircases before they assaulted the upper floor where the Chinese had dug in. He held his own pistol at the ready, running on a leg that could not hold him up and yet did, and on the third floor he was alone when the Chinese captain emerged from a room, and for one moment they stood staring at each other, the man's face burning itself into his memory, bushy eyebrows matched by wisps of black hair the consistency of straw sticking out from beneath the military cap. His mouth was half open, showing yellowed teeth, breath rasping, sour with

fear, and Ito thought crazily that he should invite this terrified man
to sit down over tea and redress their differences. But then the
captain raised his gun, just a moment too late, a fraction of a second
after Ito had already pulled the trigger on his pistol. The explosion
rang in his ears, and the man stood there as if the bullet had not
touched him. Then Ito saw the blood, which first appeared as a small
red flower in the center of the man's thick padded jacket and then
blossomed. The captain's eyes dulled and he slumped backward
against the wall, the pistol clattering on the stone floor as it slipped
from his dead fingers.

Ito remembered little after that. The darkness piled up in the
corners of his mind—he had lost too much blood—and he was unconscious for some time. He was only half conscious in the hospital as
General Honjo came personally to deliver a speech of commendation and place the ribboned medal around his neck. He was more
aware by the time his father visited the hospital to express his pride,
as if Ito had now joined a fraternity that could be gained only by
killing in battle.

Ito lay in the hospital for a week and recuperated while his military doctors brought sake into his room every day to toast new
victories as the Japanese troops moved against little opposition to
occupy all of Manchuria. Finally, Ito was able to walk with a cane
and was strong enough to board the train that carried him down into
China and eventually into North Station in the Chapei settlement,
where there was a staff car waiting to greet him. At army headquarters he was given a ceremony of commendation by his commanding
officer, as if single-handedly he had been responsible for the victory
in Manchuria.

Ito knew exactly what he was, a token of his country's victory, a
participant in the battle who could be lionized by those who had not
been there. He endured the interviews and the pop of the flashbulbs, but that one moment of confrontation had changed him,
though he knew it would take him some time to discover why.

On the day after he arrived back in Shanghai, his superiors at the
consulate informed him that he would be meeting with Vice-Consul
Cummings from the American Legation to delineate the Japanese
position, and even though he looked forward to seeing Sam again, he
was not sure he could explain what had happened to him.

Shanghai . . . October 1931

SAM STOOD AT the window of Alcott's office, looking out at the overcast fall sky while Alcott sat in his wing-backed chair, a steaming hot-water bottle easing an ache in his left side. "What do you think is going to happen?" Sam said. "What will the commission appointed by the League of Nations find in Manchuria?"

"It doesn't matter what they find," Alcott said. "We don't belong to the League of Nations and the Japanese are getting ready to pull out of it. They will have all of Manchuria with no trouble at all."

"Are they going to try to take China?"

"Yes, bit by bit. They'll set up a puppet government in Manchuria and use it as a base to take on the Chinese factions south of the Great Wall," Alcott said.

"And when that's done they'll take another piece, and I suppose there isn't a thing we can do about it."

"China has withstood centuries of battle. Let's not give up too soon," Alcott said tolerantly. "Besides, you fret too much. My wife was a great fretter, God rest her soul. Come a crisis, and she would say to me, in uncharacteristically non-ladylike language, "Damn it, Mr. Alcott, you have to do something. You *are* the United States out here after all.' " He laughed. "I would remind her that I am *not* the United States but merely a very humble representative who gets Americans out of difficulty in a foreign culture if he can." He shifted against the hot-water bottle. "You're the newest member of our team and you become less young and more burdened every day. There's no way you can afford to care this much. You lose perspective. You lose the long view, and it is the long view that you must have in this country. It is a rigid country that does not want to come into the twentieth century, and sometimes I don't blame them."

"At least if I can understand what the hell is going on," Sam said, "then maybe there's a very small chance that I can make a difference."

"And where will you begin?" Alcott said.

"With the hero of Mukden," Sam said with uncharacteristic irony. "We're meeting this afternoon."

"You're talking about Ito, the good Colonel?"

"The same," Sam said.

Alcott sighed. "I will give you a word of advice, Cummings. I understand that you have become close to Colonel Ito. You've developed a certain empathy with him."

"That's true. Yes."

"Don't expect it to last. If the Japanese truly intend to ignite a major conflagration in this part of the world, then the good Colonel Ito will be repossessed by his country, so to speak. So don't expect too much from him. Don't count on him as a friend."

"I appreciate your advice, sir. Now I must be going," Sam said.

Alcott sighed again. "What I would not give in my old age to have that marvelous energy possessed by the young."

Sam had invited Ito to his house for an informal meeting where they could have privacy. Charlotte had agreed to go shopping for the afternoon and Sam had given instructions to Majordomo to have the cook prepare tea and cakes and set up a full bar by the French doors overlooking the veranda. He would leave it to Ito to pick the kind of refreshment he wanted.

Sam was home by two-thirty; Ito was due at three, and Sam knew he would be prompt. The afternoon was overcast, the house chill despite the fire burning in the library hearth. He turned on the lamps and poured himself a drink. When the Japanese staff car pulled into the circular driveway and the Colonel emerged, Sam was strangely touched. Ito had changed.

He was much thinner and he walked with a pronounced limp and the aid of a cane. He looked tired, drawn, and vulnerable as he entered the house, shook hands with Sam, and followed him into the library, where he stood with his back to the fire.

"I received your wire at the hospital in Manchuria," Ito said. "I appreciate your concern."

"How's your leg?"

"The doctors tell me that the limp will be gone in another few months."

"What do you want to drink?" Sam said. "I can offer you tea or something stronger for a cold afternoon."

"What are you drinking?"

"Brandy. French. Good stuff."

"I'll join you," Ito said.

They toasted each other as friends and sat down in chairs fronting the fireplace. Ito eased his wounded leg straight out in front of him.

"Now," Sam said, drawing the conversation to business, "just what in the holy hell is going on in Manchuria? I thought you were going to Mukden on business."

"I was. And then one night, when the fighting started, a patrol captain was killed outside of Mukden and I took his place."

"I'm glad you're safe." Sam sipped the brandy. "The rumor's going around that your people bombed their own railway in order to precipitate the crisis so they would not appear to be the aggressor. Then they used that to take over Manchuria. Is that true?"

"I'll be honest with you," Ito said. "I don't know. Officially, I'm required to tell you that the Chinese attacked first, and I trust that you'll put that in your report. I have no idea how it happened, but I do know that a large faction of our military welcomed the opportunity."

"How soon will your armies be moving into north China below the Wall?"

"I'll give you an official position paper, which your secretary can translate. It will say that before the September incident the whole of Manchuria, except for the Japanese zone along the railway, was run by warlords and plagued by bandits. The Chinese who lived in Manchuria packed into the Japanese zones because the bandits knew better than to come within the legal range of Japanese troops." He sipped his brandy. "As of today, a Chinese can travel anywhere in Manchuria without fear of being accosted by bandits. The warlords have been contained and are no threat. All of that's true, Sam, but at the moment it's not important to me."

"All right," Sam said, "what is important to you?"

"Have you ever fought in a battle?" Ito said. "Have you ever killed a man?"

"No," Sam said. "What's it like?"

"That's the problem," Ito said. "It's taken for granted that I feel like the hero that they make me out to be."

"And you don't? You got a hell of a lot of publicity."

Ito shook his head slowly. "No. I was wounded in the fight and I didn't even feel it, except that on some rational level I knew I would bleed to death if I didn't do something about it. I knew that and yet I moved straight ahead and ignored my own welfare."

"Military training."

"Perhaps," Ito said, caught up in his feelings, as if he had to sort them out. "But that's not the worst of it. I suddenly came face-to-face with a Chinese captain. I had never seen him before, of course, and I felt no animosity toward him. I had the urge to talk with him. When he pulled up his pistol I was sure he had no desire to kill me, just as I didn't want to kill him, even when I pulled the trigger. Does that make any sense to you?"

"I think so," Sam said. "You didn't see him as an enemy."

"Exactly. He had done nothing to me personally, and I hadn't done anything to him. And yet either he was required to kill me or I was required to kill him because of something that neither one of us could control. I thought about that a good bit in the hospital. It could drive a man crazy if he allowed it. But I don't. At times I feel that it never happened at all. At other times I simply accept the opinions and feelings of all the officers around me, that I've done a fine and noble thing by killing a stranger."

Ito drank before he spoke again. "What I have to say now, my friend, is in confidence."

"It won't go any further."

"The military faction in Japan is determined to have China," Ito said. "I intend to do what I can to stop them, not out of any lofty idealism or political principle, but because I sincerely believe it's stupid to kill people instead of finding peaceful solutions."

Sam was curious. "Are you asking something of me?"

"Yes," Ito said. "Some of the Japanese officers think that the whole world is in a depression so deep that the Western nations don't want to fight."

"That's true," Sam said.

"If the Japanese military is to have its war, it will have to provoke the Chinese. I'm asking you to do what you can to keep your countrymen from encouraging the Chinese to retaliate over small grievances. And I'll do what I can to see that the grievances remain small."

"I'll do what I can," Sam said.

"Now I have to get back to my consulate." He stood up with effort. "You will know whenever provocative reports come out of my office that I've done my best to tone them down."

"I guess you know that the odds are against both of us."

"We have to try."

"When you have some free time, let me know," Sam said.

"I may be called back to Tokyo," Ito said. "But we'll keep in touch."

"Yes," Sam said, putting a hand on his shoulder. "And if there's any way I can help you, call me."

"I will," Ito said.

Sam walked him outside, and as he watched the car pull away down the leaf-strewn driveway, he had the feeling that despite their mutual good intentions, it would not be long before all of China would become a bloody battleground.

The man was not a medical doctor at all and Yuki knew it, but he was a tall, kind Chinese who had grown up in a small village and migrated to the native section of Shanghai, where he had a small house with two rooms. Now she lay on the table and the "barefoot doctor," as practitioners of his kind were known, ran his hands over her abdomen and then examined the soles of her feet.

"And your stomach is unsettled in the mornings?" he said in Mandarin.

"Yes."

"And you have missed your time of flowering?"

"Yes, three times."

He pushed the canvas drape back from the door and looked at the long line of people in the dusty street. She, too, had waited patiently in the cold for hours. He let the drape fall back into place. "You are a small woman and giving birth will not be easy. But you are young and strong and that's obviously in your favor. It is also obvious that you are not a poor peasant woman from the villages who would have her baby in the fields, so I suggest that you go to a hospital in the International Settlement."

"That won't be possible, I'm afraid."

"Even for the delivery of the child?"

"I don't know."

He nodded patiently, then went to the shelves that covered the back wall and began to mix powders. He folded them into paper packets and gave her instructions as to when she should take each one, jotting Chinese characters on the papers with the stub of a pencil while she tried to absorb what he was telling her. "You are absolutely sure, Esteemed One?" she asked.

"Of what?"

"That I am to have a baby."

He gave her a tolerant smile, displaying his bad teeth. "It is the most common condition I see. So take these herbs, which will make the birth of the child easier, and especially this one"—he held up a greenish powder—"which will increase the yin and the chances of a boy child."

She paid his fee, bowed to him, and gathered the packets of powder in her purse before she went down the dusty lane, past the line of people for whom there was no hope, children with bluish membranes over their eyes, blind, others walking skeletons with bloated bellies, adults with twisted limbs and open sores.

When she reached the congestion on the bridge across Soochow Creek, where no one would be paying any attention to her, she took the packet of greenish powder and opened it to the wind, which swept it away. A boy child indeed. She would have asked for a powder to guarantee the birth of a girl but there were no such potions. Mothers abandoned girl babies on the street every night or suffocated them before sliding their bodies into the dark waters of the river.

In the privacy of her room she took off her clothes and examined her abdomen from a variety of angles, exultant at the first faint swellings. She sat down to write a letter to her mother and suddenly froze at the reality of the facts that she would have to relay. As much as her mother loved her, she would never be able to understand why Yuki had allowed herself to get pregnant with a love child by a *gaijin,* because the baby would be a half-caste, claimed neither by the Japanese nor the Westerners and forever doomed to prejudice. And to compound the problem, neither of her parents would ever understand her desire for a girl child, an *aiko,* and the wish to give her daughter a feeling of acceptance as a female, which she had never experienced in her own childhood.

She made up a story for her parents, a fantasy of a highly ranked Japanese military officer to whom she would be married, a dashing hero in whose family the birth of boy babies was commonplace, and she described him in such detail, she had no doubt her parents would believe the story.

On her way back to the consulate, she was beset by worry about how Sam would react to the news. She would not blame him if he disowned her altogether. As she sat on the tram, nearing her stop, her heart sank. She realized that as the baby began to show, she would no longer be able to work at the consulate, because the gossips would know of her relationship with Sam and he would be disgraced.

She stood outside the consulate a long time, dreading the moment when she would have to face him. Finally, realizing she could not put it off forever, she went upstairs only to find that she would not have the chance to tell him for a while. He was upset over a policy cable, which he waved at her when she came into his office.

"This just arrived from Washington," he said scornfully. "The Secretary of State deigns to let us know that whatever the Japanese military does in Manchuria is none of our business. So we do nothing." He put the papers down on the desk, and only then did he see the concern on her face. "What's wrong?" he said.

"I can't tell you here," she said. "Can we go someplace, please?"

"Certainly." He put his hand on her shoulder, worried. "Are you all right?"

When they were in the car she suddenly began to weep, and he waited until he reached the comparative isolation of the park below St. John's University before he stopped the car and reached out to take her hands. "Whatever it is, it can't be that bad," he said, giving her his handkerchief.

Gradually her crying subsided and she dried her eyes, looking out at a pair of bicyclers on the road, aware that there was no privacy here. "I have to go away," she said quietly.

"Away?" he said, startled. "What are you talking about? Why should you have to go anyplace?"

"I don't want to disgrace you."

"There's no way you can disgrace me," he said gently. "I love you. Now tell me what happened."

"I went to a doctor this morning . . ."

"Are you ill?"

". . . in Chapei." She drew a deep breath. "And he told me what I already knew. I'm pregnant."

"Pregnant?" he echoed.

"I'm going to have a baby." She started to weep again.

"Good God," he said. "When?"

She searched his face. "In the late spring."

"I see."

"It's better that I go," she said. "I knew you would feel this way."

"You don't know how I feel, because even I don't know that," he said. "It's caught me by surprise, that's all, because I hadn't considered the possibility of fatherhood. But I love you and you're not going anywhere, and that's for sure."

"It's my fault."

"No more of that," he said.

"You haven't heard it all yet," she said. "I feel in my heart that the baby will be a girl."

"So?"

"You won't mind?"

"Why should I mind? A daughter is fine with me." He released her and smiled. "So I'm going to be a father. Well, I'll be damned. We have to celebrate. Pick a restaurant. Anyplace in the International Settlement."

"Someplace quiet and secluded," she said. "Where we can talk."

He drove into the countryside west of the city, stopped at a small Chinese restaurant, which was all but deserted. Once he had ordered, he reached across the table and took her hands in his. "I wish you would stop looking so solemn," he said. "Now, let's start at the beginning. Which doctor did you see?"

"A Chinese doctor. In Chapei."

"No more barefoot doctors. I want you to go to an English doctor friend of mine who specializes in obstetrics."

"We can't do that. We can't let anybody know about this."

"This isn't something that can be kept secret," he said. "It'll take some doing, but we'll make it. We're going to need money. I'll go to work on that."

The noodles were served but she had no appetite. It was evident he intended to risk everything to claim the child and she could not let him do that when there were so many things to consider. "You have to think what this will do to your career."

"My career is suddenly very unimportant."

"It may be now, this minute. But I want you to have time to think it over."

"This makes a hell of a difference in my life. And at the moment jobs and careers and international situations are all irrelevant."

"One promise," she said.

"What's that?"

"You won't do anything without telling me about it first."

"About what?"

"Your marriage. Your work here. Anything."

"Fair enough," he said. "And you'll see the English doctor."

"I'll think about it," she said.

"Only fifty thousand dollars apiece," Ross was saying, raising his hand, snapping his fingers to hurry along a waiter at the Shanghai Bar. "Another round here, chop chop."

He was a Commercial officer at the British Consulate and he reminded Sam of a happy and well-groomed St. Bernard, a tall, rumpled, shaggy man who patted Connaught on the arm and looked across the table at Sam and an Australian businessman named Franks. Ross raised his glass when the drinks were served, drank, and plunged ahead. "The four of us put in fifty thousand each. The money goes to Chiang Kai-shek to help subdue some northern province or another. And in return, get this, chaps, we get fifty percent of the tax collection from a major city in that province."

"Ah," Connaught said with a happy smile. "And who monitors the bloody tax collectors?"

"The Generalissimo can't afford to cheat Western investors," Ross said.

"I have to get back to the consulate," Sam said.

As he stood up Connaught joined him, but Franks stayed where he was, running his fingers through his beard thoughtfully, a glint of interest in his dark eyes.

Connaught was gleeful as he walked along the Bund with Sam.

"Ross has caught himself another one," he said. "Greed is always the best lure when you fish for money in this town."

"I've heard that scheme before," Sam said. "Sometimes it works out. I know an American who doubled his money by speculating in Chinese taxes."

"But the real winner will be Ross," Connaught said. "He uses none of his own money, you see, and with every fifty thousand he raises, he gets back fifty percent, plus a share of the taxes collected." He slowed as he neared the entrance to another bar, which had a window opening on the river. "One more drink on me," he said. "Consider the alternative, a stuffy hour or so at the office writing meaningless reports, all destined to be unread in Washington anyway." He looked at his watch. "One drink should just about put us past quitting time."

"You talked me into it," Sam said.

They sat at a table, overlooking the river and a park where the old men were practicing tai chi with the slow movements of the stylized martial arts. Sam ordered a beer and considered going back to talk to Ross about his tax scheme, but the possible profits did not justify the risks, as much as he needed money to support Yuki and the child. He sipped his beer, thought about his father and the old man's uncanny ability to make money. "Christ," he said. "I wish I had my father's zest for making money. He enjoyed it more than any man I've ever known. He used to talk about it when I was a kid, the taels of gold, the chests of Mexican silver, just waiting in the China trade for a man with nerve enough to come along and pick them up." He drank his beer.

"There's an odd paradox in business over here," Connaught said. "The more you want money, the less chance you have of getting it. To the best traders business is a game. From what I hear of your father, that was his philosophy. If he was up a million, he was in position for a bigger play. If he was broke, it was a challenge to see how quickly he could recover."

"Then why would he kill himself over money?"

"If he had wanted anyone to know why he chose to leave this world, he would have written a note, wouldn't he? And any conjecture at this point would be useless."

"Did you know my father?"

"No. I met his secretary once, however, a charming lady."

"Bright Moon?"

"The same."

"How would I go about finding her?"

"You'd ask me to do it," Connaught said with a smile. "I know the ins and outs of Chapei like no other white man."

"All right, I'm asking you to find Bright Moon."

"I'll give it a try. Do you think she might lead you to concealed assets, old man?"

"No," Sam said. "I just want to talk with her about my father, whether he talked about my mother or insurance with her in his last days." He drank. "And game or not, I'm going after big money."

"A suggestion, then."

"All right."

"The holidays are coming up. If I were you, I should take my elegant wife to afternoon teas and evening receptions, to every party where the wealthy merchants and speculators of the city spend their time. And above all I would never express the slightest need for money or any desire to make it, except as a pastime. As far as the Settlement goes, you are already set for life with an inexhaustible fortune."

"That makes sense," Sam said. "I'll give it a try."

"Do that, old man." He looked at his watch, grinned. "You see? Quitting time already. Talk of money makes time fly. And I wish you luck."

"Thank you," Sam said. "I'm going to need it."

On an afternoon a week later Sam was standing near the gangplank on the deck of a Japanese ship where he had taken Charlotte to a bon voyage party when he saw someone waving up at him from the dock below. It took him a moment to recognize the man as Dawes from the consulate.

"Can I talk to you a minute?" Dawes yelled up at him. Sam came down the gangplank. Dawes was a florid-faced model of a small-town businessman who had been with the Commercial Section for the past ten years and who, at the moment, was visibly upset as he pulled the collar of his topcoat up against the chill of the day. "I thought it was you," Dawes said with relief. "Thank God for serendipity."

"I brought Charlotte to a party. I was just getting some air. What's the matter?"

Dawes glanced at his watch. "Is there an American named Fanshaw at this party of yours?" he said, looking toward the ship. "He was supposed to meet me on the Commercial dock twenty minutes ago."

"What's he look like?"

"Porky little man, from California. He smokes a carved meerschaum pipe. He's never without it."

"He's definitely not aboard then," Sam said. "It's a small party."

"Damn," Dawes said, frustrated. He looked toward a Chinese lighter chugging into the dock, a banged-up boat pouring greasy smoke into the air, its hull a collection of rusty plates. The men matched their scow—one step above wharf coolies, crusted with dirt and sweat.

"Can I help you?" Sam said.

"As a matter of fact, you can save my life," Dawes said. "Do you happen to have your checkbook on you?"

"Yes."

"Write me a check for twenty thousand and I'll guarantee you a handsome profit by morning."

"I don't have twenty thousand in the bank," Sam said.

"You will by morning," Dawes said. "I was so certain Fanshaw would be here that I didn't bring my checkbook, and this isn't like the Shanghai Club, where signing your name is good as gold. So make me a check for twenty thousand, if you please. And I wouldn't mind if you hurried."

"Why twenty thousand? What do you need it for?"

"I'll explain later. Please trust me."

Sam hesitated only momentarily. Dawes had a good reputation at the consulate. Sam braced his book against a crate and wrote out a check for twenty thousand dollars. He handed it to Dawes, who waved it dry as they walked toward the Commercial dock.

Only then did Sam notice the Mandarin Chinese standing just inside the warehouse, wearing a long black merchant's gown.

Dawes sauntered toward the warehouse while the lighter came into dock, the crew yelling at the wharf coolies to keep back beyond a rope line, lest in the melee of their fight for the right to load or unload cargo, the cargo was stolen or accidentally knocked into the water.

Dawes gave the Mandarin the check in exchange for a black bag, which seemed to have considerable heft to it. Then the Mandarin went to talk to the Chinese captain of the lighter, who directed his men to load the boxes aboard the lighter while the wharf coolies set up a yowl behind the rope. They began to curse both the captain and his ship, urging the gods to cover his body with painful boils and to swallow the accursed boat beneath the muddy waters of the river.

When Dawes came back to Sam he was considerably relieved. "I appreciate your help," Dawes said.

"They're a damned grim-looking crew," Sam said.

"Under the right circumstances, they'd make fish bait out of me," Dawes said nonchalantly. "But not as long as we're doing business together on a public dock in Shanghai. No, I would have lost face by being caught short and it would have taken some time to restore that."

"What *are* you doing?" Sam said, openly curious.

"A more proper question would be, what are *we* doing, wouldn't it?" Dawes said with a vague smile. "It's all perfectly legal. Come into the warehouse and I'll show you."

Dawes proved very adept with a pry bar. He inserted it beneath one of the boards on a small crate, the nails protesting as he pulled them loose, raising the board just far enough for Sam to see inside. "My God," Sam said. "Pistols."

"Not just pistols," Dawes said with a chuckle. "They're Broom Handle Mausers and they come in a wooden holster that fits onto the handgun to make a shoulder weapon out of it. Big prestige to having one of these upriver. Whether you're a bandit or provincial police or warlord's footman, this gives you more status than a Rolls would give an English gentleman."

"How in the hell can this be legal?" Sam said, aghast that he was participating in an arms deal.

"It *isn't* legal for the Mandarin. Under Chinese law he could lose his head unless he had documents a mile long filled with more official chop marks than he could collect in a lifetime. But if he could do it legally, he wouldn't need me or Fanshaw. You see, it's perfectly legal for an American to sell arms."

"It doesn't bother you?"

"Why should it? I look at it this way. If I sell them, then we know approximately what arms and ammunition are going upriver. If I wash my hands of it, then I lose the money and we have no information at all." He glanced toward the deck of the Japanese ship. "I'll exchange these taels of gold and settle up with you in the morning."

The next morning Dawes called Sam to his office, closed the door, opened an attaché case, and proceeded to take out stacks of American hundred-dollar bills. He began to count them out on the desk, in piles of ten, a thousand dollars to a stack, talking all the while. "Poor Mr. Fanshaw," Dawes said while he flipped the hundreds from a large stack into smaller ones. "He was gambling at the Mexican casino and time slipped away from him." He paused, mentally calculating. "Let me see, you gave me twenty. Since you get two for one, your total is forty thousand." He slid the stacks of money across the table. "You may want to count it," he said.

Sam sank into a chair, flabbergasted. "I was just doing you a favor," he said. "Forty thousand dollars?"

"Yes. Here. You might as well take the attaché case to carry it in."

"It's incredible. Yesterday I didn't have more than a couple of thousand dollars in the bank."

"Then I suggest that you make a deposit to cover the overdraft."

"I don't know what to say," Sam said.

"If you like, I'll be glad to donate the money to a local charity in your name."

"At the moment I'm my favorite local charity," Sam said. He began to stack the money in the attaché case. "If you don't mind my asking, why don't you do all these deals yourself? You wouldn't have to share with anybody."

"There's always a degree of risk which I prefer to share with someone willing to gamble. Too, there's plenty of money to be had all around."

"My God," Sam said, regaining his composure. "Suppose I wanted to make three million dollars."

"Why three million? Why not ten, twelve?"

"I need only three. And I don't want to deal in guns. Can I make it?"

"Certainly."

"How long will it take?"

Dawes leaned back in his chair. He stared at a slight crack in the ceiling as if it were an oracle. "You have to be prepared for some reverses. One out of ten times you'll lose. The whole secret is in the pacing."

"I've got an idea. I'll give it some thought and I'll get back to you."

"I'll be here and glad to help any way I can," Dawes said.

Yuki was translating a Japanese document when the mail clerk came through the consulate with his cart and paused to leave a dozen letters for Sam on her desk. She riffled through them, excited because she had glimpsed the rough paper of an envelope used by the village scribe, and took out the two sheets dictated by her mother. But as much as she enjoyed the descriptions of the farm in late fall or the antics of her brothers, she was made unhappy by her father's response on hearing that she was to have a child.

"Your father makes daily offerings at the temple to ensure that the *kami* will give you a son. I try to reassure him. After all, in the history of his family there have been only two girls that I can remember, an aunt who died of fever and now yourself."

She put the letter away. She had opened all of Sam's mail and sorted the letters in order of importance when he came in, looking more content than she had seen him in weeks.

He glanced at the letters. "Anything important?"

"You would have to determine that." She smiled. "You look very happy."

"With good reason," he said. "But right now, since it's close to noon and a gorgeous December day outside, let's go to lunch."

"A picnic," she said, delighted.

"It may be a little cold for that," he said.

"Not at all. I know the perfect place."

And she did. As he drove she directed him to the Japanese Sector in the eastern part of the International Settlement and had him park in a street filled with food stalls.

She had never felt happier. In the narrow streets they were protected from the wind and the sunshine was warm. She collected the provisions she wanted, then led him through a back alley to an old Buddhist temple and handed him the basket. "Hold this, please. I'll be right back."

She slipped out of her shoes and entered the ancient temple, where, over the centuries, the very stones had absorbed the odor of a million joss sticks. She made her ablutions, knelt before the image of Buddha, the serene stone face reflecting a slight smile, and she chanted her mantra and said her prayers, remembering her parents and her brothers and especially the life within her.

When she came out of the temple she led the way down a path across the temple grounds until, rounding an ancient wall, they came upon a sheltered patch of yellowed grass, warm in the sunshine, with a view of the great broad river, the sampans and the junks moving lazily upstream.

She took the basket from Sam, spread a cloth on the grass, and laid out the containers of tempura and sushi, then handed him a bottle of wine to uncork. "It's a beautiful day, *desho*?" she said.

"A truly fine one." He poured the wine.

He drank. "When you pray to your Buddha, what do you say?"

"I light a joss stick to honor him," she said. "I love the Lord Buddha just as I love the Lord Jesus, but my prayers are different from time to time. I thanked the Lord Buddha for what has happened and humbly requested a girl child."

When they finished eating he stretched out on the grass in the warm sunshine with his head in her lap, and she thought it both incredible and wonderful that within inches of his head a small human creature was forming who would carry a part of both of them into the next generation.

"Are you happy?" she asked.

"At this moment, very," he said. "But we have to talk about the future."

"The long future or the short future?" she said, smiling.

"The short future first," he said.

"In the short future we go back to work, *ne*?"

"After I buy you a proper coat."

"I see," she said, touching his chin with her finger. "And then what?"

"I want you to find a better apartment, a bigger one. We'll need a room for the baby."

"Perhaps a penthouse in the Cathay Hotel," she said.

"I'm serious. I'd like it to be in the Western section, off Bubbling Well Road. That way I can check on you on my way to work in the mornings and then stop by on the way home in the evenings."

"You're really serious, then?"

"Never more," he said. He sat up. She poured another glass of plum wine for him. "I want you to hire an amah to take care of the baby when the time comes," he said. "But I'm getting ahead of myself."

"A bit," she said. "What's more important is that I must quit working at the consulate soon. I'm showing."

"I think you should quit this afternoon," he said expansively.

"You've been keeping something from me," she said. "Something wonderful, from the expression on your face."

He smiled. "It seems incredible, but it happened," he said. "I won't go into all the details, but I went into a deal with Dawes at the consulate, and I made forty thousand dollars overnight."

"Forty thousand American dollars?" she repeated, in awe.

"Yes," he said. "So I want you to retire from working and do as you please until the baby comes. But first I want you to help me find a Japanese man to work for me in the Japanese Sector."

"Doing what?" she said.

He looked out at the river where a Japanese gunboat was patrolling, the Chinese junks giving it a wide berth. "The Chinese mill hands who work in the Japanese factories are paid in Japanese yen. But they don't trust the yen and none of the merchants in the Chinese Settlement do either. So they turn the yen into dollars as fast as they can at the street exchange rate of ten yen to a dollar. I want a man to set up shop near the Chinese quarter over by the cotton mills and buy yen for me. It's perfectly safe as long as he stays inside the Japanese Sector. We might even hire a couple of guards to make the operation secure."

"You want him to exchange money for you?"

"Yes. I think I'll start with about ten thousand dollars."

She was filled with a sudden enthusiasm. "Why does it have to be a man?" she said. "I'll be leaving the consulate anyway and I'd love to do it. I'm very good with money."

"Out of the question," he said.

"Because you think I'm too young or because I'm a woman?"

"Because you're my woman," he said. "And I don't want you to work at all."

"This isn't work. There's no risk. You said that yourself. And it won't last that long. I'll rent the space and hire a guard. One will be quite enough." She laughed happily. "It's perfect. And since I'm Japanese, I'll have no trouble getting a permit."

"I'll think about it," he said.

"There's nothing more to consider," she said. "At least let me try it."

"For a week only," he said. "And just because I love you enough to humor you." He slipped his watch out of his pocket. "I'm afraid it's time to go. Especially since I want to buy you a coat before we get back to work."

He stood up, brushed himself off, then reached down and helped her to her feet. She gathered up the cloth and put it in the basket, leaving the temple grounds undisturbed. When they reached the shop where they had left the car, she saw a car from the Japanese Consulate parked in front of it. Then Ito, in full dress uniform, looking better than when she had seen him last, came out of the shop.

"It's good to see you," Sam said, shaking his hand. "You're looking well. You remember my secretary, Miss Nakamura?"

"Of course," Ito said, taking her in with a glance. "How are you, Miss Nakamura?"

"Very well," she said. "I wrote you a letter expressing my appreciation for what you did for my mother. I'm pleased to have the chance to thank you in person."

"It was nothing," Ito said. "I was pleased to be of assistance."

A transaction had taken place, she realized, so subtle that she hoped Sam had missed it altogether. She had shown Ito-san the proper respect, eyes downcast except for the one glance that demonstrated her recognition of his higher social station, and the Colonel had given her more attention than was necessary, crossing the social barrier with a gratuitous remark. But she was wrong about Sam's missing its significance. He showed no sign of it, but he knew.

"I saw your car," Ito said to Sam. "I was asking in the shops to see if you had engine trouble."

"No trouble," Sam said. "I thought you were headed for Tokyo."

"Not yet," Ito said, a rather cryptic expression on his face. "Are you going to the Italian Legation Christmas reception later this week?"

"Yes, I'm planning to go."

"Then I'll see you there," Ito said. And with a nod to Yuki, he departed.

"He thinks you're as beautiful as I do," Sam said as he held the door for Yuki and then slid behind the driver's seat.

"Are you jealous?" she asked.

"Do I have reason to be?"

"None," she said. "I'm devoted to you and I don't have the slightest interest in any other man. Besides, we have too many things in common. First, a daughter on the way, and second, we're going into business together."

He touched her cheek, smiled. "You're in business for one week only, and then we'll see about it."

She settled in beside him. His jealousy was gone. She could feel it.

On the evening of the Italian Legation reception, Sam had finished dressing in his suite at the mansion when he was surprised by a tap on the door and then Charlotte's voice asking him if he was decent.

"Quite decent. Come on in."

She came in, her Number Six girl following, bearing a silver tray with a bottle of champagne and two glasses. The servant put the tray on a low table and began her descent to the floor.

Charlotte stopped her. "No kowtow, remember?" she said.

"Yes, madame," the girl said, and, after a curtsy, fled the room.

"No wonder the servants all love you," he said. He looked her over and was startled to see how much she had bloomed in the past few months. She wore a black evening dress with a choker of diamonds and her shoulders were bare. Her hair had been swept up to a fine curl at the crown. "What's the occasion?" he asked, eyeing the champagne.

"Since we have time before the reception, I thought we might have a glass of champagne and talk," she said.

"I'd like that," he said.

She poured, handed him a glass, and then sat down. "I want to ask you a question," she said.

"Go ahead."

She ran her fingers around the rim of the crystal glass, which emitted a mournful hum. "I need to know how you feel about us, about me, our marriage." Her eyes were on the bubbling surface of the champagne in her glass.

"I'd call it a marriage in name only, wouldn't you?"

"Do you think it will ever be different between us?"

"No," he said without hesitation. "I'm sorry, but I don't think there's a chance."

She said nothing for a moment, then slowly sighed. "I appreciate your honesty," she said. "It makes things much easier. And we won't have to discuss this ever again." She changed the subject with great determination, as if forcing herself to be cheerful. "I hear rumors you're going into business."

"I've made a beginning, yes."

"I know you'll be very successful." She sipped her champagne. "Have you met the new Italian Consul?"

"Afraid not."

"He's a very funny man," she said. "Sometimes I think he parodies himself and his own accent, just to conceal the fact that he can't talk any other way."

"I may not be able to spend much time with him tonight," he said. "As a matter of fact, Connaught's going to drive us because I may be staying late and he'll be bringing you home. I hope you don't mind."

"Not at all," she said. "It was very kind of you to make the arrangements." She looked at him directly. He could detect no pain in her eyes at all now, as if she had found a way to move past the unhappiness of their relationship and leave it behind. "And once again, I thank you for your honesty," she said. "More than you'll ever know."

There was no event grander than a Christmas reception in the ballroom of the Cathay Hotel, Sam decided. The room was decorated in the national colors of Italy, dominated by the massive crystal chandelier that sparkled overhead, the banks of mirrored walls reflecting the splendor of the international representatives in their military uniforms with multicolored sashes bedecked with medals.

He went through the receiving line with Charlotte, shook hands with the new Italian Consul General, a short, fat man filled with dignity for the occasion. The Consul's wife was small, plump, shy rather than reserved. Sam welcomed them both to the community of diplomats and was embraced by the Consul General, who kissed him on both cheeks.

"Isn't he a charming man?" Charlotte said with a smile once they had run the gauntlet and were approaching the buffet table.

"He'll do very well here," Sam said. "Now, do you have an appetite?"

"At present, no," she said. "But I would love a glass of champagne."

"If I can get it without drowning, I'll be right back," he said.

Chinese ingenuity had combined with Italian art to produce a champagne fountain unlike any he had ever seen before, gamboling cherubs atop a pedestal, champagne pouring from urns with such vigor that it splashed beyond the collecting basin beneath the fountain and sent an alcoholic spray onto the ballroom floor. No one had been assigned to correct the problem. Instead, a bevy of agile waiters in tuxedos attempted to catch the champagne in carafes and transfer it to crystal glasses.

He managed to get two glasses and a bit of invigorating spray. By the time he was back to Charlotte, Connaught had finished parking the car and was standing with her and surveying the room, buoyant anticipation on his face.

"I have a great affection for such affairs," he said. "The whole community puts on its best face and it's quite a glittering show. And if you will permit me to say so, your wife is the most beautiful woman in the room."

"I agree with you," Sam said, guessing that Connaught enjoyed these evenings because they gave him a chance to wear a tailored tuxedo with a broad blue sash across the chest and a collection of medals Sam had not seen before, definitely Chinese decorations.

Ito, looking slim and handsome in his formal army uniform, approached them. He bowed first to Charlotte.

"How are you, Colonel Ito?" Charlotte said graciously, extending her hand.

"Very well indeed," the Colonel said. "Good evening, Mr. Connaught."

"And the very same to you, Colonel," Connaught said with a strained smile. To Sam it was quite evident he did not like either the Japanese in general or the Colonel in particular.

"I'd like a word with you if it would be convenient," Ito said to Sam.

"Certainly." Sam passed the champagne glasses to Connaught and Charlotte. "A word to the wise," he said to Connaught. "It might pay to keep an eye on the champagne fountain. I think it's building pressure. It will be quite spectacular if it blows." He smiled to Charlotte. "Will you excuse me?" he said.

"Of course."

Sam followed the Colonel into a corner of the hall where there was a grouping of chairs. An orchestra had begun to play on the other side of the ballroom. Sam sat down, held up a hand to attract the attention of a passing waiter carrying a tray, and managed to extract a glass of champagne for himself and another for Ito.

"Ordinarily, I mind my own business," Ito said, "but I need to ask you about your secretary. I know she's been buying yen with dollars in the Japanese Sector for the past two days. Is she doing it for you or is she buying for the American Consulate?"

"For me," Sam said. "She doesn't work at the consulate anymore. There's a lot of money to be made in currency exchange, and God knows I need it. If you're interested, I'll be glad to let you know exactly what I'm doing."

"The money is only one of my problems at the moment," Ito said. He looked out at the whirling couples on the dance floor. "There's a strong feeling that the Chinese are ready to precipitate a crisis in Shanghai to bring the fighting here."

"Which faction?"

"We're not sure. I thought that your consulate might be able to find out. Could you come back to my legation now? I'll show you some of the documents and transmissions we've intercepted."

It was going to be a long night, Sam decided. He was pleased he had asked Connaught along. "I'll be ready to go in ten minutes," he said to Ito. "Just give me time to make my official apologies."

"Certainly," Ito said.

Charlotte was having a wonderful evening. The champagne, the splendor of the uniforms, the lovely gowns of the women created a feast of color, and her brief conversation with Sam had set her completely free. The night was magic. Especially when Connaught caught her up in his commanding arms and swept her around the ballroom floor as if she were floating.

The grand climax of the ball came shortly before midnight. She had heard a hissing sound even over the music of the orchestra, most pronounced when they were dancing closest to the champagne fountain. She caught the first twitch of movement out of the corner of her eyes as the cherubs began to quiver and then quake from the increased pressure. Then the Chinese waiters scattered as the whole fountain blew up, the crowning cherub developing multiple leaks, sending streams in every direction before breaking all to pieces in one grand spray of champagne that doused the dancers closest to it. The ballroom exploded with laughter while the Italian Consul General clasped his hands together with pure bliss and went to stand in the alcoholic rain, laughing gleefully, head back, mouth open.

"Enjoy!" he shouted. "Enjoy!"

And Charlotte did enjoy, so much so that once they left the ball at two in the morning, she was not ready to go home.

"Then we won't," Connaught said, a sparkle in his eye. "I'm a night person and that's the God's truth. It works very well actually, because Shanghai is two different places, a night city as well as a day city. I'd like you to see the sights, my dear."

He showed them to her. They cruised through the local quarter known as Blood Alley, a street of garish nightclubs and flamboyant prostitutes and squads of sailors from half a dozen fleets. She watched a police raid on one establishment, with the sailors fighting back with a barrage of flying bottles, one of which bounced on top of the car before Connaught maneuvered out of range. And then they went to a small and smoky bar where Chinese hostesses sat on stools against one wall, waiting to descend on the lone males who came in for drinks.

She was surprised to find Connaught as much at home in these places as in the fine shops or at the formal reception. He chatted in Chinese with the barkeep and the girls, kidding them, shrugging at the banter he got back.

They sat at a small table in a corner with a single sputtering candle to provide light and they drank gin, the only potable in this place, Connaught said, that was not watered down. He drank the gin, then poured an amber-colored liquid into the glass from the special bottle he carried in a paper sack. He bolted it down.

"What on earth is that?" she said.

"An elixir, a potion," he said with a wink.

"Let me taste it."

"Wouldn't think of it," he said lightly. "Strictly a man's drink." He put the bottle away.

"You're very much at home here in Shanghai, aren't you?" she said.

"Yes. She's like a great lady, aging but ever-fascinating. Not another city like it in the world." He checked his watch. "Which leads me to the subject of another lady of whom I am inordinately fond. If the police should happen to raid this place, which isn't likely, I'll admit, but definitely possible, it would not be good for your reputation."

"I don't care," she said. "Not tonight." She put her hand on his. "I want to know everything about you, Harry."

"With all the time we've spent making the rounds, I'd bet you know me as well as anyone in this world."

"Only the surface," she said. "Only the grand way you have with people, the ease that you show. But that's not really knowing you, what you think and feel."

He smiled, a warm and cheering smile. "If I explain myself to you, will you believe it?"

"I think so."

"All right," he said. "Then throw away all the standard statements you hear about people like 'Still waters run deep' or 'The eyes are mirrors of the soul.' " He held his hand up, displaying the space of an inch between his thumb and forefinger. "I'm that deep," he said. "I'm exactly what I appear to be. Nothing more. Nothing hidden. All on the surface. I've made all of myself that I want to be or am capable of being. I don't aspire to more. I have freedom. I enjoy the sunlight when it's warm and the darkness when it's cold. I have a full stomach when I wish, but I don't mind hunger in the least." He shrugged. "There now, a quick tour of Connaught, enough that you could draw a map of my soul from. But the map would *be* the soul. All there is. Are you disappointed?"

"Not disappointed," she said. "Because I don't believe you."

"So there you are," he said with a smile.

"We'll see," she said. "Where do you live?"

"I can show you if you like. It's between here and there, and by there I mean your house. So we'll stop and you can examine my haunts and know that I mean exactly what I say. And then it's home before the scandal rises with the lateness of the hour."

He drove her to an old building off Seward Road near the place where Soochow Creek flowed into the Whangpoo, at the very edge of the Volunteer Corps Sector. She could hear the discordant Chinese music from the moored barges and see the lanterns flickering like fireflies.

He parked the car in a narrow alley, then took her up a rickety outside staircase, unlocked a cumbersome and ancient lock with an oversized key, and showed her into one of the most interesting apartments she had ever seen. She was utterly fascinated by the shelves of pottery, the paintings, and the scrolls with which he had surrounded himself, and in the archway to the bedroom the silk covering for a dragon used in festivals, with the head mounted over the carved teak bed. There were books everywhere, in Chinese and in English.

"My God, Harry," she said. "It's a veritable museum." She touched a vase with her fingers. "This is genuine Ming Dynasty, isn't it? And this one over here is Tang."

He established himself behind a carved teak bar and poured himself another drink from his personal bottle and provided her with a liqueur. "You approve of my digs, then," he said.

"Beautiful and worth a fortune," she said. She took the small glass from him and sat down on a velvet-cushioned divan. "Aren't you afraid of keeping all these things here?"

"In such a rough district," he said with a smile, "where they can be stolen?"

"Yes."

"If a thief broke in and took a look around, he wouldn't be interested in all the Chinese art, because if it was real, then it wouldn't be here, now, would it?" he said, sipping his drink. "No, it would be in one of the great estates out on Bubbling Well with guards around it and high walls and dogs loose on the grounds. I have these beautiful things around me only because they are beautiful and not because some ancient dynasty proclaimed them to be acceptable. And if someone broke in tomorrow and stole some of these pieces, it wouldn't break my heart. There's lots of beauty around and it isn't all in things."

"Incredible," she said. The liqueur was heady. She heard the deep-throated pitch of a ship's horn as it headed out to sea and she felt as if she were on a voyage of her own. "You're an incredible man. I've never met anyone like you."

"One's enough, I think." He laughed. "And now we've come to it, haven't we, love?" he said.

"To what?"

"We've been to bed together and had a lovely time of it. But now you're wanting more than that and you don't know whether I'm the person to give it to you, as truly insubstantial as I am. And if I take you home now, then there's hope for you, because we become friends who have been lovers. But you know that if you stay, then we end up beneath the dragon's head, making love again. That would be splendid for me, but I don't know whether it would be best for you."

She looked at him steadily. "You know that I want to do just that, don't you?" she said.

He nodded. "But you see, I'm not sure you believe that I am exactly what I seem to be. I am an emotional transient. You might call me an experience, and you can never tie to an experience."

"Then you offer nothing more than tonight and nights like this one," she said. "That's what you're saying."

"Not necessarily," he said. "I'm saying there are many kinds of love, as many as there are kinds of men. Some of them are like rock pilings you can build on. And I'm smoke."

She finished the drink, put the glass down. *I will make a difference in you,* she thought. *You just don't know it yet.* She walked over to him and, leaning down, kissed him, feeling the gentle strength in the hand that touched her back. He stood up and drew her to him and then picked her up and carried her into the room beneath the dragon canopy and placed her gently, ever so gently, on the bed, as if she were the most beautiful of all the treasures in his apartment.

The commercial space was small, an enclosed cubicle with a wire-mesh window opening into the street. A Chinese sign read PLENTI-FUL MONEY EXCHANGE, and from the moment she moved a small desk, a chair, and an ancient safe into the room, Yuki found her niche in the art of business. She had hired a very large Japanese man to sit at the desk as a guard, and she perched on a high stool at the window, her abacus at hand. Her first customer, a broad-faced Chinese mill hand, spoke Shanghainese and regarded with great suspicion her willingness to pay a dollar for only ten yen. She was so excited, she laughed out loud when the transaction had been made and the customer ambled off.

She closed at five the first evening, and when Sam drove by to pick her up she bubbled over with ideas. "I think we can do extra business by expanding to include silver Mexican pesos," she said. "The regular currency traders are robbing the Chinese laborers blind because the peso has been in circulation so long. We can give them far better rates on pesos and still make more than we can on dollars. I also think we should handle the British pound—"

He laughed. "I take it you enjoyed your day."

"Oh, yes." She linked her arm through his. "Even after only one day, I know we can make a lot of money out of it."

"Unfortunately, this has to be temporary."

"Why?"

"This market is too volatile and unpredictable for us except in the short term. How much did you trade today?"

"Nine hundred sixty-three dollars."

"Excellent," he said. "I'm taking you to a new place for dinner tonight up in the Italian Sector near St. John's. Do you like Italian?"

"Today, anyplace would please me," she said.

The Italian restaurant was dimly lit, with candles on checkered tablecloths, a violin player wandering through the main room. They sat at a table against a plaster wall beneath a garish wooden saint. Yuki was still so excited from the day that she had little appetite. Sam ordered dinner while her mind raced with the possibilities. "You wouldn't believe the unusual customers I've had today," she said. "I had a French merchant approach me with fifty ounces of gold, which he wanted to trade at very favorable rates to us, for Mexican silver, which he intends to invest upriver."

Sam tasted the wine, directed the waiter to pour a glass for her. "If it was real gold, why would he pick you instead of one of the commercial banks?"

"I suppose it's because I'm not required to keep any written records," she said.

He rubbed his chin thoughtfully. "We just might do it," he said. "I'll sound out Dawes and see if we can get around the difficulties. The gold traders may be organized under the Chinese gangs, but it won't hurt to look into it." He looked up as the violinist approached their table and conversation became impossible. After one song Sam gave him money and the musician wandered on, but she could see that something had gone awry, Sam's mood changing in the flicker of an eyelid. He was withdrawn, uncomfortable.

"What's wrong?" she said, touching his hand.

"Nothing," he said. But she became aware of a table on the other side of the restaurant and she recognized an English consular official whom she had seen many times when he called on Sam at the consulate, and now he was presiding over a loud and boisterous party. Sam had abandoned his plate of linguini.

She knew that protocol demanded that the Englishman come to Sam's table to pay his respects, but that rule had been superseded by another one, as old as the Western presence in this country, and she could imagine what Stafford would be whispering to his woman companion. *Gone native*, he would be saying. *He has a most attractive wife, you know, but he prefers to have an affair with this very young oriental girl. So we will pretend not to see him and he will have to do the same.*

She looked at Sam. *So you have become invisible, my love*, she thought. *You're afraid that the code might be broken and that they might say something to embarrass me.* She waited an appropriate time. "Do you mind if we leave?" she asked. "I seem to have a headache."

"Not at all." He raised a hand for the waiter, signed a chit, and then ushered her out into the night, never once looking toward the English party.

At her apartment she kissed him and made excuses why he should not come in, and then, once she was in the privacy of her living room, she lit a candle and sat in the big chair she had bought for Sam and thought things through, too drained of feeling to be miserable, as if she were simply examining a natural barrier, a cliff, a giant tree trunk in her path.

They avoided me as if I didn't exist and they ignored Sam as well, she thought.

Some barriers could never be crossed.

On Christmas morning Sam and Charlotte made a perfunctory exchange of presents, a cashmere scarf for him, her gift an expensive bottle of perfume, which seemed to please her. She kissed him on the cheek and in the early afternoon was off to a reception on her own while he wrote dispatches. All in all, he decided, theirs was not an unpleasant relationship. They each went their own way, without question or acrimony. He gathered up the armload of gifts he had found for Yuki and left to spend the remainder of the day with her, content to do so for the time being.

On a morning just before New Year's, Sam and Ito had a meeting with a Japanese vice admiral and Sam picked up a feeling of ambivalence the moment he entered the senior officer's stateroom. The Admiral wanted to discuss peace in Shanghai even as he moved red and blue markers representing troops across an oversized map of the city on his desk.

"We have the word of the mayor of Shanghai that Chiang Kai-shek can control the Nineteenth Route Army and General Wang," Sam said, waiting while Ito translated the words into deferential Japanese. "But we need to assure the Chinese authorities that the Japanese marines will remain in the Japanese Sector."

The Admiral listened, nodded, smiled, and continued to move his markers deeper into Chapei, chatting with Ito while studying the grid of streets, as if playing a game. "The Admiral says he is under orders not to make a first move," Ito said, "but he's absolutely certain Wang will descend on Shanghai, and the Admiral will be testing his men in battle."

The Admiral rubbed his chin, moved a line of blue markers toward North Station, smiled to Ito, spoke again. "The Admiral suggests that if the United States would care to send its marines along in this action, the Admiral will see that they get a lot of good practice."

"Why did the Admiral ask us here?" Sam said.

"This is his indirect way of advising the United States government what he intends to do."

"Let him know that the United States is devoted to finding peaceful solutions to problems here."

Ito nodded, relayed the message to the Admiral, who nodded and smiled. "The Admiral says that he, too, is devoted to peace," Ito said. "He also says that should your marines care to participate, their commanding officer should contact him as soon as possible."

Sam expressed polite gratitude to the Admiral, and once he was on the dock with Ito, he lit a cigarette, looked up at the destroyer. "He won't have to get permission from anyone in Tokyo to send his troops in, will he?"

"Technically yes but actually no," Ito said glumly. "He's under orders to limit himself to retaliation. But at the same time he has the sole right to determine when the Chinese are being provocative."

"I'll have my State Department issue a statement affirming the Admiral's promises that he won't make the first move. Not that it will do a damn bit of good."

"We'll take things as they come," Ito said. "Do you have time for lunch?"

"Sure," Sam said, and they walked down the waterfront to a small cafe on the Bund that catered to emigrés, a place that offered them privacy. After they had ordered, Sam leaned back in his chair, studying Ito. "Tell me something," he said. "What do you plan to do when this is all over? Will you stay on in the Foreign Service?"

Ito sipped his tea. "My father is a baron," he said, as if that explained everything.

"I know," Sam said.

"I followed my father's pattern for me from the moment I was born. I was educated at Tokyo University to give me the best theoretical education I can get. I became an army officer to demonstrate the valor of my family. And it was expected of me, when I had the opportunity in Manchukuo, to show my personal bravery. I have been assigned to the Foreign Ministry and in a few years I will be assigned to Europe, after taking a wife who has been selected for me because of her proper family connections. Eventually I will serve the Emperor by becoming a part of the government in Tokyo, where I'll manage my family estates. I will be obligated to have a male heir, to whom I shall pass on everything I have learned, and then I will die and he will become Baron and repeat the pattern."

They fell silent while they ate sushi, and it was only when Sam began his tea that he spoke again. "Do you believe in what you're doing here?"

"Sometimes I agree with you more than my father would be comfortable with, if he knew. Because I think there is going to be a senseless war and I would stop it if I could, when, according to tradition, that would not be my role here at all. I have been assigned to support my Emperor's wishes. And since I am not to know those wishes directly, I am to obey my superiors without question because they are above me and therefore closer to knowing what the Emperor might want. I would like to have the kind of freedom you have sometimes."

"Freedom's relative," Sam said. "At the moment it's freedom to have problems." He looked at his watch. "Speaking of which, I'm sorry, but I'm going to have to cut this short today. I have an appointment with a man named Zhu. He has some factories that interest me."

"A word of caution," Ito said. "If fighting breaks out, the Admiral won't hesitate to bombard Chinese factories. And he may act on his own so swiftly that I won't be able to warn you. So don't allow yourself to get caught in the middle."

"I appreciate the advice and I'll take it," Sam said. He took the chit from the waiter to sign. "And it's my turn for lunch."

"Thanks," Ito said. "I've enjoyed it."

Zhu was a gaunt man with hollow cheeks and trembling fingers, which came from too much opium. "I think we can strike a bargain," Sam said in Chinese after they had consumed two cups of tea at a cafe near the textile factory. "Through no fault of the esteemed Zhu, the cost of raw cotton has become too great for you to show a profit on the goods you manufacture. I wish to make a proposal, but I ask you now, with the greatest respect, if you would prefer direct negotiations or the use of an agent or comprador."

"I should be honored to conduct such negotiations myself," Zhu said, as Sam expected he would.

"Then I'll call on you again within a week."

The same afternoon Sam made an appointment with his lawyer to have papers drafted to form a closely held corporation, which, on the spur of the moment, Sam decided to call Arnold Trading Company, Ltd., the name he registered with the British Consulate. He went to the Shanghai–Hong Kong bank to check on the state of his account and managed to get back to the American Consulate before Dawes left.

"I want to offer you a limited partnership in my new company," Sam said. "I'll give you a twenty percent interest in return for your advice. I'm looking for a devil's advocate, someone who'll try to find holes in what I'm doing so I can plug them as I go along."

"All right," Dawes said. "It sounds like something I might enjoy." He leaned back in his chair, fingers laced over the vest of his small-town businessman's suit. "So why not begin?"

"Fine," Sam said. "I followed your advice and exchanged thirty thousand dollars into three hundred thousand yen. I sent those to Washington, where the official government policy is to exchange yen for dollars at one to one. I now have an account at the Shanghai–Hong Kong in the amount of three hundred and thirty thousand dollars."

"Ah," Dawes said with admiration. "And what's your next step?"

"I'll exchange one hundred thousand dollars for one million yen."

"Why not the whole amount?" Dawes said, testing.

"Because Shanghai's volatile. It can explode anytime, and when it does, I'm gambling that the American policy will shift. No more one-to-one parity of dollars to yen. There could be a devaluation and I could lose my hundred thousand. In addition, they could make it a crime for citizens of the United States to speculate in the currency of what would be labeled a 'nonfriendly power.' In that case I could be fined. I'm setting aside a hundred thousand in that event. I don't consider it likely, but I'm prepared."

"Leaving you a hundred thousand clear to begin again," Dawes said.

"Yes," Sam said. "Frankly, I don't think Shanghai is going to be stable beyond next month. So I can't count on a favorable exchange rate beyond sixty days."

Dawes beamed. "You don't need an adviser. You've figured it well."

"I'm making another step," Sam said, "And this is the tricky area. Once I exchange the yen, I'm going to invest the money in cotton. There's a bumper crop in the American South and the price is so low they're having trouble giving it away."

"What will you do with the cotton?" Dawes said, intrigued. "The Shanghai mills can't afford to buy it."

"Exactly. That increases my opportunity. I've talked to the owner of a cotton mill here. I'll contract to have it made into fabric. The price for that will be next to nothing because he's starving for business and this way he can continue to operate. Now, I look around for fabric markets, and then, if the prospects are good, I go into the manufacture of military uniforms."

"For what country?"

"If I'm right, I can manufacture and sell for less than any company in any country. If I'm not, then I can sell the fabric for a tenth of what it would bring in good times." He lit a cigarette, leaned back in his chair. "All right, poke your holes."

"There are a dozen places where things can go wrong."

"Name them."

"You're taking risks at every step because you're dealing with governments and that means possible embargoes and tariffs." He snapped his fingers. "You could be wiped out. Just like that."

"I've got options at every step," Sam said. "If the cotton deals look sour by the time I'm ready to make them, then I simply hold the cash. If I buy the cotton and there's trouble here, I can make the same deal with English mills. I'm incorporating under British law against that contingency. So even under the worst possible conditions, I won't lose more than a part of my investment. And with you to advise, to keep abreast of developments, we won't go wrong."

"How great it is to see absolutely raw ambition," Dawes said, delighted. "I had it myself when I was younger. All right, I'll take your proposition. And what's our company?"

"Arnold Trading Company, Limited," Sam said. "Named after my father, God rest him."

Early in January, Shanghai turned icy with storms sweeping in from the north and there were mornings when the streets were so treacherous that Sam was forced to make the trip to the consulate in a horse-drawn carriage. At times it seemed to him as if his whole fortune lay in elements equally as unpredictable as the weather. For he had been lucky enough to buy a whole cargo of cotton bales at a minimal price, but there were storms in the Atlantic that were holding up the cargo ship on its way to the Panama Canal, and if war came to Shanghai, it was pretty certain that the mills on the border of Chapei and the Japanese Sector would be wiped out.

And it was clear that more trouble was brewing when Alcott summoned him to his drafty, cold office. The ancient heating system worked fitfully at best. It had been designed to push heat up from the basement, and so it did, but never beyond the second floor. Alcott had a teapot whistling on a hot plate and he served Sam a mixture of tea, lemon, and rum in a cup, then caught a sneeze in a handkerchief and looked at Sam with bleary eyes. "These are terrible times," he said. "It's even worse now than it was during the War to End All Wars. At least there was a sense of grace to the Foreign Service here then. George Hilger, of the Hilger Cereal fortune, was consul general. The primary requirement for being a member of his staff was that we were all gentlemen. We maintained a steady pace and a predictable morality."

Sam sipped the hot tea, pulled his suit jacket more closely about him. "Why don't you move downstairs until the heat is fixed?"

"Because a little adversity is good for the soul," Alcott said. "I've had a complaint from the Japanese Consul that you are playing the currency game and buying up large amounts of yen."

"There's no law against that."

Alcott held his palm up as if he were stemming the flow of traffic at an intersection. "Wait," he said. After a moment he came forth with a mighty sneeze. Removing a medicine bottle from a drawer, he filled a spoon and swallowed the medicine with a grimace. "Don't try to argue with me. I'm your superior and an old man. So just pay attention. You are using your Japanese assistant to exchange the money. Since it is being done during what are loosely known as working hours, it is interpreted as an official act."

"We've been through this, Mr. Alcott. She's my personal employee. You made a great point of that. She no longer occupies an office at the consulate."

"I repeat, appearances are everything here. You have apparently forgotten that. I also hear that you have been careless enough to impregnate her."

"With all due respect, sir, I consider that my private business."

Alcott ignored the statement altogether. He blew his nose. "Let me give you some advice, my boy," he said in a softer tone. "And I trust that this will be confidential, just between the two of us. At one time Mr. Connaught had the capability of becoming a luminary here. He's a very bright man and understands the Chinese as well as any white man I know. But quite early on he forgot where his allegiances lay. He forgot that he was representing Great Britain every moment of the day and night." He dabbed at his nose again. "I shouldn't tell you this, but you have a very good chance of succeeding me as consul general. But only if your personal life is impeccable."

"I see," Sam said. "And what do you recommend, Mr. Alcott?"

"May I speak frankly?"

"Of course. Please."

"It's no secret that yours is a marriage of convenience."

"That's true."

Alcott nodded understandingly. "I would suggest then that since it's obvious that you feel some affection for this Japanese lady, that you arrange to place her in an apartment in the Japanese Sector, where she will not be quite as visible as she is at present. It may inhibit your access somewhat, but it is a small price to pay. You will be seen by the diplomatic community as a young man who has sowed a few wild oats, not a maverick."

"And my business dealings?"

"First, close down your currency exchange in Hongkew. Now, you registered as a British company and I can understand why. Nevertheless, for the sake of form, it will be politic for you to register either that company or a companion company with your own country."

"I'll need a little while to think about this," Sam said.

"Of course. I know how great is the temptation to become a full-time trader, as your ancestors were before you. But your country needs you out here. Inevitably, we will be involved in somebody's aggression and the temptation to go to war will be overwhelming. You have a cool head. So I ask you to consider carefully where your duty lies. The incredibly naive mores of the diplomatic community may seem foolish to you, but all I ask is that you are perceived to follow that which is done. Do you get my meaning?"

"Yes, sir," Sam said.

The afternoon was chill with a threat of sleet in the air, and Yuki closed the currency exchange early, knowing that Sam would be along at any moment to pick her up. She pulled her coat more closely about her and made a final accounting for the day, her fingers clicking the beads of the abacus while Kenjo, her Japanese guard, kept his eyes on the street. He had been especially quiet all afternoon, occasionally standing outside the stall near a fire in a large metal drum where he could listen to conversations on the street from workmen gathering to warm their hands.

"If you like, you can leave early," she said to him. "I'm going to be picked up very shortly."

"I think I'll stay, Nakamura-san," he said. "Everybody is uneasy on the street today. There's a rumor that the Chinese will be causing trouble in the Japanese Sector tonight despite the cold. But if you will excuse me for a few minutes . . ." He went into a store to use the toilet, and no sooner had he disappeared than she saw a ragged Chinese workman detach himself from the group at the fire and approach her window, a wild and desperate expression in his eyes, his hand holding something pointed toward her and concealed by a paper sack. "I want money," he said. "I don't want to have to shoot you to get it."

She froze momentarily, caught in a cold panic, knowing that she had to stall until Kenjo came back. "This is not my money," she said in Mandarin. "If I allow it to be stolen, I will lose face with my master."

"I don't care about face," he said, voice strained, so frightened his hand was shaking. "My family has not eaten for four days. I will kill you rather than see them starve. So give me the money now."

At that moment Kenjo emerged from the store, saw what was happening. He pulled a small pistol from his pocket, kept his voice even. "Drop your weapon," he said quietly.

The Chinese workman did not move. His eyes suddenly became hopeless. He did not even look around. "Kill me," he said. "I ask you to shoot me. I do not wish to face my family without food."

"Drop your weapon," Kenjo said again.

The man's hand emerged from the paper bag, empty. "If I had a weapon, I would have sold it for food," he said. "Now, I ask again. Kill me."

"You'll go to the police," Kenjo said.

But Yuki stopped him, her composure coming back, for there was something familiar in the man's eyes, and then she remembered the expression of desperation on her father's face the night he had sold her. This man had the same look in his eyes. She took ten one-yen notes, handed them to the man, who was so startled he did not move. "You will let him go," she said to Kenjo, and then to the man: "Your family will not be hungry tonight."

He began to back away, the single soft syllable of gratitude coming out of his mouth over and over again, a soothing sound. *"She, she, she . . ."* He turned and ran down the street.

"You should have let me capture him," Kenjo said. "A thief must be punished."

"Life has punished him enough," she said, her heart just beginning to calm. "And we will not speak of this again."

She took the money from the safe and placed the stacks of bills in a leather case, leaving the empty safe open, in full view of any potential thief who might be tempted to break in. Soon she saw Sam's car easing through the sparse traffic.

The moment she was in the car she could see that Sam was not in one of his better moods. He was always quiet when he was faced with difficult choices, and it seemed that his life was full of them lately. "Business was excellent today," she said. "Over six thousand American exchanged for yen. I did some trading in pesos as well. We can get good rates at the Mexican bank tomorrow."

"You have a real gift for business," he said. "But I'm afraid that we have to close down, as of this evening. I'll contact Kenjo and settle up with him tomorrow."

"Just like that?" she said, startled. "I think the currency market will be good for six more weeks at least. And I haven't received any notice from the authorities that what I'm doing is against any law."

He pulled in at a Japanese restaurant and parked the car. "We're due to meet a real estate agent in about an hour," he said. "I thought we might have a drink until then. And there are some things I need to explain to you."

He said nothing more until they had been seated, and she ordered a white wine while he had his usual bourbon. He looked around the almost deserted room as if to determine how freely he could talk, then he covered her hand with his. "None of this is fair to you," he said. "I know that. But I'm asking you to trust me until I can make arrangements." He sipped his drink. "I have been told in no uncertain terms to close down the money exchange."

"May I ask why?"

"Because the Japanese Consulate is unhappy with the fact that I'm doing business in the Japanese Sector."

"Even though your name is not connected with the business?"

"As far as officialdom is concerned, everything you do is strictly in my behalf," he said.

"I see," she said. He could see the disappointment on her face.

"Besides, to make the really big money, we have to go through Washington." He drank his glass halfway down and then looked at his watch. "It's time to meet the real estate agent," he said.

"Are you buying property?"

"Leasing," he said. "That is, if you like the apartment I've picked out. It's quite large and luxurious. A perfect room for a nursery and a private garden. I want you to hire some servants, an amah for the baby when she comes."

"I don't want to move," she said. "I have a real home now and I'm perfectly content where I am."

"I want the best for you," he said. "Very soon you will need a bigger apartment."

He left the money on the table, led her outside into the cold wind and the gathering darkness. Off in the distance she could hear the sound of firecrackers, and for a moment, as he slid behind the wheel, he had the most forlorn expression on his face she had ever seen. It disappeared the moment he realized she was looking at him.

"We're to meet him on Nainjing Road," he said, maneuvering the car into heavy traffic. The moment he turned into Nainjing Road she heard the yelling mobs and saw them not a block away, hundreds of Chinese in the street, carrying torches and stoning the windows of a Japanese trading company. The car was stopped by a Japanese patrolman on a motorcycle as the helmeted police brigade charged down the street, guns firing, batons beating heads until the Chinese dispersed into the side streets.

Sam was very pale. He sounded his horn and backed the car around, then inched forward until he was clear of the police and into the normal traffic, away from the fighting. "Well, that won't do," he said when they were finally clear. "The apartment house was right across the street from the trading company the Chinese were attacking. It's obvious the police can't guarantee safety in the streets."

"It's just as well. I'm truly pleased with where I am."

"I'm still going to find you another place. Then after the baby's born, we should have enough money for a house."

"Do you have time for dinner?" she said when his car paused in front of her apartment.

"No," he said. "Charlotte's having a late dinner party at home."

She was filled with a great and tender sadness. She reached over and switched off the engine. "I will hold you up only a moment," she said. "But there are things we must say to each other. Sometimes you treat me as if I'm half child, half woman, but I'm strong enough to know the truth. And at the moment I know you're trying to protect my feelings while you're doing what you feel you have to do."

He lit a cigarette in the darkness. "I love you and I want to be in a position to marry you," he said. "That's all that counts."

"I know you love me, but there are many other things that have to count. You've been told to make your relationship with me more secret, haven't you?"

"Yes," he said quietly in the darkness of the car.

"And moving me into the Japanese Sector is a way to do that." It was not a question. "Do you know the meaning of *giri*?"

"No, what is it?"

"It means "duty,' the kind of duty you owe to your wife."

"Duty is one thing I understand very well. Charlotte and I wouldn't have been married otherwise. I won't neglect my duty to her and I won't move you anywhere unsafe," he said, and then, with determination, he pulled her to him, kissed her. "If anybody causes you trouble, let me know. And forget this evening. We'll have dinner tomorrow night."

"Yes." She held him close for a moment and then released him. "Good night."

As she entered the apartment and turned on the light, she felt the baby move within her, as if prompting her to take action. She put on water for tea and rice, and then she sat down beneath a scroll on the wall, knowing with absolute and heartbreaking certainty what she had to do.

The dinner party for Colonel Ito was a great success, largely due to Connaught's presence, Sam realized. Harry was an accomplished raconteur and so expert at drawing people together that there was not the slightest tension at the dinner table, despite the presence of a British official who had made no bones about his dislike of the

Japanese and a French official who had published articles attacking the Japanese conquest of Manchuria.

Charlotte was elegant in her red gown, with a jeweled comb in her hair. Following Connaught's advice, she had placed Colonel Ito at the far end of the table with Sam and flanked herself with the British and the French at her end, with the happy Italian and his wife in the center to serve as buffers.

Sam studied Ito, who was unusually reserved. When the conversation was loud at the other end of the table, Sam seized the chance to talk with him. "You seem positively glum tonight," he said. "What's wrong?" he said.

"I owe you an apology."

Sam smiled. "For what?"

"My consul general registered a complaint against you. I tried to talk him out of it, but he's a very old-fashioned man. He takes it personally that you have been speculating in our national currency and that your assistant is a Japanese national."

"You don't have anything to apologize to me for," Sam said. "In an odd way, your consul general did me a favor because he's brought the whole situation to a head. Everything's in the open now and I have the chance to make a clean decision. Are you free for lunch tomorrow? I'd like your advice on what I'm about to do."

"Certainly," Ito said. "And I appreciate your understanding."

Sam lifted his wine glass. *"Compai,* my friend," he said.

"Compai," Ito responded.

When the dinner was over and the guests were gone, he was about to say good night to Charlotte and go upstairs to bed when she stopped him. "Would you have a nightcap with me in the drawing room?" she said.

"Of course," he said. He followed her into the drawing room, which seemed to have been changed since he last looked at it. "I don't remember the damask drapes," he said. "Are they new?"

"Yes," she said with a pleased smile. "Do you like them?"

"Yes, I do," he said. "And the settee to match."

She poured the champagne and gave him a glass before she sat down. "I thought we might talk," she said, a certain wistfulness in her voice. "I hear stories about you all the time. I have to pretend that I'm not interested and don't believe them, but of course I am interested." She sipped her champagne. "Tell me about her," she said with a smile.

"About who?"

"Your Japanese mistress. Don't look so startled, dear Sam. It's all right. I have somebody of my own."

"I'll be damned," he said. "Who?"

"It's not important 'who,' " she said. "But we don't have to walk on eggshells around each other anymore."

"What do you know about Yuki?" he said. "And how did you find out?"

"I know very little except that she's lovely and Japanese," Charlotte said. *"Très élégante.* The French decorator who did the drapes and the settee used those exact words about her, and even complimented both of us because we are so modern in the way we live our lives."

"There's really nothing to tell about her," he said, hoping she knew nothing about the pregnancy. "Are you serious about your lover?"

"Very serious but most impermanent," she said. He detected a faint wryness in her smile. "I'm not very good at maintaining permanent relationships. So I don't know where it's going to lead."

"If you're considering a divorce, it's highly possible I can pay your father back in another year."

"You're that successful?" she asked, her appreciation genuine. "I'm very pleased. It may be necessary to wait until then, because Daddy is very unhappy when something goes sour that he's bought and paid for. He's just unscrupulous enough that if we did divorce, he'd cause a great deal of trouble. I wish you well, my dear, and all the happiness you can possibly have. I also wish the same for myself."

He was genuinely touched. "I'm sorry for all the pain I've caused you," he said. "Will you forgive me?"

"You're forgiven, Sam. Bygones are bygones." She stood up. "And now I'd better go make sure that Majordomo is not being a slave driver over the cleaning up. He's something of a tyrant, you know." On her way out of the room she kissed him on top of the head. "Sleep well," she said.

He stayed where he was until he had finished his champagne, feeling an unexpected sadness at the closure. There was nothing tentative about Charlotte anymore, nothing girlish. She was her own woman at last and a beautiful one at that. He had the feeling that should she play the piano now, the melody would be strong and full of life.

The next afternoon Sam read a dispatch from Colonel Ito advising him that the Nineteenth Route Army was rumored to be on the move. He put in a call to the American Consulate in Nanking but the lines were down and telephone service was not expected to be restored for another forty-eight hours.

He received a cable advising that the cargo ship S.S. *Armbruster* had put in at Vera Cruz for repairs. He had a fortune tied up in the cotton bales aboard that ship. He could make a contract with Zhu now, contingent upon delivery, but with payment for the cotton put in escrow, just in case Colonel Ito was right and Shanghai was on the verge of a full-scale conflict. He would gamble that the S.S. *Armbruster* was going to deliver his cotton to Shanghai.

Sam called for his car and decided to stop by Yuki's apartment on the way back to the mansion. When he reached the apartment house he told the driver to wait for him and, whistling to himself, sorted through his keys and then unlocked the door. As he pushed it open he stopped dead in his tracks. The room was deserted, swept clean, as if it had never been occupied. His leather heels echoed in the bare hallway as he walked toward the bedroom and found it empty as well.

And then he saw the envelope bearing his name, thumbtacked to the wall next to the door. He had to force himself to lift the envelope from the wall and open it.

Darling Cummings-san,

Please forgive the way I write this to you, because I was taught to translate documents, but never did the missionaries teach me to say what is in my heart. I have gone to the temple three times and prayed for enlightenment from Lord Buddha, but there was no answer, and I have prayed to Lord Jesus, but he, too, has been silent, and I know that in the end the decision must come from me even though my heart breaks with it. To show your loyalty to me and to your child would cause you to lose face with your people. I think your work here would be over and that is too much for you to pay for our love.

So please, I beg of you, dismiss me from your memory if not

from your heart, and know that a part of you will live on within me until I die and with our child forever. Forgive one who loves you enough to leave that which has made my life worth living.

Good-bye,
Yuki

His fingers began to tremble, the sheets of paper rustling like leaves in a wind. He picked up the telephone, dialed the Japanese Consulate, and asked to speak to Ito, but, as near as he could make out from a clerk who spoke little English, the Colonel was not available.

He went down the hall, banged on the door of the next apartment, occupied by a middle-aged Chinese couple, and he began to question them with such force that he realized he was frightening them. He stopped, bowed, trying to control the pain spreading within him, phrasing his questions politely in Mandarin. Had they seen the lady next door today? Had they seen her leave? Did they have any idea where she had gone? And to all the questions the man gave him polite but negative answers. They had not been at home for most of the day and he was sorry he could not be of aid.

Sam made his way down the hallway, knocking on doors, asking the same questions again and again, his hope diminishing with each repetitive answer. Compulsively, he went through the entire building and down the street, then finally returned to the empty apartment and sat on the floor, his back against the wall, pain overwhelming him.

I love you. How could you leave me?

But he knew the answer even as the question formed in his mind. She meant exactly what she had written in the note. She had left him for fear that his career would be hurt, that he would lose face. He sat motionless, unaware that tears were streaming down his cheeks. She would still be somewhere in this vast and sprawling city and he was comforted by that thought.

He went to the Cathay Hotel, where he found Connaught at the bar. Connaught took one look at his face, grimaced. "Sit down. Have a drink."

Sam ordered a drink, bolted it, felt the liquor burning a path down his throat. It took a moment for him to get his breath, and even then the words came out of him with difficulty. "She's left me," he said.

"Who's left you?"

"Yuki." He handed Connaught the letter.

"It's quite true, old man. She's done what she had to do and you have to bless her for that. You were about to put yourself beyond the pale."

"I don't give a good goddamn about any of that," Sam said. "Can you find her for me?"

"I don't know," Connaught said. "If she's still in Shanghai, the odds are pretty good."

"She's here," Sam said. "I know it."

"And if I find her, old man, what do I say to her?"

"That I want to see her," Sam said, waiting for the whiskey to ease the overwhelming pain within him.

Connaught stared at the desolation in his eyes. "I'll do what I can," he said. "It may take a little time, but I'll find her for you."

She spent a little of her diminishing money to catch the tram back to the tenement in the Mouth of the Rainbow District where Mrs. Liu lived, and by the time she climbed the stairs and rapped at the door, she was freezing. It was as cold in the building as it was on the street. Mrs. Liu was startled to see her and immediately brought her in out of the cold, seating her next to a brazier that contained two glowing lumps of coal to heat the tiny room as well as warm the kettle that sat over them. She had to move scraps of cloth on which she had been sewing to make room for herself. "I didn't recognize you at first," she said, pouring hot water into a cup. "I'm sorry this unworthy person has no tea to offer you."

"I'm grateful for the hot water," Yuki said.

"I hope the blue dress pleased you. I have the fabric for another dress that would look very good on you."

Yuki held the warmth of the cup in her hands, trying to keep down the rising panic within her, afraid that the cold might have harmed the baby within her. She kept her coat wrapped tightly about her, but she was sure Mrs. Liu could see the swelling of her body.

"No, unfortunately I'm not here to buy another dress."

"We were cursed by the gods when we were born women," Mrs. Liu said, rocking back and forth slightly on her chair as if to comfort herself. "My husband was taken from the streets by the army and I haven't seen him since, and now some man has sown his seed in you. But I think I can let out the blue dress, or perhaps you would like to have it made into a looser garment. That would cost you very little."

"I cannot rely on the father of this child," Yuki said.

"*Ai,*" Mrs. Liu said. "Then if you would take the advice of this worthless person, you would spare the child you carry in your belly the agony of entering into this world."

"I am here to ask you for help," Yuki said flatly. "I can cook and help with the sewing."

Mrs. Liu blinked. Her face began to harden. "I thought you could read and write and had a job."

"I did have a job, but no more."

"Surely you must have saved some of your wages."

"I sent all my money to help my parents in Japan. They are old and very poor and cursed by bad luck."

"I, too, am old and poor and cursed by bad luck, but I have no children to send me money," Mrs. Liu said. "What do you want from me?"

"A place to sleep for a few days, out of the cold."

"You must have friends."

"I must stay out of sight from the people I know."

"Then there are people looking for you?"

Something sank within Yuki as she saw Mrs. Liu's intentions written so clearly on her face. She had stopped rocking, suddenly anticipating, as a starving animal might when it catches the scent of food on the air and begins to sniff out the direction.

"No, nobody's looking for me."

"You can trust me. I won't turn you in. I've forgotten your name," Mrs. Liu said, a bit too eagerly now.

"It doesn't matter. I'm sorry to have disturbed you." She stood up. "I hope that life becomes better for you."

"Wait," Mrs. Liu said. "You could sleep in the corner of my room. You would be my guest."

The landlords of the tenement charged by the number of occupants in a room, and Mrs. Liu would not have the pittance it would take to pay for Yuki's tenancy. And now Yuki knew that she had to get away very quickly. Mrs. Liu would be at Yuki's landlord's office within ten minutes to get her name and place of employment, and by the end of the day Mrs. Liu would be at the American Consulate, seeing if it was worth anything to them to gain even this small piece of information about a Japanese girl she was convinced was a fugitive.

"I am most thankful for the hot water and your invitation," Yuki said, trying to maintain her composure. "But I will go to friends after all."

She went back down the stairs and into the freezing street, where the sharp wind carried a dusting of snow. And she knew there was only one place left for her to go now, a place she had been avoiding.

She walked to the Japanese Consulate through the narrow side streets, where the force of the wind was broken by the wall of buildings. By midafternoon she stood in the anteroom outside Ito's office, waiting for the orderly to bring him. As she stood there she rehearsed what she would say to him so she would not disgrace herself, and suddenly he was at the door, a look of concern on his face. Her planned words fled instantly, and she was no more than in his office with the door closed than she began to weep as if her heart would break, sitting down in a chair with her face in her hands, apologizing as soon as she could talk. "I'm sorry, my lord. I am foolish. I should not have come here."

He gave her a handkerchief and sat down facing her. His voice was kind. "This is the Japanese Consulate and you are Japanese. Where else would you go except to your countrymen? You came here because you had no place else to go. Is that not true?"

She nodded, wordless.

"Connaught-san called to ask me if I knew where you were," he said.

"I have no desire to cause trouble to anyone, my lord."

"Let us not speak of trouble right now. First, let me help you with your coat." He hung it on a rack. "And you must be hungry."

"I have not thought of food."

He picked up the telephone, told his orderly to bring in tea and sugar cakes, then sat down facing her again. "I ask you to tell me what has gone wrong."

"I cannot trouble you with that, my lord. It would be improper."

"In Tokyo, perhaps it would be," he said. "But not here. I am Cummings-san's friend, and although I do not know you well, I can at least offer you understanding."

The tea and the cakes were brought in and she ate one hungrily, then drank the tea. "I think the problem is apparent, my lord."

"I will tell you what I think it is and you must tell me if I am correct. You are a young Japanese girl who has been exposed to Western ideas of love and you have taken to you a very fine *gaijin* who by chance is unhappily married. Am I right, so far?"

"Hai, so desu."

"And now you carry his child and you know how the diplomatic community will react to your having his baby. Since you know it will damage his career, you have run away from him."

"That's true, my lord. And I plead with you not to let him know I'm here."

"You have my word."

"Arigato, gozaimashita."

"Unfortunately," he said, sadly, "what you think is quite true. In Japan, if he were Japanese, it would not be this way, for a man's wife is not necessarily the woman he loves. But this is Shanghai. So how can I help you, Nakamura-san?"

"I want to go back to Japan."

He shook his head. "Things are worse there than here. And your family would disown you with a half-*gaijin* child, would they not?"

"Yes. But I need someplace to live, and work to do."

He stood up, walked to the window, thinking, hands laced behind him. "We must have an understanding," he said. "I believe Cummings-san is indispensable to peace in Shanghai and I also believe that what you are doing is correct. So I will help you on that basis."

"Wakarimasu," she said. "I understand."

"When is your child due?"

"At the end of May, my lord. But, in my family, the babies always come early."

"I own a house here," he said. "It is quite large, with a staff of Chinese servants who need close attention. I have to travel in my work and I need someone to supervise them. I can pay you a small wage with food and quarters."

"I would be most grateful, my lord."

He picked up the telephone, summoned his car. "We will find you more fitting work to do as time passes. My car will take you to the house. I will call ahead and let them know you are coming."

"Thank you for your kindness," she said as he held her coat for her.

Once she was in his car, the heater purring, it suddenly occurred to her that in the fantasy she had created to spare her family's feelings, her phantom lover exactly matched the kind aristocrat who was now saving not only her life but her baby's life as well.

Within fifteen minutes all thoughts of Yuki faded from Colonel Ito's mind, for he received a summons from Miyamoto, senior general officer at the consulate. The General was in his office, studying a large map of the region mounted on the wall. "The navy is eager to move in and make fools of the army," he said. "Do not try to tell me otherwise, Colonel. Because if we are not careful, they will do it. We need an excuse to call in General Ukeda and the Ninth Division."

"If the General will permit a suggestion . . ." Ito said politely.

"If you have a suggestion, speak it."

"We need to defuse the navy," Ito said. "We need to make it impossible for them to justify moving their marines ashore."

"I had a call from the Admiral. He has definite proof that the Chinese Nineteenth Route Army is on the move."

"What is the nature of that proof, sir? Our radioman cannot raise Nanking. That means that the Admiral cannot either."

"True."

"If the General will permit, I will go to Nanking and find out for myself."

The General looked at him thoughtfully. "You go out into the countryside in your uniform and the Chinese will cut you to pieces."

"They allow merchants on the trains. I have civilian clothes."

"And what about the bandits?"

"I will take care of everything, if the General will permit it."

"The General will permit it," Miyamoto said. "In the meantime I will tell the Admiral to stay where he is until you get back. How long will that be?"

"If things go well, I will be back by tomorrow night." *Or I might not be back at all,* he thought. "Yes, tomorrow night for sure," he said.

It took him less than three hours to prepare for the journey. He sent a lieutenant to his house to pick up the one Western business suit he owned, had the Commercial Section draw up papers for him under the name of "Kono H." and listing his occupation as "salesman for watches." They could use the sample case full of pocket watches that had been left for safekeeping in the Commercial office by a salesman who had never returned.

When he was finally ready to leave he examined himself in the mirror. He found his own image unfamiliar, for he had lost weight since he had bought the suit many years before, and it engulfed him. But it gave him a rather seedy look and lent credence to his identity as one Japanese salesman who had not prospered in China. He had five hundred yen in small bills hidden in various pockets.

Along with the sample case, he carried a bag with a change of underwear, and in the bottom of it, just as a precaution, he tucked in a Type 26 pistol, fully loaded, with a box of extra cartridges.

North Station was a large red brick terminal with a haze of smoke hanging suspended near the arch of the roof over the tracks. He stood in line to buy a second-class ticket and looked at the street peasants, who had moved inside and built small fires on the stone floor to keep from freezing. The long lines were already forming for third-class, peasants and their families carrying large wrapped bundles on their backs, all their earthly possessions. They had come to Shanghai in the hope of finding work and were now moving on, lured by whispered stories of better times in another city.

At the window a clerk peered at him noncommittally when he requested a ticket to Nanking. "I'm required to inform you that the company assumes no responsibility for your safety if you take a train," he said.

"Will there be trouble?" Ito said.

"Most trains are stopped at least once. The intruders are generally bandits who can be bought off for small cash. But often there are soldiers who demand a transportation tax and sometimes there are fatalities."

Ito shoved his money beneath the grill. "I will take the chance."

The clerk gave him a ticket and change and Ito carried his sample case and his bag to the second-class coach, which was already beginning to fill.

As far as he could see, he would be the only Japanese aboard, so he sat down next to a middle-aged Chinese gentleman who was also wearing a Western business suit. There was such a chill in the coach that his breath condensed when he exhaled. He was grateful for the hostess who passed down the aisle and distributed hot tea from a tray.

Soon the train lurched ahead, then stopped and jerked again before the steam engine built sufficient power to pull the coaches out of the station. Ito introduced himself to the Chinese gentleman, whose name was Shen and who turned out to be an auditor for the Shanghai-Nanking Railroad and made frequent trips between the two cities.

"You must be worried about your railroad," Ito said.

"How so?"

"We hear rumors in Shanghai that the Nineteenth Route Army is on the move. It seems to me they will confiscate the railroad to move their supplies."

Shen took a sip of his tea. "It has already been decided," he said. "The Honorable Marshal Chiang Kai-shek wishes to unite all of South China as far as Canton with his new government. So what is the answer? A coalition, of course, with the three warlords who control South China. He will give them posts in his government and he will allow them to bring their own armies north. Shanghai will be given to them, and of course that includes the railroad. Now, as for me, I intend to move south anyway. My son is a doctor in Canton. He has a clinic and plenty of money and he wishes to have his father come join him."

"But what of the Nineteenth Route Army?"

"They have been excluded from use of the railroad," Shen said. "But then they really do not need it. They have marched as far as Soochow, where they are camped. They have their own trucks and transport. I have heard it discussed in Nanking by people who should know. The Nineteenth Route Army will occupy Shanghai until the Honorable Marshal Chiang's coalition has been formed, then they will be withdrawn and the area given to the three warlords."

Close, Ito thought, with an involuntary intake of breath. *Much closer than any of us thought.* "I wonder if it might not be a good place to sell watches," he said aloud, but as if talking to himself.

"The Nineteenth Route Army?" Shen asked.

"Yes."

"They are a coolie army. I doubt that many of them could tell time. Their pay will consist of what they can loot."

"But their officers, surely . . ."

"If you take my advice, you will avoid them like a disease. Go on to Nanking."

"Perhaps you are correct. Have they occupied the city of Soochow?"

"No. The Honorable Marshal would not permit that. They are camped north of the city, I believe, on Tiger Hill. Do you know the place?"

"I am afraid not."

"A most pleasant place in the summer," Shen said, the disapproval forming on his face. "But it is no place for an army to occupy. Too many historical sites, tombs of emperors, ancient halls. No place for thousands of men to be defecating on honored soil. But perhaps if I were a general instead of a railroad auditor, I would see it differently."

Ito offered him a cigarette but Shen declined. He pulled up the collar of his great coat, shifted his body in an attempt to get comfortable on the hard wooden seats. He fell into silence as the train lurched through the night, the glowing cinders sweeping past the frosted windows like fireflies.

Ito sat and smoked, deciding what should be done. He would have to leave the train at Soochow and confirm what Shen had said. He had no reason to doubt him, but many a wrong decision had been made based on rumors. If he found that the Nineteenth Route Army was indeed in Soochow, he would notify General Miyamoto immediately. Possibly there would be time to call in General Ukeda and the Ninth Division before the Chinese arrived in Shanghai. If not, the Admiral could move his marines into the city.

He looked at Shen only to see that he was fast asleep. Ito closed his eyes a moment and came awake with a start as the train jerked and began to stop, all of the coaches lurching and squealing down the tracks. Through the windows Ito saw the lights of a city. Soochow.

Shen moaned. "The soldiers are stopping the train short of the station," Shen said unhappily. "They will collect a transportation tax on all passengers as far as Soochow, and then the train will be stopped again outside of Nanking for another tax."

The train had ground to a halt and Ito saw the movement of soldiers outside. On impulse he moved the bag containing the pistol beneath the seat, where it was concealed. He pulled the case of watches up onto his lap, certain that the soldiers would take them all. And then he would depart the train at Soochow station, send a message back to Shanghai, and arrange to be on the next train himself.

The door to the coach opened and four soldiers came in, led by a large corporal who wore a patched-up field jacket and multiple layers of old shirts and sweaters as well as a regulation winter cap with earflaps. He carried an old rifle, which he pounded on the floor of the car.

"Pay attention," he said in Chinese. "You will have your identification ready. When the soldier states the amount of your tax, you pay it either in money or in goods. Bank notes issued by provisional armies or local provinces will not be accepted."

The soldiers started down the aisle. Ito looked straight ahead, bracing himself so that he would not respond with anger should one of them actually put a hand on him.

Shen fumbled through his pockets, came up with a paper, then mumbled to Ito, "I suggest you have your identification ready," he said. "The soldiers are impatient."

Ito took a leather wallet from his pocket. It contained the false identification and fifty yen. He could hear the soldiers working their way down the aisle and soon he could smell them, a combination of grease and sweat and urine. And now a soldier stood by his seat.

"Japanese," he said with a grunt, looking at Ito. "Give me your papers."

Ito handed them to him. The soldier stripped the money from the wallet, handed it back. "Open the case."

The watches winked like a dozen eyes as the case lid opened. "I will take those," the soldier said.

Ito closed the latches on the case, and the soldier grabbed the handle and lifted it away. He turned to Shen. "Papers."

Shen handed a folded paper to the soldier, who glanced at it but did not notice that it was upside down. "All your money," he barked to Shen, who blinked, surprised.

"The paper explains that I am an official of the railroad," Shen said. "It explains that I am free of all transportation taxes."

"You sit next to a Japanese son of a whore," the soldier said. "All your money."

Shen fumbled through the thick layer of his clothes, fingers searching for his purse. The soldier, irked by his slowness, suddenly reached out and hit him on the side of his face with a fist. The knuckles broke Shen's skin, caused blood to spill on Ito's clothes. And suddenly, reflexively, Ito reached out and, grabbing the soldier's arm, twisted it sharply and threw him off balance. The soldier went crashing into another seat and then fell sprawling to the floor.

All four of the soldiers were on Ito in a second, two of them pinning his arms while the one he had thrown to the floor struck him first in the stomach, the force of the blow partially absorbed by the thickness of Ito's coat, and then in the middle of the face, where there was no protection. His vision blurred. His face blossomed with pain and the blood in his nose made it difficult to breathe.

A corporal peered closely at Ito's face, then picked up the wallet and examined the papers. "Your name," he demanded. When he got no answer he looked to the soldier who had been thrown to the floor. "What is he carrying?"

"Watches."

"He is a Japanese officer. Military," the corporal said. "A brown dwarf son of a whore colonel, right?" No response. He yelled into Ito's face. "Right?" And when there still was no response he hit Ito with full force on the side of his head. Ito went blank.

He came to slowly, head aching, dizzy, stomach hurting, ropes cutting into his hands and ankles. He realized that he had been slung across the back of a pony like a sack of grain. He was in a procession winding its way up a hill, a procession of Chinese soldiers, some on horseback, others on foot carrying torches. Some half a dozen Japanese businessmen were trudging along with their hands tied behind them, occasionally prodded by the Chinese short swords. *First-class,* he thought. *These must be Japanese businessmen who had chosen to ride the first-class coaches.*

They crossed a bridge, the hooves of the horses making a hollow sound on the wooden slats. He smelled the smoke of campfires and above the trees saw a sliver of a crescent moon. They rode up a steep hill, past pavilions shimmering in the moonlight, the campfires of the soldiers glowing in the hollows.

The procession came to a pavilion near a rocky terrace. It was here that the general of the Nineteenth Route Army had established his private camp. Ito was dumped from the horse onto the rocks, where he lay facing the steps of a small teahouse that glowed with lantern light and rang with the sounds of laughter.

Very soon the General himself came out, and even in the dim light of the torches Ito recognized immediately the broad Mongol face, the scars, the uniform, now dirty from too many days in the field without washing. General Wang, the man responsible for the head rolling in the dirt in Shanghai. And now Ito also remembered the corporal who had recognized him on the train, one of Wang's followers at the restaurant in Chapei.

The General reached out the tip of one boot and placed it beneath Ito's chin, raising the face so the light would illuminate the features. Then the General smiled.

"The poor brown dwarfs," he said. "They cannot pay their colonels so they send them out to sell watches. They cannot afford uniforms so they dress them in civilian clothes." He nodded to a lieutenant. "Cut him loose," he said. The short sword blade slashed through the ropes. Ito started to stand up, but a soldier shoved him down to his knees.

General Wang belched. "I showed you my politeness in Shanghai because you were my guest there. But I am on my way back to Shanghai to show you how wrathful I can be to the sons of whores. I see that you have come to spy on me so you can prepare for battle, but you will bring me information instead." He snapped his fingers and a bottle was passed to him. He took a long swig, handed it back. "So you are going to tell me how many troops you have available to fight, whether they be your miserable marines or soldiers. I want to know your aircraft. So we have a lot to talk about, brown dwarf Colonel."

"I am a Japanese officer," Ito said. "I will not talk on my knees."

The General laughed. He whipped open his fly and began to urinate on Ito's head, the yellow stream striking the hair, steaming in the cold night air while Ito gave a sudden roar and tried to lurch forward, only to be pulled back. The General was convulsed with laughter. He closed his fly and had another drink. "This is a very historic rock terrace," he said. "It is called 'Thousand People Rock' because an emperor killed the thousand workman who had constructed his tomb in order to keep it secret. So now it will be called 'Thousand and One.'" He had his soldiers hold Ito steady and then, with his own thick fingers, he reached down and held the collar away from the back of Ito's neck. He pulled his short sword from his belt. "Now, brown dwarf," he said. "Have you anything you wish to say to me?"

Ito turned his head toward the Japanese businessmen. "When it is your turn, know that the Emperor would want you to die bravely," he said.

The General raised the sword, the blade glittering in the firelight. He brought it down with great force, but checked himself at the last possible moment, so that the razor-sharp blade left no more than a slight cut across the nape of Ito's neck. The General roared with laughter once again. Ito held himself perfectly still. His mind was in the warrior's state, in which he had died but was still alive. The blood rushed through his head, but he knew he had not flinched. He had not moved away from the descending blade. He had set an example.

"At least the brown dwarfs have one brave man. You are either too brave or too stupid to be afraid." He went back up the stairs, gesturing to his soldiers to bring Ito along. Ito raised himself to his feet. His legs were weak. He forced them to move, held himself with dignity, ignoring the piss that ran down the side of his head, the ache in his gut, the lightness in his head.

I am a soldier. A soldier lives and dies with dignity.

He climbed the stone stairs. The General had installed a bed in the octagonal room of the pagoda and a brazier in which chips of pine burned and smoked the ancient decorations on the walls. He had brought in a field table with folding legs, half a dozen chairs. "Sit," he said to the Colonel, and then snapped his fingers at an orderly who put a bottle of Chinese whiskey and two glasses on the table.

Ito's vision was not clear. He saw two of everything, but he took great pains to conceal it. He held both arms of the chair before he lowered himself into it, and then he bolted down his whiskey, strong, raw.

General Wang sat down across the table from him, leaned forward, his massive face resting on large spatulate hands. "I am going to take Shanghai," he said, his breath foul. "I am going to claim the rights of undisputed warlord and two million dollars a month. And then I will equip my men with the finest weapons in the world, the greatest fighting force China has ever seen."

"You won't succeed," Ito said coolly. "Not unless you have more than ten thousand men."

"You have nothing to stop me."

"There is a Japanese fleet in the Whangpoo and an admiral anxious for battle. He has marines by the thousands."

"You exaggerate."

"And there are two army divisions ready to sail from Japan. They will throw everything against you to stop you."

"My men cannot be defeated."

"It will take too long to get Marshal Chiang's new armies up from the south."

"I do not need any armies from the south. We are enough."

Ito looked at the General's orderly and pushed the glass in his direction, aware that the orderly's eyes immediately flashed to the General's face for approval. It was given with an almost imperceptible nod. His glass was filled with whiskey.

"I have not changed my position," Ito said. "If you attack Shanghai, there will be a battle and the slaughter will be horrendous. Your troops will bleed like any other men."

"You will take a message back to your admiral for me. I have the royal blood of the Mongols in my veins and my astrologer tells me that the heavens have proclaimed my victories. I cannot be stopped. It is my pleasure to spill the blood of my enemies."

He stood up and casually ordered that Ito's hands be bound behind him. Then he ordered a truck and a driver and led Ito outside, gesturing to the troops guarding the Japanese businessmen to lead them forward. He demanded a piece of wire from one soldier and ordered another to bring the shit buckets around from the nearest encampment. Ito maintained an impassive expression. "I must warn you, General Wang. Whatever you do now, you will pay fivefold for later."

"I will give your countrymen a chance to demonstrate bravery," the General said mockingly. He was given the stiff wire, which he formed into an open loop. He approached the first Japanese businessman and, taking the sword from his belt, sliced off the man's ear, shearing it from the head with a single sweep of the sword. The blood leapt out, ran down the side of the man's head, but the man did not show his pain.

Stand fast. Do not give the bastard any satisfaction.

The General strolled down the line, cutting an ear from each, stringing it on the wire thrust through the cartilage. The blood ran down his sword blade, covered his hand. The last of the businessmen was middle-aged, and when his ear was cut off something gave away within him and he dropped without a sound. The General added his ear to the wire loop, then twisted it closed and hung the grisly necklace around Ito's neck. "You may take these to your admiral," he said.

"You had better kill me now," Ito said. "If I ever see you again, I will cut your head from your body, not just your ears."

The shit buckets were brought up, six of them. General Wang stood clear and the soldiers doused Ito with them until he was covered from head to foot, the odor overpowering. The General ordered Ito placed in the back of the truck with a guard. "Now, take this stinking brown dwarf away from here before he makes me sick to my stomach."

Ito watched in horror as Wang beheaded a Japanese businessman, the head bouncing on the rocks like a melon cut from a vine.

Ito used the skills he had learned in his Bushido training to withdraw into himself. He blotted out all feeling until he was no longer aware of the truck hurtling down the rutted road on the way to Shanghai. He dozed, came to with a start to realize that they were within the city itself, just before dawn, the streets already congested with traffic, the ricksha pullers out in full force, crying for customers.

When the truck reached the docks near the berth where the Japanese flagship was moored, the Chinese soldiers rolled Colonel Ito from the truck bed. His hands were still tied so he could not protect himself from the impact against the stones. He hit with a thump that dizzied him, and he lay there as trucks and carts moved around him, one ricksha puller calling him "a lump of shit."

He struggled into a sitting position, attempted to stand, finally made it to his feet. His head was spinning. Excrement caked his hair and his clothing, the wire necklace of ears had begun to stink. The traffic gave him a wide berth.

As the sun broke the horizon to the east, he finally saw Japanese military policemen and he yelled at them, his voice little more than a croak. The pair of military policemen approached him warily, clubs at the ready.

"*Baka,*" Ito said. "I am a colonel in the Japanese Army. So cut these ropes off my hands and get me to the Japanese Consulate."

The military policemen stared at him. "If you are a colonel, you will have papers," the corporal said dubiously.

Ito stood at his full height, livid with anger, his eyes imperious as he looked directly into the corporal's face. "If you do not cut me free this instant, I will have your head by sundown."

The corporal cut the rope that bound Ito's hands.

At the consulate Ito commandeered a bathroom and cleaned himself carefully, soaping and brushing the stink out of his hair, his ears. He piled the clothes to be burned, carefully removed the caked blood from his face, examined the bullet wound in his thigh.

Once he was purified, he lowered himself into the massive bath, the water so hot it burned away all feeling and left him floating free of his multiple pains. He dozed again, to be awakened by an aide who came to tell him that the Senior General had just arrived at the consulate. A kimono had been laid out for Ito. He climbed from the bath, dried himself, put on the kimono and slippers, then took the elevator to the Senior General's office, where the old man was supervising the setting out of tea, a fish soup, and rice.

"This is your breakfast, Colonel. We can talk while you eat."

"Thank you, Esteemed Senior General." Ito downed the food, despite the odor of offal still persisting in his nostrils.

"I think you should know that the Nineteenth Route Army is currently moving into Chapei," the Senior General said.

"*So desuka?*" Ito said, startled. "The son of a whore did not waste any time. I suggest that Admiral Shiosawa be alerted immediately. The marines have to be moved ashore today."

"We are under constraints," the Senior General said. "We have orders to search for peaceful solutions."

Ito sipped his tea. "Until yesterday that was my position. But no more. There are no peaceful solutions now. General Wang killed half a dozen Japanese citizens last night. Those were the ears I carried on me. He has declared his intentions. If we move now, quickly, we can stop him."

"The Chinese are hailing him as savior of the city. They look on him as the man who will throw out the foreign devils. What makes you think we can defeat him?"

"Because he does not have any backup forces," Ito said. "No reserves. Chiang Kai-shek has made a pact with three southern warlords. He has promised them Shanghai as a part of the alliance. So General Wang will not be reinforced. If our army does not move, then our navy will. Admiral Shiosawa wants nothing more than to test his marines."

"He has been replaced," the Senior General said. "In order not to lose face, he retains command of the First Fleet but Vice Admiral Nomura has been sent from Sasebo Naval Base to oversee operations here. He is very popular with the Western military."

"Then we give Chapei away," Ito said bitterly.

"It is not up to you to question the wisdom of orders," the Senior General said. He looked out the window. "Do you have the names of the Japanese businessmen killed at Soochow?"

"No, sir."

"We will send the ears back to Japan pending identification so there can be a memorial service. I want you to write a full report, everything that you heard, observed. Then later, perhaps tomorrow, we will have an official delegation visit the Chinese mayor and request that he ask the Nineteenth Route Army to withdraw."

"Yes, sir," Colonel Ito said. He wondered how he would describe the beheaded man, the expression on that face, as if the eyes still held some terrible comprehension of what was happening, the mouth gaping open in a silent scream.

When Ito's orderly called her in the early evening, Yuki swept through the house to make certain everything was in readiness for the Colonel's homecoming, the water in the bath steaming hot, the kitchen prepared to serve his dinner. When she heard his car she greeted him at the door, surprised to see him in a formal kimono.

"*Konnichiwa, O-Ito-sama,*" she said with a bow. "The house is ready for you. And dinner can be served at any time."

"I will not have time for dinner," he said, preoccupied. "Have my man servant lay out a fresh uniform for me." He retreated to his study, where he rolled his brush in a wet ink block and proceeded to write for an hour before he went upstairs and changed into his uniform.

When she saw him again he had packed a bag and directed a servant to take it to his car. "I may not be home for a month or two, Nakamura-san. I have arranged work for you at the consulate."

"Thank you, my lord," she said. "Your house will be ready when you return."

The house took little of her time and left her free for the job assigned to her by the Japanese Consulate toward the end of January. She was in a house listening post, a rabbit warren of booths with earphones and wires that tapped into the central telephone trunk lines of Shanghai. Her assignment was to listen to calls in and out of one section of the British Consulate, and to write down anything concerning the British intentions toward the Chinese Army, which had firmly entrenched itself in Chapei and at the port city of Woosung, which was fortified with heavy artillery to give the Chinese control of any ships entering or leaving Shanghai.

For the most part, the calls were primarily social, long discussions of what the fighting might do to the racing season, and so she was left with time to grieve for Sam. In one of those calls she found herself forced to listen to two British officials talking about Sam and her.

"Damned foolishness, when you think about it," came one male voice.

"He's too bloody romantic, wouldn't you say? Sending out people to find her when he should be paying attention to this dreadful ruckus. After all, she was just a Nip whore who contrived to get herself preggers."

Her heart ached with longing for Sam, and at times she was tempted to revoke what she had done and go back to him. Perhaps the two of them could migrate to Hong Kong, where the differences between them would not be enough to impede his career and where their child would have a chance.

But she knew she was rationalizing. To go back to him would bring ruin upon him, and she loved him far too much for that.

She was in the common room having tea and trading information with the other telephone women when she was first approached by Ryoko, who was married to an official at the consulate. It was her job to listen to calls to the American Consulate and so she managed to pass on information about Sam without ever implying that she knew of his connection with Yuki.

"Vice-Consul Cummings went with a delegation to the Chinese mayor to ask for withdrawal of the Chinese Army," Ryoko said, sipping her tea. "The mayor apologized, said he could do nothing."

And on another occasion: "Vice-Consul Cummings is still looking for his lover. That's very romantic, *ne?*"

"Hai," Yuki said. "Does he think he will find her?"

"He has a man spending all his time searching. The man hangs around the Japanese Consulate."

"Did he mention the man's name?"

"I forget it," Ryoko said. "But it's the same as a street in Shanghai."

"Connaught," Yuki said before she could stop herself.

"Yes. How did you know?"

"You are very kind to pretend that you don't know," Yuki said.

"I wish to be your friend," Ryoko said. "When is the baby due?"

"Not for a while."

"Have you seen a doctor yet?"

"No."

"You're entitled to go to the Japanese hospital. Since you work here, you're a government employee."

"I don't want to take the time of a doctor who might be treating our wounded."

"There is no shortage of doctors."

But Yuki did not want to go to a hospital where a doctor would ask the name of the father of the child. She put in her hours at the listening post, then went back to the Colonel's house, aware of the sounds of distant fighting, the Japanese bombers overhead, the greater number of ambulances in the street. She thought about the future and became increasingly frightened about how she was going to take care of the child.

Sam had a nightmare one morning before dawn. Yuki was on the far side of the Chinese Settlement, in a house with a garden full of blooming flowers, and suddenly there was a shell in the sky, fired by one of the warships on the Whangpoo, and it floated through the air with such a slow trajectory that he could see the markings on the shell casing. And he knew it was destined for the very place where she sat in the warm sunlight, for he watched it make an arcing descent toward her. He opened his mouth to yell a warning but there was no sound. He found himself sitting upright in bed, gasping for breath. Further sleep was impossible. He took a shower, and had just put on his dressing gown when there came a light tapping on the door and Majordomo entered, bearing a wicker breakfast tray and an expression on his face which implied that he also brought information, should his employer care to ask for it. "All right," Sam said, picking up the coffee cup and ignoring the runny eye of the egg that stared up at him from the plate. "What's going on? Do you have news about Nakamura-san?"

"Much sorry," Majordomo said. "But big top fellow lookee for number one girl belong one time father business, this boy been told."

"Speak to me in Chinese," Sam said, drinking the coffee. "I don't like pidgin."

And while Sam dressed Majordomo told him what he knew, speaking in a flawless Mandarin. It seemed that Majordomo was related to a man named Li, who had heard that Sam was looking for Bright Moon. Li owned some tenement houses on Kiangwan Road, up near the Commercial Press Building, and he knew where Bright Moon lived.

"She wishes to see you," Majordomo said.

"Then why doesn't she come here?"

"I don't have that information. But I have prepared a letter of introduction to my relative. This should get you through any difficulties in the Chinese sections."

"You're very thoughtful," Sam said. "I appreciate what you've done."

"It is my honor to serve you," Majordomo said.

A staff meeting called by Alcott late that afternoon convinced Sam he had to meet with Bright Moon soon.

Alcott stood in front of a wall map of Shanghai. "The latest demand from the Japanese admiral whose flagship is here"—the tip of the pointer touched the bend of the Whangpoo just east of the mouth of Soochow Creek—"is that all Chinese forces must be removed from Chapei by early this evening. Now, since we are well aware that the Chinese could not remove an army the size of the Nineteenth in such a short period of time, even if they wanted to, we can assume that hostilities will commence tonight.

"I have compiled a list of American business leaders in the community and assigned a fair share of the list to each of you. I have mimeographed a message for distribution. In effect, it will say that we have issued a warning to both sides that any random harm that might occur to American property will result in grave consequences. However, we do not believe the hostilities will spill over into the International Settlement."

Alcott paused. "I'm aware that various newshawks have invited all legation personnel to a party at the Cathay Hotel roof garden, from which the battle will be observed. Some of you will be asked for statements. That statement will be that we are neutral. We will remain neutral. We will not give the slightest hint of non-neutrality. And now Mr. Boren will pass out the assignment sheets and the mimeographed texts."

A pudgy little man who sat at the table called out names from a list, handing out papers as the persons came forward.

"Mr. Cummings," he said, and when there was no reply, peered around the room over the top of his half-moon glasses. "Where is Mr. Cummings? I saw him here earlier."

"He had to leave," Connaught said. "But I shall be happy to cover his list as well as my own."

"All right, then," Boren said.

"Remember, gentlemen," Alcott said. "We are neutral."

Sam was tempted to use his official car to go up into the Chapei Settlement, but he knew it was impractical. Chapei was composed of small lanes and alleys, many of them far too small to accommodate an automobile. So he picked a ricksha from the line of pullers wait-ing outside the American Consulate, an old man stringy as whip-cord, toothless, barefooted despite the chill.

"North Paoning Road."

The old man shook his head vigorously in protest. "Get somebody else, sir. The place is full of Chinese soldiers who might cut off this ancient and unworthy head of mine."

"I want you for the rest of the afternoon and into the night," Sam said. "I will pay you ten dollars American."

The puller stopped short, balancing the fortune of this demented man against the possibility that neither of them would return alive. "Twenty dollars," he said.

"It is agreed," Sam said, looking him squarely in the eyes. "I will give you five dollars now. When you bring me back to the Interna-tional Settlement, I will give you fifteen dollars. But should you desert me before the business is finished, your head will be cut off and your limbs from your body, and all scattered so that you will be buried in many places and lose your chance for the hereafter. Do you believe me?"

It was obvious from the mixture of fear and greed in the puller's eyes that he did believe. The old man began to trot and neared the invisible boundary line of the International Settlement. He was go-ing against the tide, for already thousands of Chinese were flooding past the temporary barriers the United States Marines had placed in staggered positions on both sides of the street. It was as if all the old women and men in Chapei had gathered their worldly goods into immense backpacks to get away from the certain destruction that was coming—hoping that when the battle was over they could move like snails in the opposite direction.

Sam's puller was waved to a stop by a marine sergeant in a steel helmet.

"I'm sorry, sir," the sergeant said. "But I've been advised to keep all Western businessmen from entering the Chinese city."

Sam handed him his identification. "This is official business, Ser-geant."

"Yes, sir." The sergeant handed the papers back. "But I'd suggest that you plan to get back across the line before dark. We hear stories that the Chinese soldiers are pretty goddamned edgy. And tonight all hell is going to break loose."

"Thank you, Sergeant," Sam said. "Which troops are covering which sectors?"

"We have the center. The Japs are on the east all the way to the Whangpoo. The British and French are covering the west, with a few Italian bluejackets thrown in for good measure."

Sam nodded and then spoke to his puller in Chinese: "Move on."

As the old man padded off the main street, Sam found himself being stared at by apathetic children with swollen bellies. At Heng Tong Road he began to see the outposts of the Nineteenth Route Army: men in rags, soldiers who had occupied buildings and thrown the people out and now had kindled cookfires with pots suspended from sticks over the flames. They eyed him with curiosity, and he was aware that it would take very little to precipitate trouble. As a foreign devil he was allowed to pass only because it did not occur to any of the soldiers to stop him. Chinese soldiers were everywhere, thousands of them, well armed with rifles and machine guns. *The Japanese will have no easy time of it in this hornet's nest.*

It was early evening before the ricksha puller reached the tenement building north of the Commercial Press Building. The lower floors of the tenement had been commandeered by the army, and in front of the building stood a lieutenant in a makeshift uniform.

"You can stop here," Sam said to the puller, but the puller only slowed.

"If they search you and take your money, then where does that leave me?" the old man said.

"Your money is safe," Sam said. "But if you don't follow my instructions, you won't be. Now, stop in front of the building."

The old man obeyed and squatted between the shafts.

Sam walked past the Chinese lieutenant and through the moon door into a courtyard, then knocked at a door, as Majordomo had instructed.

The door was answered by a young man dressed in baggy Chinese trousers with a Chinese gown hanging to his knees. A Chinese captain stood in the middle of the main room, hands folded behind his back, a scowl on his face.

"I am Vice-Consul Cummings," Sam said in Chinese. "I'm looking for the Honorable Li."

Li bowed to him with great respect. "I am Li, sir, and I welcome you," he said in English. "I knew your father well. He was one of the few decent capitalists I have ever known." He looked toward the captain with contempt. "I apologize for the presence of a fascist soldier who refuses to recognize the rights of a Chinese citizen."

Li led the way through a room stacked with piles of leaflets and painted banners on the floor, the calligraphy calling for the establishment of a Communist government. The Chinese captain who stood in the midst of the seditious literature fixed Sam with steely eyes, but there was a querulous expression on his face, and suddenly Sam knew what was troubling him. "He can't read," he said to Li in English.

"If he could, my head would be on a pike," Li said. "The ignorant son of a bitch doesn't even know how much better off he could be if he freed himself from his oppressors. He has a mouth full of rotten teeth and a foul breath as well as a lung wheeze, which probably means tuberculosis and an early death. Under a people's government he would be taken care of." He flicked his cigarette ashes on the floor.

The captain wheezed, coughed, then demanded to see Sam's papers. Sam unfolded the letter from Majordomo to his nephew Li, then handed it to the man, who examined it upside down. "My name is Cummings," Sam said in Shanghainese. "I am a representative of the American government, a vice-consul. That paper has been signed by your generals and it gives me safe passage, as you can plainly see. It is your obligation to provide me protection."

The captain thrust the paper back at him, then turned back to Li and began to berate him in Shanghainese. He wanted all the people thrown out of the tenements immediately, or he would kill Li on the spot.

Li lit another cigarette. "I'll tell you what I'll do, fellow," he said calmly to the officer. "I have a vacant building, one which I am renovating because of the rats that have taken it over. If you move your men into that building and leave my people alone, then I will arrange to provide rice and fish enough to feed one hundred men."

The officer wheezed again. "You'll give the rice and fish directly to me," he said.

"You can have it straight up your esteemed bung hole, if that's the way you want it," Li said with no great malice. "I don't give a damn."

"Where is the building?"

"The second one down from here."

"And the rice and fish?"

"I'll deliver them to you tonight."

"How can I trust you?"

"Do I look like I'm going to run away?" Li asked harshly. "Kill me now. Make me a martyr and go hungry on your way to hell. Or come back at sundown and the food will be here."

"It had better be," the officer said without much conviction, edging a pile of leaflets with the side of his worn boot. They fell over as he left the room.

Li went to a cupboard, took out an unlabeled green bottle and a couple of glasses, poured drinks, handed one to Sam. "To your father and the revolution," Li said, raising his glass.

"What revolution?"

"The one that will eventually reclaim China," Li said. "And may you prove to be as good a man as your father was."

Sam drank. The liquor was strong and raw. "I came to see Bright Moon."

"Yes, of course," Li said, with some reluctance in his voice. "But first you must know it is a dangerous undertaking."

"Dangerous?"

"She lives in a highly protected compound."

"I don't understand."

"You will, if you choose to go, realizing the danger."

"Of course I'll go."

"Then follow me. And make no sound, none at all. We will not speak again until we are there."

Sam followed Li through a maze of alleys growing ever more narrow. The smell of death was overpowering, for lining the alleys were the corpses of those who had starved to death. Li settled into a jogging gait over the wet stones and Sam tried to keep up with him, aware of the darkening sky and the imminence of the Japanese siege. Li reached a corner, signaled for Sam to stop, then looked around the edge of a building toward a high parapet.

Sam saw a guard, a black figure silhouetted against the leaden sky, a machine gun in his hands, staring down the alleys. As soon as the guard turned his back Li was off again, not even looking to see if Sam was still with him. Sam could see nothing now, could hear nothing except the distant droning of an airplane.

Li struck a match, held it in front of him a moment, shielded the flame with his hand, then let it shine out again.

Momentarily there was an answering flare of flame from somewhere ahead and Li moved forward once more, carefully now, staying close to the wall until he reached an immense moon gate with bars of steel gridding the opening. But a walkway entrance had been left ajar and Li passed through it and signaled for Sam. The two men went around a short blocking wall—erected to prevent evil spirits from following a straight line through the moon gate—and into a compound.

Sam stared in astonishment. In the center of this cruel city where people lay dead on the street was a rich pavilion in the traditional Chinese style, with houses resembling small palaces in all four corners of a separate walled city. Connecting the houses were covered porticoes, gardens in their center, the grass now browned with winter, the trailing branches of the willows bare of leaves, the water running down a fountain toward a pool where golden carp swam.

Li waited in the shadows of the wall until a light flashed again, this time from the door of the nearest house. Then he led the way down one of the covered porticoes. A large carved door swung open soundlessly and a man servant appeared, bowing low as he admitted them to a tiled hallway.

"You will speak with her alone," he said to Sam in a low voice. "I will wait here to take you back."

Sam followed the servant down a hallway to a huge carved door, and then found himself in a room lit by candles and lanterns.

The floor was white marble, the walls covered with tapestries and figures made of precious stones, and at the far end of the room, on a dais flanked by drapes of green silk, sat a woman in a massive gilded teak chair topped by an intricately carved dragon. She sat beneath the dragon, her jet-black hair all but hidden by a headdress of golden brocade.

She beckoned to him and then rested her hand against the lap of the brocaded robe, which flowed to the floor around her.

"Please come closer," she said in a soft voice and perfect English. He approached hesitantly. "Closer still, so that I can see you." He reached the chair at the foot of the dais. "Please sit down," she said, and then leaned forward and studied him intently. "You resemble him when he was younger." She clapped her hands and a maid appeared. "Bring the plum wine," she said in Mandarin, and the maid disappeared without a sound.

"You are Bright Moon," Sam said at last.

"Yes. And you are Samuel, his son."

She leaned back in her chair, caught up in her own thoughts, and when she spoke it was as if she was thinking aloud. "He was a good man," she said softly.

He heard the great sadness in her voice. "And were you part of the reason he didn't come home to stay?"

"I cannot answer that. I loved him and I never questioned what he did."

"I want to know what happened to him."

"His death, then."

"Yes."

"You can change nothing."

"I have a right to know. I'm his only son."

The wine was served in golden goblets, and Bright Moon did not speak again until the maid was gone. "The truth can cause you much despair."

"I'm willing to take that risk," he said. "And you wouldn't have allowed me to come here unless you intended to tell me what I want to know."

"Ah," she said with a prolonged sigh, "you see, I am a prisoner here and I wanted nothing more than to see Arnold's son. You are all that is left of him in this world." She sipped her wine. "So I decided to see you, knowing that it is selfish of me, for answering your questions will only cause you further pain."

"I want to know."

"Your father was an honorable man."

Tell that to my mother, he thought. *Explain to her that she did not lose her husband to China but to another woman, and then let her judge how honorable my father was.*

He said nothing. Momentarily, Bright Moon began to speak again. "Your father believed that China's only hope lay in freedom from warlords and exploiters like Chiang Kai-shek who bled the country dry. I met your father because he was supporting Comrade Li and the idea of revolution. I fell in love with your father because he had a compassionate heart and gave away almost as much money as he earned to those who needed it."

"Why didn't I know about you when I was here when I was seventeen?"

"He had no desire to hurt either you or your mother. Then, too, it had to be a secret because my father was a leader of the Green Gang. I know them all, Big Eared Tu and Pockmarked Huang, and they have always hated the Western businessmen and demanded money from them for permission to do business in China through Shanghai. I knew they would kill Arnold if they found out about our relationship. Arnold even kept a pistol on the wall shelf near his desk. He told me he was not afraid but that a wise man is always prepared to protect himself."

She paused, remembering. "But then, one night," she said, "our luck ran out. A man from the Green Gang came to the apartment while I was there."

Sam felt a tightness in his head. "And what happened?"

Her voice grew very soft, remote, as if she wanted to drain all emotion from the memory. "A coolie gangster broke into the apartment while your father was sitting reading a newspaper. The pistol lay on the shelf, and before your father could reach it, the intruder had grabbed me and put a short sword to my throat. Your father remained perfectly still, knowing that the slightest move would cause my death. Without a word the man took the pistol from the shelf, placed the muzzle against the side of Arnold's head, and pulled the trigger. He murdered so quickly it did not seem possible that Arnold was dead. Then he placed the pistol in your father's hand. Within a day's time all of your father's holdings were taken over and all of his assets disappeared."

"Why did you let everybody believe it was suicide?"

"I could not tell the truth," she said evenly, the pitch of her voice never changing.

"Why?"

"I could not."

"I want the name of the man who killed my father."

"It will do you no good. He is very powerful now."

"I want his name."

"General Wang," she said simply.

Christ. The execution in the courtyard, the string of human ears on a wire. The monster who now occupied all of Chapei. He let his breath out slowly. "I'll find a way to get him. I swear to God I will."

"You asked me why I did not tell the truth about your father's death. I will show you." She reached down and slowly began to lift her skirts. "You see, my father decided my punishment would be that no man find me desirable again." And now he could see her legs. They were encased in bandages to hide the jagged stumps left by the sharp sword that had cut off both her feet. As he looked at her pain he knew there was nothing he could say to this woman who had lost the rest of her life.

Christ, he thought, back in the ricksha again, moving through the darkened streets dotted by military cookfires. *I should never have come to this goddamned country.*

To the south he saw the fires springing up in the Hongkew District and heard the faint bleat of bugles. Occasionally a lone signal rocket would streak through the night sky and blossom into a hanging flare. He directed the ricksha down an alley to avoid the files of Japanese marines marching down the streets, their white leggings gleaming in the streetlights, colors flying. They streamed through the Japanese Sector and across the line into the southernmost part of Chapei, picking up mobs of Japanese that followed along. He saw a group of civilians looting Chinese shops and then setting fire to them. He heard occasional rifle fire from the Chinese snipers at their forward posts.

When the ricksha puller came to the blockade at Range Road, he did not even look at the Japanese sentries who stood guard but ran past them, and continued to run until he reached the Bund and then the Cathay Hotel. Sam paid him and then took the elevator to the roof garden, which was crowded with slightly drunk correspondents gathered at the ramparts with binoculars and telescopes as if they were watching a sporting event, sending up a cheer when the Chinese troops ambushed the marching Japanese troops near North Station in a hail of machine-gun fire.

Connaught looked up as Sam approached. "Enter the wrath of God," he said. "You look as if you could use a drink, Sam, my boy."

Connaught handed him a bottle and he took a long pull before he told Connaught about his meeting with Bright Moon, the involvement of General Wang.

"I see," Connaught said, considerably subdued, pouring himself another drink. "So now you are steaming to see justice done, the wrongs set right, the bloody barbarian properly punished."

"There must be a way."

Connaught waved vaguely toward the rockets bursting in the sky over North Station. "The Japanese are trying to do that at this very moment, without much success, I'm afraid. Would it surprise you if I told you that there were strong rumors in the Settlement to the effect that your father was indeed murdered?"

"It would," Sam said, startled. "Why would the police rule as they did?"

"Because it was politic to do so," Connaught said, pausing to drink. "The relationship between the internationals and the Chinese is a delicate one at the very best. It's embarrassing to the Western powers to have someone messing around in Chinese politics. It is not the done thing. And your father was aiding and abetting the Communists, not a popular place to be in with either the Chinese or the internationals. When your father was killed at least a dozen wayward sheep repented and moved their business interests back inside the Settlement and to the safety of what we all like to regard as civilized behavior."

Of course. I know the way things work, Sam thought. *But General Wang won't go free. I swear that to you, Papa.*

He stayed on the roof all night, until the battle was over. He saw the unarmed teams of Japanese marines under the protection of white flags coming to reclaim their dead. They wore gauze face masks, as if to avoid breathing the air of death. He stood up, his legs stiff. The Japanese squads were piling their dead in stacks, dousing bodies with gasoline, backing away as a lighted stick was thrown into the stack and the pile burst into an intense flame.

He took a ricksha and went home at dawn.

That same afternoon Sam met with Alcott in his ice box of an office. The old man was bundled up in an alpaca sweater and a scarf while Chinese workmen were putting a round flue in one wall of his office to vent a coal-burning stove, which would finally provide warmth to this miserable section of the building.

"I have an eyewitness," Sam said. "She was there. She saw it all."

"Perhaps," Alcott said, pausing to catch a sneeze in his handkerchief, glowering once more at the dawdling workmen. "But you have to realize that even if this bloody coolie general did indeed kill him and mutilate his lover, the Chinese courts will refuse to hear the case since the Settlement police declared your father's death a suicide. And the Settlement police, having ruled, will not reopen the case. Sam, China is indeed a cruel climate."

"But they didn't even have the facts straight. Bright Moon was not his secretary."

"What would you have her called?" Alcott asked gently. "There is a gentleman's code here that works to spare the sensibilities of families left behind. So officially she is listed on the police reports as a secretary and nobody is damaged by that euphemism."

"Still, I want a hearing in the courts."

"That will never happen, my young friend. No Settlement court will touch the case because your father operated outside Settlement jurisdiction. And even if the American court could be persuaded to hear the case, the Chinese woman's testimony would not be taken seriously. Because she *is* a woman, and Chinese at that, and was your father's mistress, her credibility would be destroyed."

"Then you're telling me there's nothing I can do," Sam said bitterly.

"I've become very fond of you, Sam," Alcott said, "but it seems that I'm always having to tell you there's nothing you can do about one terribly important situation after another. Sometimes, my boy, you are a pain in the ass. Perhaps that's because I am so ancient and you are so terribly young."

"I don't feel young," Sam said. "Sometimes I think I was forced to leap from childhood to manhood, missing everything in between."

"That's really quite too bad," Alcott said. "I remember most clearly the halcyon days of my youth." He sneezed again. "But to business of a different sort. I understand you are working with Mr. Li."

"Yes."

"A Chinese Bolshevik."

"A Marxist," Sam corrected. "He's helping coordinate relief supplies to the refugees." He interrupted himself. "What's that?" He stood at the window, staring off toward the battered Chapei Settlement, where there had been a lull in the fighting the past couple of hours. Something was glinting in the hazy sunshine of late winter, a very large metallic box that seemed to be drifting through the rail yards. He picked up the binoculars that Alcott kept handy at the window and brought the metal box into focus to discover an armored box car, beveled at the edges, with a round observation bubble protruding from the top. The front of the car was constructed of hinged partitions to accommodate the lateral movement of a cannon barrel. The car was being propelled by gangs of coolies, pushing from behind, pulling ropes from the front, their breath steaming in the chill air. "Have a look at this, Mr. Alcott."

Alcott squinted through the binoculars. "What the hell is it?" he said.

"The Chinese answer to the firepower of the Japanese ships on the river," Sam said.

"A most resourceful people, the Chinese," Alcott said.

One day in late spring when she was near her term, Yuki was sent from the listening house to the consulate to deliver a binder full of the day's reports, and no sooner had she left the papers and come out of the building than her heart sank. For standing immediately in front of her was Connaught. The expression on his face lacked either malice or judgment. She bowed to him politely and he returned her greeting calmly, but all she could think of was that he was bound to have been with Sam, talked with him, and she wanted nothing more than to ask the questions that crowded into her mind.

"I think it's about time for tea, wouldn't you say, Nakamura-san?" he said. "I know a very nice place near here where the service is excellent and the privacy is guaranteed."

"I heard you were looking for me." *How is he? Is he well? Does he look healthy?*

He led her down the street to one of the smaller hotels, which catered to business people. The dining room was light and airy, with lace curtains and spotless tablecloths. Connaught ordered from a Chinese waitress who spoke with an English accent, then poured the tea himself when it arrived. "You must forgive me for playing host," he said with a smile. "But I enjoy the feel of crockery now and again, and I enjoy doing instead of being done for, if you know what I mean. How have you been?"

"Well, thank you," she said. *Does he ever talk about me? Tell me his words, all that you can remember, and how he said them.*

She accepted the tea, and allowed herself only the simplest of questions. "How is Cummings-san?" *Does he ever talk of his child to be and wonder what the baby will look like?*

"He is grieving, but that's normal. I'd say he's doing as well as can be expected. The times demand it and he's not one to shirk his duty over private pain." He buttered a hot muffin. "You must try one of these. They're . . ."

He was talking but she was not listening, the ache was so great within her. *I hope his pain is not as sharp as mine, and please ask him to forgive me but I had no other choice. Can you get me a picture of him for my wall shrine, because I have nothing of him except for the child within me and I want to see his face, smiling, if possible.*

She listened again. He was offering her a muffin. "Would you care for one?"

"No, thank you." Her breath was sticking in her throat. *I want you to tell him where I am so he will come and force me to go with him and I will not be the one who has to make this terrible choice.* "You won't tell him where I am, will you?" she said.

"Good heavens, no," he said, putting jam on his muffin. "I respect what you're trying to do. After all, I'm a living example of one who broke all the rules and put myself above community mores a long time ago. Not that my life has been all that bad, because it hasn't. I've been able to do what I wanted because I had no family standards to uphold or escutcheons I could possibly blot. But Sam's different. You know it and I know it."

"He is very special." *I don't want to be here any longer. It makes the pain worse. Convince me that I was right.* "Can you help him?"

"Time will take care of that. I've never known a man to die of a broken heart."

Or a woman. It just feels that way. "I want you to promise that you won't tell him you saw me."

"I'll probably tell him you went back to Japan."

"Will he believe you?"

"Yes," he said, picking up her sadness. "There are things in life that one wants desperately, even though they are ruinous. He's doing the done thing, as are you, as terribly painful as that may be, because neither of you can do otherwise."

He finished the muffin, wiped his fingers on a napkin, drank his tea. "Now, I don't want to insult you," he said, "but I want to give you money for the welfare of the baby."

"I am touched by your thoughtfulness, Connaught-san. But I manage the house of Colonel Ito and I have a job with the Japanese Consulate."

"Well, then," he said, "I'm pleased that you're not in need. Tell me, is Colonel Ito kind to you?"

"Yes, he is."

"Then I'll tell you something I've overheard, but I have to ask that you keep the source secret. It's not that anybody at the consulate wishes the Colonel harm, it's just this damned fence-straddling which we call neutrality." He lit a cigarette. "General Wang has decided it was a distinct mistake to let the Colonel go, and so he's ordered a special cadre of soldiers to bring him the Colonel's head on a pike if ever they catch the good Colonel outside the International Settlement. Wang won't dare move against the Settlement."

"I truly thank you," she said. "I will warn him."

"One other thing. Should you accidentally be discovered by Sam, would you please neglect to mention that this conversation between us ever took place?"

"Certainly," she said. *Take care of him if you can, Connaught-san, and tell him I will never forget him as long as I live.* "I am grateful to you on many counts."

Connaught stood up. "You are a gracious lady, Nakamura-san, and that's the highest accolade I ever give a woman. Farewell."

"Sayonara, O-Connaught-sama," she said.

Late that afternoon Sam had a drink with Connaught. Connaught told him he had heard a rumor to the effect that Yuki had gone back to Japan.

"Shall I keep looking?" Connaught said.

Sam thought a long moment before he shook his head. "No," he said at last. "She's made her choice. And as much as I don't like it, I'll respect it."

"Very wise," Connaught said. "Very wise indeed."

At the Japanese Consulate, Yuki bowed to the male receptionist and asked to see the Esteemed Colonel.

"Chotto matte, kudasai," the young man said. "A moment, please." He rang one of the offices upstairs, grunted into the telephone a few times, and then put it back on its cradle. "The Esteemed Colonel is someplace between here and Woosung," he said.

"Could you tell me precisely where?" she said. "I'll send a houseboy with the message."

"The houseboy would become a casualty," the clerk said. "There's heavy fighting at Woosung. The Esteemed Colonel is on a motorcycle trying to find new bypass routes for the ambulances bringing back our wounded."

He did not hear her thanks. He was already on the telephone with another call.

Yuki went back to the listening post, where she had left her raincoat. The spring sky had turned gray, and rain was predicted. She could not shake her mental picture of Colonel Ito being surprised by a band of Chinese soldiers. She went to tell Ryoko what she had learned.

"The *kami* will protect the Colonel," Ryoko consoled her.

"But what if they don't?" Yuki said.

"When you see the Colonel the next time, then you pass on the rumor that you've heard," Ryoko said. "That's the proper way to do it."

But Yuki had been too long among the Westerners to have much belief in the power of the *kami*, and she knew that if the Colonel was killed for lack of a warning, she would never be able to forgive herself. The raincoat covered her swollen body as she set out for the hospital, where she found medical orderlies carrying in wounded soldiers.

She stopped a corpsman who was leaving the hospital, furling his bloodstained canvas stretcher before stowing it in an ambulance. "Excuse me," she said. "Are you going back to Woosung?"

"Hai," he said. "There's enough work for a hundred ambulances."

"I would like to ride with you. Do you know Colonel Ito?"

"Everyone knows Colonel Ito," the corpsman said. "But I'm not allowed to take anyone with me except medical personnel."

"I'm a nurse," she lied without blinking.

"With what unit?" he said.

"None," she said, summoning up an arrogance she had heard in the voices of superiors addressing her. "I'm his private nurse. He has a heart condition and I am taking his medicine to him." The suspicion was in his eyes but he was young, no more than seventeen years old, without enough experience to detect an outright lie. "I don't want to cause you trouble, Corpsman," she said. "But if you refuse me, I shall be forced to report the number of your ambulance."

He shrugged. "All right then," he said. "Come along."

As she climbed into the ambulance she felt a single sharp pain in her abdomen. It lasted a brief moment and then went away. *Please, Lord Jesus and Lord Buddha, not now.* The ambulance moved away into a twilight compounded by heavy clouds and a lightly falling rain. "Do you know where the Colonel is?" she said.

"About halfway to Woosung," the corpsman said, switching on the wipers against the clouded windshield.

"Is the fighting heavy?"

"Only at Woosung," the corpsman said. He clicked on the inadequate lights. "We send marines ashore by the thousands. Our ships in the Yangtze pound their fortifications all day and still the vermin come out of the trenches with machine guns."

He fell silent as they passed beyond the city on the road that ran inland, paralleling the meandering course of the Whangpoo. It was dark now and Yuki could see nothing more than the ambulance ahead of them, crawling through the same mud, occasionally stopping to allow a southbound ambulance to creep by on the narrow road.

They had been traveling a little over an hour when the next pain hit her. She moaned involuntarily.

"What's the matter?" the corpsman said. "Are you all right?"

"There's nothing wrong with me," she said. "I'm just worried about the Colonel."

She tried to sleep, to pretend that there was no significance to the pain, but she remembered seeing a farm woman in the fields at Towa being struck by the pains, which almost doubled her up, making her gasp for breath while she was planting rice, her legs firmly implanted in the mud. Only when the pains came with such frequency that the farm woman could not ignore them did she go back to the bank, seeking the shade of a tree, where she lay with her knees up, instructing her daughter how to help her.

Tomorrow. I will have the baby tomorrow, when I'm back in Shanghai.

They reached a crossroad where an ambulance was bogged in a mudhole, crews of men working in the rain to free it with ropes and boards and sheer force, while another squad tried to tamp down a trail of solid earth around the morass so the other ambulances could move. But the road had washed away and there was no solid footing to be had. The rain was an unabated torrent now, and the men finally attached ropes to the ambulances to drag them across five hundred meters of mud.

The corpsman cursed to himself, pounded the steering wheel in frustration. "The men will die if the ambulances can't get them to Shanghai," he said.

"If you will permit a suggestion, Corpsman," she said. "Since it takes so much effort to move the ambulances through the mud, why don't the ambulances from Shanghai stay on this side of the swamp and the ambulances from Woosung stay on the far side. It would be easier to carry the wounded across the morass than to move the vehicles."

"A good idea," he said. He was out of the truck in a second, and she could see him talking to the other drivers, who began to organize the relay of the wounded men. The driver was soaked through when he came back to the truck. "I found out about the Colonel for you. He took off on a motorcycle about ten minutes ago heading west along the footpath. He'll have to come back the same way."

"Where does the footpath begin?"

"Over there. Do you see the tree with the broken branch?" He leaned over the back of the seat, came up with an ancient tin coal-oil lantern, proceeded to strike a match and light the wick. It gave out a comforting if feeble glow. "You may have this. There's not much oil in it, but it's better than nothing. If I were you, I'd wait here for the Colonel. He's bound to come back in this direction, though it may be a long time."

I don't have the time. I have to find him soon.

"Thank you, but I have to find him," she said. "Good luck to you." She climbed out of the ambulance and was assaulted by the rain, so heavy that it took her breath away.

She waded through the water, found the footpath, broke a stick from a tree and used it as a cane in the darkness that engulfed her as she walked away from the ambulances. The small circle of light from the lamp could do little. She thrust the stick ahead of her, tapped it against the solid ground as she walked. She fell twice before she learned to keep her balance, but she managed to protect the glow of light each time she went down.

She began to talk to the child within her. *I won't let anything happen to you, chi chai.* But as she tapped her way along the path, which had become a spongy mass of overgrown grass and gravel, the despair began to grow inside her mind.

The pain hit her again, so hard this time that she had to lean on the stick. She knew if she sat down to rest, she might not be able to get up again. The pain receded, leaving her panting for breath.

She was wet through, beginning to chill. She pushed on again, counting the steps she took to provide some measure of time between pains. Her ankles began to hurt and she prayed to her twin Lords, Buddha and Jesus, to give her strength, only to realize, when she had finished praying, that she had lost count of her steps and had to begin again.

Ichi, ni, san, shi . . . .

No, in English.

One, two, three, four, five . . .

She reached five hundred and fourteen and another pain cramped her with such severity that it took her breath away. It lasted even longer than the one before. She gritted her teeth. She would not allow her baby to come into this world only to die of exposure in a dark and terrible place. She could see nothing ahead of her and she thought of turning back. In this countryside the path could go for miles and miles, skirting houses and factories no more than a few meters away to either side, concealed from her by the darkness and the rain.

But she did not know how far she had come. It seemed like hours. As the pain passed she made a bargain with herself. She would go down the path five hundred steps farther, certainly not a great distance. Should she find nothing, she would turn back and make the journey to the mudhole a little at a time. The ambulances would be there. The morass itself guaranteed that. Among the corpsmen she would find a doctor or nurse who knew how to deliver babies. She moved on, one step at a time.

Twenty-nine, thirty, thirty-one . . .

She thought about her mother and father and wondered how they had endured the hardships of their lives. But even while she was thinking a part of her mind kept count, and once she had passed two hundred and fifty, her hope began to crumble.

Four hundred one, four hundred two . . .

She sank to her knees in pain so strong that only with supreme effort was she able to set the lantern down and to place the wooden staff beside it. Then she clutched her swollen stomach. She was so frightened, she could not think, but she could pray, this time to Lord Jesus, for she knew nothing about Lord Buddha when he was a baby.

Esteemed Lord Jesus, you know that I am an unworthy woman so I'm not asking special favors for myself, because I don't deserve anything. But the child within me has done nothing. My child is pure, and if allowed to live will make up for my worthless life. . . .

The pain held on and suddenly she felt something give within her. She could go no farther. She lay down, the rain pelting her exposed face.

My mother did this, and just because this is a dark, lost place does not mean that I cannot do it too.

She would wait.

She was not sure exactly when she first saw the light down the path in the direction she had been going. She was too filled with pain to give the light much thought, but then she heard the roar of the motorcycle and saw it come to a stop very close to her, and a man in a cape materialized from the darkness with a flashlight.

"Nakamura-san?" he said. "What are you doing out here?"

"Is that you, Esteemed Colonel?" His face was hazy in the light of the lantern. "Is it really you?"

"*Hai,*" he said. "We have to find help for you." He put his hand on her abdomen. "No time for that, I see." He took off his rain cape and with it built a lean-to to cover her from the rain. "How often are the pains?"

"Every few minutes."

"Then we'll wait," he said, and knelt down beside her. "But why are you out here?"

"I heard a rumor."

"So?"

"About you, Esteemed Colonel."

"It must have been a strong rumor," he said with a slight smile.

"The Chinese General . . ."

"Yes?"

"He has a group of men . . ." She paused, gasping for air. "Who have been assigned to bring your head to him."

"Go on."

"They wait for you to leave the protection of the International Settlement."

"So you came to warn me."

"Yes."

"I thank you for that, Nakamura-san."

She reached for his hand, took it, and squeezed with all her strength against a new onset of pain that swept all words away from her.

Colonel Ito knelt between her legs and talked to her, urging her to press on, allowing her only a moment's rest before his voice began again. She felt as if she were dying, *would* die beyond doubt, *wanted* to die. Yet she did not scream because the woman in the rice paddy had never screamed, even with the same pain that had been passed from woman to woman since the beginning of time, and even the mother of Lord Jesus had not been spared.

The rain stopped. She did not notice. She strained so hard that she felt she would burst. He continued to talk to her in an even tone, urging her on, and suddenly she felt a great release and her head fell back.

He cleaned the face of the bloody child with his handkerchief, reaching out for water that had collected in a fold in the canvas. Holding the baby by the heels, he suspended it upside down and slapped it lightly on the buttocks, once, and then again. There was a choked sound and the baby began a sputtering cry.

"What is it?" she said, becoming aware.

"I'm sorry to inform you, Nakamura-san," he said, as he dealt with the cord. "But you have given birth to a girl."

She was aware that the sky had begun to lighten in the east. "Give me my baby," she said. "I will call her Dawn."

She fainted.

She came to in an ambulance on the way back to Shanghai long enough to feel her baby sucking at her breast. She passed out again and then came awake in a hospital bed with the baby still beside her on clean sheets. "You're lucky to be alive," a uniformed nurse told her.

"Is my baby healthy?"

"Perfectly," the nurse said. "We will bring you breakfast very soon."

"*Arigato gozaimasu,*" Yuki said.

The Colonel came by at noon. He was dressed in a fresh uniform but there were dark hollows around his eyes, as if he had not slept for days. "I came to say farewell for a time and to express to you my appreciation for the sacrifice you made for my welfare."

"I owe you my child's life," she said.

"I have given instructions for your care. You will be moved to my house when you are ready."

"If I may be permitted a question," she said. "How did you know how to deliver a child?"

"My father played polo when he was younger," the Colonel said with a smile. "I helped birth the foals, now and again."

When Charlotte reached the Cathay Hotel she was barely aware of the distant explosions or the smoke rising from the Chinese city to the north, for Harry was waiting for her six floors up. He would be sitting at the east windows watching the Japanese ships downriver through his binoculars. He had been assigned to make a daily report to the consulate of Japanese troop strengths as more divisions were brought ashore.

She took the elevator to the seventh floor and walked down one flight. The moment he opened the door to her discreet rapping, he took her in his arms and they kissed, their passion such that they sank down on the overstuffed sofa to make love. And only when it was spent did they speak.

"My God, how I've missed you," she said.

He kissed her lightly. "And how are you, love?"

"Fine, now."

"But in general?"

"Life with Sam is becoming more and more impossible," she said. "I need to see you more than just twice a week. I want to come to your apartment."

"It's too dangerous," he said, touching her face. "The waterfront is packed with refugees and it isn't safe." He stood up to adjust his clothing. "Now, what delicacies can I tempt you with? I can call room service and have them send up noodles and prawns, whatever fits your mood."

"I'm not hungry," she said.

"How long can you stay?"

"Not long. Sam will be home for dinner any minute, probably dragging along a dozen of his Chinese friends, all of them speaking Chinese, so I shan't understand a single word all evening."

"I envy Sam his marvelous zeal," he said, picking up the binoculars for a quick sweep of the river.

"He's all the worse for it," she said.

"Never. He cares so much about the future of China, he'll meet with anybody who might possibly improve the state of the Chinese people. And he's all caught up in the money game, in cotton mills and fabrics and fortunes." He lit a cigarette and sat down next to her to polish the lenses of the binoculars. "I think it would be bloody marvelous to be so caught up in causes."

"Don't you know that's why I love you?" she said. "You seem to have all the time in the world. You have time to see me, time to love me."

"True."

Quite suddenly the idea was full blown in her mind. "I have to go," she said.

"You just got here," he said, startled. "Why are you going?"

"I won't tell you. It'll be a surprise. Trust me."

He kissed her. "No questions. But just remember that you owe me another hour and a half."

It was dark by the time she arrived home and Majordomo informed her that Sam had called to cancel dinner. He would be working late. Fortuitous, she thought, almost as if he was confirming her decision.

"Have the car wait for me in front," she said to Majordomo. "I'll be going out again in an hour or so."

She went to her bedroom and sat down at her desk, took out a sheet of elegant stationery and a gold pen nib in an ivory holder.

Dear Father,

Please forgive me for any unhappiness this may cause you. I know that when you arranged my marriage with Sam you meant to do what was best for me. Sam is a good man and has already achieved a reputation here. He has established himself in business along with his regular duties at the consulate.

Sam has never pretended to love me, and now I have fallen in love with a man who truly cares for me, and I don't want to have to act the part of Sam's wife anymore. My leaving is not Sam's fault and he doesn't even know as yet what I plan to do. Since he isn't responsible for my decision, I hope you will not cancel any financial agreements that were made before our marriage. I want you to understand my position and please don't hold Sam responsible.

I hope you're well. I've never been better. I'll write you all the details when you tell me that you understand.

Your loving daughter,
Charlotte

She packed a few personal things in a small bag and then went through her wardrobe and separated the dresses in the closets into formal gowns and street wear, uncertain what her accommodations would be with Connaught, whether he would want to stay in the apartment on the river or find something more elaborate. She would pick up the things she needed in a few days.

As she was about to leave the house she sat down and penned a short note to Sam.

"It seems to me, dear Sam," she wrote, "that we've missed it

together. You admitted as much. No hope. Love is just not there
between us and I am very lucky to have found it with someone else.
I'm leaving. I hope there won't be any bitterness between us and
that life gives you everything you've hoped for. You are still very
dear to me."

She had trouble signing the letter. She could hardly write "Your
devoted wife," or even "Love," without seeming hypocritical. In the
end she settled for the word "Ever." And then not her name, but just
a "C" followed by a dash. She put the note in an envelope and left it
on his desk in the library, where he always spent an hour or two
before he went to bed.

She took only the small bag with her, and allowed the chauffeur to
seat her in the car. Only when she went out into the darkness, a cape
around her shoulders against the chill, did she realize that she ought
not to go directly to the apartment, even though Connaught had
provided her with a key. He was probably still at the Cathay Hotel.
She would have to be careful, as there were always a dozen social
events there at night, despite the municipal curfew.

At the Cathay she dismissed the car and then approached the
bank of room telephones off the lobby and asked for Mr. Connaught's room, only to be informed by an operator that Mr. Connaught had checked out. That settled the matter. He was certain to
be in his apartment.

She wrapped her cloak around her, engaged a ricksha boy outside,
and managed to convey the address to him in the smattering of
Chinese she had picked up. Off he trotted, past the mouth of
Soochow Creek and the street city of refugees, with makeshift shelters along every curb, dozens of cook fires, and such masses of people
that the police had cordoned off lanes for vehicular traffic to keep all
of the flat spaces from becoming one immense campground.

It was nine o'clock by the time the ricksha reached the small lane.
The ricksha boy made signs with his hands to ask her if he should
wait, but she smiled, paid him, and sent him on his way.

Home, she thought. *Far more so than the mansion, for Harry is
here.* There was a light showing in the bedroom window. She put her
bag down and took the apartment key from her pocket, then very
carefully opened the door so as to make no noise and wished as she
entered the house that she had stopped to get a bottle of champagne. She should have asked one of the servants what the Chinese
do to celebrate the beginning of a new life. The drapes were drawn,

so she could not see the river, but there was a candle burning on the teak bar. She took the time to remove two small glasses from the shelf and pour two cordials, which she placed on a small black lacquer tray and then made her way toward the bedroom.

She knew he was asleep, for he was making the little bursts of noises that occasionally had awakened her when they had slept together. There was a small crack in the bedroom door, a flicker of a light. Balancing the tray of cordials on one hand, she opened the door with the other and then stood frozen at the sight.

He was lying in the arms of a young Chinese girl whose face was partially obscured. Both of them were naked, their legs intertwined. The noises were those of passion, not of disturbed sleep. The tray fell from her hand, one glass spilling on the wool of an oriental rug, the other shattering as it struck solid wood.

Oh my God, how presumptuous I've been.

Connaught raised his head from the bed and looked at her, startled, but still gentle enough that he eased away from the Chinese girl and talked to her in a quiet voice while she reached for a sheet to cover her nakedness. Connaught sat on the edge of the bed and slipped on a pair of trousers.

I cannot breathe, she thought. *I'm going to stand frozen to this spot until I die.*

He stood up and approached Charlotte. "Let's go into the other room," he said, taking her elbow.

In a daze, she allowed herself to be guided, with Connaught closing the door behind them, limping slightly, for he had cut his foot on the broken glass. "I wouldn't have had this happen for the world." He went to the bar, brought back two glasses of brandy, handed her one. She just held it as she sat down.

"The girl," she said finally. "Who is she?"

"No one," he said.

"She has to be someone," Charlotte said. "She has to have a name."

He shrugged his bare shoulders. "I'm sure she does, of course, but I don't know it."

"How old can she be? Thirteen? Fourteen?"

"I don't know her age any more than I know her name. But you shouldn't distress yourself. I think you should drink your brandy. You've really turned quite pale."

Where is the anger? she wondered. *I should be angry enough to kill him, but there's nothing inside me except a pain which I know will never heal.* She held the glass beneath her nose until her breathing came easier and her mind cleared. Only then did she drink.

"Will you forgive me?"

"For what?"

"For upsetting you," he said.

"It's not your fault," she said. "You told me what to expect. I am the fool because I didn't believe you."

He put his hand on her arm and she felt nothing except the certainty that only moments before that same hand had been caressing the girl on the bed. "I'll send her away," he said. "Give me a minute."

"No," she said. "Don't. I won't be staying."

"Then we'll have lunch tomorrow. . . ."

"Not lunch either," she said. She had herself together now. "You are one of the dearest men I've ever met, Harry, and one of the gentlest I'm ever likely to meet. And I'm ashamed of myself, because I refused to understand something which you did your best to make clear to me. Perhaps one of these days we'll talk again, but not for a long, long time."

"Charlotte . . ."

"If you would raise a ricksha for me, I'd appreciate it."

He limped to the door, opened it, yelled into the night, then turned back to her. "What we had was something very special," he said. "It's too bad to throw it away."

"You used the past tense," she said. "Entirely appropriate, Harry. And do take care of the cut on your foot. Please express my apologies to the girl."

The ricksha appeared outside the door and she climbed in, aware that Connaught was explaining to the man where she wanted to go. But once the puller trotted away from the house, she told him to take her to the Cathay Hotel. She could not see traversing the whole of the city and taking hours to get back to the house she should never have left.

At the Cathay she called the mansion and instructed Majordomo to send the car for her. Then she went into the elaborate bar and ordered a gin and tonic.

Dear God, what a fool I've been, what a complete fool.

She listened to the piano player in the bar until she saw one of the porters carrying a blackboard mounted on a stick, twisting it slightly to cause the bells to jangle. Her name was written on the board.

She summoned him and tipped him when she found that her car was waiting. At the mansion she left the bag in the downstairs closet and then tried to figure out what she was going to say to Sam.

"Where is the master?" she said to Majordomo.

"Big bossee, him bedside go, maybe one hour, missee."

"Then have a bottle of chilled champagne and two glasses brought to his room," she said. "And some pâté and beluga caviar, with the little yellow crackers. The cook will know which ones."

Majordomo bowed and she climbed the stairs and went into Sam's bedroom without knocking, only to find him sitting at a small French desk staring at a paper he had just written. His collar was undone, his sleeves were rolled up, and he was wearing a pair of reading glasses.

"I didn't know you wore glasses," she said.

"I don't very often," he said. "I didn't realize you were out for the evening. I thought you had gone to bed."

"Am I interrupting?"

"Hell, no. Glad for the company. Sit down. I'll get us something to drink.

He had not read the note. It was as if they were back at the beginning of the evening. "You don't need to bother," she said. "I'm having some things sent up from the kitchen."

She sat in a winged chair and really looked at him for the first time in ages. There were dark circles beneath his eyes, a darkening stubble of beard on his cheeks from the lateness of the night. "Poor Sam," she said. "You've suffered so, haven't you?"

He nodded, lit a cigarette. "I'm getting used to it now."

"You didn't find her then?"

"She didn't want to be found. And she was right, of course." He sat down opposite her. "It wouldn't have worked. But how are things with you?"

"Not good," she said with a wan smile. "I have discovered that my lover was not what I hoped he would be."

He saw the pain in her eyes and reached for her. She came into his arms and put her face against his comforting shoulder and her body racked with sobs. As they began to lessen she drew away.

Sam handed her his handkerchief. "Maybe you can patch it up."

"No," she said. "Broken illusions are not patchable." She wiped her face and straightened her clothes. There was a knock on the door and a servant from the kitchen rolled a cart into the room, then departed. Charlotte poured the champagne, handed him a glass.

"So you won't be seeing him again?"

"No," she said. "What shall we toast? Is there anything left to toast?"

"Each other, perhaps."

"I'll drink to that," she said with a smile. "Poor us. But maybe a marriage of convenience is truly convenient after all. We start and end with each other."

He put the glass down and leaned over to kiss her. She raised her lips to his. He lifted her to her feet. "We're not the same people we were when we came here. We were children then. We've grown up. Had to," he said.

"True," she said.

"I don't know what there is between us, but I think it's time to find out." He took her in his arms, and her answer, given in silence, was unmistakable.

It was incredible, Colonel Ito thought, that the Chinese could continue to hold out. Flying over Chapei after months of siege, he saw the wasteland below him, piles of rubble and walls that had once been connected to buildings. No one could live in that devastation, but the Chinese troops seemed to have an incredible ability to survive on nothing, to eat dirt and drink air. And where were the millions of civilians who had lived here? They could not all have been absorbed into the International Settlement, and yet as the plane made another pass at low level, he could see nothing but abandoned cook fires, some of them still smoking, lean-to's where people had slept, and here and there a wooden door propped on rubble.

Four divisions of infantry had arrived from Japan, the first wave debarking above Woosung to swarm the Chinese garrison in a fierce battle and capture the guns that controlled the Whangpoo. Another wave moved west from Woosung, crack Japanese troops in camouflaged uniforms, making a wide circle to the south of the river to approach Shanghai from the west. Soon there would be only one narrow corridor open, the corridor that pointed toward Nanking.

From the airfield Ito went directly to the temporary General Military Headquarters. The mood there was euphoric, for a Japanese warship had steamed up the Yangtze, had fired a single shell that exploded near the city gates of Nanking. That shell could not have gone unnoticed by Marshal Chiang Kai-shek, for it proved that the Japanese had the ability to destroy Nanking just as they had pounded Chapei into oblivion. Then, too, the Marshal's coalition was falling apart; he was not able to back the Nineteenth Route Army with any further supplies or reinforcements. All traffic from Nanking suddenly ceased, though the soldiers of the Nineteenth repaired the bombed tracks by night, smoothed the rubbled roads, and waited for the help that never came.

General Miyamoto studied the map of Chapei on the wall, then looked at Ito. "I want to present this Chinese general an ultimatum," he said. "Will he honor a flag of truce if we send a delegation of officers to give him our terms?"

"He's unpredictable," Ito said. "He might be willing to trade what's left of his army to wipe out a half dozen of our officers. But he won't risk everything to kill one man. I want to deliver the ultimatum myself."

"You have my permission," the General said.

Ito was grimly pleased. Since the moment he had been dumped on the dock, covered with dried shit, he had waited to avenge the insult. And he felt the time was auspicious, for only the day before he had received what he considered a good omen from his father via diplomatic courier: a two-handed samurai sword that had been in the family for generations.

"This is the honor of your family," the note from his father said.

So Ito now set up a command post near the ruins of North Station and an ancient iron gate to the city and sent out a motorcycle courier carrying a white flag to arrange for a meeting with General Wang himself.

Shortly before sundown he heard the motorcycle sputtering back through the ruined streets. It stopped outside his tent, and the courier came in.

"General Wang presents his compliments, sir. He will meet with the Esteemed Colonel at 2100 hours in his private railroad car in the railroad yards off Nenpong Road."

"Does he agree with my conditions?"

"Yes, sir. There will be a truce and a cease-fire until one hour after the meeting."

"Did he make any conditions of his own?"

"No, Esteemed Colonel."

"Send me Major Okura," he said, and by the time his aide came into the tent, Colonel Ito had already blocked out the route. "I want one flagged car and an escort of five motorcycles," he said. He traced the route on the map. "We will proceed down Nainjing Road within the Japanese Sector, cutting up to Jinnin Road, where we enter Chapei. I want the exact location of the General's private rail car and which way the entry door faces. I want a flight of bombers to come overhead at the very moment I approach. They must be low, all running lights on, fully visible. I also want a detachment of soldiers with the national and regimental flags spotlighted so that he can see them at the same moment he sees me."

"You expect betrayal, then?" Major Okura asked.

"You will remain in the car. If he dishonors himself, you will give the signal for attack. The bombers will obliterate the railroad car and there will be a no-quarter attack on Chapei."

"Yes, sir."

At eight o'clock Colonel Ito had a bowl of noodles followed by tea and then put on his dress uniform with the freshly polished boots. He wore the scabbard and the two-handed sword. At eight-thirty he went out to the car where Major Okura and the motorcycle escort were waiting.

"Everything has been arranged, sir," Okura said. "Would you prefer the motorcycles to use their sirens?"

"No, I want the Chinese General to be listening. I want him to hear the faint roar of motors coming toward him."

He entered the car and it moved off. He knew that atop all the major hotels there would be parties tonight, with field glasses and telescopes trained in the direction of the procession. The whiskey would flow while the dance bands continued to play. War had become one of the major entertainments.

Sitting in the car, moving through the darkened streets, Ito felt no resentment for the European community but instead how distanced he was from them. He was now moving in the direction of his own culture.

They reached the rail yards. The private railroad car was bathed in light, making it a perfect target for the half dozen bombers that came swooping down now from out of the night sky.

Colonel Ito left the car and walked across the tracks toward the delegation of Chinese officers who stood near the steps of the railroad car. Wang was not among them. Colonel Ito entered the car to find the General standing over a table examining a water-cooled machine gun. It was not until Ito approached that Wang looked up. His truculent eyes were not those of a defeated man suing for peace.

"It surprises me," Wang said, "that your forces could find nobody better to send than an officer whom I last saw covered with shit."

"I was delighted with the assignment," Ito said. "Better to be covered with shit than to have to eat it."

The General drank from a bottle, wiped his mouth on his sleeve. "And does the Colonel intend to live up to the warning he made when last we met?"

"That would dishonor my sword," Ito said. "I kill only men, not animals. I am not here to ask for your surrender, General. I don't believe you could give it if you wanted to. Your men are scattered in the ruins. All discipline has broken down."

"Then why are you here?"

"To point out what you are too arrogant to face. You are completely surrounded except for one small corridor to the northwest. You are out of favor with your own government. If we attack, then all civilians in Chapei will be killed along with your soldiers. It's impossible to tell the difference between them."

The General smiled. "Have a look at this new machine gun. My army is being supplied with them. They will enable me to shit on your forces as I pissed on one of their leaders."

Ito whipped the sword from the scabbard and, raising it over his head, brought it down with such force that the blade went through the machine gun, cleaving it in two pieces and collapsing the table with such a clatter that General Wang jumped back involuntarily. He stood facing the tip of the sword that now hovered in front of his face, making small circles. Ito's eyes bored into him. The General's mouth opened but Ito silenced him.

"Shut up. One word and I cut you to pieces and then there will be nobody to issue the orders. At dawn we move into Chapei. One of your soldiers left behind, even inadvertently, and we kill everybody. No. Don't speak. I don't want words. Your words are worth as little as your machine guns. Personally, I hope you stay, General, because I will deliver orders that no one is to be allowed to kill you except me."

The General's face was flushed, but he did not speak.

Ito turned and went down the steps and back to the car. As they drove away he managed to calm his rage enough to tell the Major, "I will lead a company from the Ninth Division in at dawn. You will deliver that message to General Headquarters."

The Major asked no questions.

Colonel Ito slept little. He waited until the first rays of the sun broke over the horizon to the east, and then, leading a procession of troops in an armored car, he drove back to the railroad yards. The General's private car was gone. There was no sign of a Chinese soldier.

All day long the reports came in from scouts of soldiers streaming to the northwest. General Wang was gone. His army had been routed. Ito did not worry. His day with Wang would come.

Yuki awakened with a start, seized by a minor panic when she could not hear the baby's breathing. She was out of the bed quickly to lean over the crib in the semidarkness just before daybreak, and she placed her hand on Dawn's chest, felt the life. She picked her up without waking her, then sat down in the rocker, trying to calm herself. The baby was a month old and the war had swept away from Shanghai, and still Yuki took nothing for granted, as if the good fortune that had given her the child would turn bad.

She sat and rocked, feeling the warmth of the baby against her, looking down at the tiny face, the shape of the features, the delicate curve of the eyelids. *Just like your grandmother, chi chai,* she thought, and she had a sudden longing for her mother to be here now, to share this fragile and wondrous time. *I will save my money and take you to your grandmother,* she thought, and then she looked closer at the sleeping face and knew that would never happen. *You have your dear father's nose and your chin is much like his and you can never see your grandparents because you are half gaijin.*

The child moved, came awake, made sucking noises. Yuki rang the bell to summon the Japanese wet nurse who also served as amah for the child, a woman who had survived Ito-san's tyrannical interview for the position when Yuki's milk had dried up prematurely. The short and stocky woman came into the room now, bowed, took the baby, and, baring a breast, offered the child a nipple. She was only half awake, instinctively gentle with the baby as she cradled it in the crook of her arm while it suckled.

"May I say something, Nakamura-san?" she said.

"*Hai, dozo.*"

"I think you should give the child a Japanese name. People won't understand what this English name means."

"I know what it means. The coming of the sun. The beginning of a new day. And you know what it means."

"I was thinking of people in general."

"I don't care about people in general."

The amah nodded, resigned. "Shall I take her to the park in the pram today?" she said. "It should be a very warm afternoon."

"No, I don't want her to be that far away for a while. You can sit with her in the garden. You can take her to the park when she's older."

"So desu."

The same night Yuki was in her sitting room, the baby having been put to bed, when the Colonel came in, dressed in his formal kimono, his face thoughtful.

"I want to talk to you if you're not too tired," he said.

"I'm not tired at all," she said. "It's been a pleasant day. Let me bring you some sake. I have some warmed."

"I would like that," he said, and when she brought him the rice wine he sipped it slowly, considering his words. "The world is all awry sometimes, I think," he said. "If I had stayed in Japan, I would never have had confusion in my mind because every action would have been set out for me and I would have known what to feel in every situation." He looked at her, studied her delicate face. "We're all in the same place, aren't we?" he said. "You and Cummings-san and I. If these were normal times, he would still be a very young man just out of university in America, not having to think such weighty thoughts, and you would be a happy schoolgirl in Japan, and I would be learning my father's business, selecting a geisha at night in the house on the river and preparing for the marriage my family has arranged for me." He drank another shallow cup of sake. "But none of us has been allowed to enjoy being young."

Yuki shook her head. "You forget, my lord, that I come from a very poor peasant family where the girls are required to grow up very quickly if they are allowed to live. I am very grateful for what I have and where I am. If we were in Japan, I would never have known you and Cummings-san."

"And what are your feelings for Cummings-san now?"

"I believe in the Lord Buddha and the Lord Jesus. Everything has happened as it should."

"Things are not that simple for me," he said.

"How so?"

"We have given the Chinese reassurance that our government wants no further military presence in China than the number of troops we were granted after the Boxer Rebellion. But the Chinese are going to keep fighting until all Japanese are gone, and so they will give our military factions who want to expand in China a reason to do so. And Chapei will be only a beginning."

"So what will you do?"

"Try to end the fighting. And to do that I need your help."

"Anything."

"The battle in Chapei has turned many of the Western nations against our government. Some of the Western press are calling for our military to leave China altogether."

"I have read such things."

"I need an informal listening ear to let me know what's going on."

"Similar to the listening house?"

"No. I want you to put a shop in the International Settlement, perhaps a flower shop, to cater to the foreign legations. You will pick up news and rumors and report them to me directly. Do you think you can do that, Nakamura-san?"

"It will be a pleasure, my lord," she said. "I would enjoy having a flower shop."

"Then it's agreed," he said. "You will have all the money you need, both for the shop and for you personally as well." He finished another cup of sake and his face softened. "I trust our baby from the storm is doing well."

"Very well, my lord," she said. "I will forever be grateful to you."

"And I will always stand by you," he said, putting his hand on her arm. "I want you to be certain of that."

She felt the warmth in his fingers, but his touch was tentative, an overture without demands, and she covered his hand with hers. *Forgive me, Lord Jesus and Lord Buddha, and if it were possible, I would be comforting Cummings-san tonight, but it has been a long time since I have felt a man wanting me.* He looked into her eyes and saw the acceptance. And he put his arms around her. As they came together on the bed he was far gentler than she had imagined him capable of being. And she felt loved and loving.

Afterward they lay together without speaking as her hand caressed his hair, soothing him, and it occurred to her that the fantasy lover she had described in the letters to her mother was now marvelously real.

Yuki was due to meet the real estate agent at ten o'clock, but she went to the cathedral first, lighting a candle in front of the wooden figure of Jesus on the Cross, intending to pray. She found herself distracted by her memories of last night, the gentleness of the Colonel's lovemaking. She had awakened once during the night to look on his face with a feeling approaching awe. For he was the embodiment of an aristocratic warrior, and had they been in Japan, she knew the chasm between them would have been so wide that she would never have dared speak to him. Even now she could but marvel at what had happened between them, for the limits of their relationship were bound to be set by his social rank. She felt a great attraction and a profound admiration for him, but she told herself she would never be able to be as free with him as she had with Cummings-san.

She should not stay in his house any longer than was necessary. She had organized his Chinese staff so that everything was running smoothly, and she was no longer needed. Once her shop was open, she would find a small house for herself and Dawn.

He is so much like Cummings-san in many ways, she thought, kneeling in the church, and then forced Sam out of her mind, looking up at the quiet passive suffering depicted by the statue. *I am sorry, Lord Jesus. I should not bother you with such small problems, and I am unable to pray today.* So she lit an extra candle, hoping that the Lord Jesus would excuse her, and then went down the marble steps to take the first ricksha in the line of waiting pullers.

She was filled with excitement as she turned into Nanking Road and the heavy traffic, and from the moment she saw the empty shop she knew it would be perfect. There were broad windows for floral displays facing two streets, a showroom where she could put her cases to keep fresh flowers cool, a workroom behind that, and even an extra room with an adjacent courtyard where an amah could take care of Dawn during the day.

The agent for the property, a stout, red-faced Englishman named John Paxton, stood in the middle of the shop, which had been empty for six months, and with a pleasant smile manufactured an outrageous untruth. "In all honesty, Miss Nakamura, there is quite a battle between merchants for this outstanding space and that means it will go at a premium sum. I'm willing to entertain an offer, of course, which I will convey to my client, but unless it's substantial, I'd suggest that we cast an eye for something more modest."

"Who is your highest bidder and what does he offer?" Yuki said.

"It would be unethical for me to give you his name, but he's a Hindu lawyer of considerable means," Paxton said. "He's willing to pay fifty pounds sterling per month, a most reasonable sum I'd say, wouldn't you?"

"I think your Hindu might be distressed," Yuki said, returning his smile.

"How so?"

"By the meat market two doors from this place. Wouldn't it disturb his religious beliefs to pass animal carcasses hanging on open display in the window?"

Paxton did not even blink. "He's a reformed Hindu, I believe."

After making one last inspection, she removed fifty pounds from her purse in ten-pound notes. "I am prepared to lease this place for one year at twenty-five pounds a month," she said, keeping her voice under control so he would not know how nervous she was with such a large amount of money. "I will pay you first and last month's rent."

"I appreciate your gesture, indeed I do, but I'm sure my client won't even consider that. You certainly won't be able to crowd out our Hindu lawyer with such a low offer."

She put the money back in her purse. "Thank you for your time, Mr. Paxton."

She started for the door while he stared after her with an expression approaching pain on his face. "You're missing a bargain, madame," he said. "I'm sure my client would be willing to take the fifty pounds a month, which was the Hindu lawyer's offer, seeing as how you're here and he is not."

"Mr. Paxton, we both know there is no Hindu lawyer," she said. "I know what I can afford and I've offered it. If you can't rent it to me for that, then I'll find another shop."

"Well," he said doubtfully, "could you possibly go thirty?"

"Twenty-five is the very best I can do."

He seemed to groan, as if in physical pain. "All right, then. I'll draw up the papers, Miss Nakamura, and prepare to suffer the wrath of my client."

Days later she was taking measurements of the main room when there was a light rap on the lintel and she looked around to see Connaught smiling at her from the open doorway.

"I'm delighted to see you," she said. "But how did you know I was here?"

"A certain Mr. Paxton has been moaning around the Shanghai Bar about a beautiful young Japanese lady who has taken advantage of depressed times. I put two and two together," he said, coming in to look around. "An impressive location, I must say. Flowers, is it?"

"That's what I'm planning, yes."

"Is your lovely daughter with you?"

"She's at home with her amah."

"Then you're free to abandon your work and come with me," he said happily. "There's something I think you absolutely must see, a veritable serendipity, I believe. And it can't wait. I have a car outside. Will you trust me enough to come along?"

"Of course," she said. "But where are we going?"

"That will have to be a surprise." He seated her in the car, took his place behind the wheel, and drove like a madman through the congested streets, tires squealing, until he reached the edge of the French Concession, where he slowed abruptly. "Their gendarmes are not as tolerant of my driving prowess as they once were," he said.

"Have you seen Cummings-san lately?" she said.

"Daily," he said.

"And you never told him of our meeting?"

"No."

"How is he?"

"Fine as rain," he said, peering through the window as if looking for an address. "But that's not really what you're asking me, is it, Nakamura-san?"

"No," she said candidly.

"Someone told him you were in Shanghai and he knows you're living at Colonel Ito's."

"Only until I locate a house."

He glanced at her. "He also saw the baby from a distance once when your amah wheeled her to the park for an outing." He paused and she said nothing. "I'm sure this can't be easy for Sam, but he's making the best of things. He's back with his wife." Then he saw tears in her eyes. "And I can see it's not an easy time for you either."

"You are a good friend and I thank you," she said.

"We all recover, don't we? And life goes on. Fortunately, a broken heart is not a terminal illness."

He turned the car into a narrow lane so sheltered by trees that it could be found only by somebody who already knew it was there. Shortly a small shop came into view, the name MADELEINE in separate gilt letters above the diamond-pane windows. The windows displayed the latest European fashions as well as a dress line she had not seen before, a design combining bright Chinese colors with flaring skirts.

Connaught held up a key that glittered in the cold afternoon sunlight. He opened the door and followed Yuki into a showroom with dresses on racks and boxes in various states of being packed.

"All right," she said. "Why did you bring me to this place?"

He lit a cigarette, pulled a white sheet cover from a wicker chair, and sat down, making himself comfortable. "A business proposition," he said. "A dear friend of mine, gender female, status married, got bored and poured a small fortune into this shop only to find herself absolutely unsuited to the world of business. Witness her choice of location, for instance. Only someone lost in the bush could possibly stumble across this salon. So she's selling everything at a pittance and looking to place her staff elsewhere. She will lose a small fortune in the process, which bothers her not at all because she is outrageously wealthy."

"And you think I should buy this stock?" Yuki said.

"Absolutely. It's a marvelous opportunity."

"I could never afford such grand clothing," Yuki said. The memory flashed across her mind of the hot summer afternoon in the missionary school when she had sketched the dress worn by the American woman. *I want this,* she thought. *Oh, how I want it.* "And I plan to sell flowers, not gowns."

"Why not both?" he said. "I think such a combination would do very well. And dear sweet Madeleine will let you buy this stock on any terms you can manage."

"How do you know that?"

"I asked her on the vague chance that you might be interested."

"Of course I'm interested," she said, excited. "Everything is so beautiful."

He stirred from the chair, ground out his cigarette in a brass fish. "Then consider it arranged," he said. "She trusts me in matters of this sort. So now, let's consider the services of the designer. Do you like her creations?"

"I think they're splendid," she said. "But I won't have the money to hire her right away."

He smiled tolerantly. "Her name is Yvonne Chen," he said. "She is half Chinese and half French and she has been married sequentially to half a dozen wealthy old men who have passed to their rewards in heaven while leaving her overburdened with earthly goods. She designs for the joy of it. Eventually she would expect to be paid handsomely for her work, but I'm sure she would be amenable to other arrangements in the beginning."

Yuki's mind raced through the possibilities. She had no business taking on such debts at this point, and she knew that she should start small and grow only when she had the cash. But certainly the Lord Jesus and the Lord Buddha had conspired to offer her this opportunity, and to refuse it from a lack of faith would be to doubt their wisdom.

"All right," she said. "I don't know how, but I'll do it."

He looked very pleased. "I knew you would," he said. "I've always known you were a very bright woman, Nakamura-san, and I guarantee you'll never regret this move."

Yuki entered into negotiations with Madeleine within the next week and bought the stock with a small down payment, the remainder to be paid off as her business prospered. She also met with Yvonne Chen, who was large, easygoing, and wore so many golden bracelets that she clanked when she moved to fill the ever-present wineglass near her drawing board, which held her new batch of sketches.

"You'll have no trouble selling my designs," she said. "And if I were you, I'd hire the seamstresses for alteration work on the stock you already have. They're twins in their sixties, Chinese ladies I call Yin and Yang because they're always at odds with each other, but they can work from my sketches and put the gowns together as you need them."

Yuki was ecstatic at her good fortune.

Sooner than she thought possible, the windows in the shop had been cleaned, floors carpeted, walls painted, contracts placed for the supply of flowers, a Japanese girl hired to make flower arrangements and bouquets, furniture placed in the back room, and the courtyard filled with blooming plants and hanging vines, with space for the amah to sit in the sunshine and take care of the baby.

She found her own household in the French Concession, a charming old cottage, rather small but well built, with a long-term lease. She moved Dawn and her amah into it with a pair of servants and acquired her own car and driver to take her to the shop and out to the legations, where she hoped to be in demand for parties and weddings.

She dressed her staff in the gowns so they would serve not only as salesgirls but as models, and she placed three of the more elegant Yvonne gowns on wooden mannequins among the banks of flowers, with no price tags showing.

She wrote personal letters to all the consulates offering the services of her shop, which she had named Blossoms, and beneath the letterhead she included the word *couture* in very small print. Within two months she had to hire a regular delivery man to take care of the orders. And she decided to extend her lease. The women from the legations often came in person to make selections of bouquets or to tell her the kinds of flowers they wanted at a wedding. They wanted to look her over because she had become a part of diplomatic folklore, having almost thrown that wonderful Samuel Cummings off the track when he had first arrived out here, and then leaving him for the favors of a dashing Japanese colonel, the hero of Mukden.

And then they discovered that Blossoms carried fine and unusual apparel, and by the end of the first year that part of the business was bringing in more money than the flowers. The European fashions did not sell as briskly as Yuki had thought they would, because all of the shops on Joffre Avenue specialized in European imports, so she discounted her stock of European gowns and sold them out within a month for enough to pay the rest of her debt to Madeleine. Thereafter she limited her dresses to Yvonne's designs.

In her third year she converted one corner of her flower shop into an elegant arrangement of French chairs and delicate tables where, when the diplomats' wives came to order flowers or have a gown modeled, they were invited to have a cup of tea or a glass of wine while they waited. And to be in fashion for such tête-à-têtes, Yuki went to Yvonne to have distinctive gowns made for herself, and twice a week she went to a hairdresser in the Central District. One day, as she sat in the tea area with a client, she saw a reflection of herself in the glass of the case and she marveled at how far her Lords had permitted her to go in this life, for there was no longer any sign of the village girl who had come to Shanghai to seek her fortune. Instead, the mirror showed her a lady of poise and beauty.

She was able to send her mother a monthly check, which grew larger as she prospered, and she considered herself fortunate indeed. But there were many times when she felt envious, especially when society girls her own age visited her shop and she overheard their chatter about this young man or that, and whether Alicia was going to the King's next birthday ball with the new staff member at the British Consulate, and how Georgina had cut her hair. It seemed as if the realities of life had not touched them yet, while there had never been a time when she had been truly free from trouble.

On a summer evening in 1935 she stopped by the Colonel's house in Hongkew, as she had most Friday evenings since the shop had opened. They had dinner and then sat on the terrace in the moonlight while she gave him what information she had been able to pick up during the week.

"Not much has happened that is worth repeating," she said. "There was to be a farewell reception for Captain Dunning at the British Consulate. It was to take place on Monday and I had orders for three hundred dollars' worth of flowers."

"So desuka?" he said with immediate interest. The coal of his cigarette glowed in the darkness. "You use the past tense."

"Yes. Today all of the orders were canceled. And two women who came in for a fitting said that Captain Dunning was not leaving after all."

"Are you certain? Perhaps his transfer has just been delayed."

"No, my lord. One of the women was unhappy because now there will not be a party at the British Consulate until the King's birthday."

"That is most intriguing," he said. "I thank you for the helpful information."

"May I ask you a question, my lord?"

"Certainly."

"How can gossip like this possibly make any difference to you?"

"Most of the time it doesn't," he said. "But Captain Dunning is the naval attaché in charge of British trade on Chinese rivers. He is a pleasant man to invite to parties and he looks splendid in his dress uniform and speaks five languages, but he has never been an efficient officer. I have been expecting the British to replace him with a more aggressive man and a tougher trade policy."

"I still don't understand."

"The fact that he is staying is a clear indication that the British do not intend to change their policy for a while. So your information is useful."

"I am happy to please you," Yuki said. "Especially since what I am about to say now may not meet with your favor."

"And what is that?"

"I have no right to ask, my lord, but I say it anyway. I have known for some time that your marriage has been arranged."

"Yes."

"And when will it take place?"

"No date has been set."

"But when it does happen your wife will be coming here."

"Perhaps," he said. "But from what I have been told of her, she is a retiring woman who does not like travel. So there is a better chance she will stay in Tokyo."

"I presume on our relationship, my lord."

"Are you asking if my marriage, when it happens, will change things between us?"

"Yes."

"I realize that my future might seem threatening to you," he said. "But when my marriage takes place I will owe my new wife no more than *giri*, the traditional obligations of a husband, and that has nothing to do with my feelings toward you and Dawn."

"I do not want to take anything that is hers."

"You will not," he said. "She will not be concerned in any way with my life here."

"I am glad." She smiled. "There is one more important thing I want to mention to you," she said. "I have kept a strict accounting of the money that you gave me to start the business. In another few months I will have enough to pay you back."

"That is not necessary."

"You have a generous heart, my lord. But it is absolutely necessary for me to repay this money. It is a heartfelt obligation and a duty. I want to know that I have accomplished something on my own and then the information I give you can be a clear gift. Is it selfishness on my part to feel this way?"

"No. I admire that in you."

"And it will not change anything between us?"

"It will change nothing between us."

There will be changes, she told herself on her way to Blossoms the next morning, because as reassuring as Ito-san was trying to be, his marriage to another woman was bound to affect his relationship with her. Over the years a way of life had developed between the two of them in which he was her lover and her benefactor, as well as a surrogate father to her daughter, but he never demanded anything of her, only requested, and she made no claims on him. As much as she craved a feeling of permanence, she knew she would never have it with him, for he was a wave on sand, and as easily as he had swept into her life, he could slip out again. He was an aristocrat with a predestined life, and were he called back to Japan tomorrow for a permanent posting, he would have to go and she could not follow.

Once she reached Blossoms she found everything on the brink of pandemonium. Yin and Yang were screaming insults at each other in the workroom, and when she tried to intervene they both glowered at her and retreated into a hostile silence. Elder Sister informed her that two of her girls had called in sick and there was a message from her delivery man that a wheel had flown off the truck while making a delivery up near St. John's. He would be out of service all day. Yuki steeled herself for an onslaught. And when she called Yvonne Chu she half expected to find that Yvonne had eloped with a seventh husband or been taken ill with a summer flu, but Yvonne came to the telephone bright and cheerful.

"Can you do me a great favor?" Yuki asked. "Yin and Yang are fighting and they have a gown to finish this afternoon."

"I'll straighten them out," Yvonne said instantly. "And one of these days I'll teach you to swear in Shanghainese. Sometimes it's the only way to get their attention."

"I'm grateful to you," Yuki said. She severed the connection and summoned Elder Sister to her. "We are going to need at least one other girl in the salesroom this afternoon. Do you know anyone with experience who might come in?"

"I have a cousin who worked in a shop one summer, madame. I think you would find her more than satisfactory."

"Fine," Yuki said. "Now, for the deliveries we need a young man who can read and write, somebody trustworthy."

"My younger brother would be delighted to serve you, madame."

"I'm pleased you have a large family," Yuki said. "I want him to hire a ricksha to make the deliveries, one of the newer ones, freshly washed, since it will be representing Blossoms."

"Yes, madame."

Once Elder Sister was gone Yuki rang for a cup of tea and then tried to concentrate on the sheaf of bills, but the specter of the future continued to haunt her. There were no guarantees in life and she would have to prepare herself to stand alone, to see after her business and her daughter with no help other than that which she could hire. She sipped her tea and listened to Dawn playing in the courtyard with her amah, then wrote checks until eleven, when she was interrupted by Elder Sister, who told her that a customer in the salon had asked to see her.

She went out into the salesroom and glanced at the back of a well-groomed Western gentleman looking at a silk gown on a plaster mannequin, and she was about to introduce herself when suddenly he turned and his features came into focus. Her knees almost gave way with the jolt of recognition.

Sam.

She had no words, no polite greeting, nothing. It was as if she had never expected to see him again. And yet here he was.

"I would like to talk to you," he said at last.

"Yes," she said. She glanced toward the tearoom and saw a group of women who had not yet detected his presence. If they saw him, the gossip would begin again. "Please wait for me outside," she said. "I'll be with you in a minute."

"I understand."

She told Elder Sister she would be back shortly and then joined him on the crowded sidewalk. He walked down the street toward the Cathay Hotel and she fell in step beside him. *He is even more handsome,* she thought. She looked at him, fighting her feelings and the memories he evoked in her.

"Do you want something cold to drink?" he asked. "It's a hot day."

"No, thank you."

He found a bench in the small park overlooking the river near the hotel. He watched her as she sat down. "I didn't know it was going to be this difficult," he said, turning his face toward the river.

"Why did you seek me out?"

"Because I'm a person who has to finish things. No loose ends, nothing left unresolved."

"I hear many lovely things about your wife," she said.

He glanced at her. "Don't play Let's Pretend."

"Please," she said, the ache so strong within her, she thought she would be ill. "Don't do this. Go back to your world. I'm no longer in your life."

"There's something I want to discuss with you."

"This is very painful for me."

She saw his fists clench in frustration, then relax. He lit a cigarette. "I don't want to upset your life, or mine. But you don't know the number of times I've passed by your place and wanted to come in and talk to you. Or the number of times I've wanted to ask Ito about you. But what do I say?" His voice became bitter. " 'Tell me, Colonel, how's my daughter? And how's the woman I was ready to chuck everything for who walked out on me?' "

She had to blink back the tears. "Please stop it."

He sat down on the bench, oblivious of the crowds of Chinese in the park. "Why didn't you talk to me before you left?"

"I left you a note."

"Everything for my own good."

"Yes."

"Why didn't you let me decide that?"

She wept quietly, looked at her hands in her lap. "I wouldn't have been able to leave if I had talked to you."

He looked at the birds in the branches. "I guess I knew you couldn't have. It's a confused world, isn't it? I loved you so much I would have thrown away everything for you. And you loved me enough that you did throw everything away, didn't you?"

She stopped crying. "It had to be done."

"I'm happy with Charlotte now," he said. "But a part of me will go on loving you as long as I live." He rested his arm along the back of the wooden bench, his fingers brushing her shoulder. She felt the electricity, did not move.

"And I you," she said softly.

He sat in contentment, his eyes following a junk under full sail on the river. "Remember the day we went sailing and you bopped the man with our binoculars?"

"It was a wonderful day," she said.

He was silent a long time. "The Colonel treats you well?"

"We're good friends. But I no longer manage his household. I've had my own house for some time now."

"I hear that you're very successful."

"I knew what I wanted from the time you let me set up the currency exchange. I knew I wanted a business of my own."

"Tell me about my daughter."

"She's a very happy and inquisitive three-year-old. She likes bright colors and she asks 'Why?' to everything. You would be very proud of her."

"What will you tell her about me when she's old enough to understand?"

"I don't know," she said honestly. "Whatever is best for her, I suppose. Whatever will not hurt her."

"I've talked with Charlotte about her."

"I don't want your wife to be unhappy because of me."

"She accepts the way things are," he said, and Yuki could hear the admiration in his voice. "She's a lot like you in that way, in her willingness to accept. But I want to do something for Dawn."

"Dawn has everything she needs."

"I want to set up a trust for her."

"No," she said instantly, as if she had no power to stop the word.

"Hear me out. A million dollars. She'll never lack for anything."

She searched his face, looking for any sign of what she knew must be there, the thought that would eventually occur to him if it had not already. Sooner or later he would come to believe that he had the right to influence the life of his daughter because of the money he had given her. Yuki could not have that. "She will never need anything I can't give her," she said. "You've always been a generous man, but this time you must trust me on this. I will look after her."

"Think about it."

"Her future is in the hands of the Lord Jesus and the Lord Buddha, who have placed her in my care," Yuki said.

"I'd like to see her sometime."

"When I think she's ready."

"At least consider the money."

"If I change my mind, I'll let you know." She stood up. "I have to get back to Blossoms."

"I'll walk you there."

"No, I'll go by myself."

"If that's what you want."

"We don't often get what we want," she said. "But we take what is best at the time and continue to hope."

"And you won't forget."

"No." She took the hand he offered and then hurried away without looking back, half running through the crowds to her shop, regaining her poise long enough to cross the showroom to the privacy of her office before the panic seized her and she knew why she was running.

Ito-san will be married and I will lose him and someday Sam will decide he wants his daughter and he will be such a powerful man I will not be able to stop him. And then I will be alone. Abandoned.

Her body ached with longing and her pain and grief were intense. She went into the courtyard and gathered Dawn to her and hugged her fiercely, tears streaming down her face. And when she had finished weeping she dried her eyes and comforted her bewildered child, her own fears quieting.

We have everything we need today, she told herself. *And when the time comes, if ever I am faced with calamity, I will have the strength to meet it.*

By the end of her third year Mr. Paxton came around to see her, looking at the splendid furnishings in her office with an attitude of appraising awe. He accepted a cup of tea and sank into a soft leather chair with a placid smile on his face. "You have accomplished miracles here, madame," he said. "And that's a fact. And you have opened my client's eyes to the full value of this splendid property, but he's not out to take advantage, no, and even though this lease is now worth a fortune, so to speak, I have been instructed to allow you to continue your tenancy for the paltry sum of an even one hundred pounds a month, plus utilities, of course. You must admit that this is a most generous offer, madame, considering the inconvenience of relocating as well as all that lost revenue."

She took the news with equanimity. "I thank you, Mr. Paxton, because you've helped me make a decision. Blossoms has generated such traffic on this corner that all the shops on the block have benefited and I've had many offers from other block owners who will *give* me space just for the traffic I bring in. So please inform your client I will be out by the end of the month."

Paxton blanched, fingers trembling enough to spill tea from the cup before he could set it down. "Let's don't be too hasty here, madame," he said. "I mean, after all, surely you'd want to be fair about this. My client has been gracious enough to give you a minimum rate for all this time. My client deserves consideration, you have to admit that."

"All right, then," Yuki said. "Since your client owns the whole block, and since it has been upgraded by my presence in the past year, then it seems to me that a reasonable lease rate should be fifty pounds a month. And I want that guaranteed for the next ten years."

Mr. Paxton, moaning that his client would be so outraged as to dismiss him altogether rather than ever agree to such a proposal, was back within the hour with the papers drawn up. Yuki was guaranteed a lease for ten years.

On a brilliantly cold day in January, Yuki came home at noon to give herself time to enjoy Yvonne's latest batch of sketches. She put the portfolio on the table in the living room and sought out Dawn in the upstairs playroom only to find the amah sitting by herself, the expression of awe on her face that was always there when she had been around the aristocratic Colonel.

"The Esteemed Colonel came to take your daughter out for the afternoon," she said. "He said that you should be prepared for a surprise at four o'clock."

"What kind of surprise?"

"He wouldn't say, madame."

"Tell the cook that the Colonel will be here for dinner," Yuki said happily. "I will have tea in the living room and then I don't want to be disturbed."

"Yes, madame."

She spread out Yvonne's designs over the back of the sofa and the chairs and wondered at the miracle of the woman's genius, each of her designs more tastefully flamboyant than the one before, as if Yvonne were responding to the bleakness of winter and rumors of imminent war with a particularly gorgeous array of colors. Yuki surrounded herself with swatches and bolts of fabrics, clicking off sums on the beads of an abacus, figuring costs.

She was so absorbed in her work that when the whole house shook it took her a moment to realize that an airplane had swooped down very low over her roof just as the mantel clock was striking four. She ran outside into the garden, ignoring the cold, her breath steaming, as the biplane banked out across the river and came back again, wings waggling, and she waved, laughing, as she saw one end of Dawn's red scarf streaming like a banner from the front cockpit, which she shared with Ito-san. The plane made another pass and then seemed to shoot straight up in the cloudless sky, making a roll before it disappeared to the west toward the airfield.

An hour later Ito drove up and Dawn popped out of the car and flew into her mother's arms. "Did you see me, Mama? I saw you."

"Of course I saw you," Yuki said. "How did the world look from up there? Did the people look like ants?"

"No," Dawn said. "They looked like people." She ran back to help Ito carry the packages in from the car. "We went shopping," Dawn said. "Everything is for me except one gift for you." She brought the packages into the house, set them on the floor, and opened them carefully, one at a time. Dresses, skirts, a coat, a pair of fur-lined boots, a porcelain doll, an origami bird of bright blue paper, which she carried to Ito-san. "Show Mama how it works," she said.

"You do it," Ito-san said. "You know how, remember?"

Dawn held the body of the bird in her left hand and tentatively pulled the paper tail with the fingers of her right hand. The wings wiggled and began to flap as Dawn giggled gleefully. "See, I *can* do it," she said.

"Of course," Ito-san said. "There was never any doubt."

"Where's amah?" Dawn said. "I must show her."

"Upstairs."

And Dawn was off at a run while Yuki gathered the sketches from the furniture and put them in the portfolio.

"I brought a present for you," Ito-san said. "But you have to sit down before I can give it to you."

"It would be impossible for me to be happier than I already am," she said. "Dawn adores you, and when you flew over the house this afternoon, I thought my heart would burst with joy."

"You have made my life very rich," he said. "At times when I am in a grim meeting with men who can think of nothing but weapons and strategy, I picture you and Dawn in this house and know that I will be seeing you soon and that the things that happen around me are not nearly as important as they seem."

She sat down next to him. "I am grateful to you."

"There are some things I want to say to you," he said. "They are difficult for me to put into words but they must be said. But first I will tell you that the past three years have been joyous ones for me, and if it were possible I would marry you and adopt the daughter who already belongs to me."

"I am content," she said. "I told the cook you will be staying for dinner, and it is my fervent wish that you will spend the night."

"Now the gift," he said, "and the words that go with it." He took a small box from his pocket, held it in his hand. "There is a tradition in my family that was given to me as soon as I could understand words. My father told me that in times of adversity I was not to be afraid because true success came only from what seemed to be defeat."

His eyes were downcast, the velvet box turning in his hand. "This is a token," he said, handing her the box. "I am sharing my belief with you."

She opened the box with trembling fingers. The circle of jewels glittered against the black velvet. It took her a moment to recognize the design of the brooch, a bird with wings spread to the limit of the circle on either side. "It is a phoenix, my lord," she said. "Are you trying to tell me that we face a time of ashes?"

"It may seem that way," he said. "I received word this morning that my father has suffered a stroke."

"I am very sorry."

"Since he is feeling very mortal, he wants the comfort of knowing that there will be a male heir to continue his line. So my wedding has been scheduled in February and I will be going back to Tokyo next week."

She was suddenly cold. She looked toward the door to see if it had come open, but it was firmly closed, and she knew the chill was from inside herself. She sat very still, not wanting him to see her feelings.

"We have talked of this day many times," he said.

"Yes, my lord."

"I will be gone no longer than a month or so. And when I come back everything will be the same between us."

I want to believe that with all my heart, she thought, running her fingertips over the sparkling surface of the diamonds, emeralds, and sapphires, but she could not. *You will make love to another woman, who will bear your child. The gift you hand me is one of farewell and remembrance.* And she was certain in this moment that once he left, she would never see him again.

Tokyo . . .
February 1936

LATE ON THE afternoon of his wedding day, Ito sat in the Western-style library of his father's house, across the table from his father's business manager, a round little man named Otani who handed documents to Ito one at a time.

"Since the Esteemed Baron's illness," Otani said, "he wants you to examine those properties which you desire to keep, those which you would like to sell, and those which will merge with the businesses of your new wife's family."

"I understand," Ito said. "I will go over the properties. And now you must excuse me, Otani-san."

"Certainly," Otani said apologetically. "I would not disturb you at all on your wedding day, but the Baron's astrologer advises that these decisions should be made by the second of March, and that leaves you something less than a week."

"*Arigato,*" Ito said just as the telephone rang and Otani departed with a bow.

Ito picked up the telephone to find his friend Major Hirota of the military police, the *kempeitai,* on the line. "I do not like to bring you trouble on your wedding day," Hirota said. "But I need to know your schedule for tonight."

"We'll follow the traditional schedule with some changes," Ito said. "Watanabe-san will leave her family home at nightfall. My mother insists on a brief ceremony at the shrine, and then we will come back here for the banquet and the *san-san-kudo.*"

"It's snowing very heavily."

"I believe the trip to the shrine will be made by horse carriage."

"Will your father be along?"

"He's not well enough for that. Do you think the threat of a *gekokujo* is that real for tonight?"

"I have nothing definite, but I believe the young officers will start their rebellion tonight. And I know for a fact that your father is on the list of government officials they intend to murder. So I am pleased your father will stay home tonight."

"I am grateful, Hirota-san. Please keep me informed."

He put down the telephone, listened to the sounds of activity in the house, the preparations for the great feast. He stood at the window, watched the heavy flakes drifting down, the mantle of white on the roof tiles and the heavy beams of the house, the unbroken layer of snow to the massive wall and the trees that surrounded the estate. Then he turned and picked up the small portrait of his prospective bride, which had been presented to his mother. Ariko, this slender twenty-year-old with a pretty face and large eyes, was more of an unknown to him than the manufacturing plants controlled by his father. The shyness of this delicately boned aristocrat made her seem remote and austere, and Ito could feel nothing toward her one way or another. He looked forward to the wedding itself with neither anticipation nor dread, already thinking past it to the things that must be done before he returned to Shanghai.

The wedding evening was pretty much of a ritualistic blur. Ito wore his dress uniform rather than formal clothes, endured the carriage ride through the snow-filled darkness to the shrine for the prayer before Ianagi and Izanami, the two mythical beings who had given birth to the ancestor of Japan, the Sun Goddess, Amaterasu Omikami. Ariko's face was barely visible through her thick white veil, shielded by the large round hat designed to conceal the horns of jealousy, as her hand touched the ceremonial knife suspended from her neck by a cord, the knife with which she would take her own life should she dishonor him.

When the ceremony was finished and the wedding party emerged from the shrine, the snow was heavier and the old-fashioned carriages and horses were already waiting, the families seated according to strict protocol. The Colonel was edgy. During the ride back to the mansion he watched the streets for the least sign of any unusual activity, but the veil of snow and the darkness obscured his vision and the lights from the large houses were dim and distant. As the carriage turned into the gate of his father's mansion, he glimpsed the bowing gatemen and realized that the house was totally unprotected.

At the dinner he tried to participate in the joy of the *san-san-kudo* as he and Ariko drank from three wine cups each, in turn, the three times three, nine-sips pledge, but he was very much aware of his father sitting at the table, dressed in a formal kimono, physically present though part of him was lacking. The right side of his face was drawn down, as if by an invisible string. His right eyelid drooped, his speech was still slurred, although his mind appeared to have regained its former sharpness. A middle-aged retainer sat with him to assist him in his eating.

After the ceremonial dinner the Colonel excused himself and asked for Major Hirota.

"What news do you have?" Ito said.

"We have the possible ringleaders of a *gekokujo* under surveillance," Hirota said. "But there are so many of them, we can't guarantee that we can stop any attack before it starts."

"What other precautions are you taking?"

"We have flying squads ready to move the moment there is trouble anywhere in the city."

"Can you give me two soldiers for my front gate and two for my back?"

"Can't you arm your servants?"

"They're not professional fighting men."

"I'm trying to stretch too few men in too many directions," Hirota said. "But I can give you one *kempei* for each gate."

"*Arigato gozaimasu,*" Ito said. "You are a good friend."

"I'll have them there within the hour."

He went back to the celebration, the toasts, and the congratulations of the family friends, the repeated references to the good luck he would have since his wedding day was a *tai-an* as well as a *kichi-jitsu*, a good-luck day according to the calendar and a day of great peace as cast by an astrologer.

Before the guests embarked for home the Colonel called his friend at the *kempeitai* again.

"All quiet so far," Hirota said.

When the gates had closed behind the carriages carrying the guests, Ito saw his bride depart to be prepared by the maids for her wedding night, his mother going along to counsel her. He stayed in the Western drawing room with his father, who sank into a leather chair and then dismissed his retainer with an abrupt wave of his hand. In a thick voice he asked his son to pour them each a brandy.

"You pay far too much attention to rumors," the Baron said, once he had the beaker of brandy in his hand.

"You know what's being said, then?"

"Of course," the Baron said. "Every year there's a suggestion that the young officers are going to have a *gekokujo* and oust the old guard. But it hasn't happened so far. And who are the soldiers at our gate?"

"I didn't think you would notice. They're *kempei*."

"I only had a stroke. I'm neither blind nor senile," the Baron said. "This is still my house and you should have asked my permission."

"I apologize, Honorable Father," the Colonel said. "I'm about to incur more of your wrath by my suggestion, but I intend to make it anyway."

His father said nothing. His right eye, glassy from the stroke, seemed to reflect the light.

"I have been informed that should there be a *gekokujo* tonight, that you have been marked for assassination because of the stand you took against the military budget."

"So?" the old man said. "I would feel slighted if I had been excluded."

"I want you to sleep in the guest quarters tonight, in the east wing."

"I sleep where I please. I don't like the east wing or I would have made my bedroom there in the beginning."

"If they make an attempt on your life, they will know where to find you."

"Then I'll sleep with a pistol at my side."

The Colonel sighed. "I mean no disrespect, Honorable Father," he said, "but you cannot now defend yourself. So you must allow me to make these decisions."

"When I'm dead you make the decisions in this house. And now I don't wish to talk about such matters anymore."

"But—"

"I mean what I say," the old man said sternly. "Now, I'll tell you what I want from you. A grandson. So tonight, when you are putting your seed into your wife, you think of battles, successful battles, and you remember the face of the Emperor at the very moment your seed shoots forth. Can you remember that?"

"Hai, so desu, Honorable Father."

"Then I am going to bed now," the Baron said. He struggled to rise from the chair, using his one good arm to push himself upward, and as if by magic his retainer materialized through the door to be at his side. "Remember," the Baron said. "The Emperor's face."

Once his father had gone down the hallway, Ito put on his greatcoat and went out into the snowstorm, which was so heavy now that even the light he carried seemed shut down to a glow in a white fog. He tramped his way to both gates, found his gatekeepers and sergeants from the *kempeitai* at the front and back, admonished them to be especially watchful, and then went back into the house.

Ariko had not yet come into the bedroom but the futon had already been rolled out on the mats. In the storage closet a few feet from the bed, Ito put his loaded pistol as well as his sword. Then he took a steaming hot bath, attempting to free his mind from the potential violence of the night.

In his night kimono, he came back to the bedroom and found himself alone with his new bride to repeat the *san-san-kudo,* and then Ariko, in her shy but eager responsiveness, seduced his mind from all the problems of the night. He made love to her with tender aggressiveness, aware that she was still virginal, and he took great pleasure in her, knowing from her responses that she shared the same feelings. And when at last he knew that he was out of control, he almost laughed aloud, for at the moment of ultimate release the face of the Emperor came floating into his mind, and he thought how obedient he was to his father's wishes after all.

Afterward, as he lay by her side in the darkness, he heard her voice, soft, gentle, assured. "I know that I will give you a son," she said.

"And how do you know that?"

"You will think me foolish, but at the exact moment I knew that a son had been planted within me, Honorable Husband."

He reached out to pull her to him, and just at that moment he heard a shriek of alarm from somewhere in the house. He had grabbed his robe and retrieved his weapons when he heard his mother's agonized cry, unmistakable.

He ran down the corridors of the great house, the screams echoing, until he reached the door to his father's bedroom, where he found his mother holding on to the arm of a young Japanese soldier with such force that the man could not shake her, though he struck her in the face repeatedly. The soldier was making one more attempt to break free, to reach his pistol, when with a cry of vengeance Ito lunged at him with the sword, the blade entering his chest.

Ito's mother was weeping, unable to speak, but one hand gestured toward the bedroom. He rushed inside to find the outside screens broken away, the snow blowing into the house, the body of the dead retainer sprawled over the threshold.

In the snow, like a woodprint, he saw two soldiers dragging his father, leaving a trail of blood that made a brilliant red pattern in the snowdrift immediately outside the house.

He raised the pistol swiftly and focused on the soldier to his father's left. The bullet caught the soldier in the middle of his back, spun him around. He fell in the snow, lifeless.

The second soldier was left to bear the entire weight of the old man but he could not, and the Baron sagged into the snow. Ito fired again. This time the bullet only wounded. The soldier limped away and was lost to sight within a short distance.

Ito leapt out into the snow, barefooted, and ran to his father. He was staggering back with him toward the house when servants materialized to help him carry the Baron into a warm room. The Lady Ito ordered one servant to call a doctor and another to bring her basins of water and clean cloths.

But Ito knew that his father was dying. He had been stabbed repeatedly through the chest and then slashed by a sword.

Ito covered his father's body to the neck while his mother gently wiped the blood at the corner of his mouth, making soothing sounds, as if her husband were a small child in need of comforting. And Ito felt a terrible pain of his own.

The Baron whispered something, words that were garbled by the blood in his throat. Ito knelt with his ear close to his father's mouth. "Do not take revenge."

And then, without another word, the Baron died. And his son gave forth a great cry of despair.

As soon as he could, Colonel Ito made a tour of the grounds. The assassins had come in through the back gate. One of them had scaled the wall to come up behind the *kempei,* cutting his throat. The servant had been run through the chest. The two bodies lay where they had fallen, already covered with a mantle of snow. The men at the front had been killed as well and the gate left open.

The Colonel ordered the servants to carry the body of the soldier in his father's bedroom out to the yard. They laid it beside the soldier he had shot. The wounded soldier had reached the car and escaped.

A call from a distraught Major Hirota gave him the names of the other victims of the night. "I don't know how many are dead," Hirota said. "They attacked the War Minister and the Prime Minister, the Finance Minister, the Grand Chamberlain, and the Lord Keeper of the Privy Seal."

"You have failed my family," Ito said. "You should have sent more *kempei.*" The rage was apparent in his voice. "I will not forget this, Major."

"I had no more men to send. We were spread too thin."

"What action is to be taken now?"

"Shirinai," Hirota said. "I don't know. All is chaos."

"I'll talk to you again when I've been to the Foreign Ministry," Colonel Ito said. "In the meantime, find out what you can."

At dawn he tried to reach the Foreign Ministry and found that barricades had been erected around a square mile in the center of the city where the government officers were housed. Guards from the First Division handed him a printed copy of a manifesto.

He went to a hotel on the Ginza and called the Foreign Ministry, and was informed that none of the senior officers were available and that a blanket order had been given for all personnel under the jurisdiction of the Foreign Ministry to await further developments.

Ito was filled with a deadening fatigue at the thought of how his life had been irrevocably changed, not only in the ways in which the attempted coup would influence his future with the government, but personally as well. For with the death of his father, he had now become the Baron Ito, in charge of the vast business interests belonging to his family and personally responsible for the estate and the grounds. He told himself he could not consider that now. He went to a hotel tearoom, the rebel pamphlet still clutched in his hand.

The pamphlet was concerned primarily with *kokutai,* the national essence of the country, and its corruption by the conservative old men who surrounded the Emperor, men who urged moderation and nonexpansionism. It was the younger army officers who had revolted.

From the window of the tearoom he could see the barricades in the snow near the Diet Building. Nothing moved. He was certain that the senior naval officers would not accept this army bid for power, and it could very well result in a battle between the two services.

The Colonel went home and called in the Shinto priests for the preparation of his father's funeral. He told his grieving mother and his frightened wife that the funeral would be held in two days, without any display of public acclaim; there was still no certainty that the violence was over.

He called the Foreign Ministry again and finally got through to a vice minister named Yonai, but Yonai had nothing concrete to report. The Emperor had just made a pronouncement that was so vague as to be meaningless, and the government had just placed the center of Tokyo under the official control of the rebels.

"The navy will be the key," Ito said. "What do you hear of naval movements?"

"The Combined Fleet is steaming for Tokyo. They're within a couple of days."

"And the outlying army units?"

"They can't agree on what should be done."

That afternoon the priests arrived. Ito's father's body was cleansed and purified, then dressed in a formal kimono and laid out, with the head to the north, a white cloth covering the features, the hands clasped together. The offering to the gods had been placed on a small table near his father's head, the specially washed rice called *semmai* and a bowl of clear water, along with a small spray of flowers. The Baron's ceremonial sword was also on the table against the invasion of evil spirits. Ito paid his respects to the body and the spirit of his father and then left the house.

He walked in the snow back to the barricades. A corporal stopped him, the bayonet on the end of his rifle fixed at ready.

"You cannot pass, sir," the corporal said, his voice edgy.

"Then run me through, idiot," Ito said, and shoved past him and asked for Captain Anami, one of the ringleaders of the *gekokujo* who had signed his name to the manifesto. The Captain had headquartered himself in the Sanno Hotel, and when Ito entered the building he saw soldiers painting the tablecloths into rebel banners. He found Captain Anami sitting at a table where he was writing with a brush on a piece of paper. The Captain looked around, irritated, to find who had admitted this intruder into his presence.

"Do you sit in the presence of your superior officers?" Ito demanded.

Anami stood. "I would advise you to leave this place, Colonel. I cannot be responsible for your safety."

"Nor can I be responsible for yours," Ito said. "Your forces killed my father, the Baron Ito."

"*Ah, so desuka?*" Anami said. "It was regrettable."

"Then you don't deny that this was on your orders."

"I take responsibility for the actions of my group."

"In that case, I could pull the pistol from my belt and shoot you through the head and win merit for it."

"There would be others to take my place."

"But none quite so daring," Ito said. "I don't intend to kill you, not because I lack the desire or the courage, but because you are going to see reason before this is finished."

"The Emperor will support us. We have that assurance."

"You have piss in a sake cup," Ito said. "You have nothing except a watered-down reflection of what someone thinks the Emperor might feel. This is 1936 and not a time for you to be playing the part of a rogue samurai. And if you think the Emperor will permit you to weaken this country, you're mistaken."

"We also have popular support."

"Only because opposition has not yet been marshaled against you. When the warships pull into the bay and when the army divisions converge on the capital, then see how much popular support you have."

Anami sat down again, took off his thick glasses, and polished the lenses with a handkerchief. "If you wish to take vengeance, Colonel, then do so. Otherwise, I'm very busy. I will send official condolences to your father's house this afternoon."

"My father instructed me not to take vengeance," Ito said. "But I will stay here until you surrender to the proper authorities."

"We *are* the authorities now," Anami said. "If you stay, people will think you have joined us."

"No one would believe that."

"Then I ask you with all due respect, Colonel, not to attempt to talk any of my men into surrender. The feeling is running very high here. What we do is for the national essence. We will not be dissuaded."

Ito removed himself to a corner of the lobby where he sat in full view of Anami, and there he remained for hours, waiting for the moment when Anami would be forced to give in, for he could not believe that this act of gross insubordination and mass murder could be allowed to go unpunished.

The Colonel watched the gradual dissolution of the spirit of victory that had prevailed when he first entered the hotel. He heard the radio reports from men in the field as army tank units rumbled into the capital. From where he sat he could see one of the tanks at a street barricade, parked, engine smoking.

The outside loudspeakers had begun to blare, urging the rebels to give up and stating that any man who did not would be considered a traitor by the Emperor. Through the window Ito saw an advertising balloon rising with a trailing banner that proclaimed in bold red characters: IMPERIAL ORDER ISSUED. DON'T RESIST THE ARMY FLAG.

When Captain Anami came out of his office and asked Ito to have tea with him, Ito knew the moment had come. He rose from his chair, stiffly, and followed Anami into the office.

"You have no idea, Colonel, how many of my men have wanted to kill you," he said, handing him a cup of tea. "Most of them were sure you were a spy, here to observe and remember names and actions should the time come when the tide might turn against us."

The tea was balm for Ito's parched throat. He said nothing.

Anami's face was weary. "So I ask you, Colonel, what are you doing here?"

"I am here exactly for this moment," Ito said. "You have brought me in to ask a question. So ask it."

Captain Anami picked up a pencil in his two hands as if gauging the length of it. "There are destroyers in the bay. The navy has landed men in a number of positions. I know of your experience with the navy in Shanghai. So I ask you, Colonel, what will the navy do if we hold to our position?"

"They will rejoice," Ito said, his voice rasping.

"Rejoice?" Anami said, puzzled.

"Your men have killed or tried to kill three of their senior admirals, Suzuki, Saito, and Osada. Your men are in direct disobedience to the will of the Emperor. With every minute that you delay, the chances improve that they will be able in all conscience to use their naval guns to demolish this building and a dozen others you occupy." He sipped the tea again. "They would enjoy destroying you because they can blame the whole army for not disciplining you sooner. And in the end, the navy can take control."

Anami looked at him directly, sternly. "Are you telling me what you truly believe?"

"If you are calling me a liar, Captain, then I have the right to kill you despite my father's advice."

"I apologize."

"I am an army colonel. I don't want to see the navy take control any more than you do."

Anami nodded. "We cannot hold. It is not right that we should try." He called in an orderly, dictated a statement.

During the afternoon the rebels began to drift away from their positions, and Ito made a call on General Araki of the Imperial Army to tell him that there was no need for a final military action against the rebels.

The General agreed and included Ito in the small party of officers who went to the Sanno Hotel to confront the rebel leaders who had stayed behind. The General walked into the ruins of what had been the dining room and stared straight at the officers who stood at attention. "I can understand that you acted according to your consciences," the General said. "And I admire the courage and spirit that you've shown, as misguided as it has been. I therefore give you the chance to die like samurai, to take your own lives and spare yourselves and your families the shame that you have created for yourselves."

Captain Anami stepped forward, bowed slightly. "We have considered hara-kiri, Esteemed General," he said. "But we choose to submit to courts-martial where we may make public statements regarding the corruption we see in our beloved country."

"That is your choice," the General said.

Ito spent another week in Tokyo. He went through his father's businesses, decided to sell none of them for the time being, and assigned Otani-san to meet with representatives of his new father-in-law to discuss appropriate mergers. He saw his father cremated, the form carried out, watched the city return to normal with the threat of the *gekokujo* now resolved, at least temporarily. But he knew the matter had not ended, for the public was dramatically fickle, and by the time the trials were held the Emperor might well have withdrawn to his marine studies and allowed the spark of expansionism to burst into flame once again.

The new Baron had a final dinner with his mother and his wife, who had paid the *osatogaeri*, the obligatory first return to the home of her parents, and had now settled in to keep the Lady Ito company. They both wept at his parting.

It was only on the train, as it steamed toward Yokohama and the ship that would take him back to Shanghai, that he thought of Yuki and the child and allowed himself the pleasure of contemplating a reunion.

Shanghai . . .

YUKI WAS SITTING in her office going over some designs with Yvonne when she received a call from one of her friends at the Japanese Consulate. She listened without saying a word, and then put down the telephone.

"You look very pale," Yvonne said when Yuki had finished the call. "What's happened?"

She took a breath, and said as calmly as she could, "There's a report that Colonel Ito was killed by assassins at his house on his wedding night."

"No," Yvonne said, genuinely shocked. "Is that definite?"

"Nothing in this world seems to be definite anymore," Yuki said.

Yvonne stood up, the gold bracelets jangling on her thin wrists. "You don't need to be worrying about business at a time like this." She closed her leather portfolio over the sketches. "We'll talk another time, my dear."

"The designs are beautiful," Yuki said. "There's really nothing to talk about. We'll go ahead with all six of them."

Yvonne leaned down, pressed her cheek against Yuki's. "If you need me, call me."

"Thank you," Yuki said.

Yuki could not move from her desk. She was aware of the babble of voices from the busy shop, and she knew she should call Yin and Yang and tell them to take on more seamstresses to produce Yvonne's new designs, but she was frozen where she was, and she tried to imagine what life would be like if the rumors were indeed true and Ito was dead. She opened the large drawer of her desk, removed the money box, and looked at the bundles of bank notes she had saved to pay him back for his investment in the shop, as if to convince herself that he must be alive, for there were so many things unfinished.

She heard Dawn's laughter from the other room, and she knew she could not face her daughter without breaking into tears. She put the money back into the locked drawer and summoned Elder Sister.

"I will be out for a while," she said. "Please take care of everything."

"I will, madame."

Yuki walked through the cold streets in a daze, without seeing, stumbled into a Buddhist temple to kneel and ask that Ito-san be returned to her alive. *He is the only father my child knows. Please do not allow him to be taken away from us.* She took a ricksha to the Japanese Consulate in the hope there would be further information by now, but the door was surrounded by a mob of people waiting to read a hastily written communiqué tacked to the wall, which told her little more than she already knew. There had been an army uprising, casualties. More details would be released through the newspapers and the radio stations when they were available.

She took the ricksha back to Nanking Road and stopped by a shop to buy a *daruma*, a doll with blank eyes and a weight in the round bottom, and then she composed herself before she went back to Blossoms. She did not want to upset Dawn. She forced herself to check all the orders due out that evening and then managed to tell Yin and Yang about the new designs. She saw that Dawn and her amah gathered up all Dawn's toys to put in the car. And once they were at the house she told the cook to prepare dinner and then took the *daruma* to Dawn's room, where the child examined it with fascination.

"Where are the eyes, Mama?" Dawn asked.

"It is a *daruma* doll for Ito-sama," Yuki said. "We will fill in one eye and then make a wish that Ito-sama will have a safe return from Japan, and when the wish comes true we fill in the other." And she rolled a brush in a *sumi* block and guided Dawn's hand to place a black pupil in one eye, feeling that the petition had more power since the eye had been filled in by an innocent child.

After dinner she sat with Dawn and allowed her to paint with the brush and ink while Yuki listened to a Japanese broadcast, frustratingly aware that the authorities in Tokyo were holding back any details of the military uprising until it was resolved. That night, in the darkness of her bedroom, she decided that until she had definite news, she would continue to believe that Ito-san was alive and would come back to her when he could. He was a military officer, after all, and he would certainly be pressed into service against the uprising and be so occupied he could not get in touch with her. Too, the rumors were notoriously unreliable; the story of the Emperor's death had been corrected. The confirmation of Ito-san's safety was just a matter of time.

By the next morning she felt confident. She went through an ordinary day filled with faith that the telephone would ring at any moment and the word would come to her that he was alive and well. Two more days passed in silence and she changed the story she told herself. After all, he had just been married and it would not be fitting for him to contact her so soon. She wanted to call Sam to see if he had any information, but she could not bring herself to do it. Finally she called Ryoko, who still worked at the listening room and this time was given some halfway specific information.

"The rebellion has been contained," her friend said. "But there were a number of casualties among high-ranking officials."

Yuki's mouth was dry. "What about Colonel Ito?"

"Hold on a minute. I'll check the list I have. Yes, here it is. There was an Ito-san killed. But there's no mention of his rank."

"Can you find out for me?" Yuki said. "I want to know whether it was the Colonel or his father, the Baron."

"It's hard to get information, but I'll try."

That night she was at home reading to Dawn from a book when the call came.

"I have some information," Ryoko said unhappily. "This is unconfirmed, but it was given to me by an army captain who just called from Tokyo. The man who used his influence to persuade the rebel officers to surrender was Baron Ito."

"Baron Ito," Yuki echoed. Hope died within her. "The Baron lived."

"That's what I was told."

"*Domo arigato gozaimashita.*" She replaced the telephone on the hook.

"Read some more, Mama," Dawn said.

"Later, perhaps," Yuki said. "Mama doesn't feel well."

Dawn turned the page. "I am going with Ito-sama tomorrow," she said. "He is going to give me a ride on his motorcycle."

"Not tomorrow," Yuki said numbly.

"When, then?"

"I don't know, *chi chai.*" She put her arms around her daughter, feeling that they were quite alone in the world now. For the past few days she had kept him alive in her mind, breathing. Now she knew it had all been an illusion. He was no longer on this earth. The ceremonies had already taken place and he had been reduced to ashes in a burial urn. The thought was unbearable.

The next morning she called Blossoms and canceled her appointments for the next four days, until the night of a reception at the Cathay Hotel, which would require her presence. Then she booked passage for herself, Dawn, and the amah on a steamer going upriver, and by noon they were moving against the swirling yellow waters. She sat on the deck in the thin sunlight on the lee side of the boat and endured her grief without expressing it, wondering as the settlements on the bank grew more primitive if the soul of Ito was now on a journey too.

Which world are you in, my lord? Where does your spirit dwell?

She debarked upriver and checked in at the walled compound of a country hotel where she could see nothing from her window but bleak winter fields, and while the amah saw to Dawn she walked in the cold countryside until she was exhausted. She returned to her room and unpacked. She caught a glimpse of the phoenix pin, the diamonds catching fire, *ashes,* and she collapsed into bed, where she wept until she could cry no more.

On the morning they were to return to Shanghai for the reception, she knew her life was ended and yet she must go on. The boat pulled into the dock at four o'clock and she went home and had a hot bath, then went down to Blossoms to see that the right flowers had been sent to the Cathay Hotel. She wore a gown Yvonne had designed for her, blue, the color of loyalty, the phoenix pin worn for his memory. She wanted to wear white to show that she was in mourning. But then, she thought as she studied her face in the mirror and applied powder and rouge to hide the signs of grief, she had never had any claims on Ito-san, no formal ties to him, only the love that had been shared between them. She had no right to mourn him publicly.

The reception was in honor of a French vice-consul returning to Shanghai after a six months' leave. She went to the ballroom a half hour early with Elder Sister to make sure the flowers had been properly placed. Elder Sister had seen to everything, the center-pieces of roses on the table, the sprays of flowers brought in from the southern provinces to grace the bandstand, where the musicians, in black tie, were tuning up. Yuki decided to stay long enough to give her greetings to the French vice-consul's wife, who was one of her best customers.

"We'll have a glass of champagne, I think," Yuki said to Elder Sister, "while we wait."

"I don't think that would be proper, madame," Elder Sister said shyly.

"You have been responsible for making the room beautiful," Yuki said. "You deserve the credit and some of the pleasure." She stopped a waiter and handed Elder Sister a glass from the tray and then took one for herself. The guests had begun to flow into the room, and she was looking toward the door and waiting for the vice-consul's wife to appear when she saw the apparition. She could not hold on to the champagne glass. She handed it to Elder Sister quickly, then leaned against the wall to keep from falling.

"What's wrong, madame?" Elder Sister said, alarmed. "Are you ill?"

"I have seen a ghost," Yuki said. She closed her eyes and then opened them slowly. Not a ghost. Ito-san was alive, standing there in his full-dress uniform with the diagonal sash across his chest. Alive. Safe. Surrounded by people, chatting, laughing. She took the cham-pagne glass back from Elder Sister and drank it down. "I'm all right now, Elder Sister," she said. "You can go home now. And take a holiday tomorrow. You deserve it."

"Are you sure you're all right, madame?"

"Oh yes," she said. "Perfectly all right now."

Elder Sister murmured her thanks and Yuki watched her leave and stood where she was, unable to move until she was sure she would not disgrace him by weeping or throwing her arms around him.

She crossed the ballroom at the edge of the dance floor, avoiding the whirling dancers, and when she knew he had seen her she stopped, allowing him to free himself from a conversation and seek her out.

"I heard you had been killed." She flushed with excitement and there was a tremble in her voice as she spoke.

"I'm sorry for the confusion and pain I caused you. We have much to talk about," he said. "Will you be at home later?"

"Oh yes, my lord. How soon?"

"An hour or two. No longer."

She went home in a daze and, kneeling down, put her arms around Dawn. "Ito-sama will be here soon," she said. "I want you to have your bath now and eat your dinner. He will want to see you."

"Will he take me on his motorcycle?"

"Not tonight but soon." She kissed her daughter, sent her with her amah to the far wing of the house. Trembling with excitement, she warmed the sake that Ito liked and then sat in a chair by candlelight to wait. She heard the bell as he came into the house and then she could restrain herself no longer. As he entered the room she ran to him and wept without restraint, the words pouring out of her while he held her to him, one hand stroking her hair, comforting.

"I was so afraid, so terrified, because I thought you were dead, and I cannot live without you."

"The reports were confused. I took my father's title on his death. I have been trying to get a message to you for the past three days."

"I was gone, not here." She stopped crying. "I apologize to you, my lord. I am most humbly sorry that you should have lost your father, and I have been weeping for myself. Please sit down. I have sake ready."

He held her a moment longer and then sat down and accepted a cup of sake, stretching his feet out to the log fire in the hearth. Then he started telling her things he would say to no other living person.

"When my father died I killed two men," he said, the sake cup in his hand. "The first I stabbed with a sword and the second I shot. And when I carried my father back into the house I was filled with such anger that I wanted to destroy the two men all over again, and when I sat quiet in the hotel to bring reason to the rebels, there was a part of me that wanted to see them all beheaded for what they had done to my father. And yet I sat, knowing that sooner or later my voice would be needed. But I don't know which was the Japanese part and which the Western. Did the desire for blood and greater vengeance come from my ancestors? Or was it the desire to take action that was Western and the infinite patience that was Japanese. I don't know."

"Is it important to know, my lord?"

"Most important. I must be totally Japanese, without the contamination of any Western thoughts. Yet when I sat in the Sanno Hotel I found myself wondering what Cummings-san would have done in the same position."

"And what was your answer?"

"I did not allow myself to proceed to an answer."

There was a light rap on the door. Ito waved at Yuki to stay where she was while he opened the door. Dawn stood there in her nightdress, the one-eyed *daruma* in her hands, and Ito picked her up joyously and held her in his arms.

"I wondered where you were," he said.

"Mama has been crying," Dawn said. "You won't go away anymore?"

"Not if I can help it." He saw the doll. "What's this?"

"Since you have come back, the *daruma* needs another eye, I think," Dawn said.

"So she does," the Colonel said, putting her down. "We need a brush and a *sumi* block." And when Yuki had provided it he rolled the brush on the wet ink block and then handed it to Dawn. "You fill it in, please," he said.

Dawn put in the other pupil with great care and then gathered the doll up, allowing nothing to touch the wet eye.

"Now, off to bed," Ito said. He gave her a kiss. "And I'll play with you tomorrow."

Once the child was gone the Colonel looked after her with great fondness. "I have missed her very much. She is as my own," he said.

"Yes, my lord."

"Now, what have you been doing?"

"Living in fear and prayer," she said. "And now that you are safe and home, I want nothing more than the chance to make love with you and watch you sleep."

She looked at the phoenix pin, the jewels alive in the candlelight. *All true after all,* she thought. *My life has come back from the ashes.*

Washington, D.C. . . . June 1937

AFTERNOON IN HER town house and Adele had settled down with a glass of white wine. She finished reading a letter from Sam filled with everything that had happened during the spring of 1937, then she picked up the telephone and called Roger Cummings, who was now the Under Secretary for Far Eastern Affairs. He seemed delighted to hear from her.

"How are you, Adele?" he said. "You're surviving the hot weather, I trust. I hear of you now and again."

"Good things, I hope."

"The word is that you've recouped your fortune. I wouldn't be surprised if the Secretary of the Treasury called on you shortly to discover your secret."

She ignored her brother-in law's attempt at humor. "I was wondering if you're free for dinner this evening," she said. "I know it's terribly short notice, but I'm having a few senators and congressmen in."

"I suppose I could make it," Roger said. He knew well the advantage of rubbing shoulders with some of the men who controlled his destiny. "What time?"

"Why don't you come early, around six-thirty? We'll have a little chat, the two of us."

"Six-thirty it is, then," he said.

He was on time, peering at his watch as Adele answered the door. He accepted a scotch and soda and then sat down on the powder-blue divan in her large living room, squinting up at a painting on the wall. "Interesting painting," he said.

"It's a Picasso. Do you like it?"

"I always have trouble with paintings when I don't know what they're supposed to be."

"They're supposed to be worth a lot of money," Adele said with a smile.

"A good point," Roger said. "I appreciate the invitation this evening, Adele, but I can hardly believe that I suddenly came bobbing to the surface of your mind just in time for a dinner party."

"I want to talk about Sam. I have a letter from him about the consul in Shanghai, a Mr. Alcott."

"Eugene Alcott, yes," Roger said. "Very much a legend in Asia. He was a close friend of Sun Yat-sen, you know, as well as the famous Sassoon. He's the last of a breed of men."

"I understand he's currently ill."

"Yes," Roger said, nodding. "There's no secret about that. When a man reaches his age something always gives way."

"I'll get directly to the point," she said, cutting off his reminiscences. "I want Sam appointed consul there when the current consul dies."

"No, I won't appoint him."

"Why?" Adele said, stunned by an answer she did not expect. "He's competent. You know that."

"I could have brought you a copy of the last full report on Sam," he said. "It would have saved a lot of time. But I'll try to summarize it for you. I intended to give Sam the spot, you see, but I had to make routine inquiries, and when they came back I decided to let the matter drop for the time being."

"Let what drop? I don't understand."

"I never collect facts the first time around, only rumors. And in this case the rumors around Sam are negative. Everybody in Shanghai thinks the world of Sam, both professionally and personally, but he doesn't have a chance of being the top American there."

"I don't understand what you're talking about."

"To put it bluntly, a consul general has to be a man above reproach."

"You're saying Sam is not?"

"According to unofficial reports, Sam had an affair that resulted in a child born out of wedlock. The mother and the little girl are still living in Shanghai. The woman in this alleged affair is Japanese, and there's a strong current of anti-Japanese feeling in Washington at the moment." He drank the scotch, spilled some on his vest, dabbed at it with his handkerchief. "So I haven't carried it any further. That way it doesn't get entered in the official records."

She was stunned. Her hands were suddenly icy. The past intruded for a moment and then she set it aside. "You mean he's being denied a promotion on the basis of a rumor?"

"I don't think it's best for him to be promoted at this time."

"That's ridiculous," Adele said. "The whole thing could be malicious gossip."

Roger seemed to be studying the shape of some ostrich plumes feathering from a tall vase. "There are times, Adele, when it's circumspect not to ask questions—since there's every chance of getting an answer you don't want."

"Then you're saying that you know these rumors to be true."

"To my satisfaction, yes," Roger said. "Otherwise, I would have ordered a complete investigation. After all, he *is* my nephew."

"And he's my son," Adele said. "If I can bring you proof that there's nothing to it, will you reconsider?"

"Of course," he said, and only then did what she had said strike him. "Bring me? Did I hear you correctly?"

"Yes," she said. "I'm going to Shanghai myself."

Shanghai . . . July 1937

As THE SHIP turned up the Whangpoo, the Chinese delta, green with crops in the summer heat, brought a wealth of memories to Adele's mind. They were not welcome.

She had been on a similar ship just before the War to End All Wars, with Sam and Arnold at her side. Arnold's enthusiasm had been boundless.

"My God," he had said, putting an arm around her shoulders. "Look at *that*, Del. Have you ever seen anything like *that*?"

She had thought, at the time, that there was something lacking in her because she did not instantly know what *that* referred to. For her, Shanghai was a stinking city filled with filth and poverty.

As the months passed she reached the point where she could no longer understand Arnold at all—he had become a different man. At first she thought she was imagining things. After all, it was only natural that his business should occupy all his time at this point. He was making money hand over fist and all of their friends seemed to adore him.

"Del, darling, you must feel like the luckiest woman on earth to have him as a husband."

The American Consulate had occupied a mansion on Bubbling Well Road, where they stayed because Arnold had done business in the Chinese trade with the consul general, a large, expansive man named Hilger. They drank a good bit together and played billiards in the billiard room while Adele entertained herself by reading in her room or sat watching Mrs. Hilger do needlepoint of the Chinese character for "good luck" in multiple versions and colors to send to her nieces and nephews in the States for Christmas.

At night Arnold would come to the bedroom smelling of scotch and wanting to make love. She couldn't respond. But she felt that her dissatisfactions were abnormal. The people around her seemed to be having exciting, happy lives.

She tried to adjust as the years went by, and then, one morning in early summer, as she sat at an open window of the old consulate looking down into the gardens, she watched a Japanese gardener, a strong, handsome man, trimming a hedge. And then she heard laughter and saw a young Japanese woman in a floral summer kimono playing hide-and-seek among the banks of flowers with a little girl, catching her up and swinging her in the air while the child squealed with laughter. Adele was transfixed, moved by the tableau of the mother and daughter and, on the terrace, beaming down at them, the husband. They were so beautiful and unrestrained in their feelings, so complete in each other.

Romantic nonsense.

She closed the window with a bang and drew the curtains. But she could never again persuade herself that a life of pervasive boredom was natural. She could not tolerate the thought of gliding into old age, needlepoint in hand, while her husband went his own way, adventuring, as if her preferences were nonexistent. And then the great indignity had occurred, and when Sam was twelve she had taken him back to live in the States.

Now, standing on the deck of a ship approaching the same wharf, so many years later, she was convinced that the way to survive was to reshape those things about her which she found so terribly imperfect. And she was not about to allow Sam's future to be ruined by romantic nonsense. He would have to be tough to rise in the world. If she could do nothing else for him, she would force manhood upon him.

A steward walked along the deck ringing a gong. She looked down from the railing to see if she could spot Sam on the dock, but she could not. Only when she reached the bottom of the gangplank did she see the blackboard with her name on it, carried by a handsome if slightly dissolute-looking man in his early forties who recognized her instantly and came forward with a broad smile.

"I'm so sorry, Mrs. Cummings," he said. "But your son is up-country at the moment, very sticky times here, you know, and he sent me to take care of you. My name is Connaught, but I've never been one to stand on formality. Most people call me Harry."

"And where is my daughter-in-law?"

"Indisposed, I'm afraid. But if you'll allow me to retrieve your luggage, we'll get you through customs and be on our way."

She watched him operate as he moved her through the customs house, knowing where to give bribes of money and where to smooth the way with jokes in Chinese. She had the strangest feeling that she was going to need his services before she was through.

When Sam came back to Shanghai in mid-July he found the city in turmoil, the Chinese Settlement networked with trenches and sandbags and a flotilla of warships from a dozen different countries strung out like a fence in the middle of the river. He checked in at the new quarters of the American Consulate, which occupied three floors of a modern hotel, and was on his way to see Consul Alcott when Dawes popped out of his new office.

"What the hell is going on?" Dawes said. "All I get is rumors."

"There's been a large-scale confrontation between the Japanese and the Chinese at the Marco Polo Bridge outside Peking," Sam said. "Each side is blaming the other, but it really doesn't make a hell of a lot of difference who's right. Everything's upside down. Nanking is calm and everyone seems to be going crazy here."

"I've taken the liberty of changing money again," Dawes said. "The traders on Szechuen Road are frantically upping the Chinese dollar one minute and the Japanese yen the next. When you have time we might decide on a cutoff point."

"Use your own judgment for now," Sam said. "I haven't been home yet, and I want to check in with the old man."

Dawes shook his head. "Just don't be surprised at anything."

"What do you mean?"

"You'll see for yourself."

There was a nurse in attendance at the suite that served as Alcott's quarters. And there in the sitting room, which had been outfitted as an office, Alcott sat at his desk, smoking a thin cigar and looking like a specter of death, as if his flesh had shrunk away from his body, leaving only skin and bones. His translucent skin had a yellowish cast to it, and when he looked up from the paper he was reading, there seemed to be a pall over his eyes, as if he were seeing everything from a great distance.

"There you are, Cummings," he said. "Come and sit down and tell me how things are in Nanking. I hear the Chinese and Japanese are at it again." He placed one frail hand against his robe over his breastbone. "They will always be at it, don't you see? Because both have civilizations and cultures based on the denial of the value of individual human life and a belief in supernatural credit for dying properly in battle for the homeland. And you can't really have the honor of that kind of death without a war, now can you? Have you read the glorification of the three Japanese soldiers who made themselves into a human bomb to demolish some barbed wire? Foolishness, of course, because they actually started to drag a pipe bomb and the damn thing went off, but who's to say they wouldn't have blown themselves up if they'd had the chance?" He waved his hand for the nurse, told her it was time for his medicine and for her to serve Cummings some refreshments. "Well, there we are, aren't we?"

The nurse gave Alcott an injection in the arm, which he accepted as a blessing. He smiled when the feeling of relief spread over him. He pulled his sleeve down. "Tell me something, Cummings. How do I look to you?"

"Terrible," Sam said.

"Ah, thank you," Alcott said with a bright smile. "You have no idea the number of people who are constantly telling me how very well I look. Christ, I'm dying. I know that." He pulled his glasses up on his nose and peered at Sam. "I have recommended you for my replacement," he said, "but you probably won't get it because you couldn't keep your dong in your pants. I have never thought there was much correlation between the two because I've never seen a man run a legation with what he had below the belt. It's what's between the ears that counts." He looked around. "Goddamn," he said. "She didn't serve you tea."

"It's all right," Sam said. "I just stopped by on my way home, Mr. Alcott. I'll come back in the morning and give you a full briefing."

"Take care of your health," Alcott said, eyes burning. "The whole of the Orient is teeming with bacteria that take advantage of any break in the skin. You can't afford to minimize. Death can creep up on you over here without your knowing it."

Sam had a staff car take him home through streets already beginning to pile up with refugees. He could not shake the image of the dying Alcott from his mind. For the old man, time had collapsed. Sam knew the incident of the three Japanese and the pipe bomb had happened five years before. He was suddenly very weary. And there was still his mother to face when he got back to the mansion.

She was there waiting for him as the car drove up. He looked at her standing at the door and thought what a handsome woman she was. But not beautiful, because beauty to him required some softness, and there was none to be found in her.

Had there ever been a streak of gentleness there?

The moment he was out of the car Adele took charge of him— dismissed the driver, called Majordomo to take care of the luggage, gave him a brief embrace, and then led him into the drawing room.

"I want to let Charlotte know I'm home," he said.

"She'll see you soon enough. I've come all the way across the Pacific and I deserve some time with my son." She surveyed the carved teak liquor cabinet. "I had your liquor restocked," she said. "Charlotte didn't seem to mind."

"I think you've finally come to the right country, Mother," he said, amused. "If we could just persuade the Japanese and Chinese to let you take charge, you could sort the whole damn thing out in three days."

She took two glasses from the cabinet, poured scotch into them, handed him one.

"For God's sake, sit down, Mother. Light someplace."

She perched on the edge of a leather chair. "Now," she said. "We need to have a frank talk."

"How was your trip? How's Noble?"

"I don't want to talk about either my trip or Noble. Why didn't you write us that Charlotte is pregnant?"

"Because we just found out about it the day before I went to Peking."

"It seems that you're proving your virility all around," she said, and he could feel the weight of the sarcasm.

"Meaning what?" he said.

· 269 ·

"You know what I'm talking about. Is it true that you have a child by a Japanese woman?"

His sense of amusement began to evaporate. "I don't think that's any of your business."

"None of my business?" she said, startled. "Who took care of you, reared you, provided your education? It wasn't your father. He was never around. So don't tell me it's none of my business."

"I'm very tired, Mother," he said, rubbing his forehead. "But I'm glad you brought up the subject. I want to talk about Father."

"There's nothing to say."

"I think there is," he said, looking directly at her. "Do you know all the facts of his death?"

"As much as I want to know. It makes no difference."

"It makes a hell of a lot of difference," he said. "I have every reason to believe he didn't kill himself but was murdered at the orders of the Green Gang by a Chinese general named Wang."

"There's nothing to be gained by pursuing this," Adele said. "Arnold's dead. And my relationship with him is ended."

"Didn't you hear me? Father did not commit suicide. He was murdered." He could see no change of expression on her face, no sense of surprise or shock. "Ah," he said. "You knew about his relationship with Bright Moon a long time ago, didn't you?"

"I don't intend to discuss your father's past," she said evenly. "There's nothing to be gained by going over a situation that is beyond all possibility of change." She swirled her glass, the ice ringing against the crystal like wind chimes. "But we are going to deal with an area where changes can be made. I won't allow you to ruin your life."

"I'm not ruining my life. Whatever happened is in the past. It's over and Charlotte and I are very happy together," he said.

"And what about your career?"

"I'm doing all right," he said. He stood up, carried the drink to the French doors that opened onto the terrace. "I have a separate business going and I'm making a lot of money. My work at the consulate is fine."

"Fine?" she said, as if he had just uttered an obscene word. "Do you really believe that what you've done is regarded as 'fine' back in Washington, where it really counts?"

"I damn well do," he said. "I've received no complaints from the Foreign Service."

"Only because your uncle has spared you," she said. "Nothing derogatory is ever forgotten in Washington. You may think you can afford to be cavalier about having a bastard, but your uncle can't even investigate because he knows it would be confirmed as true. It would go on your record and ruin your chances for promotion."

His anger simmered just below the surface. "We'd better put this talk off for a while, Mother," he said. "You've been through a long trip and I've had a hell of a jolt seeing Alcott so sick. I don't want to get involved in a battle with you at the moment."

"All right," she said. "I apologize. I understand you've done a good job here, that you've kept Washington well informed about what's going on."

"I think I've been effective in my job, yes," he said.

"Couldn't you do more to bring about a peaceful settlement if you were the American Consul General?"

"Mr. Alcott is the Consul General."

"And Mr. Alcott is dying."

"Unfortunately."

"Death is a fact of life," Adele said calmly. "We know he's dying and others know it as well. So there will be competition for the post."

"I'm not going to scramble for the position held by a friend who's still alive, for God's sake."

"I'm not asking you to," she said. "I just want to know about the child you had by that woman. There are steps we can take to neutralize any adverse effects caused by your indiscretion."

Majordomo appeared at the door, rapping on the doorjamb with his knuckles to announce his presence. "Big master catchee callee by telephone?"

"Yes. I'll take it in the study."

"Think about what I said," she said as he left the room. She stood at the open door to the terrace and drank the scotch without tasting it, reminded of Arnold by the way Sam walked, the ambling stride. Sam was like his father in many ways, but she would see that in his case Sam turned himself around.

The following day she called Connaught and arranged to meet him at the tearoom of the Cathay Hotel. She had investigated Connaught shortly after her arrival, using the services of an English lawyer.

Connaught was already at a table when she arrived. He stood up, smiling, handsome, dressed in a white linen suit befitting the heat of the season. He took her hand with the finesse of a man who loved women.

"I'm delighted that you called, Mrs. Cummings," Connaught said. "I was hoping you would accept my offer to show you around the city, especially at such an exciting time."

She smiled coolly. "I want to hire you, Mr. Connaught," she said.

"I'm at your service, Mrs. Cummings," he answered with a gracious smile. "But as a friend, not as an employee. I already have a situation, as they say."

"I don't require any continuing work," she said. "I just want your signature on a piece of paper admitting that you fathered Yuki Nakamura's child."

Her words eroded his smile. "I'm afraid, madame," he said in a quiet voice, "that you have either over- or underestimated me. In any event, you have most certainly selected the wrong man for what you have in mind."

"On the contrary," she said confidently. "I'm sure you're the right one. I'm willing to pay handsomely for it, exactly seven thousand three hundred twenty-one American dollars, as a matter of fact. That is the right figure, isn't it?"

He looked at her evenly over the top of his glass. "That's a familiar figure, yes, Please go on."

"I'd suggest you pay very close attention to what I have to say," Adele said. "I've had some research done on you, Harry, and although the American Consulate must suspect parts of your history, they certainly don't know it all or you wouldn't be retained. In the first place, you drink absinthe, which will guarantee that you don't need to conserve your resources for your old age because you won't have one. You have seduced every eligible woman in sight. You owe the seven thousand three hundred and twenty-one dollars in gambling debts at the Mexican casino and you have absolutely no financial resources."

Connaught sipped from the glass, rolled the wine around his palate before he swallowed it. "I truly love women and that's a fact," he said. "Some people may consider that a weakness, but I've always known it to be one of my stronger suits. I have always loved them, *and* I have yet to take a penny from any of them."

She ran an index finger around the rim of the crystal wineglass and studied him carefully. "I'll even pay you a bonus of five thousand dollars above the gambling debt."

He seemed to ignore her as he snapped his fingers for the waiter, an elegant-looking white Russian in formal clothes. "Boris," he said. "Would you be so kind as to find out what my tab is as of this date?"

"Certainly, sir."

He watched Boris make his way through the tables, and then he looked at Adele. "You're a bitch, madame, there's no escaping that fact. But generally I find that a woman becomes a bitch only because she's been badly hurt and doesn't know how to be anything else."

Boris returned, handed him a pad on which a figure was written. "I have no secrets from this lady, Boris. Please tell her how much I owe here."

Boris squinted at the figure on the pad. "I believe, sir, that it is something in the range of eleven hundred American dollars."

"Is the management worried about my payment of the bill?"

"On the contrary, sir," Boris said, flustered. "If you would like the manager to tell you the same thing himself . . ."

"That won't be necessary," Connaught said.

"May I bring you anything else, sir?"

"No, thank you, Boris."

Connaught leaned over the table, clasping his hands in front of him. "I'm sure you won't mind, Mrs. Cummings, if I make a few suggestions. This isn't Washington and things are done differently here. I have always owed gambling debts and the casino is not the slightest bit concerned about eventual payment. I can continue to play with house money there as long as I am capable of signing a chit."

"You do value your job at the consulate," she said. "I know that. And you must know that I won't hesitate to have you fired. I have that power." She opened her purse, took out a paper. Then uncapped a fountain pen and handed both to him. "Just sign your full name on the line. And if there's any questioning of the signature, I will expect you to verify the information in the statement."

He shook his head. "In my own way, Mrs. Cummings, I make life easier for everybody at the consulate. There's no difficulty they can get into in Shanghai that Harry Connaught can't take care of. They all know precisely what I am and they accept that. And if you were to have me fired, they would simply hire me again under a different category." He glanced at the sheet of paper, then shook his head with a pronounced sadness. He capped her fountain pen and handed it back to her. "You're trying to do quite a terrible thing, Mrs. Cummings, but I suppose you know that."

She folded the paper, put it back into her purse. "I won't give you another chance, Mr. Connaught."

"Nor I you, madame," he said. "There are few unforgivable things in my lexicon of sins, but a cold heart is one of them."

She stood up, removed a handful of Chinese dollars, and placed them on the table. "For the wine," she said.

"The money will be a handsome tip for Boris," he said with a slight smile. "As for the bar bill, I always pay by signing."

She left the hotel, with rage, but she had not given up. There remained now a confrontation with the Japanese woman herself, one that the whore could only lose. She set off down the street for the Japanese woman's shop.

She was startled at what she found. She had expected a hole-in-the-wall establishment, but instead there was a large shop with an elaborately decorated sign in script: *Blossoms*. She opened the door to find herself in a combination garden and tearoom, a clientele of fashionable women, the oriental waitresses in fashionable gowns. She asked for Yuki Nakamura and presented the hostess with a calling card.

The hostess disappeared momentarily, then came back and indicated with a bow that Adele should follow her down a hallway to an office that opened through French doors into an outside garden. Adele was momentarily ill at ease, for the young woman who presented herself was not at all what she had expected. She had seen whores before, all the way from street girls to courtesans of high-ranking officials, and Yuki did not resemble any of them. She was a delicate woman with porcelain skin, hair the blue-black color of a raven's wing combed back and held in place by a ruby-studded comb. She was wearing a tea gown with a pattern of boldly colored flowers on the flaring skirt.

A parrot sat in a cage over a small French desk, talking to itself in Chinese.

"I am very pleased to meet you," Yuki said in flawless English. "May I offer you tea?"

"My business here won't take that much time," Adele said.

"I think I know why you're here," Yuki said, and before Adele could stop her she had called out for Dawn, who came in from the garden dressed in a spotless frock, a beautiful little girl, all knees and elbows. There was something about her eyes and her smile that reminded Adele of Sam. "Darling," Yuki said to her daughter, "this is Mrs. Cummings. I wanted you to say hello to her."

"How do you do?" the little girl said gravely.

"Very well, thank you," Adele said. For a moment something within her felt as if it might break. "How old are you now, my dear?"

"Five or six, depending," Dawn said.

"Depending on what?"

"On whether you're Japanese or American," Dawn said solemnly. "Since you're American, then I would be five to you."

"You can go back to the garden now, dear," Yuki said, and Dawn curtsied and went out the door while Adele stared after her, transfixed, remembering the mother and child in another garden in Shanghai.

"I think I will sit down after all," Adele said. "And I will have tea."

Yuki rang a silver bell, gave orders to a servant, and then sat down in a chair across a glass table, pouring the tea herself when the tray was brought in. "Do you take milk, lemon?"

"Neither," Adele said. She accepted the fragile porcelain and breathed deeply, trying to sort out the confusion of her feelings, frightened at their strength.

"I've heard a great deal about you," Yuki said. "I'm pleased to meet you at last and to give you the chance to see your granddaughter."

"I didn't come here for that," Adele said. She drank her tea, gauged the delicate opulence of the room while she gathered herself up and made adjustments in what she was determined to do. "I came to discuss Sam's future."

Yuki's eyes were puzzled. "Perhaps you don't realize, Mrs. Cummings, but Sam and I haven't been together for a long time."

"I'm aware of that."

"I have no effect on his future."

"But you do. The fact is that your daughter stands in the way of Sam's becoming the American Consul General here."

"I see. And where is your information from, Mrs. Cummings?"

"From Washington," Adele said. "I'm a very rich woman, Miss Nakamura, and I have some power as well. Sam's father was a trader in the Orient and I have extensive contacts here."

"I'm pleased for you. But that has nothing to do with me."

"More than you know," Adele said. "I'll pay you fifty thousand dollars."

"I beg your pardon?"

"That's what I will pay you the moment you move back to Japan with your daughter. By the time you sell this business here, you should be quite wealthy. And my contacts in Tokyo will help you establish any kind of business there you would like. Perhaps another fashion shop."

"I am very content here," Yuki said. Her tone was harder now. "I have no desire to move."

"If it's a matter of the amount, I will pay one hundred thousand. If I were you, I would take it. If you think you can establish a claim against Sam's inheritance or his fortune somewhere down the line, you're sadly mistaken," Adele said.

"I think we have nothing else to say." Yuki's soft voice trembled with emotion.

"I have a great deal to say. I am going to protect my son, one way or the other. I will also pay you fifty thousand dollars if you sign a paper to the effect that my son is not the father of your child."

"If that's what Sam wants, he has but to ask me. It will cost him nothing."

"My son is a very stubborn man sometimes. So it has to be enough that I say it's necessary." She removed the paper from her purse and handed it to Yuki. "I can obtain an affidavit from another man to the effect that he fathered your child."

Yuki glanced at the paper. "Connaught?" she said with some surprise.

"Yes."

"The paper isn't signed."

"I can find a dozen men who will agree to sign this paper. And what do you suppose that will do to your daughter's future, to have something like that hanging over her head?"

"Nothing," Yuki said. "It is not such a sin here to have a love child."

"You don't want to make an enemy out of me," Adele said. "As a friend, I can be most generous."

Yuki stood up with great dignity, but her face was flushed with anger. "I am not for sale," she said. "Not for one dollar, not for one million dollars."

Adele wanted to smash the porcelain on the floor and throw a crystal vase through the window, but she did not. "Then we have nothing else to say to each other. Good day, Miss Nakamura."

Out on the street, she calmed herself with the realization that there was no problem here. She could have a paternity certificate signed by any male and sworn to in a court of law. And in this godforsaken city she would have no trouble finding a thousand men willing to swear to carnal knowledge with the Japanese woman.

With Alcott incapacitated, it fell to Sam to see to the thousand and one details of running the consulate. He attended innumerable meetings with consuls from the other legations, but the meetings ended in fruitless letters to Chiang Kai-shek and to Prince Konoye, who had formed a cabinet in Tokyo, urging a peaceful resolution of their differences.

Early one afternoon when Sam stopped by to see Consul Alcott, he found him struggling to get into his formal clothes while the Chinese nurse stood weeping at the side of the room. Alcott stood propped against the footboard of the carved Chinese bed in which he had slept for almost half a century trying to raise a shrunken leg to insert it into his trousers. When he saw Sam come into the room he immediately brightened. "Ah, friend Cummings," he said. "Just the man. Come and help me."

Sam looked at Alcott's face for any sign that he had finally slipped beyond rationality, but the old man's eyes were unusually bright. "It looks to me as if you're doing a fine job of terrifying your nurse," Sam said, steadying the old man's arm as he put his pants on.

"Pay no attention to her," Alcott said. "The Chinese are great ones for using tears to try to get their way. This inscrutable Oriental business is absolute nonsense."

"If you don't mind my asking, sir, just where in the hell do you think you're going?"

"That's quite apropos," the old man said with a smile. "Although you have no way of knowing it. Now, I have to rely on your steady hands for the waistcoat and the tie and particularly the shoes. I have always been one for observing the proper form and I think you should remember that. I had a conversation with the Empress Dowager a long, long time ago in which I explained to her very carefully why I could not kowtow to her. As a man, of course, I could stand on my head in her honor, and as a private citizen I undoubtedly would have, but as a representative of the United States of America, as the physical embodiment of my country, I simply could not do it. She understood, of course. She pretended not to hear it at all, but I was aware that protocol demanded that. By hearing but *not* hearing, then no one loses face." He sat down on a bench. "I should regard it as a great favor if you would put my shoes on for me. I have reached the point where I cannot manage that at all."

His foot was so thin that Sam had to draw the laces tight to keep the shoe from falling off. "Where are we going, sir?" he said.

"You'll make a worthy successor," Alcott said. "You'll help me?"

"Of course," Sam said. He called for a car to wait at the hotel entrance while Alcott, putting his weight on an ebony cane with an ivory head, forced himself to his feet.

"If you would be so kind," he said. "My card case is on the dresser. I shall need that."

Sam handed it to him and Alcott put it in his vest pocket. "I am really combining business with pleasure," he said as they descended in the elevator, his hand resting on Sam's arm. "I want to see my fine city once again."

Sam seated him in the car very carefully, for the old man was frail, brittle, with no substance to him at all, as if the lightest of breezes would waft him away. "I shall leave the route up to you," Alcott said to Sam. "I intend to visit all of the major foreign legations and I want to drive along the Bund and through the Chinese cities, and finally to the cemetery. You know the one."

A bright, sunlit day, and Sam was grateful that there was a cool breeze off the river. The old man rolled down his window and, closing his eyes, filled his lungs. "Can you smell that, son?" he said, exultant. "Quite unlike any other smell in the world, a great city, life and death, growth and decay, all the opposites crammed together. A wonderful stink, the true smell of life."

As they turned up the Wei Nalloo, flanking the river, Alcott called for the car to stop. He peered at the line of Chinese junks and sampans, freighters and houseboats maneuvering across the muddy yellow waters between the South Suburb and Pootung on the other side of the river. There was a dull explosion and smoke from one of the junks. It began to settle slowly into the water while the crew scampered along a plank to the next boat in line.

"Ah, poor ignorant souls," Alcott said. "They'll sink their own boats in the hopes of stopping traffic on the river." He told his driver to move on. "That's one thing you must remember to convey to

Washington repeatedly. We can never think of China as we do of the United States. They are an upside-down, inside-out people. And I have loved them so."

They drove through the Japanese Sector, the streets filled with disembarking marines and trucks carrying supplies to military depots, and when they reached the Japanese Legation, Alcott insisted on getting out of the car by himself. Obviously in great pain, he made his way up the short flight of marble steps one by one, ringing the bell to be admitted through the polished door, reappearing a moment later, his top hat firmly in place, only the beads of sweat on his ashen forehead showing what the effort had cost him.

The car moved away, and now Alcott wanted to go through the great steel gate near the North Station, crossing from Hongkew, where the Japanese were erecting barricades, to Chapei, where the Chinese were trenching the streets and putting up sandbag walls.

"Light a cigarette for me, if you please," Alcott said with a thin smile.

"A cigarette's the last thing you need," Sam said.

"Almost. But provide me with one anyway." And when the cigarette was lit he blew the smoke into the warm air. "Someday when the history of this coming war is written, I believe it will be shown that neither the Chinese nor the Japanese wanted it. I also believe it will be shown that the volleys of bullets fired at the Japanese troops at the Marco Polo Bridge came not from the Kuomingtang Forces but from a delegation of Communists who wished to provoke the war we are about to have. I should say *you* are about to have, not I."

He managed to make it through the doors of the French Legation and out again, and this time, as he sank into the car seat, it was evident he had no energy left. "I am afraid, young Cummings, that I have the energy for but one last stop, and you know where that will be. I have never talked much about my wife, the grand darling woman, but let nobody lead you to believe otherwise, when you part with a mate of a lifetime, the heart falls in upon itself with a grief that knows no bounds and cannot be communicated. I was grateful that she went first, because she allowed the thought of death to terrify her, especially mine, and sometimes in the dark of the night she would say to me, 'Promise that you shan't go first.' And I promised and God, whether he be American or Chinese, allowed me to keep that promise, because it wouldn't have done, you see, for her to have stayed here by herself, to have been left alone."

The car went northwest into the countryside past the university and finally to an Anglican cemetery with a black cast-iron fence and a gate with a cross worked into a fanciful circle. Alcott stopped the car again, nodded toward the cross with a smile. "I was on the committee to put up the gates," he said in a voice that was now barely audible. "We had a metal worker named Feng who kept making the bottom leg of the cross too short. He did that about three times and finally I drew him to one side and explained the significance of the cross, that it represented the place where Jesus was crucified. And Feng explained to me, 'I Christian boy. So when thisee boy build cross, makee damn short so big-time Jesus can climb down easy.' " He laughed, remembering. "So the cross has been left that way, and I'm sure that metal-worker Feng, God rest his soul, entered into heaven on the strength of that one glorious statement." He peered through the window. "Left at the next turn, and up the rise about twenty yards."

When the car stopped he reached up and took a flower from the limousine vase. "I can make it from here by myself, thank you," he said. Departing the car, he walked across a stretch of grass beneath a tree to a rugged stone with only a small rectangle polished to contain the name and date incised in both English and Chinese. He sat down on the grass and Sam could see that he was talking to his wife, running his fingers over the rough surface of the rock that had endured a million years. And then he seemed to fall over, and Sam was out of the car in an instant, running across the grass to where Alcott was lying on his side. "Help me sit up, please," he said.

Sam lifted him to a sitting position, and Alcott, almost frantically, pulled his card case out of his pocket and with a pencil began to initial the cards. "You must deliver these cards for me," he said. "All the legations. Proper form. Sorry I cannot in person fold the corner to pay my respects." His strength gone, the cards fell in his lap and he looked into Sam's face. "I wish to be buried here. With her. Chinese fashion. My hair is not to be cut. No nails trimmed. Everything just as it is." He gasped for breath. "That's a prayerful order . . . young Cummings."

"Yes, sir."

Sam thought of signaling the driver, who stood by the side of the car anxiously awaiting orders, of a mad rush for help, to try to stay death awhile longer from a man who had readied himself for it. Instead, he knelt beside Alcott and cradled him in his arms and

Alcott nodded and with a sigh accepted the touching and looked up with fading eyes at the sunlight flickering through the foliage of the tree. "Not . . . so bad," he said in a last audible whisper. "Nothing . . . to fear." And then his breath drained from his body and he died.

Sam continued to hold him, and with a free hand picked up the card with the elaborate raised printing containing Alcott's name. And written in pencil were the letters *p.p.c.*

A diplomatic necessity.

An abbreviation of the French inscription:

Pour prendre conge.
I bid you farewell on leaving my post.

And sitting there in the grass with the old man in his arms, Sam began to weep.

The protocol officer threatened to cable Washington, but Sam was stony in his firmness. "You may do so if you wish, Mr. Nedwin," he said. "But I must tell you that if State doesn't uphold you, which they will not, then I will ask for your immediate transfer."

Nedwin ran a hand over his thinning hair and looked around at the disorder of Alcott's office as it was being sorted out. "We were friends, the old man and I," he said, as if everything could be justified by that remark. "And if he personally requested it . . ."

"He did," Sam said.

So the old man was given a Chinese funeral procession for which Sam paid the costs himself. The coffin was the most ornately carved teak that could be found in the Chinese city, painted in the most garish colors, and it was placed atop a motorized palanquin that resembled a pagoda on wheels. He hired a hundred professional mourners to precede the hearse, banging gongs to drive away the evil spirits, and to follow along behind, wailing with such sincerity one might suppose they knew the man whose procession they formed.

The Anglican priest did not bat an eye, for he was an old China hand, as Alcott had been, and the mourners lined the back of his church and punctuated the formal service with cries of such forlorn pain that the stained-glass windows of his church shook in the steel forms that contained them. And finally, at the cemetery, there were two ceremonies, Anglican and Buddhist, and Alcott was lowered into the ground, his name and his Chinese chop already engraved on the smooth plaque in the ancient stone next to his wife's.

There had never been such a funeral, Sam thought, with representatives from all the legations, including the Japanese, and a hundred or more Chinese children scattered around the cemetery to witness the shooting off of the firecrackers.

Sam was the last of the mourners to leave, aware that the Chinese gravediggers were waiting respectfully in the trees, ready to fill in the gaping hole in the earth.

His prayer was a short one, nonspoken.

Please makee walls of heaven damn short one time only so your servant Alcott can climb over easy.

On the evening after the funeral Sam called a meeting of the members of the American Legation in a conference room on the third floor of the hotel.

"I realize that I don't have the proper credentials to call this meeting," he said, in deference to the presence of the protocol officer, who nodded his head wisely, as if to say that the verbal caveat was sufficient to excuse the violation of the rules. "I have sent the following cable to Cordell Hull, Secretary of State, with a memorandum to Roger Cummings, under Secretary for Far Eastern Affairs.

" 'We, the members of the American Legation at Shanghai, China, wish to inform you, sir, that as of this day, Mr. Horace Eugene Alcott, Consul General, has died after a long illness and we have conducted funeral ceremonies for him in accordance with his wishes. It is out of no lack of respect for Mr. Alcott that we have decided not to observe an official period of mourning. We feel that these are critical times indeed, that what appears to be an impending war is taxing the capacity of our personnel here to the limit, and that there is no time to pay proper homage.'

" 'We therefore request the immediate assignment of a replacement for Consul Alcott, at least on a temporary basis until the State Department has selected a Consul General.' "

He put the paper down on the table. "I took the liberty of signing this dispatch. Now, I consider it necessary to come to a consensus about what we should do next. We all know how slow Washington can be. So I think we should discuss those problems which concern us all."

Gradually, over the next hour and a half, Sam, who at twenty-seven was the youngest man in the room, gave the section chiefs full permission to do what they felt was right, knowing all the time that such permission was not his to give.

And when the meeting was over Dawes rode the elevator with him to Alcott's combination office and sitting room, where Chinese maids were packing all of his personal effects into trunks. "Did he have any survivors that you know of?" Sam asked.

Dawes shook his head. "Last of the line."

"Then I think we'll give what's left of his earthly possessions to missionaries to disperse among the Chinese."

"I think he would approve wholeheartedly of that," Dawes said.

Once Dawes was gone Sam studied Alcott's worn leather chair for a long time before he sat down in it, gingerly, looking around the room. No man, however capable, would be able to take Alcott's place.

The same afternoon, as he was going over correspondence that needed to be answered, Mrs. Worthington buzzed him from the outer office. "Colonel Ito is here to see you, sir."

"Thank you. Send him in, please."

He stood up as Ito came into the room, wearing his full-dress uniform. From the moment Sam shook his hand he was aware that something had changed between them, but he could not be sure that it wasn't due to the jealousy he felt toward this man who was now a father to Dawn. "It's good to see you again, Colonel. Would you care for a drink?"

"No, thank you. I will not be here that long. I'm here to offer my personal condolences for the death of Consul General Alcott."

"Thank you," Sam said. "At least sit down for a few minutes. A lot has happened to both of us." Ito sat down. "I hear you're about to be promoted to brigadier."

"Yes," Ito said. "And when that happens I will have to assume new responsibilities and new attitudes, whether I agree with them or not." He took a cigarette from his gold case, lit it. "So I wanted to use the excuse of this condolence call to talk as friends, off the record."

"All right. Nothing goes out of this room."

"I find what I have to say very painful. If I had come here as senior general from my consulate, I could be indirect and give you the speech that I may be obligated to make very soon outlining my government's position."

"Which is?"

"There must be no outside interference between China and Japan."

Sam sighed. "That says it all, doesn't it? Then a wide-scale war is definite."

"I'm afraid so."

"And there's no chance of third-party mediation?"

"No. I hope to make an official appeal to my government after my promotion, but I have little hope that it will be successful."

"If there's anything I can do to help, personally or officially, you know I'll do it."

"I thank you for your understanding," Ito said. "The time may come very soon when I will not be able to speak to you with any candor at all, and if that should happen, I ask you not to take it personally."

"I won't."

Once Ito had gone Sam stood at the window with feelings of sorrow and frustration, sorrow at the possibility that very shortly he and Ito would be unable to talk with any freedom, and frustration because the new Japanese insistence on no interference in their war with China was unnecessary. The American government would set no limits. And the war would be a bloody one indeed.

The whole procedure was far simpler and much less expensive than Adele had thought it would be. Her English lawyer, Yardley Adams, a young man with black hair slicked back against an aristocratic scalp, had a sullied reputation that was not wholly of his own doing. His mother had died in childbirth and his father had maintained an unsavory practice as a lawyer in Shanghai until he was finally shot to death by an unsatisfied client. Yardley had never been able to shake the reputation his father had left behind and now was well known himself in Shanghai as a practitioner in the gray areas of jurisprudence, passing no judgment on anything he was hired to do.

One afternoon Adele went to his office after telling Charlotte she was going shopping. Sitting there sipping a gentle green tea, she interviewed one at a time the dozen young men whom Adams had gathered. The applicants had been told only that a large stipend for an unnamed task would be given to the first man who proved suitable.

She rejected three English sailors and an American marine, none of whom had been in Shanghai at the time of the child's conception, two white Russians who spoke poor English and no Japanese at all. But when prospect number seven came through the door, she had a strong feeling he would do nicely, despite the fact that he was Chinese. His name was Ching. He spoke excellent English and could have been a handsome man five years ago. But now there was a tremor in his fingers, which held the brim of his Western-style hat, and a grayish pallor to his face above the collar of his Western shirt and tie.

Opium, she thought, remembering her early days in China.

"Do you speak Japanese, Mr. Ching?" she said.

"Yes, very good Japanese."

"Do you like Japanese women?"

Which way do you want me to answer? his eyes were asking. He shrugged, looked to Adams, found the answer in the lawyer's face. "Yes," he said. "I do."

"Have you worked with Japanese women, seen them socially? Since you speak Japanese, perhaps you've worked as a translator."

"Yes," he said quickly. "A translator."

"And I would imagine you have had many Japanese women in your time?"

"Had?" he said blankly, looking to Adams, who explained the word in Chinese. Then Ching nodded eagerly.

"Yes. Many Japanese women."

"Including Yuki Nakamura."

It was not a question and he knew it. He could smell success now, project himself past the sea of words that had to be crossed before he could lie on a narrow wooden shelf in a dark room and cook the round gummy ball and light the pipe. He allowed himself to be led, admitted the picture they drew of his life, aware that he was being guided, steered, gently directed, aware, too, that a Chinese stenographer had come into the room with her ink and brush to take down what he said.

I met Yuki Nakamura, yes, at a Communist meeting, at a time when the Chinese and Japanese Communists were working together, trying to expel the Western capitalists. She was new to Shanghai, I think. Yes, she was just here a few weeks, and we slept together many times. . . . Where? Many places. Once, when we were drunk, in the park along the river where we were nearly caught by the police. I brought her presents, and she liked me, and then she came to me and said she was going to have a child, my child, and I told her I could not allow a personal relationship to interfere with my work for the Party. I told her to choose an American vice-consul. Why an American? Because she was working there by this time as a translator. I heard her mention one by name and I thought it would do him damage. He was a capitalist. I would have picked the consul general himself, but he was an old man then. Dead, now. But even then it wasn't likely he had seed in his loins. Yes, I am the father of the child and I make this admission freely.

Quicker than it seemed possible, Ching was presented two copies of a statement in Chinese to which he affixed his name, holding the brush very steadily. Shortly, after a typewriter had finished its clicking, he was given an original and five copies in English to which he signed his name in romanized letters.

When he was finished the lawyer called in two secretaries to witness the signatures and then he affixed his own chop mark in red wax on each. He counted out five hundred dollars in American money into Ching's hand. Ching put the bills in the inside pocket of his suit coat and left the lawyer's office, his mind already moving on to the sweet smoke.

Adele paid Adams, then picked up one English copy of the affidavit, wrote across the bottom of it with her pen, "You have twenty-four hours to contact me before I make this public." She folded it in half, handed it to Adams. "See that this is delivered to Yuki Nakamura right away."

"She'll have it this afternoon."

"Can we prove this statement?"

"I can have fifty credible witnesses to anything in a day's time."

"Fine. Will you send a cable for me?"

"Of course. Write it down and I'll have it taken around the corner to the cable office immediately."

She addressed the cable to Roger in Washington:

I HAVE DISCOVERED THE TRUTH AND SAM HAS BEEN VINDI-
CATED. SINCE THE VACANCY LEFT BY THE DEATH OF MR.
ALCOTT REQUIRES FILLING, I NOW SEE NO REASON WHY
SAM SHOULD NOT BE PROMOTED. I WILL FILE A COPY OF

THE CONFIRMING AFFIDAVIT WITH THE PROTOCOL OF-
FICER, H. NEDWIN, AT THE CONSULATE. PLEASE CONTACT
HIM IMMEDIATELY FOR VERIFICATION.

ADELE

Outside, she could hear the sound of distant bombings from the
north part of the city. She gave the explosions little thought. Her
personal battle had been won.

The large room at the consulate that had been set up for the
processing of visas was full by nine o'clock and a long line wound
down the street. A rumor had passed among the street people, a sad,
false promise that the Americans, having seen the extreme disaster
of the 1932 war in Shanghai, had stocked provisions for this one so
that no Chinese child would go hungry. Now they were in line by the
hundreds, filing into the visa room one by one to be told that the
story was false. There was no rice to be given away, no special
evacuations from a war zone being planned.

Standing at his window, looking down into the street, Sam
watched his employees walking the lines, telling the Chinese that
there was nothing to be gained by waiting, but nobody abandoned
his place. Hope was the cheapest of commodities and the people had
nothing but time.

Then he heard the shelling begin from the river, the Japanese
warships opening up on Chapei from the south, joining the sporadic
artillery to the north of the city. He was handed a report that the
Chinese battalions were converging on Shanghai from the countryside. He knew he could wait no longer. He had to locate stores of rice
before it was too late to move around the city.

He made inquiries among the rice experts in the Commercial
Section and then ordered his driver to take him out to the home of
an English trader named Owenby near the university. St. John's was
at the edge of the city and Sam was surprised to find that the Englishman had a Tudor country estate, with a manor house on a
rolling slope that passed for a hill.

Owenby was in the midst of entertaining, his guests having tea
and small sandwiches on the lawn behind his house where they
could see the explosions rising from sections of Chapei.

Sam was greeted warmly and taken in tow by a British consulate
official named John Mandrake, who was dressed in formal clothes

and carrying a golf club on his shoulder as if it were a rifle. "We have a little pool going, Mr. Cummings," he said cheerfully. "The ante is ten pounds and you simply guess when the Commercial Press Building will be hit by shellfire."

"I'll consider it," Sam said. "In the meantime, can you direct me to Mr. Owenby?"

"Quite," Mandrake said, peering through the crowd. "Yes, he's over there, actually, the tallish chap with the mustache and the terrible golf swing. But don't wait too long for the pool. The latest report is that shells are already hitting structures a hundred meters from the Commercial Press."

Sam nodded and walked away. He approached Owenby and three other men who were dressed in golfing knickers and caps, driving balls down a long slope where a whole platoon of Chinese boys ran to hold up banners where the golf balls came to rest.

"Ten pounds on this shot," Owenby said, planting his feet, looking off down the slope. "The boy in the red shirt is at one hundred meters. The boy in green is not more than five meters from him. So I shall put the ball between them."

"Hate to take your money, old chap," Smythe said with a smile.

"Let me have five pounds of it," Murray said.

Owenby concentrated. The club came back and with a rush descended, clipping a piece of turf from the ground, sending the ball off in a shower of dirt. It curved off to the left, as if trying to escape into a grove of trees, bounced twice, and disappeared into the brush.

"Bad luck, old man," Smythe said sincerely.

"It's the damned club," Owenby said sullenly. "The shaft is all askew. I should have thrown it away months ago, but it was a Christmas gift from my wife. And what can one do?" He turned to Sam and smiled. "Ah, Mr. Cummings, how delightful to see you. You don't know me, but I know you, of course. I'm Oliver Owenby." He shook Sam's hand and then introduced him around. "Gin's the drink of the day, but Americans don't prefer gin as a rule, do they? What is your pleasure, sir?"

"I think I'll pass, thank you," Sam said. "And may I take you away from your guests for a moment, Mr. Owenby?" he said.

They walked along the top of the slope to the edge of a terrace where umbrella-covered tables had been set up for the elegant women who sat in the shade. There seemed to Sam to be no connection between this house with its manicured lawns and perfectly tended gardens and the lines of desperate Chinese packed into the street.

Owenby led the way into the formal garden, examined the roses with a frown. "Not a good country for roses," he said. "They require cooler weather. The summers are too damned hot. I'm really delighted that you came up. Your mother's here on holiday, isn't she? I've been wanting to have you and your wife for simply ages, but we all have our dog paths, don't we? I take it this isn't a simple social call?"

"I took the liberty of investigating the stores of rice in the Pootung godowns," Sam said. "You have thirty tons just across the river."

"Indeed and rotten luck," Owenby said. "You don't happen to have any upriver transport free, do you?"

"No," Sam said. "I'm here to offer you wholesale price, out of my own pocket, for distribution to the refugees."

Owenby shaded his eyes, the better to see Mandrake's swing and the glint of the ball in the light. "I wouldn't mind, of course," he said absently. "I'm not in favor of setting up such charities myself, but I've never been one to interfere with another man's beliefs. Wholesale it is, and I'll even provide transport if you can get word to my lorries at the godown." He shook his head as the Chinese boy waved a flag to signal a good shot. He smiled suddenly. "I have just had the most marvelous idea, old man. Why don't I send a car around to fetch your wife and mother for dinner? The bombardment will be really quite spectacular from here, and in case it falters, I've arranged for quite an exorbitant fireworks display."

"You're very kind, but regretfully we are already committed for tonight."

"I am sorry. Indeed so. Please convey my best to your family. And we shall have to arrange a little get-together. Very soon."

"Thank you," Sam said. "I'll send your comprador a check for the rice."

He left with a feeling of unreality. *My God, the British,* he thought. *They've made a game of war. Mad as hatters.*

As he rode back to the consulate he looked at this city he loved and thought how it had seemed to Charlotte when first she saw it, and how much she had changed since then. She was content now, loving, beginning to swell with his child, and one part of his life had ended as another had begun. For even as a part of him mourned the loss of

Dawn, knew that he would never hold her in his arms as her father, another part of him loved Charlotte and rejoiced in planning for the birth of their baby.

As he reached the consulate and the third floor, he put his personal thoughts aside. Dawes was on the telephone, checking the latest currency quotations, making a date with a broker for dinner tonight on the roof garden of the Cathay Tower to watch the fireworks. Nedwin was worrying over a party of United States congressmen who were determined to take the tour of the front offered by the Japanese military to journalists and any government officials who wanted to see the fighting close up. The tour was perfectly safe because the Chinese had yet to mount a significant offensive and the cordial Japanese offered a buffet at the briefing that followed the tour, complete with a free-flowing bar of fine Western alcoholic beverages, but Nedwin was concerned that the congressmen would be unduly influenced.

There was a strange atmosphere in the consulate today, Sam decided. Everyone was quiet, courteous, overly polite to him, and distant.

He ran into Connaught downstairs. "What's going on around here?"

"In what way?"

"You know what I'm talking about. It's as if the whole staff has something against me and I don't know why."

"Let's discuss this in my office. We're less likely to be disturbed there," Connaught said.

Sam followed him down the corridor to a cubbyhole littered with papers, memos in Chinese, a gallery of photographs on the wall, and a single open window, which looked down into an alley behind a restaurant. The sound of a shrill argument between two Chinese cooks mingled with the honking of geese confined to a bamboo cage. Connaught removed a stack of papers from a chair. "Sit down, please," he said. "And pardon the clutter, but I'm not really in the office all that much and I know where to find what I want."

"I don't have time for your notorious tact," Sam said. "What's going on?"

"There aren't any secrets in a consulate like this," Connaught said. "Too small and it's easy for things to be misinterpreted."

"What in the hell are you talking about?"

"Washington has chosen this time of all times to open a probe into the character of one Samuel Cummings in the form of an inquiry to Nedwin, who, quite by coincidence, I'm sure, received this by special messenger." He opened a drawer, removed a carbon copy of a deposition, which he handed to Sam, who read it with the conviction that the world had gone suddenly crazy. Here, on the letterhead of one of Shanghai's shyster lawyers, was a confession and an indictment of such outrageous proportions he could not believe it. A Chinaman named Ching was claiming to be the father of Yuki's child and labeling her a Communist in the process. Sam slammed the paper down on the desk.

"The son of a bitch is lying," he said. "Dawn is my daughter. I've never claimed otherwise." He looked at Connaught with sudden anger. "Does the staff believe I'm behind this?"

"They haven't said so, but I believe they do. If so, don't be too hard on them. Look at it from their point of view. The Consul General's position is open and it's no secret that old Alcott was fond of you and recommended you for the spot. It's also no secret that you would never get the position because of your sexual indiscretion. But now there appears a sudden affidavit, a deposition, whatever you want to call it, and Washington chooses this moment to question your character, which, after this cleansing purge by some well-paid wretch, will emerge pure and washed clean."

Sam stood up. "This is obviously a carbon. How many of these are there in existence?"

"I have no idea."

"How many have been circulated here in the consulate?"

"Only this one."

"Then how do you come to have it?"

"Because I told Nedwin I would talk with you about it."

Sam uncapped a pen and began to write.

I, SAMUEL CUMMINGS, STATE THAT THE CHING AFFIDAVIT IS A LIE. FURTHERMORE, I CLAIM PATERNITY OF THE FEMALE CHILD BORN TO YUKI NAKAMURA AND ASK THAT MY NAME BE REMOVED FROM CONSIDERATION FOR THE POST OF SHANGHAI CONSUL GENERAL.

He signed it, handed it to Connaught. "Have Nedwin cable this to Washington," he said. "I'll wait here for a copy, and I want you to notify the lawyer who issued this that if one more copy is circulated, I'll have his head."

"Ah," Connaught said, glancing at the statement and then to Sam with a thoughtful expression. "I think, old man, that there is something you should know, but I approach the subject with great trepidation."

"If it sheds any light on this, please tell me."

"I was approached by a certain person, whose name I am reluctant to reveal, with an offer to sign such a paper in return for a large sum of money."

"Why?" Sam said. "Who in the hell would profit by my advancement?" He put the palm of his hand to his forehead. "My God, *she* did this, didn't she?"

"I wouldn't even attempt to probe her mind for the 'why's' of anything," Connaught said.

"Why didn't you tell me she approached you?"

"We had what you might call words over this. I was rather certain she would abandon the whole idea." He looked out the window, where a row had developed in the alley, with the cooks from the kitchen beating back a family of refugees who were trying to steal the geese. "But you've solved the problem with your statement, I believe," Connaught said. "Since you've set things straight and withdrawn from the running, she's bound to let the whole thing drop."

"I'll deal with her," Sam said. He looked out the window at the flailing sticks, the fleeing refugees, the cooks in full pursuit. He was filled with a cold, and deadly, anger. "Indeed I will."

Yuki could hear the shelling of Chapei in the distance. She sat in her office, going over a stack of orders, while Dawn played with her paper dolls in the garden. One of Yuki's American customers had brought Dawn a Betty Boop cut-out doll with paper clothes and Dawn stood in the sunlight imitating the salesgirls at Blossoms, standing back and telling Betty how superb she looked and how she should have the dress in red as well as blue, pretending to write up the order while her amah sat in the shade, her crochet hook looping thread. Yuki thought of Ito and prayed for his safety, and as if the two men were joined in her mind, she thought of Sam as well. She had heard he was working with the Chinese. If only he stayed out of the battle zones . . .

Elder Sister entered, bowed deeply, and placed a letter in Yuki's hands. It took no more than a glance for Yuki to know what the document was and to read the scribbled message on the bottom of the single sheet. Furious, she crumpled the paper and threw it in the wastebasket.

Then, drawing a deep breath, she recovered the wad of paper and smoothed it out against the black lacquered top of her desk and read it again carefully, looking at the chop and the signature. So Adele had found someone. A Chinaman named Ching? The father of Dawn? The Communist Party? Impossible. No one would believe it. Abruptly, she leaned back in her chair, despair creeping in. *Wrong. They will believe it,* she thought. And even a story as preposterous as this could be damaging enough to ruin her.

She had been at a gala thrown by the British only last week when Mr. Smythe was expounding on the China problem. "The Communists are the real menace, don't you see? The ruin of all we've stood for in this country. Cancer in the body politic of China. All invisible, agents everywhere."

And should this monstrous piece of gossip, so crudely put together, gain widespread circulation, the first cancellation of an order would come directly from Mrs. Smythe herself, her telephone voice sweet and evasive. "I've been thinking . . . my dear . . . about the voiles . . . and let's put them off a bit, shall we?" And then another cancellation and yet another, all of them polite, no real explanations. There was no way to extricate herself from such a web of suspicion.

She picked up the telephone and through the Settlement operator got the number of Sam's house. She dialed it, spoke to a man servant who asked the question of Adele and then relayed her answer. Madame did not care to come to the telephone but Madame would be receiving until five o'clock. Yuki called for her car, told Dawn she would be back shortly, left the store in the capable hands of Elder Sister, and gathered her wits about her as she was driven down Bubbling Well Road. Adele already had her affidavit freeing Sam from his paternity. Obviously she wanted something further.

Sam was so furious he could not concentrate on his work. He sat at his desk and waited for confirmation that his message had been dispatched. In a few minutes Nedwin came into his office and, to Sam's astonishment, patted him on the back. "That cable of yours," he said. "It was a damn fine thing to do. You've proven yourself to be a gentleman."

A gentleman, Sam thought wryly. It was incredible that anyone should give a damn whether he was a gentleman or not while thousands of people within a radius of five miles were being blown to pieces or suffering from starvation and disease.

Mrs. Worthington appeared at his door. "This just arrived for you by special messenger, Mr. Cummings."

"Thank you," he said, taking the envelope. When she had gone he sat down to examine it. He opened it to discover thin sheets of paper covered with writing and a photograph, which fell into his lap. The picture sickened him. A Chinese man in the bloody tatters of a Western business suit. Dead. Tied to a wooden post the girth of a railroad tie, his face bloated, tongue bulging from the mouth, eyes protruding and ruptured, a thin line apparent on the neck from the garrote. Hung around the dead man's neck was a thin board inscribed *Han chien.*

Enemy of the people.

The first written sheet was from Comrade Li, a message short and to the point. "The enclosed is self-explanatory. The man's name was Ching. He was a member of the Party overcome by greed and the need for opium. He perjured himself for money and disgraced the Party. I humbly beg your pardon for his actions."

The other sheets were typical of Chinese confessions, row after row of Chinese characters admitting his betrayal of the principles of the Chinese Communist Party and the twelve brave men who assembled in Shanghai in 1921 to bring the Party into being, at great risk to themselves. He confessed all the sins of a misspent life, his headstrongness as a child, his weaknesses as an adult, which had led him to opium and alcohol, and specifically for this most recent weakness, to lying against a person unknown to him and accepting money from an American woman and a British lawyer for his perfidy.

Sam looked at the picture of Ching again and was filled with horror. His mother had caused the death of this man just as certainly as if she had killed him with her own two hands. *My God,* he thought. *I've got to get her out of this country before she destroys us all.*

He found a ricksha and began the slow, tortuous trip through the crowds of people to the docks. *The first ship, any ship,* he thought. *And you'll be on it, Mother.*

The car turned up the long, curving driveway to Sam's house and stopped beneath the porte cochere. No sooner had Yuki's driver opened her door than Majordomo emerged from the house, bowed to bid her welcome, and led her through a sitting room toward the terrace where Adele was waiting.

Yuki looked in vain for any sign of Sam as she walked through the room and she wondered if he ever sat by the small ornamental fireplace in the winter reading a book, or if he ever had a drink in the leather chair overlooking the lawns through a great diamond-paned window.

Then Majordomo opened the French doors onto the marble terrace and she saw Adele. Her instant thought was how well this older American woman blended with the riches that surrounded her, the Italian marble of the polished balustrade and the winged cherub balancing on the rim of a birdbath while water flowed from a vase in his stone hands.

Adele was dressed for summer in a light blue linen dress, her fair skin protected by the wide brim of a straw hat. She stood by a table, making a composition of pink hydrangeas in a cut-glass vase. She glanced at Yuki, then took the time to place one more stalk in the composition before she wiped her hands on a cloth and studied her work.

"It's very difficult to get the right amount of bloom with the greenery," she said. "But then, flower arranging is one of your many gifts, isn't it?"

Yuki looked out over the garden. Above the billowing tops of the trees was the long smear of smoke from the Chapei fires, riding the wind. "What do you want from me, Mrs. Cummings?"

"I want you out of China," Adele said simply.

"I see. Then the letter signed by this Ching was not enough?"

"No, I don't want any reminder of Sam's foolish mistakes left in Shanghai." A flame leapt out of Adele's golden lighter, touched the end of a cigarette. She exhaled the smoke into the warm afternoon air. "You really should have listened to my offer, my dear."

"How many copies of this man's statement have you circulated?"

"None," Adele said. "Otherwise, there would have been no point in asking you here, would there?"

Yuki touched one of the hydrangea stalks in the vase. "You put too much effort into the arrangement when the secret lies in simplicity." She paused, studying the flowers. "The man's statement is simply not true." She removed a flower from the vase.

"It doesn't make a damn bit of difference what *is* true, it's what *seems* to be true that counts. I happen to know there's a strong anti-Japanese sentiment among Westerners in Shanghai. And all I'm doing is giving the locals *one* Japanese to be against. You must realize that you're highly vulnerable or you wouldn't have come here."

"I came here to make you the same offer as I made before. If Sam asks me to do it, then I will make a statement that he is not Dawn's father. But he has to ask me himself." Her hands continued to work with the flowers.

"Sam doesn't have to do a damn thing. You'll do it because I demand it."

Yuki looked at Adele, saw her face, the ashen white of rice powder, filled with an angry pain. She sensed the real battle was not over Sam's career or his fathering a child. It came from somewhere so deep in the past that it was beyond her knowing.

"You are the grandmother of my child," Yuki said. "So I will leave this in Sam's hands. He is bound to find out what you've done. If he does nothing to interfere within two days, then I will take this to be what he wants and I will issue a statement that he's not Dawn's father. But I will not leave China." She turned back to the arrangement, moved the center stalk into balance, her voice even and unafraid. "There, I think you will like that better." She looked at her watch. "I've been here long enough," she said.

She did not go back through the house but instead went down the marble steps that led to the driveway and her car. *The die is cast,* she thought. *I will let Sam make his choice.* As the car door closed behind her and the chauffeur pulled the car around the driveway, she knew she could not have done differently.

Charlotte had been standing in the drawing room watching the mirrored reflection of what was happening on the sunlit terrace. From the beginning she was certain the two women were locked in a desperate battle and she wanted no part of it, and yet so compelling was the confrontation, she could not bring herself to leave it.

Only when the elegant Japanese woman had gone down the terrace steps and driven away did Adele, with one sweep of her arm, knock the flowers in the cut-glass vase off the table to shatter into a thousand glittering pieces. She breathed deeply and then picked up the small silver bell to ring for Majordomo, her eyes wild, just beginning to calm as she turned her face toward the French doors. "You might as well come out and join me, Charlotte," she said.

Charlotte emerged into the sunshine. "How did you know I was there?" she said.

"I just saw your reflection in the glass. Did you hear the conversation?"

"No," Charlotte said. "It was like a silent movie without subtitles."

"I'm trying to save your husband's career." She rang the bell again, with a vengeance this time. "Where in the hell is he?" she said, and at that moment Majordomo came onto the terrace. "I want all of this cleaned up," she said, pointing to the flowers and shards of glass. "And I want a gin and tonic with ice," she said. "And I want it damn chop chop."

Majordomo looked to Charlotte. "Bling big missee what please?"

"Nothing, thank you, Majordomo," Charlotte said, disturbed by the vengeful fire in Adele's eyes. Adele took her drink from the ornate silver tray, drank it straight down, sent him off to bring her another.

"Would you care to tell me what's happening?"

"Have you no capacity to hate?" Adele said.

"Who? The Japanese woman?"

"Who else? She stole your husband."

Charlotte watched a squirrel moving along a high branch in little jerks of movement. "As a matter of fact," she said reflectively, "she *gave* me Sam."

"I don't believe that."

Charlotte displayed a tolerant smile. "I have some regrets, of course, but they're not big ones. If Sam hadn't gone his way and I mine, we never would have found each other, not really. It's ironic, but we're together only because we were both so desperately wounded when we were separated."

Adele's second drink arrived. "I want you to do something. I want you to talk to Sam."

"Oh?"

"He is to take no action regarding the Japanese woman."

Charlotte laughed despite herself. "If you're worried about his reputation, it's a waste of time. Scandals are of short duration in Shanghai. One follows on the heels of another."

"She had Sam's child. That must bother you."

"I'm carrying Sam's child now."

Adele finished her drink. "You won't help me, then?"

"I make it a rule never to interfere. Sam's his own man and I trust him. He'll decide what's right." Charlotte could tell that Adele was no longer listening to her. Charlotte studied the branch, looking for the squirrel, but he had become successful, invisible.

The truth in Adele was like that squirrel.

Now you see it and now you don't.

"You look terrible," Charlotte said as Adele finished her drink. "Would you like to lie down for a while?"

"No," Adele said. "When Sam gets back tell him I want to talk to him. He's not to go back to the consulate or anywhere else until I see him. I'll be upstairs in the sunroom."

Adele turned and, as if sleepwalking, slowly climbed the stairs.

Majordomo was visibly relieved. "Tea now, missee," he said. "Time for tea is here."

Sam stormed into the house and called for Majordomo, who appeared from the drawing room, a tray in his hand. "There's no time to waste, Majordomo," Sam said. "Where's my mother?"

"Upstairs thinkee."

"I want you to call for the car and driver to be here in fifteen minutes. Then get all the upstairs maids and send them to my mother's room to pack her things. I've booked passage on the S.S. *McKinley* for her and it sails in two hours. That doesn't give us a lot of time. I want you to put her on board that ship and make sure she leaves."

He saw Charlotte in the drawing room as he made for the stairs. There was no time to talk now and he had no desire to explain anything. He went into his mother's room, yanked open the closet doors, and tossed out garments until he came to a beige linen traveling suit. He chose shoes, purse, and hat to match and threw them all on the bed. Suddenly she appeared in the doorway, a threatening expression on her face, the pinched and angry scowl he had seen so often in childhood. "Just what do you think you're doing?"

It won't work, Mother. Not this time.

"How dare you touch my things? Sit down," she commanded. "I want to talk to you."

He ignored her, turned to the maids, who came silently and fearfully into the room. "You are to pack all the clothes in the closets," he said in Mandarin. "All the toiletries from the bathroom. Everything."

"You can't do this," she said. "I'm your mother."

He pulled the papers from his pocket and laid them all in front of her one by one, the photograph of the dead Ching on top. She looked at the picture, glanced at the paper, then brushed them all to the floor with the back of her hand.

He picked them up. "You can burn the papers but the truth won't go away," he said. "You wasted your time. I sent a cable to Washington today and I put the lie to your whole scheme. I claimed the paternity of my child."

"How stupid you are," she said. "Tell these maids to get out of my room."

He laid the steamship ticket on the table by her side. "The maids are following my orders. You have fifteen minutes to get out of my house and with any luck you'll clear the China coast by nightfall."

"You can't tell me what to do."

"You'll either walk aboard that ship of your own free will or you will suffer the indignity of being carried aboard and locked in your stateroom until the ship sails. But you're going, by God, one way or the other. So get yourself ready."

He turned on his heels and went downstairs to mix himself a drink, aware that Charlotte was looking at him with myriad questions in her eyes.

Shortly, Majordomo came through the hallway, followed by the upstairs maids carrying luggage to the front door. Sam watched them load the bags into the car and retreat to the back of the house while Majordomo stood by the door. Adele came down the stairs, her heels clicking on the treads, eyes someplace between defiant and frightened as she poured herself a stiff drink from the side bar and downed it. She turned to Sam. "I wish I'd never seen this barbaric country. It's cost me both men that I've loved the most." She waited a moment. "Have you nothing to say to me?"

Sam turned to face her. "Yes, and it's that I never want to see you again."

Adele squared her shoulders, lifted her head high, and went out to the car, followed by Majordomo.

"Now," Charlotte said quietly, not wanting to provoke him further. "Not that I have the slightest objection to what you're doing, but would you tell me what prompted the eviction?"

Without a word Sam pulled the papers out of his pocket and handed them to her. She sat down to read them, beginning with Ching's affidavit and ending with the photograph of his body. She looked up at Sam with tears in her eyes and a sense of horror she could not express.

"She caused this?"

Sam nodded.

"Oh, my dear . . ." she said. "I'm so sorry."

He put his hand on her shoulder, listening to the faint sound of the motorcar passing the gate at the end of the long drive before it moved out into the traffic. "It's over now," he said with great finality, as if a door had been closed that could never be opened again.

Sam had to jostle his way through the crowds of Chinese in front of the hotel housing the American Consulate. Dozens of sick or injured babies were held up to him while old women wailed and men begged in singsong Mandarin. "You feed sick babies, sir? Feed my child." He made sympathetic noises as he went into the hotel, past the marine guard, and up to the office, where he sat down at his desk and wrote a blistering note to Comrade Li:

"You've done your Party a great disservice by this monstrous and bloody barbarism. Is your code of justice really as primitive and cruel as you make it out to be?"

He handed it to a Chinese messenger and told him to deliver it chop chop and then rang Dawes on the house telephone and awakened him from a sound sleep. "I'm sorry to disturb you, Mr. Dawes," he said. "But first thing in the morning, I would like you to make an assessment of our business ventures."

"Certainly," Dawes said. "Is something wrong?"

"No. I've decided to pay off some large debts. So we will be dissolving our partnership."

"As you wish. A proper accounting may take a little time."

"I understand." He put the telephone back on the cradle. He sat back in his chair, tapping the end of his pen staff against the palm of his hand. He decided to write a note to Bright Moon:

"I'm concerned for your safety every time I watch the shells falling in Chapei. I want to offer you the protection of the American

Consulate with my personal guarantee for your safety. Please take advantage of it."

He sent the note by messenger to the residence of Big Eared Tu, playing a hunch that the Green Gang would welcome this unofficial American recognition and might allow Bright Moon to accept the sanctuary offered her.

Then, all urgent work done, he poured himself a brandy and soon thereafter was dozing in his chair. He was jarred awake at three o'clock by a messenger returning from Comrade Li. He yawned, opened the folded paper.

"No political gains can be made if corruption is allowed to exist in any revolutionary organization. Ching was one of our members and it was up to me to use whatever discipline I considered strong enough to discourage any similar crimes on the part of those men who have pledged their lives to the cause."

Sam folded the note over, edged it away from him. Christ, not a dent in Li. Sam suddenly felt he could spend a lifetime here and make not one damn bit of difference in this culture.

Toward morning the cables from Washington were delivered by a code clerk and Sam deciphered the one addressed to him and marked "Private." It was from his Uncle Roger.

YOUR ACCOUNTS OF THE SHANGHAI DEVELOPMENTS HAVE BEEN MUCH APPRECIATED BY THE SECRETARY OF STATE, AS WELL AS YOUR INITIATIVE IN KEEPING THE CONSULATE ORDERLY DURING THIS MOST DIFFICULT PERIOD. YOU ARE ADVISED THAT THE OFFICIAL POLICY OF THE UNITED STATES TOWARD THE COMBATANTS ON BOTH SIDES IS ONE OF STRICT NEUTRALITY. HOWEVER, THEY ARE TO BE ADVISED THAT ANY ATTACKS ON AMERICAN INTERESTS THERE WILL NOT BE TOLERATED.

I HAVE RECEIVED THE CABLE FROM NEDWIN AS WELL AS YOUR OWN. I REALIZE YOUR PROPENSITY TOWARD GALLANTRY. AS WORTHY AS YOUR EFFORT MAY BE TO REDEEM THE LADY'S REPUTATION, I HAVE ACTED UPON AN OBJECTIVE REPORT OF THE SITUATION THERE WHICH NOW REMOVES ALL IMPEDIMENTS TO YOUR ADVANCEMENT. THIS CABLE WILL SERVE TO INFORM YOU THAT AS OF THIS DATE

ROBERT L. DUNCAN

YOU ARE NOW APPOINTED TO THE OFFICE OF CONSUL GEN-
ERAL OF THE UNITED STATES IN SHANGHAI.

> ROGER B. CUMMINGS
> UNDER SECRETARY OF
> STATE
> FAR EASTERN AFFAIRS

He read the dispatch with a sense of irony. So be it, he thought. To hell with everything. He would begin again later. Perhaps in the light of day everything would make more sense. He called his car to take him home.

"You and Sam simply *must* come," Molly Pearson was saying over the telephone. "You won't believe it, darling, but it turns out that the Palace Hotel ballroom is suspended on giant springs and one can actually feel the bombs exploding in Chapei. Really *feel* it in your legs. Uncanny. The party is for Reggie."

Charlotte held the receiver against her left ear while she nodded to the irate Chinese cook who stood before her, face grimacing with anger and indignation. "Sounds fun," she said lamely. "I have to go, Molly. Household emergency."

"Only if you promise to be there," Molly pouted.

"If Sam's free." More chatter and she hung up the receiver, the act releasing a torrent of words from the cook. Charlotte waved her hand as if to smooth the air. "You speak too fast, Number Three," she said, pronouncing each word distinctly. "Slow down." But he went all the faster, waving a handful of paper. Fortunately, Majordomo materialized to translate, and she found herself following the trail of the marvelous Chinese logic. Cookie was incensed that relatives of the house staff had been raiding the kitchen for leftovers as well as some provisions that had not yet had time to become leftovers. Cookie demanded the right to say who took what from the kitchen.

But Charlotte had seized one word from the translation and hung onto it. "Relatives," she said. "What relatives, Majordomo?"

"Runaway from Chapei, missee."

"Refugees, then. And where are they staying?"

"On grounds."

"Where on the grounds?"

"Big plenty room sleepee."

"And how many relatives are there?"

Majordomo stared unseeing into space, his fingers working an absent abacus. "Some" was the best that he could do.

"I see," she said. "Missee want look-see. Tell cookie missee talkee later. He Number One in kitchen. Now, show me the relatives."

In the warm, soft, humid air of the afternoon, she smelled the cook fires the moment she stepped outside and set off across the vast back lawn, Majordomo at her side. Once past the screen of trees along the potting shed, she came into the camp, the lines of shelters made of canvas tarps against the rains. Children were playing in the pathways and an old man, all bones, smiled and nodded to Charlotte while he filled buckets, pots, pans, cups, jars, and bottles with water from the gardening faucet. She shaded her eyes with her hand. Three hundred people at least, camping among great mounds of belongings, clothes, bedding, small furniture, anything that could be carried on a strong back. The latrines were trenches in the sandy soil at the back perimeter of the property, modesty preserved by sheets and blankets hanging on ropes between bamboo poles. As she wandered down the paths Majordomo padded along behind her with the most profound of silences.

"These surely can't all be relatives of the staff," she said.

"Muchee kin, missee."

She stopped, knelt by a small child, ran her fingers over the thin face. "You're not getting enough to eat, love," she said to the uncomprehending child, who wiggled free. She looked at an old woman who was boiling water in a pot. "Who is this woman, for instance?"

Majordomo did not hesitate an instant. "Great-aunt of Number Six housemaid."

"And this gentleman here with what appears to be a family of six children?"

"Him Second Cousin Wa of myself personal," Majordomo said.

"I see," she said, and when she was back at the house she had Majordomo wait while she went over her personal moneys, which she had promised Sam not to touch. "There is no way that these people can get enough to eat from our kitchen. I want fresh milk for the children, plenty of rice and leafy vegetables, oranges if you can find them, and fresh fish. I also want a promise from you," she said, writing out a check. "I will contribute as much money as I can for the feeding of these people. But you will be responsible for the shopping yourself so there is not one cent of squeeze or baksheesh. Cookie will dispense the foods so he won't lose face. Agreed?"

"Absolute yes, missee," Majordomo said, accepting the check. "Blessee by God."

Which God? she wondered, but she did not ask.

"I don't understand it fully," she said to Sam at dinner that night, a special Shanghai dinner that came as a gift from the grateful cook.

"Understand what?"

"Now here is the line between the Japanese and Chinese sectors." She traced a path across the linen tablecloth with her fingertip. "The Japanese cross the line all the time with their hit-and-run attacks, but the Chinese come to the line and stop. Why?"

"Fear," he said, taking more potatoes from the bowl the maid held for him. "They don't want to provoke retaliation from the other powers that share the International Settlement."

"Perhaps I'm not meant to understand these things," she said. "But it doesn't seem logical to me. Suppose the Chinese attacked the Japanese Sector?"

"Then the rest of us would be duty-bound to take the Japanese side."

"Would we actually go to war over that?" she said. "Would the British?"

He laid the knife across the top of his plate, put down his fork, then leaned back in his chair with his coffee. "No," he said thoughtfully. "The Chinese don't know what would happen so they won't take the chance. We have warships on the river. The British do too. But neither we nor they are going to get tied up in a war. We would growl a lot, rattle sabers, demand apologies, but that's all." He stifled a yawn with the back of his hand. "I'm sorry, dear," he said. "But I have to go to bed. I'll be home early tomorrow though. We need to go over the finances."

"I don't want you worrying about money."

"I'm not."

"I'd like to ask your permission for something."

"Certainly. What's going on?"

"I'd like to use some of my personal money to help the families of the staff who have come across from Chapei."

"I'm all in favor of it," he said. "As a matter of fact, I've set up a rice station downtown. Now, I'm gone. I'll be up and out before dawn." He stood up. "We haven't had any time to talk at all. Are you all right?"

"Fine."

"Politely fine or really fine?"

"Really fine. But missing you."

"We'll make up for that." He kissed her on the top of her head. "Sleep well."

After dinner she went into the library to look at the latest fashion magazines, which had been given to her by the wife of the French *chargé*. She needed some new gowns, now that the baby was expanding her waistline. But the dinner conversation still disturbed her enough that she could not keep her mind on clothing.

She knew that Yuki was at her shop every day with Sam's daughter, as she had come to think of Dawn, and Nanking Road was very close to the edge of the Settlement. Sam seemed to be certain the Chinese would respect the line, but what if, as the battle progressed, one of the uncontrollable Chinese warlord generals got carried away and stormed across the line in force?

The time had come, she decided, for Sam to get acquainted with this daughter of his. There was plenty of room in this mansion, and it would hurt nothing if Yuki brought Dawn to stay for a few days until the fighting in the Chinese districts fell into a predictable pattern. She wouldn't have to tell Sam about it before she asked Yuki for her permission. If she refused, there was no point in bothering Sam at all. If she said yes, it was almost a sure thing that Sam would go along. She wanted Sam to have a chance to protect his children—the born as well as the unborn. She was sure of his love now; the past was the past for both of them.

Besides, she had long wanted to meet Yuki and see the salon she had heard so much about. She decided she might have some gowns fitted while she was there. She thought it through as she undressed and lay beside her sleeping husband. There was no need for any jealousy or regrets. She had seen Connaught today from a distance and there was not the slightest twinge of pain. She could feel the new life stirring within her. *I feel you. I know you're there.* She felt smug. She laid the back of her hand against Sam's leg, ever so gently, just for the contact, and shortly she drifted off to sleep.

When she awakened the next morning Sam had gone for the day. Charlotte summoned Majordomo and made a tour of her own small refugee camp and found everything in good order, the fires kindled, the rice pots boiling, the smell of raw fish in the air. She was surprised to hear so much laughter, to see such cheerfulness. An old and toothless woman smiled at her and made the sign of the cross. When she was back at the house she asked Majordomo about the religious gesture.

"No harm, missee," Majordomo said.

"You always say that when you've done something you're not sure of," she said. "Something that might get you in trouble."

"Chinee people much all time afraid," Majordomo said. "They say, 'What happen big missee pitchee everybody out?' They say, 'Yankee missee all time changee mind.' I say, 'Other missee maybe, this one special missee.' " He paused, as if trying to find a way to exhibit extreme tact in a language he only partially understood.

"And how did you tell them I was special?" she asked, to prompt him.

"I say, 'This missee special missee because she going to become again Jesus baby mother.' "

"What?" she said, startled beyond belief. "You told them what?"

"How you say, Vigin Malee? Makee right, yes?"

"You told them I am the Virgin Mary?"

"Makee feel whole lot better, missee. All trustee Vigin Malee."

"I understand what you're trying to do," she said. "But tomorrow I want you to tell them the truth."

"Sure, missee," he said without hesitation.

"You *will* tell them."

"First-class true, missee."

"Then why do I have the feeling you're not telling me the truth?"

"Funny people Chinee, missee. You givee food, sleep place. You say 'I helpee' when Yankee missee other place no helpee. You come down lookee, makee everything okay. So makee big sense you baby Jesus mama. If I say was lie, they smile."

"In other words, they believed your story then and they won't believe any new story."

Majordomo nodded.

"Then don't tell them any more," she said, feeling buoyant and happy inside. "If the Virgin Mary gets the credit, that's fine with me. But what if I give birth to a girl? How will you explain that?"

"Big surprise," he said, eyes bright. "Jesus now got new missee baby sister."

She made the call rather awkwardly, and when Yuki came on the line she wanted to apologize for the way Adele had treated her, but she did not know where to begin. "This is Charlotte Cummings, Miss Nakamura," she said in her most friendly voice. "I don't quite know how to say this, but I'd like to get acquainted with you and I wonder if you would mind if I dropped by your salon."

"That would please me very much," Yuki said.

"I'll be there as soon as I can," Charlotte said.

It was noon before she was able to get away, before a second car could be sent from the consulate for her use, and even then it took her no more than a few minutes to realize that traveling by car into the downtown area along the Bund was going to be impossible. Chapei was being shelled again, and every street and road south into the Settlement was clogged with slowly moving lines of Chinese refugees, some of them in rickshas piled high with personal belongings, others pushing wheelbarrows with bundles and babies intermingled, and finally the refugees on foot who carried old people or the sick on their backs or on stretchers made from wooden doors with handles nailed onto the four corners.

When an hour had passed and they were no farther along than the Avenue Joffre, she spotted an idle ricksha and had the chauffeur engage the thin young man and his conveyance for the whole afternoon, promising to pay him double wages. The chauffeur made the deal and helped Charlotte into the bamboo seat. "He speaks little English, madame," the chauffeur said. "But he does know the names of all the places you could possibly want to go."

"Thank you," she said. "We'll do fine."

The puller looked at her with darkly curious and accommodating eyes.

"I want to go to a shop called 'Blossoms,'" she said, pronouncing each word distinctly. "It's on Nanking Road. Do you know the place?"

He nodded and set off at a trot, and at first she was about to correct him for going the wrong way until she saw that the street ahead was clogged with a minor vehicular accident and thousands of refugees waiting patiently for the Sikh traffic policeman in his turban to clear the roadway so they could move again.

He padded to the south and then came up the Bund itself, where the breeze off the water made the warm afternoon more bearable. Ordinarily the lawns that fronted the river held an occasional European lying in the shade, but today it reminded her of a human anthill, for there was not an inch of space unoccupied, and some of the trees had been stripped of their lower limbs to fuel the cook fires. She could smell the cooking rice and knew that the water must be from the contaminated river itself.

Beyond the walkways and the lawns the river was dark brown under an overcast sky, and she saw the great blue-gray bulk of the Japanese flagship, the *Idzumo*, moored in front of the Japanese Consulate General. Its artillery fired holes into the clouds.

The puller brought the ricksha up to the Cathay Hotel and turned up Nanking Road, no more than a block or two from Blossoms. She began to rehearse what she would say to Yuki and to plan the logistics of getting Dawn back to the house. There would be no point to delay, for the streets were growing more congested by the second.

She looked at the tragedy all around her and had to close her eyes. It was too much to take in; she was overcome by a sense of helplessness.

She heard the roar of aircraft now, and she turned and looked behind her just in time to see the four Chinese bombers swoop down out of the clouds and begin to release their bombs along the river while the flak from antiaircraft batteries splattered in the sky around them. Then, as if everything had slowed to a snail's pace so she could examine it, she saw bombs continuing to drop from the Chinese planes as they flew inland, and she told herself this could not be happening, because this was a protected area.

Eggs falling from four gray birds.

The Cathay Hotel lobby exploded from the inside, the glass windows flying out in a million tiny shards, followed by dust and debris and a roar that drowned out the screams.

She looked up as the bombs came straight down toward her. Incongruous thoughts. *No little sister for the baby Jesus. Never again the touch of Sam's dear face.*

Our father who art in heaven . . .

Yuki sat in the rear of the crowded church, feeling very much alone, listening to the organ playing the hymns she had heard the Thompsons play in the mission in Tokyo, only now Sam's wife lay in the polished ebony casket at the front of the church. All of the legations had turned out in force, and when the Japanese officials were conducted down the aisle, she was close enough that by reaching out she could have touched Ito-san on the arm. He was resplendent in his new brigadier's uniform as he strode into the church with the Japanese Consul General in his morning coat and an admiral who had come to represent the navy.

She saw Sam seated at the front of the church and her heart ached for him. His face was gray stone, and all during the ceremony his expression did not change, as if with the death of his wife a part of him had disappeared from the earth as well.

The minister droned a eulogy against the immense banks of flowers, and then as the line began to form to file past the coffin, she slipped out of the church and sought out her ricksha among the ranks of chauffeured limousines. When her puller reached the edge of the churchyard, she had him wait, and she sat weeping as the pallbearers carried the coffin into the tiny Western cemetery, Sam walking behind it, so caught up in his grief that his life seemed suspended.

She forced herself to tell the puller to move on.

When Sam came home from the funeral he could not go into the house, not yet, knowing that Charlotte would not be there. With Majordomo at his side, he made a tour of the refugee camp on the back of the property, walking through the compound. Firecrackers popped all around him as the people Charlotte had sheltered held their own memorial service.

"They are expressing much sadness," Majordomo said in Mandarin. "She was much beloved by them."

"Yes," he said, realizing as he spoke that his voice was wooden with shock. *Charlotte is dead and I am alive.* He was caught up in the nightmare, but there was work to be done. "I'll be relying on you even more now, Majordomo. You'll be in charge of providing rice to the refugees outside the consulate as well as the people in this camp. I'm doubling your wages. And for the time being you will tell the servants that nothing of Charlotte's is to be touched or moved."

He knew that sooner or later he would have to pack her clothing and sort out her things, but not yet. He was not ready.

He went to the consulate to find Connaught waiting for him, working from a chair at the side of Sam's desk, sorting out piles of paper memos. "What do we have?" Sam said.

"Nothing that you should concern yourself with."

"I need to work."

"And God knows I could use the help," Connaught said. "Are you all right?"

"As right as I'm going to be."

"Then here's the situation," Connaught said as Sam sat down in his chair. "The American news services have dispatched *beaucoup* reporters to cover the glamorous war in Shanghai. And the calls from the bureau chiefs are not falling upon us softly as the gentle dew from heaven. They're demanding that the consulate provide suites at the Astor or in the undamaged sections of the Cathay or the Broadway Mansions. They don't want the hotels in the French Sector, where there's plenty of room. They want a rooftop view of the war with an open bar."

"Draw names out of a hat," Sam said. "Assign the first ones you pick to the best places you can get and the rest to accommodations any damn place you can find them. Arrange with the hotels to provide roof bars and telephones for everybody."

"Will do," Connaught said.

Connaught left the office and Sam sat down and wrote a dispatch to Washington chronicling what he saw as a slow decline of Japanese power. It seemed to him as if this might be one time that a great coming together of the Chinese armies could overwhelm the more efficient firepower of the Japanese.

He was interrupted by a somber young man from the signal room with a cable. It was a reply to a cable he had sent Noble shortly after Charlotte's death.

YOUR CABLE MOST INADEQUATE. I WANT ALL THE DETAILS OF THE DEATH OF MY BELOVED DAUGHTER. AT A LATER TIME I SHALL WANT TO DISCUSS THE POSSIBILITY OF BRING-ING CHARLOTTE BACK TO THE STATES FOR BURIAL. RE-GARDS.

NOBLE

He stayed late at the office, and only when he got home that evening did he set about writing a reply. He fortified himself with a bottle of brandy at his side, the tasseled lamp turned on over the leather chair that he had brought home as a remembrance of Consul Alcott. He unscrewed the silver cap of the inkwell to discover that the glass bottle was still half full. He raised the pen staff to the light to examine the point and make sure the nibs were not sprung. Then, pouring himself a glass of brandy, he began to put the pain into words.

Dear Noble,

The responsibility for the incident has been fixed but the reasons are still in doubt. The Chinese government has issued a formal apology for the dropping of the bombs, claiming that their bomb racks had been damaged by Japanese antiaircraft fire and they were trying to reach the racetrack before they jettisoned the bombs but did not succeed. The Cathay Hotel was bombed and the area just west of it along Nanking Road, killing dozens, injuring hundreds, and leaving craters thirty feet deep. I was at the consulate at the time and did not know of Charlotte's death until a couple of hours after it happened, when the police were able to make an identification. I don't know what she was doing there but I think she was shopping

He could write no more. He left the sentence hanging and called for the car to take him back to the consulate. He decided to spend the night there, for sitting in this semidarkened room he expected to hear Charlotte's voice at any moment, asking him if there was anything he needed, or the sound of her singing in the bath, or the click of her high heels on the parquet floor of the hallway. He screwed the cap back on the inkwell, put the letter in the drawer. He carried the brandy decanter and his glass with him.

His driver, Shen, was a young Chinese who was not as wedded to the formalities of the old ways as some of the more mature drivers, so tonight Sam sat in the front passenger's seat and poured himself a brandy to drink on the way. The sky glowed with the fires in Chapei and the steady rumble of the artillery was a constant background noise.

"Do you wish to speak in English or Chinese tonight?" Sam said.

"English, if you please, sir."

"You don't need the practice. I think you speak it very well."

"Thank you, sir. I wish to extend the condolences of myself and a friend of yours, Mr. Li, who said that whenever the opportunity presented itself that I should apologize for his inability to attend the funeral. He said you would understand."

"You can tell him I understand. Are you Communist too?"

"Yes, sir."

"Tell me what you think." He gulped the brandy. "Are the Chinese going to win this go-around with the Japanese?"

"No, sir," Shen said.

"Because?"

"I am just a driver, sir. My opinions are not worthwhile."

"Nonsense," Sam said, feeling easier now that the brandy had begun to take hold and he had distanced himself from the reality that squeezed the breath out of him. "Obviously, Mr. Li has you here to report to him. So that means that you're a good observer or he would have gotten somebody else."

"I don't spy, sir," Shen said adamantly. "I give him my impressions only."

"Then give *me* your impressions only."

"The Chinese will appear to win at first, but the Japanese have greater resources. They landed an army of thirty thousand on the south side of the Yangtze this afternoon."

"If you're Communist, that shouldn't bother you too much, should it?"

"How so?"

"These are Nationalist troops that are getting wiped out. Isn't that the Communist strategy, that the Nationalists should exhaust themselves against the Japanese? Then, later, there will be fewer of them the Communists will have to fight?"

Shen did not answer. The street was so packed with refugees that the truck ahead of them was having a hard time getting through. The truck stopped every few feet for workers wearing hospital masks, who handed small bundles up to the men stationed on the truck bed. Sam squinted, peering through the windshield. "What are they doing?" he asked.

"It is one of the baby wagons, sir," Shen said quietly.

"Christ," Sam said, more of a prayer than a curse. He sank back against the seat. He had seen reports of the baby wagons that picked up hundreds of small children every night, the casualties of the day.

"I want to drive you past the Shanghai Benevolent Association, sir."

"Very well."

As Shen drove through the winding streets Sam smelled the stench even before he saw the flames rising from behind the walled-off courtyard where the small bodies stacked like cordwood were burning. "Drive on," he said, sick to his stomach.

"The babies are neither Communist nor Nationalist, sir, if you don't mind my saying."

"Your point is made," Sam said.

"I was asked to relay one other message to you, sir, and Comrade Li hopes you will not take offense."

"Over what?"

"He knows that you meant well when you offered sanctuary to Bright Moon. Big Eared Tu had Bright Moon removed to Peking very quickly. Comrade Li doesn't know why."

"But she's safe."

"Yes, sir."

"Tell Li I have not taken offense," Sam said.

At the hotel he moved into Alcott's quarters, adjacent to the office, but no sooner had he ordered the servants to put fresh linen on the bed than the telephone rang. Dawes was on the line. "I've been informed that you're spending the night," Dawes said. "So, since your daylight hours are limited, I wondered if you might not like to talk business awhile."

"Yes," Sam said, grateful for the interruption. "Don't bother to knock. I'll be in the office."

He was pouring the brandy when Dawes came in carrying a sheaf of papers. "I always picture you with a ledger in one hand and a portable adding machine in the other," Sam said. "Or maybe an abacus."

Dawes was wearing his business suit without a tie. His eyes were tired, red-rimmed. It was obvious he had been working on his accounts all evening. He took the brandy glass, then sat down on a worn brocaded sofa and drank. He removed his spectacles and pinched the bridge of his nose. "This isn't the time to cash in," he said. "We'd do better to hold off another month on this."

"I don't want to wait," Sam said. He sat down, propped his feet up on the desk. "How much cash can I get hold of?"

Dawes replaced his glasses. "The cotton venture really worked out. Half the cargo went to mills in Hong Kong and the rest to mills south of Shanghai. In both cases the mills already had outstanding contracts to produce table and hospital linens, industrial uniforms, and a cheap line of women's wear for European countries. I arranged to buy the contracts, pay for the piecework, collect from the buyers." He squinted at the adding-machine tapes. "The money due you is in a dozen different currencies. Part of that comes from the countries where we have been doing business and part from the currency futures we have been buying. But I take it you will want your money in dollars."

"Yes."

"Then your share is approximately three million three hundred and eighty-three thousand dollars."

Sam drank his glass of brandy, poured another. "So I'm a very rich man, it seems."

"Quite," Dawes said. "I think we did very well together."

"I want you to do something for me," Sam said. "There are hundreds of Chinese children dying every day, disease, starvation, a dozen other causes. So I want you to take a million of that money and spend it for food, milk, medical supplies, doctors. My majordomo will be in charge of the distribution."

Dawes looked at him with sad eyes. "Do you know how many refugees are on the streets now?"

"That has nothing to do with anything."

"A half million of them," Dawes said. "You can't save the children without saving the grown-ups. In the first place, there are so many goddamned desperate adults out there that very little of the food would get to the children. In the second place, there's no way we can bring the adult diseases under control. We have a thousand people going blind every day, thousands more with rickets, scurvy, tuberculosis, and the real chance of a cholera epidemic."

"Don't get practical with me now, for God's sake," Sam said. "You don't have to use an adding machine to show me that if you have a half million people and only a million dollars, that's only a couple of dollars apiece."

"Facts are facts. We might be able to take care of them a few days, providing we can get doctors, providing we can find food, everything provisional. But in the end, sad as it may be, the money all goes down the drain, and the children still die."

"If I buy any extra life for those people, then it's worth it to me. Will you do it?"

"Yes, of course. I'll do the best I can."

He left. Once Sam was alone again he went to bed, knowing the futility of what he was doing but unable to stop it. He lay for a long time staring into the darkness and finally drifted off to sleep only to find himself climbing over a mass of people, desperately looking for someone. The faces were dim in the darkness; the air was filled with smoke. A peal of thunder rolled across the sky and a streak of lightning crackled to the ground and gave him enough light to see faces. Christ, all children, with wide eyes staring at him, so still he could not tell whether they were alive or dead, and he called out Dawn's name, but there was no answer, and he tried to call the child that would have been born of Charlotte, but sweet Jesus, that baby had no name and he would never be able to recognize the unborn features. He cried out, sat up in bed. The rain was drumming against the windows; he could hear the shelling, which would never stop. The tears ran down his face with a grief that threatened to split him in two.

He did not go back to sleep that night.

Ito's hands roamed her smooth back, caressed her breasts, touched her gently in all of the sweet and sacred places until Yuki was on fire with wanting him. He entered her and she was consumed with the pleasure he gave her. When it was over she lay in his arms treasuring the peace and contentment while she drifted off to sleep, only to come awake during the night to find he had left the bed and was standing by the open window in the moonlight, dressed in his kimono, staring out at the trees of the garden.

"You should sleep, my lord," she said to him.

"I can't sleep," he said.

She prepared tea for them and went back to the bedroom. "Would you like to talk?" she asked, filling a cup for him.

He raised his face to the sky, as if listening for any sounds of battle carried on the night air. "I have a decision to make," he said.

"And what are your choices?"

He studied the tea as if looking for answers. "The Foreign Ministry has offered me the chance to become consul general for Shanghai. Do you know what that would mean, how much Cummings-san and I could accomplish with both of us in key positions? We might bring about a peaceful solution, at least in Shanghai."

"Congratulations," she said. "Why should you hesitate?"

"I received word today from Tokyo that my petition for a change in military duty has been granted. They have offered me command of a Japanese division landing at Woosung."

"And you must choose only one of the positions."

"Yes. Neither the Foreign Ministry nor the army wishes to offend the other."

"Which do you want?"

"I can't consider that now. I have to decide how I can best serve my country, how my father would have counseled me, were he still alive."

"Finish your tea and come back to bed," she said. "You'll make a better decision with a clear mind."

She drowsed before daybreak, came awake to see him putting on his uniform.

"Please don't get up," he said. "My transportation is waiting for me outside."

"When will I see you again, my lord?"

"I do not know," he said. "I have decided to take the military command for the present."

Her heart sank. "Yes, my lord."

"I will be back when I can. Give Dawn my affection."

"I will."

He leaned down, pressed his lips against her forehead, and in a moment was gone, the rattling truck engine slowly fading in the distance. *Lord Buddha and Lord Jesus,* she thought. *I beseech you. Bring him honor but do not let him die.*

A bomb had blown a crater in Nanking Road and brought down the south wall, which joined Yuki's property to that of Brookings, an English jeweler who was prowling through the rubble. He was a short, pudgy man well past his prime, and it was evident that the devastation of the street had overwhelmed him. He poked at a brick with the tip of his cane, nodded to Yuki, and then peered back at his shop, the windows shattered and the stonework reduced to rubble. "A terrible bit of business," he said. "I hope you haven't been quite as smashed as myself. I was telling the wife just this week past. I was intending to sell out and retire, you see? Afraid something like this would happen. And underinsured. But that's the fate of us all in the end, isn't it? More than a bit of bad luck. Tests the character, doesn't it?"

She stood at the front of the space that had been his shop. "You have a lease, Mr. Brookings?"

"I own the place outright, I do," he said. "I've been here forever, haven't I?"

"I would be very much interested in buying your property from you," she said. "I've been wanting to expand and add a dress salon."

The thatch of his eyebrow lifted slightly. "As is?"

"Of course. I'll have to remodel anyway. How much would you want for it?"

"That would be left to the agents, don't you think?"

"I'd prefer not, if it's all right with you."

He rubbed his chin with a pudgy forefinger, studying the rubble that had been his life. "I'll be fair with you," he said. "I have insurance that covers my stock and fixtures and some of the destruction. There's a sturdy wall or two left, and the price of the ground. Should we say, then, twenty thousand pounds sterling?"

"That's fair," she said instantly. "Can you have the papers for me this afternoon?"

"Aye, I can do that," he said. "I'll drop in for tea. Now, what terms would be convenient for you?"

"Cash," she said.

He smiled. "A word to delight the heart," he said. "Four o'clock then?"

"Four o'clock." She found the foreman directing the Chinese construction crew who were cleaning and stacking the bricks from the collapsed wall. "I'll be making some changes in the rebuilding," she said. "I'll want to extend this workroom six feet and put a door through into the shop next door. But I'll have plans for you in a day or two."

She went into her office, and after she had locked the door she removed a board from the floor and took out the tin box. She removed twenty thousand pounds from it, then replaced the box next to the gold she had hidden away in the hollow of the floor. Daily there were new scandals in the Shanghai financial institutions that made her less secure about depositing her money in them. She kept a balance in the Shanghai–Hong Kong bank sufficient to the daily needs of her business, but she felt safer with the bulk of her money close at hand. She replaced the board and put the pound notes into an envelope.

At three o'clock she met with Yvonne and told her of the plans to enlarge Blossoms, then inspected some of Yvonne's new designs. "One of these days," she said as Yvonne was putting her sketches back into a portfolio, "I would like you to go into a partnership with me if you would want to."

Yvonne hugged her. "You're a dear. I'd love it," she said. "Let me know when you want to talk about it."

Yuki took a sketch pad and went into the tearoom, sat at a private table exclusively hers, separated from the other tables by tall plants and next to a window covered with butterfly paper. As she started to sketch the plans for the new salon, she became aware of women talking at a table on the other side of the screen of plants. She found herself listening instinctively, although she had long since stopped reporting gossip to Ito-san.

"He's completely changed, much more reserved and serious."

"It's quite ironic what's happened to him, wouldn't you say?"

Englishwomen, Yuki thought. *In their thirties.*

"I'm not sure I know what you mean."

"He went quite mad after his wife's death . . ."

Sam. They're talking about Sam.

". . . and he tried to give all his money away to the starving Chinese. But he inherited quite a sizable trust, everything in non-negotiable bonds, so he's still quite rich."

Yuki stopped listening. *Poor Cummings-san,* she thought. *No better off than Ito-san, both searching for something they will never find.*

At four o'clock Mr. Brookings arrived with the papers and was shown to her table. He handed her the file, and after a quick reading she handed him the envelope with twenty one-thousand-pound notes in it.

Brookings did not quite know what to do with himself. "I must admit, Miss Nakamura, I feel somewhat at a momentary loss for words."

"How so, Mr. Brookings?"

"To be frank, I had heard from a Mr. Paxton, the real estate chap, that you are a very hard bargainer."

"I'm very particular with Mr. Paxton because he is not trustworthy," Yuki said. "But I do trust you. And I hope that you and your wife will be very happy in your retirement."

She did not go into Blossoms the next morning for she had heard that the Chinese were preparing a counteroffensive. She tried to call Blossoms to tell Elder Sister to take charge, but the telephone lines were out so she sent the amah with a written message. She spent the morning reading to Dawn in a corner of the garden among the flowers. Shortly before lunchtime it seemed that the rumble of artillery from across the river had grown louder. It sounded as if the

Chinese batteries had moved southeast along the river and were now almost opposite South Station on the far bank of the Whangpoo.

"You've stopped reading, Mother," Dawn said.

"Where was I?"

"The dragon was almost at the village."

"Yes, I remember now." She lifted the book again but she found it difficult to concentrate. Japanese military trucks were rumbling down the lane, and in a few moments a servant girl came running into the garden.

"Excuse me, madame, but there's a Japanese officer at the door who wishes to speak to you."

"I want to see the soldier too," Dawn said.

"You stay here and keep the place in the book," Yuki said, handing it to her.

The officer was a marine captain. "I am warning all residents of this section," he said. "The Chinese artillery is moving upriver and their shells may fall in this area. We suggest that you evacuate."

She saw the trucks moving down the lane, the cannons towed behind them. They stirred the dust in the street. Each caisson seemed like a bead on an endless string. "Do you expect an invasion, Captain? Will they attempt to cross the river?"

"They won't cross the river," the captain said, "but they're using some heavy artillery. I'd suggest that you leave here until morning. We'll have them under control by then."

"*Arigato gozaimashita,*" she said, and gently closed the door, her mind already cataloguing those things she would need to take to the restored Cathay Hotel for the night. She summoned a servant and told her what to pack. She stopped briefly by the study, picked up the sketches she had made for the remodeled salon, put them in a canvas carrying case along with Dawn's drawings and colored pencils, something to keep her occupied.

She had just gone out into the garden to get Dawn when she heard the first shrill scream of a shell in the distance and the hollow whomp of an explosion. Then there was another whistling scream and a closer blast and she waited no longer. She opened the wooden door to a stone shed.

"Get inside quickly," she said to Dawn. The child looked up from the book on her lap.

"Why?" Dawn said.

"Do it now," Yuki said, trying to stay calm. She heard the scream of another shell and knew instinctively that this one was going to be very close, and she pushed Dawn ahead of her into the stone shed and closed the door just as the garden exploded with a deafening roar that left her head ringing. She held her mouth very close to Dawn's ear. "Put your hands over your ears," she said. "Then sit down and pull your knees up and your head down."

Another blast shook the stone shed, jarring loose a shower of rocks, threatening to collapse the walls. But the next explosion was farther on, like a malevolent giant walking away, shaking the earth, and the following one was even more distant. Her hands were trembling. The concussions had left her half deaf. She was frightened but still in control. Dawn was on the edge of hysteria, about to wail.

Yuki fixed her with a stern look. "You are not to cry, understand?" she said firmly. "You are to stay exactly where you are. Not a peep from you."

The hysteria receded. The child stayed motionless. Yuki brushed the dust out of her hair and then opened the door into what was left of the garden. She stepped out just as a half dozen Japanese bluejackets, wearing armbands that showed them to be medics, ran through the demolished walls. A truck had taken a direct hit on the other side of the wall and was burning intensely, sending black smoke pouring into the sky, while three marines struggled to unhook the caisson and wheel it away before the fire ignited the ammunition. There were dead men littering the alley. Others had been blown into the trees. The branches were littered with scraps of clothing and pieces of bodies.

A medic ran up to her. *"Mizuwa kudasai,"* he said. "We need water."

"The kitchen," she said. "Through there." He darted away. She was torn between the desire to help the wounded men in the lane and the need to get her daughter away from the danger of exploding ammunition. Breathing a prayer to Lord Jesus and Lord Buddha to take care of the wounded, she opened the door to the shed and pulled Dawn to her feet. "Listen to me," she said. "We are going to the house. When we leave the shed we will look only toward the door of the house. Only toward the door. Do you understand?"

"Why?" Dawn said.

"Because I say so. Come. Walk ahead of me." With Dawn leading, Yuki followed her toward the house. She was aware of a human foot, still in a bloody boot, which had been blown beside the path. She did not want Dawn to see it. "Eyes straight ahead," she said. "That's it. You're doing well." They made it to the steps and then into the kitchen. A medic shoved past them with a bowl of water. Another dull thump sounded from the alley.

The gas tank on the truck, Yuki thought. *Not the ammunition.*

She left Dawn in the main room and examined the walls closest to the garden, both upstairs and down. Cracks ran from the corners of most of the windows outward in diagonal patterns, like spider webs. She pushed against a wall with the flat of her hand. It was sound. Some of the panes had been blown out of the windows and the servants had already begun to sweep up the glass.

She went outside again. As she listened it seemed to her that the sound of the Chinese artillery was fainter than it was before, and when the Japanese guns answered they were at least a mile to the west. She summoned the servants to the main room.

"I have decided to stay here," Yuki said. "I think the danger has passed. But I give you my thanks and tell you that if you wish to leave, to make sure your families are safe, then please take the rest of the day off. For those of you who will stay, the wounded marines need your help. The kitchen staff will prepare hot food and the rest of the staff will help the medics. I thank you for your loyalty."

In the other room Dawn was holding the book opened to the illustration of the multicolored and garish dragon. Yuki turned her attention to Dawn and sat down beside her on the tatami, suddenly exhausted.

"Did you see the foot?" Dawn said matter-of-factly.

"Which foot?" Yuki said, not wanting to get involved in the complicated subject of death.

"The one in the garden. You must have seen it. It was a man's foot in a shoe."

"Yes," Yuki said. "I saw it."

"Was it the dragon?" Dawn said, wide-eyed.

"What dragon?"

"The one in the book. The one that breathes fire and eats people. I think he swallowed the man in the garden, all except the shoe. Do you think it could have been the dragon?"

Yuki nodded grimly. "In a manner of speaking, the man was consumed by a dragon, yes," she said. "A terrible, terrible dragon."

By that night the sound of the cannons had faded and Yuki could hear the crickets in the underbrush. The bodies and the debris had been removed from the lane, the truck hauled away, and in a pale wash of moonlight the ruins of the garden with its collapsed walls had the charm of antiquity, as if this was something that had happened in another lifetime. She saw the lights of a car coming down the lane and went back into the house as the car stopped and one of the servants went to the door.

Ito stood in the shadows. She heard his voice and she wanted to run to him, but she showed him her respect by waiting as the servant helped him remove his boots. When he came into the light she bowed to him, her heart sinking. His uniform was torn, bloodstained. His face was gaunt, cheeks sunken, eyes dull, as if he had not slept in days. He turned, gave instructions to the driver outside the house, and the car moved off. Yuki sent a servant for brandy, then ran to Ito and put her arms about him, gently, with as much support as affection. She led him to the pillows by the low table.

She took the bottle from the servant and filled Ito's glass. As he reached out to take it she saw that the back of his hand was raw, caked with dried blood. He drained the glass, put it on the table to be filled again.

"I was told your house was shelled," he said.

"Just the garden. None of us was hurt. Are you wounded?"

"Old wounds, new wounds," he said. "It doesn't matter. We've beaten the Chinese, routed them from the city. But we lost thousands of men, fifty thousand, a hundred, I don't know. Tomorrow, we mop up Chapei. Burn everything."

She poured him more brandy, called another servant, ordered a bath drawn. "You can talk to me later," she said. "Right now, you need a bath and sleep."

"I've left a call at headquarters. When they need me they will come for me."

"They have to give you time to rest."

He emptied another glass of brandy. Then he slumped down on his elbow, and in a moment had put his head on a pillow and was asleep, his mouth slightly agape. She took a coverlet from a closet and put it over him, then sat back to watch over him as he slept.

After twelve hours he came awake with a start. She was still sitting there, watching him as he sat upright, looked around, took a moment to get his bearings. "It's dark," he said. "What time is it?"

"You don't need to worry about time now," she said. "Everything's quiet."

"I would like to eat," he said. When the food was brought to him he ate ravenously. "Now I am ready for a bath."

She summoned a servant, told her to have the bath filled with the hottest water possible.

"It has been a bad time for you, my lord," she said.

He lit a cigarette, blew smoke into the semidarkness. "Yes," he said. "I don't see the point of this war. I'm not supposed to question, and yet I do."

"It will be all right in the end," she said. She touched the side of his head.

"Only when I stop questioning," he said.

She saw that his bath was steaming hot and then helped him into the bathroom, where she cleaned him before he immersed himself in the immense porcelain tub with the four claw feet. He sat up to his neck in the water and she soothed him. There was a fresh cut on his shoulder blade and scrapes and abrasions on his arms and legs. But the hot water soaked away the pain, and he dozed fitfully. After a time she dried him off and fitted him with a sleeping kimono and put him to bed in the softness of a Western-style mattress raised from the floor.

She sent his uniform to be cleaned and pressed and put a boy to polishing his boots. Even as she watched Ito sleep she knew that Dawn needed her attention, and that important decisions awaited her at Blossoms. But she felt that Ito was only on loan to her for a brief time. Shortly after dawn he awakened and reached out a hand to her. She came into the warmth of his bed. They made love, tenderly, as if this was a final gift they could give to each other.

"I have no words," he said afterward.

"Words are not necessary, my lord."

"You have given me life again."

"I am grateful to the Lord Jesus and the Lord Buddha for bringing you to me."

By eight his uniform had been returned and the orderly was waiting in the staff car outside. Still he took the time for a cup of tea and then, almost formally, returned her bow, adjusted his cap, and departed.

In the staff car Major Futsu was waiting to take him to see the extent of their victory and to judge what was left to be done. The car crossed the single open bridge over Soochow Creek into Chapei. *The landscape of the moon,* he thought, piles of mud, rock, and debris as far as the eye could see, narrow ridges rising where there had once been walls, paths littered with debris where there had been wide streets. The stink of death permeated the scene.

Across the way the ruins of North Station looked as if some giant hand had rammed the roof inside the walls. General Ito asked the major to stop the car beside a group of officers waiting in the street.

He told them what he wanted. Within minutes the trucks began to pull the artillery pieces into position along the edge of the border with Hungjao. He waited for the signal from the wall of troops moving down from Yangtzepoo to the north of the city to keep the Chinese troops from escaping in that direction. He invited the marines to augment his troops on the south, forming a rectangular corridor. The Chinese had no aircraft, no artillery. Foot by foot his artillery moved forward, yard by yard, muzzles belching fire, another line of partial buildings exploding in front of them, collapsing to rubble. And still the Japanese bombers swooped down from the other side. He kept his batteries firing until nightfall and then ordered a cease-fire. He set his picket lines well forward, machine guns to cover a lighted zone with such heavy fire that the Chinese would destroy themselves if they tried a counterattack. The enemy remained silent.

Ito visited his signal center before he had dinner. He listened to the reports of the Chinese armies fleeing to the south and there came into his mind the thought that if a small corridor could be opened out of this death square, the battered survivors would limp out and southward during the night, the majority of them so wounded they could not fight again. And he could then call the Western journalists together and explain that even with the ability to annihilate the enemy, the Japanese could show mercy.

The thought was no more than a fleeting one. In the officers' mess all the talk was of jubilant vindication, fortified by sake. The Chinese had caused the Japanese military great embarrassment by fighting such a prolonged battle here in Shanghai, by killing so many Japanese troops and causing the Imperial Forces to lose face in the eyes of the world.

"They've been taught their lesson," one colonel said happily. "This defeat will end the war. They'll know better than to try to fight us again."

Multiple toasts to victory, bottles consumed, confidence soaring. And General Ito's vague thought of clemency evaporated.

The next morning at dawn the artillery began its barrage again while the hawks of the Japanese Air Corps continued to lay down the patterns of explosions. By noon there was no further resistance. Ito sent out patrols to scout the wreckage. There was no gunfire, no sound at all except the moan of the wind through the ruins. Hours later the patrols came back one by one, all with the same report. In that wasteland there was not one person left alive.

Sam's secretary popped her head into the door of his office. "It's Luke Hawkins," she said. "From Associated Press."

"Tell him I don't know anything about the Japanese attack on our gunboat that he doesn't already know," Sam said.

"He witnessed it, sir. He was aboard the *Panay*."

Sam picked up the phone. "You saw it?" he said.

"The whole goddamned thing," Hawkins said. "Their aircraft assaulted the British gunboat *Ladybird,* and then they sank the gunboat *Panay* and three boats belonging to Standard Oil. They even strafed the lifeboats. I had to swim for my life."

"With no provocation."

"None. There wasn't even time for a defense."

"When you write your story send me a carbon for my official report."

"We can't let this one go unanswered," Hawkins said. "The *Panay* was evacuating American Embassy personnel and the Japanese knew it. You'll have my story within the hour." He hung up.

They're testing, he thought. *They want to see how much we'll take.*

When Hawkins's firsthand account arrived Sam immediately fired off a coded cable to State, stating that the attack on the American gunboat was an unequivocal act of war. Then he called General Ito's office and was told that the General would call him back shortly. The return cable from State arrived within hours.

ROBERT L. DUNCAN

WE HAVE REGISTERED AN OFFICIAL PROTEST WITH THE
JAPANESE GOVERNMENT OVER THE UNCONSCIONABLE
ACTS OF DECEMBER 12, 1937. PLEASE PROVIDE ANY FUR-
THER DETAILS AS SOON AS POSSIBLE.

R. CUMMINGS

His office was besieged by local correspondents seeking an explanation. They had already attended a news conference given by
Major General Harada Kumakichi that had turned into a shouting
match between officers of the Japanese Army and Navy who first
accused each other and then joined forces to accuse the *Panay* of
initiating the attack.

By the next morning there was still no word from General Ito. Sam
was visited by a stocky missionary from Iowa who had served in
Nanking for twenty years and was now leaving China. Miller sat in
Sam's office and stared at the floor. In a flat voice, as if he had
exhausted all emotion long ago, he described what the Japanese
troops were doing to the people of Nanking. Executions by the
thousands. Tortures. Japanese troops dragging women into the
streets and raping them. Blood everywhere. Perversity. Slaughter.
When he had finished his recital Miller continued to stare at the
pattern in the rug, lost in his own thoughts.

"I don't know why I'm telling you all this," he said.

"Something will be done about it," Sam said. "I promise you that."

"That was my first thought," Miller said, raising his eyes slightly,
very matter-of-fact now. "I thought that something would have to be
done. But I thought the same thing twenty years ago when the
warlords were cutting off heads of peasants who refused to give up
everything they had. They're all barbarians on both sides, no, not all,
most, and even the ones who aren't can easily revert. No one can do
anything about it." He stood up, wobbly on his feet. He had not slept
for days. "I want someone to look at my passport and see if it's still
good. I'm going home, back to a little church in an orderly world
where the people are full of small sins I can cope with." He shook his
head. "Have you ever seen a young girl eviscerated, sir? You
wouldn't want to. It does something to the mind. So just the passport
and I'll be going home. And as time passes, with any luck, I'll learn to
remember only the good times."

Sam called in Johnson from Passports and told him to make sure
Miller was given food and a bed while his papers were being

checked. Then, brooding, Sam sat at his desk and addressed the pile of cables just in from Washington, growing more impatient with each new inanity that demanded his attention, queries about the use of storage space, comparison statistics on the efficiency of stenographers in all Far Eastern consulates, and finally he gave the whole pile to a subordinate and drafted a cable to his Uncle Roger.

I BELIEVE THE AMERICAN LACK OF RESPONSE TO JAPANESE ATROCITIES AT NANKING IS NOT ONLY INAPPROPRIATE BUT ENCOURAGES THE JAPANESE MILITARY TO BELIEVE THERE IS NO LIMIT TO OUR TOLERANCE. SO DOES OUR REFUSAL TO TAKE ANY MILITARY REPRISAL FOLLOWING THE PANAY ATTACK. ADVISE ME OF ANY PENDING AMERICAN ACTION I CAN USE TO COUNTER THE WIDESPREAD FEELING THAT WE WILL PERMIT THE JAPANESE TO GO TO ANY LENGTHS WITHOUT OUR INTERFERENCE.

He sent it classified "Urgent" and within twelve hours had a reply marked "Personal," which he decoded at his desk.

THIS CABLE IS UNOFFICIAL. DESTROY AFTER READING. THERE IS A CLEAR DIVISION HERE BETWEEN THOSE WHO CONSIDER THE SINO-JAPANESE WAR A DISPUTE IN WHICH WE HAVE NO BUSINESS INTERFERING AND MY FACTION WHICH WOULD REFUSE TO ACCEPT THE CURRENT JAPANESE APOLOGIES FOR AN UNPROVOKED ATTACK ON AN AMERICAN GUNBOAT AND THE MURDER OF AMERICAN SAILORS.

THE SECRETARY OF STATE IS PREPARED TO ACCEPT JAPANESE APOLOGIES WITH APPROPRIATE COMPENSATION. THE NEUTRALISTS HERE CONSIDER THE REPORTS FROM NANKING UNRELIABLE PROPAGANDA SINCE THE EVACUATION OF EMBASSY PERSONNEL FROM THERE HAS DEPRIVED US OF OUR OBSERVERS. CAN YOU GIVE ME ANY HARD EVIDENCE TO USE IN FORCING A REEVALUATION OF AMERICAN POLICY?

Sam burned both the coded and deciphered versions of the cable in a metal wastebasket, then coded a request.

I ASK OFFICIAL PERMISSION TO GO TO NANKING ON A FACT-
FINDING MISSION.

The next cable was sent in the open from Washington and was
exactly what he wanted, phrased in official language.

THE AMERICAN CONSUL GENERAL IN SHANGHAI, THE HON-
ORABLE SAMUEL CUMMINGS, IS HEREBY AUTHORIZED AND
REQUESTED TO PROCEED TO NANKING UNDER THE CUR-
RENT PROTOCOL AGREEMENT BETWEEN THE UNITED
STATES OF AMERICA AND THE EMPIRE OF JAPAN WHICH
PERMITS FREE AND PROTECTED ACCESS TO THOSE AREAS
CONTAINING AN ESTABLISHED DIPLOMATIC MISSION OF EI-
THER COUNTRY. THE UNITED STATES OF AMERICA,
THROUGH THE STATE DEPARTMENT, HEREBY REQUESTS
THE COOPERATION OF ANY AND ALL JAPANESE OFFICIALS,
CIVILIAN AND MILITARY, TO FACILITATE CONSUL GENERAL
CUMMINGS'S MISSION TO NANKING.
A COPY OF THIS CABLE HAS BEEN FILED WITH THE JAPA-
NESE EMBASSY IN WASHINGTON, D.C., AND ANOTHER SENT
TO THE JAPANESE FOREIGN MINISTRY IN TOKYO.
                                    ROGER CUMMINGS
                                    UNDER SECRETARY OF
                                    STATE
                                    FAR EAST

On a December Thursday morning, early, Sam called General
Ito's office and requested a one o'clock meeting. Ito agreed.

He had not expected the wave of personal feeling that swept over
him as he entered Ito's new office at Japanese Military Headquarters
and found the General relaxed and surrounded by solicitous subordinate officers. In his brigadier's uniform, his boots impeccably polished, his hair combed straight back and close to the skull, Ito had
never looked to him in better form. And as they shook hands Sam
could not keep from thinking how much Ito had prospered.
*You've ended up with everything, haven't you? My wife and baby
are dead, you have the woman I loved, and you have my daughter,
and I can't even ask about them.*
"I am very pleased to see you," Ito said, sitting down at his desk. "I

am so sorry I had no chance to speak to you at your wife's funeral. Did you receive my personal message?"

"Yes, thank you. And you received my note congratulating you on your promotion?" Sam cleared his throat, blinked against the reflection of the sun on the glass of a framed portrait of the Emperor on the wall. "I have a request to make of you."

"You have but to ask," Ito said reflectively. "We are finally in a position to have mutual influence in Shanghai. And there's no problem here we cannot solve between us."

Sam removed the cable from his pocket, laid it on the desk. "This goes beyond Shanghai."

Ito was thoughtful as he read the cable. "I hear terrible things from Nanking myself. But it is beyond my jurisdiction."

"Surely you can make arrangements for me to go there."

Ito removed a gold cigarette case, and when Sam declined, decided against having one himself and returned the case to his pocket. He looked around the room with a slight discomfort, as if inhibited by it. "Would you join me in a walk to stretch the legs?" he said. "I've been sitting too long."

"Certainly."

They left the army compound and walked along the river, the air cold. Ito's gloved hands held a leather swagger stick; his breath condensed into steam. "It is easier for me to think in the open air," he said. "I walk along this river quite often."

My wife was killed by bombers that overshot your ships on this river. And somewhere near here I had a picnic with Yuki before my daughter was born. Sam pulled his collar up against the cold. He knew there was no time for bitterness now, and yet it stirred within him.

"Your forces have gone too far," he said.

"You will get no disagreement from me," Ito said. "Our Japanese military commanders decided that if they terrorized Nanking, the Chinese would lose any will to fight. Your government has decided that by accepting apologies and money that our military will somehow become pacified. And they are wrong."

"And what in the hell could the American government do that would make a difference?"

"Perhaps pretend that you are ready to fight for the sake of a principle." Ito lit his cigarette now, the gold case flashing in the sunlight. He exhaled the smoke into the chill air. "The British did nothing when their gunboat was sunk. The Americans did nothing. So my General Staff feels that it has carte blanche."

"How can you be so frank with me about this? Does your General Staff know your position?"

"They know that I have fought in battle and will continue to do whatever my country requires of me. I am not required to have any official position beyond that. I make my views known in a tactful manner. But please do not think that because I may differ with what is happening in China that I am in any way disloyal to my country."

Declarations, Sam thought. *Just words.* He looked at the flocks of white gulls wheeling over the fantails of the ships anchored in the muddy water. They would still be flying here when the last ship was gone. "I'm tired of all the diplomacy that does nothing," he said. "I want to go to Nanking and find out if the stories I hear are true, then I intend to do my damnedest to force some action from my government to stop it."

"I will do what I can."

"Which means you may not help me get to Nanking."

"You do not understand the Japanese method of command," Ito said. "General Matsui commands the armies that occupy Nanking and he answers only to the General Staff for the actions of his troops. He releases very few reports about what is happening there so I have little more evidence than you do, just a great many stories, which may or may not be exaggerated." He dropped his cigarette, ground it out beneath his heel. "If you have no objections, I will go with you to Nanking."

"Why should you?"

"In the eyes of my superiors I will be your official escort to keep you safe. There can be no objection to that. And when I return I will file a full report of what you saw and experienced, because my superiors will want to be forewarned about anything you might have to say. They know that if the atrocities are indeed true on the scale they are rumored to be, you will make an official report to your government concerning them. So they will then take some action to bring them to a halt."

Shrewd, Sam thought. *You always were.* "Matsui's in town, isn't he?"

"Briefly, yes. I think I can get you an immediate appointment."

"A meeting that you will attend."

"Of course," Ito said. "The official meeting of the American Consul General with a distinguished military commander requires a high-ranking translator."

General Matsui was a pale, soft-spoken little man who conversed with such a measured and deliberate slowness that Sam had to restrain a strong desire to hurry him along. He read Sam's cable in English, asked Ito for a translation, and then clarified the translation word for word, looking directly at Sam all the time he was listening to Ito. Then he made a long speech, pausing every few seconds to sort out his thoughts. When he finished he looked to Ito to translate.

"To condense what General Matsui says," Ito said. "He knows why you want to go to Nanking and he admits that there have been irregularities there in the past."

"Irregularities?" Sam said.

"An unusual kind of hostility," Ito said. "He says that his men were very unhappy with what happened in Shanghai and for the resistance along the way because the Chinese burned everything in the path of our army. They also committed atrocities. So when Nanking was captured some unfortunate things happened and some illegal acts occurred. But he says that he issued orders the moment he became aware of such irregularities and that such incidents stopped."

"Then he will have no objections to my journey?"

"He says that you should take his word that everything is in order there."

"I have been instructed to inspect American properties."

"He says that even though Nanking is rapidly becoming pacified, it still must be considered a dangerous area."

"Tell him I will assume responsibility."

Ito entered into a quietly intense and strangely formal conversation with General Matsui in which neither man broke eye contact, almost as if each was assessing the other for any sign of weakness. Finally, General Matsui accepted a cigarette from the gold case with a grunt and looked at Sam's face while Ito explained.

"I told him I would accompany you," Ito said. "He wanted to know why I would waste my time in this manner and I explained it would be inappropriate to allow you to go to Nanking by yourself. He has informed me that by my taking you, he will be absolved from any responsibility. But he will countersign your pass. His chop will ensure the cooperation of his local commanders in the field."

"Please thank him for his courtesy."

Once they were outside Ito checked his watch. "What time would be convenient for you?"

And for a moment Sam's mind played tricks on him and he thought that he would need to talk to Charlotte before he scheduled the trip. Then he felt the sharp pain of reality. "Anytime," he said. "The sooner the better."

"There's a late afternoon train," Ito said. "About four o'clock."

"Fine," Sam said. "I'll be ready."

The train to Nanking was crowded with troops. At the first sight of General Ito a sergeant hurried through the coach and rousted soldiers out of a compartment, belaboring them with a stout wooden stick. The compartment stank of beer and sweat-stained uniforms.

"Troop trains all smell alike," Ito said. He offered Sam a cigarette, lighting it before he lit his own. He listened to the blast of the train whistle as the coaches lurched and began to move forward.

"Are you ever homesick?" he asked.

"No," Sam said. "Are you?"

"Sometimes," Ito said. "A Japanese man changes when he goes abroad. He doesn't know how he fits into the order of things. But in Tokyo I never even have to consider it. I know exactly who I am and what I'm required to do."

The order of things, Sam thought, looking out at the ruins of Chapei in the twilight. *In the middle of chaos, order is being restored.* Already shacks were going up, lean-tos, cook fires glowing in the angles of ruined walls, ants returning to the anthill, patiently beginning to build back a city razed to the ground. How many times, he wondered, had this section of the city been destroyed and rebuilt in five centuries? How many times would the Chinese continue to come back and begin again? *Forever,* he thought. This ground could be pulverized annually for a thousand years and still, within hours after the last bomb fell, the people would begin to sift back into the ruins again.

The city became countryside, and he realized he was looking at the China of three hundred years ago. Even this close to the cities all of the amenities of the modern age were lacking, no electricity, no running water, herbal medicine dispensed by barefoot doctors.

He studied Ito, who was absorbed in a Chinese newspaper. *My God, we're both in the same boat,* he thought. *He's as much out of his element in China as I am.* Both foreigners, trying to make do. And Ito, he thought, was not faring well here, trying to walk the very narrow line between East and West.

Shortly after dark an orderly brought tea. Very soon Sam found himself nodding, lulled by the clacking of the wheels on the rails, the swaying motion of the coach, the occasional wail of the whistle as the train hurtled through the dark chill of the Chinese night. He came awake when the train braked and came lurching to a stop. He looked through the window but there was nothing but darkness outside, no sign of Nanking Station or even a temporary military depot.

An orderly came bursting into the compartment to bring information to the General.

"Chinese soldiers have removed some of the rails and thrown them into a creek, sir," he said. "Fortunately, we have a company of Japanese army engineers aboard the train. They can repair the line."

"How long will it take?"

"Eight hours, sir."

"How far back is the nearest town?" Ito said.

"There's a small village about five miles east, sir."

"How far ahead to Nanking?"

"About ten miles, sir."

Ito looked at Sam. "I do not think it is a good idea to try to reach Nanking in the darkness. The train can take us back to the nearest village and we can proceed in the morning when the track is fixed."

"Are we close to a road?" Sam said. "Is there any other kind of transportation?"

Ito asked the orderly. "Cavalry horses," he said. "The cavalry discovered the missing rails and flagged the train."

"I'd like to go into Nanking," Sam said. "If you're up to it."

"I trained with the cavalry," Ito said.

Arranging the ride into Nanking was no simple matter. The cavalry patrol, suddenly faced with the presence of a general officer, decided after much conferring that two lieutenants would give up their mounts to the General and the American Consul while the captain accompanied the visitors with an escort of a dozen troops. Sam was given a spirited bay, and as he swung into the Japanese saddle he remembered the times he had gone riding as a boy with his father in China. The horses trotted through the chill darkness, following a path through the hills, and Sam sensed that the cavalry captain was nervous about something.

The captain spoke to the General in a subdued, apologetic voice, as if afraid of Ito's wrath, but Ito merely nodded. "The captain informs me that the troops in Nanking are drunk and out of control," he said to Sam. "Apparently, General Matsui's orders have not been followed."

"What are you going to do about it?"

"I have to go into the city and do what I can to restore order. But there's an inn near here where you will be safe."

"I'll stay with you and take my chances."

"Then keep close," Ito said. "I have no specific authority in Nanking, but if we can make it to command headquarters, I think I can take charge as a ranking officer."

Less than five miles from Nanking, Sam saw fires burning in the distance. As they approached a temple he heard the sporadic sounds of gunfire, laughter, and the barking of dogs, more like a celebration than a battle. Riding into a square, he found himself in the middle of a crowd of Japanese soldiers gathered around a campfire, passing bottles of sake. A dozen dogs milled around the center of the square, yelping and snarling, and some of the soldiers were putting money on a betting board. At first they appeared to be gambling on a dog fight, but as Sam rode closer he could see in the torchlight two frantic and bloodied Chinese men, buried to the waist in the middle of the square, each armed with a short stick. They were trying desperately to beat off the wiry dogs that circled them and darted in to attack while the Japanese soldiers laughed and yelled encouragement to the dogs.

Suddenly, Ito spurred his horse into a gallop and, drawing his sword, charged into the middle of the camp. With one swing of the blade he cut a mongrel in half and scattered the rest of the pack. The dog's blood flew on the night air and the soldiers fell back, stuporous, muttering, until they realized that the apparition on horseback was a general officer. Instantly they began to fire their rifles at the dogs and chase them with sticks while a drunken corporal tried to gather up the money. He was spun around by a black hound that darted past him, teeth bared, to attack one of the half-buried men, ripping his throat before he disappeared into the darkness.

Ito fired his pistol into the air, his face flushed with anger. "You are Japanese soldiers," he yelled at them. "You are not butchers. I command you to go back to your quarters."

But the soldiers were too drunk to be controlled. In the confused melee of dogs and horses, with a sergeant yelling at the corporal who had scattered the money in the dirt, they paid little attention to the shouting General. A large column of soldiers came marching into the square, herding twenty to thirty Chinese civilians who were roped together like a giant bundle of grain waiting for threshing. As they passed Sam's horse reared and fell and he was thrown into a shallow ditch while his mount galloped away into the night. Dazed, his head bleeding, Sam scrambled backward to keep from being trampled as Ito's escort troops dispersed to allow the marching column to pass by.

Sam stayed on the ground until the last of the soldiers had passed, and then, dazed from the blow, unable to locate Ito, he fell in behind the soldiers at a distance with a vague plan in mind. Eventually he would run into an officer, show him the pass signed by General Matsui, and request a guide to command headquarters.

He staggered down a lane flanked by large animals carved of stone, the approach to an emperor's tomb. The light of the torches glinted on a marble lion, a granite elephant. Slowly his senses returned and he began to think logically. He should have stayed where he was. Ito would be looking for him in the vicinity of the square. But there was no great harm done, he told himself. Undoubtedly the Chinese prisoners were being taken to a detention center where there would be senior officers in charge to set things straight. He would follow them.

But the soldiers did not stay on the road. Instead, they moved the Chinese prisoners onto a path and up to the edge of a ravine, prodding them along with bayonets. He concealed himself behind a stone elephant and watched with horror as three noncoms circled the civilians with cans and sloshed them with liquid, matter-of-factly, and then another soldier stepped forward and thrust his torch at the nearest prisoner. The flame swept across and around the bound men in a spiraling wreath of fire. The prisoners screamed, struggled to get free, but those nearest the ravine lost their footing and fell, pulling the others over the edge with them. Then the Japanese soldiers, in no particular hurry, lined up along the ravine and fired their rifles into the burning targets.

Sam sat down heavily against the stone leg of the elephant, fear pulsing through him. Christ, no written paper would protect him here, not from soldiers who stood cheering at the edge of the ravine until the last screams died away and then staggered back down the lane in uneven ranks, singing.

Sam moved deeper into the shadows. He touched the aching side of his head, felt the blood on his fingers. He could not stay here.

As soon as the soldiers were gone and he could no longer hear the echo of their singing, he stood up, light-headed, dizzy, and began to walk back toward the square, only to find it deserted except for hungry dogs chewing on the bodies of the half-buried Chinese. No sign of the horses. The campfire smoldered beneath a layer of dirt. He went down a narrow lane, past a line of men hanging upside down against the side of a building, gutted, their gray entrails spilled out onto the cobblestones.

He had been pushed into a nightmare where nothing seemed to make sense. He wandered in search of air that did not stink and eventually found his way into the trees of a park where he sat down heavily, tired, dazed. He watched from his place in the woods as three more columns of Chinese males were marched down a side road near the walls of the houses by Japanese troops. When one prisoner stumbled and fell he was bayoneted by the nearest guard and left to die while the column moved on. Sam closed his eyes, gave in to the pain.

Dawn came after many hours and with it a glimmer of hope. In the cold, clear daylight he was sure he would be recognized as American or European, and the soldiers who were drunk last night would certainly be sleeping it off. Ito would have put himself in command by now. Sanity would have been restored to the city.

Shivering from the cold, cramped and stiff, he stood up, deciding to look for the nearest headquarters unit. He heard running water in the park and he walked toward it, found a shallow stream emptying into a natural stone basin. Cupping water with his hands, he drank and saw his reflection in the surface of the pool. The blood had caked on the side of his head, matted the hair, covered the side of his neck.

The greatcoat he wore was filthy, bloody. He washed his face as best he could and with his fingers smoothed his hair into place. It would have to do. He stood up, brushed some of the dirt and leaves off his coat. He heard a slight rustle, which startled him, and he turned to confront an old Chinese woman and ten young girls in their early teens. They stared at him with terrified eyes.

The old woman bowed to him. "Honorable sir," she said in Chinese in a voice that was barely louder than a whisper. "Are you English?"

"I am American," he said.

"These are the girls of the Sacred Heart School," the old woman said, bowing again. "Since they are Christian and you are American, I humbly ask for your protection."

"I am honored at your request, Esteemed Grandmother," he said. "But you can see my condition and the respect that has been accorded me."

"The teachers have been killed," the old woman said. "The girls have not eaten for three days. The nights here are very cold and some of the girls are already sick. If it is possible, Honorable Sir, that you are able to save yourself, I would ask you to intercede for these worthless girls. I ask only for passage across the river where we can find a way to a Christian community that is five hours walk from there."

Christ, he thought. *Why not?* There had to be a vast difference between drunk enlisted men and sober and responsible officers. "I will do my best to aid you," he said. "But I ask you to keep the girls here, Esteemed Grandmother. Keep them out of sight until I have a chance to find the right officer. If I am not back by midday, you will know that I did not succeed."

The old woman bowed again. "This worthless person is not Christian but I am almost led to believe by the fact that a savior has been sent for my girls."

He patted her on the arm. "I'll do the best I can, but you must keep the girls hidden."

He walked out of the woods and passed a large stone beast with the head of a hawk and the body of a lion. One side of its head had worn away with the centuries and a part of the stone flank was missing. Close to a royal tomb, he thought, but the knowledge did not help him get his bearings. Nanking was one vast mausoleum of a city, emperors, nobles, had been interred here for thousands of years. A city of massive stone memorials, a city of death.

He entered a residential neighborhood, almost every building bearing the mark of bombs, no one around. He could see smoke in the distance but there was no sound of a battle, not even the distant pop of rifles.

He saw two Japanese soldiers making their way down the street, their rifles in sling position, and he approached them, waving the pass signed by General Matsui. They studied the pass and then, in broken English and sign language, managed to convey the location of their headquarters to him. He thanked them in Japanese and walked away, patting his pockets for his identification card and his diplomatic passport. He approached a doorway at which a well-groomed Japanese stood guard.

He half expected the guard to stop him, but the soldier merely came to attention as Sam went inside. A Japanese sergeant seated at a desk eyed him suspiciously.

"I am the American Consul General in Shanghai," Sam said imperiously in English, presenting his papers. "I want to see your commanding officer."

The sergeant looked at him blankly, took the papers, then stood and went to a door, disappeared for a moment, and reappeared to beckon Sam into the room. An army captain with a thin mustache patted his mouth with a napkin. Obviously his breakfast had been interrupted. The remains of soft-boiled eggs, soup, and daikon pickles littered the table in front of him.

"I am Captain Sumoda," he said, in stiff, textbook English. "Did I hear you tell my sergeant that you are American?"

"I'm the American Consul General in Shanghai. As you will see, this pass is signed by General Matsui."

The Captain waved his hand. "I believe you. The proof is unnecessary." He saw the dried blood on Sam's head, pursed his lips disdainfully. "I will have one of my medics look at your head. You do not want an infection." He barked in Japanese at his sergeant and sent him flying. "Would you care for something to eat, sir? An egg, perhaps?"

"Tea would be fine," Sam said, beginning to relax. "Please go ahead with your breakfast."

The Captain poured tea for him, then neatly tapped the end of a soft-boiled egg shell with a knife. "What are you doing in Nanking, sir? It was my opinion that there are no American diplomats here now. I have studied English, as you can tell, I believe. I thought that a mastery of English and a knowledge of business methods would make a large difference in my life after my return to Japan." He peeled the top off the egg, examined it critically, and finding that the exposed end was not large enough to admit a spoon, began to tap around the shell again. "Of course, it made no difference," he said with irony. "I was made an officer in the army and allowed to serve my country."

Sam sipped the tea. "I came here last night with General Ito. Do you know where I can find him?"

"I am afraid not," Captain Sumoda said. "I have not had the privilege of knowing about this general, much less his whereabouts."

"Do you have a telephone here? I want to call Shanghai."

"Unfortunately," the Captain said, "our telephones are not functioning. If I want my company surgeon, who is not even a hundred yards from here, I cannot telephone for him. I have to send a messenger." He picked the pieces of cracked shell off the surface of the egg with great dexterity.

"Then I will write a letter and ask you to send it to Shanghai with your battalion dispatches, Captain. You must be aware of what's going on in this city. Chinese civilians are being slaughtered in the north part of the city, burned alive."

"Was that where you received your wound?" the Captain said.

"I fell from a horse."

The company surgeon knocked on the side of the open door, bowed to the Captain and then to Sam, introducing himself in a polite whisper of a voice. He washed Sam's wound with warm water and a medicinal soap. He clipped the hair around it and then covered it with salve. He applied a bandage and departed.

"I apologize to you for the fact that you were wounded and also for the inferior medical treatment I have been able to offer you," Captain Sumoda said. He inserted the spoon into the top of the egg and pried loose a small bite. "There have been unfortunate breakdowns in communications, but I must say to you, sir, that there have been many Chinese provocations that have not been reported. I would advise you, sir, to allow me to provide you with an escort to the railroad line, where you may have transport back to Shanghai."

"I need to take care of something first," Sam said. "There is a group of schoolgirls in the care of an old woman hiding in the woods. They're Catholic and they want transportation out of the battle zone to the other side of the Yangtze, where they have people who will take care of them."

Captain Sumoda had another bite of egg, scooped out the yoke with the tip of his spoon, then followed it with a loud slurp of tea. "That can be arranged," he said. "If you will tell me where they are, I'll send men to take care of them."

"I'll take your men there myself," Sam said. "I will also stay with the girls until they're safely aboard a transport to the other side of the river."

"You should accept my word," the Captain said.

"After what I've seen here, I want an absolute guarantee that they will be safe. It's no reflection on you personally, Captain, but it's obvious that some of the officers have lost control of their troops."

"You are welcome to be an observer," Sumoda said.

Within fifteen minutes his orderly had rounded up a detail of a dozen men under the leadership of a corporal to accompany Sam to the place where the girls were hiding. As they walked the young corporal slapped a willow switch against his thigh as if to count cadence for the scraggly troops, many of whom looked as if they had neither slept nor bathed in days. They walked through the streets and Sam heard the intermittent popping of rifles firing somewhere off to his right, people yelling, screaming, so far away that it did not seem real.

Jesus, he thought. *How vulnerable I am, how goddamned presumptuous.* He was assuming that Sumoda was really in charge, that these men would follow his orders, that he, as a representative of the American government, counted for something here—that the girls in the woods would indeed be safe. The corporal spoke English but there was no conversation.

It was almost noon by the time they climbed the slope into the park. The corporal looked around and then yelled at his men to spread out and search the woods for the girls.

"No," Sam said firmly. "Call your men back, Corporal. These girls are frightened. I don't want them upset even more."

The corporal shrugged, countermanded his order. Sam called out into the woods. "You have nothing to fear, Esteemed Grandmother," he said in Chinese. "These men are here to conduct the girls across the river. I'll be along to guarantee your safety."

Time passed. The soldiers stood where they were. The corporal was clearly irritated by the delay. Sam watched the birds at the top of one bare tree, chattering in the thin sunshine of the winter day. After a while he spoke again, almost conversationally. "I understand your fear, Esteemed Grandmother," he said. "If you choose to stay hidden and leave here on your own, then I will respect your wish and take these troops back to the city. You don't even need to reveal that you're here. I'll wait another three or four minutes and then leave." He noted the time on his watch, then nodded to the corporal. "We'll go back to the city, Corporal," he said.

The corporal had turned to give orders to his men when Sam heard the thin voice of the old woman.

"Wait," she said. "Please."

She came out of the bushes by herself, studied the Japanese soldiers, who had stopped a few feet away. Her ancient face was screwed up in intense thought as she tried to make a decision. "Are you sure of these soldiers, Esteemed Sir?" she said.

"I wish to God I could say that," he said quietly. "I think they can be trusted. Their captain seems to me to be a reasonable man. But I can't see that your girls have any other choice."

"Do you think the Japanese will give food to my girls?"

"I'll ask on your behalf when we get back to command headquarters."

The old woman made up her mind, nodded toward the woods. The girls came out single file. They wore the dark blue coats of their school uniforms. The corporal regarded them with disinterest.

"We'll take them back to your command headquarters," Sam said. "They've had nothing to eat in a long time."

The corporal nodded. He deployed a half dozen men at the front of the column of girls, the remaining six at the rear, and they all began to move back toward the town. Sam could feel the fear in the girls, so intense that they walked without making a sound. When they reached the edge of the business district and rounded the first corner onto the boulevard, they were suddenly in the middle of what appeared to be a skirmish. The corporal moved the girls and his troops into a small alleyway. In the street a squad of Japanese troops was pouring rifle and machine-gun fire into a row of buildings as another squad stormed the doors and minutes later emerged with half a dozen Chinese males, all of them old or very young. They were prodded out into the middle of the street with their hands atop their heads. Abruptly one teenaged boy broke from the group and tried to run. A soldier raised his rifle and carefully squeezed off a shot that smashed the boy's right knee and sent him careening into a wall.

From the mouth of the alley Sam watched the bickering between the shooter and another soldier who, half drunk, was trying to make a bet with him. The grimacing Chinese boy was thrashing in pain against the wall, trying to get to his feet, an impossibility with one knee shattered. The bet was whether or not the shooter could hit the boy's left hand, which flailed the air. The shooter raised his rifle, the muzzle waving to and fro, the moving hand an almost impossible target. But the rifle tracked it and the shot was fired, the boy's hand exploding red.

I have to do something. Christ, the bloody barbarians.

But the boy was beyond Sam's help now. A final shot through the head had put him down. Another soldier moved around the clump of Chinese with a rope, binding them together, a bundle of sticks to be burned, and Sam looked around the alley for a place to hide the girls but there were no doors in the wall, no place to go. One of the girls was weeping quietly, tears running, no sound.

Sam approached the corporal. "You are responsible for the security of these girls," he said quietly. "And you will find a way to get them to safety."

The corporal's eyes were on the street. "There is a sergeant out there. He outranks me."

"But you're under orders from your captain."

"I'll talk to the sergeant," the corporal said. He went out into the street and walked up to the sergeant, who was yelling at the soldier winding the rope around the Chinese men, telling him to raise it so the men could walk. Sam could not understand the conversation but the sergeant produced a bottle, offered it to the corporal, who took a long drink before he handed it back. The corporal talked a long time and then stayed where he was while the sergeant approached the alley, a broad smile on his face. He was a squat, seemingly good-humored man, not drunk enough to be red-faced or slurred in his speech. He glanced at the girls and the old woman and nodded, then in broken English asked Sam to see his papers.

He glanced at the pass, nodded as he folded it, and handed it back. Then he called the corporal to come and translate. "I explained the situation," the corporal said. "The sergeant will give you a man to take you back to Captain Sumoda. The sergeant will assume personal responsibility for the girls and the elderly woman."

"Tell him that won't be necessary," Sam said. "I've given my word to see these girls safely across the river and that's what I'm going to do."

The sergeant's smile was constant as he spoke to the corporal, who translated for him. "He says that you are a *gaijin* after all. You have no influence in this place. He is in charge of this street patrol in the middle of a battle zone where he has enemies all around him. He thinks it would be best if you follow his instructions." The sergeant turned and called one of his men, who came to him at a dead run. "This soldier will take you back to Captain Sumoda," the corporal said.

"No," Sam said. "Tell him to send a man to bring the captain here."

Suddenly, with such quickness he did not see it coming, a fist struck Sam in the side of the face and spun him around against the wall.

"Run," he yelled to the old woman. "Take the girls and run."

The girls tried to run but the soldiers were too swift. A burly recruit grabbed the old woman, who began to claw at his face, and the recruit struck her sharply. In that moment Sam grabbed a knife from the recruit's belt and drove the blade into his chest, but as the soldier's body slumped away, Sam saw the old woman lying on the cobblestones, dead, a rifle still balanced on the thin spike of a bayonet in her chest.

Angry, yelling, he grabbed the rifle and pulled the bayonet free, fired at a soldier who had caught one of the girls and had thrown her to the pavement, and was prying her legs open with a knee. The bullet caught the soldier in the neck, threw him onto his back. Just as another soldier raised his sword, Sam turned and hit him in the head with the rifle butt, knocking him against a wall. The sword clattered away. But then he felt a numbing blow in his back, a sharp pain so intense that it knocked him to the ground. He realized he had been bayoneted, the wound pushing him toward shock. He stayed on the edge of consciousness, willed himself to get up, commanded his fingers to hold on to the rifle. But his fingers disobeyed. A boot kicked him in the side. He saw a soldier with a two-handed sword standing above him, ready to cut him in two.

The sword did not descend. The sergeant's face, smiling. Better not to kill a man with a pass signed by a general. That unforgettable smile. Very even teeth, one of the incisors half gold, divided diagonally, metal sparkling in the sunlight. Sam moved his mind away into the comfortable and unfeeling darkness.

He stirred. Pain. All enveloping, his back on fire. He wanted to drift away from it again, into sleep. It was after twilight, darkness piling up in the corners of the streets. A raging fire in the distance, backlighting the ruins of the buildings demolished by the Japanese during the afternoon. A street full of ghosts, people moving silently from the bombed-out piles of stone into the open. Not ghosts, no, the local women picking up the bodies of the schoolgirls he had tried to protect that afternoon. Pain on ancient faces, but not a sound to bring the Japanese back again. Bodies. One girl ripped wide open from the throat to the stomach.

He saw, closed his eyes. He knew what was happening to him. Bleeding to death. Little time left if he did not get help. He had to do something. *Force yourself.* He dug his fingers into splintered brick. With all of his strength, he pulled himself to a kneeling position. Head spinning. Weak. Now the legs. Holding on to the wall, he inched up the side until he was standing. He let go and lurched down the street, kept his balance, listened to the far-off screams, the chatter of machine guns. Short bursts.

He looked for something. He had shot a Japanese soldier in the act of rape. No dead body left. They had hauled him off. He was not interested in the body. He wanted the rifle.

The girl's body was still there. The street women had not yet come to get her. He stood over her, looked around for the man's rifle in the street. Taken away, obviously. A glint of something metallic near the curb caught his eye. In a pile of leaves. The bayonet. Jarred loose, kicked away, overlooked. He picked it up. Metal cold against his hand. He knew what he was going to do.

Could not stay alive, no, the wound too deep, blood still coursing out. The papers in his pocket, the official chop mark of the general, the diplomatic passport, no talisman could save him. He could not escape this city. He was in the midst of men gone mad.

He staggered down the street, practiced walking. Mind fresher from the cold night air. Past a burned-out trolley, the shape of an animal, long thin neck raised to graze a wire. Down the street toward the headquarters. He made the picture in his mind, held on to it, kept moving. First conceal the bayonet beneath his coat. Fingers fumbling, stiff-jointed. Bayonet now out of sight. He would go into headquarters. Captain Sumoda waiting. Rice bowl held beneath his chin, chop sticks shoveling food. Sumoda looking up. Astonished eyes. No words. No need for words. The point of the bayonet would say all. Sumoda's mouth open. A question? A protestation? A cry for help? No sound at all. No time. The bayonet driven into his chest.

My life not wasted. One for one.

He rounded the corner. Military cars in front of the headquarters, three or four soldiers standing outside, breath steaming in cold air. Drivers, maybe. Waiting. Laughing? Did one of them laugh? Obscene.

He leaned against the wall. Giddy. So light-headed it was hard to think. Changes. Captain Sumoda beyond him. Fingers fumbled for a cigarette. Lit a match. Sucked smoke into his lungs. Dizzier for a moment and then clearer.

It did not have to be a captain. Any soldier. All killers. He stood, watched. Three soldiers standing together. The fourth wiping the fender of the car with a rag. The man was short, faceless. Leggings perfectly wrapped. He wore his hat at a precisely correct angle. A good soldier. He would do.

On down the street, legs still holding him up, the pain a furnace in his back. Fingers on the handle of the bayonet. The soldier did not turn around as Sam approached. His jacket drawn taut over his back as he reached up over the top of the car with the cloth. Perfect. The blade to go left of the spine. Through skin and bone and tissue. Into the heart.

One of the other soldiers saw him coming, paid little attention. Now was the time. He drew the bayonet and thrust it forward. Awkward. Thin air. Almost fell. Someone grabbed his arm.

"Cummings-san? Is that you?"

He turned, tried to pull free, wanting to kill. Words like bullets. "Bastards. Safety. I promised. You killed them all. You sons of bitches. You butchered young girls, old women." Out of breath. Dizzy. "All dead. My wife. My baby." All gone now. His strength. Everything. He gave a deep sigh and fell forward into blackness, Ito catching him in his arms. A soldier took the bayonet, dropped it on the ground, and helped Ito with Sam.

Sam came to, blinked. He was inside the warm headquarters. A jolt of brandy to warm his stomach. His coat was peeled off, the shirt torn away. A team of medics this time, cleaning his wound, staunching the flow of blood. Crazy. From vengeance to gratitude. Killers as saviors. Insane.

Not dead after all.

Someone came into his view. Really Ito? Yes, not an apparition. And for a second Ito's face blurred and he looked like all the other soldiers and Sam remembered the sergeant grinning at him with his gold tooth. *Are you one of them, Ito-san?*

Stitches and a bandage and Ito looking at him intently, concerned. "I've had men looking for you since last night. What happened to you?"

Very much has happened to me. Human bonfires. People as carrion. Mutilation. The rape of schoolgirls. Wild animals.

Very weak, but the head was clearer. He forced himself to sit up. "You didn't stop the carnage," he said.

"No," Ito said sadly. "But it is coming to an end. And I will see that some of the men are punished." He asked his aide a question, turned back to Sam. "There's a train out in an hour," he said. "The tracks have been repaired."

Sam said nothing. No words. Ito handed him the flask again and Sam took another long pull of brandy.

The enlisted man Sam had wanted to kill helped him to the car. Very strong arms. Sam in the backseat, Ito beside him. The car moving away, threading through the bomb craters in the street. He shivered. Feverish with infection. Detached. Listened to Ito. "The Chinese committed atrocities as well. They slaughtered the Japanese patrols they captured."

Bestiality on both sides? All unforgivable. Nothing can be canceled out.

Suddenly the car stopped. A ragged column of cavalry rode out of a side lane, leading a Chinese general, his uniform in rags, his face set, his expression superior even in captivity.

Wang, yes. The son of a bitch. Wolf of Shanghai.

Sam looked at the face of the Chinese general, saw the arrogant eyes, the glint of evil, and suddenly General Wang was the essence of all slaughter and cruelty. *The first dinner in Shanghai. A human head rolling in the dirt. Jesus, he killed my father, cut off Bright Moon's feet.* Sam held out his hand to Ito. "Give me your pistol."

Ito put it in his hand and Sam left the car, his legs rubbery as he weaved through the soldiers toward Wang. *Is the bastard really smiling? Doesn't the son of a bitch know I'm going to kill him?* He lifted the pistol with a shaking hand. Pulled the trigger. Fired. Missed. Dropped the pistol. Collapsed to all fours to grope around for it. Looked up to see Ito with the pistol, speaking to the General in Chinese. "I do this for the crime against the American as well as myself. I should never have let you escape from Chapei the first time."

General Wang was smiling. "Free me and I'll piss on you again."

Ito leveled the pistol at Wang's forehead, pulled the trigger. A round black hole centered above the junction of the eyebrows. Wang jerked slightly, eyes dulling, face going slack, and then his knees gave way and he collapsed into the dirt.

Finished, Sam thought. *Enough dying, enough revenge.*

With Ito's help, he stood up, returned to the car, sank into the seat. The car moved on. "Jesus Christ, all too much."

He lay in the Shanghai hospital bed for two weeks, alternately burning up and chilled, aware of the nurses who hovered over him and the American doctor who studied the chart at the foot of his bed.

Gradually his mind began to clear, and he saw that Connaught was checking the clanking radiator to see if it was functioning properly, giving orders to the Chinese nurse to keep the water pitcher filled at all times, and only when it seemed that he had the room well in hand did he sit down beside the bed, smiling.

"Well, old boy, it seems that you're finally on the mend."

"What's going on?" Sam said.

"I would like to tell you that God's in His heaven and all's right with the world," Connaught said, "but the Japanese armies are pushing to the south and west. Are you warm enough? Is that radiator doing any good?"

"I can feel it. I vaguely remember firing off a cable about Nanking before I came into the hospital. What's State doing?"

"Our men at State have had tea with their envoys in Washington. 'Excesses on both sides' I believe was the phrase used in the final reports."

"And the schoolgirls?"

"All whiffed under the rug, I'm afraid," Connaught said. "A Catholic girl's school was destroyed early in the fighting and there was no way to tell whether the shells had come from the Chinese or Japanese artillery."

Sam groaned. "I want you to send another cable in my name protesting the wide-scale slaughter in Nanking and demanding that the United States issue a formal reprimand. I can understand individuals being carried away in the heat of battle, but I refuse to accept an official policy that approves torture on a mass scale."

Connaught put a hand on his arm. "I would strongly advise against it."

"For what reason?"

"Your country has already made its feelings clear on the matter. If anybody catches hell now, it will be you. Not the Japanese."

"I want you to do it anyway."

"So be it."

Three days later Connaught was back, nodding approvingly that the radiator was continuing to function properly. "Well, I've done it, reluctantly I must admit. Here is the reaction from Washington." He handed Sam a sheet of paper, an open memo to all personnel at the consulate general.

FROM THIS MOMENT FORWARD, NO STATEMENTS CONCERNING AMERICAN ATTITUDES TOWARD ANY OF THE COMBATANT POWERS WILL BE MADE PUBLIC BY ANY EMPLOYEE OF THE UNITED STATES GOVERNMENT STATIONED IN ASIA WITHOUT EXPRESS PERMISSION IN WRITING FROM THE SECRETARY OF STATE. ANY PERSONNEL VIOLATING THIS RULE WILL BE SUBJECT TO SWIFT DISCIPLINE AND REMOVAL FROM SERVICE.

R. CUMMINGS
FAR EAST

"There is now no stopping the Japanese." Sam crumpled the paper and dropped it into the wastebasket.

Tokyo . . . January 1938

WHEN HIS GOVERNMENT car passed Tokyo Station, General Ito glanced at the dozens of giant banners welcoming the troops home on leave and exhorting them to fight even harder for the national essence when they went back to the front. The banners were proof of high morale, a colorful flowering of the military spirit, which was also evident in the traffic on the street, the mass of military vehicles, the voluntary decrease in the use of private cars.

He had left Shanghai as soon as he learned that Cummings-san was going to be all right and had been home three days now, long enough to get acquainted with his infant son, Kanao, and to hear his wife's complaints.

"Some of the rice we are forced to buy is very coarse," she had said. "And I have to send the kitchen servants all the way to the country to find vegetables that are even edible. My father said yesterday that many of the golf courses are to remain closed this spring because of whatever goes into making golf balls is no longer available . . ."

His mother had been delighted to see him, but he could tell that all was not peaceful in the large house. Not that his mother complained about Ariko, but she let him know, indirectly, that she had not found a companion with whom she could talk and play mah-jongg. For Ariko had been quietly miserable throughout her pregnancy and had preferred to stay by herself, making appearances only as custom and etiquette dictated, occasionally sharing a meal with her mother-in-law. Instead of leading a life of contemplation, his mother said, Ariko was brooding.

"I would never make suggestions to my esteemed son about his career," his mother said, eyes tactfully averted, voice carefully modulated so that no forcefulness exhibited itself. "But if your esteemed father, the Baron, were still alive, I believe he would advise you to give serious consideration to coming home."

The flea runs the dog, Ito thought. Were he to take a post in Tokyo, he would soon bring his wife into line. It was possible, of course, that he might be returned to Tokyo against his will, for he was being highly presumptuous in making an appointment to see Prince Konoye, the Prime Minister. His father had been a friend of the Prince and so his visit could be interpreted as simply a paying of respects, but Ito knew the true reason would be guessed in military circles and considered an affront by the General Staff.

The car pulled into the circular driveway at the Prince's house, and Ito was led into a waiting room furnished Western style, with wooden paneling and a coal fire burning in an English fireplace. Through the leaded-glass windowpanes he saw a delegation of ambassadors in frock coats leaving by another door.

In a moment a door opened into a spacious office and Prince Konoye himself came forward to greet him. He was an unusually tall man with an air of unshakable confidence. He dismissed his male secretary before he closed the door behind them and went immediately to a teak bar, where he poured two beakers of brandy.

Prince Konoye handed him one, then raised his own. *"Compai,"* he said. "To your health."

Ito sipped his brandy as Konoye waved him to a couch and then sat down in a leather chair opposite him. "I knew your father well," the Prince said. "And I hear of you now and again from many sources. I congratulate you on the birth of your son."

"Thank you, Excellency."

"I also hear that you have a tendency to be outspoken, General. Is that true?"

"Unfortunately so, Excellency."

"Outspokenness is a virtue here. I hope you will give me an objective and frank report on what is happening in China."

"I am sure you are briefed, sir."

"I am not talking about which army moved here or there, or casualties, or prisoners taken," Konoye said. "You are as close to a civilian general as the country has. So I am asking you for a candid assessment of what we are doing in China and your recommendations."

"China is a swamp," Ito began. "And daily we bog down further. Everybody in the military knows that, and yet there is a never-ending contest between the army and the navy as to which service will be in the ascendancy, and that leads to more battles as each service sets out to prove superiority. But may I ask you a question, Excellency?"

"Please do."

"Is it the policy of our government to test the American and British military forces to find their limits?"

"There are some who interpret that as our policy. I do not."

"It is so interpreted by the military in China."

"And what is your recommendation, General?"

"I would bring the fighting to an end. I would consolidate that area north of the Yangtze River into an autonomous region similar to Manchukuo." He searched the Prince's face for a reaction but he could see none. He could not tell if he had gone too far.

"That is more easily said than done." Prince Konoye stood up, paced the room with his hands clasped behind his back. "Our government was against the extension of the war after the incident at the Marco Polo Bridge. But it was the Chinese who insisted on pushing the conflict. They were given many chances to detach without losing face."

"It has been suggested, Excellency, that the Chinese would have withdrawn except for a faulty communication system. Given a chance, I believe the Chinese would welcome an end to the hostilities, and I recommend that the British be asked to serve as mediators between our forces and the Kuomingtang government."

"Our military would never agree to that, I'm afraid. As you said, the British have been tested along with the Americans, and both countries demonstrated a great lack of national character. Japan could never align with weakness."

He has already decided on an action, Ito thought. *He is about to let me know what it is and it won't be anything that will please me.*

"I ask for your confidence now," the Prince said. "The Emperor, in his imperial and divine wisdom, deems it proper to take no position contrary to the General Staff. And the military wish to strike an alliance with Germany as further insurance against Western intervention in Asia. It will be done."

"Then I apologize for taking your time, Excellency."

"I ask for your support, General Ito."

"You have it, sir."

They went through the ceremony of departure, and the secretary came to conduct General Ito to the door. The secretary's eyes were large and black, as if they absorbed everything they saw. He was probably the one who would report the conversation to the General Staff, Ito thought.

As soon as he reached home he called for his accountant. Otani arrived within the hour and, kneeling by a low desk in the Japanese-style office, removed an abacus from his briefcase and went to work, his brows furrowing as the beads clicked in his fingers. The rifle plant was showing a healthy profit and, with the investment of more capital to modernize the machinery, it could bring in a net of two million yen a year within two years. The long-term, established industries were sound and needed no current adjustment. Otani recommended further investment of capital in a merger with the Watanabe shipyard in Kagoshima; it was common knowledge that the navy was about to enter into an accelerated freighter-building program.

Ito listened and nodded and watched the figures being written down, but he found his mind wandering to Yuki and Dawn in Shanghai. If the military expelled him, he decided, he would simply stay in Shanghai and come home only when it was necessary.

He thanked Otani profusely, escorted him to the door, and then went to the Western-style sitting room, where his family was gathered. His mother was bent over a table, brush in hand, practicing calligraphy by copying one of her late husband's haiku. Ariko was arranging flowers in a vase, a bored expression on her face, while Kanao was being tended by his amah.

Ito dismissed the amah. "I wish to speak to you both," he said. "I have to leave for Shanghai immediately. I do not know how long I will be gone this time, but Otani-san will take care of things while I am away. You have but to tell him what needs doing."

"There are some things about the house that need repair, Honorable Husband," Ariko said. "Not in the physical sense, but in many other ways."

"Then you may write them all down and send them to me in Shanghai and I will let you know what to do," he said. "Now, I would like you to supervise the packing of my trunk."

He was gone within the hour, certain that his wife would be weeping with frustration and anger while his mother would be governed by her resolve to say nothing. He was glad to be going.

Yvonne came in from the salon, her face ashen. "I just heard some Japanese women talking in the salon," she told Yuki. "They didn't know I could understand them."

"So?"

"One was saying what a shame it was that you would be leaving Shanghai and wondering what would become of Blossoms. And the second said that just because the General was in disfavor and being transferred didn't necessarily mean that you would be going too."

"Transferred?" Yuki said. "Disfavor? What were they talking about?"

"Something your General did in Tokyo," Yvonne said. "Something to do with the Japanese Prime Minister. You're not leaving, are you?"

"Of course not," Yuki said cheerfully. "You know how rumors are in this city."

"Forgive me for troubling you," Yvonne said, much relieved. She held up a red silk gown she had been carrying. "Don't you think we should switch this one for the blue cotton in the lineup? The red is really spectacular, don't you think?"

"I couldn't agree more," Yuki said, and for the rest of the afternoon she maintained her smile as the ladies of the diplomatic community came in for champagne and the informal fashion showing. But in midafternoon she slipped away to call Ito's office, only to find him in a meeting. She left a request for him to contact her and then, at four-thirty, walked the short distance through the congested street to the Cathay, where she had taken a suite.

She reached the sidewalk in front of the hotel just as the black Packard coupe drove up with Dawn. She was wearing a blue jacket and gray skirt, the uniform of her school, with a pert red tam on the side of her braided hair. She gave her mother a quick kiss, and as she crossed the sidewalk she voiced her unhappiness.

"I want to take the tram to school like the other girls do," Dawn said darkly. "I don't want to be driven there."

"We'll talk about that later," Yuki said. "Now, go upstairs and change out of your school clothes and we'll have tea."

"I really mean this, Mama."

"I know you do."

Dawn disappeared through the revolving door and Yuki turned to the chauffeur. She had hired him to drive Dawn to school every morning and spend the day outside the fenced grounds where he could watch the doors to the school and the playground and bring Dawn home when she was dismissed.

"Tell me something, Shumate," she said. "Dawn doesn't want to be driven to school anymore. Do you know why?"

"May I be candid with you, madame?"

"Certainly."

"Your daughter is a beautiful child, but I see her on the playground, isolated from the rest. She pretends to prefer it that way, that she doesn't like the other children or the teachers. Or sometimes she tells me that if I didn't drive her then she would be like the rest of the children, but of course that's not the case. The truth is she can't face things as they really are."

She knew the answer before she asked the question, but she had to have it confirmed. "And what is it that makes her so different that she's isolated?"

"The fact that she's half-caste, madame. The children make fun of her, despite the efforts of the nuns to stop them."

"And what would you do if she were yours?"

"Exactly what you're doing, madame," Shumate said sincerely. "It's no secret that you don't have the same protection that the consulate parents have. You're wealthy and there are plenty of Chinese who would take her for ransom if they had the chance."

"Thank you," she said. "I appreciate your honesty."

She took the elevator to the suite high in the hotel. Dawn had already changed her clothes and was wearing a cotton dress as she sat in the small kitchen having tea.

You look so grown-up for six, my chi chai, Yuki thought. "Would you like me to brush your hair?" she asked.

"After a while," Dawn said, biting into a sugar cake. "How long will the war last, Mama?"

"I don't know. Why? Have you been discussing it at school?"

"Yes. The Sisters say we should give thanks that there is no more fighting in Shanghai. But I would like for one more airplane to come over the city and drop one more bomb."

"And where would you have the bomb drop?" Yuki said.

"On the school," Dawn said with perfect aplomb. "On a day when everybody was in the chapel. Except for me, of course. Because I would be ill and have to stay home that day." She took another bite of the cake, nodded to herself with satisfaction. "Yes," she said. "About eleven o'clock some morning. And perhaps there should be two big bombs instead of one."

Ito came to the Cathay suite at ten o'clock, long after Dawn was asleep. He kissed Yuki briefly, took off his uniform jacket, then sat down on a sofa overlooking the lights of the river. "I am sorry I could not come sooner," he said. "But there have been meetings all day over whether we are pushing too far or whether we are not going far enough."

"Would you like something to drink?"

"Tea," he said. "No, coffee if you have it. I need to stay awake tonight because I have to prepare for the morning meetings."

She brought him coffee and then sat on the carpet at his feet, resting her head on his knee. And she wished that she could preserve this one moment of contentment.

He sipped the coffee. "What led to your call?"

"I heard a rumor today, Ito-san. Concerning you."

"And what was said?"

"That you had offended the Prime Minister in Tokyo and that you would be transferred away from here as punishment."

"Ah," he said, an exhalation of breath, almost a sigh. "And who said this?"

"Two ladies from the Japanese Consulate. I didn't see them myself so I don't know who they were."

"It does not matter," he said. "It was no accident that they were there today or that they said what they did. They knew with great certainty that you would get word and then you would tell me." He put the coffee cup down and lit a cigarette, leaned his head back against the cushion of the divan.

"Why would they go to all that trouble?" Yuki said. "Why not tell you directly?"

"They will allow me to save face," he said. "There was a discussion of a general command in Manchukuo today, who would be the best man to fill the post. They will now expect me to volunteer for that position."

"But why? What have you done that's so terrible?"

"I questioned my government's commitment to the war in China. I suggested the English as mediators when it turns out that we have signed a pact with Germany." He jabbed his hand at a cloud of blue cigarette smoke hanging in the still air. "I described China as a swamp into which we would all sink." He nodded to himself. "His secretary had to be listening, to report the conversation to the General Staff. And now they will have to discipline me, remove me from my position here. But since I am a baron, their action will have to be a judicious one, most subtle. It cannot seem that there is any connection between what happens to me now and what I said in that room because it might appear that Prince Konoye was indiscreet and they do not want that."

True, then, she thought, and she knew instantly that her world was about to be turned upside down.

She ran her hand along the calf of his right leg. "What will you do?"

"I do not know," he said. "I cannot fight a cloud, and the campaign against me if I stay here will be as subtle as a whisper and as deadly as a spider bite. If I do not volunteer, then day by day my duties here will be decreased. There will be policy meetings from which I will be inadvertently excluded until the whole world will know that I am in disgrace. So I have to decide whether to take the Manchukuoan command as my form of apology to the General Staff or to suffer the humiliation here."

He put away his coffee, reached down, and pulled her up beside him on the divan, smoothing her hair away from her face. "And you have to think about yourself and Dawn."

She put her fingertips against his lips to silence him.

He moved her hand. "Listen to me. If I go to Manchukuo, you must stay here. You have Dawn's education to think of. No one will bother you. And when the time comes, I will return to Shanghai."

She was weeping now, quietly, the tears moving down her cheeks. "You have taken such wonderful care of me. May I not show how much I care for you? I could help make Manchukuo less painful for you. I don't want to be here without you. I might never see you again."

"I will never give you up, Nakamura-san. You mean too much to me. Dawn is my daughter. And I want you both safe."

"No more talk tonight. Come to bed."

"I cannot. I have to get back to headquarters to show them that they have not upset me with the calculated gossip of two women in a dress shop." He held her tightly to him. "I ask only that you think about what I said."

"I will."

After he was gone Yuki stood by the window, looking down at the street far below. *Perhaps Dawn will be better off in a Manchukuoan school,* she thought, and in that moment realized that her decision had been made.

Connaught spoke in English to the naked Chinese girl who lay beside him in his bed, knowing full well that she could not understand a word of it.

"The world has gone mad," he said. "Especially our part of it."

She smiled at him, accustomed to his rambling.

The telephone rang and he picked it up, turning his back on the girl. "Connaught-san?" the voice came. It was Yuki.

"How are you, Nakamura-san?" he said.

"I'm fine, but I'm in what I think you would call a dilemma. I need to pass some information to Cummings-san about Ito-san, who would like to arrange a meeting but is not permitted to contact him directly. But if Cummings-san were to meet him accidentally, then that could not be held against Ito-san. Do you think you could arrange it?"

"When?"

"Anytime. Even tonight."

"At someplace discreet."

"Yes."

"I can think of a dozen places where God himself could make an appearance and the regular patrons wouldn't give a damn one way or another. There's one in particular, a White Russian bar near the Soochow Bridge called the Moskva."

"Could you arrange for Cummings-san to be there at eleven o'clock?"

Connaught checked his watch. "If I can find him in the next three hours. Where are you?"

"At the Cathay."

"I'll give you a ring if he won't be there."

He hung up and called the consulate. It was after hours and he was surprised when Dawes picked up the call. "Connaught here," Harry said. "Working late are you, Dawes?"

"Waiting for a cable from Washington."

"Put Sam on, will you?"

In a moment Sam was on the line. "If you're agreeable to having a circumspect drink with Ito, I'll pick you up shortly," Connaught said.

There was a lengthy silence. "I've got nothing to lose."

"A half hour, then." He put the telephone back on the hook. The Chinese girl raised one dimpled knee slightly and shifted an arm across her stomach beneath the slight mounds of her breasts. "You were talking about me, weren't you?" she asked in Shanghainese. "To believe that the whole world revolves around you," he said to her in English. "Such a fine and marvelous feeling, but it belongs to youth, you know. When you get older the feelings of mortality begin to creep in." He slipped his trousers on, his shoes. "But of course none of us is immortal, and it's just as well, my dear, because it wouldn't do to live forever. How would one have a sense of perspective?"

The girl reached out to clutch his arm, her lower lip pouting slightly as she had trained it to do, studying her face before a mirror for hours to achieve the effect. "Come back to bed," she said in Chinese. "Stay with me."

"I have something to do," he told her in Chinese. He put on his coat. "But if you wish to stay and wait for me, then please do so. The apartment is warmer than the street and I will pay you many Mexican silver pesos."

"I will be as constant as the sea," she said, relaxing on the bed.

He smiled. "You should know, dear child," he said, "that if you lie to me, I have a flying dog that I keep in the basement. If you steal anything from this apartment and leave, then I shall give my flying dog your scent and he will find you out wherever you go."

"You don't have a flying dog," she said, but the tone of her voice and the expression in her eyes were doubtful. "There is no such thing as a flying dog."

"There is only one way you can find out," he said. "But if I were you, I'd accept my offer, which will bring you more money and no danger at all."

Once outside, he hailed a taxi to take him to the consulate. The girl will stay, he thought, as the taxi moved off into the traffic. After all, he told himself, the Chinese are very superstitious people, even those who have spent a lifetime in the cities, for to all of them the world is run by spirits, and there is a great dragon that sleeps beneath the ridges of the earth. If one can believe in a large sleeping dragon, it is simple enough to accept a flying dog.

At the hotel he told the taxi to wait. He passed the marine stationed at the floor entrance and went directly to Sam's office. There were papers spread out on the polished teak of a coffee table, which Sam was sorting into piles. He did not look at all well. Connaught knew the bayonet wound in Sam's back had not healed properly and continued to pain him, and that Charlotte's death had squeezed all the breath out of him. And now he was being rejected by his country. The office was in disarray, half-filled boxes on the floor.

"I get the distinct impression that you are a man preparing for departure," Connaught said.

Sam nodded. "I'm being transferred," he said.

"I'm sorry to hear that, even though I suspected it was coming," Connaught said. "But it's not such a bad time to be leaving here. Shanghai's changing right before our eyes and we're all too drunk or preoccupied to know it. Bit by bit all of the familiar lunacies are being replaced by the Nipponese grimness. It used to be unthinkable to foul the nest, but no more. A Japanese soldier killed a shopkeeper last week because he wanted money to play the slot machines. The Japanese will eventually take it all over, you know, all of Shanghai." He lit a cigarette. "It's ironic, isn't it, that they should be tossing you out for telling the truth about the Japs."

"I've gone further than that," Sam said. "I sent State a long message yesterday lambasting the Chinese as well. Nobody is acting in good faith anymore. So I let them know my feelings about the Kuomingtang. As long as I'm being forced out, I'm sending them a final truthful dispatch, which tells them on the record far more than they want to know. They stopped wanting the truth a long time ago, when Chiang Kai-shek took twenty million dollars in gold for the protection of Shanghai and put it all into his personal coffers. Yet the

Americans support him because he has a Methodist wife. That's what it boils down to."

"Who will replace you?"

"I'm not at liberty to say."

"I can tell you what he'll be like," Connaught said. "He'll be so conciliatory he simply won't exist as a person. He won't offend the Japanese or the Kuomingtang or the Communists. And the presence of the United States in Shanghai will become vaporous."

"It's already become that," Sam said.

"No," Connaught said earnestly. "Do you know what the Chinese call you on the street? 'The Man Who Feeds the Birds.' A genuine tribute. Because talk is cheap in this town and positive actions are rare. Everybody is arguing political nonsense and you're feeding people."

Sam looked at his watch, put on his coat. "I'm pleased that Ito-san wants to get together but we've got to be careful. I've been put on alert that I'm to be totally circumspect in every way or I will be out of the Foreign Service instantly." He paused a moment. "Ah," he said. "Since Ito, too, wants an out-of-the-way meeting, the rumors I hear are probably true. He's being transferred as well, isn't he?"

"I believe that's an accurate statement," Connaught said.

Connaught took him to the waiting cab and rode with him as far as the Russian cafe. "I'll leave the taxi with you," he said. "I'm no more than a five-minute walk from here."

"Won't you come in for a drink?"

Politeness. Connaught shook his head. "No, thanks. I'll see you tomorrow."

Sam paused just inside the bar, letting his eyes grow accustomed to a darkness broken only by the candles on the tables. A balalaika was playing somewhere, and Ito was sitting at a table in a far corner. He stood as Sam approached. "I am very pleased you could come," Ito said. "I wanted us to have a chance to say good-bye." He signaled for the waiter.

Sam ordered a drink. "It's fitting," he said to Ito. "We've been through a lot together."

"Far more than I ever anticipated when I first came to this country. We have both worked hard, hoping for different results."

The waiter brought the drink and Sam lifted his glass. *"Compai,* Ito-san."

"And *compai* to you."

"And where are you to be posted?" Sam asked.

"I have been given a command in Manchukuo, as far from Shanghai as they can find for me," he said. "And you? Where are you going?"

"The most conservative bastion of Western influence in the Far East," Sam said with an ironic smile. "Singapore. They really enjoy their military parades there, all spit and polish, strictly ceremonial. I will be put in a subordinate position for speaking out. At least you're not being demoted. When will you be going?"

"The next day or two." Ito smiled wryly. "They don't quite know what to do with me," he said.

"We gave it a good try," Sam said.

"Yes, we did that."

Sam looked at the balalaika player, a man with a ragged beard and a frayed red satin shirt. "We've never talked about Yuki, you and I."

"No," Ito said. "That's true. I always felt that if we wanted to work together, there were some subjects that could not be mentioned."

"But now that I'm at the end of something and God knows what's going to happen in the future, I want to know about her. Is she well? Is she happy? And how is my daughter?"

"I believe Nakamura-san is very happy with her work," Ito said. "Her health is good and the child is a delight."

"Are they going with you to Manchukuo?"

"I have tried to persuade Nakamura-san to stay here."

"Then she's going."

"Yes."

"I have no right to ask you this question."

"Please ask what you will."

"Do you love her?"

Ito held his glass before his eyes. "That is a difficult question," he said. "I am married, as you know, and I have a son. That means I have a duty and an obligation, which I will meet. But I care for Yuki-san as I do not care for my wife, and I care for Dawn in the same way." He sipped his drink.

"And does Yuki love you?"

"It gives me much happiness to believe she is fond of me."

And the two of you make love, Ito-san. But I don't want to think about that. He was silent a long time. "It's damned ironic how much you and I have shared," he said finally. "And now we're both being punished for the same beliefs. We won't be seeing each other again,

I'm sure. I wish you well in Manchukuo. And if ever I have the chance to do you a good turn, Ito-san, know that I'll do it."

"I pledge the same to you. And may you find happiness in Singapore."

A handshake and bows, and Ito departed. Sam had another drink before he went back to the consulate, knowing that he had things to finish before he left Shanghai. Tomorrow he would meet with Dawes, who had been appointed to succeed him. Dawes would be exactly the kind of man Washington wanted in the post. He was one hundred percent business-oriented and he would never do anything to rock the boat.

And Sam would go to Singapore and everything that had happened here would be behind him. But he was determined, sitting in this darkened bar in a city that would soon be a part of his past, that he would see his daughter at least once more, talk to her, collect some memories of her to take with him before he left, never to see her again.

When she put down the telephone after talking with Sam, her hands were shaking. She rang for Elder Sister, told her to bring tea in fifteen minutes, then walked around the room, touching the back of a gold brocaded chair, trying to convince herself that her anxiety came because she was having to give up Blossoms, the elegance of her life here and the familiarity of her surroundings, the Hiroshige woodcuts against the golden damask wall coverings. She saw her face in a mirror and was startled at her own youth when she felt so much older. She composed herself.

Elder Sister appeared at the door with a bow. "A gentleman is here to see you, madame."

"Show him in, please. And you may serve the tea."

Yuki turned toward the door as Sam came in and her first feeling was one of concern. He had lost weight, was almost wiry, and despite his expensive suit he looked ill groomed, as if with the death of his wife he had stopped caring for himself. She was concerned for him, wanted to touch him and ease his pain. She pushed the feeling aside.

"I'm glad to see you, Yuki," he said.

"Thank you." Elder Sister rolled the tea cart into the room, set out the cups and napkins on a low table, then poured before she left. "Please sit down. Do you still take your tea plain?"

"Yes."

She picked up her cup. "It seems we follow parallel ways, doesn't it?" she said. "We came to Shanghai at the same time and endured the maelstrom, and now we leave. My Chinese friends would say that we are caught in the forces of Yin and Yang, arrival and departure, happiness and sorrow, all beyond our control."

"Sometimes I feel as if I've lost more than I've gained," he said, half to himself, not looking for a response. He took a silver cigarette case from his pocket. "Do you mind if I smoke?"

"No, not at all," she said. She started to light his cigarette but he did it himself, automatically, breathing the smoke in as if hungry for it.

"I want to ask you a favor," he said. "And I hope you won't say no."

"I'll grant it if I can."

"I want to talk about Dawn."

"If it's about the trust . . ."

"No," he said reassuringly. "I apologize for the last time we met. I had no business pushing so hard when that wasn't what I wanted to say at all. I just wanted to do something for her and now I know there isn't any need."

"I was threatened," she said. "And I'm touched that you should explain." *Your tenderness upsets me; your sweetness makes me uneasy. Is it because you're free again and I'm not? Ito-san, forgive me for these thoughts. I owe you so much.* She looked at a woodcut on the wall, travelers crossing an ancient bridge in the rain. "I think Manchukuo may be good for her."

"I wish you both all the best," he said awkwardly. "I thought of so many things I wanted to say to you about Dawn and I can't remember any of them." He smiled wryly. "I even thought about taking out an ad in the newspaper. It would have said 'I am the father of Dawn Nakamura' in very large type, with my signature beneath it. I thought about making it a whole page so you could take it with you, and when the time comes that she asks who her father is, you could show her the page." He tapped the cigarette ashes into a concave bronze fish. "But I honor your right to tell her whatever you please when the time comes. The diplomatic community knows she's my daughter, God knows, after the battle with my mother. But I'm here to talk about something else."

"What favor do you want?"

"I'll be leaving for Singapore at the end of the week. And I'm aware that the odds are very great that I'll never see Dawn again. So

I'd like to be with her for a day. You can introduce me to her as an old friend of yours, anything you want to invent. The day can start at noon and I'll have her back by nine o'clock."

She looked at the sunlight reflecting on the serene face of a golden Buddha sitting on a pedestal. Her heart ached at this final parting. *I have always known that I could see you again if I wished, Cummings-san, and now that time is coming to an end. When we part this time there will be no turning back.* But there was a difference in her now and she could feel it, for she had reached the end of her youth, and as much as she had loved this man, her loyalties now lay elsewhere.

"I'll have her ready tomorrow at noon." She managed a smile.

"Thank you," he said. "With all my heart, thank you."

She was exhausted by the time he left. She finished her tea, looked upon the shining face of the Buddha with gratitude. *I do not fully understand what is happening to me,* she thought. *But I will make it.*

It was an afternoon for magic, unseasonably warm for winter, and he devoted himself to the enchanting little girl who met him at Blossoms, radiant despite her shyness.

"Darling," Yuki said to her. "I want you to know an old friend of mine, Mr. Samuel Cummings, who wants to take you out for the afternoon."

Dawn's expression was very solemn. "How do you do?" she said, extending her hand.

Sam took it. "Very well, thank you," he said. "Are you ready to go?"

"Yes," she said. She kissed her mother and then moved toward the waiting limousine, where the driver was holding the door for her.

"I'll have her back here promptly at nine," Sam said to Yuki.

"Enjoy yourselves," Yuki said.

"We shall."

When they were in the car she looked up at him with large brown curious eyes. "You must be somebody very important," she said.

"What makes you think that?"

"This is the longest car I've ever seen. And we are told at school that if American flags are flying on the fenders, a very important man is riding inside."

"Let's just say that some people look at me that way."

"This is a very nice car."

"Thank you."

"I would like to drive by my school," she said. "Do you know where it is?"

"I think I do," he said. He gave instructions to the driver and the car pulled out into traffic. "Do you like school?"

"No," Dawn said matter-of-factly. "Some of the children in the school say that I'm only half Japanese. I asked my teacher which half of me was Japanese and she became very upset and said I wasn't acting on my best behavior." She looked at him soberly. "Would you say that I'm acting on my best behavior?"

"I don't know," he said. "You seem just fine to me."

"I seem all right to myself too," she said. "But I don't know whether it's my best behavior. Do you mind if I sit on my legs? I'm too short to see out of the window very well."

"Not at all," he said.

She sat on her legs, and as they neared the brick structure of the school, he saw the children in the fenced yard, undergoing calisthenics. "Do you think your driver could slow down and honk his horn?" she said.

"I suppose so," he said, and then he saw her purpose. "Why not?" He leaned forward and instructed the driver, who kept his hand on the horn and slowed the car to a snail's pace, watching the children turn and look as Miss Dawn Nakamura rode past in regal splendor, her face turned to the front, never deigning to cast a glance in their direction. After they passed the school Dawn sat down in the seat in a regular fashion.

"Do you suppose anybody missed seeing me?" she said. "Do you think we should do that again?"

"I think you did that quite well," he said without cracking a smile. "I'm sure everybody saw you, including all the teachers. Now, is there anything else that you would especially like to do?"

"It's only polite for me to let you have a turn," she said.

"I'll take two turns later. What would you like now?"

"I should be honest with you. My mother says I should be honest with everyone. I have a list."

"Of things you'd like to do?"

"Yes. Is that all right?"

"Of course. The day is yours."

"My mother talks about the ox on my grandparents' farm. I've only seen pictures of an ox and I would very much like to see a real one."

"Then so you shall," he said.

They drove out into the gray countryside. The scars of war were everywhere, the craters in the ground now growing over with winter grass, the old peasant houses showing new mud where the walls had been reconstructed. And there in a field stood a female ox, a calf sucking at her full udder, butting against the bag to coax her to give down. Dawn uttered a squeal of delight, and once the car had stopped was out of it in a flash, climbing through the fence as Sam tried to keep up with her, afraid that the cow would do her harm. But the ox merely looked at the little girl and continued to chew her cud, breath steaming in the winter air, the calf's muzzle covered with milky foam.

When Sam caught up with Dawn she was standing there entranced. "She's *really* big, isn't she?" Her voice was full of awe. "Just absolutely *huge.*"

The Chinese farmer was out of his house now, a bony man, dressed in a bulky coat and barefoot except for wooden sandals. He had a concerned expression on his toothless face. "How can this unworthy person be of service to you, sir?" he said to Sam.

"The little girl has never seen an ox."

The farmer looked puzzled, as if he could not understand why any little girl would want to see an ox. "She is welcome to look at the unworthy ox all she wishes," the farmer said.

Sam gave him some Chinese bank notes and the man bowed gratefully, bobbing like a cork.

"Why did you give him money?" Dawn said once they were back in the car. "Is it all right if I ask you 'why' questions? My teacher says that adults don't like children to ask why."

"Why not?" he said.

She laughed. "You're being humorous, aren't you?"

"Yes," he said.

"That is very funny. 'Why not?' I like that."

"I gave him money because he was kind enough to allow us to look at his cow and calf."

"But mostly you gave it to him because he needed it, right? I mean, if he had been very rich and somebody had been driving him around, you wouldn't have given him money."

"That's right. Now, where would you like to go?"

There was a snake charmer one of the children had told her about in a crowded street in the old city, and they managed to find the man, an Indian with a flute and a snake so sluggish in the cold weather, it rose lethargically from the basket in which he kept it.

"You gave that man money too," Dawn said when they had moved on.

"He makes his living that way."

"It's really the snake who does the work," she said. "What does the snake get out of it?"

"A mouse or two for supper, I'd guess."

Dawn's nose wrinkled distastefully. "He must like mice more than I do."

They went to one of the last of the private zoos in Shanghai, took a boat trip on the Whangpoo, during which time Dawn tried to catch her own shadow, raising an arm suddenly in the hope that the shadow on the water would not be paying attention. "Shadows must be very smart," she observed. "Very smart and very quick."

They ate noodles in a stall shop and then went to a Chinese music hall to watch the acrobats and the singsong girls. In the car on the way back to Blossoms, he realized she had gone to sleep beside him in the backseat, her head resting on his arm, and for a moment he was so saddened by the thought that he would never see her again that he felt a strong physical pain in his heart.

He carried her into the side door at Blossoms to find Yuki waiting for him. He smoothed Dawn's hair and kissed her forehead, and then passed the sleeping girl into the arms of her amah, who took her into the private rooms.

"May I offer you a drink before you go?" Yuki said.

"No, thanks," he said. He was not sure he could deal with their final good-bye. "I appreciate what you've done, letting me have her for the day. I want you to know that should either of you ever need help, you'll have it. Just get in touch with me."

"Thank you," she said. She leaned forward and kissed him very lightly. "Good-bye, Sam."

He was grateful for the darkness and the privacy of the car.

Manchukuo . . .
February 23, 1938

SHE SAT AT the rear of the darkened railway coach, shivering despite the fur robes pulled up around her and the sleeping Dawn huddled in against her, so cold she thought she would freeze if she could not move, but there was no place for her to go. The coach was only a dozen yards long, but as far as she was concerned the distance was impassable, for at the forward end were General Ito and a few high-ranking officers seated close to the coal stove, which glowed a cherry red with heat and occasionally belched smoke and ashes when a down draft struck the tin vent poking through the roof.

She looked out the window at the darkness over the rolling plains and the lantern light at occasional crossings where Manchu men, completely covered with fur except for a slit across the eyes, waited for the train to pass. *How far to Mukden now? An hour perhaps, no longer than that.* She could stand it, had endured the cold in the three days and nights since Shanghai, the interminable stops at small stations, the delays on sidetracks, the discomfort of a roadbed that all seemed to be under repair. And most of all she had endured the humiliation. For though the forward part of the coach was comfortable, befitting the rank of the officers who graced it, the rear was piled high with luggage, much of it her own, and across the aisle and a bit forward were four Japanese girls destined for the brothels of Mukden, brash, experienced young things who occasionally looked at her openly and then tittered to themselves, wondering who she was.

She had been given the same physical status as a whore and she knew there was nothing Ito-san could do about it. He had raised hell with the transportation office to get her on this train at all, and the rest of the coaches were filled with enlisted troops and supplies. There was no other place for her and Dawn. She withdrew into herself, pulled Dawn closer to her, knowing that within a few hours at the most, the ordeal would be over. The sale of Blossoms to Yvonne had been a simple financial procedure but a costly emotional one, and she had dismantled her cottage in a hurry, trying to keep her mind away from everything she was leaving behind, concentrating on the future.

Ito-san had been able to get her a house in the Russian quarter, and the housing officer in Shanghai had described it as modest but pleasant. Within a week or two she would begin to look around for an empty store in which to establish a salon. She had read of the White Russians who had formed a colony to escape the Revolution, and in her baggage she carried the latest patterns of Yvonne's designs as well as an ample stock of fabrics so that all she needed were seamstresses.

The train began to slow; lights were more frequent in the dark square of the window. Dawn moaned, shivered slightly as she came awake. "Are we there?" she said.

"I think so. A very few moments at the most."

Dawn looked over the edge of the fur robe, saw the stove at the front of the coach and Ito-san sitting close to it. "I'm going to go up by the stove with him."

"No, darling. We can't do that."

"Why would he mind?"

"It's a kind of game," Yuki said, knowing there was no way she could explain this to Dawn. "Since he is a general, he has to pretend not to know us now. There will be someone at the station to meet us, and we'll see Ito-san later at the house."

A game, she thought as the train pulled into a modern station, the platforms aswarm with troops waiting along the multiple tracks. *A game and I had forgotten the rules.* When the train stopped a team

of officers came aboard to welcome Ito and the other officers, the
ceremony full of bowing and honorifics, and then Ito-san was gone.
She was filled with a sense of desolation, emptiness, of being abandoned, which she had not felt in years. Another soldier came aboard
the coach for the girls, and Yuki rose from her seat, folded the fur
over her arm, took Dawn by the hand, and led her out onto the
platform. There a squat little man dressed in furs and cossack boots
grinned at her, spoke in Russian, which she did not understand, but
she had heard her name in the deluge of words. She spoke to him in
Japanese. His smile was uncomprehending.

"Do you speak English, by any chance?" she said.

"Most perfectly, of course," he said, touching his mustache, which
was long and tapered, waxed at the points. "You must be Madame
Nakamura, of course, and this is your daughter. I am Alexi. You
would not be able to pronounce my last name so I save you embarrassment."

"I'm pleased that you're here," Yuki said. "We're very tired. Can
you take us to the house?"

He looked puzzled, but only for a moment. "Soon," he said. "But
first we must have your baggage checked, yes?" He snapped his
fingers and four men went into the railroad car and began to emerge
with her luggage and the boxes, which they piled onto the broken-
down hand trolleys. They followed along as Alexi led the way
through the doors into the warmth of the clean station, lowering his
voice as he talked to Yuki under his breath. "The officer in charge is a
Major Yamashita," he said with dislike. "He is, English expression
now, son of a bitch, madame. He suffers from great frustration because at one time he was big *kempeitai*—so I pronounce correctly?—
and he is sent to this place considered by him as well as most to be
miserable because of one mistake or another, and his bitterness
make him very harsh. Understand?"

"I understand."

"Conceal nothing from him. Perhaps he will be mercifully brief."

They went to a deserted counter, empty because they were the
only civilians arriving on this train, and Alexi directed the men to
put all the baggage and the boxes on the wooden tables. Shortly two
men in uniform came out of a door to open all the boxes and cases
and prepare them for the Major, who stalked out of the door, a stick
under his arm, his cap squared precisely on his shaven head, his
boots perfectly polished, his uniform pressed in knife creases. He

was a short man of forty, and he stood directly in front of Yuki, legs slightly spread, as if taking a stance and waiting for something. She was momentarily confused, and then it came to her: *He is waiting for me to bow.* And she folded her hands one over the other in front of her and bowed while Dawn watched and imitated her mother.

But Yuki knew she had waited too long, and with a sinking feeling in her heart, she turned to Alexi, spoke to him in English. "Is there a place where you can buy my daughter something to eat?" she said, wanting Dawn out of there.

"The hotel connected to the station has a cafe," Alexi said. "When you are through here just say 'Alexi' to any of my men and he will bring me." He took Dawn's hand, led her off.

"Your papers," the Major said, extending his hand to Yuki.

She gave them to him and he flipped through them, eyes flicking from the papers to her face and back again. "Your occupation?" he said.

"It is listed there."

"A servant?" he said with a curl of incredulity. "Are you entering Manchukuo as a servant?"

"To General Ito," she said.

"Ah, so desuka?" the Major said. "A servant, but all these are your possessions? All this luggage, boxes, crates?"

"Hai, so desu," she said, something within her bridling now. *I don't have to take the sarcasm of some bureaucratic customs officer. I had one of the finest businesses in Shanghai.* She stopped before she spoke. She was no longer in Shanghai but in the customs section of a drafty railway station at the end of the earth, trembling from fatigue and frustration, wanting nothing more than to get past this man to the warmth of the house waiting for her and the comfort of a bed. He poked his stick into a box, pulled up the edge of a bolt of cloth. "What's this?"

"Fabric."

"For what?"

"Dressmaking."

"And this box here?"

"The same."

"And this and this and this and this? All dressmaking fabrics?"

"Yes."

"You make dresses professionally?"

"I had a salon in Shanghai."

He glanced at the paper again. "So you are a servant and you make dresses as well."

"Yes."

"So these bolts of cloth are commercial items. Why are they not entered on the form as commercial items?"

"Because I have no dressmaking business in Manchukuo."

He nodded, tapped the lid of a finely fashioned wooden box with his stick. "You have declared gold on your form."

"Yes."

"How much?"

"The number of taels is on the paper, I believe."

"How many taels?"

"Fifteen hundred, I believe."

"And Japanese yen?"

"I have fifty thousand yen, in my purse."

"Are you aware of the new law?"

"I checked the laws before I left Shanghai. Or General Ito did."

He reached out his hand and an aide put a book of regulations in his fingers. "Have you read this?"

"I'm sorry, but I can't see what it is."

"You couldn't have read it because it just came in from Tokyo today." He put a cigarette in his mouth and an aide provided a flame. "The official currency here is the yuan but yen can also be taken in and out of the country without penalty. However, there is a new tax on foreign currencies and precious metals." He opened the small book, isolated a column of *kitagana*. "We will weigh the gold and then figure the tax on it."

"How much tax?"

"The rates vary. There will also be an investigation of the commercial fabrics to determine their status. And this box . . ." The stick lifted the flap. "What is it?"

"Dressmaking patterns."

"Commercial."

She could restrain herself no longer. "I am a Japanese citizen and you will not treat me this way any longer. I am under the protection of General Ito and you will answer to him for your rudeness to me."

The instant the words spilled out of her, she knew she had made a terrible mistake, because the Major's subordinates stood perfectly rigid in their silence, recognizing the fury in their superior. She was a lowly woman and she had confronted him. He held his stick in two hands, his arms trembling with tension, and she knew he could strike her if he wished, for no more reason than the blatant lack of respect she had shown him. He would seek to regain face now and she would be the loser for it. "No one here is above the rules," he said in a tight voice. "If General Ito wishes to contest the regulations, then all your possessions will be impounded for years. As it is, you may take your two bags of personal luggage, no more, and you will be notified when I have made a ruling on the rest."

She stood struck dumb, unable to speak or to bring herself to apologize. *I have to learn to do better,* she told herself, watching the major spin on his heel and disappear into his office. *Tomorrow, I will write him an official letter of apology. I'll make everything all right. Tomorrow.*

She sent a man for Alexi, who appeared shortly, still chewing, wiping his mouth on his sleeve, holding on to Dawn with his other hand. "I hear he has been ruffled by you," he said, then shrugged. "But perhaps everything will be fine. Not to suggest unlawfulness to you, madame, but certain people who are not so honest or lawful as yourself would have sent gold by carriage or by wagon. So much traffic, you see. Such terrible roads that perhaps no one would have cared to examine. But all is spilled milk," he said. "Come along. Carriage is outside. No automobile for us, you see. Too costly by far."

"Are you all right, Mama?" Dawn said quietly.

"Yes."

"You don't look all right."

"Put the robe around you," Yuki said as they moved toward the door. The moment they stepped into the night the blast of frigid air took her breath away. She held on to Dawn until they were in the enclosed carriage with Alexi, who shouted orders over the howl of the wind to the porters, who lashed down the luggage atop the carriage. Then Alexi climbed in and rapped on the panel behind him to get the driver moving. The frost had hoared his fur hat, laced his mustache and his eyebrows with white. He crossed his arms, stuck his gloved hands beneath his armpits, and looked at both of them appraisingly.

"It is matter of greatest survival," he said. "Do not submit yourselves to the cold outside for long time because it has been known to happen to men, women, and child as well that shoes of regular nature have frozen to the ice, causing calamity. With soles frozen, the man, woman, or child cannot move and so freezes quickly. Or the man, woman, or child takes off shoes and feet freeze and have to be removed."

Yuki was only half aware of his voice. She was listening to the wind howling like a wolf, the creaking of the carriage, the clopping hooves of the horses. She had never been colder in her life. *A few minutes at a time. I can endure anything if I can see an end to it.* The horses turned up a narrow lane, partially sheltered from the wind, and Alexi rubbed a clear spot on the frosted window with his forearm, peered out, then pounded the planking above the seat with his fist. The carriage stopped immediately.

"Stay here until I open the door," he said, and bracing himself, he darted into the wind and in a few moments was back for them, holding Dawn's arm with one hand and Yuki's arm with the other, his grip surprisingly strong as he helped them through the gale into the open door of the small house, then yelled at the driver to get the bags inside while Yuki stood shivering and stunned by what confronted her. The room was small, filthy, dominated by a giant cast-iron stove resting on brass feet, shaped like a barrel, with slots at the top to emit the heat when there was a fire inside. There was none now. The furniture was ancient, heavy, and overstuffed, covered with dust, stinking of coal dust, cabbage, and stale onions. She touched a cheap tapestry on the wall and her hand came away grimy. She looked into the small kitchen, where an icicle hung from the single water tap. *Lord Jesus, I can't stay here.*

But Dawn was looking at a picture of a uniformed man on the sideboard. "Who is he?" she said to Alexi.

"He was Czar," Alexi said proudly. "Ruler of all Russia before Revolution."

"What happened to him?" Dawn said.

"If he ever visited Mukden, he froze to death," Yuki said.

"It is good to joke," Alexi said. "I did not build fire before because if train had been late, coal would have wasted itself. We have ration. Only what is in scuttle for each day." He got a fire going, closed the metal door with a clang. "Will warm soon."

"Is there water?" Yuki said.

"Will melt soon," Alexi said, tapping a brass kettle sitting atop the stove.

"And food?"

"Only bread now in kitchen. Tomorrow, Alexi will arrange things for you."

"How far are we from the school?"

"Is with Japanese military, you understand? I will take little one there tomorrow."

"I'm not so little," Dawn said.

"And what do you call yourself?" Alexi said.

"Dawn."

"Most descriptive name. Cheerful." He looked to Yuki. "Can I be of more help tonight, madame?"

"No," she said. *We're beyond help.* "I thank you, Alexi."

He shrugged. "Tomorrow, then." And he was off, out the door, slamming it behind him while Dawn looked around, exploring the single bedroom, the toilet with the slot in the floor and foot tiles on either side. She came back into the living room, where Yuki was pulling an ancient love seat closer to the stove.

"I don't like it here very much. Do you?" Dawn said with great seriousness.

"It will get better," Yuki said. How difficult it was to lie: *Your mother has made a terrible mistake by bringing you here.* "I want you to go to bed now. Don't undress, just keep your clothes on. I don't think the house will be warm before morning."

"Shall I wash my face?"

"No." She led her daughter into the bedroom, helped her to take off her shoes and climb between flannel blankets. She put the fur robe atop her for warmth. "I'll be along shortly," she said. "I'll leave the door open." She went back to sit by the stove, which was just beginning to cast off a slight warmth. She wanted to clean the room, to wash the walls and beat the dust from the furniture and remove the carpets to hang on a line in the wind while she scrubbed the floors. But there was no water, no soap, no broom, only the terrible cold, the fatigue, and the despair that coursed through her.

She opened one of the traveling bags, looking for the bottle of brandy she had brought along for her first dinner with Ito-san. She needed it now. It was crystal, encased in leather, with a silver cap that could be used for a cup. She poured it full, drank it down, the fiery liquid burning in her throat, then filled another and drank it more slowly, feeling better. She would display the virtue of *gaman*. She would suffer without complaint for the present. She was a rich woman after all, having sold Blossoms to Yvonne (with Yin and Yang to have a share) for a hundred thousand dollars in gold, and even if the new tax took half of that, she would have plenty of money to begin a salon here and an opportunity to find a larger house with adequate heating and plumbing.

She drank two more brandies and, encouraged by the surge of hope, fell asleep.

The next morning she found tea in a kitchen cupboard, along with a loaf of black bread, and after breakfast she was able to provide Dawn with enough warm water to wash herself before she dressed for school.

"How long will I be in school today?" Dawn asked.

"I have no idea. Alexi will take you and find out what you will be doing. Then he will pick you up when classes are finished."

"Why can't you take me?"

"I'll explain that someday, when you're old enough to understand."

"It has to do with O-Ito-sama, doesn't it? He's angry with us. That's why we couldn't sit with him on the train."

"No, he's not angry. He's in a delicate position." She shrugged, decided not to attempt an explanation. "Once we're all settled, I'll be able to take you to school."

Alexi arrived at eight o'clock, radiating good cheer and carrying a basket, which he put down on the table. "Maybe not usual food," he said. "But later, we shop. For now, beets, potatoes, onions, more bread."

"Thank you, Alexi. I want you to take a note to General Ito for me," she said. "Have some tea. It will only take a minute or two."

She found her writing paper and her pen, thought carefully about the phrasing of the note should it fall into the hands of a subordinate before it reached Ito-san.

My lord,

Your house will be cleaned and ready whenever you should require it. I trust that your journey was pleasant and that you will be pleased with what I have done.

Your Faithful Servant,
Nakamura-san

She folded the note and gave it to Alexi. "I have some things to do so I want you to come back for me after you deliver Dawn to school," she said as she helped Dawn into her coat and wrapped the scarf around her face until only her eyes were showing in a slit beneath the fur hat.

"Good to have warm clothing," Alexi said. "Last night, old emigré fell while coming from tavern. Friends find him quite soon, within minutes. Frozen like wooden board. Stiff. Dead."

"I think we can survive without the horror stories, Alexi," Yuki said.

"Is vital to frighten children of the cold," Alexi said. He examined Dawn, approved the way she was dressed. "Alexi will return soon."

And he took Dawn out the door into an overcast day, the wind down, a heavy snow falling.

Yuki was prepared to go by the time Alexi was back with the carriage. She was startled to see the twisting lane of the quarter of the city in which she was housed, tiny houses of Russian architecture all jammed together. "Why are all the houses built so close together?" she asked.

He fiddled with his mustache as if considering the wisdom of something. "I will ask you question," he said. "I have been engaged as servant for you and you are Japanese and Japanese now own Manchukuo. So shall I speak plainly to you, without punishment, or shall I exhibit all politeness?"

"I want you to speak plainly, please."

He nodded. "This is Japanese city now. Military wishes to keep all Russians together so have allotted small space only. Most Russians live in Harbin. Some exceptions, certainly. Very rich counts and royalty with estates. And native Manchus all together, and a few Englishmen, the same."

The carriage pulled out into a wide avenue, heavily trafficked with army trucks moving slowly through the snow, the buildings modern. It was as if she had moved from a past century into the present. "I want to rent a store," she said.

Alexi looked at her as if she had suddenly gone mad. "A store?"

"I had a salon in Shanghai, flowers, a dress shop."

"Impossible, I think," Alexi said.

"There are bound to be wealthy women here who like elegance."

"Perhaps," Alexi said. "But is necessary to have permit from Manchukuoan government for store. Then, with permit, could rent except that there is nothing available."

"Then I shall build one."

"All labor is used by Japanese military."

"Then I want to rent a much larger house," she said. "I'll have a salon in my home. There's no law against that, is there?"

"No, madame. I do not want you to think that Alexi is contradictory man," he said. "But housing very difficult to obtain. First, must have permission to move. When that happen, must find other house, which is impossible. Where you live now was very difficult to find, possible only because old grandmother dies."

I will not be frustrated, she thought. *I will find a way.* "Then take me to the bureau where I make my application for shop space, and after that, I want to go back to customs."

The commerce building was imposing, made of polished stone, the office she sought heated by steam radiators that hissed and gurgled along the walls. She dealt with a Manchu clerk who spoke passable Japanese and had her filling in forms while through a half-opened door she saw the Japanese head of commerce, a portly little man in a business suit, sitting relaxed behind his desk, drinking tea and listening to scratchy music from a gramophone.

When the clerk carried the paper into his office, the door closed for a long time, and when it reopened the round face of the Manchu clerk was full of apology. He found a new set of forms in a file drawer, put them before her on the counter. "It will be necessary for you to apply for a change in classification, Nakamura-san," he said. "You enter the country as a household servant."

"Are you saying I will not be permitted to open a shop?"

"I am just saying that you must apply for reclassification before it can be considered."

"Who will make the decision?" she said. "Your superior? The man in the office?"

"That's correct."

"Then I'll talk to him now," she said. She stood up and in that moment realized that the clerk would not let her pass.

"That's impossible," he said.

"And how long will the decision take once the papers are filled in?"

"Six months," the clerk said.

"I think it will be done much sooner than that," she said. She picked up the papers and walked out.

At the train station she found that Yamashita had gone on vacation for two weeks and she was rejoicing at that happy circumstance until she found that she had been assigned to a Lieutenant Takemoto, who, at the age of twenty-six, had already mastered the example provided by Major Yamashita and had been fully apprised of the case. He sat at a desk with four sheets of paper spread out in front of him and he was constantly plucking at the edge of one and then another, looking down through his half-glasses at the forms and then over the rims at Yuki.

"I am here for the gold taels that were impounded on my arrival last night," she said.

"Hai, so desu," he said, his upper lip bulging as he ran his tongue over his teeth. "Do you have proof of your ownership of the gold? Can you demonstrate that the gold belongs to you and that you are not bringing it into the country on behalf of somebody else?"

"I sold a dress salon in Shanghai," she said. "I can show you papers concerning that transaction."

"Yet you're listed as a household servant on your papers."

"I am here to serve General Ito."

He pursed his lips, tapped a cigarette on the desk before he finally lit it. "Was the gold assayed?"

"The taels are stamped, I believe, by the Shanghai and Hong Kong Bank."

"I understand that. But do you have an assay certificate?"

"No."

"Then the gold will have to be assayed to determine its value."

"And how long will that take?"

"I can't say."

"Then I want to pick up the bolts of cloth. Tell me how much duty I owe and I'll pay you now."

"Were the fabrics manufactured at a Japanese mill?"

"No. British."

"But run by Chinese, employing Chinese workers?"

"I have no idea," she said. "The mill could have employed Japanese workers."

"You have no certificate then?"

She restrained herself. "What kind of certificate?"

"Proving that this material was not manufactured by an enemy of Japan."

"It came from the International Settlement."

"That proves nothing," he said. "There is a law that prohibits the import of manufactured goods from a nonapproved company."

She blinked. *The world has gone mad,* she thought. *I had forgotten the way my countrymen think. I have to get around him.* But she could not. Her mind was blank with frustration. Finally she found words. "What can I do now to clear these fabrics through customs? I wasn't told I needed a certificate."

"It is a new ruling. The goods will be confiscated."

The anger boiled within her and she shifted into honorifics to dispel it. Anger would forever close off her chances. "Then I ask you, Lieutenant, where I must go to appeal this decision."

"At Changchun," he said abruptly. "But it will do you no good. I tell you this to save you the effort. You would be wasting your time. There will be rules against British-manufactured goods very soon, I believe."

She watched the blue cigarette smoke wreathing around his close-cropped head, his fingers continuing to pluck the corners of the paper like the strings of a harp. *If I had the power, I would kill you here and now,* Yuki thought. "There is one more thing, Lieutenant. The patterns I brought with me."

"Patterns?"

"Dress patterns. They're very important to me."

The third sheet of paper received the attention of his probing forefinger. "Yes," he said. "Notations in Chinese."

"That could be. I don't know."

"There is also a Chinese chop mark. Yvonne Chen." He looked up at her and his single word was not a question. "Chinese."

"She's the dress designer. Half Chinese. Her mother is French."

"Her name is Chinese. The chop is Chinese."

"Surely you have no rules against dress patterns."

"These are perilous times," the Lieutenant said, tapping his cigarette ashes into a dish. "We know that the Chinese armies are plotting every moment against Manchukuo."

"In all politeness, sir, what do dress patterns have to do with any Chinese plot against Manchukuo?"

He sucked on his cigarette again, looked at her without emotion. "We have no way of knowing what is a dress pattern and what is not," he said. "But there is a rule against papers written in Chinese being brought into the country except by an authorized official. In this case there is no point to questioning the matter. The papers have been declared seditious."

She was stunned, all words driven out of her. She stood up, bowed politely, and left.

The snow was drifting in the lane by the time she reached the house. When she opened the door she found Dawn in the living room, sitting by the stove, but before Yuki had a chance to speak Dawn threw herself into her mother's arms and began to weep.

Yuki looked at Alexi, who stood by the door with great sympathy. "Would you please have a cup of tea in the kitchen?" she said. "I need to talk with my daughter."

"Certainly," Alexi said.

Yuki let Dawn cry herself out, holding her tightly against her, soothing her hair until the child could talk. She dried Dawn's eyes with a handkerchief. "Can you talk now?"

"I think so."

"How did you get here?"

"A Japanese soldier brought me in a motorcycle sidecar."

"I see. And why did you leave school?"

Dawn blinked back the tears. "They wouldn't let me stay."

"Because?"

"I don't know. I think it was because I caused trouble. The other children hit me. They said I was only half Japanese and they called me a *gaijin* bastard. What's a bastard?"

"It means that your father and I weren't married when you were born."

"I don't think fathers are so important. I can always say Ito-san is my father."

"You can't say that because it isn't true."

"Then who is my father? And where is he?"

"He was an American, killed in Shanghai." *Forgive me, Cummings-san. I just made my decision.*

"Then I don't see how I can be blamed for that."

"You can't, darling. I want you to read one of your books for a while. I have to write a letter."

"But what will I do about school?"

"Don't worry about that now." She sat down by the stove, full of a calm resolve that had been building within her all day. The doors had closed in front of her, one by one, and now she had no choice. She took out a sheet of paper.

My lord,
I am sorry to disturb you now but it is essential that I talk with you today or tonight at the latest. I would not be writing this to you if things had not become desperate. Please tell Alexi if you can come.
Your faithful servant.

She called Alexi from the kitchen. "Did you deliver the other note directly to the General?"

"No. Captain took it."

"Can you put this letter directly into the General's hands?"

"Yes."

"And when you do, then find out when the next train leaves for the south."

"Connecting Shanghai, yes?"

"Yes. And one more thing. If the General tells you he's coming here this evening, I would like for you to take my daughter out to dinner."

"Will take her to my house," Alexi said happily. "I have many children."

"That will be good for her," Yuki said. "She needs other children to play with." *Children who won't hit her and call her names.*

She went out in the snow when she received word the General was coming and she found a small meat shop in the Russian Settlement where she bought some lamb and then she spent the rest of the afternoon cooking awkwardly on the small coal-burning kitchen stove while she rehearsed what she was going to say to Ito-san. He was due at six-thirty, but by five o'clock darkness had set in, the sun going down, the weather worsening, the snow streaking past the windows to drift in the lanes. She was not sure he would be able to make it from military headquarters across town, but shortly after Dawn and Alexi left at six-fifteen, Yuki heard the sputtering engine in the street and looked out to see Ito stepping down from the running board of a military truck.

She closed the door behind him. He sat down to remove his snow-crusted boots and her heart sank as she saw his face, the dark hollows around his eyes, the taut muscles in his jaws. She put her arms around him, held him to her for a long moment. "I was so afraid you couldn't come, my lord. Come and sit by the stove. You're like ice."

She brought him a steaming glass of tea in a holder, Russian style, and he warmed his hands against the glass. "It was difficult riding in the same railroad car with you all the way from Shanghai and never being able to speak," he said. He sipped the tea. "Do you have any alcohol? I feel chilled to the bone all the time." He accepted the brandy gratefully. "I made a great mistake by allowing you to come here."

She sat by him, looking at his face, his skin chapped and red from the cold. There was a slight blue tinge to his fingers. "You don't look well," she said. "I've prepared dinner, and while we're eating I'm warming the bed with hot stones."

"I can't stay for either," he said bitterly. "The truck will be back in thirty minutes. I'm being punished. My superiors refuse to think of it in that way. They would say I am being disciplined as an example to other general officers. I have been assigned to training recruits as if I were a lesser officer. This is the staging area for the China campaign and the extension of the war into Indochina. And the Russians are continually testing our borders and killing our men to let us know they can do it. The Russian troops are barbarians and thrive on this weather. But I am forced to train young men in archaic ways." He took her hand in his. "Never mind that. I have been restricted. I don't know when I will be able to see you again."

"Then you make it easier to say what I must," she said. "Dawn is not to be allowed schooling here. All my materials have been confiscated and my patterns destroyed. They won't allow me to go into business in Mukden. So I am going to take Dawn back to Shanghai, just as soon as the gold taels are assayed and the tax assessed and I get what's left. But I may need your help to intercede with the customs officials."

He stood up, restless, walked around the room, his body tensed, his hands clasped behind his back, stopping to look at the portrait of the Czar, who had posed for the camera with his royal dogs lying at his feet. "Manchukuo is a dumping ground," he said. "A place for soldiers who have antagonized their superiors in some way that requires a different punishment. And there is a strong hatred here for aristocrats because we can't be broken in the simpler ways, beaten with wooden bats or sent to freeze patrolling the northern border." He lit a cigarette, inhaled the smoke, still studying the picture. "You can see it in the Czar's eyes, the sense of being invulnerable. He doesn't waiver for a moment in his belief that he will prevail since that is his right. But he wasn't and he didn't." He drew on the cigarette again, not looking at her. "I wish I did not have to tell you this, but I am very vulnerable and you are a part of my punishment."

"I refuse to be, my lord."

"You have no choice. My superiors know of my attachment to you."

"I don't understand."

"Customs was told to treat you as they did, to confiscate your fabrics and destroy your patterns. And none of your gold will be returned."

Her heart stopped for a moment, began again. "There is a point beyond which they can't go, my lord. Under Japanese law I have the right of appeal. They can't confiscate my gold."

"You forget," he said. "This is Manchukuo, declared to be a separate country with its own emperor to make it legitimate. So the laws can be anything the generals in power want them to be. They can enforce Japanese law when it suits them and shift to the laws of Manchukuo when they want to abandon Japanese law."

"You're telling me they *can* take my gold, then."

"Yes."

"Very well," she said. "I still have fifty thousand Japanese yen. And there's a train for Shanghai tomorrow afternoon."

He took her in his arms as if to protect her with his body. He kissed her tenderly then, softly, and withdrew. "I'm sorry for the pain I have brought you. I must ask you to be strong," he said. "I registered a protest this afternoon when I heard your gold had been confiscated and I requested space for you and Dawn on tomorrow's train."

She said nothing, not wanting to hear what he was about to say.

"I was told that since you came to Manchukuo as my servant, if you should try to leave this country with your remaining money, your actions would be interpreted as an attempt on my part to send currency out, something which I have been forbidden to do."

"I don't want to endanger you in any way," she said.

"You don't understand," he said patiently. "They would take every yen you have, confiscate it all, should you try to leave the country. You wouldn't even have enough money for a ticket."

"I don't understand," she said, confused.

"You can't leave Mukden."

"I can't stay here. Dawn has no school." *I can't exist here, confined to dirty rooms that cannot be cleaned, in a world where I know you're close but can't see you.*

"You have no choice, at least for the present." He raised his head as the horn sounded outside. The truck was back. "I will do the best that I can for you. The punishment can't last forever." He kissed her. "Be brave."

"Yes. I'll try."

He slipped on his boots and his heavy coat and waded through the snow to the truck, which swallowed him up and took him away, leaving her more alone that she had ever been in her whole life. She put the last of the coal into the stove, knowing that there would be no more until morning, knowing that once the coal was exhausted after midnight, the frigid cold from the Manchukuo plains would seize the house. The lights flickered twice, went out, leaving her only the light from the burning stove. She began to wail with a weeping that could not be stilled. Trapped in darkness. Sentenced to life in a cold hell. Unable to pray.

Trapped.

Perhaps there are such spirits as the kami, Ito thought, walking through the intense cold of the military compound, through the trucks filled with wounded waiting at the hospital, hundreds of wounded soldiers mangled by the Russian savages in battles along the border. General Kato had been wrong in his tactics, murderously so, and he might have tried to kill himself had not the command car in which he had been riding skidded on an icy road and overturned three times. At the hospital Ito pushed past the doctors into General Kato's private room.

The base surgeon bowed to General Ito from Kato's bedside, a stricken expression on his face, which meant that Kato was dying and the surgeon did not want to be held responsible.

"He hangs onto life by a thread," the surgeon said. "His legs were broken and his skull was fractured. In addition, he suffers from internal bleeding."

Ito looked at the man on the bed, legs splinted, head bandaged, his breathing a shallow rasp. "How much longer will he live?"

"Until morning, perhaps."

Ito walked back to the headquarters building in the premature darkness of the winter afternoon wondering how life would change with Kato's death. After his talk with Prince Konoye he had been prohibited from any direct contact with Tokyo for fear he might foment unrest. And here in Manchukuo all of his orders had been cleared through the very man who lay unconscious. But soon he would be in command.

The General Staff in Tokyo had prohibited Ito from seeing any active duty against the Russians, had assigned him to the training of troops instead. Ito had personally stayed with his men through their training exercises in the subzero cold. When they ate starvation rations he went hungry as well, and he turned them into zealots and gave them killing skills as keenly honed as a sword. And now, as ranking officer, he was determined to use the toughness his field command had developed in him.

When he reached his office he told his aide to bring him a bottle of cognac, all the written reports on the latest military disaster, and then to summon the four colonels of the training regiment to an immediate meeting. He sat at his desk in his unheated office, his overcoat collar pulled up around his neck as he absorbed the details of the battle and sipped at the cognac. He summoned his aide again, told him to get the best calligrapher on the base. Very shortly a bandy-legged sergeant, face white with fear at being summoned before a general, bowed at the door.

"Have you ever written a scroll of official apology?" Ito asked him.

"No, sir. But I was taught to do so."

Ito gave him orders and the sergeant scurried away just as the colonels began to arrive. They were all good men, Ito thought, but they were ashen-faced and bleary-eyed now. There were a thousand recruits due in tomorrow to begin a training cycle and two of the barracks had been pressed into service as an overflow medical facility.

Ito stood up, his leather swagger stick beneath his left arm. There was no softness in his words, not a trace of sympathy. "I do not intend to ask your opinion of what has happened in the past two days," he said, "because I know why our men were massacred, and as I take no responsibility for it, neither will you. The training procedure was dictated by the Esteemed General Kato, but he is now incapacitated, and I intend to change it."

He looked out the frosted window at the campfires burning on the drill field to warm the walking wounded. "There is not one hospital in all of Manchukuo that is not filled tonight," he said. "Over twenty thousand men died in the past week, and I will tell you now that it is only the *kami* and poor Russian planning that keep the enemy's armies from sweeping down and wiping out every man we have." He whacked his swagger stick into the leather glove of his left hand. "The Russian foot soldier is an ignorant barbarian who has never seen an electric light and drinks blood. He can fight on half rations and withstand the cold. But foremost, he can drive a tank. They meet our infantry with organized tank battalions and you see the result out there."

He began to spew out orders. Colonel Inukai was to put the new recruits in tents, on immediate half rations to toughen them up, and begin forced marches in the icy weather to bring them to the point where they could match Russian endurance. Colonel Miyazawa was to get every remaining tank into Mukden and Colonel Sajima would be assigned to help him, while Colonel Mogi concentrated on the logistics of supplies and tankers to carry diesel into the field.

"Within thirty days we will have a tank corps capable of engaging and defeating anything the Russians can throw at us, and I will so inform the General Staff in Tokyo when that privilege is allowed me. I say thirty days, gentlemen, which means that if thirty-one days from now there is a Russian attack and we are forced to endure the kind of carnage that exists right out there beyond that window, then the five of us will commit seppuku."

He dismissd them, then continued to sit in the freezing office, knowing the enlisted men believed that he did not suffer the feelings of ordinary men. *Let them think that if it makes them better soldiers,* he thought.

Shortly after dawn he was informed that General Kato was dead.

By noon the sergeant calligrapher had brought the finished scroll for his examination. He studied it carefully, approved, sent a regimental messenger to hand carry it to Tokyo.

His sense of timing worked perfectly. In the confusion of messages to the General Staff reporting the disastrous battle with the Russians, no thought had been given to the training division. And then his scroll had arrived with its request that his shortcomings, perceived or real, be forgiven so that he could communicate matters of extreme importance to the General Staff. He received an immediate permission.

And so he wrote a masterly paper outlining the training program that was already under way. His training paper was circulated among commanders in the field and he was given any supplies he requested.

He had been forgiven and returned to power.

A letter was delivered to Yuki by special messenger from Lieutenant Takemoto asking her to stop by the train station at her convenience. The note was so worded that it could be interpreted as an apology, but the fury that she had managed to control came back again and she stormed through the house thinking of ways to get back at this arrogant officer.

She dressed in a kimono, Japanese style, and layers of outer garments against the cold. She wrote a note to Dawn, who would be home midafternoon from a session with her tutor down the street, and then she had Alexi drive her to the train station, which was filled with soldiers in battle gear being sent to the frontier as replacements. Lieutenant Takemoto greeted her courteously and invited her into an office furnished with two straight-back chairs and a decrepit wooden desk, a dwarf tree, perfectly shaped, sitting on the windowsill.

The Lieutenant sat down, gestured toward the other chair, and indicated that she should sit. His attitude was stiffly formal. "A determination has been made in your case, Nakamura-san," he said. "Under the current laws of Manchukuo, a private citizen is not allowed to keep taels of gold. However, you are entitled to compensation for the value of the gold, which has been fixed by regulation, minus the tax, which I mentioned at our last meeting. Your compensation may be had in Japanese yen or in the currency of Manchukuo, the yuan."

"I would prefer yen."

"Very well." He lifted a telephone, summoned another lieutenant, who came into the office carrying a cash box while Takemoto filled out a receipt. "You are entitled," he said, "to eleven thousand four hundred and sixty-three yen and seventeen sen."

She sat motionless, surprised that she could feel such a destructive inner rage and allow none of it to show. They were stealing her gold and she was powerless to stop them. She did not even argue, knowing that it was possible to lose the eleven thousand yen if she contested the decision. The Lieutenant counted the money from the cash box, snapping each bank note before he put it on the table before her, placing each coin with a precise click. She signed the receipt Takemoto handed to her, and then gathered up the money, murmuring her thanks.

The other lieutenant departed and Yuki was about to leave when Takemoto lifted a cardboard box to the table from the floor. "It has also been determined that the Chinese papers you presented are indeed dress patterns, and it has also been determined that they are for your own personal use." He pushed the box forward. "You may take them. But the cloth that you brought was confiscated because it was in a commercial quantity."

She showed her joy no more than she showed her wrath. "*Arigato gozaimasu,*" she said politely, and gave him the slightest of bows as she left the room.

That evening as she was preparing dinner she found herself waiting for a message from Ito-san or, far better, a visit to let her know what had happened. But time passed, and she was aware that it might be days before she heard from him again. In the interim there were decisions she had to make.

As she put the rice on to cook she watched Dawn struggling with her arithmetic at the table, and she looked over the small house with a critical eye. It was not unattractive, now that the tapestries and the overstuffed furniture were gone, and she had scrubbed the smells from the walls and whitewashed them. The carpet would do. A splendid icon hung on the wall, a triptych she had bought from a family forced to sell their belongings. But the house would be turned into a decent salon only with great difficulty because rich women would never appreciate Yvonne Chen's designs against such a setting.

And there was the problem of sewing machines and materials, of women to do the work. She now had thirty-six thousand yen, including the eleven thousand from the gold, in a tin box beneath the floorboards in the bedroom. It would be a gamble.

Dawn put down her pen with a sigh, stared at the paper in front of her.

"Can I help you with something?" Yuki said.

"Arithmetic," Dawn said.

"What's the problem?"

"My tutor says that one half plus one half equals one."

"True."

"So if we are sharing a bowl of rice, my half is the same as your half."

"Yes."

"But my one halves are not the same."

"I don't understand."

"If I'm half American and half Japanese, then what am I altogether?"

"You are my very dear daughter," Yuki said.

"I know I'm that," Dawn said, frustrated. "But I've decided that I don't want to be one half *gaijin* and one half Japanese anymore."

She sat down beside her at the table and put her arm around her daughter. "And what would you be if you could choose?"

"All American."

"How would that be better?"

"The day I was at the school here, I couldn't even whisper without permission. And the head of the school, I don't remember his name, gave a talk. He said all the boys should be ready to die for the Emperor when they were needed. And he said that all girls were lucky to be alive because we were useless. He said we must always do exactly as we were told."

"Not like Shanghai," Yuki said, eyes misting over.

"No. I could hit back there if somebody hit me first. Can we go home, Mama?"

I have made such mistakes, Yuki thought. Home to her daughter was Shanghai. She had never been to Japan.

"This is our home now," Yuki said. "Home is where we are together."

"Then I want us to be together in Shanghai."

"Perhaps someday," Yuki said. The rice was ready and she stood up, pleased at the distraction. "But for now we are here and we will make the best of things. All right?"

"If I have to," Dawn said.

We both have to. And tomorrow she would begin to look for sewing machines and everything she needed to go into business, knowing that only through the amassing of money would either she or her daughter ever be truly free. And whatever it took to get that freedom, she would do it.

The next morning she saw Dawn off to her tutor and worked for an hour on an official document before she dressed in her kimono.

She summoned Alexi and the carriage and shortly was rattling off down the street toward the commerce building, where she entered with all the decorum of a proper Japanese lady, placing the document and the clearance papers from customs in front of the same Manchu clerk who had been so unpleasant before.

"I would be most grateful for the opportunity to talk with your superior," she said.

"I will see if he is available," the clerk said, disappearing into the office occupied by the portly man, and as she listened to the muffled melody from a scratchy gramophone, she was sure that they were placing a telephone call to determine why customs had suddenly reversed policy in her case. Despite the large number of troops in Mukden, the Japanese military was a small and closed community, and the rumor would have passed around by now. She was the General's woman.

Momentarily she was ushered into the commerce chief's office and he rose to lift the arm from the gramophone before he asked her to have a seat. He rubbed his chin thoughtfully while he went over the document that she had written character by character. "Perhaps you can explain to me exactly what you have in mind, Nakamura-san."

"There are many women who wish to support their country and have no way of doing so, sir," she said. "My proposal is a simple one. I wish to set up a factory for the repair of uniforms."

He looked at her cautiously. "Do you currently have a contract with the military?"

"Not yet," she said. "I can't very well offer the services of a factory that doesn't exist."

"*So desu,*" he said, nodding. "But I fail to see specifically what you are requesting of this office."

"First, a reclassification of my status from 'household servant' to 'seamstress.' "

"I see no difficulty in that," he said. "But how will you support this effort, even if you find women who are willing to join you?"

"You will find that in the second part of the document," she said. "I will buy the sewing machines myself and convert my home into a factory. And we will start by repairing uniforms and other clothing, thereby conserving materials that the military may need, and perhaps soon we will be able to make uniforms."

"Ah," he said with a nod, realizing the gamble he was taking. He felt he could not turn down a project that looked so patriotic on paper, and yet if he were reversed at a higher level, he would lose face. Finally he signed the document. "I commend you for your patriotism, Nakamura-san," he said. "And I will grant your request. Unfortunately, there are no uniform manufacturers in Manchukuo at present, but I will certainly forward your proposal to Tokyo should there be any plans to have such work done here."

"*Domo arigato gozaimasu,*" she said. "I think I will need a permit to buy sewing machines, is that not so?"

"The clerk will provide you the papers. How many will you need?"

"I just wish to buy two at the present time," she said. "But should the need arise, I would like permission to buy a dozen."

"Fine," he said. "And I wish you the best of luck in your undertaking. But you must remember that any army work will have priority."

"I would not want it any other way."

As soon as she was in the carriage with Alexi, he questioned her. Her excitement was contagious. "Why such happy?" he said.

"Because I no longer fight battles that cannot be won," she said. "I have learned to bend like the willow, to become Japanese. Do you want to go into business with me, Alexi?"

"Is not allowed," Alexi said with great patience. "Not for you. Not for me."

She showed him the papers stamped by the commerce office. He was incredulous. "How you do this?" he said. "You have magic?"

"No," she said. "I have common sense, which was lacking when I arrived here. So, now I have a proposition to make you. You won't become fantastically wealthy, but you will have enough money to live much better."

"Alexi will listen," he said. The stubborn expression on his face gradually yielded to joy as she talked. "Will work, dear lady," he said happily. "Will work."

"Then you'll do it?"

"With exquisite and profitable pleasure," he said.

"How soon can we find sewing machines?"

"Today," he said. "One hour. Maybe two. Will be expensive. Perhaps five hundred yen."

"That's fine. And we are going to need material, the finest fabrics we can find."

"Leave to Alexi. And workers?"

"We shall have to start looking soon," she said. "But the other things come first."

Before the afternoon was over Alexi had led her to two treadle machines, both old but in excellent condition, and had arranged to move them into her house by the following Saturday.

Two evenings later his carriage drew up in the lane outside, and two men began to carry in pieces of fabric of every description, which Alexi had bought from White Russian women who had brought their finery with them to Manchukuo. Damasks and silks and velvets, fabrics that had been used in ball gowns and drapes or which still remained wound in bolts.

Yuki held up a piece of silk to the light, golden and iridescent, felt its softness against her cheek.

"How much did you have to pay?"

"Seventy-six yen," Alexi said gravely. "With some conditions."

"What kind of conditions?"

"Much came from Madame Cherenko," he said. "On condition that from green velvet she wishes gown for which she will pay sixty yen. Will not get rich quick like that."

"Every future begins someplace," Yuki said, and then to Alexi: "Please arrange a suitable time for us to call on Madame Cherenko. We are going to give her the finest gown Manchukuo has ever seen."

"Are you going to make more dresses, Mama?" Dawn said.

"Yes, darling. We're starting all over again."

Ito lay naked on the bed, his golden body motionless while she moved down its length, her long black hair caressing him like a shadow. His body was like iron from his weeks in the field. She brushed over him like a butterfly, and when at last she settled on him, ever so slowly, she drew him into her with a small cry and he could lie quiet no longer. He pulled her head down to his and rolled her over on the bed and brought them both to the moment of release.

Soon she lay beside him ready to talk. "Does everything go well with you?" she asked tenderly.

"I do what I have to," he said. "The men training in my tank brigade are passionate to pursue the war, and the officers whip their passions. They believe that the Japanese essence will bring us victory against any enemy and that to die in battle is a glorious death.

When my officers get together, their eyes shine with belief. They actually envy the young men who have been killed, and when they get drunk enough they weep because the Russians have quit fighting and give them no chance for glory."

"How does that trouble you?"

"Because I do not feel the same way. I lead my men in the field until they are ready to drop of exhaustion, just as I am, and then I force them beyond pain. I do that to make good soldiers of them so that they may live. Dying against the Russians is a terrible waste of young men."

"So the fighting with the Russians is ended?"

"For now. No one is certain how long it will last. But plans exist to divert the men into China and Indochina if the Russians decide to stop testing the borders. The General Staff must have a place to fight to justify the country's spending so much money." He looked around the room as if to clear his mind. "You work miracles," he said. "This room looks different."

"We painted it. No miracle, just a lot of hard work. I'm going into business again." she said. "As a matter of fact, I've made an agreement to buy the house next door, which I'm going to turn into a small salon."

He laughed. "Unbelievable."

"I have no fear that I won't succeed in business," she said. "But I need to talk with you about Dawn's future."

"You worry too much," he said. "She is a bright child."

"Too bright sometimes, I'm afraid. I have taught her to read and write Japanese as well as English, and she already knows as much Chinese as I do. And every day she goes to a tutor, a young Japanese woman who drills her in arithmetic and tries to set an example to Dawn of what a young Japanese woman should be like."

"I do not see what you are worrying about."

"Dawn doesn't think of herself as Japanese."

"Ah," Ito said with understanding. "Her life here is much more difficult than it was in Shanghai, isn't it? She has always been outspoken, from the time she learned to say her first word."

"The rejection she receives from Japanese children is real, Ito-san."

"I have no doubt it is," he said. "But perhaps as she grows older and follows Japanese traditions, she will be tolerated. We will arrange for her schooling in Japan later on, at a place that will help her learn to conform to Japanese customs."

He sat staring out the window at the thin light. She marveled at the strength of his profile. "I am sure things will be all right for her," she said. "But I worry about you."

He covered her hand with his. "I have survived the enemies in my own camp," he said. "And that is the first rule of a successful military man." He glanced at the clock. "And speaking of my work, my transportation will be here in fifteen minutes." He reached out to embrace her, then rose to get dressed. "I will be able to have dinner with you two weeks from now, on a Sunday. Perhaps Dawn could be with us."

"She would love that. What would you like for dinner?"

He looked at her with surprise. "Our quartermaster has trouble getting anything except dried fish. And you can offer me a choice?"

"The White Russians are very clever. I can offer you beef, pork, mutton . . ."

"Anything except fish," he said. He took her in his arms again, his uniform rough against her skin. "Your strength sustains me more than you know. They took everything away from you and still you did not give up."

"I was taught never to give up," she said. "To give up is to die."

He kissed her lightly as a horn sounded in the street. "Two weeks. And do not worry about Dawn. She will be fine."

He was gone. She watched the truck disappear down the lane, and she knew that she had not pursued her belief any further because Ito-san, despite the love he felt for Dawn, would never understand her predicament. For Dawn was not only half-*gaijin* but female as well, and Yuki could not forget how poorly she herself had fared in Japan such a short time ago. *My daughter is worth more than a beast in the fields*, she thought. She would not allow Dawn to be so little valued.

She wrote a quick note to her mother, enclosing a few yen, and then went back to work.

On the day she scheduled Madame Cherenko's final fitting, she stopped to pick up Inga, the seamstress who was doing part-time work for her. She was an elderly woman who lived in the attic of her son's house, where in the waning weeks of winter she sat very close to a coal-oil lamp in order to see her stitches. She wore clean white gloves from which the fingers had been cut to allow her to hold a needle. But now that spring was here she worked outside the house on the stoop when the afternoons were warm enough. As Yuki's carriage drew up she was waiting in the yard, dressed in a starched white smock.

"This will be our final fitting," Yuki said as Inga climbed into the carriage. "You've done beautiful work."

Inga nodded her gratitude. "It is rare to work from such a beautiful design."

In a few minutes they reached Madame Cherenko's house. A servant girl was scrubbing the white marble steps with soapy water and a brush. The brass plate backing the bell glinted like a mirror. Alexi waited in the carriage. A starched maid answered the door, conducted them into the parlor, where an ancient icon graced the stark white wall. Soon thereafter Madame Cherenko swept in, and from the set of her fine-boned face Yuki could see that she brought trouble with her.

"Good day," she said with a nod in Yuki's direction. She brushed back the edge of the lace curtain with her hand, frowned at the servant girl scrubbing the steps. "In St. Petersburg we had a hundred servants at the main house, all vying with each other to become perfect. And we had perfection then, in so many ways." A touch of calculated melancholy. "Well, let's proceed, shall we?" And the maid placed a small box like a platform in the center of the room and Madame stepped daintily onto it while Yuki supervised the putting on of the new gown.

It was a perfect fit, but Madame Cherenko was studying herself in a three-paneled mirror the maid had brought in. "Does the hem seem off to you?" she asked the maid, whose opinion was not visible on her face. "Does the bodice seem a bit too full? And the sleeves . . . I simply don't know."

"I have never seen a finer fit, Madame," Yuki said. "And the bodice is exactly as it was when you approved it at the last fitting."

"Fabric changes," Madame said vaguely. "I know that you've done the very best you can, but there's something missing. *Je ne sais pas.*" She shook her head with finality. "No, it simply won't do," and then, almost in the same breath, " . . . at least not at the exorbitant price we agreed on."

"I believe the price is sixty yen," Yuki said, trying to cut off her anger before it began. "This gown was designed by Yvonne Chen. In Shanghai it would sell for two hundred and fifty American dollars."

"Not to me," Madame said. "And this isn't Shanghai, is it? We do have a problem as I see it, because technically the material does belong to me."

"Alexi bought the material from you."

"Only on the condition that a satisfactory dress be made for me. And the dress is not satisfactory."

"How much does Madame propose to pay?"

"I would not be required to pay anything according to the law," Madame said. "But I recognize the time and effort that you and your seamstress have spent and above all else I want to be fair. I will return the money you paid for the material and give you an extra ten yen. I may be able to get some wear out of the gown." She told the maid to bring her purse. She counted out ten one-yen notes, handed them to Yuki. "Perhaps another time."

"I'm sorry the gown does not please you," Yuki said.

In the carriage Inga began to cry, burying her face in her handkerchief. "It's all the same," she said. "So many of them cheat. I will never be able to move from my son's house."

Yuki smoothed out the yen notes and pressed them into Inga's hand. "I agreed to pay you thirty yen and I will bring you twenty more tomorrow."

Inga's crying stopped abruptly. "But you will lose money."

"I always honor my agreements. It is my responsibility," she said. When they let Inga out at her son's house and drove on to pick up Dawn, Yuki was thoughtful. "Did you know that might happen?" she asked Alexi.

"Very selfish people," he said with a sigh. "They cause the Revolution, people like Madame."

She will cause a revolution in my life, Yuki thought. The house next door was already undergoing a slow renovation as civilian workmen spent any time not used by the military to create a single long room for a salon, with a smaller room to store supplies and serve as a workroom. All the building materials had been bought on the black market at ten times what they were worth. Yuki had counted on women like Madame Cherenko to become walking advertisements so that she could charge more as her reputation grew, but she had suffered a setback. She knew now that she could not rely on the society trade and yet, at the moment, she could see no other. It was highly possible that she would have to default on the house next door and pay off the remodeling debts out of what remained of the fifty thousand yen. And she would be worse off than when she had first arrived.

The next morning Yuki walked the few short blocks to deliver the money to Inga, only to find her barring the door, her frail arms stretched from lintel to lintel while she glared at her thirty-year-old-son, Josef, a handsome man with a glossy mane of hair, an expensive suit, and dove-gray spats buttoned over his patent-leather shoes. He carried a gold-headed cane, which he raised as if to strike his mother while he shouted at her to get out of the way. Behind him, one step down, was a pretty girl in her late teens, shabbily dressed in a cotton frock, patiently awaiting the outcome of the battle, which obviously concerned her.

Inga was wailing that he was not going to bring another of his whores into the house where his own mother lived while he yelled at her to stand aside. Finally, Inga dissolved in a flow of tears, moving back while her son conducted his girl into the house. And Yuki led Inga down the street to a tea shop, taking a table in the corner where Inga's tears turned into a narrative of complaint.

"He shows no respect for his mother and I almost died when he was born," she said. "He makes his living off his girls, he calls them *girls*, his whores and hostesses, and sometimes he lives with one in the house and I tell him that God will strike him dead"—she made the sign of the cross—"but he won't listen to me. And his poor mother freezes, *freezes* in the attic, *freezes*, while his girls share his bed and the rest of the house."

"I don't quite understand," Yuki said. "Is your son a pimp?"

"A devil," Inga said. "He breaks the laws of God and his mother's heart."

"I mean, exactly what does he do for a living?"

"Read the Ten Commandments. He breaks them all." Inga slurped her tea, blew her nose. "He provides bar hostesses for a dozen different places of the devil. His whores sell drinks and get a commission and *he* gets a share of that. And they sleep with soldiers and civilians alike. *Sleep,*" she snorted derisively. "Ten, twenty men a night at ten yen apiece, and the prettier ones charge twenty yen, and my son, the bloodsucker, may God forgive him, takes thirty percent from each girl. He makes a fortune from their sins while his mother *freezes* by winter and never has a breath of cool night air in the summer."

Yuki sipped her tea and looked out the window. It was level with the sidewalk; she could see nothing but feet and shoes and boots. "I want to make an offer to you," she said. "But it's only fair that you should know that I can fail. And if I do, then you may be in worse circumstances than you are now."

"I couldn't be worse off," Inga said.

"First, I will pay you one hundred yen a month," Yuki said. "If I'm able to find work for us, then you may be very busy, but you'll get the money whether there's any work or not. The only condition is that you work for me exclusively."

"That's most generous," Inga said. "But you saw what happened with Madame Cherenko. Many of the aristocrats are like that."

"Yes," Yuki said. "Eventually our patrons will be the very wealthy, but until then we will do work where we can. Now, another condition. The house that is being remodeled into a salon has a workroom. You can live in it if you like. There's plenty of light and there will be heat in the winter."

"A room," Inga said with rapture.

"We will have to take whatever work we can get," Yuki said. "And there will only be enough money for three months unless we find work."

"God bless you," Inga said, on the verge of weeping again. "When can I move in?"

"By the end of the week," Yuki said.

That night Yuki went for a long walk through the twilight streets and found what she expected, more or less. At night there was no life in the streets except in the bars and restaurants patronized by Japanese soldiers, men from the White Russian community, and native Manchus. The one thing all the places had in common was women—hostesses of every age from young to old, most of them poorly dressed. Yuki sensed the feeling of inevitable doom that Ito-san had planted within her. For the soldiers this was the last oasis before the Chinese front. Inga's son had become prosperous by providing a few girls for bars, but there were literally thousands of women working here.

She went home to find Dawn sitting at the table, staring at an empty cup.

"What are you doing, *chi chai?*" Yuki said, hanging up her jacket.

"Why do I have to learn about tea?" Dawn said.

"What do you mean?"

"My tutor says that if I want Japanese people to like me, I have to learn about tea. And I really don't even like tea without sugar."

"I don't know the answer," Yuki said. "But preparing tea is a Japanese ceremony."

"Then I'll do it," Dawn said. "I'm boiling water now. Is it all right if I practice on you?"

"Certainly."

"I liked the way it was in Shanghai," Dawn said before she disappeared into the kitchen. "If you wanted tea, you asked one of the servants to bring it."

No more Shanghai, Yuki thought. *And no more servants.* She sat down with one of Yvonne's patterns and with her pen she began to redesign it for bar hostesses, sketching three separate versions that could be done in red velvet, since she had twelve yards of the fabric.

The first sketch seemed incomplete, so she put more ruffles around the neck and sleeves and a longer slit in the side of the skirt.

In a few minutes Dawn carried a tray in from the kitchen and then poured a pale liquid into a cup and, with an awkward bow of her head, handed it to her mother. "Be careful," she said. "It's very hot."

Yuki sipped from the cup. "I don't think you put in enough tea, darling," she said.

"That's not important," Dawn said. "You're supposed to look at the cup and admire it." She tasted the tea herself, made a face. "That's pretty awful. I think I can admire the cup and still have sugar." She brought a sugar bowl in from the kitchen, sweetened the tea, then looked at her mother's sketches. "Are you going to make these dresses?"

"I plan to," Yuki said. "I just hope I can sell them."

"You'll sell lots of them, Mama," Dawn said. "They're beautiful."

The next morning she went down the street to talk to Alexi. "What is the most expensive bar in the Russian Section?" she asked him.

"Most expensive is Ivanov's."

"Do they have hostesses?"

"Most beautiful," he said, lowering his voice slightly so his wife would not hear him.

She asked him how to find Ivanov's and that afternoon put on her finest dress and commandeered the carriage. Even in these hard times Ivanov's Bar shone with prosperity and expensive discretion, all marble and brass on a side street, and her carriage was momentarily blocked by a car disgorging Japanese military, three men, all colonels, one wearing the insignia of a Tokyo command. She went into the cool dusk of a long room lighted by candles, dominated by the polished wood of the bar, just in time to see the Japanese officers greeted by three hostesses, all of them young and pretty, but none of them particularly well dressed.

Yuki took a table and was approached by a hostess who asked first if she spoke French and then took her order for wine. By the time she had come back with the glass on a tray, Yuki had spread the three sketches in front of her and was pretending to study them. The girl put the wine on the table. She was Russian and young, nineteen or twenty perhaps, blond hair, a good figure, but she carried herself as if she were plain compared with the three beautiful girls laughing with the Japanese officers.

"I would like to ask you a question," Yuki said. "Which of these three dresses do you think would look best on a cafe hostess?"

The girl leaned over, beamed at the dress with the ruffles. "This one, of course. Do you have a shop?"

Yuki had rehearsed in her mind all the things she could say to interest a girl like this, only to find that she needed none of them, for the girl was immediately captivated, especially when she learned that it could be made in red velvet. "How much?" the girl said.

"Two hundred yen."

They had the first fitting the next day. The girl was delighted with the dress and within a week Yuki had orders for three more at three hundred yen each. She moved Inga into the room of the renovated house, brought in the first of the sewing machines, sent Alexi on a frenzied search for more fine material, and learned what she could of the tea ceremony of *o-chan-o-mizu* to help Dawn, who was getting better at it day by day.

And when she had dinner with Ito-san again in two weeks, Dawn wore a kimono and served tea to Ito-san with awkward grace, and when no one was looking, added sugar to her own.

Singapore . . .
Summer 1941

"I'M AS TOLERANT as the next man," General Percival was saying to the American Consul as he stood by the polo field watching the horses flash by in the brilliant sunlight. "But at the same time, Donaldson, old man, there is such a thing as going too far, isn't there? He's been here three years after all."

"I can hardly tell him what or what not to say," Donaldson said.

"I shouldn't think that would be too difficult." General Percival paused to pat his white gloves together as the goal was made. "It's a bit much to have a Cassandra around all the time, wouldn't you say? All this talk of the coming war, it does tend to depress one. It upsets the ladies, don't you know? A word from you should do it, old man. You have the position, don't you? I mean, he is subordinate, is he not?"

"Quite," Donaldson said, feeling slightly uncomfortable that he had fallen into the British vocabulary, the intonations, but then in this British colony the heavy influence was only natural. "Well, if you'll excuse me, General . . ."

"You're not leaving, are you, old chap?" General Percival said. "You'll never see a finer demonstration of horsemanship than our chaps are showing. The Australians are forceful, to be sure, but they lack the finesse, wouldn't you say?"

Ah, the finesse, Donaldson thought as he wandered off down the side of the grounds toward the white wicker tables and the brilliantly colored umbrellas protecting the English ladies from the broiling tropical sun. *That's all that's required of the government in dealing with the Germans or the Japanese, wouldn't you say? It's just a matter of the proper finesse.*

And down near a bar that had been set up on the grass stood the current source of Donaldson's troubles, Sam Cummings, talking to a couple of British businessmen in white linen suits.

"It's quite obvious," Sam was saying. "They've taken Indochina so they have their bases ready there. We're next, without a doubt."

"I heartily disagree," Lacewell said. He was a businessman who had been in Singapore for most of his fifty-five years. "We've had rumors about the little yellow people for half a century now and, frankly, I find such projections absurd."

"Good afternoon, gentlemen," Donaldson said, and after the proper exchange of remarks about the match and the horses and the Australians, he looked at Sam with a forced smile. "Time for business," he said pleasantly. They drifted off together. "I suggest we stroll down to Raffles and have a drink at the bar," Donaldson said. "It will be private enough, since everybody's watching the polo match."

"I saw you talking to General Percival," Sam said.

"Splendid," Donaldson said with only a slight sarcasm. "Then you know the subject of our upcoming conversation."

They walked in silence through the city to Raffles, entered the bar, a cool twilight with fans stirring the air overhead and a surly Chinese waiter who approached the table with a towel draped over his arm. "What's your pleasure?" Donaldson said.

"Whiskey and water. With ice."

"A mineral water for me," Donaldson said. And when the waiter had gone: "I received word this morning that your Uncle Roger is dropping in soon to pay us a visit."

"Any particular reason?"

"He wants a firsthand view of the situation," Donaldson said. The drinks were served. He sat back and studied Sam. "I don't understand you," he said. "Or let me amend that. I do understand you but I don't. You've been assigned here as a first Commercial officer and you do a bang-up job of it. The community likes you. The local businessmen think you're a whiz. But I had a similar chap assigned to me when I was in Canberra. He would maneuver American businessmen through the most intricate areas and then, when most men were content to reward themselves with a 'Well done' and a cold drink, he would say, 'Now I want to talk to you about Jesus Christ. Are you saved?' "

"This is hardly the same thing," Sam said. "I don't care how you cut it, the Japs are preparing for war. We're high on their list here and General Percival insists on sticking his head in the sand."

Donaldson sighed, drank his mineral water, blotted his tanned forehead with a linen handkerchief. "We'll go through this again. General Percival is in charge of the British Forces here. He is a distinguished military man with a spotless career. Now don't you suppose that there is just the smallest possibility that he knows more than you do about military affairs?"

"I don't think he wants to see the problem," Sam said. "He's too happy with the status quo."

"Which means?"

"He doesn't want to go to the trouble of fortifying Singapore against Japanese attack."

"Do you know that the majority of people in the English-speaking world consider Singapore to be damn near impregnable, just as she sits? The major naval base of the Far East. More firepower than you'll find concentrated anywhere east of Gibraltar."

"It's still vulnerable. The Japanese will take it."

"You're not leaving me much of an alternative," Donaldson said.

"You're telling me to keep my mouth shut. Right?"

"Not exactly. You're free to write all the cables to State you like and all the articles for magazines you want. You may state your beliefs in great and colorful detail, with all your examples, whatever they may be. But it's been made quite clear to me that if you continue to upset the local population with your theories, then you will no longer be welcome in the British community. And for a Commercial officer, that is the equivalent of the kiss of death."

Sam picked up his glass, downed it. "You don't believe me either, do you?"

"Not the tiniest whit," Donaldson said. "I believe that the Japanese would be very foolish to take on Singapore when they already have their hands full elsewhere. You know, if you relax more, you may come to enjoy it here."

"I won't talk defense again then," Sam said. "I'll write it but I won't talk it."

"That's all I ask," Donaldson said amiably. "And now I'm going back to the polo match to see if the Australians have advanced into the twentieth century yet with their finesse. And I feel so agreeable, I'll even pay for the drinks."

He bought himself a small sailboat, which he kept at a dock west of the causeway on the Johore Strait, the narrow ribbon of water that separated Singapore from the long thin peninsula of Malaya. On most afternoons, when his work was finished (and all work was done by tea time in Singapore), he would load the ice chest with cold beer into his Morris Minor and roar out of the city proper into the forested rubber plantations that covered the western and northern sections of the island. Once aboard his sailboat, he would use his gasoline motor only long enough to get free of the docks and then cut it off and revert to the silence of sail, the wind billowing the canvas, generally sailing south and west until he cleared the island, at which time he would lash the tiller and run with the wind while he opened a bottle of beer and sat back to study the clouds, the sun warm on his face and his shirtless back.

There was something healing about the sea. There were times, when he went out far enough to escape the sight of land, when he had had enough beer, that he no longer worried about the Japanese, when the whole slaughter at Nanking seemed like a bad dream, and when his memories of Charlotte did not evoke the nightmare of her death.

One Wednesday, when he sailed into the middle of the Strait, he heard the sound of an orchestra on the far side, near the Sultan of Johore's Palace. He tacked his sailboat close enough to see the ladies in their pastel dresses and the gentlemen in turbans and pith helmets, then he struck his sail and threw out a sea anchor to keep him in place while he drank a beer and listened to the music.

He was about to doze off when a motorboat went roaring by, and he looked up, startled at the speed. It was an open boat with two Chinese men and their ladies, all of them quite drunk or close to it, laughing as they cut a snakelike path through the water, leaving a wake that rocked his boat and sent swells beneath the rowboats at the pier on the Sultan's side.

As he watched a boy climbed into a red rowboat at the Sultan's pier, a small chap no more than ten, dressed in short pants and a white short-sleeved shirt. To Sam's mild astonishment, the kid cast off the line and, grabbing an oar, pushed away from the dock. It was obvious that he intended to stay close in to the shore and that he would have difficulty doing it. He did not know how to work the oars and so the slight current was pulling him farther out into the Strait with every passing minute.

Sam retrieved his sea anchor, started his outboard, and began to putt along in the general direction of the boy. A woman had come down to the pier now, an attractive woman in a pink dress and a broad-brimmed organdy hat, obviously the boy's mother, because she was yelling at him, telling him to turn around and come back to shore while the boy was moving his oars the wrong way and becoming more helpless by the moment. Then the woman screamed, and at that moment Sam saw the Chinese motorboat cutting through the water on the far side of the Strait, the bow so high that the driver could not see what was immediately in front of him. Quite suddenly the motorboat hit the wooden rowboat at full throttle, smashing it to pieces and throwing the boy into the water.

Sam opened the throttle on his outboard and then, in less than a minute, killed it and went over the side, swimming in a steady crawl toward where the boy had disappeared. He filled his lungs, dived. By sheer luck he saw the boy on his way to the surface. He grabbed him around the neck and pulled his face into the daylight, the boy fighting him in blind panic. Sam slapped him across the face, yelled at him, and then decided to swim back to the boat, a good ten yards closer than the Sultan's dock.

He reached the side of the sailboat, looked at the boy's face. The kid was crying now, blubbering, sputtering water.

"Shut your mouth," Sam yelled at him. "Stop the crying or I'll let you sink. You hear me?"

The crying stopped immediately. "Good," Sam said. "Now, it's going to take both of us to get you into the boat. On the count of three I'm going to shove you up and you're going to grab that line and pull yourself aboard. You ready?" The boy nodded. "All right. One. Two. Three." He pushed the boy up and the boy caught hold of a line and pulled himself into the boat. When Sam joined him the kid was doubled up, retching seawater.

Sam kicked the small outboard into life and pulled aside the pier on the Malaya side where a crowd had gathered, Australian officers in their whites, ladies in tea gowns, even a small rotund man Sam took to be the Sultan. Sam picked the boy up and handed him to one of the officers on the docks who stood him up as he went into the arms of the woman, who proceeded to check him over to make sure there were no broken bones. And then she stood up and extended her hand to Sam.

"I'm grateful, Mr. . . ."

"Cummings. Sam Cummings."

"I'm very grateful, Mr. Cummings. They could have killed him. Did you happen to see their registration number?"

"I have it down," an Australian officer said, and then, to Sam: "You'd better come and have a drink, mate."

"Thank you, no," Sam said. "I need to be getting back."

He took one final look at the boy, who was very pale now, but otherwise all right. "When you're ready for a rowing lesson, son, let me know."

"Thank you, sir," the boy said.

It was only when Sam was under way again, halfway across the Strait, that it occurred to him that he had not even bothered to get the name of the boy or his mother.

It was on a Thursday morning a week later that Sam had a call at the consulate from a Mrs. Morgan, obviously Australian. "I didn't have the chance to show proper appreciation when you rescued Byron. My sister is really quite grateful and she'll be writing you from up-country."

"Your sister," he said, with a slow dawning. "Byron is not your son, then?"

"My nephew, visiting on holiday. But I was calling to ask you to lunch since I'm in town."

"I would like that," Sam said. "Where shall I pick you up?"

"It's the other way around," she said. "I invited you. I have a car. Shall we say twelvish?"

"Twelvish it is," he said.

The rest of the morning was a total loss as far as Sam was concerned. He had just received a dispatch that the Japanese were massing on the eastern Thai border and yet the Brits visiting him at the consulate were discussing cricket scores.

By noon, when the red coupe came to pick him up, Sam was fuming. He tried to disguise his feelings in the presence of what turned out to be quite a lovely woman in a blue silk dress. The top of the car was down, and her long blond hair was blowing. "I know a perfectly delightful place on Tanglin Road," she said. "American food as well as Chinese."

"Fine," he said.

"The owner is Mr. Lu. Delightful man. His wife was eaten by crocodiles last year."

"Yes," Sam said.

"The specialty of his restaurant is roast elephant."

"Fine," Sam said, and then he realized what she had said and broke into laughter. "I'm sorry. I deserved that."

She turned into Orchard Road, avoiding the bicycles and the pedicabs. "I had no idea when you pulled my nephew out of the water that you were a local celebrity. The rest of the afternoon was spent in arguments between those who agreed with you and those who didn't."

"And where do you stand, Mrs. Morgan?"

"Among the hopeful," she said. "My husband died five years ago in an accident and so I've been running our plantation in Malaya since. When it comes to war and rumors, I take things a day at a time. Does your wife like Singapore, Mr. Cummings?"

"My wife died in the fighting in Shanghai."

"I'm sorry." She turned off on a side lane flanked by trees. "Ah, here we are," she said. She left the car with a valet and another servant opened the door to the restaurant, where they were met by an elderly Chinese in a Mandarin gown who welcomed them and personally led them down a corridor to a screened porch surrounded so closely by forest that the brilliantly colored birds were flying only feet away.

"Crocodiles," Sam said wryly as they sat down at the table.

"That was terrible of me," she said, smiling. "But my sense of humor is sometimes rather bizarre."

They had curry for lunch, and wine, and very shortly he was calling her Lydia and she was calling him Sam, and for the first time in months his mind was free of the political and military situation.

She was quite straightforward about herself. "I loved my husband very much and we were married twelve years," she said. "When he died I considered suicide and wrung my hands and blamed God and then decided that there were things to be done to keep the trees in shape and I simply went about doing them."

"You run the plantation by yourself, then?"

"It took a while but I came to enjoy it. I even supervised the building of a room onto the house, which overlooks the Straits of Malacca from the west side of the peninsula. I have over a hundred workers and I stay busy. In all, I'm reasonably content with my world."

"You're a remarkable woman," he said.

"You have a reputation as something of a pessimist, you know, and my friends in Singapore sometimes call me 'Lady Sunshine' because I'm an incurable optimist. But I had to be or I wouldn't have made it when my husband died. There were bookmakers actually taking odds in Singapore that I wouldn't last six months."

"People can be cruel sometimes," he said.

"I went to the Chinese bookmakers and asked what the odds were against me and they said ten to one. So I put a thousand pounds on myself and it was a good investment. I was ten thousand pounds richer."

He laughed. "I like your style. And I'd like to know you better."

"Would you like to see the plantation?"

"Yes, I would, very much. You say you're right on the Strait?"

"Yes, we have a small dock, actually."

"How far?"

"About thirty-five miles. There's a sign on the dock. Morgan Plantations. You can't miss it. Would Sunday be convenient?"

"Perhaps a picnic on the water and a tour of the plantation?"

"Splendid. Shall we say noonish?"

"Noon it is."

On Sunday morning he navigated the Johore Strait and set sail up the Straits of Malacca, having no difficulty in finding the place because Lydia was already sitting on the dock waiting for him. He helped her aboard and pushed out into the Strait, pleased to find that she was a game and fearless sailor who, once she took the tiller, could read the wind and tack with little trouble. In an hour he dropped anchor close to shore, and they enjoyed the awkwardness of close quarters as he spread a blanket on the deck and opened the wicker basket of roast chicken he had brought along.

He could not remember having a more pleasant afternoon in a long time, all light conversation with lots of laughter, and finally the late-afternoon sail back to the plantation.

She ordered the car brought around and they rode through the great rubber estate, which extended inland for miles, the trees standing in rows like soldiers. They came to an inland village where many of her workers lived, all of the people along the road giving a *wai* and a bow of respect to the woman who ran this plantation.

When they were back at the long wooden house with its wide verandas, they found that the cooks had prepared an early dinner. They had wine with the curry and then went out to the veranda that faced the west. Sam reached for Lydia's hand and they watched the sun set over the water.

"Will you have any trouble sailing back after dark?" she said.

"Not at all," he said. "But I'd better get under way shortly."

"It's been a fine, fine day, hasn't it?"

"We'll do it again, soon."

But once he was alone on the water, crossing into the downstream shipping lane, watching the stars pop out of a jet-black sky, the afternoon with Lydia fell into place for what it was, a visit between new friends, no more than that. He had lost two women and learned to live by himself, without the intimacy but also without the pain. Perhaps it was his destiny never to marry again.

He held the tiller to a following sea, lit a cigarette, watched the running lights of somebody's warship far ahead of him down-channel. And the thought occurred to him that if he was to be a friend to Lydia, he would have to advise her to sell her plantation while she could, for the time would come, and soon, when the Straits of Malacca would be filled with warships and her land would be worthless.

Sam watched the developments in Tokyo very closely, listened to the Japanese broadcasts, and read their official pronouncements in the Japanese-run *Singapore Herald*. He detailed his beliefs to Washington and decried the false confidence that pervaded Singapore.

More than once a British officer would try to provoke an argument with Sam as a way of passing a dull afternoon, but Sam remained silent. For there were a number of American correspondents in

Singapore who were now asking all the questions he had asked before, who fought vehemently against the military and civilian censors who kept them from reporting anything that might tend to depress civilian morale. Instead, there were false reports of aircraft squadrons due to arrive any day, airfields being built down the length of Malaya to prevent any Japanese from moving in that direction. Then came reports in the local papers that the fighters and bombers had arrived and been deployed to the Malayan airfields.

But when he had been at the plantation he had talked to workers who had been north and seen no such airfields, no such aircraft. Morale in Singapore reminded him of the atmosphere in Shanghai in the International Settlement, the feeling of invulnerability that came from being American or European.

No small country, it was felt, would ever have the gall to challenge the power of England, as exemplified by the fifteen-inch guns set in concrete facing out to sea at Changi. And the *Prince of Wales* and the *Repulse* were anchored at the naval base, along with assorted destroyers and smaller craft, the men anxious to see action, frustrated at being pulled away from the real war, which had seen the English armies pushed out of Europe to start fighting the long way around from the deserts of North Africa.

In late November, Uncle Roger arrived by Clipper from the United States, and when Sam picked him up in a rented convertible to transport him to the American Consulate, he was surprised to see his uncle's face so heavily lined. It was obvious he was under great strain.

"It's great to see you again," Sam said, pulling the car out into heavy traffic. "I hope I had something to do with bringing you here."

"In a way, yes," Roger said. "But primarily I'm here to have a firsthand look at the political and military situation myself."

"Then I feel no need to point with panic or view with alarm," Sam said. "You have a keen and dispassionate eye and a nose for bullshit."

"Is there someplace we can stop for a cool beer and a breeze to match?" Roger said. "Once I'm officially logged into the consulate, you and I won't have time to visit."

Sam pulled in at a small restaurant overlooking the ocean, and when they were seated in the shade he ordered cold beers while Roger took off his suit jacket and stared out over the water. "Family business first," he said. "I understand that you're at odds with your mother."

"That's the understatement of the year."

"Would you care to give me the details that led to the rift?"

"I think you know enough about it."

Roger shrugged, drank from the bottle when the beer was served. "I despise family battles," he said. "But Adele seems to have settled down since she and Noble got married. He's a most attentive man. As soon as he knew I was coming here, he asked me to try to patch things up between you and your mother."

"Believe me, they are unpatchable."

"Then I will let that matter rest. Do you think you'll marry again?"

"No. I have a very good friend here, a widow, and we see each other quite often. But it's no more than that." He sipped his beer. "Now, what other minor items do you bring me?"

"You remember General Ito?"

"Of course."

"He's stationed in Mukden. He asked one of the British chaps up there about you, how you were doing, that sort of thing. He was out of favor for quite a while, but they needed him too much not to use him. He's in the training end of the army."

"Yuki? Dawn?"

"Still with him as far as we know."

"He's a good man," Sam said. "He's as much against a general war as I am. But we were both yanked out of our positions before we could accomplish anything."

"He was as much a pain in the ass to his people as you have been to us," Roger said without malice. "So now I'm going to reverse myself and ask your bedrock opinion. Your reports and memos have nettled our British cousins and literally raised hell in the department. One faction in Washington is certain you're right. The other damns you offhand because they want to avoid unpleasantness and accept the official British dispatches, which are downright rosy." He looked at his nephew evenly. "I want your opinion straight out. Will Singapore hold if the Japanese attack?"

Sam shook his head unhappily. "No," he said.

"Why?"

"Stupid, blind prejudice," Sam said. "The British refuse to acknowledge anything positive about the Japanese as fighters. In their opinion the Japanese are braggarts and cowards. The British refuse to cooperate with the Chinese, who know better. The British are even at odds with the Australians stationed in Malaya. It's a goddamned frustrating business. The British officers in charge are imbued with the spirit of the old empire. A lot of them served in India, where the brown skins waited on them hand and foot. They simply cannot believe that God would allow such an unthinkable thing to happen to an Englishman."

"I can see how you brought the wrath of officialdom down on your head," Roger said with a wry smile.

"I'm relatively popular these days," Sam said. "I'm playing the game according to their rules. I'm going to bat for the American tire companies, which are trying to sell their product in Malaya despite British opposition. At the same time I'm trying to persuade the British to allow us to buy more rubber from a country they control quite effectively because they handle all the transport."

Roger finished his beer. "Can you predict the outcome of your negotiations?"

"That's the irony of it," Sam said. "It makes no difference what I do. Malaya will be overrun by the Japanese, who will take the rubber and make their own tires. So this is all one grand mental exercise."

"There's always the chance you could be wrong, isn't there?"

"Of course," Sam said.

"Have you given any thought to what you're going to do with your future?"

"That depends. Will the United States get into the war?"

"Roosevelt wants to help the British in Europe."

"Will America fight over Singapore?"

"I don't think so," Roger said. "But why don't you come back to the United States? I can use you in Washington."

"Sooner or later, I'll do that. But I don't have this part of the world out of my system. And I want to get back to China someday."

"You have a lot of your father in you," Roger said thoughtfully. "But if I were you, I'd keep as many of my assets liquid as possible, just in case you have to leave in a hurry." He stood up. "And speaking of hurry, you'd better get me to the consulate. I'm scheduled to fly out in twenty-four hours."

By the early days of December, Sam was spending much of his spare time putting his finances in order. He had spent over a million American dollars on the refugees in Shanghai and paid back his debt to Noble in full. But he still had some two hundred thousand dollars in an account at the Shanghai–Hong Kong Bank, and he wired

Dawes to have that account closed and the money sent to a bank in San Francisco. There were accruing profits from investments he had made in Hong Kong, which were more difficult to change over, but he sold out all his remaining interest in a Chinese cotton mill for an even quarter million dollars and had it transferred to another bank in Los Angeles.

He was suddenly much in demand by Americans with property in Malaya who wanted to sell, and he maintained a list for the convenience of British investors who wanted to buy. On a Thursday afternoon he took a call from David Caldwell, a British plantation owner who expressed interest in discussing properties and invited him for stengahs at the Raffles bar. Caldwell, a bronzed man who wore white shorts and a natty straw hat, owned considerable property up-country, which he allowed overseers to run while he saw to business in Singapore. He drank his stengah, leaned back in a wicker chair.

"I know your views on the political situation here, of course," Caldwell said with a smile. "You're still convinced that the Japanese will overrun Malaya, I take it?"

"Yes, I am. And I assumed you disagree or you wouldn't want to expand. I have a list of American properties if you'd like a look at it."

"Actually, old man," Caldwell said offhandedly, "it isn't an American property I'm interested in."

"Then I'm afraid you've come to the wrong person."

"I don't think so. It's the Morgan plantation I have in mind. If you're right in your view of the military situation, Mrs. Morgan will be left in a bit of a dilemma, won't she? She has a thousand acres, roughly ninety thousand trees, which produce something over two hundred tons of rubber a year. She also has her own rubber presses and smoking sheds." He offered Sam a cigar and, when Sam declined, lit one for himself, rolling it between his fingers. "What will happen to her crops and stock on hand if the bloody Nips do come rolling down the peninsula?"

"In this case I think you're doomed to disappointment," Sam said. "Since she's a friend, I have advised her to sell out, the same advice I give to anyone who will listen, by the way. But in her case, she's intransigent."

"My offer would be a bit different, I think," Caldwell said. "I would like to buy her next year's crop, and I suggest a *leasing* arrangement for the entire plantation, should she decide to evacuate. I have a spotless reputation if I must say so, Mr. Cummings. I knew her husband and I've met her on many occasions, although I really can't say that I know her well."

"Then why didn't you go directly to her?" Sam said.

Caldwell snapped his fingers, brought a Malay waiter running with two more stengahs. "Ordinarily, I would have, since she has been running the place, but candidly, sir, I know your view on this subject and I know that you two are friends. It occurred to me that you might suggest the possibilities to her."

"Where are you staying in Singapore?"

"I have a permanent apartment here at Raffles," Caldwell said.

"Then I'll get back to you."

"What do you think of David Caldwell?" he asked, driving the car beneath the majestic canopy of the groves to inspect a drainage ditch.

"A fine man," Lydia Morgan said. "He treats his trees as if they're his children. Why do you ask?"

"We had drinks Thursday. He wants to buy your inventory and lease your whole operation for the next year," Sam said. "The pressing mills, the smoking sheds. I believe he would be agreeable to a longer lease, as a matter of fact."

She looked at Sam as if he had taken leave of his senses. "You know how I feel about this. Why are you bringing it up again?"

"Because we're friends and because I don't want to see you hurt."

"I happen to love what I'm doing." She climbed out of the car and stalked across to a silt bed and began to instruct the workers in Malay, telling them to dig out the silt and move it to the north forests where the topsoil was thin.

"I know how you feel about your plantation and you have to make your own decision about it," he said when she was back in the car again and they were under way. "But you can't ignore the facts. Time's running out. I've spent the past few days transferring every cent I have in the Far East to the United States. I'm that sure of what I believe."

Her face was troubled. "If there is an invasion, what will happen to my plantation?"

"The Japs will use it as long as they can hold it. When they retreat they'll burn the house and the processing buildings to the ground."

"You can't be a hundred percent sure."

"In this case, I am."

"I don't want to believe any of this."

"There are lots of things I don't want to believe," he said. "But that doesn't change the facts. And there's still a decision to be made."

She allowed Caldwell to come out the following week. He made a tour of the facilities and was happily surprised to find that the plantation was equipped to turn out crepe as well as sheet rubber, and that the warehouse contained bales of both awaiting shipment.

She talked with Sam on the telephone that night. He could tell that she was torn. "I'd like you to be there when I talk with him," she said. "It wouldn't hurt to have a specific offer from him, would it?"

"Not at all," he said.

He made an appointment for them to meet Caldwell at Raffles on Wednesday and they had dinner together on a screened veranda. The night air was warm. And over brandy Caldwell broached the business that had brought them here. "I must tell you how much I like your plantation, Mrs. Morgan," he said. "You've done a top-drawer job of it, and I take it that you're willing to entertain an offer or we wouldn't be here, would we?"

"I'm certainly willing to listen," Lydia said.

"Then what would you say to a five-year lease on all the property and equipment and an outright purchase of the inventory in the warehouse at current market prices?"

"I wouldn't want to include the house," Lydia said.

"That would be perfectly agreeable. And I'll also hire your field Malays at the going rate if they want to stay."

She looked from Caldwell to Sam and then back to Caldwell again, a rather sad expression on her face. "It's possible that the plantation you propose to lease may not even exist a month from now."

"That's a gamble I'm willing to take," Caldwell said. He wrote a figure on a piece of paper. "This is my offer, Mrs. Morgan. I would appreciate an answer as soon as possible."

Lydia looked at the figure and handed it to Sam, who studied it thoughtfully. A hundred and fifty thousand pounds. Roughly half a million American. "It's your decision, of course," he said to Lydia, "but if you decide to accept it, I think you should require cash. No long-term payments."

Caldwell shrugged. "I would be willing to do that, yes."

"I'd like to think about it overnight," she said.

"Fair enough. Just ring me when you decide."

Sam took her up to his apartment to talk, and she put the paper on the coffee table and quite casually, as if they both had known it would happen one night, they kissed and ended up in bed together, their lovemaking sweet, nurturing, a coming together with mutual caring but no all-pervasive passion. And when they were through she lay naked on the bed beside him, her small breasts pale in the dim light, and they shared a cigarette.

"A bloody shame, really," she said.

"What is?"

"That we won't have more time together. I think eventually we would have really got on, don't you?"

"Yes. I do."

She blew smoke toward the ceiling. "But I'm just freshly healed from my loss, love, and you haven't even begun. Such a long, long time it takes." She rolled over to face him, her weight on her elbow. "I don't really have any choice at all about the plantation, do I?" she said. "I've always prized myself for having no illusions. Is his offer truly fair?"

"From the deals I've seen, it's generous."

She took a final drag from the cigarette. "Would you call him for me?" she said. "We'll settle tomorrow."

"Certainly," he said.

The next afternoon she signed the papers and then accepted the briefcase with the hundred-pound notes in neat stacks bound with paper bands while Sam signed the agreement as a witness. She shook hands with Caldwell. "I wish you good fortune," she said.

"Thank you, Mrs. Morgan. And know that I shall take good care of your property."

By midafternoon Lydia had deposited the money in her bank and they had a final drink before she had her driver take her back to the plantation.

On Sunday he went to his office, the building all but deserted, using the quiet time to catch up on his paperwork, and then he had a late supper in the Raffles dining room before he went to bed. Sometime after midnight he came awake with the ringing of the telephone. There was the drone of aircraft overhead and a series of distant explosions. He grabbed the telephone. "I think you had bet-

ter get over here, Mr. Cummings," he heard. "The Japanese are
bombing the city."

Sam put the telephone back on the cradle, clicked on the lamp.
He checked his watch. Four in the morning. He dressed and went
outside. The city was ablaze with light. Smoke and dust were rising
from Raffles Square immediately across the street. There was a surreal quality to the night. The bombs had done no real damage and
nobody he met on the street seemed particularly upset.

At the consulate there was a gathering of employees outside the
signal center. They were waiting for the official cables from Washington while one of the secretaries fiddled with the dial of a short-
wave radio, trying to get a broadcast from the States.

A signalman poured Sam a cup of coffee, filled him in. "The Japs
have landed in northern Malaya," he said. "They got in on the beach
at Patani and we're told they've captured the airfield at Kota Bahru.
We don't know how much damage their bombers have caused here
in Singapore."

"They hit some of the outlying districts, then?"

"Yes, sir."

"I've got San Francisco on the radio," someone yelled, and the
talking ceased and the voice came crackling out of the static.

My God, Sam thought with mounting disbelief, *the ignorant sons
of bitches have attacked the United States.*

The Japanese had bombed Pearl Harbor in the Hawaiian Islands.
They had attacked the Philippines, Hong Kong, made a sudden
move into Siam.

"Is there any news of Shanghai?"

"The Japs have taken over the International Settlement, the
French Concession," the signalman said.

It's here, Sam thought, *the goddamned war,* but far more widespread than he had ever imagined it could be. Never for a moment
had he believed the Japanese would be foolhardy enough to attack
the British and the Americans at the same time. *Absolute madness.*

Sam found the British reaction to the war quite maddening. In the
days before Christmas the quality of life in Singapore became even
more surreal. The local news was totally unreliable. Up-country
sources reported that the Japanese were making rapid progress
down the length of the peninsula, but neither the radio nor the
newspapers mentioned it. He talked to Lydia daily by telephone,

and she said that none of the local planters seemed particularly concerned, interpreting the Japanese move toward Malaya as a diversion.

The frequent air raids on Singapore did only limited damage and thereby convinced the local population that the myth of Japanese incompetence was true. At night searchlights caught and held on the perfect V formation of the Japanese bombers until they disappeared in the distance, but the antiaircraft fire was as ineffective as the Japanese bombs.

It seemed that the war was to be ignored as much as possible. The tea dances at the local hotels lost none of their popularity and long lines formed nightly at the motion-picture houses. And when Sam drove up to the plantation to insist that Lydia make immediate plans to evacuate, he found her walking among the trees with Caldwell, earnestly discussing the different ways of tapping the rubber trees.

Lydia linked her arm in Sam's the minute he joined them and Caldwell smiled at him pleasantly. "It's good to see you, old man," he said. "I'm on my way up-country to calm my Malays. They're dreadfully superstitious and they tend to panic easily."

"They panic with good reason," Sam said, startled at the man's total disregard for the situation. "Don't you know what's happening? The Japanese are moving down the peninsula. They're making eighteen miles a day."

"I wouldn't believe all that propaganda if I were you," Caldwell said, settling into his car. "It's needlessly upsetting. The fields have been flooded in the far north. The Japs can't move in all that muck."

"For God's sake, be careful," Sam said. Further talk was useless.

Caldwell touched his hand to the edge of his hat and then drove on.

Back at the house, Sam sat down with Lydia on the veranda, looking out at the Straits, a few warships in the distance moving northward through the afternoon haze.

"I think you should come into Singapore as soon as possible," he said. "It's no longer a matter of wait-and-see. The situation's going to get dangerous here very quickly."

"Nobody around here is worried. Singapore radio is very calming, and we don't even see Japanese aircraft out here. I don't think the Japanese will get this far down."

"There's nothing to stop them," Sam said. "This is the damndest case of bureaucratic stupidity I've seen. The Japanese are landing thousands of fresh troops in Malaya every day."

"How much longer do you think I have here?"

"No more than three or four days at the plantation. And I want to book you to Sydney ten days from now."

"That soon?"

"Yes."

"What are you going to do?"

"I can't leave my post now. The Americans have to be convinced to evacuate, and the local government's making no effort to get the word out. As a matter of fact, they keep assuring everybody that there's no danger."

She rubbed his arm, as she often did when she was trying to sort things through. "I don't see how I can possibly pack the furniture in ten days."

"You won't have to. There won't be any room for furniture on the ship," he said. "Only clothes and a few personal possessions."

"If it has to be done, then it has to be done," she said.

She spent three days going over her house, trying to convince herself that she was simply leaving for a month's vacation, but it didn't work. She drove down to the main highway to watch the Asian refugees streaming south with their pushcarts piled high with their possessions and she knew the enemy was moving inexorably in her direction, despite the reassuring radio broadcasts from Singapore.

When she went back to the house she broke into tears and caught herself quickly. No more self-pity. She had survived the death of a husband; she would survive this. And when the maid served dinner in the dining room, she could not help but picture this gracious room transformed. Instead of the colorful painting of the Australian outback on the wall, there would be battle maps in Japanese, and their army cooks would take over her perfect kitchen. Their troops would swarm through the house like termites, sleeping in her bedroom and her bed. She could not endure the thought.

The next morning Caldwell was back again with his number one Malay to inspect the machinery in her working buildings.

"Actually," Caldwell told her, "I'm going to take a few bales from the warehouse in the next week or two and set my contracts. There's a good bit of talk that the government at home is going to put ceilings on rubber, but there are still buyers at rather inflated prices. I feel at times as if I've taken advantage of you, Mrs. Morgan."

"I'm satisfied," Lydia said. "And that's all that matters in the end, isn't it, that both parties to a deal be pleased?"

"Quite," he said.

Caldwell's indefatigable confidence in an untroubled future eroded her confidence that she had chosen the right course. But she had made her decision.

She followed Sam's advice and in the end took nothing more than she could pack in two suitcases. She gathered her household staff together and spoke to them in Malay.

"I am sure that you understand what is happening far better than I do," she said, finding it difficult to keep her voice even. "But I will be closing the house for a while and going across the waters to the south to Australia. I have prepared envelopes for all of you with three months' wages, and I have asked cook to divide all the food stores among you equally. This house has sheltered us all and I have been happy here, but the time has come when we all need a different kind of shelter. I hope I will see you all again and I wish you the blessings of Allah and a long life if He wills it."

She embraced the women servants one by one and then exchanged respectful bows with the men. While the suitcases were being loaded in the car, she went up the stairs again, trying to fix in her mind the glow of light on the polished teak, the exact angle of her bedroom windows, which overlooked the Strait on one side and the forest of trees on the other. In the end she knew she could not hold all these memories, any more than the suitcases could hold all the possessions she considered indispensable.

On her last night in Singapore she and Sam made love and then afterward talked far into the night. Her ship would be leaving the next day.

"I want you to do something for me if you can," she said as she lay on his arm.

"Anything."

"I can't stand the thought of the Japanese living in my house. After I'm gone, if there's no hope, I want the house to just not be there anymore, if you know what I mean."

"Yes, I understand," he said.

"Will we ever see each other again?"

"I'm counting on it."

She went to sleep on his arm. He lay awake for a long time, grateful that this was one night the Japanese bombers had decided not to fly.

Everything was confusion at the dock, despite Sam's advance preparations. During all the farewells he was aware that the stewards were trying to clear the ship of visitors because the captain had heard rumors of Japanese warships to the south and was anxious to get out into open waters.

Sam kissed Lydia good-bye and then watched from the crowded dock as the ship moved away from the pier. He felt strangely alone again.

Weeks passed. Christmas came and went and then New Year's. He received a letter from Lydia, who was safe with her family in Australia after a hair-raising trip. Never for a moment did he doubt the wisdom of her leaving. The Japanese bombing accelerated but Singapore radio still announced that the Japanese had been contained in Malay. Each day Sam went out to talk to American families who had opted to stay behind, lulled into a false feeling of security despite an ever-increasing danger.

In late January, with the streets outside his window filled with Chinese leaving the city for refuge in the smaller villages on the island, and Malays streaming into the city in front of the Japanese advance, Sam made his decision to leave. He called British naval headquarters and requested space on a British destroyer going to Batavia in two days.

He was working his way through the crowded streets heading for his suite in Raffles when he was approached by a distraught young Englishwoman outside the Raffles bar.

"Are you Mr. Cummings?" she said.

"Yes," he said. "Do we know each other?"

"In a sense," she said, looking around as if seeking some place where they could have a little privacy. "I wonder if you would be so kind as to buy me a gin. I'm really feeling quite faint."

"Of course," he said. And he managed a table behind a potted palm and sent a Malay waiter scurrying for a gin and a stengah.

"David said you were a man of great conviction," she said, a smile barely clinging to her face. "But he never believed a word of what you said."

"David?" he said. "I'm afraid you have the advantage, Mrs. . . . ?"

"Caldwell," she said.

"Ah, Caldwell," he said sadly. "I heard the rumor about him."

"No rumor. It's true. He's dead," she said, shrugging off his sympathy, reciting the basic facts of his death in a rote-like manner, as if to keep her emotions separate. "The Japs came across the river. There was a small firefight but the British soldiers pulled back. David decided to see if he couldn't talk to the Japanese commander about allowing us to evacuate. He had a white flag on a stick and he walked out, waving it, and the first Jap soldier he saw, an almost naked man wearing a loincloth and boots and cap, simply shot him. No questions, nothing. He just shot him in the head."

"Do you have a place to stay?" Sam said.

"It's not important," she said, eyes dull. "They're going to evacuate us in another week or two."

"I'm leaving tomorrow. I have a suite here and you're welcome to take it over."

"That's very kind."

"Do you have children?"

"No. We planned to."

He saw her established in his suite, ordered dinner sent up. She picked at her food.

"He leased my friend's plantation," Sam said.

She nodded. "Yes, I know. It's lost. It's all lost and I just don't bloody care. I never want to see a plantation again."

He spent all night at the consulate, keeping track of the Japanese Fifth and Eighteenth divisions, which were sweeping down the west side of the peninsula, and he realized that the promise he had made to Lydia was a foolhardy one. The possibility that he could reach the plantation by car was slight. The main highway was clogged with refugees; there was no guarantee he would be allowed across the causeway. Finally he decided that his only chance lay in sailing, though the odds of making it by daylight were slim indeed. Japanese patrol planes, insufficiently armed to take on larger vessels, were strafing small craft in the Malacca Straits. He would have to make the voyage after dark.

He slept little. The next day he cleaned out his desk and left instructions for his replacement should he not make it back. A couple of hours before sunset he changed into dark clothing and went down to the dock where he kept his boat and checked the gas tank on the outboard. Almost full. That would do for any direct maneuvering, and there was a brisk east wind that would work in his favor. He was about to cast off when a British soldier came bustling down the dock.

"What in the bloody hell do you think you're doing there?" he demanded.

"I'm going sailing, Corporal."

"That's out of the question. Let me see your papers."

Sam handed him the diplomatic passport. The corporal's mood softened as he glanced at it and handed it back. "If you plan to sail that boat all the way to Sumatra or Java, sir, I'd recommend against it," he said.

"I appreciate your advice," Sam said. He pulled the outboard into life and made his way through the maze of small-boat traffic down toward the west end of the island. Once he was in the open water, he shut down the motor and lay to, waiting for nightfall. Directly the sun slipped behind a cloud bank in the west, then plummeted like a stone, leaving him the shelter of darkness. The wind fell calm. He could not use his sails. He started the outboard and followed the familiar shoreline, watching the shadowy shapes of the great ships with which he shared the lane. He paralleled the shore at a hundred yards distance, lighting a cigarette, trying to relax, the tiller nestled under one arm. He heard the drone of a small aircraft, flipped his cigarette into the water, eyes straining against the sky, certain it was Japanese, but he could not locate it. He was grateful that his sails were furled, no great expanse of white against dark water to serve as a target.

The sound of the aircraft faded away. He lit another cigarette and occasionally used the light of the coal to illuminate the dial of his watch.

Eight twenty-seven.

Then nine oh-three.

He glided in toward the shore, peering into the darkness, moving slowly just beyond the shoaling water. And then he saw the white boards of the dock, and the shape of the dark house through the trees. He killed the motor, let the boat slip toward the shore, and came alongside the dock.

He fetched the flashlight and some matches from the cabin, then made his way down the dock, pausing every few moments to listen. He heard nothing except the night birds in the trees. By the time he had passed the house and reached the building that sheltered the rubber press, his nervousness had dissipated. He was obviously ahead of the Japanese advance and beyond any current Australian or British defensive position. The door to the building was unlocked, and he flashed on his light and found a five-gallon can, which he filled with gasoline from the outside pump.

He began with the warehouse, filling two smaller cans with gasoline and setting them near the door while he doused the wooden walls.

He moved from building to building, splashing gasoline on walls and floors, and finally moved to the house, where he carried two five-gallon cans up and down the stairs, dousing the curtains and the floors, the veranda where he and Lydia had watched the sunset. And finally, when everything was ready, he moved to a lumber pile and selected sticks that were used to prop up young rubber trees. He clustered half a dozen in a clump and poured gasoline over one end of them, then struck a match and lighted them.

He threw a burning stick into the entrance of the warehouse and watched as it exploded into flame. He torched the machine sheds and smokehouses, and their fires lit up the clearing as if the sun had risen prematurely. The billowing smoke from the burning rubber clouded the night sky.

He approached the house and paused for a long moment before he threw the final firebrand in a great looping arc onto the veranda. The flames raced in all directions, through the doors and up the stairs, catching at the drapes, bursting out through the windows to climb toward the roof.

He heard a shot from the trees and spun around in time to see Japanese troops running toward the house and the burning buildings, perhaps a hundred yards away, yelling to each other. They had not seen him. He ran into the shadows, following a trimmed hedge down toward the dock and burst onto the wooden pier only to stop short.

A Japanese patrol boat was anchored beside his sailboat. Three Japanese soldiers stood on the dock. A light flashed on and froze him where he was. He put his hands over his head and waited for them to fire.

Manchukuo . . . 1944

"I BROUGHT YOU the latest reports, sir," Colonel Mogi said, standing in front of Ito's desk, eyes straight ahead, back straight, at attention.

"Sit down, Colonel," Ito said, knowing they were not favorable but not yet sure what his decision would be.

He glanced through them and now he could interpret the tragic fire in Colonel Mogi's eyes, for he knew that many of last week's casualties had been trained by Mogi. "I believe that many lives could have been spared in the South Pacific last week if there had been more experienced leadership," Mogi said. "And I would like to have my request seriously considered, Esteemed General."

"I have been thinking about it," Ito said, leaning back in his chair. "But I ask you to reconsider what you are asking, Colonel. It is a natural thing to grieve for the young men you have trained who fall in battle." *No,* he thought. *Not fallen in battle. Blown to pieces by bombs or dying an agonizing death in the searing breath of a flame thrower, or holding a live grenade to the belly rather than surrender, an explosive hara-kiri.* He cleared his throat. "You are one of the best officers I have been privileged to command. You are able to inspire raw recruits to do the impossible and season them as soldiers in a very short time. And if you go into battle yourself, who can possibly replace you?"

"I believe the *kami* will provide, Esteemed General," Colonel Mogi said. "I believe it is my duty to fight directly for my Emperor and the national essence."

"And nothing can dissuade you?"

"If you order me to stay, then of course I will."

Ito looked at a map mounted on the wall, the red-flagged pins marking the slow pulling back during the three years since the first attack on the American Fleet. "Do you prefer the tanks or the infantry?" he said.

"Infantry, sir."

Ito tapped the casualty report with his finger. "You know what is happening on the islands. They are forcing us back, regaining these little specks of jungle one by one."

"It will be an honor to die for the Emperor if I must."

"Let me consider this further," Ito said. "I will let you know by tonight."

"Thank you, sir," Colonel Mogi said. And he was up and out of the office in an instant.

Ito sighed, lit a cigarette, called his orderly. "Lieutenant, I want you to make another inquiry about the American prisoner for me."

"Cummings-san, sir?"

"Yes. Send another wire to the commanding officer at the Changi Prison in Singapore. Tell him I am not satisfied with the slowness of any response from him. Also tell him that if he does not respond within one month, the whole business will be turned over to the *kempeitai.*"

"Yes, sir."

Ito walked outside, blinking against the bright sunlight of summer. His driver snapped to immediate attention beside the car, but Ito passed him to go to the motorcycle with the sidecar, which he used when he wanted the opportunity to be alone and think. In an hour he was due to pick Dawn up, and she had liked the motorcycle since she was a little girl.

First, he drove through the camp. There were shortages in every area, including the number of recruits. He had empty barracks here now for the first time, and the carpenters were tearing them down and stacking the wood. The officers believed that there was new construction in the offing that would use the lumber. He would not disillusion them. But in the back of his mind he was aware that next winter would see a severe shortage of coal, and if so, the lumber would be used to keep them warm.

He drove through the city. All civilian cars and buses were banned and there were very few military vehicles crawling through the congestion of horses and wagons and, occasionally, bicyclers. He felt much better when he turned down Yuki's lane in the Russian District and marveled anew at the creative energy of this woman he loved. For now she owned three adjacent houses, one as a residence, one as a showroom, and one as a veritable factory, a collection of workrooms where eight women worked full-time.

Dawn was waiting at the door when he arrived and he smiled fondly at her and told her to hop in the sidecar. Twelve years old, he thought, almost a woman, and she was ripening into a beauty, a tall girl with all the best of Yuki's features and some of Cummings-san's fairness as well, the hair that was deep brown instead of jet black, the flecks of hazel in her brown eyes. She settled herself in the sidecar, her sketchbooks on her lap, and then looked up at him.

"I'm not sure about this at all," she said soberly. "Now, just exactly who is this man again?"

"He is highly recommended by my aide, whose father is an artist. He's a master of the brush, a *sensei*, and your mother says you have all the makings of a fine designer but you need to learn how to use the brush."

"Have you met him?" Dawn said.

"No, but I have a strange feeling that you will get along with him very well, since he is as outspoken as you are. My aide tells me that many years ago a major went to see the old man to order him to paint military signs, road signs, things like that. The old man drew himself up and said he was an artist. The major was not used to having his orders questioned, so he told the old man that during these times even the highest of men were going to have to do those things which had to be done, without any thought of pride. So the *sensei* said that he would begin to paint the signs on the same day that the major came around personally to empty the daily shit buckets for the house."

Dawn laughed. "What did the major do?"

"He didn't bother the *sensei* again."

"All right," Dawn said, bracing herself. "I'll give it a try."

Ito kicked the motorcycle into life, and after ten minutes of nego-
tiating the twisting lanes, came to a stop in front of a small Russian-
style house.

"Is he a true master?" Dawn said nervously.

"That's his reputation. His name is Shiozawa."

When Ito rang the bell a Russian woman with coarse features
opened the door a crack and peered out at her, then spoke in Chinese.

"What do you want?"

"I want to see the honorable *sensei,*" Ito said in Japanese.

"I don't speak Japanese," the Russian woman said, but she was
interrupted by a male voice that commanded her to speak Japanese
and find out what the intruder wanted.

"I want the honorable *sensei* to teach my adopted daughter the art
of the brush," Ito said in a loud voice, not waiting for any further
comments from the Russian woman.

"If I decide to teach her at all, it will cost you twenty yen for each
lesson I give her."

"That's satisfactory," Ito said.

The Russian woman admitted them to a small sitting room filled
with heavy furniture. "He will want to see your daughter alone," she
said to Ito. "So you will have to come back later."

"Does he have to go?" Dawn said.

"You are the one who is to be taught," she said.

A curtain parted and a bearded face peered out at them. He gave
Ito a polite but cursory nod. "The girl may come in," he said. "With
her drawings."

"I'll be back in an hour," Ito said.

Reluctantly, Dawn pulled back the curtain and walked into a
Japanese room with tatami mats on the floor and a skylight that
flooded the white room with brilliance. The old man was sitting with
his ink block in front of him and he gestured to her. "Come here," he
said in Japanese. "I can't see your miserable efforts from this distance. Give me your drawings."

She handed them to him and he took them out one at a time, held
each against the light. "What's this?" he said, pointing to her name
printed in English below each drawing. *"Nan desuka?"*

"My name," she said. And then, in English: "Dawn."

He rolled his brush on the *sumi* block, then drew a character with such swiftness and grace that it took her breath away. "You must sign your name in Japanese."

"I'm not Japanese."

"You dress Japanese. You speak Japanese. Why do you deny being Japanese?"

"My father was American and I've never been in Japan."

"What family name do you carry?"

"Nakamura."

"Of course you're Japanese."

"If I have to use ideograms instead of English, then make them Chinese. I'm a China Dawn, not Japanese."

"What an ignorant, stubborn child you are," the old man said. He rolled his brush again and this time his brush swept two characters onto the paper. "Li Ming," he said. "That's Chinese for Dawn."

"I do not mean to be disrespectful, O-Shiozawa-sama," Dawn said. "But now that you've seen my work, I want to know whether you're going to teach me or not."

"And if I don't?"

"I will have to find someone else."

He looked at her crossly. "The discipline is very hard, perhaps too hard for young girls."

"I'm more than just a young girl," Dawn said. "Just as you are much more than just an old man."

"Ha," the old man said, an exhalation of breath. "I will give you an opportunity. But if you don't work and do as you're told, then I will beat you with a stick."

Dawn gathered up her drawings. "I offer you the greatest respect, Honorable Sensei," she said. "And I will work very hard and do everything that you ask of me and more. And if you are displeased with what I do at any time, then you can stop teaching me. But in my whole life I will never give anyone permission to beat me with a stick."

The old man pretended he had not heard her last statement. "When can you begin?" he said.

"Anytime, sir. Now, if you wish."

"Then we will begin now," he said. "And the first thing you must do is learn to sit correctly in relationship to your paper, to show great respect to your brush, and to mix the proper consistency of ink from the block."

At the end of an hour Ito came back for her and found her waiting for him, glowing with pride. "It went well, then?" he said as she climbed into the sidecar.

"Very well. He doesn't tolerate foolishness, but I don't either, so we have that in common."

"I think you work too hard," he said. "You are still a child, after all. You have to learn to play."

"Sometime I'll do that," she said.

He drove her home and told her to tell Yuki that he would call her when he was going to have a free evening, now that she had a telephone.

As he approached the headquarters building and parked his motorcycle, his depression set in again. The clouds were towering cumulus nimbus, shaped like smoke rolling into the sky from a distant fire. Madness, he thought, that his country had ever attacked the Americans. Madness that so many of his men, including Colonel Mogi, lived on faith when the facts were so dismal.

He had dinner in his office and then summoned Mogi, who stood before him expectantly. "I know that you want to serve your Emperor and your country," he told the Colonel. "And because I have such confidence in the future, I will allow you to transfer to any division that you pick."

With a great sign of relief, the Colonel expressed his gratitude, bowing again and again until he closed the door behind him on his way out. And General Ito had his sake, knowing he had lied to the Colonel, but it made no difference. He had allowed him to leave because he had no confidence in the future and each man would have to do what pleased him most.

Josef came through the door to Yuki's salon and smiled seductively at the salesgirls, who greeted him politely and then summoned Yuki from her office. They went into a fitting room. His black hair was perfectly combed, his dress shirt heavily starched. He sat down on a needlepoint chair, leaned forward on the gold head of his cane, and looked approvingly at the paintings of St. Petersburg and Moscow as they had been in the days before the Revolution.

"Lovely," he said musingly. "It must have been very pleasant to have been so rich without doing anything to earn it."

"But it cost them everything in the end," Yuki said.

"True." He clipped the tip from a cigar, held a flame to it. "My mother wanted such a life and she blames me because I didn't provide it. But she wouldn't have been happy. No matter what, she has always managed martyrdom." He could not get the cigar going. He lit it again. "She refuses to see me anymore, you know. How is she?"

"Very happy here," she said. "If you would like to see her, I'll be glad to send one of the girls to ask."

"Not today," he said. "But I want you to know that I never mistreated her. My attic was the place where she crucified herself because she enjoyed being a martyr. She refuses to see the world as it is." He nursed the cigar. "I think your daughter's designs for the new dresses are excellent," he said. "How long has she been studying?"

"Two years," she said. "And I'm pleased you like her work. So which of the designs do you want us to make?"

"The one that is similar to the first dresses you made for me. My girls loved those. Such a long time ago." He exhaled a blue cloud. "Very few of the same girls work for me anymore," he said. "There's such a turnover. And I have one hundred and sixty girls now. Can you believe that?"

"I may have trouble getting enough material for a hundred and sixty identical dresses."

"I'll supply that," he said.

"And where will it come from, if you don't mind my asking?"

"A number of the Russian merchants think that the war is all but lost," he said. "It's February. They expect a defeat by fall, so they're willing to turn loose a lot of goods they have no way to take away from here. And since I'm supplying the fabric, I would expect to get these at a price of two hundred apiece."

"You can have them at the equivalent of two-fifty a gown," Yuki said.

"The equivalent?"

"I don't want yen. I'll take English pounds, American dollars."

"Ah," he said brightly. "You feel it, too, then, the coming collapse. But perhaps we'll have another good six months or a year. And I can make a lot of money in that time." He drummed his fingers soundlessly on the head of the cane. "I'll give you the equivalent of two hundred."

"Two and a quarter."

"Fine," he said. "I'll have the first dozen of my girls here for a fitting in the morning."

Yuki half expected Inga to refuse to have anything to do with her son's order. "I know how you feel," Yuki said to her in the workroom. "So if you prefer, you can work on the gowns for Madame Berenko or any of the other quality orders."

"And you say he asked about me?" Inga said, continuing to repair a rip in a dress due for delivery in the late afternoon.

"Yes."

"He is sorry now for how he treated me and now he hopes I will relent in my feelings against him, but he will have to beg forgiveness on his knees before he gets it from me."

She was interrupted by the bell jangling in the salon, and Yuki's first thought as she went down the corridor was that she would need to reschedule the girls in the factory to take care of the new orders. It was possible she could use another dozen temporaries to get the work done quickly.

A Japanese private, no more than a boy, stood just inside the door of the salon, his motorcycle still running in the street. He bowed uncomfortably, handed her a letter, bowed again, and left. The cough of his motorcycle diminished down the lane.

She sat down at a glass-topped table to read the letter from Ito, expecting that he had to delay their next meeting or tell her he was off to Tokyo. But as she read his precise vertical rows she turned to ice inside.

"I ask you to be strong! I have learned that sometime last month an American bomber was hit by antiaircraft fire and dropped its bombs into the countryside. Your brothers were visiting at home. Your whole family was asleep, your mother, your father, as well as your brothers, so they did not know when the bomb hit the farmhouse. It is certain that they all died instantly."

No, impossible. There has been a terrible mistake.

"The Village Association has already sorted through the ashes of the house and interred the remains in your family's tomb and assigned farmers to continue cultivation of the land since food is in such short supply."

I do not believe it. Any time now a letter will come from my mother as usual, dictated to the village scribe.

"How I hate writing these words that will cause you such pain. I will be with you soon." It was signed "Ito."

She folded the letter carefully until it was a small and compact square and then put it in the drawer of her desk.

With every passing day Yuki was more on edge, trying to deal with a hundred things demanding her attention. She interviewed girls, finally hired a White Russian named Eva, who spoke six languages, to take charge of the factory. Yuki supervised Dawn's sketches for Josef's order, then helped Inga make the patterns.

She was alone at the house when the letter from the village scribe came. She picked it up, her heart rapid as her finger dislodged the almost glueless flap. She unfolded the paper, stared at the standard, formally phrased letter of condolence, and then let the page fall from her hands.

She went to the storeroom, lifted the lid of a trunk, and found the kimono her mother had given her in parting. She held it up, the colors still lovely. She buried her face in the richness of the color while the tears flowed. When her grief was spent she folded the kimono tenderly and returned it to the trunk. She closed the lid. Her family was gone. That part of her life was over.

Manchukuo
and Tokyo . . .

IN LATE JANUARY of 1945, General Ito made an inspection of
the trucks in the presence of Major Mitsunaga, a tall lean man with
knobby knees and elbows. The Major's eyes were downcast, his
voice a whisper, his drivers standing at attention in front of their
trucks, eyes fixed firmly ahead, staring at nothing. On the manifests
the trucks were listed as "renovated," the implication being that
they were operative. Yet now, as he walked down the line, one truck
lacked an engine, another wheels, a third was sitting on flat bald
tires. General Ito switched his leather swagger stick against his leg.

"How many of these trucks run, Major?" he said.

"All of them, sir," the Major said in a hushed voice. "Just as soon as
we receive replacement parts and tires."

"How many of these trucks are capable of carrying troops at this
moment?"

"Two, Esteemed General. But I have been promised the parts by
next week."

"I see," Ito said, having no wish to shame him. "Are there any
parts you can remove from one truck to get another running?"

"We have already done that, sir."

Ito walked back toward his office. It was as bad as he had expected.
His new aide was a young captain who had lost a leg at Guadalcanal
and now wore a polished wooden peg yet who insisted on standing
whenever the General came into the office. Ito went to his desk, his
despondency like a fever as he looked through the window toward
the drill field. A scattering of new troops were under the command
of a sergeant who had lost a hand. The recruits were practicing with
wooden sticks in place of rifles and they would have no more than a
week of training before they went to the battlefield. All a pretense,
Ito told himself. On paper his training force in Manchukuo was a
model of modern efficiency, but in reality the recruits had to take
turns handling a real rifle since weapons were needed at the front;
all his machinery lacked parts, and petrol for it was in very short
supply.

*My aide has only one leg and even the ink in the bottle on my desk
is ersatz. Local orders are written on scraps of paper while full sheets
are saved for the falsely optimistic reports to Tokyo.*

Ito brewed himself a cup of tea from local herbs and then sat down
to deal with the collective craziness usually contained in the dispatches. Only last year one of the dispatches had boasted that Japanese troops had landed on American soil, setting off a great rejoicing
until Ito discovered that the soil in question consisted of two small,
rocky islands in the Aleutians and that news of the victory had
crowded out the report of a major Japanese naval disaster.

Among his mail was a letter with a battered envelope, a letter
from Changi Prison Camp, and he knew he had finally received an
answer to a query he had been making for years. He took his time
opening it, not certain it would contain any news at all, hoping that
Cummings-san had been evacuated before the fall of Singapore.

But the letter from Changi Camp confirmed that they had a prisoner named Samuel Cummings and the commandant was honoring
Ito-san's request and transferring Cummings-san to the custody of
the *kempeitai;* he was being sent to Tokyo. Ito looked at the date
Cummings-san had been put on a troop ship for transfer, three
months ago. He called out for the Captain. "Telephone the
kempeitai in Tokyo. I want to know if an American prisoner named
Samuel Cummings has arrived there. My name would be on his
transfer file. I want to speak to the officer in charge."

The Captain set about putting through the call and Ito shuffled
through the rest of the papers: routine reports from the Russian

watchers along the border, increased activity now with the collapse of Germany, concentrations of tanks along the Amur River. Another official form, this from the General Staff in Tokyo: a request for explanation of failure to meet quota of trained troops as replacements for casualties in the Ryukyus. For once he wanted to write the truth. *There aren't enough young men to meet the quota, and even if they existed, they would be as untrained as the boys you now receive. Most of my able-bodied training officers have gone to the front and I am left with the walking wounded.* But he answered with standard politeness. The replacements would be sent any day now. They were simply awaiting transportation.

The door opened and the Captain stuck his head in. "I have a General Haneda on the line in Tokyo if you wish to speak to him."

"Yes," Ito said. He snatched up the telephone, leaned forward in his chair to concentrate on the words that filtered through the poor connection, cracking with static. Cummings-san was safely in Tokyo and in custody. Ito said he would be in Tokyo as soon as he could catch a flight.

He caught a transport plane that same afternoon that overnighted in Chosen and put him in Tokyo the next day. There were few automobiles on the street; the shop windows he passed were bare. The crowds of people were poorly dressed and all of them wore gauze surgical masks against disease. The car crawled through a street where a swarm of workers were clearing by hand the mountain of rubble that had once been an office building. "When was this building destroyed, Lieutenant?" Ito said.

"The day before yesterday, sir," the Lieutenant said cheerfully. "One of their bombers got through while dozens were destroyed through the heroic efforts of our antiaircraft batteries." Ito recognized the recital of the official line—the bright side of disaster even if it had to be invented. "The people are clearing the streets by hand because they understand that all the heavy equipment is needed at the front and this is their way of defeating the enemy."

Ito stopped listening.

When he reached his house and went through the ceremony of greeting his wife, his mother, and his small son, he soon learned that civilian life was even worse than he had observed on the streets. The lines on his mother's face were much deeper than they had been before. Ariko looked as if she had aged twenty years since he had last seen her. But as they sat down to dinner together the servants were still efficient; it was apparent that his mother had maintained her dominance in the house.

It was only when he was alone with Ariko in their rooms that the words came out of her in an unstoppable monotone, as if she had been pressed down for so long that even her words were flat.

She poured his sake and then sank down on her knees. "The best families are all sending their children to the country and my honorable father has a villa at Kurizawa in the mountains, where other small children of the family are being taken by the wives to preserve the future. Everybody knows that Tokyo will be destroyed, district by district, and I want to make every effort to preserve your heir, since you are the last male of your family."

He drank the sake, felt the chill in the room. He would not ask about the heat. He knew there was little coal left for residences. "You do not look well," he said. "It is a hard time for you."

"Your honorable mother does not wish to distress you with the truth. But since you are a general in the military, I am sure you want all the facts so you can make the proper decisions."

He sipped his sake. "What is troubling you?"

Her lower lip was trembling. "We have been saving from our rice rations for months just so you wouldn't know how little we are given to eat. There's a black market in food out in the country but the military runs the trains and I can't send any of our servants into the countryside." Her hands fluttered like wounded birds. "There are shortages of everything, of soap and paper and food, of radios and automobiles and doctors."

"Are you ill? Do you need a doctor?"

"No, but there are outbreaks of typhus and cholera all over the city and I live in fear that Kanao will get sick and perhaps die because there is no medical treatment available."

"And there are doctors at Kurizawa." It was not a question.

"Plenty of doctors. Plenty of healthy food. And no dangers."

"I think that is an excellent idea," he said. "I want Mother to go with you." He looked at his watch. Time was running short and he knew he needed to report in to the War Ministry. "We'll decide the details later."

At the War Ministry he went to General Haneda's office, where the official paper requesting personal interrogation of a prisoner was ready for him. He put his signature on it, then sat back while Haneda made the necessary telephone calls.

"It will take a very short time to make the arrangements," Haneda said. "I understand you worked with this American in Shanghai."

"Yes," Ito said. He looked at the face of the older general, found it contemplative.

"It may come to that," Haneda said unhappily. "Finding a way to talk with the Americans. I wish you well."

"Thank you," Ito said.

Ito was taken to a small Western-style house at the bottom of a hill near the Diet Building. As he arrived the sky rumbled and a heavy rain began to fall. The living room was furnished with heavy chairs and a patterned couch confiscated from the closed Western embassies. He looked at the *kempeitai* captain who had been assigned to him. "I have made a list of some things I want immediately. Can you get them for me?"

The captain glanced at the list. "Yes, sir."

When Sam was ushered into the room Ito was shocked by his appearance. He was gaunt, his hair ill kempt, and he wore old and poorly fitting clothes. There were sores on his hands, cuts on his face where he had been shaved by an inept barber. He squinted at Ito as if he could not quite bring him into focus, and then there was a slow dawning of recognition. "My God, Ito-san," he said. "Is it really you?"

Ito embraced him, felt the bones of the back. "I have been looking for you a long time but I really did not want to find you like this. I hoped you had gone home."

Sam sank into the sofa as if something had let go within him for the first time in years. "Jesus, it's good to see you. I've had so many hallucinations over the years, I'm no longer sure what is real and what I invented. I asked a guard at Changi about you. He said he thought you were dead."

"I was out of favor for a while. As good as dead, officially. But we have both survived," Ito said. "It seems very strange to speak English after such a long time. These have been terrible years for you, I know. I apologize to you."

"You didn't start the war. You didn't take me prisoner."

"But I can make it up to you now." He picked up the telephone, barked an order. There was a knock on the door and the captain came in, followed by two corporals carrying trays, which they placed on a small table. The captain had done well, Ito decided. The trays contained a bowl of fresh fruit, three slices of ham and cheese, and what appeared to be fresh bread. There was also a pack of American cigarettes and two bottles of Japanese beer.

Sam's face lit up. "I haven't seen anything like this since before the war." He reached for the apple, took a bite while he surveyed the second tray. "How did you arrange this, my friend? I heard that your country's in a bad way. I was able to see something of the streets when they brought me here."

"I never approved the war but I have never gone against my country," Ito said. "And you are here as my own small victory, my accomplishment in the face of frustration. I have at least saved a friend of many years."

Sam picked up one of the packs of American cigarettes, shook out two, and waited while Ito lit them. "It's about over, isn't it?" Sam said, leaning back, dizzied by the smoke.

"I do not know," Ito said, sitting down, savoring the cigarette. "I have learned to accept the days as they come, one at a time."

Sam finished the apple and then reached out for a beer. "I've thought a lot about the old days since I've been a prisoner. Yuki," he said. "Yuki and Dawn. How are they?"

"They are doing very well now," Ito said. "It has not been an easy time for them. Your daughter is beautiful and very mature for thirteen."

"Does Yuki know I'm here?"

"No. Do you want me to tell her?"

Sam took another long pull at the beer. "No," he said. "Will they be all right in Manchukuo if the Russians come in?"

"Nobody will be all right. I will get them out before that happens."

"I know you'll take care of them. You have—from the beginning."

"They suffered in Manchukuo because of me," Ito said. "And even when I was in favor again, things were not easy for Nakamura-san. But on her own she has built a substantial business, very prosperous for a place like Mukden. You would be very proud of her."

"I am proud of her," Sam said, and for a moment he saw the sunlight on the yellow waters of the Whangpoo and in his mind turned the sailboat upriver and kept going, her face smiling at him. *We should have left Shanghai and never come back, love,* he thought, and then he pulled himself back to this moment. No more escaping into what might have been. *Be grateful for now.*

Sam finished the first beer, offered the second to Ito, and when he declined, took it for himself. "So what happens now?" he said.

"I think I can arrange to have you kept here for the rest of the war," Ito said. "I may be able to get a cable through to Washington to let your family know you are safe. Your Uncle Roger is there, if I am not mistaken."

"Can you do this without getting yourself into trouble?"

"I think so, yes. Through the Swedes."

FEB 1, 1945 (CODED CABLE VIA SWEDISH FOREIGN MINISTRY)

TO: ROGER CUMMINGS, DEPARTMENT OF STATE
　　WASHINGTON, D.C.

FROM: SAMUEL CUMMINGS
　　TOKYO, JAPAN

I AM HEALTHY AND SAFE. CANNOT EXPLAIN FURTHER.

FEB 8, 1945 (CODED CABLE VIA SWEDISH FOREIGN MINISTRY)

TO: SAMUEL CUMMINGS
　　TOKYO, JAPAN

FROM: ROGER CUMMINGS

WE RECEIVED INFORMATION 12 FEB 1942 THAT SAMUEL CUMMINGS WAS KILLED IN THE FIGHTING IN SINGAPORE, HIS BODY BURIED IN A MASS GRAVE. TO ESTABLISH YOUR IDENTITY: GIVE ME YOUR MOTHER'S MAIDEN NAME, THE LAST PLACE WE MET, THE NAME OF YOUR IMMEDIATE SUPERIOR IN SINGAPORE ON YOUR TRANSFER THERE.

FEB 10, 1945 (CODED CABLE VIA SWEDISH FOREIGN MINISTRY)

FROM: SAMUEL CUMMINGS

TO: ROGER CUMMINGS

(1) ADAMS (2) SINGAPORE (3) DONALDSON.

ROBERT L. DUNCAN

FEB 15, 1945 (CODED CABLE VIA SWEDISH FOREIGN MIN-
ISTRY)
FROM: ROGER CUMMINGS
TO: SAMUEL CUMMINGS

JOYOUS NEWS TO FIND YOU ALIVE. YOUR MOTHER IS IN
EXCELLENT HEALTH AND SENDS HER LOVE.

The next morning Ito walked with his mother on the grounds of the estate, where dozens of workmen were digging trenches within the boundaries of the cast-iron fences.

"There is a rumor that the heavy air raids will begin very soon," his mother said. "I have been told by the servants that there are insufficient trenches for people to conceal themselves in the city, so I have given permission for such shelters to be dug here."

"You are a generous person, Honorable Mother."

She examined the grass at the edge of one shallow pit, turned away to walk toward a clump of fir trees. "Your wife spoke to me about going to the country with her and the child."

"I think you would be much better off there."

"I know it is my duty to follow your will. But I seek your permission this time to make my own decision. I am a very old woman and I have spent all my life here and I have no desire to be in the mountains when the end approaches."

"Of course I will honor your request," he said.

"I am most grateful." She breathed deeply, as if she had difficulty getting enough air into her lungs. "My astrologer tells me there will be a few losses and things will look very dark and then, suddenly, there will be a burst of great victories and the national spirit will prevail. But I have heard that the government has ordered all astrologers to give favorable predictions to keep morale high. As your mother, I ask you for the truth if you are free to give it to me. There is an old saying that the blind man does not see the snake. So I ask you. Is the snake now at hand?"

Ito nodded. *"Hai,"* he said. "The snake is now at hand. But it makes no difference. I send young men off to battle, knowing that most of them are going to die. It is my duty to send them and it is their duty to go. In the end, what is unthinkable will become unavoidable."

She nodded. "I thought as much," she said. "But it has been a good life and I will leave behind a son and a grandson. Your father's line will survive. And I'm sure that his spirit will be pleased that I stay here to the end."

Ito received a cable from his adjutant in Mukden that the Russians were moving along the border again, and he knew he had stayed as long as he could in Tokyo. He called and secured a place on an aircraft leaving for Mukden in the late evening and then he went back to the house near the Diet Building.

He was cheered by the improvement in Sam's appearance. The sores on his hands had healed and he was regaining some of his lost weight. "I see that you are better today, my friend," Ito said, "and it makes it easier to say what I have come to say." He offered Sam a cigarette and sat smoking, thoughtfully. "I have to go back to Manchukuo tonight. I have told the *kempeitai* to keep you here and to treat you well because you are my prisoner and have information I need. You will be moved from a cell to a more comfortable room, but you will still be closely guarded. They will honor my orders, but I ask you to do one thing to guarantee your safety."

"Certainly. What is it?"

"You will be given paper and a pen. Every day you need to fill the page with writing, anything that comes to mind. But you will put this 'report' in a sealed envelope with my name and the date on the front. No one will violate the seals on the envelopes."

"How do I thank you for saving my life again?" Sam said.

"Let us hope that someday we will meet in peace."

"You *are* a man of peace, General. You deserve a good life." He put his arm around Ito, a wordless embrace, and then Ito was gone. Neither man was sure they would ever meet again.

After her son's departure Lady Ito went to Ariko's quarters and was amazed to find the main room decorated with small pieces of paper folded in knots, good-luck symbols hanging from strings. She informed the servants to tell her daughter-in-law that she was here. Shortly, Ariko came into the room, taking very short steps, descending to her knees in a formal bow.

"I am honored by your visit," Ariko said.

"I think the time has come for you to take Kanao to the safety of the mountains," Lady Ito said. "I understand that your father still has a motorcar which will run."

"Yes, my lady."

"The telephone no longer works, but if you will write him a note, I will have one of the servants deliver it on his bicycle and wait for an answer. I would suggest the servant start early in the morning because it will take all day to reach the mountains."

"Again, I beg my esteemed mother-in-law to join us."

"I thank you again for your concern," Lady Ito said. "When you know your plans I would most appreciate your informing me. I would like to spend some time with my grandson before you go."

"Domo arigato de gozaimashita," Ariko said, making a deep bow of respect.

Two nights later Lady Ito received Ariko, who said the answer from her father had just come. The car was being converted to burn wood instead of coal and it would arrive at about noon. Lady Ito asked to spend the final morning with her grandson, and although she did not say it, she knew it was a final good-bye.

That night the sirens began to wail, and were followed by the drone of bombers coming in low. And the nightmare began. Waves of bombers swooped across the city, by tens at first, then twenties and fifties, finally hundreds, lines of planes flying wing to wing, dropping incendiaries, spreading flames into the wooden houses and the paper screens, into the reed floors, until the whole of the city's center was laid out ready for kindling.

Four square miles.

Explosions, solid flame. People were cooked, incinerated, choked to death by smoke, dying from lack of the oxygen being consumed by the giant firestorm that rose like a thermal cyclone into the night sky.

Lady Ito heard the sirens and ran outside to see what was happening. Off to the east was a solid wall of flame, and the whole city was exploding.

She directed the servants to soak futon and bed coverings in water and then she ran to her daughter-in-law's room to find Ariko wrapped in good-luck strings, holding her son to her, hysterical with fear.

"Get up," Lady Ito said, a command. "Follow me."

Ariko whimpered. Lady Ito reached out and slapped her across the face.

"I said get up and follow me. The fire is coming."

Only then did Ariko rise, and Lady Ito yelled for the servants to wrap both of them in the wet cloths and then flee to the west, toward a canal flanked by a park, which might break the progress of the fire.

When they reached the door to the house Lady Ito felt a sharp pain in her chest and she stopped momentarily. She watched the servants half carry, half lead the terrified young woman and her child across the lawns and through the gate, into the mob of people running down the street toward the park.

One servant stopped to help Lady Ito, but she urged him away. "It is my wish that you go," she said, and when he hesitated: "Follow instructions. Go." And when he left she stood alone in the entryway of the house in which she had spent most of her life. Embers carried by the wind had just reached the east wing. She sank slowly to her knees, watching the flames. They seemed to be as alive and beautiful as the phrase that had been coined to describe them:

The flowers of Edo.

Her ashes would be mingled with the ashes of the house, impossible to separate. She closed her eyes and found departure before the flames reached out to greet her.

Manchukuo . . .
March 1945

ITO COMMANDEERED a reconnaissance bomber for a flight across the Amur River along the border. The plane made a slow, almost lazy bank, and the pilot pointed with his leather hand. Ito nodded. Far to the left was a Russian column on the road, a thin trickle of men that stretched for miles. Ito raised his binoculars, took a closer look, saw the men plodding along, breath steaming, over-sized packs on their shoulders. Few vehicles. A truck here and there. Nobody in any great hurry.

Ito noted that the Russian troops had brought with them no heavy winter gear, since spring was approaching. That meant that they did not intend to stay beyond the end of the short summer. Whatever battles they had in mind would come before the first snow.

He could not fault the Russian logic. They surely knew the state of the Kwantung armies, and their spies could observe that there was little training being conducted now. The few able-bodied men remaining in Japan were being pulled into the army and shipped immediately to the south to fight the advancing tide of Americans. There was not even sufficient fuel to send regular troop ships to Chosen or Tientsin anymore.

The pilot touched the instrument panel with a thick leather finger and pointed to the petrol gauge, which was showing low.

General Ito nodded. He had seen all he needed.

When he got back to his headquarters there was a message on his desk from Tokyo. Since the training headquarters was no longer needed, General Ito was to report to Kyushu within the week to help prepare the island for the American invasion.

He drove Yuki into the countryside on a midsummer day. Ordinarily farmers would have been in the field, making the most of the short growing season, but horse carts piled high with household goods were moving south. Ito drove past a military outpost, sandbags piled high around a pair of cannons pointing to the north.

"They all know the Russians will be swarming down any day now," Ito said, peering through the windshield in search of a side road, where he turned off to drive across the rolling plains toward a ridge of land in the near distance. "I am trying to persuade the local commanders that it is senseless to fight the Russians when we are going to need everything we have to defend Kyushu."

"Can you not command them to go, Ito-san? You're a general."

"I'm not in charge of anything here since the training is discontinued," he said. "I can consult with local commanders. I can tell them that Russian armies are poised just across the river, waiting for Moscow to declare war on us. And once they invade, nothing we can do will even delay them." He stopped the truck on top of the rise and led the way to an ancient mound shaped like a small ship. He made a sweep of the northern horizon with his binoculars, shook his head. "There's no natural barrier on these plains, nothing to fortify."

They sat down in a hollow of the mound, and Yuki took a bottle of wine out of her bag, opened it, and offered it to him. He took a long pull, nodded his gratitude. The hollows around his eyes were dark; his body was thin. He put his arm around her. "I would like nothing better than for us to live together in a peaceful time with our daughter," he said in a weary voice. "But you already know that, do you not?"

"Yes," she said.

He lit a cigarette, breathed out the smoke, put a hand on her arm. "There is little time left. Exactly how much I do not know, but you should begin to liquidate your holdings. Your real estate will be worth nothing, of course. But settle your affairs and collect any debts owed to you." He lay back with his head in her lap, looking at the clouds in the sky. "There is an airfield south of Mukden," he said. "It does not look like one because there are no landing lights, no wind sock, and the men who operate it are housed in a small barn with a radio."

"I know the place."

"I will send you a message forty-eight hours before the arrival of the evacuation aircraft. I will try to come for you myself, but even if I cannot, the aircraft will bring the two of you to me in Kyushu."

"Yes, Ito-san."

He looked up at the sky a long time. His eyes closed and he dozed off. She did not move for fear of waking him.

She heard the wail of a train and from a distance saw the plume of gray smoke trailing from a steam engine chugging south toward Mukden. Very shortly, she told herself, the trains will stop and the weeds will grow over the rails and the land will be deserted.

At dusk Ito stirred, then came awake with a start. "I have to go," he said reluctantly. "I have to take a plane to Kyushu tonight." He put his arms around her, drew her to him. "When I see you next time, we will be leaving Manchukuo."

She said nothing, clinging to him, fixing forever in her mind the way his body pressed against her, as if the memory had to last the rest of her life.

Dawn was sitting by the front window of the salon staring absently at the street, where the traffic was heavy, wagons piled high with furniture, elegant carriages packed full of people from the great households.

"I heard that Madame Berenski left this morning," Dawn said. "It took four wagons just to carry the personal things she couldn't live without. I wonder where she can go. Will it be any better for her in China?"

"Anyplace will be better than here," Yuki said. She saw Alexi at the front window. He pushed the door open, nodded to Dawn, then took off his hat as he approached Yuki, an almost desperate expression on his face. "I must speak to you in private, madame," he said. She led the way into a small office.

He lowered his voice. "Have you heard of bomb?" he said.

"What bomb?"

"Dropped on Japan, some city, I don't know. The city there one minute and after bomb is dropped, poof! No more. I hear many rumors but this I believe. Also that Russia is now in war. So I am taking family south, but I had to warn you."

"I don't know what we would have done without you, Alexi. I'll pay you for your share of the business."

"Most kind," he said, "but Alexi's family has all that is needed." He took her hand, kissed it, eyes moist. "If I believed in God, I would ask blessings for you. Good-bye, madame."

She told Dawn to lock the door leading into the street. "Ask Inga and Eva to come in here, please," she said to her daughter, and while she was waiting she opened her tin cash box and then uncapped a bottle of cognac, setting out the crystal glasses. When Inga and Eva came into the room she poured them each a drink.

"There is a rumor that a new and terrible bomb has been dropped on Japan," Yuki said, trying to keep any sense of panic out of her voice. "And another rumor that the Russian armies have invaded Manchukuo."

Eva's hand began to tremble, but Inga merely regarded Yuki with unhappy eyes. "I knew this would happen," she said. "I knew that my luck wouldn't hold. But I will not go back to my son's house for any reason."

"I would advise you not to stay in Mukden at all," Yuki said.

"I spit on the Bolsheviks," Inga said. "They don't frighten me."

Abruptly, Eva began to cry, her cheeks flushing a bright red. "I don't have anywhere to go," she said.

Inga put an arm around her, clucked at her soothingly. "You'll stay with me. I've always wanted a daughter, and in the eyes of God I hereby trade my son for you, if you'll stay with me. I'll keep the Reds away from you." She raised her glass. "To the fine business we shared together. It has been the best time in my otherwise miserable life." She downed the cognac in a single draft.

"I want to help you as much as I can, my dear Inga," Yuki said. "We've done a very good business. I want you to have what you would have made for the next three months, in gold. And I will write you out a deed to this property. There is still money owing on it but there won't be anybody left to collect it and there's a chance you might be able to hold on to it, if you're set on staying."

"God bless you," Inga said.

Yuki counted out the money. "You can also have all the fabrics, the stock, everything in here. We can't carry it back to Japan."

"Thank you for your generosity, madame," Inga said. She wrapped the gold in a cloth. "We'll go into the country for a few days and then come back when things settle down. Will there be fighting?"

"I don't know," Yuki said. "I wish you well."

They all embraced in turn, and once the Russian women had gone, the salon felt strangely empty.

But Dawn looked at her mother with large brown eyes. "We're in more danger than you're telling, aren't we, Mama?"

"Yes, but we'll survive." She locked the door for the last time and, linking arms with her daughter, stayed close to the side of the buildings and out of way of the horse carts. As they approached the house Yuki was not surprised to find a motorcycle with a sidecar and driver in front of her house, and a Japanese colonel waiting to talk to her. She unlocked the door and invited him into the house, aware that Dawn was listening with a solemn face.

"I have brought you a message from General Ito," the Colonel said. "Everything at headquarters is bedlam, Nakamura-san. We have orders to evacuate on the one hand, and on the other we are to stand fast and wait for an announcement of surrender from Tokyo. And then there is a third set of orders that says we are to disregard any announcements from Tokyo and fight to the last man."

"And what will you do, Colonel?"

"I have specific orders from General Ito himself. I am to fly to Kyushu to become a part of the army that will make a stand against the invasion. I'm instructed to inform you that the General has been wounded, that he has broken a leg in the landing of an aircraft that ran out of gas in Kyushu, and he orders me to convey his profound sadness at his inability to come himself."

Her breath caught in her throat. "Is he badly hurt?"

"I don't know."

"When will the plane arrive?"

"There are further difficulties," the Colonel said. "The Russians have moved past Harbin. We have nothing in the field to stop them. They should reach Mukden by late tonight. But the plane cannot be here until Wednesday."

"Three days," she said.

"It will arrive at the airfield at exactly 2200 hours to take advantage of the darkness. It can stay on the ground no longer than thirty minutes."

"So my daughter and I will have to survive until then," Yuki said, almost to herself.

"I would offer you the protection of the army except that I don't believe there will be one," the Colonel said. "In any event, they will attack our military headquarters first. Do you have a place to hide for three days, Nakamura-san?"

"We're prepared for that, Colonel."

"I'll greet you myself on Wednesday night if luck is with us," he said.

"I am profoundly grateful to you, Colonel. And what time will the Russian troops be here tonight?"

"By midnight perhaps. An hour either way."

"*Domo arigato gozaimasu,*" she said.

She listened to the sound of his motorcycle trail away in the distance, and for a moment she was overwhelmed, knowing that her beloved Ito was wounded and there was no way she could get more information. He could die and she might never know it.

Dawn stood near the door, doing her best to hide her bewilderment and fear. Yuki patted the sofa cushion next to her and Dawn sat down. Yuki put her arm around her daughter's shoulders. "It will take both of us working together to get through the next three days. Whatever we do outside must be finished by this afternoon."

"What can I do?" Dawn asked solemnly.

"Make an inventory of the food and water we have under the floorboards in the bedroom. You'll have to get whatever we need as quickly as you can and get back inside the house."

"What will you be doing, Mama?"

"Finding the closest route to the airstrip where the plane will pick us up." She pressed one of Dawn's hands between hers. "We will have to avoid the Russian soldiers at all costs. I want you to find the worst and most foul-smelling clothing that you can. I believe there were peasant *mompei* in one of the parcels of cloth we bought from the Russian lady near the station."

"The padded clothes with trousers?" Dawn said.

"Yes." She ran her fingers through her daughter's long hair. "Now, before you find the clothes, it is necessary that we cut your beautiful hair."

Dawn brought the scissors and Yuki steadied her hand and forced herself to make the first cut and then the second, hacking away until the hair lay close to the head, an ugly thatch. "I can truly say, for the first time in your life, daughter, that you look terrible," she said with some humor. "Now, you must do the same to me."

"I love your hair," Dawn said. "I can't do it."

"Of course you can. Make a game of it. Pretend there's a prize to be won for the ugliest haircut."

"Do you mean it?"

"Of course."

Dawn picked up the scissors. She cut a long swatch of her mother's hair from the back of her head at an angle, and then, horrified at what she had done, she dropped the scissors, covered her face with her hands, and began to weep. Yuki put her arms around her daughter, tried to soothe her. "The game, darling, remember?"

Dawn nodded silently and began to clip around on her mother's hair, leaving a patch here, a bush there, nothing at all in another spot. Yuki heard a giggle, smiled. "That bad, is it?"

"I used to see a dog at the park in Shanghai," Dawn said, snipping away with abandon. "A Chinese woman clipped it and made such terrible mistakes that she finally gathered up the little bunches of hair that stuck out all over the poodle and tied little satin bows on them."

"So you're making me look like the poodle."

"Oh, much worse." A final snip of the scissors. "There. I'm through."

"The mirror," Yuki said. "Come sit beside me." She had never felt such great love for her daughter as she did in this moment, their faces side by side in the mirror. Dawn stuck her tongue out at her image.

"I think I'm uglier by far," she said.

"Never," Yuki said. "Now I want you to get the *mompei* ready. There's mud in the garden behind the house. Get a pail of it and smear the clothing and then keep another pail for us."

"The dirt in the garden stinks," Dawn said. "Somebody has used night soil on it."

"All the better. Check the supplies. I should be back in an hour or so."

"Where are you going?"

"To the airfield. When the time comes we will have to get there in total darkness."

"Please be safe," Dawn said. "I can't survive without you."

Yuki touched her daughter's cheek with her hand. "Oh, but you can," she said. "You won't have to, if the Lord Jesus and the Lord Buddha are willing, but you must keep the thought firmly planted in your heart that you will survive despite anything." She kissed her on the cheek. "I'll hurry."

Yuki had never seen the city so deserted in some places, so frantic in others. Residential areas were empty, trash piled at the doors, but the streets that fed into the main road toward the south were congested with military traffic and long lines of refugees. She stayed away from the heavily trafficked roads, followed a lane into the open country until she arrived at the airfield, where a cow grazed contentedly on the winter grass in the middle of the pasture. There was no sign of life, even in the barn with its rich smell of rotted straw and manure. She checked the time.

Forty-seven minutes.

And she had not run. They could if necessary do it in half the time.

She patted the pocket in her skirt. She had the equivalent of fifty dollars worth of gold with her. She would buy a pistol from one of the retreating soldiers. They would be destroying the ammunition in the arsenal anyway.

She approached the center of the city, turned a corner, and then pulled back quickly, her heart beating wildly. A Japanese guard at the door to the city prison was turning loose the scores of men who had been detained there. The felons of every nationality scattered into the side streets. Yuki knew they would be looting the city before the Russians arrived.

She ran down a back alley, and when she arrived at the house she found Dawn sitting in the sunshine in the garden, smearing the *mompei* with mud.

"Did you check the supplies?"

"We have plenty of food and water."

"Come inside the house." She locked the back door behind Dawn and took up a position by the window where she could see down the lane.

"What is wrong, Mama?"

"They've turned the prisoners loose from the prison. They'll be looking for food, weapons, whatever they can find."

"Maybe they won't come here."

We won't be that lucky, Yuki thought, and, as if to confirm her fears, she glimpsed the shadows of three men down the lane and heard the crash of glass. She picked the sharpest knife she could find and put it in the bag of supplies Dawn had prepared. She put a hand on Dawn's arm and without a sound led her to the bedroom, where she had prepared the floorboards. She pried them up.

"We have to get down inside," she said.

Dawn looked at the shallow crawl space. "There isn't room."

"There's room. I've tried it. Lie on the ground with your face up. We'll stay there only until the looters pass by."

Dawn inched her way beneath the floorboards and Yuki handed her the bag of supplies. Dawn winced as Yuki followed and reached up to pull the boards back into place, leaving the last one open so she could catch the edge of a small rug and pull it over the loose boards before she put the last board into place.

"Are you hurt?" Yuki asked.

"I cut myself on the knife," Dawn said in a low voice.

"How?"

"It was sticking through the cloth."

"Is it bad?" Yuki whispered. There was no chance for an answer. At that moment the two front windows crashed inward in a shower of glass and the front door burst open, to the sound of boots on the wooden floor, and Yuki knew there was nothing to stop them now: no police, no law, nothing.

She heard the crash of dishes in the small kitchen, the sound of a cabinet ripped open, whoops of delight. They had found the liquor supply. Soon they came down the hall, one of them singing a tuneless melody. She prayed that they would take what they wanted and leave.

But they did not. One came into her bedroom and clicked on the radio. A military announcer was urging everybody in the city to keep calm.

"It is considered expedient at this time for the Emperor's armies to disengage. Be prepared to set fire to your abode to show the barbaric Russians entering our city that we will leave them nothing, no food, no beds in which to sleep, and in that deprivation will be a victory." The voice stopped to be followed by the national anthem.

Yuki heard the sound of boots on the floor, the creak of bedsprings, and soon he was snoring. *Perhaps he was drunk and they could slip out.*

"What are we to do, Mother? My arm hurts. Where will we go if the fires come?" Dawn asked, the fear in her voice.

"I will take care of it. Be patient, *chi chai.*"

She stroked her daughter lightly on the cheek and soon she heard Dawn's gentle deep breathing. Her daughter was asleep. Then she heard voices in the kitchen. She would wait. Time dragged by. Silently she lifted the board and an edge of the rug. It was dark in the room. Then she heard glass breaking and a chair fall over in the front part of the house. She lowered the board. She heard nothing more for a long time.

She was awakened by a blast of music from the radio in the bedroom above her. She felt Dawn move just as the bedsprings creaked. "He's still here. I think it must be morning. The station is broadcasting again," Yuki whispered.

The music stopped abruptly. The man had unplugged the radio. Then she heard him moving around.

Why doesn't he leave?

He was standing immediately over the space where they lay and the loose boards rattled beneath his feet. *My God, he suspects something.* She groped around, dug in the bundle, and found the handle of the knife, gripped it tightly. As soon as the first board was ripped up, she would lash out at him with the knife.

A loudspeaker truck blared forth from the street, and the man ran down the hallway as the tinny voice urged all Japanese residents to evacuate. The loudspeaker faded away. The house was silent again.

Yuki thought she heard the back door open and close but she could not be sure. She waited, counting to herself, first to a thousand, then to five thousand. She heard no sound.

"Do you hear anything?" she whispered to Dawn.

"No."

Yuki could hear a tremble in her daughter's voice. Carefully she pushed up on the first board again, peeled back the rug, and then removed enough boards to be able to sit up and look into the room. A layer of tobacco smoke hung in its center.

She climbed up into the room and it was then that she saw the red stain on her fingers and the handle of the knife. Blood. She gave a small cry of alarm, helped Dawn up, saw the gash in her daughter's forearm. The blood had already soaked the fabric of her sleeve. Dawn was crying softly and Yuki could see blood on her lips where she had bitten them to keep from crying out.

"Mother, it hurts," she said between sobs.

Yuki opened a drawer, grabbed a piece of cloth, began to wipe the arm to determine the extent of the cut. It was deep. She could see that Dawn was petrified at the sight of the wound. Dawn needed a doctor, stitches, but there were no doctors, no hospitals, and time was running out. She had to stay calm for her daughter's sake. "We need to take care of your arm. Come into the bathroom."

She washed the wound with water, found a bottle of antiseptic, doused the arm, and then wrapped gauze around it. Control, she thought, she must control the hysteria that welled up in her.

"Does it still hurt?" she said.

"Yes, Mother."

"You must be very brave because we have to leave here as soon as possible."

"Can't we hide here until it's time?"

"You heard the loudspeaker. They're calling for all evacuees to set fire to these buildings before the Russians come. We have to find a place closer to the airstrip." She took a bottle of aspirin out of the medicine chest, put it in her pocket, then tightened the cap on the bottle of antiseptic, wrapped it in gauze, and took it as well.

In the bedroom she began to take things out from beneath the floorboard. "We'll take only what we have to have. You get the *mompei.*" She decided to take the bottle of water, the rice, and the dried fruit, as well as the gold and jewelry she had hidden there. She wrapped them all in the bedspread and tied the corners, then cut off the excess with the knife.

Dawn brought the padded coveralls into the room and Yuki helped her daughter get into the shapeless garment before she slipped her own *mompei* over her clothes. Yuki made two slits in the midsection of her baggy trousers and then slipped the blade of the knife through the cloth loop she had formed.

Dawn picked up the bundle. "Where are we going, Mama?" she said.

"I don't know," Yuki said. She went to the front windows, pushed the drapes aside with the back of her hand, looked out into the street. "They're gone, but that doesn't mean we're safe. We'll go out the back and through the garden. When we're in the alley just stay close to me. We'll be heading for the airstrip, but we'll be looking for a place where we can spend the next two days away from the city."

Dawn hoisted the bundle, but Yuki took it from her. "We don't want to strain your arm." At the back door she took a long time to examine the garden, but she could see nothing awry. A column of smoke was rising to the west. They had begun to burn the city. She pushed the door open and ran through the garden with Dawn behind her.

As Yuki ran up the first side lane the cloth bundle swung and hit against the edge of a wooden gate and the ancient bedspread ripped and spilled everything onto the cobblestones. The bottle of water shattered against the pavement. Yuki grabbed up the containers of rice and dried fruit, handed them to Dawn, picked up the cloth that held the valuables, moved through the first doorway into a deserted building, then hid behind a bare stone wall, listening for any sound from the streets. She looked at the sky, knew it must be afternoon by now.

She heard distant gunfire, men yelling, then nothing.

She moved more carefully now, swiftly but cautiously, following a zigzag trail through the houses, making a turn at every corner, into alleys, lanes, pathways, crossing a bridge over the running water of a creek. They ducked under a dry overhang from the bridge, ate some of the rice and fruit, rested for a while. Yuki looked at her watch. It was already four o'clock; the evening would be getting chilly shortly. It would not be too long before they lost the sun altogether.

They must hurry. Finally she saw a stone building ahead of her, and she went through the door to find that they were in a deserted factory, the machinery still in place. She looked at her daughter. Dawn was trembling. "How do you feel, *chi chai?*" Yuki asked.

"Dizzy, Mama. My arm aches. I'm sorry."

"It will be all right. We'll stay somewhere in this building for the night," Yuki said. "In a drain, storage compartment, anyplace looters are not likely to look."

They found a heavy metal grate in the floor but it wouldn't do because they could hear water running beneath it. Then Yuki saw a concrete staircase to the second floor, but beside it was an old elevator. Its door was open and on the floor a cast-iron plate with a ring welded to it. It took both of them to raise the plate. Yuki struck a match and lowered herself into the shallow bottom of the elevator shaft. There was enough room for both of them.

"This will have to do," Yuki said. She looked around the factory until she found a small stick, no more than five inches long, and once they had lowered themselves into the area beneath the elevator car, she used the stick to prop the iron plate up slightly, to give them fresh air and allow her to hear any sound in the cavernous room of the factory.

It was only when she sank down that she realized that the effort of straining at the grate had started the blood flowing from Dawn's wound again. She used the knife to cut away the sleeve of the *mompei*. In the semidarkness she wrapped the last of the gauze around her daughter's arm.

"Is it all right to talk here?" Dawn whispered.

"If you keep your voice very low," Yuki said. "Is your arm hurting badly?"

"It doesn't hurt more than I can stand," Dawn said.

Yuki cradled Dawn in her arms and watched over her until her daughter slept. Then she allowed herself to drift off. She came awake abruptly, to the sounds of trucks in the street and the loud clatter of machine guns. It took her a moment to realize that there was no battle taking place, that the Russian troops in the trucks were either drunk or crazy because they were strafing the sides of buildings while laughing and singing. As she peered past the raised end of the metal plate, she saw a half dozen poorly clad Russian soldiers come into the factory with lighted torches. One of them flipped a switch and an electric light bulb came on at the end of a cord. Another soldier howled with glee and tried to push him away from the light switch. In a moment they were fighting and grappling on the floor while a third soldier flicked the light off and on, fascinated. Yuki found it incredible that they had never seen an electric light before.

They were Siberian peasants, with large heads and broad spatulate noses flattened against round faces, eyes like Mongolians, stocky men, young, ignorant.

An officer came in, a tall man wearing boots and carrying a braided swagger stick. He barked out orders in a dialect Yuki had not heard before. Soon wrenches were being unloaded from a truck and carried into the factory, and another soldier had built a fire at the open door and hung a cooking pot on a tripod over the flames. The soldiers set about dismantling one of the pieces of machinery bolted to the floor, chanting as they put their weight to a long wrench to loosen a bolt.

Yuki nodded to Dawn. They both held the metal plate while Yuki removed the smooth stick. They let the plate down slowly, so that it made no sound. Then Yuki leaned back against the wall in the darkness, exhausted, grateful that Dawn could not see her despair. She soothed her daughter back to sleep, but now there would be no sleep for her.

Over the hours she touched Dawn's forehead, felt the fever climbing despite the chill of the hole. *I ask you to help us, Lord Jesus and Lord Buddha,* she prayed. *Unless the Russians leave soon, we're never going to make it out of here alive.*

The sun came up, the sky lightened in the east. Yuki knew it only because one small crack at the edge of the plate allowed the light to leak through.

Dawn had grown worse. She would thrash her head back and forth, her lips moving as if she were talking with someone, and then she would fall into a deathly quiet, her face flushed red with fever.

The factory became filled with a clamorous clanging, and Yuki was frightened out of her mind when the soldiers discovered the elevator. The gears turned with a loud clank as the cage ascended, moving ponderously up to the second floor, then came back down so relentlessly that she was afraid it was going to push right through the restraining bars and crush them both to death. But it did not.

She used the moments of light to try to help her daughter. She took the knife and cut all the cloth away from the arm. The flesh around the wound was puffy and yellowed with infection. When she inadvertently jarred her, Dawn moaned, a low sigh of pain, and Yuki had to put a hand over her daughter's mouth. She poured more antiseptic into the wound and cut Dawn's blouse into strips to make a dressing.

The infection was far beyond the point where the antiseptic could help. She crushed an aspirin tablet in her fingers until it became powder, then put it in Dawn's mouth, but she couldn't swallow it. Her mouth was too dry. Yuki crushed another and mixed it with her own spittle and placed it on Dawn's tongue, but that, too, was useless. They needed water.

Yuki ate a little rice from one of the containers, did not touch the dried fruit because she knew it would only increase her thirst. Darkness came, and with it the end of work for the Russians, time for the building of the cook fires.

Dawn was unconscious. The fever was consuming her. Yuki strained against the metal cover, raised it enough to slip the stick into the crack. She could see the Russians camped just inside the open doorway.

The transformation of the factory was amazing. In a short time much had been removed: machines, overhead belts, electric lines, down to the bare concrete. There was not a scrap of metal, a stray nut or bolt to mark where they had been.

The soldiers were drinking beer from plain green bottles. She saw one with a water canteen suspended in a canvas webbing from his belt. Her own mouth was leather.

Late that night something happened so grotesque that it seemed unreal. All of the soldiers were asleep except for one sentry, who sat by the fire with a rifle propped against his knee. As Yuki watched, Inga's son, Josef, came into the factory with both hands full of money, the bills spread out into fans. The sentry trained the rifle on Josef, who continued to shake the fans of money. He was speaking Russian in a low voice, obviously trying to strike a bargain. He had decided not to go south; he was not afraid; he could be of great use to the comrades of the military.

A couple of soldiers came awake, stretched, stood up. Josef shook the money at them, too, more confident now, certain that they would accept the deal he was offering, and for a moment Yuki wondered if he was here as an answer to her prayers. If the soldiers accepted him, she would take the chance and make herself known in the hope of getting help for Dawn. But her hope was short-lived.

One of the soldiers moved behind Josef and with a swift, dispassionate blow of the rifle butt smashed the back of his skull and sent him sprawling forward on the concrete floor, the bank-notes fluttering into the air.

Two more soldiers came awake and some began to grab up the money while others took off Josef's clothes, almost gently, so as not to tear the fabric. One soldier put a leather shoe next to his own foot, decided it was a match, and discarded his boots, while another soldier took a watch and a third a pair of eyeglasses, which he propped on his own nose. When Josef was quite naked the same soldier who had hit him before swung the rifle butt against his head to make sure he was dead. Then two soldiers dragged the body outside by the heels and the camp settled down again.

In the small hours of the morning, Yuki felt Dawn's forehead again. The fever had risen even further. Yuki had to find water for her. Now. Yuki looked through the crack, saw one sentry wake another soldier to stand guard while he turned in. The new sentry stood up, tried to shake the sleep from his mind. He uncapped his canteen and drank, then lit a cigarette and walked outside into the cold night air.

With all her strength, knowing she could afford neither a mistake nor a sound, Yuki put her back against the metal plate and raised it slowly, caught it with her fingers, and leaned it up against the wall of the elevator. She concealed the knife in the folds of her *mompei*, then crawled out of the hole, keeping to the shadows. She went outside through a rear door, weak, nauseated, her legs so stiff from the hours of sitting on the cold concrete that she could barely walk.

She made her way to the corner of the building, where she took off the *mompei* and ran her fingers through what was left of her hair. She tried to remember the Russian words she had learned in her business, but now they escaped her. No, one word was there. *Tovarich.* Carrying the knife under the *mompei* over her arm, she rounded the corner. The guard was standing just outside the open door.

She summoned up her nerve, spoke.

"Tovarich."

He looked around, said something softly in Russian. She knew he was questioning, asking who she was. She said the one word again.

"Tovarich."

He came down the wall, the cigarette dangling from the corner of his mouth. He smelled of garlic and diesel. He grabbed at her and one of his hands sought her breast. With all her might she drove the knife into his chest. He staggered backward but did not go down. He glared at her, his mouth opening as if to call out, before he slumped against the wall and slid to the ground. She pulled the knife out of his chest and then slashed the canteen free and ran back around the side of the building, just as a voice called out from the door the sentry had been guarding.

She reached the elevator and slid into the crawl space, her heart pounding. There was shouting at the side of the building where the dead soldier lay. She grabbed at the metal plate and carefully lowered it. Then she turned to her daughter. She coaxed Dawn to drink, then mashed aspirin in the canteen cap, mixed it with water, and managed to get her to swallow it.

She had killed a man. There was a smear of his blood on her hand, and yet she felt nothing except gratitude. She now had a chance to keep Dawn's fever down until it was time to go to the airstrip.

· 461 ·

Dawn came awake, in such pain that she moaned aloud. Yuki handed her the length of stick that had been used to prop up the metal panel.

"I know you hurt," she whispered. "But they're still out there. So when it hurts the most, hold on to the stick, but don't make a sound."

She could not tell whether Dawn heard her or not, but her daughter made no more noise.

The Russians were in the shaft above the elevator now, stripping out the cable. Yuki held the knife ready, determined that if one of them pried up the metal panel, she would kill him before she killed her daughter and herself. But truck horns blared outside the factory, and she heard the Russian soldiers yelling at each other as they ran for the transports.

The building and the streets outside were silent. She pushed open the metal panel and cautiously rose to look into the factory. She saw a completely stripped room, nothing left behind except the walls, the floor, and the ceiling.

She looked at her watch. It was two o'clock in the afternoon. In her exhaustion, she had slept, lost precious hours. She sank down again. Dawn was dull-eyed, feverish, whispering incomprehensibly to herself.

"You have to listen to me," Yuki said. "The plane will be coming tonight and we have only a few hours to get to the airstrip. We don't know where the Russians are or how far we're going to have to go to avoid them. Can you hear me? Can you understand me?"

There was no sign of comprehension on Dawn's face.

She reached out to take her daughter's hand and the piece of wood fell to the concrete. She picked it up and saw the row of bloody indentations where her daughter's fingernails had dug into the wood as she endured the pain without making a sound.

Yuki put the wood into her pocket. She stood up, pulled on the *mompei* again, then reached down and pulled her daughter up out of the shaft. She held Dawn upright and helped her to the door. She half carried her daughter down a narrow pathway, moving with excruciating slowness, aware of the flames in the distance where the city was burning. By the time they reached the country, Dawn's legs could hold her no longer. She fell unconscious to the ground.

Yuki washed her daughter's face. "It's not much farther," she said. "You're going to do this."

Dawn's eyes opened again and Yuki helped her to her feet. It was two more hours before they reached the barn. A frightened Japanese woman's voice came out of the darkness. "Stop there. We have guns. Don't come any farther."

"Please. My daughter is badly wounded. I need help," Yuki said in Japanese. Two young boys, no more than twelve, came out of the shadows and helped carry Dawn to the side of the barn where a half dozen people were waiting while a Japanese soldier watched the skies through binoculars.

When he heard the drone of an aircraft he whistled sharply. A half dozen other soldiers moved out of the darkness, down the meadows, to set fire to oil pots that marked the boundaries of the makeshift runway. The Japanese plane descended, taxied up to the barn. A hatch opened and an officer began to load the waiting people.

When Dawn was carried to the hatch the officer shone a light into her face, pulled back one eyelid with the side of his thumb. "She's dying," he said. "We'll leave her here."

Yuki confronted him, knife in hand. "I killed a Russian soldier to get my daughter on this plane," she said. "And she's going to go."

"I have no time to argue with you. Hurry up and get her on board if you're taking her." He looked into the darkness where he could see truck lights approaching. He closed the hatch and the plane spun around and picked up speed down the runway, lifting into the black night sky just as the Russians moved in force onto the empty field.

Yuki sat on the floor of the plane, holding her daughter in her arms. "You must not die," she whispered into her ear. "You must not die."

Yokohama . . . September 1945

COLONEL YATES WAS wearing summer khakis as he sat across the table from Sam in the makeshift officer's club and ordered another couple of beers.

"The doctor says that you're suffering from some malnutrition," he said. "But there's no reason that with proper care and a good diet, you won't be right as rain."

Sam blinked, having trouble holding this tanned, vigorous officer in focus, as if at any moment this reality would dissolve and he would find himself back in a Japanese cell. *Fish heads and rice,* he thought illogically as he tasted the cold beer.

"I do have one bit of bad news for you. Roger Cummings at the State Department—he was your uncle wasn't he?—anyway, he died of a heart attack about a month ago."

Dead, he thought. He remembered his uncle's face as he last saw him in Singapore just before the attack on Pearl Harbor. *Incredible. A thousand years ago.* "Did he live long enough to know of the peace?"

"Yes. He died the day after the Japanese surrendered."

"He deserved to know." He began to believe that the chair, the table, the Colonel himself were real. "How soon can I go home?"

"Whenever you feel well enough to travel. But in honor of your uncle's long service to his country as well as the ordeal you've gone through, we would like to invite you to attend the official surrender ceremonies."

The end of hostilities, he thought, and for a moment the sound of the Emperor's voice on the radio echoed in his ears, thin, reedy, a courtly language that few of Sam's captors understood. But they knew, by God, they comprehended the meaning, and through the door that separated him from them, he heard them weeping.

"I'd like that. Thank you." He looked at the Japanese waiters poised near the bar, waiting to fill a water glass or replace an ashtray. *Men who would have cut my throat a month ago converted to docile servers in white coats.* "You met no opposition at all?" he said to the Colonel.

"Incredibly, no," the Colonel said. He glanced at the waiters. "These boys were all would-be kamikaze pilots for whom the divine wind never blew. No planes, no gas. I understand there was a good bit of effort on Kyushu to organize maverick soldiers into suicide squads and resist the end of the war. Even the commander of this base was refusing to accept defeat. Two months ago everybody was armed with bamboo spears and determined to die for the Emperor in one grand charge against the invading Americans. But now you'll find no more cooperative, friendly people any place on the face of the earth."

"For the moment I've had too much of the oriental mentality," Sam said. "When is the surrender ceremony?"

"Two days from now. September the second."

"And how long before I can get military transport home?"

"I've already begun that process," the Colonel said. "Three days, tops. You'll go by air. Should be home within a week."

The day for the ceremony aboard the USS *Missouri* was cloudy and Sam stood in one of the front ranks on the crowded deck, astonished by the silence, the sense of ceremony, the lines of generals and admirals from many countries, including the emaciated General Wainwright, everybody waiting in the soft breeze. The launch approached and the Japanese dignitaries began their climb to the deck, looking diminished in defeat, with Foreign Minister

Shigemitsu groaning as he dragged himself up the gangway, propping himself on his cane, his wooden leg threatening to give way.

Christ, Sam thought. *Is this really the enemy, this collection of tired old men trying to preserve their dignity? Could a handful of men like this have caused so much misery in the world?* Yet now they stood uneasily on the deck, ashen-faced, tired beyond emotion, for what seemed like hours, waiting while the newsreel cameras whirred, their shame recorded. Only when the delay seemed unbearable did the cabin door open and General Douglas MacArthur come out onto the starboard quarter deck, a stern expression on his face.

The Supreme Commander read a statement into the cluster of microphones and then gestured for the Japanese leaders to approach the table and sign the surrender documents, one in Japanese and the other in English, while he stood with his hands laced behind his back and watched impassively.

Sam saw Ito-san at the back of the group, wearing his general's dress uniform. Ito's presence startled him. *How old are you now, Ito-san? Forty, perhaps, or forty-one? No more than a few years older than I am.* Ito-san looked like an aide to these old men in their military uniforms and outdated formal clothes, some with top hats, leaning over the table to put a formal end to the war that seemed to have lasted forever.

One of the Japanese generals had trouble with the pen—the ink would not flow. He shook it. *All the paperwork,* Sam thought. *Sheets and reams and tons of paperwork, proposals, agreements, treaties, all the way back to Shanghai and hours with Ito-san over drinks. It could have stopped then if we could have gotten anyone to pay attention, Ito-san.* Useless to think about it.

General MacArthur declared the proceedings closed.

The ceremonies were over and now, with perfect timing, the sky began to fill with a roar as wave after wave of carrier planes and B-52's swept overhead, hundreds of them, as if to show these old men and their exhausted country the inexhaustible resources of the victors.

The sun broke through the overcast.

Over, Sam thought. *No, not quite.* He turned his mind to the deposition he wanted to write, one which would return a life for a life.

He finished the document that afternoon and then sought out Colonel Yates at the officer's club after dinner. "I want to ask you about the war crimes trials," Sam said. "What's the procedure going to be?"

"That's being worked out now, I hear," Yates said. "There will be a tribunal here, of course, and trials in other countries that suffered under Japanese domination."

"Will General Ito be prosecuted?"

"I'm certain he will." The Colonel leaned back in his chair to allow one waiter to light his cigarette while a second poured hot coffee. "Do you want to testify against him?"

"No, *for* him," Sam said. "I've written a deposition on his behalf. I know him very well. I've worked with him since the early thirties in Shanghai."

The Colonel accepted the envelope with reluctance. "Personally, I'd like to see the bastards hang."

"He was against the war," Sam said. "But if you don't want to hand my deposition to the proper authorities, I'll do it myself. I intend to come back for his trial and testify in his behalf."

The Colonel shrugged. "That's up to you. I'll see that your deposition is properly routed. But the trials are a long way down the road. I suggest you get as much sleep as you can, because you're going to have the rare privilege of going home in the morning."

Washington, D.C. . . . 1947

"WE CAN OFFER you South America," Jennings was saying. He was a lean man with a distinguished mane of white hair and a trace of New England society in his voice. "Frankly, there doesn't seem to be anything out east at the moment, unless Bangkok, I suppose. But if I were you, I think I would stay put here. You've been back two years now and you'll be in line for the Far East desk eventually."

"I'd like to join MacArthur's staff in Tokyo," Sam said.

Jennings took a loose-leaf notebook off his shelf, turned the pages until he found what he was looking for. "There's a slot open. Do you know anything about agriculture?"

"I know MacArthur's plans for agrarian reform," Sam said. "Put me in for it."

Jennings kept his eyes on the page. "It's a full grade below your level."

"Whether I'm offered the slot or not, I have to be in Tokyo in three weeks. I'll go as a civilian if necessary," Sam said. "But I would prefer to go in an official capacity."

"Well," Jennings said with a sigh, a distasteful expression on his face. "I suppose there's no avoiding the issue, is there?" He pushed back from his desk and stood up to pour coffee from an electric pot, placed a cup in front of Sam. "It's no secret that you've been sending letters to the Supreme Council of Allied Powers on behalf of General Ito."

"It was never meant to be a secret."

"For your sake, we've played down the resultant inquiries at State."

"Who could possibly object to what I'm doing?" Sam said.

"I'll give it to you straight. General Ito is being tried as a Class A War Criminal by a tribunal of judges from eleven countries. He's right up there with Tojo and Doihara. It may or may not be fair, that's not for me to say, but the world expects the Class A's to be convicted and the selection of the judges was made toward that end. Now, if Ito were a Class B or C, it wouldn't be any problem."

"What's the objection?" Sam said flatly.

"It's a simple reality," Jennings said. "If you let things rest here, then there's no harm done. If you insist on testifying at the trials, then you flush a promising career down the drain. Look at it from the point of view of the countries invaded by the Japanese. How do you think their governments are going to react to having a diplomat assigned to them who has publicly supported a major Japanese war criminal? And believe me, Cummings, your efforts won't make one damn bit of difference. In the end they'll still hang General Ito, and you'll be left with all your dirty laundry in full public view."

"I appreciate the advice," Sam said. "And I'll give it serious thought. But I want the Japanese assignment anyway. I wouldn't be of any help in South America." He stood up, extended his hand, and from the relief on Jennings's face he realized that Jennings thought he had capitulated to reason.

"You'll hear within the week," Jennings said.

He went back to his apartment in Georgetown at eight o'clock and he put his briefcase on the kitchen table, opening the French doors to the bricked-in garden to catch the summer breeze. He heard the music from the restaurant down the street. This was his worst time of day, the transition from the office to the loneliness of the rooms here where he would work until midnight.

There were a couple of letters on the floor beneath the mail slot in the front door, and he put them on the table after glancing at the return addresses. One was from Lydia in Australia, the fifth he had

received in their exchange of letters since she wrote to the State
Department to learn that he had survived. In her second letter she
had told him about her marriage to a banker in Sydney and invited
him to write and tell her what he was doing, which he had, and then
there had been more letters, photographs, one of husband Horace
grinning in the Australian sunlight, a hearty and pleasant-looking
man, and another of the baby, Phillip, when he was a month old, and
as Sam hefted this latest envelope in his hand, he knew there would
be more pictures, which would only serve to increase the distance
between now and that remote past in Singapore when they had
known each other fondly and briefly.

He poured himself coffee, reluctant to open the briefcase quite
yet, thinking about what he would write to Lydia if he could be
candid. *There is something missing in me now, Lydia, that was not
absent then, and at times I think it must have been the war and then
the suffering that gave me such a keen desire to hold on to life, and
which, in some dreadful way, offered my soul an excitement that
peacetime can never match. And your letters depress me because
they remind me that I am thirty-seven years old, with a daughter
living God knows where, no friends, a stranger in my own country,
far more like my father must have been than I ever thought I would
be. So I won't be writing to you again, and I wish you well in your
efforts to reclaim your plantation one day, and happiness with Horace and your son, but you are a part of the time that was, and I have
to get on with the "now."*

No, he would never write that letter. Instead, the relationship
would die by attrition, and he would scribble a note saying he was
terribly busy and would write more later, and then a Christmas card,
and after that, nothing.

The second letter was from Noble, with the same refrain as a
dozen prior approaches: "Please don't let your mother know that I
am writing you because she says that you will call her on your own
when forgiveness has taken place, but she is not well, and we are
having a small dinner party on November 2, and it would mean a
great deal if you could simply drop by for a while, a few minutes, just
to pay your respects. I am certain that she deeply regrets what she
did in Shanghai, actions that were the result of caring too much and
of stress brought on by an overtiring journey halfway around the
world, and she wants the opportunity to show you, over a period of
time, the contrition she feels. She has suffered quite enough from

the rift between you, I believe, and if you could only see your way clear . . ."

He abandoned the letter, phrased another honest mental note to Noble: *This isn't a matter involving forgiveness of a grudge or anything quite that easy to solve, Noble, because in Shanghai my mother showed me that even though I am her son we are so enormously and totally incompatible that the most that can be hoped for between us is politeness or civility, but never any understanding or affection. I have long since passed the point of having any real emotion toward her; as a matter of fact, I would welcome the opportunity to hate her, because it would at least be a departure from the indifference I feel now. If you hope to reestablish the filial bonds, you're really wasting your time. I learned too much about Pavlovian responses in the prison camps to pay the slightest attention to a family bell when I know there is no reward at the end.*

He would send his regrets to Noble's invitation. He made himself a ham sandwich and sat down at the table to eat it while he went through the papers he had brought home from the office, a bundle of neatly typed descriptive statistics about rice production in the Philippines that he was supposed to work into a report that would eventually be incorporated into a larger recommendation to be made to Congress and perhaps influence an appropriations bill.

He finished a first draft of his report shortly before midnight. He mixed a bourbon and water and drank it slowly. He went to bed and allowed himself to think of escaping the claustrophobic world in which he found himself. The job in Tokyo would be offered to him because he was qualified for it and no one at SCAP would turn down a former prisoner of war who wanted to help the Japanese. And on his way he would stop in Shanghai and gather material and visit the past. On that note, he drifted off to sleep.

Shanghai . . .
October 1947

FROM THE MOMENT the plane landed in Shanghai, Sam felt the change. It was as if he had never been in this place before. Where once Shanghai had been almost mercurial in its moods, now it existed in a somber grimness. There were long lines of people in front of the stores, street vendors everywhere, peasants from the country with their onions and chickens and other produce spread out before them. The prices on their cardboard signs increased a dozen times in a single day as inflation devalued the Chinese yuan.

The taxi taking him to the old Cathay Hotel, where he was to meet Connaught, passed the place where Charlotte had been killed, but he could no longer locate the exact spot, for the street had been paved a dozen times since, curbs moved, old landmarks transformed. One of the original glass doors at the Cathay had been replaced by a piece of wood that had been in place for so long that it had weathered gray; the other was cracked and braced with tape.

The lobby was makeshift now, furnished with chairs and divans that did not match. From one of them rose a spectral man he did not recognize at first, but the smile was there on that emaciated face and the spark of charm had not been extinguished from the hollow eyes.

When Connaught saw Sam he threw his arms around him with open delight. "You have no idea how good it is to see you again, old chap," he said. "We must go into the bar and have a drink and talk. And forgive the way I look. It's calculated, of course, to elicit pity in the eyes of any creditor. A good front." He snapped his fingers at a waiter in the old manner, headed for a table near the window overlooking the river. He ordered a bottle of scotch and two glasses. "That's not true, of course, all that business about a calculated appearance. The absinthe and the Japanese have accomplished reductive miracles on my insides," he said. "The Japanese broke bones and the absinthe ruined the liver and other vital organs. And the Japanese and the absinthe both disappeared about the same time."

The bottle was served. The waiter stood there with folded arms while Connaught looked embarrassed. "No more signing of chits, old man. I do hope that you have five dollars American. It would take a wheelbarrow full of Chinese bank notes to pay for a bottle of scotch."

Sam gave the money to the waiter, who departed with great indifference. "So the white man's Chinese domain is no more," Sam said.

"You noticed his scarcely concealed contempt, I take it," Connaught said. He uncapped the bottle, poured a shot into each of the two glasses, lifted his. "Absent friends," he said.

"Absent friends." Sam drank. "Were you able to contact Comrade Li and pass the message?"

"Indeed," Connaught said. "And we shall look him up presently, after five o'clock." He pulled back the tattered sleeve of his linen suit and looked at his bare wrist, then shrugged with an embarrassed laugh. "Force of habit. The watch disappeared last week," he said.

He looked around the room at the Chinese, many of them military. "They are such cocky sons of bitches," he said, pouring himself another drink. "The Communists have Manchukuo and they will have all of Shanghai very shortly, without even having to fight for it. The city will simply self-destruct because the money isn't solid. When a merchant sells something he sends a man to buy something tangible within the hour before the price goes up again. That's the way I've been making my living lately, doing a swift business in exchanging money for goods, and when I say swift, I mean literally so." He drank again, reached out with the bottle to pour into Sam's glass but Sam put his hand over it.

"I'm cutting down," Sam said.

"I'm glad somebody is," Connaught said. He grimaced as he downed another shot, then capped the bottle. "We'll take this with us if there's anyplace you want to go before we meet your Comrade Li."

"I would like to go to the cemetery."

"Quite. One of the few places that has not changed. Are you well fixed for dollars?"

"Yes."

"Then we'll take one of the motorized three-wheelers." He flagged down a three-wheeler and there immediately began a tirade in Chinese, with the wiry driver yelling at Connaught and Connaught accusing him of every crime against nature from buggery to selling his own sister. Finally, Connaught looked at Sam with a calm smile. "Two American dollars," he said. "One now. The other at the end of the evening. He knows he has a good deal because he won't have to rush to spend the money before it goes bad."

They climbed into the cramped compartment and the three-wheeler chugged off down Nanking Road past the building that used to house Blossoms.

"They sell genuine ersatz rhino horn and other aphrodisiacs in a shop there now," Connaught said as if reading his mind. "Ironic that such an elegant place should disappear. But for a while I bought ox horns in the countryside and ground them up myself and then represented myself to some of the rhino-horn merchants as a white hunter direct from Africa with the real goods in such quantity I could sell quite reasonably. Eventually they caught on and began to buy their own ox horns."

A military car sounded its horn, swept around the three-wheeler with such speed that it almost hit a pair of bicyclers who had to scramble out of the way. The car had Chinese flags on the front fenders.

"High brass?" Sam said.

"The trials are still going on," Connaught said. "They've become a regular sport here now, a chance for civilians to harangue Japanese officers who formerly harangued them. There are occasionally executions, some beheadings, some shootings, and there's been pressure from various foreign governments for hanging, for what reason I cannot imagine, except perhaps to make them consistent with the

Tokyo trials. But they're having trouble in Japan keeping the generals from killing themselves and opting out of the trial proceedings."

"Not Ito," Sam said, suddenly alarmed.

"Not that I know of."

They reached the cemetery and Sam moved through the tall grass looking for Charlotte's grave only to run across Alcott's stone, obscured by weeds. Connaught reached down and pulled the weeds from in front of the large rock, then opened the scotch bottle and took a long pull. "Those were good days," he said. "And we did have the good sense to enjoy them. What happened to Yuki and your daughter?"

"I don't know, but I intend to find out now that I'm back."

Sam found Charlotte's grave, ran his fingers over the rough stone. He took out his pen knife and began to cut the weeds around the base.

"Are you sure you don't want another drink?" Connaught said. "Shanghai is much easier to take these days if you keep a little alcohol in the system at all times." He walked through the weeds. "Now, this is my plot over here," he said. "I decided I did not want my mortal shell to be launched into the muddy waters of the Whangpoo as food for fish. I hope you don't mind my spending eternity within a reasonable distance of your Charlotte."

"You'll be in good company," Sam said.

"Yes, the best."

Sam traced the lettering on her tombstone with his finger, remembering the day she died. *Let there have been flights of angels,* he thought. Time was passing and he knew he had to leave. He stood up and checked his watch. "We can meet Li now," he said with a sigh.

"Yes, it's time," Connaught said. When the three-wheeler was under way again Connaught began to ramble. "I don't remember him, you know. I have trouble with my memory. Absinthe does that. But there's not much I really want to remember anymore, who's alive, who's dead, who's here and who's not. The only thing that's constant is my little Chinese bird, my girl who lives with me. Her face may change and her name, but they're all exactly the same, you see, so they provide continuity to my life. We were talking about Li, were we not?"

"He's still Communist, I take it?"

"A high factotum among the Reds. It's rumored he'll be in the government when the Nationalists are all gone, which should be soon."

They reached an old godown along the river, a warehouse in the last stage of decay, so frequently patched with tin sheets that it looked as if it would collapse. Connaught directed the driver to stop near a flight of wooden stairs. "His office is up there."

"I'll be back shortly." Sam climbed the stairs, found the door open and Comrade Li inside, blinking at him through thick glasses, smiling as he extended his hand. Incongruously, he was dressed as a peasant, despite the Western-style haircut. He had a box of papers in front of him.

"How pleased I am to see you," Li said. "How pleased I was when you sent word you wanted to meet with me."

"I was afraid you wouldn't be amenable. My government is supporting the Nationalists."

"That was expected," Li said. "But I don't think that you and your government always see eye to eye."

"No," Sam said. "You can't do any worse with China than the Nationalists did."

"I can't even offer you refreshments," Li said. "But I did get the depositions you wanted. I did this only as a favor to you, although I found a lot of Chinese willing to attest to Ito's fairness and the quality of his peacefulness. I even found some of General Wang's men who verified the great cruelty he displayed toward his own men as well as to the enemy."

"I'm in your debt," Sam said.

"I also have a message for you from Bright Moon."

"Oh? Is she here in Shanghai?"

"She died many years ago, in Peking. But when we last talked she told me she was touched by your concern for her."

"I appreciate your telling me," Sam said. "Hers was a splendid spirit and I'm sorry she's not among us anymore." He stood up. "How can I repay you for helping me?" he said.

"Just speak of what you have seen in this unhappy city," Li said. "And speak what you believe. That will be payment enough."

Sam transferred the depositions to a suitcase. That night he had a final dinner with Connaught, who had indulged in a haircut and a shave and was now wearing a fresh linen suit for the occasion.

They ate on the roof garden of the Broadway Hotel, looking out at the lights of the boats on the Whangpoo. Connaught ate little, content to be with his friend, a bottle between them.

"You have rights, you know," Sam said. "You don't have to live like this."

"What rights?"

"You were an employee of an American Consulate when it was seized by an enemy force. That entitles you to back pay for all the time you were imprisoned by the Japanese. There's also every chance that I can get you on in Tokyo. You know the Orient as well as any man alive and that's invaluable."

"I would have to leave Shanghai," Connaught said, as if that answered everything.

"There's nothing left here anyway," Sam said. "You said it yourself."

"It'll last as long as I do," Connaught said, as if he were describing a street beyond repair. "I have been given by Chinese doctors— what a foolish word, *given,* as if they have it in their power to grant time to me—a year at the outside, and were I forced to make a prognosis for this marvelous city, I would give it about a year of life before the dragon wakes and everything we know here is devoured. And I think it entirely appropriate that the city and I should go out together. I have really had quite a good life, no regrets."

"You can't ask for more."

"One could," Connaught said with a wry smile. "But one wouldn't get it."

"I will see that the government sends you back pay."

"That would be appreciated, yes," Connaught said. "There's becoming less need for the kind of services I provide as each day goes by. Speaking of which, what time does your plane leave?" And he rolled his wrist and looked at bare skin, embarrassed again, but taking it with humor. "Old habits die hard."

Sam took off his wristwatch, extended it to Connaught. "Present," he said.

"I can't take your watch," Connaught said.

"I insist," Sam said.

"You have been a true friend," Connaught said, strapping the watch onto his lean wrist. "I shan't forget you."

"Nor I you."

"I don't think I'll go to the airport with you," Connaught said. "So I would leave you with one wish."

ROBERT L. DUNCAN

"Name it."

"When you hear that the Communists have taken Shanghai, know that I am on my way elsewhere, on a journey from this world, and drink to my voyage."

"I shall," Sam said. "Old friend."

Tokyo . . . November 1947

HE WAS ASSIGNED a house with servants on a lane in Senda-gaya, a suburb slightly north and west of the center of the city, and he had just entered it for the first time when he heard a telephone ringing. He found it on a teak stand next to a window overlooking a sand garden. "Mr. Cummings," a deep rumbling voice said in a broad Texas accent. "This is Custer."

"You got my letter then?"

"Of course, and I got to tell you right off, it's raised my hopes. How soon can we meet?"

"Now, if it's convenient."

"That's fine with me. I have an office in the Dai Ichi Building, but it might be best if we meet in Hibya Park. It's my kind of fall day and I could use the walk."

"A half hour?"

"Fine. There's a tea pavilion. I'll be the only fat Texan wearing a white Stetson."

The November leaves had turned into flaming colors and were piled along the paths of Hibya Park, despite the teams of Japanese men in faded army uniforms sweeping the sidewalks. He saw Custer at the corner of the tea pavilion, a short heavyset man with a Stetson on his head. His suit was rumpled and his pudgy fingers fumbled with something in a brown paper bag.

"Roast chestnuts," he said as Sam approached. "Have one, Mr. Cummings."

"No thanks," Sam said.

Custer ate the last one, crumpled the bag, and threw it into a wastebin, then wiped his hands on a fresh linen handkerchief. "Maybe we'd better find us a park bench for a while," he said. "And I better explain the ground rules right off because you may not want to play the game once you know the stakes." He found a bench facing the street, offered Sam a cigarette, and then lit one for himself. "We have two teams of lawyers in town," he said, smoke trailing out of his nostrils. "And you can't tell the good guys from the bad by the color of their hats. First, you have your prosecutors, and they're sharp as hell and have the big advantage because the judges want them to win and give them special rules without any pretense of playing fair. They will accept any kind of evidence from the prosecution and keep us from introducing the same kind of evidence if it's helpful to our clients. Needless to say, I'm on the downside team, the defense attorneys. And we have a tendency to drink a lot and get mean because we're frustrated."

"You represent Ito."

"Among others. He's my big one, my Class A, and then I have a handful of Class B's and C's."

"How is he?"

"Different," Custer said with a sigh. "And that ain't necessarily good. The rest of the Class A's are tired old men, some of them so out of it they don't know what's going on. Some speak no English and the translations are so botched, the defendants often don't recognize the written transcript of what they're supposed to have said. One of them has really gone crazy. He smacked Tojo on his bald head in court the other day and proclaimed himself to be the next Emperor of Japan. He may have the right idea for a defense after all."

"Ito," Sam said, reminding him.

"Ito's the only young man in the lot. He's in his forties, speaks perfect English, and unfortunately he's the only one who looks like a samurai warrior. Webb, the President of the Court, is an Australian who has taken a particular dislike to Ito." He paused, crossed his legs, blew smoke into the autumn air, and watched a group of elementary schoolgirls in their uniforms being herded along a path by a nun. "I hated all Japs," Custer said. "I was in the European theater and I thought they were all buck-toothed cannibals. But back to Ito. You need to know what you're getting into before we start. That's the reason we're meeting here. The prosecutors have spies everywhere."

"I was warned by the State Department before I came."

"I'm not talking political trouble, career trouble," Custer said. "I'm talking a skin-you-alive attack. They'll turn you inside out if they can and hang your carcass out to dry."

"There's nothing that troublesome in my past."

"Is that right?" Custer said with a crocodile smile. "You mean to tell me you're pure as the driven snow? I like to remind clients with your attitude that sweet Jesus was the only sinless man, and look what the prosecution did to him."

"How can I help you?"

"By repeating the things you told me in your letter. You worked with him in Shanghai and found him devoted to peace. He yanked you out of an infamous prison camp to save your life."

"And that's it?"

"I hope to hell that's it. Just a good solid character witness. Maybe the prosecution won't take out after you, but you have to know they're able. From the moment you filed those Chinese depositions, they've had their investigators all over your past."

"Are you trying to convince me to quit?" Sam said.

"Hell, no. I want to win this case, and when I say win that means I keep Ito from hanging. They'll find him guilty. I take that for a given. But I've never lost a client to the hangman and I don't intend to start now. I've got my pride. And I'm telling you that unless you're hard as nails, I don't want you in that courtroom. If you can't go the distance, then drop out now."

"Underneath all that colloquial bullshit, you're one mean son of a bitch, aren't you?" Sam said.

"Oh, I try, and you better believe it. I learned from my daddy that this is a mighty hard world for anybody and especially hard for bullheaded people who assume they're right and expect the world to pat them on the back for it," Custer said. "My daddy gave me a hurdle right off. He could have named me Howard or John or Paul. Most of the time I go by my initials, G. A., because he named me

George Armstrong Custer, one of the biggest losers of all time, and if you don't think I had to work my butt off to live that down, you're not very bright." He sucked on his cigarette and his eyes were ice cold when his smile faded. "All right, Mr. Samuel Cummings, I need an answer. Are you out or in?"

Sam looked off across the park. He ran the risk of having his whole life dragged through the mud. He was silent a long time, and when he spoke he was surprised at the sound of his own voice.

"In," he said.

Early on the morning of the seventeenth day of November, Yuki went to her boutique in the arcade of the Imperial Hotel to find Takae waiting for her. He was a child, no more than ten or eleven years old, but he was wiry and street-smart and from the gleam in his eyes it was obvious he had been successful. "I have tickets to the trials for all this week, Nakamura-san," he said. "But they were expensive for me to buy. I have to have thirty dollars apiece, American."

"Ten dollars each," Yuki said, unlocking the door, leading the way inside. "American."

"Twenty-five."

"Twenty."

"If you take all five."

"Wait here. I'll be right back." She left him in the salesroom and went back to her small office, where she kept the American dollars behind a drawer in the desk. It was forbidden to deal in dollars or military script, and even the yen was closely monitored, with frequent changes in the design of the currency to control the black market, but she felt she could trust Takae not to inform because he made too much money off her as it was, scrounging the city for materials in short supply.

She brought him a single hundred-dollar bill, which he snapped between his short fingers and held to the light, back turned to the corridor so he could not be seen. He handed her the five white cardboard passes to the gallery at the War Ministry Auditorium, the date for each pass stamped on the face. "Do you have anything else you would like me to do for you, Nakamura-san?"

"Locate tickets for next week," she said. "I'll let you know by Wednesday if I'm going to need them."

Dawn was in the shop by eight o'clock, and Yuki smiled at how beautiful her daughter looked in her blue silk. She was mature for fifteen and still as outspoken as she had been at five. Dawn began to lay out the Western-style kimonos and arrange them on the front displays. "I don't want you to go to the trials today, Mother."

"If you need to be at design school, just close the shop."

"No, it's not that at all," Dawn said. "I love Ito-sama. I always have. He's the kindest man I know, but the Russian judge has told everybody that he expects to see all the Manchukuo generals convicted and executed."

"So?"

"You will suffer through this with him for no reason at all. I think you've had enough pain."

"I would suffer more if I didn't go," Yuki said. "At least I can see him. Perhaps he will be able to see me and take comfort from my being there."

"Do you think he would want me there too? Would it help him?"

"I will go for both of us. But pray for the man who loved you as a father," Yuki said, embracing her daughter, tears in her eyes.

She caught a steam-powered taxi on the street, an old car with a wood pile lashed to the top and a boiler in the trunk so that the driver had to stop every few blocks to stoke the furnace.

Yuki spent the long ride praying. *I thank you for your great mercies, Lord Buddha and Lord Jesus. I thank you for allowing my daughter to live and now I pray for Ito, that he be spared. If he cannot be free, may he be given a life sentence and, in your wisdom, may such a sentence be commuted in a few years.* Free. To have him free. She thought of their last moments together in Manchukuo and the feel of his arms around her. Safe. Her reverie was broken by the voice of the taxi driver. They were there.

At the War Ministry, American guards with rifles and perfectly polished boots stood examining the passes to the balcony. Yuki was not fortunate enough to have a front-row seat. Instead, she sat five rows up, on an incline, but her view of the court was unimpeded. She slipped on the earphones provided and experimented with the settings, three separate positions on a dial that would allow her to listen in English, Japanese, or Russian.

The prisoners were marched in by white-helmeted military police, and each defendant took a seat behind one of the waist-high desks that rose at the rear of the large, dark-paneled room like stair steps, four tiers high. When Ito entered the room her hands turned cold. She willed him to look up, to see her, but he kept his eyes straight ahead, walking with a military bearing, taking his seat on the first tier, putting the earphones on, and she wondered which language he would be listening to. *I am here. I am here, Ito-sama.* At that moment he raised his head and looked directly at her. She held herself still as he took her in, as if there were no years or distance between them, and then he seemed to force himself to look away.

Suddenly there was a stir at the front of the court as the batteries of attorneys took their places. The eleven robed judges filed in and the President of the Court banged his gavel to begin the proceedings.

Yuki dialed to the English-language setting, heard the long list of charges read against Ito, a string of generalities, as if Ito, in some ill-defined way, had helped cause the aggression of Japan's military faction, not by any definite action on his part but simply because he was a high-ranking member of the military. He was described as helping plan the war in China while serving in Shanghai, of the murder of a Chinese general in Nanking, of being warlike against the Russians while providing continual oppression of the Chinese province of Manchukuo.

As she listened she became aware of a Japanese woman sitting in the front row of the balcony, a thin, willowy woman dressed in the traditional kimono of a matron. Her eleven-year-old son sat next to her, wearing a school uniform. *Ito's wife and son,* she thought instantly. *The boy looks like his father, the same nose and eyes and cheekbones. The woman is beautiful and graceful, not at all like the nagging shrew you described to me, Ito-san.*

Custer stood up, made a series of motions for dismissal, all of which were denied, then entered a plea of not guilty. The prosecution presented its case, witnesses, and depositions while Yuki switched the earphones to the Japanese translation only to find that it did not match the English at all. The plump American lawyer stood with his thumbs hooked in his belt, objecting to everything, being overruled again and again.

A game. No, a ritual, leading toward a predetermined conclusion.

Ito was called on to testify and he took the stand, a microphone in front of him, removing his earphones while the American lawyer addressed the court. "If it pleases the court, the defendant wishes to testify in English."

The President of the Court leaned forward. "Why would he want to do that, Mr. Custer?" he said.

"Perhaps we should ask him, your honor." Custer turned in Ito's direction. "Would you be kind enough to explain to the court why you wish to testify in English, Mr. Ito?"

"I am at home in English," Ito said. "And I am aware that the translations from Japanese to English are totally inaccurate as well as misleading. I want my testimony to be understood exactly as I give it."

"Objection," said one of the prosecutors. "I move that the remark concerning the accuracy of the translation be stricken."

"Sustained," the President of the Court said. "Mr. Ito may use English if he is so inclined."

"Thank you," Ito said. "I have a written statement to submit to the court in English as well as Japanese to ensure a proper translation."

"Objection."

"Overruled. The translators will examine both statements to see that the meaning is the same. The court will accept the written statements without oral presentation, Mr. Custer. Do you wish to examine your client, Mr. Custer?"

"Not at this time, your honor. I would like to call my first witness, Mr. Samuel Cummings."

Yuki's breath caught in her throat. She had not known whether he was still alive, had not seen him since that summer day he had spent with Dawn in Shanghai. Now here he was, being ushered to the witness box, sworn in while she sat transfixed in her chair, as if he were an apparition.

"Your full name, please?"

"Samuel Adams Cummings."

"What is your current occupation, sir?"

"I have been assigned to head the Agrarian Reform Section of SCAP."

"And prior to that assignment?"

"Consultant on Far Eastern Affairs, State Department. Before that I was a prisoner of war in Singapore and Tokyo. Before the war I served in Shanghai as Consul General and in Singapore as First Commercial Officer."

"Would you tell us, sir, when you first met the defendant?"

She listened to Sam's recital of life in Shanghai and found herself remembering their months together, the day he helped her move, the first time she was in his arms, the sweet love they had made in the apartment they had shared, her excitement at being pregnant with his child. And then, the day she left him. And she wondered what would have happened had she never left the apartment. Perhaps they would have gone to Australia together, or someplace else where life would have been easier and less complicated. She stopped the drifting of her mind; he was answering questions about Nanking.

"Did you see the alleged murder of the Chinese general, Mr. Cummings?"

"I did."

"What if anything did you see and hear?"

Sam paused. He knew he was on shaky ground. He'd lost so much blood. Horror piled on horror. The evil face. He remembered the gun falling from his hand. Wang's voice to Ito: "Free me, and I'll piss on you again." The bullet in the forehead. Revenge for all. How could he make this court understand the times? Custer had told him to keep his testimony short. "We were leaving Nanking when we came upon General Wang. He threatened General Ito and Ito-san shot him."

"Would you call it an act of self-defense, Mr. Cummings?"

"I would, yes."

Yuki watched Ito's son lean forward in his seat, watching his father, openly curious.

The testimony was now on Cummings's transfer from a prison camp in Kyushu to Tokyo. *You never told me he was there, Ito-san,* she thought. *Was that your idea or his? Did he ever ask about Dawn and me?*

"Copies of the substantiating cables have been entered in evidence, your honor," Custer was saying. "Defense exhibits one thousand four hundred sixty-three through seventy-four." He turned to Sam. "Would you say, sir, from firsthand knowledge, that General Ito was putting himself at risk by saving your life?" He paused slightly, as if waiting for an objection, but there was none.

"I believe so."

Custer checked his notes, looked toward the tier of seats where Ito sat. "And how would you characterize Mr. Ito, sir, from your personal knowledge?"

"If his views had prevailed, there would have been no war with China in the first place, and if his later efforts had been successful, no war with the United States either. General Ito was a man who desired peace and worked for it."

"Thank you, Mr. Cummings." He looked to the prosecution bench. "Your witness, Mr. Gunther."

Gunther resembled a young bulldog, and when he spoke he sounded as if bad temper and irritation lay barely controlled just beneath the surface, ready to break loose at any moment. "I have a question or two of you, Mr. Cummings." He smiled at Sam. "It's been quite an ordeal for you, Mr. Cummings, and my sympathies are with any man who has had to suffer as a POW. A lot of good men died in those camps. The mental wards are still full of survivors. Would you mind telling us, sir, how your experience in those camps has affected you?"

"I have put all of that behind me," Sam said.

"How fortunate, sir, that you're able to. I take it then, that aside from malnutrition and a skin disorder, the items mentioned in your initial physical after being released from a house in Tokyo in August of 1945, that you were in reasonably good physical shape?"

"That's true."

Gunther was constantly in motion, glancing at the papers in his hand, wandering away from the witness box and then back again, tapping the eraser end of a pencil against his clipboard. "You puzzle me, Mr. Cummings, I have to admit that. You are here to testify in behalf of a Japanese general because you think he is in no way responsible for any of the terrible things that happened during the war, because he is a peaceful man who, at one time, shot a Chinese officer at point-blank range for reasons that you characterize as self-defense. But I'm wondering, sir, whether you are seeing things accurately. Most prisoners of war suffer from mental aberrations for some time after their release."

"Objection," Custer said patiently.

"Sustained," the President of the Court said. "You have not demonstrated that Mr. Cummings suffers from any mental aberrations."

"But on the subject of General Wang's death," Gunther said. "You did interpret the killing as self-defense, is that not so, Mr. Cummings?"

"Yes."

"And you're certainly aware that other witnesses might have interpreted the same events differently."

"I would imagine so, yes."

"Fortunately, we don't need to imagine," Gunther said, glancing at the paper. "We have depositions from half a dozen soldiers, Chinese and Japanese alike, who witnessed the same incident. They say that there were harsh words between Ito and the Chinese general. They also say that you were in very poor physical condition, that you had been wounded and were staggering, almost incoherent. You really didn't know what was going on, did you?"

"I was aware of what was happening."

"How many shots did General Ito fire into the body of the Chinese officer?"

"One, I believe."

"You believe?" Gunther said with incredulity. "This isn't a matter for belief, Mr. Cummings." He shrugged. "But let's move on. What kind of hold does Mr. Ito have on you, Mr. Cummings?" Gunther said abruptly.

"I don't understand the question."

"Let me see if I can clarify, then," Gunther said. "When you arrived in Shanghai you were assigned as liaison with the Japanese and, according to your testimony, you worked very closely with General Ito to preserve a delicate balance. Then you went with him on an inspection trip to Nanking and you came back with such an absolute hatred for the Japanese that you could not control it and were transferred from Shanghai to Singapore for your continued verbal and printed attacks on the Japanese in Shanghai. In Singapore you were reprimanded eight times officially and continually unofficially for your verbal assaults against all things Japanese."

Gunther was sweating now with the intensity of his effort; Yuki could see the perspiration on his face glistening in the light. He was ready to pounce. She could feel it. She looked at Ito and back at Sam. So much depended on whether Sam could win this encounter. "Yet even now, after your humiliation at Nanking, your injury to the point that you were staggering, you continue to defend Mr. Ito."

"I was—"

"Please don't interrupt, Mr. Cummings. You know what I'm talking about, don't you? You know exactly why, to this day, you will continue to perjure yourself. I ask you now, of your own volition, to tell the truth, before I have to make public something which you don't want to discuss any more than I want to bring it to light. It involves, sir, a Japanese woman and a child . . ."

It's all right, dear Cummings-san, she thought, as if her message could reach him. *Don't try to protect me or Dawn.* She could see that Sam was angry; his face was white.

Gunther laid his clipboard down on the prosecution table as if he was beyond the need of any more facts, his last statement hanging in the air, waiting for an answer. And then she watched, horrified, as Ito-san rose to his feet. He looked at her for a brief moment and began speaking into the microphone, in Japanese, and Custer was on his feet at the same time with an objection while the President of the Court banged his gavel and demanded order.

"I request a recess, your honor," Custer said. "I need to confer with my client."

The President raised his hand slightly, as if suspending time while he listened to a translation through his earphones. "It is my understanding that Mr. Ito wishes to change his plea."

"I think my client wishes to make a statement, not change his plea."

"Enlighten us, Mr. Ito," the President said. "Which is it?"

Ito spoke in Japanese, and the English-speaking judges on the bench reached for their earphones. *Lord Jesus and Lord Buddha,* she thought. *Don't let this happen.*

"I am Japanese and I made a mistake by not testifying in my own language," Ito said, his voice loud, his words crisp. "I wish to make a statement and to change my plea at the same time. I apologize to all my countrymen for seeking life at the cost of my honor. I commanded troops who died for the glory of their country and the Yamato way, and I can do no less. I admit to the execution of the Chinese General Wang for the brutalities he demonstrated in Chapei and Nanking. I admit to doing my best to defeat my country's enemies. I apologize to my beloved Emperor for my lack of success and plead guilty to all the charges against me."

"I want to speak," Sam said. "I'm not through."

The President ignored him. "You make this change of plea freely and without duress?" he said to Ito, waiting impatiently until the question was translated.

"Hai, so desu." Ito bowed once before he sat down.

"An official translation will have to be made of the defendant's remarks," the President said. "But the court is satisfied that the essence of the statement is a change of plea. Since the examination of the current witness is now irrelevant, it will be stricken from the record unless you can show cause, Mr. Gunther, why it should not be."

Gunther shrugged and made a slight flutter of his hands, signaling his willingness. "You may stand down, Mr. Cummings."

Yuki watched Sam leave, shaken and defeated, as though he were the prisoner. Ito's wife was weeping silently into a handkerchief. Her son turned slightly, glanced once at Yuki before he turned away. *Does he realize that his father has just sentenced himself to death?* she thought. *You're trying to save me, Ito-san, and Sam. And we can do nothing to save you.* She was so numb she could not move from her seat.

They were allowed to meet at Sugamo Prison in a sterile concrete room with one barred window, small, open to the blue sky, a pair of chairs bolted to the floor in direct line with the small watch window in the door. Sam was conducted into the room first, and shortly he heard the door being unbolted and Ito came in, dressed in his gray prisoner's uniform, which, being too large for him, seemed to dwarf his frame. He looked at Sam, nodded, and then sat down.

"How is the day outside?" he asked.

"Almost clear," Sam said.

"Any clouds?"

"Off to the southwest."

"Is it possible to see Fujiyama today?"

"Early this morning," Sam said. "Then a haze set in."

"Is there any snow on the mountain?"

"Yes."

"Ah," Ito said, as if the thought of the snow on the mountain gave him pleasure. He sat squarely in his chair, his palms resting on his knees. "I would like to climb Fuji again. When I was young I went once with my father. I carried a stick all the way to the top and it was stamped at each of the resting stations. It was cloudy that day, and at the top the sun was glorious, the light brilliant over an unbroken sea of clouds. My father said at such a time one could believe in the Sun Goddess."

"You shouldn't have pleaded guilty," Sam said quietly. "That was what the prosecutor wanted you to do."

Ito shook his head. "He made the price of silence far too high. He would have ruined your reputation, and Nakamura-san's as well."

"She's in Tokyo then?" Sam said. "Is Dawn with her?"

"They have a shop at the Imperial Hotel."

Sam took out a pack of cigarettes, offered one to Ito, aware that the guard's face materialized instantly at the watch window, then disappeared as Sam clicked a flame from his lighter.

"I was prepared to ride out anything the prosecution could bring up," Sam said. "Anyway, I think there's a chance that you won't be sentenced to death."

Ito ran his hand over his short-cropped hair. "If . . . ?" he said, looking directly into Sam's eyes.

"Your lawyer and I talked to one of the judges, who is opposed to wholesale executions. He'd like nothing better than to spearhead a move in the court to give you life imprisonment. We've drawn up a draft of a statement that Custer will bring here for you to sign. You've already pleaded guilty. This statement is just pro forma, an admission of remorse, a request for clemency."

"Remorse?" Ito said.

"General Wang's character was a matter of public record. Not even the Chinese authorities are upset that he's dead. But you know the form of these things a hell of a lot better than I do. You make a statement, the court is then allowed to be generous, and in a few years it's all forgotten."

"You have been a good friend to me," Ito said. "Under circumstances that my father would never have understood."

"As your good friend, I ask you not to be stubborn," Sam said. "You have nothing to lose by taking my suggestion."

Ito puffed lightly on the cigarette. "If the positions were reversed, if you had been successful in killing the Chinese general, would you make a public apology now?"

"To save my life, yes, I think I would, especially if I were being prosecuted by a court that is patently unfair and more than a little political. Think about it. You sign a statement and you can have a full life. A few years in prison and then parole."

"It wouldn't be a good life," Ito said.

"It would be whatever you decided to make it."

Ito tapped the cigarette ashes into the cuff of his uniform. "I am not sure you will be able to understand what I am about to say, but I want you to try. I was convicted because Japan lost the war, and I am both Japanese and a general officer. But in a way my conviction is not really important. When I first came in here the other Japanese officers bowed to me out of politeness, but I could hear them talking sometimes, after the lights were out. On this corridor a whisper is easily heard. The first thing I learned was that they did not consider me one of them. As a matter of fact, there was a nickname for me. I was known as the *gaijin* Japanese, the outside Japanese, a soldier who wore the Japanese uniform but whose loyalties were divided. And then, when I put an end to the defense and made my statement in court, I proved myself in here. All the generals speak to me now, and we talk about the weather and other unimportant things. And for the first time I am not fighting what I am. Japanese. They all understand exactly why I did what I did and I have gained great respect from it. Not only respect from my peers but self-respect as well. Now that I have it for the first time, I do not want to lose it."

Sam dropped his cigarette to the concrete and ground it out beneath his heel. "And what about Yuki and Dawn? Have you considered what you mean to them?"

"Nakamura-san will do well by herself," Ito said. "Your daughter was half dead in Manchukuo and her mother brought her home, nursed her to health, and took care of both of them. She will understand my decision."

The guard's face was at the small window again. Sam's time was up. He got to his feet, reached out, and embraced Ito. "I understand, but I don't want to accept it, Ito. You are my friend. Please think carefully about what you are doing."

Ito smiled and on his way from the room turned to bow deeply with respect, and Sam found himself bowing back to this man he wanted so much to save.

During the end of November and all of December, he was allowed to circulate freely in the exercise yard, talk with the few remaining officers, reminiscing about the China campaigns and the long Manchurian winters when the air was so cold, it forced a man to keep moving just to stay alive.

He allowed his hair to grow longer.

One morning he asked for a brush and an ink block and began to practice his calligraphy. He wrote poems, which he gave as mementos to his American guards, who had begun to relax with him because he could speak English and would talk about anything during the long hours of the night when they were required to continue their close watch on him.

Late in December, as the Christmas season approached, Ito knew that the time had come for him to complete his plan. One day when he was rolling his brush on the ink block, he stopped and went to the door of his cell and asked the guard outside for the use of his penknife for a minute so that he could trim uneven hairs from the brush. The guard was a young man who liked the General, and so he came into the cell and handed Ito the penknife and waited while the General trimmed the brush. Ito gave him a pack of cigarettes for his trouble.

The next day the General requested some clean white cloth to clean his brush, and the day after, the penknife again. This time he kept the penknife in his cell for three hours and just before the young guard went off duty called to him and returned it, giving him more cigarettes as well. The next day Ito borrowed the penknife again and trimmed his brush before he wrote a letter to his wife and son, asking that the boy be raised in the finest traditions of the country, holding no resentment toward the past, carrying on the family name by assuming the obligations of his position.

Then he put another scroll in front of him and began a letter to Yuki:

I believe you will understand what I have done, for you have been closer to me than my own breath, dearer to me than my own life, and very often you have known the secrets of my heart even before they were revealed to me. In these days when I walk the exercise yard and look at the sky, I remember many things, and most of them are times that we shared together, wondrous times that sustain me now in memory. I remember Dawn's birth in the rain, a child who has been mine, in my heart. And when the sky is overcast and presses down on me, I remember some of those times in Manchukuo when I came to the house to sit by the fire in the hearth and then to share your bed, and the low clouds no longer exist for me.

In times of bright sunshine, I remember the walks we took together when first we met, before we had truly come together. Even then I think we both knew what was destined to happen between us.

Seeing you at the trial, knowing you were sharing my pain, made me want to reach out for you, to comfort you as you so often have comforted me.

I do not know where I am going because I do not know the

resting place of the soul, but I know you believe in Lord Buddha and Lord Jesus, and I hope that what you believe is indeed true, that there is someplace beyond this world where we will be re-united.

I am so sorry that I cannot leave you physical riches. But I can tell you what I have never told you, since it is not a Japanese custom to do so. I love you with a love that is strong enough to conquer death.

He pulled up a lock of his hair and clipped it with the penknife and rolled it with the scroll. He sealed it and left a note in English addressed to Sam, asking him to see that Yuki receive one scroll and Ito's wife the other.

Then he tested the edge of the penknife against the pad of his thumb and found it dull. Patiently he began to grind the blade against the concrete floor with one hand while he sang aloud to cover the noise. He held the brush in his other hand so that when the young guard looked through the small watch-door he would see nothing unusual. At the end of an hour the blade was still not very sharp, but Ito knew his time was running out. Very soon the guard would be changing.

He knelt down on the floor and pulled his shirt out of his trousers, then exposed his abdomen. He wrapped the white cloth around himself, faced in the direction of the Imperial palace, breathed deeply for a few moments as if to free his mind of thought, then drove the knife into his abdomen. The pain was overwhelming, but he forced himself to cut across his lower stomach and then, with his last strength, to pull the knife up sharply in the final cut. He doubled over, suspended between life and death.

He could see Yuki's face, smiling, eyes alive, but the image began to fade as he was aware of the yelling, the clanging of the door being pulled open, the hands that seized him. But he knew that when they rushed his body to the hospital, he would no longer be at home in it, for he saw the rectangle of blue sky, and rose toward it, past the bars into a light.

"By tomorrow certainly." Yuki hung up the telephone and saw that Dawn was closing out the cash register. "I'm going to stay awhile. I promised the colonel's wife I'd have the kimono ready for her by tomorrow."

"I don't mind doing that if you're tired," Dawn said.

"I'd rather have you go home and put on the rice. And do take a taxi."

She watched her daughter leave and considered putting the kimono off until the morning, but she had given her word. The colonel's wife was much too large for the patterned kimono, and Yuki knew that even when it was a perfect fit she would do no more than have her picture taken in it and perhaps wear it once or twice to show her friends back in the States before it went into a box to be stored away as a souvenir.

Yuki was about to turn off the salon light and go into the back to use the sewing machine when she heard a rap on the glass. She turned and froze at the sight of the man in the corridor. It was Sam, his face solemn, a small parcel in his hand. *Why has he come—and at this time of evening? Certainly after all these years, it was not to see Dawn again.*

"Yuki . . ." His voice broke. He breathed deeply. "Let's go upstairs and have a drink."

Ah, she thought. *I have wondered what I would say to you if we ever met again face-to-face.* "Only a quick drink," she said, putting the kimono on a hanger. "I have some work to do."

He took her upstairs to the elegant bar, which had survived the war unscathed, and she sat down across from him, studying his face by candlelight. He still carried a haunted expression in his eyes. *We're both refugees,* she wanted to say to him. *We have paid a terrible price for the past and can't reclaim what we lost.* "I'll have a bourbon double," Sam said to the waiter. "And bring the lady a cognac." He sat back in his chair, obviously ill at ease. "All right," he said when the drinks came, "drink it down. You're going to need it."

She smiled slightly. "I've survived a great deal without cognac."

"Drink it anyway."

She tasted it, looked at him. "It's very strange," she said, "sitting here with you after all these years."

"I wish we could talk under different circumstances," he said. "And one day, perhaps we can." He cleared his throat. "It's about Ito. I told him I thought I could get his sentence commuted to life. A few years and he would be out."

Suddenly she knew where he was heading, and she willed her ears not to hear, but the noise in the room did not stop, the babble of voices, the distant music.

Don't say another word. No more talk. I will blink my eyes and you will be gone.

She would thank him for the drink and go back to the shop and work on the kimono. *No more words.* She tried to remember where she had put the new spool of gold thread. Her thoughts leapt around but she was fixed to the chair and could not move, waiting for the dread words and phrases and sentences to come out of his mouth, for him to say what he had come to tell her. She would not make it easier for him. He could circle around it but she would not shape that dread center for herself.

The pain began to rise like a flush on his face. "If only he had listened to me," he said. "But the acceptance of the damn Japanese generals meant everything to him." He reached across the table, put his hand on hers, looked straight into her eyes. "He killed himself this morning. He cut himself open and they thought they could save him but they couldn't. I brought you a letter."

"I see," she said.

"Do you understand what I'm telling you? Ito is dead."

She nodded dumbly. She drank the cognac all at once and then stood up, picking up the parcel. "Thank you for being so kind, Cummings-san."

"Please sit down. We have a lot to talk about."

But she turned and threaded her way through the tables quickly. He tried to signal the waiter for a check, and when he realized he did not have time to wait, he threw down a wad of yen from his pocket and went after her.

But she was already out of the hotel, into the darkness and the cold rain, feelingless, certain there had been a terrible mistake. There were many generals in the prison. Cummings-san had been wrongly informed.

She went past the food stalls along the street, the flaps of canvas spread out like wings against the rain, and she stumbled blindly along until, soaked to the skin, she reached the train station and darted into a coach, sinking down on a hard wood seat as the train lurched forward. Clutching the parcel in one hand, she looped an arm around the chrome pole to steady herself as the wave of anger and belief crashed down over her.

True. Dead. A knife in that goddamned precious flesh of his. Bastard!

And she spoke to him in her mind, hoping that he had become an earthbound spirit who could hear her words.

Damn you . . . coward . . . goddamn you for your false pride. You have stolen from me . . . from your daughter. Abandoned . . . no need . . . you had the chance to live. May your soul burn in hell if there is a hell, and may you be condemned to another life if there is a nirvana. She caught herself. She had been rocking in the seat with the swaying of the train, banging her forehead against the chrome pole. An old man across the aisle was watching her.

Can you see my hatred, old man? I'm angry enough to kill you with my thoughts if you provoke me.

The old man turned his attention to his newspaper.

She left the train at Shinanomachi Station, walked beneath the bridge to the row of apartments, the cold rain heavier, aware when she came through the gate that Dawn was home, the light leaking through the wooden shutters outside the paper shoji. She removed her shoes in the entry, put on the hall slippers, and, taking the parcel with her, went upstairs. She slid back the door and sank to her knees by the small table. Her teeth were chattering, her body trembling beyond control.

Dawn ran to her mother, flinging a blanket around her. "What happened? What's wrong? Are you sick?"

Yuki shook her head.

"I'll get the brandy. It will help warm you." She brought it to her mother and put the glass on the table, talking as she poured. "You'll feel better soon."

"I have some things I want to say to you. Don't ask questions. Just listen."

"Yes, I will."

"I have always been pleased that I had a daughter, but I did you no favors bringing you into this world where women don't count. Did I ever tell you that my father sold me into the Yoshiwara? He got enough money to buy an ox. So my value was set. I wasn't worth any more than an ox. And I ran away, to a man who would protect me, a missionary, and my owner at the Yoshiwara tortured him and I had to go to Shanghai since I couldn't go home because my father would have had to return the ox." She drank again, grateful for the numbing that had begun to take place. "And in Shanghai I met the man who was to become your father and then I left him when I was carrying you so that I wouldn't disgrace him, because I was always taught that the man comes first. And then Ito-san became my protector, or so I believed, because he was kind to us." She drank again. "But we made our own way. You and I. Our dependence on him was a myth." She looked straight at her daughter. "You must always be proud to be a woman and you must know that you can survive, no, not just survive, but prosper. We will become the richest women in Japan, on our own, because the Lord Jesus and the Lord Buddha gave us the brains and the courage to do it." She emptied the glass, started to fill it again.

Dawn stopped her. "You need to get dry and into bed," she said.

"Not until I know you heard and understood everything I said."

"I understand, Mother."

"Not all," Yuki said. "Ito-san is dead."

"Dead?" Dawn said with a sharp intake of breath.

"Today. He killed himself. Seppuku."

"Dear God!"

"He abandoned us. But we don't need him." She stood up, unsteady on her feet, but managed to put on her night kimono as Dawn spread the futon on the floor and helped her lie down beneath the comforter.

Yuki awakened sometime in the middle of the night to find that she had been crying in her sleep. She got up and searched frantically for the parcel, opened it. She read the letter through, and started over again, every word dear to her, tears flowing freely. It was as if his voice was speaking to her from beyond the grave.

Dearer to me than my own life. Yes, Ito-san, it is so for me too. I love you. May you find peace, my dearest one.

Tokyo . . .
1961

IT WAS FROM THE old women who tatted lace in the small family shops that Yuki first learned of the trouble in the House of Itsugi. Itsugi was the leading couturier in Japan, but, according to an elderly lacemaker with the most agile fingers in the world, he was in great trouble now. "He is flamboyant, *ne?*" she said to Yuki, her fingers never pausing. "He had an assistant named Aiko who created most of his designs. She came to work for him three years ago, in 1958. And not one month ago she stood right where you are standing now, Nakamura-san, weeping, crying at the abuse she has taken from him, and then last week she quit. She left him to go to Kyoto as a pattern designer for a silk company."

From this scrap of information the plan formed in Yuki's mind. She considered all of the ways she could make it work, figured possible profits, checked the numbers again and again. Then she stopped by the offices of the English version of *Asahi Shimbun* to consult with Matsu-san, the most unlikely fashion editor in the business, an ancient man with the curiosity of a fashion historian and the ability to synthesize a hundred small pieces of gossip into the truth. He poured coffee from a pot that had not been cleaned in months. The smell of it was bitter, sour.

"Itsugi is a genius at spectacle, an absolute magician at staging and selling," he said to Yuki, tasting the coffee with a grimace. "He's besieged by writers and photographers from the minute he hits Paris because he is so outrageous. Last year he insulted the English Queen with such panache, it was carried around the world, and he licensed dozens of things to people anxious to take all the risk and pay him outlandish sums for the use of his name, for the notoriety. He has also loved a series of willow boys, some of them talented, others not. The talented have left to work for themselves and he's made bitter attacks on them. He has a gift for being vicious that's equal to his penchant for publicity. Are you thinking of allowing your daughter to work for him?"

"Perhaps."

"It would be a great coup for him but not for her. His talent for design can be contained in a thimble for a very small seamstress. But your daughter is a splendid designer, and she can count on no credit and no percentages with him."

"I want to know about his organization."

"Terrible." Matsu-san grimaced at the coffee again as if it were his enemy. "His accounting system is atrocious and he spends money on everything except his employees. He lacks efficient management and his licensing agents cheat him with exorbitant fees and lousy accounting. The only reason he does so well is that the flood of money coming in is large enough to cover the mistakes and the thievery."

"Can you provide me figures, Matsu-san?"

"Approximations." He sorted through a stack of papers on the corner of his desk and then moved to a larger pile on the windowsill, squinting as he riffled through it, and extracted five pages stapled together. "I'm going to do a story on the economics of the business one day," he said. "So I did research on the House of Itsugi. Not that I would ever use his name. I admire some things that Itsugi does, even though I can't say I like him." He handed her the paper.

"Thank you, Matsu-san. This is most generous."

"You're welcome," the old man said. "Just keep in mind that Itsugi operates *gaijin*-style in his business. Get him to put any agreement in writing. He'll honor it if it's written. But otherwise he has a very selective memory."

Yuki went back to her office and, working with Matsu-san's papers, went over her figures one last time to be sure that she had made no mistakes. The new small Blossoms on the Ginza, which had been hers for the past ten years, was far more complicated to run than her salon in Shanghai had ever been.

She went across the salon, a large, well-furnished room full of mirrors and light where her two salesladies were waiting on customers, turned down a corridor to Dawn's atelier. The walls were covered with sketches pinned to corkboard, the best of her daughter's designs. Dawn looked up briefly, then added a final touch to a sketch, washed out her brush, and leaned back in her chair to pick up a cup of lukewarm tea.

"What's on your mind, Mother?" Dawn asked.

"Money," Yuki said.

"I don't understand. Business has been very good."

"We show a handsome profit, enough to keep up with the mortgage on the farm, the house in Shinanomachi, and the lease here."

"So what is your concern?"

Yuki poured herself a cup of tea and looked out at the morning traffic. "You're thirty years old and you have little social life except for the young royals who are also your customers and that's part of your work because you design for them. It seems to me that you have very little pleasure."

"My work is my pleasure. I love what I'm doing. Now, out with it. What's bothering you?"

"This isn't enough," Yuki said. "I want Paris and the reputation you deserve. There's no designer in the world who can touch you. I want so much money that we'll have trouble knowing how much there is. And I think I know a way to get there, but it will involve risk. And I have to be certain you want the same thing before I take the gamble."

Dawn's face was totally serious now. "Yes," she said quietly. "That's exactly what I want. And the name that goes with it, the reputation."

"Then I'll go ahead. It's drastic, a different approach. But I think it will work."

"I'm dying of curiosity."

"I need a few days, and then I'll tell you all about it."

The next day she gathered a portfolio of her daughter's best new designs and walked down the crowded Ginza to Itsugi's salon, a small establishment presenting the elegant perfection of a black onyx cube to the street. She paused outside the door long enough to breathe a prayer and gather her determination about her as a glass door outlined in gleaming chrome was swung open for her by a handsome young man dressed in a golden robe. She gave her business card to another young man, who would take it to Itsugi-san himself.

Very shortly she was conducted past a fitting room where a Filipino woman stood on a pedestal in a long gown ill-suited to her, through a maze of corridors into Itsugi's private studio, a chaos of colorful furniture and photographs of European women. Itsugi himself was sitting in a modern leather chair, black, and he stood up as Yuki entered the room. He was a tall, thin man wearing a black silk shirt and black trousers with golden thongs on his sockless feet. He wore his hair long, bound together in back by a golden cord, and on close inspection she was sure he was ten years older than the thirty-five he claimed to be.

He bowed and then took her hand. "Come have a look," he said with a charming smile. "If you stand just so at the window, you can see your salon down the street. A fine location. Better than this one actually, but when I went into this business it was not available. Please sit down and have tea. My work would drive me crazy without an occasional pleasant interruption." His telephone buzzed and he instructed his secretary to shut off all calls and to have tea brought in. "I'm really quite pleased to meet you," he said. "Your daughter is an excellent designer."

"Thank you," Yuki said.

A young male servant brought in the tea and departed, leaving Itsugi to pour. "What can I do for you?"

She placed the folder in her lap. "I brought a portfolio of my daughter's designs."

"Of garments she has already completed."

"No. Of gowns and dresses she intends to make."

"This is very unusual," he said, openly curious. "A designer never reveals his private vision of the future."

"Which leads me to my proposition," Yuki said. She felt a sudden caution. She would have to avoid threatening his ego in any way. *I know that your assistant left you,* she wanted to say. *I suggest you need what I am about to offer as much as I need you to accept it.* She sipped her tea, nodded at the street. "They are the reason I'm here," she said.

"They? I don't understand."

"Look at the next ten women who walk by. Five will be wearing traditional kimonos. Four others will be dressed very sedately in Western clothes and will work in jobs that don't pay them enough to dress any better. And the tenth woman might be a potential customer for my daughter's designs except that the odds are overwhelming that she will be buying at a better-known salon."

"True," Itsugi said reflectively. "But what does all this have to do with me?"

"You're rich and successful because you design for a world market, because you license your designs worldwide. My daughter's customers are all the young royals, the women who would be the aristocrats of Japan except that the titles were all abolished. I want my daughter to have a broader horizon. I want her to design for you."

He opened a brass box of cigarettes, inserted one in a black onyx holder, lit it with a gold lighter. "Let us be frank with one another," he said. "I know your salon turns a good profit. So I am naturally suspicious that you should come to me. What reason could you possibly have? Do you think I am going to pay your daughter some outlandish fee?"

"Oh, she'll come to work for you for nothing," Yuki said matter-of-factly.

"Nothing?"

"And her new designs, you're free to use them."

The cigarette holder rested lightly between his thumb and forefinger. "And what would you get out of this seeming generosity?"

"She gets experience in Paris and exposure to a world clientele. If you use her designs in your Paris showing in October, she will get a percentage share of the licensing of those designs. If you decide not to use them but put her to work developing your ideas, then at the end of the third month you must either fire her or pay her the equivalent of fifty thousand American dollars a month."

"Absurd." The word came out on a puff of smoke.

"With all respect, Itsugi-san, you lose nothing," she said. "If in three months time you don't think she's worth that amount of money, simply let her go."

"And what would you do without her?"

"For the time being I'll turn Blossoms into a boutique for the other nine women on the street. I'll handle kimonos of every price range, low-priced wedding dresses, and I'll carry Western ready-to-wear and accessories."

"You think you can make that pay?"

"Of course. I know my business."

He snubbed out his cigarette and stood up. "I've heard that your daughter is very outspoken. It's a rule in this house that no one talks back to me."

"Ah, so desuka?" Yuki said, this moment already planned, rehearsed, as she picked up the portfolio, stood up. "Then I won't take any more of your time, Itsugi-san."

"What are you talking about? Where are you going?"

"She would be entirely useless to you under those circumstances," she said. "She is discreet in her outspokenness, but she will never lie to you or agree with you when she thinks you're wrong. You may accept or reject what she has to say, but she won't agree with you simply because this is your business."

"Please sit down," Itsugi said. He inserted another cigarette in the holder. "You came past a fitting room where one of my darling ladies from Manila was being dressed. Did you see her?"

"Yes. Only a glance in passing."

"And what do you think your daughter would say about the gown she's wearing?"

"I think Dawn would say that the gown did not suit the woman. She is too short and plump for the full skirt and it makes an otherwise attractive woman look squat."

"So that would be your daughter's opinion?"

"I think so."

He tapped his ashes into a modern ceramic bowl, looked at her thoughtfully. "You're right. The gown is for her daughter's wedding. I argued for simplicity, for straight lines, but she insisted on the organdy monstrosity you saw in there. And thus it is my duty to make my client pleased with her decision." He looked at her shrewdly. "The question in my mind is, how much is the talent of the daughter and how much the management of the mother? Suppose I were to suggest an arrangement that would include both of you?"

"I have my own business."

"Which, when you convert to ready-to-wear, as you say you will, you can manage in two hours a day. I'm right down the street.

Besides, I'm developing an inexpensive line that you might like to carry in your shop on an exclusive basis."

"Let me think about it."

"I'll think about it as well," Itsugi said. "Meanwhile, I'll look through the portfolio."

"When we come to some agreement," Yuki said, "then you are welcome to it. Shall I call you tomorrow?"

He took a *meishi* out of a card case, wrote a telephone number on the back. "At four o'clock. This is my private number here."

"Four o'clock then," she said. "You'll hear from me."

Yuki was in the garden of the house in Shinanomachi when she heard Dawn arrive. She went to meet her daughter on the polished wooden terrace overlooking a miniature cove of sand raked to imitate waves, with two volcanic rocks jutting from the surface like islands.

"The red silk came in from Kyoto," Dawn said.

"Good, but now I want to tell you about my idea," Yuki said. She told her everything that had happened at Itsugi's, as well as about the conversation with Matsu-san. "I would like you to think about the idea," Yuki said. "All the advantages. All the disadvantages."

"I know all about Itsugi," Dawn said. "He has the morals of a snake. Any designs I originate, he will take credit for."

"All the people in the right places will know differently."

"That doesn't build a clientele for us."

"Eventually it will."

"Are you seriously considering working for him, Mother?"

"Yes."

"There might be some advantages," Dawn said. "The exposure to Paris might be worth the gamble." She stood up. "But right now I'm going to change into a summer kimono and tell the maid that we're ready for dinner."

Yuki dreamed of Ito-san that night, a strange dream in which she sat across a table from him in Shanghai and tried to speak to him in endearing words, but the words came out as numbers and he listened to her with a forlorn expression on his face and said nothing. She came suddenly awake, sat up on her futon in the twilight of the room.

The meaning of the dream was evident to her. *I apologize to you,*

Ito-san. You honor me by coming into my dream and my mind is so full of numbers I can't appreciate it. She could not sleep. She slid open the shoji and went onto the terrace by the garden, but before she could sit down she heard the jangle of the telephone and picked it up quickly, speaking in a hushed voice so she would not awaken Dawn.

"*Nan desuka?*" she said. "What is it?"

She heard the voice of a man, full of honorifics, and it took her a moment to realize what he was talking about. He was an officer in a fire brigade, and even at this moment Blossoms was aflame, the fire so extensive that the whole block was involved. He was offering his most profound apologies. It was his job to put out fires and he was profoundly sorry he had failed.

She was on the Ginza within three quarters of an hour, Dawn beside her, the fire lighting up the sky as if it would set the low-scudding clouds ablaze, the flame leaping through the gutted interior of Blossoms, sending billows of black smoke skyward. They could not get close to the block itself, the heat of the fire was too intense. Yuki had to listen to the roar of the flames, the directions being given through bullhorns to firemen on towers, while she tried to hear the quiet voice of a brigade officer intoning the details of the disaster.

"The fire began in a restaurant behind your store, not the usual kind of grease fire we find in blazes like this, but an electrical short circuit. Fortunately the restaurant was closed at the time and therefore no loss of life or injuries were incurred. There was no visible fire for the first hour so the flames ate through a wall into your storeroom. We thought we might have to destroy parts of the block, but fortunately some of the fire walls were thick enough that . . ."

She stopped listening to him and looked at the barricades that had been erected a hundred yards down the street to hold back the mobs, most of them just onlookers. A woman reporter spoke very softly into a microphone while the camera lens glowed red with a reflection of the fire.

Yuki returned the bow of the brigade fire officer, who had to get back to work, and only then saw the absolute defeat in Dawn's stricken face.

"The fire took everything, Mother," she said. "Everything."

"Not everything," Yuki said. "We're still alive."

A young man came up to them in the semidarkness. "Nakamura-san?" he said to Yuki, and when she nodded he handed her an envelope. "Itsugi-san asked me to give this to you. I am to wait for an answer."

She opened the envelope. The light of the fire was bright enough for her to read the words. "Tell Itsugi-san we are most grateful."

The young man bowed, moved off into the night. Dawn looked after him. "What does the note say?"

"Itsugi-san has offered us office space at his salon for the time being, until we decide what we're going to do. He asks nothing in return. I have accepted his most gracious gift."

It was two days before Yuki could go through the charred ruins. There was absolutely nothing left other than the still-smoking remains of some bolts of silk. Only the shell of the building was left, the romanized letters on the marble facade melted away. Dozens of shop owners were sifting through the disaster area along with a platoon of firemen.

An old man approached her in the company of a younger executive. He had owned the restaurant where the fire had started and he was abject in his apology while she completed the ritual and forgave him.

All right, she told herself. *It is now time to move forward.*

As she was picking her way through the wreckage toward the street, a young man in a business suit, after addressing her, took a letter from his attaché case and gave it to her with a bow. She walked down the street to a morning cafe and over a cup of coffee opened the envelope. She was not surprised by the formal letter inside. Some months ago K&I Development, with headquarters in Yurakucho, had bought the building in which Blossoms was housed. The letter asked her to drop by company headquarters to discuss the lease.

She called Dawn at Itsugi's salon, told her what she was doing, then took the train back to Shinanomachi, and once home took out a tin box from the closet that contained her personal papers. She changed into a Western-style suit with low heels, put the papers in an oversized purse, and then took the train to Yurakucho. She found that K&I occupied the whole of a modern ten-story building of glass and steel.

She approached the receptionist and asked to see Sakomizu-san, the man who had signed the letter. She was directed instead to the tenth floor, where she was led to a massive corner office with modernistic polished wooden furniture from Scandinavia. But on one wall was a classical *kakemono,* a scroll so old and breathtakingly beautiful, she could not read the stylized poem. And on the corner of the desk sat a small ceramic vase, hundreds of years old, of a cerulean blue that looked as if the potter had been able to capture a piece of the sky itself. A young man in a business suit stood waiting for her. She had a strange feeling that she had seen him before, knew him and yet didn't. He was taller than the average, probably mid-twenties. "Nakamura-san," he said with a slightly formal nod. "I am very pleased to meet you. I apologize for the change in your plans. But I wanted to talk to you myself."

"So desuka?" she said, puzzled that the head of this corporation should occupy himself with such a minor matter.

He handed her his business card and with a start she realized that he was Ito Kanao, the general's son, and the memory flashed into her mind of the boy at the trials, his quick glance at her when his mother's attention was diverted. "Please sit down," he said. "You will find that the chair next to the window has a pleasant view."

"Ah, I never thought to see you again," she said gently.

"You remember the awkward boy at the trial then? My mother warned me not to look at you under any circumstances or I would be struck dead. But I managed to catch a glimpse of you and I lived through it." He smiled briefly and Yuki caught a hint of his father's smile. "The war did strange things to my mother. She was a very bitter woman who held my father responsible for all the misfortunes that befell us, including the loss of the war."

He waited until the tea was brought in and then sat down with his back to the view.

"How is your mother?" she asked.

"She died two months ago."

"I am very sorry for your loss."

"She was ill a long time. And I must tell you in all fairness that my mother's spirit will not rest until you have nothing," he said. "And until your daughter has nothing."

She looked out the window at the heavy layer of yellowed smog over the city and she refused to let him see the weakness she felt, as if she had already endured more battles than she could survive. She took a deep breath, steadied herself, looked directly into his face as she drank her tea. "And how are you going to accomplish this?" she asked.

"I'm in the process of doing it," he said. "I have arranged to buy the mortgage on your house and also the mortgage on the land in Towa when you default. Since the fire has destroyed your business, you will not have the means to pay your debts."

Forgive me, Ito-san, she breathed. *But I am beginning to feel a great anger toward your son.* "You assume too much," she said.

"Like my father, I never say anything I do not mean."

"I loved your father," she said. "I do not want to engage in a battle with his son."

"Then perhaps we can reach a compromise," he said. "The farmland is worth considerably more than the mortgage on your house. I will take over the land and you can have the house in Shinanomachi free and clear, plus a modest allowance to live on. I do that in memory of my father."

"You lack your father's cleverness," she said. "He never underestimated anyone."

"I don't think I'm underestimating you, Nakamura-san."

"But you are," Yuki said. "You assumed that I don't know business and that you can take advantage. I read the original lease again last night. Since it was made so many years ago, when everything was being rebuilt, it gives me the right to buy the building and the land on which it stands for the equivalent of a million dollars American, which at the moment is about three hundred million yen."

He looked at her sharply. "There is no building for you to buy. It was burned to the ground."

"The building was destroyed, but not the land."

"You are being foolish," he said. "The land isn't worth a million dollars."

"I have thirty days to buy it from you."

"If my reports are right, your financial resources can't handle a cash payment like that, and no bank will lend you twice what the land is worth. I withdraw any compromise I might have made in the name of my father. I'm going to take everything you have."

"Perhaps," she said.

He leaned back in his chair. His voice was strained. "You've made a terrible mistake with your attitude," he said. "I will follow my mother's wishes."

"Then I hope you will consult your mother's spirit again before you take any further action," Yuki said. "If you want, I will go to your mother's burial place and speak to her, but under no circumstances will I allow you to jeopardize my daughter's future."

"I repeat. I am sorry to have to take such actions against a woman, but you leave me no choice."

Yuki stood up. "I think you will find that it is not necessary for a Japanese to be male to show bravery. And I warn you, in advance, that you have a great deal to lose."

She gathered her papers and left.

She went into comparative seclusion for a week in an office that Itsugi had provided for her in his building. Dawn had begun to consult with Itsugi on his designs, and quite often now Yuki could hear Itsugi's inquisitive and abusive voice through the thin walls followed by Dawn's calm defense of her position. Yuki surrounded herself with business papers and an abacus, threading her way through an analysis of his operation while trying to sort out her own financial position as well.

But her energy was sapped by her inability to sleep soundly and without dreams, for ever since her interview with Kanao she had had a continuing dream, night after night, in which she saw the face of Kanao's mother, alive, filled with hatred, even as the cremation fires leapt up around her fine cheekbones and shot through the sockets of the malevolent eyes.

I apologize to you, Yuki said in her dreams. *I never believed that I had the power to take what was truly yours.*

But the eyes still glared at her.

Finally, when she was fully prepared, she came out of her office to intercept Itsugi-san on one of his circuits down the corridor. He was not in a good mood. She had the feeling he had been arguing with Dawn again.

"Now that you've come out of hibernation," he said to Yuki as they approached his office, "I am going to rely on you to control your daughter. She may be talented but she is also insufferable."

"What I want to talk to you about now is far more important than my daughter," Yuki said. She did not wait to be asked but sat down in a chair beside his large desk. "I have some papers I want you to see."

"If it's about money, talk to one of the accountants," he said, sinking into his chair and lacing his fingers behind his head. "Money bores me."

"Fine. Then you should be feeling happy, because in a maximum of five years you won't have any."

"What?" he said, startled.

"I want to know how much it's worth to have someone say yes to you all the time. A million dollars a year? Two million? And how much are you willing to pay to be protected from all the unpleasant realities of life? Another ten million?"

He looked at her darkly. "Don't go too far with me, Nakamura-san," he said, a warning.

"Your agents in London, Paris, and New York are robbing you blind. In some cases they are taking seventy percent of the proceeds of licensing your name. Last year alone that cost you thirteen million seven hundred and ninety-six thousand dollars."

He leaned forward in his chair. "Prove it."

She pushed the papers across the desk. "No one's trying to hide it. You signed these agreements yourself."

"*Baka*," he said. "Crazy. Why haven't my accountants caught this?"

"Because they're afraid of you." She picked up another sheaf of papers. "You've given them reason to be. And you're losing money in this salon only because of gross mismanagement. Your location is far too small for one thing, and you're paying out far too much money for every service you hire, every piece of material you buy, all because you act too much on whim."

He studied the pages, looked up at her. "If this gets out, it will make a fool of me."

"Everybody makes too much money off you to call anything to the public attention."

He put a cigarette in his holder. His fingers trembled slightly. "I want you to become my business manager," he said. "I want you to fire the firm of accountants, quietly, and then, as the licensing agreements come up, I want you to negotiate them."

"I'm honored at your display of confidence," she said. "But I would have conditions."

He shrugged, made a vague and expansive wave of his hand. "Pay yourself any salary you want," he said. "You'll be keeping my company from bleeding to death."

"That leads to my first condition," Yuki said. "I have a great respect for you, Itsugi-san, and I know the concentration that talent requires. But if I take the position, then you must set aside one hour

a week to sit down with me and go over the budgets I have arranged.
So you will know at any time where you stand."

"Agreed. What else do you need?"

She looked out the window at the street. "I have an enemy and I
must show him that I cannot be threatened without his paying a
terrible price. And I need your help."

"I will help any way I can," Itsugi said.

"Fine," she said. "You can begin by lending me one million dollars,
interest free, for a period of one month."

For a week Yuki watched the charred ruins of the buildings down
the street from her window at Itsugi's salon. The bulldozers were
already at work, leveling the whole middle section of the block,
trucks hauling off the debris. In the evenings she wandered the side
streets around the Ginza and heard the same story so often she knew
it must be true. Kanao had capitalized on the fire, relocated the
restaurant, paid the other tenants to move elsewhere, and was planning a luxury office building, with high-priced shops on the ground
floor.

You're making a great mistake, Kanao-san.

On the morning of the first day of the month, she watched from
the window while a black limousine disgorged Kanao and a party of
businessmen, all of them dressed in expensive Western business suits
and yellow hard hats emblazoned with the company logo. A team of
lesser officials had set up a table and were weighing down the blueprints of the new building against the disruptive breeze.

She examined herself in a full-length mirror, pleased with her
plum-colored Italian silk dress. Her hair was shining, her eyes untroubled. She put the necessary papers in her bag and walked down
the street, pleased at the mildness of the day.

Kanao was standing with the other men at the table, looking at the
blueprints while photographers circled like birds of prey. She stayed
well beyond the range of the lenses, but she was aware that he had
seen her because he seemed to stiffen where he stood. Soon he
wandered over to her, his face flushed. "I do not want you here," he
said. "My astrologer warned me against disturbing influences today."

"You have two choices," she said evenly. "I will meet you at the
small cafe down the street in ten minutes or I will conduct my
business with you in the presence of your associates."

"I have no business with you," he said in a low voice. She started to walk past him toward the table. He put a staying hand on her arm. "All right. The cafe."

"I'll be on the second floor, overlooking the street," she said.

He was there within ten minutes, minus the hard hat, his face filled with a dark and terrible impatience. "I'm having tea," she said. "It might do you good to have some refreshment."

"I'm here to warn you," he said. "I have alerted our security people. If you even come close to the site, I'll have you removed."

"You should have consulted me, Kanao-san, before you did so much work on the site. Although it would have had to be done, sooner or later."

"I have no more to say to you."

She opened her bag, placed the million-dollar check before him on the table. He did not touch it. "It's not real," he said. "There's no way it could be."

"I have the other legal papers here, referring to the original agreement, attesting to the presence of the funds in the Chase Manhattan Bank in New York City that are ready for transfer to your account with the Sumitomo Bank in Tokyo."

"Who would lend you the money? The land isn't worth half a million."

"It's worth far more than that since you have to have it," she said. "It's right in the middle of your development."

He was ashen-faced now. "You can't do this to me."

"I gave you fair warning," she said.

"We can come to some agreement," he said, forcing himself to be rational. "I'll cancel the mortgage on your house and on your farmland. I think that's a very generous offer."

"But I've had a better one," she said. "It seems that this is a very desirable location and a colleague of mine has offered to trade me another building on the Ginza for this site. In addition, he will pay off all my existing debts."

Kanao was sweating now despite the air-conditioning in the cafe. He dabbed at his upper lip with a handkerchief. To have to cancel everything at this point would shame him beyond redemption. He was paralyzed. His words came out from between clenched teeth. "What do you want?"

"First, you must make a journey to your mother's burial place and tell her to stop appearing in my dreams."

"What else?" he said with burning eyes.

"By no later than four o'clock this afternoon you will deliver to me a legal paper transferring to me a share of the building you will be erecting plus an equivalent interest in the ground beneath it. This paper will say that you will build a ground-floor salon, facing the Ginza, with thirty thousand square feet of space, to my specifications. You will also cancel all of the debts I owe you."

"Do you think I'm crazy?" he said. "Do you think I'll give you all of that for a million dollars?"

"Oh, you won't get the million," she said, picking up the check, putting it back into her bag. "Not unless you decide to cancel your project and give me the title to my site."

She was enjoying watching him as he tried to work his way out. "I'm only part of the company," he said.

"The head of the company," she corrected.

"I still can't agree to this without the approval of my directors."

"I don't care about your problems," she said. "You either agree or you don't. You either show up at the address I will give you by four o'clock with the proper documents or I will exercise my option."

Music was blaring from the loudspeakers at the site. *"Hai, so desu,"* he said. "But I promise you, Nakamura-san, that sometime in the future I will get my revenge. And not for my mother's sake, but for my own."

He came to Itsugi's salon promptly at four o'clock, his face so blanched and stiff it seemed to be covered with rice powder. He waited while she read the documents, and when she nodded her approval he turned and stalked away without the slightest pretense of politeness.

In her first week as financial manager at the House of Itsugi, Yuki found herself caught up in a maelstrom of activity while she dealt with suppliers and set up a central purchasing department, which reported to her daily.

She spent some time with the clippings of his reviews in the Paris press, his work characterized by such adjectives as "bold," "stark," "simple yet powerful," and she pored over the photographs of his models on the runway. He had made his reputation by going against the postwar trend toward billowing skirts and puff sleeves. Itsugi had worked with straight lines, a severely tailored look that said, in effect, "Now the war is over and it's time for women to consolidate the new positions of equality that wartime gave them."

As she leafed through the pages of mounted clippings from later collections, she could see that he was always ahead of his time, setting trends. She was pleased with what she saw and looked forward to what she and Dawn might accomplish with this new affiliation with Itsugi.

It soon became apparent to Yuki that the creative side of the House of Itsugi was now dependent, to a large degree, upon a diminutive wisp of a woman named Myoko. She was the organizer, the coordinator in this bedlam, constantly in motion, her wooden getas clattering down the concrete corridors of the atelier, getting the swatches of material he wanted, making sure everything was arranged for Itsugi-san's convenience.

One morning when Itsugi-san was in Yokohama on business, Myoko approached Yuki and Dawn and invited them to witness something that she thought they both should see. She led them into his atelier, where she had put out the secret sketches intended for use in the fall.

Dawn moved from one to the next, while it took Yuki no more than a glance to find that she could see nothing but disaster in what Itsugi was planning. It was as if, having no new ideas, he had made a composite of what he considered the best of a dozen of his past collections. There was no innovation in his work. And Yuki knew that very few women would consider the unflattering look that Itsugi seemed determined to impose upon them.

"I need your honesty, Myoko-san," Yuki said. "You have been with him since the beginning. How much of the designing has he actually done and how much has been done by his assistants?"

"He has provided all the spirit," Myoko said. "He has inspired everything, but the people who work with him have done the drawings and the samples."

"And you have shown us these sketches in an attempt to help him."

Myoko looked at Dawn. "I hope that you will be inspired by his greatness," she said with all sincerity.

"I hope so too," Dawn said, challenged by the opportunity to show what she could do.

ROBERT L. DUNCAN

The next day, as Dawn walked along the Ginza studying the decorated windows of the competition, she was accidentally caught up in
a crowd of political protestors, hundreds of people in the street in
front of a bamboo platform where a man was speaking, his deep
voice amplified through loudspeakers. He and his followers wore
loose-fitting jackets with full sleeves, like a *happi* coat, with the red
character for banzai emblazoned on the back and a white headband
with the same red character.

Dawn nodded to a woman in a kimono. "What is the name of this
group of protesters?" she said.

"They represent the Banzai Movement," the kimonoed woman
said. "They want Japan to take back its former glory."

When she went back to the House of Itsugi and secluded herself in
the small studio that had been provided for her, she found herself
rolling her brush against the paint block and allowing the forms to
take shape on the paper. In an hour Myoko appeared at her door and
bowed.

"If it is convenient," she said, "O-Itsugi-sama would be pleased to
have a conversation with you."

"I will look forward to such a conversation," Dawn said, her brush
continuing to move. "Would you be kind enough to tell him that I am
unfortunately delayed for an hour or so?"

"Hai," Myoko said, bowing with her palms pressed flat against the
front of her thighs. Dawn could hear the clatter of her wooden clogs
down the hallway. As the sound diminished she forgot Itsugi altogether. She was caught up in her work, and she occasionally left her
drawings to get a color chart or a scrap of material from the bolts of
cloth piled in a bin. And when she was finally finished she looked at
her watch and realized that it was seven o'clock in the evening. The
building was quiet around her and she put a kettle on her hot plate
and then made tea. Pouring herself a cup, she sat down, as tired as
she had ever been in her life.

She heard a sound in the hall and recognized Itsugi's footsteps.
She had forgotten him. She went immediately to the door and threw
it open. "Oh, Itsugi-san, I apologize to you. I meant no disrespect. I
forgot everything in my work."

"When you did not come I looked in on you and I decided to wait
you out," Itsugi said, his voice steely.

"Please enter. I have made tea."

"I have waited to tell you that you have now gone too far. You will not treat . . ." His eyes fell on the sketches spread on the drawing table, floor, tacked to the wall.

He moved from sketch to sketch. "Ah"—as he picked up one after another—"and this is what you have been doing?"

"Yes," she said. "All of the designs are adaptations of the costumes worn by the members of a political movement."

"I know the group. Continue, please."

"The originals are all silk, but the designs will be produced in synthetics as well. An overblouse with large three-quarter sleeves, simple gold bracelets on each arm, and either culottes, pants, or skirts, all in the same lines, to a point midway between the knee and the ankle." She sipped her tea. "The key is in the headband. It has to be wide enough to display a Japanese character in a bold color, preferably red, and long enough to knot and drape down the left side of the head. You can echo the motif in a sash for formal wear."

"And what ideogram would you have on the headband?"

"Where they have the character for banzai," she said. "I think we should use the character for the House of Itsugi."

"Inspired," he said.

"You like them then?"

"Very much." He sighed, drank his tea. "I would make some changes, of course, minor ones."

"This is your house and I would expect you to," she said. "There's genius in what you do."

"Not in this year's designs," he said. "I knew that when you and your mother gave me no personal response after Myoko showed them to you. But never mind. You have more than redeemed yourself."

"I want two things of you," she said. "I want to go to Paris for the showing. And I would also like my salary to begin immediately."

"Certainly," he said. But his eyes were still on the sketches, which stood out against the wall. "Inspired," he breathed, almost to himself. "Inspired."

Yuki had retained a single accountant from the firm that had so badly mishandled the Itsugi account. His name was Megura, a small athletic man who was about to be retired at the age of fifty-five when Yuki hired him for the House of Itsugi. As she read the weekly financial report he had given her, he stood eyeing her carpet, as if measuring the distance between his feet and some imaginary spot.

She looked up. "What are you doing, Megura-san?"

"Mental putting," he said. "I have had great success with my woods and even my pitching irons, but my game is poor on the greens."

"You saved us a quarter of a million yen this week," she said. "Why don't you take a few days off and play on a real golf course?"

"I'll take time after Paris," he said. "But in the meantime, I am training my eyes." He turned to go back to his office. "Oh," he said, "I received the building plans from Ito Kanao this morning. They need your approval by the end of the week."

"Has he lived up to the space agreement?"

"I would say so," Megura said. "Perhaps a hundred square feet short, but that's to be expected in any large project."

"Please call Kanao's project manager," she said. "He's not to be one square foot short. This has become a matter of principle."

"*Hai, so desu,*" Megura said. "The agreement is almost ready for transferring this building to you on the day Itsugi takes possession of the new salon. You need to think of creating a corporate shell, Nakamura-san. I need a name for the agreements."

"The House of Dawn," Yuki said without hesitation.

"And you will be listed as president, your daughter as vice president."

"Yes. And I would like you to be listed as treasurer. There will be no conflict of interest, Megura-san, because the corporation will be inactive for a while."

"I'm honored by your trust."

When he was gone she glanced at her letters and sat back contented. Kanao's mother had not come back to haunt her dreams again, a sure sign that Kanao had surrendered, at least for the moment.

McLean, Virginia . . .
Spring 1962

As Sam pulled up in the car he had rented at the airport, Noble came out the front door to meet him. Noble was tanned, dressed in a pale blue sport jacket and golfer's pants, with a jaunty cap on his head, and there was something incongruous to Sam about the grave expression on his face. "I just want you to know how grateful I am that you agreed to come out to the farm," he said. "I know your time is limited. You'd better come into the library and have a drink before you see Adele."

Sam glanced around him at the green fields and the expanse of lawns, the white-columned house that would have been perfect for antebellum Georgia. Inside the foyer was a winding staircase that led up to the second floor, but Noble led him into a room that was more bar than library, with one wall in glass shelves containing hundreds of bottles. "I'm having scotch," Noble said. "But as I remember, your drink is bourbon, isn't it, son?"

"I don't want anything," Sam said wearily. "I'm just off one jet from Paris and I leave in two hours for Southeast Asia."

"I hear mighty fine things about what you're doing," Noble said, dropping two cubes of ice into the amber liquid in his glass. "Are you about to get everything squared away out there?"

"Nobody will ever get everything squared away out there," Sam said. "The message you left for me concerned my mother."

Noble downed the drink and poured himself another. "There's no way I can soften this," he said. "She's dying."

"I see. And how long does she have?"

"Another month or two. Perhaps three. The doctors have all agreed on the prognosis. They—"

"I don't mean to be unkind, Noble, but I don't want the medical details. Where is she now?"

"Out in the back garden," Noble said. "She no longer has the use of her legs."

"How do I find the back garden?"

"Through the living room," Noble said, "but let me finish my drink and I'll take you."

"I'll find my way," Sam said.

He wandered through a large living room furnished with American antiques and went through French doors onto a terrace from which he saw his mother sitting in a wheelchair in a rose garden near a stone bench and fountain, and he was amused to see that she was making notes on a legal-sized pad and ignoring his presence altogether.

He went down the steps. She had become frail, almost birdlike, her face pinched as she squinted through her glasses at her writing. She did not look up as he approached. He lit a cigarette. "Admit something, Mother," he said. "You saw me from the moment I came through the French doors."

She put the pencil down with great deliberation, and with her head cocked to one side at a slight angle, looked at him. "Why should I admit anything? You've taken your own sweet time about coming to see me. You're looking terrible," she said.

"That's lack of sleep," he said. He sat down on the stone bench, looked at the water spilling from the pitcher held by a water nymph into a basin below. "Are you really dying, or is this another one of Noble's ploys?"

"It's no big thing," she said. "I have no fear of it but it does tend to put things into perspective, though. I was just making changes to be incorporated in my will. Is there anything you want?"

He sat down on the bench. "I see the changes you've already made," he said.

"I wondered if you'd notice."

"It's impossible to miss," he said. "Not a hint of the Orient in the house. What happened to your collection?"

"I wanted to destroy it but Noble insisted on giving it to some museum. Tax purposes, I believe. But anything you want from the collection is still available."

He shook his head. "I don't want anything." He looked out across the field, which seemed to stretch for miles, unbroken. "What are you doing out in the country? I thought you were a committed city woman."

"I wanted the opposite of Shanghai," she said.

"It's certainly that," he said. "There would be room here for a thousand Chinese farmers."

"The doctor said I should have fresh air and sunshine. So it gave Noble an excuse to buy this monstrosity where he can raise Arabian horses and entertain a hundred and fifty guests if he wants to. And it's close to a country club and a golf course." She studied him in silence. "I didn't think you'd come," she said. "Why did you relent this time? Did you know I'm dying?"

"I guessed it," he said.

"Most people shy away now that I'm terminal. Sometimes I think they believe I might take them along with me. And I've outlived most of my enemies who are close enough to know about me. So I get neither sympathy nor rejoicing. What do you feel?"

"Sadness," he said. "You and I have never agreed on one damn thing, as far back as I can remember, but I only threw you out of China. I never meant for you to leave this world."

"We've never really gotten along, have we?" she said.

"No, we're different people."

"Let me have one of your cigarettes."

He lit one for her, handed it to her. "Life has not been all that splendid for me," she said. "I never had what I really wanted."

"Which was?"

"A faithful and ambitious husband in the beginning," she said. "And failing that, a son who was on my side, who was as much like me as he was like his father."

He drew smoke from his cigarette. "I'm a good bit like you," he said. "I inherited your stubbornness, I think. I certainly matched you as far as carrying grudges is concerned. My grudge against you lasted almost as long as your grudge against poor, long-gone Father, God rest his soul."

She smiled slightly. "You have that," she said. "And your staying away for all this time has been just as mean-spirited as I've ever been. Is your grudge still active?"

He shook his head. "It eroded away a long time ago."

"I don't suppose that you're ready to admit that you've been one hundred percent wrong."

"About what?"

"None of this would ever have happened if you hadn't followed in your father's footsteps and gone to China. You have to admit that."

He reached out and took her hand, the fingers slight, cold. "I could admit anything and everything and nothing would be changed by it," he said. "I could damn China until I was blue in the face and admit that my life has been full of wrong turns, and we'd still be sitting here on a warm summer day with nothing changed."

"True," she said. "But China's beyond both of us now."

"Only for a while," he said. "It's ironic, isn't it? The only descendant either of us will ever have is a half-Japanese girl who will never know that I'm her father or that you're her grandmother. Doesn't that disturb you sometimes?"

"A little. The Japanese woman ruined you, but I don't have to tell you that."

Now it was his turn to smile. "Nobody ruined me, Mother. I would never have made one of your exalted bureaucrats and I never wanted public office. I work in Southeast Asia. Sometimes I feel like a fireman who is called in only when the flames have consumed the structure and there's no hope. But maybe one of these days I'll do some good."

"I won't apologize to you for anything I've done," she said. "Given all the same conditions, I would do everything exactly the same way."

"Good for you," he said without irony. "No quarter asked or given. That's the spirit."

"Are you making fun of me?"

"Of us both," he said. "The battles are long past, Mother, all the wrangles over passion and ambition and what might have been. I lost some people very important to me and so did you. So I guess without knowing it, I came here to strike a truce."

"A truce?"

"That's my business, after all. I've been doing it for years. There's no reason why I shouldn't negotiate a final truce with my own mother."

"Even lacking love?"

"You don't need love to have a truce," he said. "Maybe all we need is a desire not to fight anymore, and we do have a bond, after all, because as hard as I have tried to deny it, I came from you, and as much as you might wish it otherwise, I'm your child."

"Perhaps so," she said. She put her other hand over his. "A truce then, but only that. Because there's been too much disagreement between us for real peace."

"I'm satisfied with that," he said. "And now, as I knew when I came out here, I have to go. I have a plane to catch to Saigon."

"I always preferred traveling by boat," she said. She was quiet a long moment. "I suppose there is too much bad feeling between us for you to kiss me good-bye?"

"I think we can manage that, don't you?" he said. He stood up and leaned down to put his arms around her and he felt the strength of her frail arm embracing him. He kissed her. "Good-bye, Mother. I'll see you when I get back."

"Call first," she said, eyes misty. "It might not be convenient."

"Yes," he said. "I'll do that."

Six weeks later he was sitting at a conference table in Saigon, discussing military advisers with a small and nut-brown man when he felt a cold chill move through him despite the heat of the day, and although his ears did not miss a syllable of what was being said, he knew at that moment that his mother had died.

Paris . . .
Autumn 1962

FROM THE MINUTE Yuki landed in Paris, she was faced with a series of impossible tasks, the first of which was finding some way to cut back on Itsugi's personal spending. She took a suite at the Georges V, spread out her cost projections on the polished top of a Louis XIV table, and began making a last-minute check with the aid of Megura, who studied the columns of figures and shook his head unhappily.

"I think the production costs are realistic," he said. "And we should come in on budget. But I checked the records for last year. There's no way to force him to cut back."

"You can leave that to me," she said.

But over the next twenty-four hours she came to the conclusion that Itsugi's spending was as calculated as the appearance of full-blown lunacy that he affected on his arrival in Paris. He could be seen departing a rented limousine dressed in a black brocade gentleman's kimono, wearing sunglasses, a crowd of reporters and photographers in tow. He picked up the bills at expensive bars in Montmartre and had an eternal open house for the press in his suite at the Ritz. He was always good for an acid comment.

Of X: "He designs perfect clothing for a mother of five."

Of Y's new "net" look: "It should protect one against mosquitoes."

He took as good as he gave. There was still an undercurrent of prejudice in Paris against the Japanese for what had happened in French Indochina during World War II, and there was some pressure on Chambre Syndicale de la Couture Parisienne to boycott Japanese designers, though the government would not hear of it. But what could not be officially permitted was converted to sarcasm in the press.

In *Le Figaro:* "The Japanese are back again this year, led by their chief clown, Itsugi. If they follow their usual custom, they will simply prove the old truism that East is East and West is West and never the twain shall meet. Japanese fashion, like good wine, simply does not travel well."

Yuki found Itsugi totally unaffected by such comments. He had a male secretary with him who read French, English, and German and he scoured the daily papers to clip any stories that mentioned Itsugi, however briefly. And Myoko, in her kimono, met and entertained buyers and fashion writers at the Ritz suite, offering them champagne and no hints at all of the new style that Itsugi was going to introduce this year. She was incorruptible. She spoke no French and little English, so what seemed like a charming and knowing smile was in reality total incomprehension.

He knew what he was doing, Yuki realized, so she dropped the matter of money and let it be known that she would be handling the licensing for this year's collection and then concentrated on the showing. She obtained permission from the municipal government to erect a very large circus tent on the lawn sheltered by the wings of the Louvre. Then she realized that neither Itsugi-san nor any of his willow boys was going to be responsible for supervising the construction of the catwalk and the placement of the changing rooms as well as of the two long champagne tables on either side of the tent. As usual, Itsugi had left such matters to a union steward who could be counted on to steal Itsugi blind.

Two days before the show, when the tent was supposed to be fully in place and was not, Yuki and Dawn went to the site. Yuki located the union steward, a heavyset man whose eye held a barely concealed contempt as he saw the Japanese women. He sat down on a box to light a cigarette, breathed smoke toward the sagging canvas overhead.

"Let me handle this one, Mother," Dawn said, fire in her eye.

"Certainly," Yuki said, standing back to observe.

"Do you speak English?" Dawn asked the union steward, looking around the tent at a dozen men who just seemed to be waiting.

"Non," the man said with some sarcasm. *"Parlez-vous français?"*

Dawn stopped another man, somewhat younger, who was carrying a box. "Do you speak English?" she said.

"I speak some," the young man said. "I try."

"That's fine," Dawn said. "That's all I ask. Now, please inform this gentleman that there is a strict rule against smoking in the tent. And secondly, inform him that he is no longer working here. He's fired. He's to be out immediately."

The union steward glowered at Dawn as the young man started to speak. "If I don't work," he said in broken English. "Then nobody works."

She glanced around the tent. "Nobody's working now, are they?" she said. "So it doesn't make any difference, does it? You're fired, and you," she said to the young man, "are the new foreman. You can tell the other men that if the tent is finished by tonight, then they will be on the payroll until we leave Paris. If not, we'll hire an entirely different crew."

"Perfect," Yuki said under her breath.

That night the tent was finished. The union steward who had been fired had made a formal protest to the union and the *Chambre,* and Yuki saw Dawn being interviewed in the bar of the Georges V by a middle-aged French journalist who seemed to regard the whole episode with wry good humor.

"You seem to have set officialdom on its collective ear," the man said. "I suppose you know that you risked the wrath of the people who control the business of haute couture in Paris. They could have shut you down over the incident if they wanted to."

"We appreciate the courtesy extended to us by the city of Paris," Dawn said. "Just as I'm sure that the city of Paris appreciates the very large amount of money that the House of Itsugi spends to come here to exhibit."

"Do I hear a vague threat?" the journalist said with a smile.

"You may describe it any way you like," Dawn said.

"I suppose you know that some of the French papers will rip you to pieces."

"Fortunately I don't read the French newspapers," Dawn said.

"We're here to exhibit a new line and that's all. Let the new designs speak for themselves."

"I love it," Itsugi said to Yuki the next day at the Ritz when his boy handed him the paper with the picture of Dawn on the front page.

"How do you know?" Yuki said. "Have you learned to read French?"

"A little. I know how to spell *Itsugi,*" he said. "And I can count. *Itsugi* is mentioned ten times in the article. And though I can't read it, I know exactly what it says. I had a call from the labor unions this morning demanding an apology."

"And you gave them one?"

"Of course. I apologized to their union that one of my women designers should have had to do what a lazy foreman could not."

Yuki accepted another cup of coffee from the waiter in the restaurant. "I told you Dawn was outspoken," she said. "And I think details of the collection have been leaked. I have seven appointments already following the showing."

"Of course," he said. "I leaked information myself. Not all, but some. There's very little reality to any of this business anyway. We create an illusion and if we're lucky then we make a lot of money off it and everybody else gets rich as well. You're very good at this game yourself. You haven't chided me once about the expenses."

"For every dollar you spend, we'll get back a thousand," Yuki said. "You have an excellent collection but you also make everyone happy when they're around you, especially the press. You have a very particular genius."

"For the time being," he said. "Let's hope it lasts." He inserted a cigarette in a black holder, lit it. "Did your daughter like the Count?"

"What Count?"

"She didn't know? The man who interviewed her is the Count Emile Riboud. He is very influential, a member of the Syndicale."

"If he's a designer, what's he doing conducting interviews?"

"He's made his fortune in men's clothing. And he owns a newspaper or two, I believe." He looked up from his tea as one of his charming boys brought him a sheet covered with Japanese characters. Itsugi gave him an adoring smile and then scanned the paper and broke into laughter. "This is a translation of the Count's story about Dawn. It's really quite marvelous. He says that if the collection of the House of Itsugi has as much fire as one of its beautiful employees, then the city of Paris is in for a treat."

"Fire?" Yuki said.

Itsugi read on. "Did you suppose she really made the threat that the House of Itsugi might decide to bypass Paris."

"It wouldn't surprise me," Yuki said.

"Your daughter is priceless," he said, handing her the sheet. "As long as she's around, we won't be ignored, that much is certain."

On the night of the showing Yuki could tell that Dawn had stage fright even though she would never pass beyond the curtains to the catwalk. "What if the designs aren't accepted?" Dawn asked her mother. "What if the first model out is received with catcalls?"

"She won't be," Yuki said. "You've done beautiful work."

Reassurance was useless, Yuki thought, and Dawn's only cure would come from the night's experience. By the time the music had begun, Dawn had no time for nervousness. When she adjusted the headband of the first model and sent her through the curtain, she was only vaguely aware of the rising chorus of applause because she was already inspecting the second model. Down the line a missing headband had created a crisis. Dawn sent Myoko scurrying to a reserve rack, bringing her one just in time to drape it around the forehead of a model before she went out through the curtain.

Yuki knew the show was going well from the energy and the rising enthusiasm of the models as they came back through the curtains.

And finally, with applause ringing through the tent, the models surrounded Itsugi, who examined himself in a large dressing mirror, adjusted his black cape, and affixed an expression of false modesty to his face before he went out to meet the people who had both created and witnessed his triumph.

Tokyo . . . November 1962

BY THE MIDDLE of November, Yuki was back in her Ginza office, besieged by telephone calls, cables, contracts, and a new problem now that the world media had begun to take Itsugi seriously. Myoko came into Yuki's office for advice. "I have a hundred requests for interviews," she said, "and Itsugi-san doesn't have time for any of them."

"He'll have to learn to take time," Yuki said. "But I think we should also hire a public relations firm to put out releases. That should take off some of the pressure."

On her third day home, Dawn called from her workshop. "Can you break free for an hour?" she said.

"Certainly," Yuki said.

"It's a cold day but I'd like to take a walk."

There was a strong chill wind from the north and a hint of snow in the air as they walked down the Ginza to the site of Kanao's new building, where the giant land movers were excavating a very deep basement while government archaeologists went over every foot of ground to make sure that no historic site was being disturbed.

"What is our financial position, Mother?"

"Excellent," Yuki said. "Why?"

"I realize this is probably ungrateful on my part," Dawn said. "I was really awed when I first went into Itsugi's salon. But something happened I didn't expect. I created a basic design and he was supposed to have changed it, enhanced it, made improvements on it, but he didn't. That was my victory on the runways in Paris. Those were my designs out there, totally untouched by him. They may have had his name on them, but they came from my imagination."

"And you feel cheated."

"Yes."

"That's the way the world is," Yuki said. "If you expect everything to be fair, then you will always be disappointed. Especially in Japan."

"Then I intend to change things," Dawn said. "I want credit for my work. How long have you promised to stay with Itsugi?"

"No definite time," Yuki said. "But we won't move until the time is right."

"I trust your instincts, Mother," Dawn said. "But I don't intend to wait forever."

That afternoon Yuki received a letter delivered by messenger and took it straight to Itsugi's office, where he stood at a window looking down at the street. A hundred members of the Banzai Movement were creating a public demonstration, carrying banners, chanting, condemning Itsugi-san. "What do they want?" Itsugi asked. "Why are they here?"

"They just delivered a letter, Itsugi-san," she said. "They want an apology."

"For what?"

"They consider your new fashion line a corruption of their uniform. If I were you, I would invite their leader in for a cup of tea and donate money to their movement. It would be excellent public relations."

"Absolutely not," he said. "Itsugi-san apologizes to nobody. I wouldn't give them that satisfaction." He lit a cigarette, turned away from the window. He walked around his office, trailing blue smoke behind him. There was no contrition in him. "They take themselves far too seriously. Ignore them."

She went back to her office, but she found that the crowd on the street could not be ignored. For even as she worked with Megura on contracts, she was distracted by the sound of drums, and when she checked the street again the original crowd had quadrupled and the Tokyo Metropolitan Police were beginning to assemble in the side streets and patiently erecting crowd-control barriers. Colorful signs and banners were raised, popular slogans from the war, slightly altered. "All the world under the eight-cornered roof of heaven!" "The spirit of Bushido shall prevail!" "No contamination of the Japanese spirit!"

Behind the police barriers the number of officers increased rapidly. The chanting began, a snake dance winding up and down the block in front of the building, and Yuki began to feel the same way she had when the sirens wailed in Shanghai—a terrible dread.

Yuki punched the intercom, summoned Myoko, who appeared at her door, terrified, speechless.

"Is Itsugi-san in his office?" she said.

"Hai," Myoko said.

"I want you to do something for me," Yuki said quietly. "Take all the staff out the back door. There may be a riot here and I don't want to see anyone hurt."

She rang Dawn's line. "Meet me in Itsugi-san's office in five minutes," she said.

She stormed down the corridor and into his office without knocking, paying no attention to his disapproving scowl. "You don't have any more time," she said. "Now either you call in a representative and make an apology, or I want you to go out the back way and get into a car and leave. This is no ordinary political rally. You could be in great danger."

"I'm in no trouble," he said. "Have you seen any sign of the television crews?"

"You called the television stations?"

"Of course," he said. "This is a happening, after all."

"You've gone too far this time," Yuki said. "You can't turn this into a media event."

"Itsugi doesn't have to flee before the rabble," he said.

Dawn burst into the office, her face pale. "The security officer recommends that we leave immediately," she said.

But there was no more time, as on the street a thousand men surged forward as one, *collectively,* overwhelming the police line, catching the backup police units off guard, pinning them in the side streets. The sirens were screaming, lights flashing, crowds chanting. The hail of rocks began.

They burst through the windows of Itsugi's office, and he froze, as if he could not believe this was happening. Yuki grabbed Dawn and pulled her into a sheltered alcove as more panes shattered under the barrage. The crowds broke through the front door and began to smash everything in sight, yelling, spreading like ants into the workrooms, upsetting boxes, ripping bolts of fabric to pieces, surging up the stairs.

To Yuki's great surprise, Itsugi did not choose to hide but instead grabbed up a stout, three-sided measuring stick and stepped out of his office to meet the rioters, his face ashen behind the dark glasses. He managed one swing with the stick before a bamboo pole caught him off guard across the face and he went down, dazed. Blows from bamboo poles rained against the side of his face, his sunglasses shattering, the pieces flying away like a thousand tiny brown insects.

Yuki saw Itsugi's young man, the willow boy, rushing along the hall with Megura. They hurled themselves forward, trying to protect Itsugi from the mob, but they were struck down instantly.

Yuki ordered Dawn to stay where she was and stepped out of the office only to be sent reeling against the wall by a blow from a stick. She managed to crawl over to Itsugi, who was all but unconscious, his willow boy stroking his face, trying to bring him around. Megura was dazed. He held on to the wall as he stood up.

The fighting had whirled through the building and out again, down the stairs into the street, where the reserve police had finally taken control, tear-gas canisters flying, a squad pushing through the smoke with clear plastic shields in front of them to break the ranks of the rioters.

Yuki made her way into the street and found an emergency medical team, which she led back to the second floor, where she stopped short. For there was Itsugi standing against a smashed door, the twisted frame of his broken sunglasses in his fingers as a prop, a camera whirring, the lights flooding him as he was interviewed by a television newsman.

"I simply refused to give in to the pressures of the past," Itsugi-san was saying. "I was attacked by a reactionary group because my designs are accepted internationally. I truly believe that I represent the new and progressive Japan."

"Can you believe this?" Dawn whispered incredulously, coming up beside Yuki.

Yuki shook her head, directed the medics to the willow boy and

Megura and sent Dawn with them as she waited for the television crew to finish. Then she followed Itsugi-san into his office, where he opened a drawer and found another pair of sunglasses, which he slipped on before he examined himself in a mirror, smoothing his hair, running a fingertip over a welt on his cheek where a bamboo pole had caught him.

"What a fine public relations job," Yuki said, close to awe.

Itsugi grimaced at the mirror and examined his teeth. "We'll have media coverage all over the world in places where fashion coverage isn't even carried. The public always sympathizes with one man standing alone against a mob, and I would project an increase in sales of this year's line by at least twenty-five percent." He took a flask of brandy out of a drawer, filled two fragile porcelain teacups, handed her one.

"You could have been killed," she said.

"One has to take risks to make millions," he said. He held his cup out to her. "To success," he said.

She drank.

Tokyo . . . 1964

ON A COLD DAY in December, two years later, Yuki was at her office when Itsugi called her. She could tell from the tone of his voice that he was in one of his melancholy moods, his unhappiness compounded perhaps by some slight, real or imagined, on the part of the willow boy who had become his favorite. "I had a call that the new salon is now finished," he said. "I thought we might have a look at it, the two of us."

"I would be honored," she said. "Shall we walk?"

"I make it a rule never to walk anyplace," he said. "It spoils the effect of an elegant arrival."

The driver seated her in the limousine and Itsugi settled back against the leather seat, looking out the tinted window at the face of his old building. "I've worked in this building a long time. I'm reluctant to leave it. It's become an old friend."

"You're free not to move," Yuki said. "If that pleases you."

He tapped the glass with his gold ring. The driver pulled out into the traffic. Then Itsugi turned his face toward her with a thoughtful smile. "I'm under the impression that we have a contract," he said. "I have all of this wonderful space. And in exchange you will have my building. How soon will you start Blossoms again?"

"A few months."

He looked out at the traffic. "I was very lucky when I made you and your daughter part of my company," he said. "The new line is every bit as good as last year's and will make even more money. And you've increased my profits by a half billion yen."

"Thank you," she said. "We have been fortunate."

"Not fortunate, shrewd. I always feel a bit uncomfortable around people who are shrewder than I."

"You flatter me," she said.

The limousine pulled to a halt by the curb and they got out. The bamboo scaffolding had been removed from the eight-story building and now they could see the modern steel and glass structure. Itsugi's magnificent salon dominated the lower floor, faced by marble with the letters of his name in bronze. The doorman opened the heavy glass door to admit them and they made their way into the main salon. The room was large enough for catwalks and the showings, the workrooms all glass and light, carpeted in quiet shades of green. At the end of a corridor was Itsugi's personal office and workshop, bare of the furniture that would enhance it except for a couple of canvas and wood director's chairs and a very large television set built into a low dividing wall.

Itsugi sat down in a chair beneath a skylight, looked at his watch, and then took a silver flask from his pocket, had a long drink, and offered it to Yuki, who declined. He leaned back in the chair, looked through the skylight at the clouds. "I am uneasy," he said.

"About what?" she asked, sitting down in the other chair.

"I understand the owner of this building hates you because you outwitted him. Are you outwitting me?"

"He is a different matter, Itsugi-san. He made the mistake of underestimating me."

"And it cost him a fortune."

"Yes."

"Which leads me to our personal relationship," he said. "I have never had much trust in women, as you may have guessed. But I have to think of the future. I know I don't look it, but I'm over fifty years old and I have to think of the survival of my line. Do you have definite plans for your future?"

"Yes," she said.

"Will you marry?"

"No. But I think that Dawn will, one day. Perhaps the French Count."

"And regarding the House of Itsugi?"

"The year will come, not for a long time, but certain to arrive, when I will start a house for my daughter," she said. "The House of Dawn."

"I thought as much," he said testily. "You will abandon me, then."

"We are only your employees, Itsugi-san," she said.

"You have made a lot of money out of my business," he said.

"Nobody is abandoning you, Itsugi-san."

"But you will eventually, and the contemplation of that time is as bad as the reality." He stood up, restless, pacing on the expensive carpet. "All right," he said. "I'll make you my offer anyway. There are a thousand designers in Tokyo today who would sacrifice a leg for the honor and the opportunity. And I don't want an immediate answer. Talk it over with your daughter." He drew a cloud of smoke into his chest, exhaled it in a burst of air. "My health is terrible. I smoke too much and my blood pressure is astronomical. The doctors advise me to stop drinking because my liver is almost nonfunctional." Another puff, a hanging cloud of smoke thinning in an unseen current of air. "I will adopt your daughter and she will take my name. Upon my death the House of Itsugi will belong to her, and to you as well. She will not be forbidden to marry, but she must retain my name." He stopped abruptly, studying Yuki's face for any sign of rejection, but she showed him nothing except gratitude.

"We both owe you a great debt, one that cannot be easily repaid. I wish I could do as you ask but I cannot."

"Do you not know what a great honor I offer her in this country where the man is everything and the woman is insignificant?"

"I'm very aware of that."

"Give it as much thought as you like," he said. "And take as long as you want. But there is something else I must tell you so you will understand me fully." He paused, lit a fresh cigarette from the remains of the first. "To the degree that I can be a great benefactor, so I can also be an enemy." He puffed on the new cigarette until the uneven coal caught. "And I will tell you now that if you or your daughter ever desert me, *ever,* you will face a cruelty like you have never seen before." His eyes studied her face as if he could see into her soul.

I believe you, Itsugi-san. But in this world we all do what we must.
She said nothing. He expected no answer. It was only when he
headed for the door to return to his old salon that she rose quietly, to
follow.

Saigon . . .
April 1975

SAM RAN ACROSS the embassy roof in the darkness, struggling to keep his footing despite the blast of air from the spinning rotors, and swung into the helicopter with the aid of a sergeant. He could hear the pilots yelling above the roar of the engines, and there was a scrambling of people helping the Ambassador across the roof. Looking out the open hatch, Sam saw hundreds of people waiting in the courtyard below, the Vietnamese who had been promised evacuation, and quite suddenly his eyes caught on the shining black hair of two oriental women.

My God, how did they get here? he thought. *I've got to get them out.* He tried to push past the marine just as the Ambassador was being brought aboard and the engines were revving up.

"I've got to get off," he yelled at the sergeant who had helped him into the helicopter. The machine had begun to lift. "Get out of my way."

"No can do, sir," the sergeant yelled, and as the helicopter rocked slightly, pulling up and away from the helipad, Sam saw the two women again, their faces illuminated by car lights. Two Vietnamese women. Not Yuki and Dawn. The chopper gained height. He could see the streets around the embassy packed with waiting people, and the whole nightmare of the city stretched out before him. He was leaving and thank God for it.

Shortly the lights gave way to the darkness of the South China Sea, and he used the time to make notes for his report to Jennings at State, short bursts of words so he would be able to remember.

"Finally out. Great relief. But Christ, the cost!"

He turned to the sergeant. "What's the schedule, Sergeant?"

"There isn't any, sir. The fleet's about an hour offshore. We'll be landing on a carrier."

And in less than an hour, with the sky lightening in the east, he saw the ships below, not only the American Navy but the thousands of civilian craft, riding low in the water and crowded with refugees. The helicopter sat down, engines off, rotors winding down. *The last trip,* Sam thought.

Sam followed the sergeant across a crowded flight deck past a briefing area and into an officer's lounge where he recognized Townsend, a young man with red hair and eyes to match who had served as an assistant in the Saigon Embassy news section for the past year. He made room for Sam on the divan.

"Stinks, doesn't it, sir?" Townsend said, and it was only then that Sam realized he was drunk.

"It was inevitable," Sam said.

"I don't mean the getting out," Townsend said, his speech slightly slurred. "I mean leaving all those people behind. They'll end up dog meat."

Dog meat, Sam thought. And he remembered the dogs circling the Chinese buried to their waists in Nanking. "How long have you been over here, Townsend?" he asked.

"Second year. I had friends. Even there in the goddamned compound, I mean. Vietnamese friends. They kept yelling at me, not angry, no, but like they didn't understand. They had worked for me. How come they weren't going to get to go? And I kept saying, 'Don't worry. We'll get you out.' And they're still there. No more evacuations. You have influence," Townsend said. "Any chance of your getting more choppers in there?"

"No," Sam said.

"I didn't think so," Townsend said. "So that's all over and done with. No use trying to make sense out of it. Just over, that's all."

It took Sam two weeks to get back to Washington, and as he sat in Jennings's office he felt temporarily displaced, as he always did at the change of cultures when he came back from the Orient. From *tuk-tuks* and pedicabs on the tropical streets of a city to a building so soundproof that he could hear nothing except the muted clicking of a distant typewriter and a secretary telling her boss that she was leaving for the day.

"It's all so damned civilized," Sam said, realizing even as he said it that Jennings was the epitome of all things civilized, even now pouring coffee into an official State Department cup, his gold cuff links properly monogrammed, his suit dark blue, as unrumpled at the end of the day as it had been at the beginning.

"Cream or sugar?" Jennings asked.

"Neither, thanks." Sam tasted the coffee. "The reports are so damned civilized," he said, suddenly obsessed with the word. "The reality is jungle and mosquitoes and American boys dead on their feet from lack of sleep or too much grass and diplomats more anxious to protect their individual asses than to find real solutions. Not to mention abandoning thousands of people we swore to protect. And I turn in a hundred pages that analyze and probe and try to draw conclusions."

"I read your report. It was quite cogent, I thought."

"As a young man said to me on the aircraft carrier just off Vietnam, 'No use in trying to make sense out of it.' I was in Shanghai when the Japanese moved into Southeast Asia, and they couldn't make a go of it any more than the French could in Vietnam. We couldn't either. We could never find a solution because we always became a part of the problem. Now we've done what we should have done. We got out."

"Time has tempered you, Mr. Cummings."

"Time has made me a realist."

"We need to discuss what you would like to do now," Jennings said. "You can continue to be an ambassador at large if you like. There will be a lot of mopping up to do in Southeast Asia."

"What do you have in China?"

"That depends," Jennings said dryly, leaning back in his chair.

"I know that look of yours," Sam said. "When you have something in mind, why do you always beat around the bush?"

"Because what I have in mind would require you to take a demotion."

"I don't give a damn about rank, Charlie. You know that."

"Suppose we do it this way. I want you to read a position paper and tell me what you think. If the project appeals to you, you can let me know."

"I'll take it to New York with me," Sam said.

"Good enough," Jennings said. "And let me know as soon as possible."

As he had his bags carried into the New York penthouse, he wondered why he had kept it all these years, but as he wandered through the rooms he knew why. Adele had left it to him in her will, and although it had been repainted many times over the years, the old Tabriz carpets were the same, and the books on the library shelves, which his father had never read. And he stood by the Chinese piano, and ran his fingers over the intricate inlay work with a smile. Ah, that damned Chinese piano, and it would have made the perfect story to have been handed down in the family, with some unknown voice generations from now awe-struck with the details.

And your great-great-grandmother had to have the whole wall taken out just to get this piano into the room.

Except that there would be no great-great-grandchildren.

He could always give the piano to the Smithsonian but only God knew what use they could make of it, or he might send it back to China, to Comrade Li, and ask that young musicians be trained on it. Arnold would have liked that idea.

He settled down in his father's old chair to read the position paper and from the first sentence he was gripped. Before the end of the first page he knew why he had been picked and what Jennings wanted him to do.

For China was still in the grip of the Cultural Revolution and the situation was highly unstable. One of the men on the periphery of power was unclaimed by the hierarchy but of sufficient power to remain unpurged, an old man named Comrade Li. Included in the papers from Washington was a picture of a gathering in Beijing and the unmistakable features of the lean man Sam had known in the thirties. The camera had caught him in a characteristic scowl of contempt. If Mao represented the soul of the new China, Li represented the reproving Marxist conscience, violently opposed to the intrusion of the West.

Sam picked up the telephone, called Jennings in Washington.

"Well," Jennings said. "You read the material. What do you think?"

"I'll be frank with you," Sam said. "I'm tempted, but it may not be in the best interest of the United States to send me to deal with Li."

"If we didn't think you could do it, I wouldn't have suggested it," Jennings said. "I have all your background with him during the thirties. You got along well together."

"It's apparent you don't have everything," Sam said. "I developed a great respect for Li and his convictions. And if he's opposed to what we're offering, you can be damned sure there's something wrong with the deal."

"Precisely what are you saying?" Jennings said.

"I can't guarantee to be a team player in this one," Sam said. "I can't go to China and try to change his position until I know what he's thinking. And I can tell you now, the odds are better than even that I'll agree with him."

"But you can't know that until you talk with him. Correct?"

"True."

"I'd like to make arrangements for you to meet him in Shanghai. Just talk to him. If you decide that you can work to modify his position toward the West, then by all means stay and work with him. If you can't, come home. How soon can you leave for Shanghai?"

"How long do you need to set up the meeting?"

"Thirty days."

"Then set it up."

Shanghai . . .
July 1981

HE HAD MEANT to stay in China no more than a year at the outside, but on a hot summer day six years later, as he rode with Comrade Li through the streets of Shanghai in the backseat of a small car, with the latest dispatch from Charlie Jennings in his pocket, he realized that the time had passed in a blur and his work here was finished. Li sat beside him, thin as a stork's leg, suffering from emphysema and still puffing a cigarette.

The car moved through streets crowded with bicycles making way for a yellow and white electric tram, and the masses of people all seemed to be dressed in the unofficial blue uniforms of the People's Republic. So much was unchanged and so much was dramatically different, he thought.

"It's hard to recognize the Shanghai we knew in the thirties," Li said, as if reading his mind.

"You accomplished your miracle," Sam said. "You preserved the city just as it was, a museum piece, and you changed the lives of all the people in it. No more starving poor, no refugees freezing to death on the streets. You've brought stability here."

"Nothing is stable," Li said, crushing out his cigarette. And at that moment, as if to illustrate his words, the car went past the entrance drive to the mansion where Sam had lived with Charlotte a lifetime ago, and a sign identified it as a CHILDREN'S CULTURAL PALACE. The lawns were filled with young boys doing calisthenics, but for a moment he imagined he could see the ranks of servants gathered at the front portico, Majordomo at the head of the line.

The car pulled beneath the porte cochere of the Jinjiang Hotel, a newer hostelry far removed from the Bund. "Come in and have tea with me, Ha Li," Sam said in Shanghainese, using the expression of friendship.

"I might as well," Li said, and they entered the richly appointed lobby and went up to Sam's suite, where the servants brought tea and rice cakes. But Li contented himself with another cigarette. "I suppose you know I am retiring from the government," he said. "I helped the country survive the Gang of Four and there are good hands taking care of things. And I will write my memoirs and warn against the capitalist drift I see in China."

"Face it," Sam said with a smile. "You helped save your country from starvation. And capitalism is no threat to China. You will simply absorb those parts of it you need and spit out the rest."

"Perhaps you're right."

Sam sipped his tea. "I've been offered the position of American Ambassador to Japan."

Now it was Li's turn to smile. "A strange world," he said. "You destroyed the Japanese in war and then taught them a new civilized kind of competition, which will see your country swallowed up if you're not careful." He was quiet a moment. "Personally, I will miss you, Ha Cummings. You are one of the few Americans who understand that we are noted for more than Ping-Pong and acrobats."

"I haven't decided to take the position yet," he said. "Perhaps I have grown accustomed to arguing with you."

"It is a sign of trust and affection that I will argue with you," Li said. "Personally, I prefer to smother foreigners with politeness. It takes less energy away from my real work."

When he was alone Sam read the cables again and remembered Alcott and the old man's love for China. And Sam was half tempted to get in touch with Jennings before the week was out and ask to spend the last assignment of his professional life here, for it was rare to be present at the rebirth of a country and he felt very much at home in China.

He sat down by the window to browse through the *Asian Wall Street Journal*. And then his eyes fell on a story datelined Tokyo, a piece about Japanese fashions and a mother-daughter team that had broken away from the House of Itsugi and would be showing their first collection in Paris in October. And for the first time in years a bit of the irrational crept into his thinking. *Yuki never could quite throw off the belief that the kami were real, and perhaps she was right.* He picked up the telephone, placed a call to Washington. Hours later the call came through and Jennings was on the line.

"Are you going to take Japan?" Jennings said hopefully.

"I am going to leave this in the hands of the *kami*," Sam said. "How soon can I get Senate confirmation?"

"September," Jennings said. "The only hitch might be your opinion on the trade balance."

"That's simple," Sam said. "Something for something, a quid pro quo, no dumping, no unfair advantages on either side."

"When would you be prepared to take over in Tokyo?"

"October. On my way to take my post, I want to go to Paris. I want to throw a party for a new Japanese designer making her debut there as well as for other designers and the press."

"No better way to start than with positive public relations. You'll want to invite the Japanese Ambassador to France, I'm sure. Let me put protocol on it."

"Fine," Sam said.

"I'll let the President know and set the whole thing in motion," Jennings said. "Congratulations and thank you."

"My pleasure, Charlie," Sam said.

Paris . . .
October 1981

YUKI STOOD ON the third floor of the mansion in Montmartre and looked down on the lights of the city shining through the chill October night. *I am finally here on my own,* Yuki thought. *Dawn's collection is being put together on the stage of the Opera House and I will get past the enemy who is trying to stop us.* And once again she sat down at the table and listed the three names. ITSUGI. KANAO. ARMAND. The names loomed large in her mind. But there was no new meaning to be found in them.

She would talk to Armand again, and if it took more money to free her order from the mill, then she would pay it. And if it meant using Dawn's new friend Trish Devane to follow her journalistic leads in search of the small crack that had to exist somewhere in this scheme to ruin her, then she would do that. She would find a way.

She finished the scheduling sheet she was working on and was downstairs walking past Segawa's computer room when he called out to her. "Hong Kong is on the line," he said. "Do you want to take it?"

It would be Liu again, she thought, asking about the delayed

· 546 ·

shipment of the materials. It took very little to worry him to distraction.

Yuki took the telephone from him, spoke in Chinese to a distraught Mr. Liu. "I regret having to disturb you," he said. "But I have obligations to many employees, and if I have no work to keep them busy, the unskilled will go hungry and my irreplaceable cutters will immediately go to work for my competition."

"I don't understand," Yuki said. "Why are you worried?"

"Because of the item in the *International Herald Tribune* this morning," he said.

"What item?"

"A story that you will not be filling orders for your collection."

Her heart skipped a beat. She kept her voice even, strong. "I see. Did the newspaper state a reason?"

"Only that the fabrics had been accidentally ruined."

"I'm glad you called," Yuki said. "I can put an end to the rumors. I will be late with my orders, but to make sure that you won't lose your people, I'll transfer two hundred fifty thousand American dollars to your bank in the next three hours."

Liu was immediately calmer. "I apologize for disturbing you," he said. "I hope you understand that my responsibilities forced me to call."

"Think nothing of it," Yuki said. She put down the telephone, aware of Segawa's disapproval.

"It's not customary to pay so much before any work is done," he said.

"Someone is saying that we won't be going into production. Paying so much in advance will put an end to the stories in Hong Kong. Now we have to take care of it here before it kills all our orders. I want you to get a copy of today's *Herald Tribune* and, whatever the story is, issue a denial."

"I will," he said, subdued.

She called Trish, arranged to meet her at Le Petit Chien, and Trish arrived bursting with information. "I've been hoping for a chance to meet you," she said. "I was about to call Dawn when you called me," she said. "I located the reporter who did the story. He said Armand called him personally to say that a water leak had ruined your order but that customers could be reassured that there was no other damage."

"Armand?" Yuki said, shocked. "Why is he speaking for the mill when he said he had sold it and had nothing to do with it anymore?"

"Does he have anything against you personally?" Trish asked.

"Nothing."

"He must have some reason."

"What used to be his mill produces most of Itsugi-san's fabrics."

"Would Itsugi put that kind of pressure on him?"

"I don't know," Yuki said. "But I think I've waited long enough. I'm going to get a lawyer."

"Can you give me anything to counter the story with in the meantime?"

"You can print that I've paid the factory in Hong Kong a quarter million dollars in advance with the full assurance that we will go into production."

"Fine," Trish said. "It'll be a holding action until you have something more definite. I'll be seeing Armand tonight, at a party. I'll see what I can find out."

Yuki stopped by the Opera House to find Dawn occupied with rehearsal, but Emile was sitting in the back row and she told him everything that had happened.

"And what are you going to do?" Emile said.

"Arrange to fight," she said. "Get me an appointment with a good lawyer as soon as possible."

Sex and money, Trish thought. *They run through the whole industry like an undercurrent. Money is most important, of course, but sex runs it a close second.* She had no doubt that both would be involved in the answer to this riddle. She decided to make a few discreet telephone calls.

After the showing that night Claude picked her up to drive her to a party at the Georges V, where Trish was prepared to pull a bluff on Armand. The gala for the evening was a benefit for some obscure disease, a Monte Carlo night when dinner cost a thousand American dollars a plate and the guests were given a million dollars in play money to gamble at roulette, chemin de fer, craps, poker, and blackjack. At the end of the evening there would be an auction of exotic donated gifts with bids in bogus money won at the tables. She was there to do a column on the celebrities present.

She entered the ballroom on Claude's arm and her eyes swept the crowd until she located Armand in black tie, his aging wife in a white

Valentino gown that matched her hair. On the other side of the room, dressed in a voluptuous red gown and accompanied by its designer, was the divine Sakura. *Fascinating*, Trish thought, for again and again Armand's eyes drifted toward that fiery red dress.

Claude noted her interest in Armand. "It's rumored he will be given the Legion of Honor next month."

"How marvelous," Trish said. "I'll see how much he wants it."

"Can you tell me what's going on?" Claude said.

"I'll let you know by the end of the evening."

They were seated at a table with American jet-setters from Texas. Ordinarily, Trish would have found them amusing, especially the blond wife of an oil magnate who was always good for a quote or two. But tonight Trish was more interested in watching Armand making a special point of ignoring Sakura, who was also going out of her way to avoid him.

After dinner was over and the obligatory speeches had been made by the charity officials, the golden envelopes were distributed to each of the diners, filled with a million dollars in elaborately engraved bogus bills. Each envelope also contained a pledge card for the charity and a list of the prizes to be auctioned promptly at midnight.

This was Paris at her best, Trish thought, as she surveyed the glittering crowd, the rich and the famous, the most beautiful women in the most elegant gowns the world had to offer, the sleekest men, groomed from birth to deal with inherited riches. As she wandered among the gaming tables she knew the code of the very rich: Their secrets would be treated as such, they would protect each other. Trish knew her job was not to question anything but simply to report the glittering surfaces.

She spoke to dozens of people, sat down at the blackjack tables to play for a while, but she managed to keep an eye on Armand, who had drifted away from his wife and was sitting at the roulette table, a stack of chips in front of him. And nearby, at a poker table, Sakura had possession of the dice and was on a run.

I have a feeling that this isn't going to be your evening, Armand, Trish thought.

Trish was dealt a pair of aces, split them with a hundred thousand dollars on each, nodded to the dealer, who dealt two cards facedown atop the aces. She held her breath as if she were playing with real money, exploded with inward joy when the cards were flipped over to reveal two blackjacks. She was now a half million ahead.

She drifted to the roulette table, where Armand was having no success at all. He grew angrier with each spin of the wheel as the rake removed his chips from the table.

"No luck, I see," she said right behind him.

He glanced up at her sourly, then played another fifty thousand dollars on four numbers while Trish simply placed five hundred thousand on the red. The wheel was spun, the ball flipped into the opposite direction to skitter across the holes until the wheel was finally slow enough for it to settle.

"*Cinq, rouge,*" the croupier called out. Trish's money was doubled. Armand's was raked away.

"Why don't we have a drink?" Trish asked Armand, but he did not even bother to look at her as he concentrated on the numbers.

"I don't have time," he said. "I'm down by half a million and I want to recoup my losses."

"Gambling bores me," Trish said. "I'll give you a half million of my stake just to get me a champagne and talk a few minutes."

Armand thought a moment, then pushed back from the table. "All right," he said. "But only because they're going to auction off a childhood picture of Coco in a silver frame. My wife was a close friend of hers and I'm determined she's going to have the picture."

"That's very sentimental of you," she said.

She found a quiet corner away from the tables, sat down on a love seat near a screen of living plants to wait for him. Armand came across the polished wooden floor carrying the glasses of champagne. He gave her one and accepted the half million with a nod.

"What do you want to talk about?" he said.

Trish leaned back, sipped the champagne, smiled. "How much money do you think the picture in the silver frame will bring?"

He shrugged. "The bulk of the money will go for the big prizes," he said. "The picture should go for a million or less."

"Then you won't have any problem," Trish said. "I'll give you the rest of my money. That's another million and a half. More than enough."

His eyes narrowed. "Why?"

"Because there are no prizes I want," she said. "I've been to Tahiti and I don't care for the tropics. The Concorde is simply transportation. I consider the million and a half to be a carrot."

"What are you talking about?"

"The money is the reward for the information I want," she said cryptically. "Which means, of course, that there will be trouble for you if you don't give it to me."

He snorted derisively. "This is play money you're dealing with. And you can't make trouble for me."

"I'm not playing," Trish said soberly. "And you've already made the trouble for yourself." She looked toward the crap table, where Sakura was laughing. Obviously winning. "Let me tell you what I know about her, Armand. I made a few calls today to confirm a suspicion. You've given the divine Sakura a fortune in jewels, furs, and money in the past month. You had to sell your mill to keep your wife from finding out what you're doing, because if she knew, she would divorce you, and you wouldn't have any family or fortune left. Your Legion of Honor would fly out the window." She paused for effect. His face was very pale. "Is Sakura blackmailing you?"

"It's all a lie," he said quietly. "There's not a word of truth to any of it. You can't prove a damned thing."

She finished the rest of her champagne. "If she's not blackmailing you, then all your gifts have been voluntary."

"I don't have to listen to this," he said. He started to rise.

"If you leave, then I'll interview your wife and get her reaction to the list of gifts you've made to this very sensual and expensive young lady."

Armand sank back into his chair, sweating now, subdued. "Why are you doing this? What do you want out of me? Money?"

"Of course not," Trish said. "I told you what I want. Information."

"About what?" he said, blotting his face with a handkerchief.

"What prompted you to release a story about the House of Dawn?" Trish asked. "What do you have against them?"

"Nothing," he said.

"Then why set out to ruin them?"

"I hope they will not be ruined."

She leaned forward, her face only inches from his. "Who bought the mill?"

He shook his head unhappily. "I have never wanted anything in my life as much as I want Sakura," he said. "You can't know how it is."

"I don't care how it is," Trish said. "I want to know what's going on, Armand."

He folded the linen handkerchief, replaced it in his pocket. "I sold the mill because I need the money and now I have to make sure I can collect it."

"I want the name of the buyer."

"If I reveal it, I lose the deal on the mill."

"If you don't reveal it, you lose your wife."

"I need time to think."

"How much time?"

"Forty-eight hours."

"That won't do. Twenty-four. Do we have a deal?"

"I'll let you know tomorrow."

"All right."

She handed him the golden envelope with the auction money in it. "I'll talk with you tomorrow."

"I can promise nothing," he said.

She watched him go back to the tables and realized that she pitied this man. *You'll cooperate with me because you haven't any choice. But you'll lose in the end because the divine Sakura will pick you clean before she moves on and who's to say whether your wife will be content with what is left?*

At midnight a bell rang, ending the play, and the auction commenced, with dinners at Tour d'Argent going to men who had chefs every bit as good in their own kitchens, and Concorde excursions to families who had fleets of jets, and diamond solitaires to women whose maids spent one day a week cleaning the family diamonds.

Armand bought the silver frame with Coco Chanel's picture for a million five.

You're not in the clear yet, Armand, she thought. *Not until you give me what I want.*

She had an early breakfast with Yuki the next day at a cafe in Montmartre and told her of the evening. "I'll hear from him by tonight," Trish said. She lit a cigarette, looked out at the street and the unexpected mildness of the autumn morning. "He'll come through with the name because he has no choice."

Yuki drank her tea. "I'm not powerless," she said. "I've asked Emile to arrange for a lawyer and I'll talk to Armand this afternoon."

"Fine." Trish checked her watch. "I have to run," she said. "I have three interviews before the first collection of the day. I'll call you this evening. I'm dying to know what you find out."

Yuki watched Trish dashing off toward her car, but her thoughts were on Armand.

Who was he fronting for? Kanao, out to avenge his father? Perhaps, for vengeance was a virtue of the old Japan Kanao loved. Or Itsugi. Hate mixed with love there, an explosive mixture.

Yuki found a large bouquet of flowers in her office at the Montmartre house and a note in a handwriting she recognized instantly. "I couldn't find anything as beautiful as the Shanghai blossoms," it said. "As the new American Ambassador to Japan, I want to invite you to a party at my hotel following your collection. Please call the number below. I want to hear your voice." It was signed "Sam."

She held the note pressed between her hands as if it warmed her. *I never thought to hear from you again, Cummings-san.* She sat down and composed herself, then dialed the number. He answered.

"Cummings-san," she said.

He laughed. "I hoped it would be you," he said.

"The flowers are beautiful."

"I'm so pleased you like them," he said. "Now, I won't take no for the party. It's all arranged."

"We will be delighted," she said. "Dawn and I."

"And lunch, the day after tomorrow. I'll pick you up at your Montmartre house at twelve. Please don't say no."

"Thank you for asking me," she said. "And I'll see you then."

When she put down the telephone she found her hands were trembling slightly. She stood in front of a full-length mirror and wondered how she would look to him. He had thought of her as beautiful when she was young. But now she was in her sixties. She thought she had aged well, but would he?

Vanity, she thought briefly, then shook her head. *Not simple vanity, no, far more than that.* But she did not have time to think about him now. For very shortly she would be seeing Armand and that meeting would require all the calm she could muster.

Sakura stood against the background of the Seine, waiting, smoking a cigarette. A young director with a white Chiclets smile and barely tolerant eyes was lining up his shot, gesturing toward the photographer with the heavy minicam saddled over his shoulder and the battery pack around his waist to move farther to the right.

The director clapped his hands to get the attention of the men holding the rectangular aluminum reflectors. "Okay, guys, let's get into position. A little more to the right, André. Right there. Yeah. Hold it. Now, Sakura, just come down along the sidewalk, and when you get to the lamppost look out toward the river, then make a full, slow turn, pensive, and walk right toward the camera."

Yuki watched from the sidewalk cafe. She picked up her glass of wine as they started the music from the tape recorder and Sakura came down the sidewalk wearing one of Dawn's most elegant creations, shoulders back, floating rather than walking, the folds in the blue silk dress hanging perfectly.

Yuki raised the glass to her lips, watched Armand as he sat on the terrace of the next cafe, his eyes never leaving the willowy girl, and she felt a great pity for him. He had lost weight since she had seen him last, slimming down radically in order to wear a modish Italian suit without lapels, and he had spent a fortune on a hairpiece so skillfully done it had a perpetual ruffled look built into it, as if it had just been touched by a breeze. He was trying to relive his youth through that gamin who now stood by the lamppost, no expression on her perfect face to distract from the dress as the photographer moved the minicam in for his pickup shots.

Yuki left the money on the table for the wine, threaded her way through the tables and up the stone stairs to the terrace where Armand sat, concentrating on the shoot. When at last she stood at the table, her presence unavoidable, he flinched slightly, startled, then looked back toward the river, as if he did not want to face her.

"I'm sorry," he said flatly. "Business is business. There's nothing I can do."

"May I sit down?"

"Suit yourself."

She sat, ordered coffee from the waiter. "She's a very beautiful girl," she said.

"If you're here to threaten me, it won't do any good," he said. "I love her."

"I have no doubt that you do," Yuki said. She looked straight ahead, watching the photographer coaxing a fresh pose. "But love is no excuse for dishonor. And I don't intend to pay for your obsession."

"You can't—"

"Listen to me. My whole life is at stake and I won't accept what you're offering. So if you hold to your position, you had better be ready to uproot yourself completely. Because I will see that Sakura has so many lucrative assignments in Asia that she can't turn them down. So you can prepare to leave your children and your grandchildren as well as your wife."

"I'll do what I have to. I intend to marry her."

"Take a good look at her," Yuki said. "A realistic look." Sakura's face was backlighted now, a perfect profile. "You have no chance unless you have an endless stream of money. Because your wife will clean you out with a divorce settlement and you will have my suit to deal with as well. So you can lose everything, including Sakura."

He glanced once more at the girl standing by the water and then, with a heavy sigh, looked down at his old man's hands. "What do you want from me?"

"The truth. Are my fabrics truly damaged?"

"I don't know," Armand said. "I was told to make the statement to the press."

"By whom?"

He picked up his glass, his hand unsteady. "If I tell you the truth, will you leave me out of it?"

"If I can."

"Kanao," he said quietly. "But there's more to it than you might think. He wanted to buy the mill to revenge himself on you, but the selling price was far too steep for him to handle by himself. So he went to Itsugi, who was bitter against you and your daughter, and Itsugi agreed to buy the mill with Kanao for six million dollars. Kanao made the contract with me but suddenly it became apparent that Itsugi's collection was in trouble and he didn't have the money. So now it's strictly Kanao's deal."

"I see," Yuki said.

"He's paid three million so far. And I need the rest of the money." He was forced to set the glass down; his fingers were trembling. "I have nothing against you. I apologize that I have caused you trouble. Will you forgive me, madame?"

"You have cost me far too much for that. You have my pity but not my forgiveness."

"I must ask you a question. Does that woman have any love for me?"

"My opinion is unimportant."

He looked toward the Seine again as the sun broke free of the clouds and the water turned instantly blue. "I want it anyway."

"You know the answer or you wouldn't have asked the question,"

Yuki said. "You can't claim her with love. As a model she's more aware of the passage of time, more afraid of it than even you are. Your gifts are payment and she flatters you. But she knows there are immensely rich men who can spend a million dollars a week on her and never run out of money, men who are just as anxious to collect her for their reasons as you are for love. And your money won't last that long."

"That's an answer without mercy," he said.

"Life is a process without mercy."

"And what will you do now?" he said.

"Anything I must," she said.

At the Opera House, Yuki ran into Trish on the steps as she was just coming out. "I was looking for you," Trish said. "I left a note with Dawn."

"And what did you say in it?"

"Delicious gossip," Trish said. "I found out this morning. Sakura has another man she sees when Armand is exhausted and has to have his rest. He's an Italian count, young, rich, handsome, and sexy. Armand has become a running joke with the in crowd. Claude's putting together pictures, facts, all the when's and where's."

"I just saw Armand. He told me Kanao bought the mill."

"My God," Trish said. "Would you like me to tell Armand that he's being cuckolded? He deserves it."

"No," Yuki said. "Nature will take revenge on him. But if it's possible, I would like to know Kanao Ito's current financial condition."

"There's something terribly frightening about that man," Trish said with an involuntary shudder. "He's like ice."

"No," Yuki said. "Ice melts with warmth."

"Caution noted," Trish said. "I'll get back to you."

Onstage, Dawn was working with the director to get a particular amber glow to one scene. She waved at her mother from a distance as Yuki sought out Emile in the fifth row back. She told him what had happened with Armand. "I would like you to keep this to yourself for the time being," she said.

"All right. I've talked with my lawyer," he said under his breath. "He will meet you at his office as soon as you can get there."

"Now? It's after five."

"Henri will see you."

"I need to go by my house for records."

"Segawa sent a printout by messenger to Henri this afternoon." He put his hand on Yuki's arm. "Henri is the best lawyer in Paris, but even with your new information, your problem is not going to be easily solved."

"I don't expect miracles," Yuki said.

"Would you feel more comfortable if I went with you?"

"Thank you, no," Yuki said. "I appreciate the offer, but I prefer to handle it alone."

Henri Broussard occupied a suite of offices in a modern building near the American Embassy, and when Yuki first saw him she knew she was in excellent hands. He was a tall, lean, restless man in his forties and his whole attitude seemed to deny the possibility of failure. With an elbow resting on his desk and the pads of his fingertips touching the sides of his face, he looked directly at Yuki. "Now, madame, I read the material you sent to me and I know some of the rumors that are floating about, but I would like you to tell me precisely what happened between you and Armand."

"It's very simple," she said. "I entered into a contract with Armand's textile factory in Lyon to produce thousands of yards of fabric to be sent to a factory in Hong Kong."

"I see. And you have a legally executed contract?"

She took it from her purse. He unfolded his reading glasses, put them on, glanced at the pages of the contract. "All pretty standard."

"Yes."

"And you gave him a check, a down payment?"

"I did." She gave him the canceled check.

"And then the fabric was not delivered on schedule."

"That's correct. He told me today that he sold the factory to Kanao Ito. He claims that the contracts are no longer his responsibility."

"That's questionable," Broussard said. He made a note on the paper. "But that's one of the things we will have to find out." The pen was poised to write again. "Now, the deposit for the order was given to him?"

"No. It was made out to Guillam et Cie in Lyon. And last week I received the deposit back." She removed it from her purse and gave it to him.

He examined it carefully. "I can't make out the signature. But apparently the signee is the company treasurer. You've done well not to cash the check. In effect, you would have nullified the contract."

"I don't believe that the fabric was water damaged," she said. "I want Kanao forced to open the warehouse to inspection."

He capped his Mont Blanc, put it in his shirt pocket, then leaned back in the chair and stared at the paper thoughtfully. "We will file suit against both Armand Meyer and Kanao Ito for this failure to honor a contract."

"Excuse me, Mr. Broussard," she said. "But how long will all this take?"

"We can't be sure of that," he said. "French justice moves with excruciating slowness, but I think you will find that it is a system that guarantees fairness."

"And suppose that at the end of all this litigation, we win. Exactly how much money are we talking about?"

"I can't say for sure," he said. His shoulders made a slight Gallic shrug. "There's no way to determine this in advance."

"But there is no way it can cover the amount of money I have put into promotion, or the lost sales on a line that can't be produced. And I take it that you work on a contingency basis?"

"In this case, most certainly," he said. "But you're quite correct. It is doubtful that compensation will be adequate to cover all the areas you mention."

She thanked him for his time, told him she would be in touch, and when she reached the lobby of his building she used a public telephone to call Emile at the Opera House. And while she was waiting she had difficulty containing the fury she felt, and the desperation. *You will not defeat me, Kanao,* she thought. *I will not be defeated by some technicalities of the law.*

Emile came on the line. "How did it go?" he said.

"Not well," Yuki said. "I want you to do something for me. Hire a private investigator. I want to know if our fabric exists and if it has been damaged in any way, and I want the answer by tonight."

"I'll arrange it."

"I want to talk with this investigator personally and privately. If you will arrange some discreet place."

"Certainly. It will be done."

Yuki had a confidential meeting with H. Chyka, the private investigator, at a small bistro near Les Halles where their privacy was assured. He wore a rumpled wool suit and thick-lensed glasses. He sipped black coffee across the table from her. "I think I have the answers that you want," he said.

"My fabrics . . ."

"Your order was completed and is quite safe," he said, lighting a cigar. "I sent a man posing as a government inspector who wandered about the place quite freely, asking questions about production. It always panics the mill directors to think that tax information is being collected."

"Has Kanao made himself known to the mill managers?" she asked. "Do they know why my order is being held there undelivered?"

"No one there has the slightest idea what has happened except that the ownership of the mill has changed hands and the employees are uneasy about their jobs. And no, Kanao has not visited the mill or made himself known."

"What do you think will happen to my order? What will they do with the material?"

"I can only guess, madame," Chyka said. "If I were Kanao, I would hang on to the fabrics long enough to make them useless to you. And then, when you filed suit against me, I would have the material delivered to you, and in any court battle I would be properly repentant for the unhappy situation that resulted from a change in ownership. And I would pay whatever penalty the court imposed, knowing that it would be insufficient to help you."

"Have you seen the mill? Can you describe it to me?"

He shrugged as if unsure how to answer. "Typical, I would say. Headquartered in an old château with a former *salles d'impression* used now by the designers to form their printing blocks for hand work, a courtyard showroom for remnants, and the mill itself producing a million yards a year, mostly fine fabrics. And then there is a shipping warehouse. That's about it."

"And my fabrics are in that warehouse?"

"Yes."

She was silent a moment. "And what would happen if I hired someone to steal my own fabrics?"

"You would risk going to prison," he said, lighting his cigar. "Your enemy can always claim mitigating circumstances. But there are no excuses for larceny in the eyes of the law."

"If I decide to do it, can you arrange it for me?"

He tapped an index finger against the cigar. He thought it through. "How much do you owe them for the fabrics?"

"About a half million dollars."

He pinched his nose. His forehead wrinkled with thought. "The fabrics would need to be taken from the warehouse, put through customs at some airport, and shipped to Hong Kong. Is that approximately correct?"

"That's exactly correct."

He exhaled little bursts of smoke between pursed lips. "It would be expensive to try. With no guarantees."

"I face certain ruin otherwise."

"For my fee I would need a quarter million francs up front."

"I want you to prepare for it," she said. "But you are not to follow through until you hear from me. I'll give you a check now."

"No checks. Cash. Tomorrow."

"Very well."

She did not tell Dawn what she was doing. She did not even see her daughter before she went to bed. She lay there and listened to the drumming of an autumn rain on the mansard roofs. *I am gambling everything again,* she thought. *I've spent my whole life gambling on one thing or another, just ahead of calamity. But this time, if I fail, I could go to prison.*

During the showing of the Saint Laurent collection in a Tuileries pavilion, Trish surveyed the seating sections of the Americans, British, and French. Immediately across the runway and to one side was the Japanese contingent, and she recognized Kanao and his wife sitting close to the runway. Trish could not read Kanao's face, but his wife was excited and in constant motion, using opera glasses, occasionally touching her husband's arm when she saw something she liked on the runway.

The last item was, as always, a wedding gown, lacy yet modern, and, to the applause and shouts of a standing crowd, the designer was coaxed out onto the runway by his bevy of mannequins and the show was over.

When the lights came up Trish remained seated, watching the Itos as they headed backstage. Obviously they had been invited to the champagne reception. She took the time to open the envelope Claude had thrust into her hand just before she came in.

Word from my banking people has it that friend Kanao is about to lose his ass. A large deal gone sour, they think. Scrambling to recoup.

C—

She folded the note, put it in her purse.

She moved backstage, where the buyers were having a look at the mannequins and the garments. She fixed her attention on the Itos as they stood examining a layered silk frock, the diminutive wife asking questions in Japanese that Kanao translated into French. It seemed to Trish that there was at least fifty thousand dollars on her arms, her back, and her shapely neck, perhaps fifteen thousand for the couture Yamamoto frock, custom shoes, spike heels, solid gold fingernails and glittering necklaces and multiple bracelets. She turned slightly and Trish saw the marquise diamond in one ring, and the chinchilla cape draped over one arm, and she abandoned her calculations altogether.

There's a part of the Japanese iceberg's financial problem, she thought.

Trish examined Kanao. He was a fiercely handsome Japanese, a tall man with an almost samurai aspect to him, wearing his expensive navy-blue business suit as if it were armor. *You're right, Yuki. Not ice, cold steel,* she thought as she approached him, addressing them by name, introducing herself while the wife looked at her with inquisitive eyes, the pupils such a deep brown they appeared to be black.

"I'm very pleased to meet you," Kanao said in clipped English, and then explained to his wife who this *gaijin* woman was. The wife's eyes flashed instant respect and an overweening vanity, which Trish had encountered so often that it had become commonplace.

"If you have the time, I'd like the two of you to join me at the Crillon for cocktails," Trish said. "I'd like a Japanese view of the collections."

"I don't have a great deal of interest in fashions," Kanao said. "But I'm sure that Yoriko will be delighted to answer any questions for you."

The wife chattered all the way to the Crillon. When they were seated in the bar, Trish asked her a series of questions meant to disarm her and get the words flowing, and then she dropped in a question designed more to evoke a response from Kanao than his wife. "Do you look forward to the House of Dawn collection?" she said.

She fancied she saw a slight flicker in Kanao's eyes but she could not swear to it because he immediately translated the question for his wife, who went into a flurry of words, obviously urging him to ask a question that he was reluctant to translate, nudging his arm with her bejeweled hand. He tensed, moved his arm away from her, and made Trish wonder what happened when Yoriko pushed this volatile man once too often.

"My wife is determined to attend the House of Dawn collection," he said. "But we have heard that tickets are very scarce."

"I should think a man of your standing would have no trouble getting invitations," Trish said.

Yoriko was chattering again and Trish saw the spark of irritation in his eyes. Trish was sure Kanao was being pushed to ask Trish to get invitations for them, and Trish was equally certain that a man of Kanao's pride would never put that question into English.

"Are you here just for the collections?" Trish asked him, allowing him to avoid his wife's demands.

"No," Kanao said. "I'm here on business, but my wife came for the fashions."

"May I ask what kind of business you're in?"

"Investments," Kanao said. "Real estate."

"Fashions change but real estate endures," Trish said lightly. She gave a subtle sign to her waiter, who immediately informed her that she was wanted on the telephone. She used the opportunity to excuse herself, thanking the Itos for their time and leaving them with a bottle of champagne.

She did another collection in the afternoon, that of a minor French designer whose collection was mediocre. She skipped drinks with some writers from Rome and went back to her apartment and wrote the first draft of a column on Saint Laurent, along with the lead paragraph on the mediocre collection. She looked up as Claude came in and shed his coat, then mixed martinis, placed one in front of her, and carried his to the long divan.

He waited until she signaled that she was available for conversation by abandoning her work and moving to her favorite chair with her martini. "What calls today?" she asked.

"At least a dozen invitations," he said. "I've penciled in those on your calendar I thought you'd take, regretted a couple, put the rest on a check list."

"Tell me everything you know about Kanao's finances."

"My contact at Suissebanc says that Kanao had a credit line of five hundred million yen there and that he's used it to the limit. He's applied for more but it's not immediately available to him. She says that he's overextended himself in Tokyo and here as well."

Of course your contact would be a woman, she thought. "Interesting," she said. "Then if he still owes three million dollars on the mill, he may be hard put to come up with it."

"My contact says he is really scrambling around," Claude said. "But she's convinced he'll come up with it one way or another."

"That's too bad," Trish said. "We can't count on his defaulting." She looked at her watch, moaned slightly. The time had evaporated and she had only a half hour to get to the next collection. She put on her shoes, checked her makeup, refreshed her lipstick. And thought of Kanao's eyes.

When they arrived back at their suite in the Plaza Athénée, Yoriko stopped in the spacious sitting room, one golden fingernail poised on her shapely chin. "You'll have to call the manager again," she said to Kanao. "He promised me a peach-colored chair that would not clash with the wallpaper." She draped her fur on a divan, went over to a small and elegant desk, pushed a couple of papers aside until she found what she was looking for. "I just wish that my esteemed father were here," she said. "There was no door he could not open for his family."

Yoriko handed him a list of the collections to which they had not received invitations. "The Valentino and the Kenzo are the most important of the regular shows I want to see," she said. And then, with no change in the pitch of her voice: "For the House of Dawn collection, I want the seats to be on the aisle and near the runway, where the turns take place," she said. "I don't want to be at the back of the house."

Leaving the suite, he stopped at the floor desk and handed the list to a middle-aged French concierge. "I would much appreciate your handling this for me," he said. "Confidentially, if you can't find more than a single good seat for most of these collections, I won't mind. But I do want two excellent seats for the House of Dawn collection."

The concierge squinted at the list, nodded, then frowned again. "I can get good seats for Valentino at four hundred apiece. The Kenzos will cost seven hundred and fifty for the pair."

"Please take care of it."

"The Dawn collection is an entirely different matter. There are no tickets available for that showing."

"Have the invitations been issued yet?"

"I don't believe so," the concierge said. "They will be delivered by messenger when they're ready. But considering the rumors about the collection, the magnitude of the showing, if and when anybody decides to sell an invitation, it will probably bring at least three thousand American."

"I don't care how you get the tickets or what they cost," Kanao said. "You get them for me and I'll give you a bonus of five hundred dollars."

The concierge was not impressed with the figure. He shrugged. "I'll do my best, sir."

Kanao went for a walk through the *arrondissement,* enjoying the fall colors in the trees and the elegance of the district, but his mind soon moved back to business. He stopped at a telephone and dialed a number.

The telephone was answered by a woman. He identified himself and asked to speak to Itsugi, then waited an uncomfortably long time before the woman came back to the telephone, her voice apologetic. "I'm sorry, sir. Itsugi-san does not wish to speak to you at present."

"He doesn't wish to speak to me?" he repeated, incredulous. "Tell him to pick up the telephone now, this moment."

"He doesn't wish to speak to you, sir," she said.

He slammed down the telephone, headed back to the hotel, trying to control the rage within him. He was met by the concierge. *"C'est fini.* I have the other tickets, but I called the House of Dawn's business office and was told that unfortunately neither you nor the Lady Ito are on the list and that there will be no additional seats."

"Impossible."

"I should think that for such a popular collection, there will be standing room. I imagine I might get two such spaces for two hundred apiece."

"See what you can do," Kanao said, frustrated, and prepared himself to face his wife.

She was dressed in a red silk robe, her hair bound up in a turban. She sat at her dressing table examining her eyes in the mirror, putting on artificial lashes. She glanced at him briefly.

He poured himself a scotch over two cubes of ice. "I have the tickets to Valentino and Kenzo," he said.

With the steady fingers of a surgeon, she affixed lashes to her left eye. "They're simple to get. But what are the seat numbers for the House of Dawn showing?"

"Seats for that collection are not available," he said. He sat down by the window.

She fixed the second strip of eyelashes into place and blinked at herself to make sure they were secure. Then she turned to face him. "Not available, *ne?*" she said. "So the Baron is unable to get tickets that anybody else can get."

"Let it rest," he said.

She stood up, unwrapped the turban, let it fall to the floor while she began to brush her long black hair. "I should have known better than to ask you in the first place," she said, the tempo of the brush increasing. "You have too much pride to follow through like ordinary people. I told you to make a request of the fashion writer. But I know you didn't do it."

The rage was rising within him. He made one final attempt to control it. "I don't want you to say another word," he said, his voice as cold as the ice rattling in his glass. "You will not mention this again."

She was closer to him now, the brush flying through her hair, crackling with static electricity. "You'd really like to have a Tokugawa wife, wouldn't you? You could do as you please, couldn't you, with no one to question you. But I've been around men of real power, so I can't be deceived—"

He sprang at her, managed to grab her left wrist even as the right hand swung the brush at his face. He pinioned the right wrist, shook the brush free while she yelled at him. He was beyond hearing, so caught up in his rage that he forced her back to the bed. He threw himself on top of her while she thrashed wildly, swearing at him in languages he did not speak, rolling her head from side to side, trying to bite the hands that pinioned her wrists to the bed.

She broke free momentarily, hit him on the shoulder, but he grabbed her again and the robe fell away from her. He held her with the weight of his shoulders while he freed himself from his trousers. Then he fell upon her, and as she writhed beneath him she planted him more firmly within her. He thrust at her as if to pound her into submission. But his anger converted her into a frenzy of passion.

She freed her hands and pressed her fingers into the small of his back as if to drive him deeper. And then, abruptly, he stopped moving while she cried in his ear, pounded on his back until he began again, slowly at first, then gradually increasing his speed until she was jarred each time he rammed against her. He raised his shoulders slightly, elevated her knees, and then thrust straight down into her until with a wild spasm her body moved of its own accord and she cried out, throwing her arms back on the bed.

Then he stood up and looked down at her. Her eyes were dazed, just beginning to focus. She reached out her golden-tipped fingers and stroked him erotically. *"Dozo,"* she said in a whisper. "Please."

He ran his hand along her silky thigh, eased her around until she lay sideways on the bed, open to him. And began again.

When she was in her bath he refilled his drink and sat at the window overlooking the city and knew he had to finish that which had brought him to Paris.

Yuki spent two hours making certain her hair was exactly right, and she tried on three dresses before she found one she thought would do, a modern version of a cheongsam in memory of the days in Shanghai. She was filled with anticipation as she watched his chauffeured limousine pull into the driveway of the Montmartre house. She met him at the door with hands outstretched and he caught her in a brief embrace.

"Yuki, my dear," he said, holding her hands. "Let me look at you." *And what do you see, dear Sam?*

"A lovely lady," he said as the chauffeur opened the door for them. The limousine pulled out onto the street. "You look splendid to me."

"I imagined what it would be like to be with you again. You've changed."

"Time will do that," he said with a smile.

"The smile's the same, still very dear, but you're not driven anymore. You look quite distinguished." She studied his face. "You have no idea how nervous I've been about seeing you."

"You too?" he said, laughing. "I feel the same way I felt when I took Dawn out for the afternoon in Shanghai. I wanted to impress her then just as I want to impress you now."

"I can't imagine your being nervous."

"Nevertheless, I am. I've waited so long for this moment. I almost came looking for you six years ago."

"Oh?"

"When I was boarding the last helicopter out of Saigon, I saw two women in the compound, just a glance, and I tried to get off but a sergeant held me down. I was convinced the two women were you and Dawn, then I chanced to see their faces and realized I was mistaken."

"That touches my heart, Sam," she said. "Sometimes I thought about writing Washington to find out where you were."

"Why didn't you?"

She interlaced her fingers in his, looked away. "I was afraid I might find out that you were no longer on this earth. My heart could not have stood that loss."

His hand tightened on hers. "Now you've touched me, my dear."

"Where did you go from Vietnam?"

"China. I was there until this spring. And then I saw your name in a newspaper, a story about you and Dawn coming to Paris, and I knew I had to be here. I had to see you again." The car turned down a lane near the river. "We're going to a very special restaurant, not on any of the tourist itineraries yet."

They pulled into a walled courtyard next to a Chinese restaurant built like a traditional teahouse, with green tiled roofs curled like bird wings, the massive red door opening into a room overlooking the river. A bowing waiter conducted them to a table separated from the main room by an intricately carved teak screen, and for a moment she felt that they had stepped back in time and that she was looking at the Whangpoo instead of the Seine. "How lovely," she said. "It reminds me of the day we had our picnic."

"A different life," he said. The waiter brought a bottle of Kao Liang wine. Sam lifted his glass to her. "Your success," he said. They drank.

"Why are you really in Paris?" she said.

"To throw a party for you."

"Seriously. You're not here on business?"

"No. I came to Paris to see you. So I'll ask you the important question, straight out. Are you married, engaged, tied up in a special relationship?"

"No," she said.

"Thank God." He glanced at the hovering waiter. "I took the liberty of ordering in advance."

The waiter brought in platters of white-cut pork, shreds of ham and chicken, and "happy family" stew. Yuki laughed with delight. "All Shanghai foods," she said. "How marvelous this would have been when I was seventeen and first in China, and how wonderful it is now." She began to sample the pork. "Did you marry again?"

"No."

"And you survived the grief for Charlotte?"

"The heart has a way of healing," he said.

"How could I have forgotten?" she said suddenly. "I meant to congratulate you on becoming Ambassador to Japan. That's marvelous."

"I hope you really think so."

"Truly. And I want you to approve of me, sitting here, everything I am, all I've done in this world."

"I do approve, believe me. With all my heart."

"How is your mother?"

"Dead," he said. "We struck a truce at the last, but never a peace."

"I forgave her a long time ago," Yuki said.

"I'm glad you could, but tell me about Dawn."

"She knows she's half American and she's proud of that. But she thinks her father died a long time ago."

"I will never tell her otherwise," he said. He looked at her with longing, reached out to touch her hand.

"I remember the touch of your fingers," she said. "That hasn't changed."

He refilled her wineglass. She drank. "Do you truly realize how different I am now from the girl you knew in Shanghai?" she asked.

"Yes, I think I do."

"I'm pleased that my lords have seen fit to send you back to me," she said. "I've always been pleased that you're Dawn's father, and perhaps one day it will be time for her to know it. But not yet. I would like to introduce you to her at the party as Ambassador Cummings, a friend of mine."

"Of course," he said. "I understand."

The next morning Yuki had her driver take her to the business office Segawa had opened on the Rue St. Honoré. He had rented a suite of offices, had the walls painted off-white, the House of Dawn logo on the wall in a dramatic splash of red, and he had hired a former model as a receptionist.

Segawa sent his receptionist on a break and seated Yuki in a wing chair before he slumped down on a leather divan. "The eye of the hurricane," he said. "It's usually a madhouse in here, but there are two big collections in the pavilions this afternoon. Not that anybody's anxious to write our line. The buyers stop in out of curiosity, wondering what's going to happen next."

"I want you to put Kanao and his wife on the invitation list," she said.

"Consider it done. Have you found a way out of the dilemma?"

"I don't know," she said. "But it's vital that the buyers believe I have."

"I'll do my best," he said.

As Yuki was on her way to the Opera House, she made the decision to protect her daughter until the show was over. She found Dawn and the Count in one of the dressing rooms studying a feather boa wrapped around the neckline of a mannequin dressed in a long silk gown with draping sleeves. Dawn looked up as Yuki approached and the Count nodded to her.

"We can use your opinion, madame," he said.

"You know this gown, Mother," Dawn said. "Do you think the feather boa enhances it or not?"

"I know your tastes," Yuki said. "You like things simple and elegant. So you would not like the boa. I also know that the Count usually knows what will sell from the runway. So I say have the mannequin wear the boa halfway down the runway and then remove it and carry it in her hand. The buyers will be able to see the possibilities both ways."

"Thank you, madame," the Count said with a smile.

One of the mannequins came up to Dawn, bowing slightly. "You had a telephone call," she said. "I told her you couldn't be disturbed but she was very upset."

"Who was it?"

"She said her name was Myoko. She was crying. She asked if you or Madame Nakamura could come to her place as soon as possible."

"Is she still on the line?"

"No, madame."

"Thank you," Dawn said.

"I'll go," Yuki said.

"Why bother, Mother?" Dawn asked. "He wouldn't help us."

"Oh, but he did for many years," Yuki said. "And so I will do what I can for him now."

In the back of the limousine, Yuki found herself suddenly fatigued. She had no heart for a confrontation with Itsugi and yet it would inevitably come to that.

She remembered the last days she had spent in Tokyo in his great rich space of a workroom where there was perfect light, where not a whisper of noise leaked through the insulated walls—an ideal studio except that the talent had fled from the man who occupied it. He had depended on Dawn for the designs that continued his reputation and upon Dawn's mother to manage his money. But on that day last year, with all of the designs set for the fall line and with the books in better shape than they had ever been, when Yuki told him that they were leaving him, he had refused even to look at her.

He had sat in front of his drawing board, brush in hand, without making a mark on the paper. "The whole world is against me," he said in Yuki's direction. He threw the brush in the wastebasket and began to roam the room as if in a prison. "I should never have taken you into my business. You have learned all my secrets and now you are not only abandoning me but are going into competition with me."

"It's a very big world," she said. "There's room in it for all of us."

"I'll ruin you," he had said, cigarette smoke boiling from his nostrils. "I'm not without influence in the fashion world."

She had not seen him since then. She had hoped he would mellow toward them, but his cooperation with Kanao was proof he had not. When the car pulled up in front of Itsugi's atelier on the Rue Montaigne, the rain was heavier. Myoko was waiting at the entrance to the narrow three-story building that housed his Paris salon and his small apartment on the top floor.

"I don't want you to think that I am disloyal, O-Nakamura-sama, but he has been raging through the workshop, terrifying the new girls, and the models are threatening to leave."

"Is he drunk?"

"*Hai,*" Myoko said hesitantly. "He is also calling out your name."

Yuki could hear the roaring of the old man from the fitting room. She pushed past Myoko and the covey of seamstresses and models who stood clustered in the doorways.

She went into the main fitting room. Dresses were all over the floor, as if caught in a whirlwind. Itsugi himself, barely able to stand, was trying to rip a pinned dress from a dress form, yelling incoherently. His ponytail was undone, his hair long and uncombed, his face gray and puffy, his eyes wild. He grabbed at a bottle, then stopped in the act of drinking and looked at Yuki.

"You," he said. "How dare you come here and spy on me?"

"I was called," Yuki said. "But I should have known better than to come. You were foolish when I worked for you and I see you haven't changed a bit. You're almost seventy years old. You know better than to get drunk. You have a showing tomorrow night."

"I should kill you," he said. "I should have killed you long ago." He held the bottle as if prepared to throw it at her, but his eyes rolled upward and he crumpled in a heap on the floor.

Yuki called Myoko to her. "Have him taken to his apartment and put to bed."

"*Hai,*" Myoko said. Four of the girls managed to raise Itsugi to his feet and half walk, half drag him down the hallway toward the stairs. Myoko began to weep quietly. "He will kill himself, O-Nakamura-sama," she said. "When tomorrow comes and he has nothing to show, he will be disgraced. And considering his state of mind, he will certainly commit seppuku."

"He may destroy others," Yuki said, "but he's much too vain to destroy himself." She turned her attention to the dress on the form. It was not impossible. "Get me your fitting model," she said.

When the girl came in Yuki had her put on the dress and then stood back from it. The blouse looked like a bubble, with another bubble around the hips. "He went too far, that's all," Yuki said to Myoko. She began to tuck in the extra material around the shoulders, to bring it into shape. She took another swatch of the same material to wrap around the neckline, leaving a line of cloth falling down the front. Then she went to work on the skirt section, again reducing the size of the billow around the hips, tapering the skirt toward the ankles.

"Do you see what I'm doing?" she said to Myoko. "Itsugi-san has always been known for tapered skirts, for scarves and headbands."

"I do not have the experience to do that," Myoko said in a soft and hesitant voice.

"Because he's never allowed you to have it. But you know the shape he's in. So either you take over now or you call the newspapers and cancel the showing."

"I could not face that disgrace," Myoko said.

"Then you don't have much time." Yuki picked up a teapot and found it cold.

"I'll send for more, Nakamura-san," Myoko said.

"No, don't bother."

Myoko stood shaking her head. "I hope you will forgive him. Sometimes he gets very angry, Nakamura-san. You know him, the way he is. But the *kami* have been testing him for the past year. Most of his money is gone. Even when he was talking about ruining you, he did not have the money to do it."

"How could that be? He was rich when I left."

"When you and your daughter left he decided to adopt his willow boy to carry on the House of Itsugi. But there was a big argument after the adoption had occurred and the willow boy stole hundreds of millions of yen and disappeared. O-Itsugi-sama was heartsick. And when I suggested that he go to the authorities, he swore at me. He was sure the ungrateful willow boy would come crawling back. And when I made the suggestion that we could find a way for expenses to be more modest, he swore at me again."

Yuki went upstairs. The girls had laid Itsugi on his bed. He was cognizant again but still so drunk that he was not sure where he was.

"Bring me a raw egg and tomato juice and strong tea," Yuki said. "And a little grated daikon radish. Until then, leave me alone with him."

She closed the door behind them, then opened the drapes and looked down at the street. "Ah, we've come a long way, you impossible old man," she said in a soft voice. "We had such high hopes, both of us." He lay there in his misery, eyes half open, mind half aware. "Of course we'll both survive. Myoko is very bright despite her timidity and she will salvage what you've done. You may or may not find your willow boy. If you're lucky, he'll be gone forever."

The girls came back with the tomato juice in a glass and she broke the egg into it and stirred it with a fork, whipped it to a froth before she added the grated bitterness of the daikon and stirred it gently.

"Now, prop him up," she said. She managed to coax at least half the mixture into him before he began to choke. She let him rest, then took a cup of the tea herself and sat beside the bed, aware that he was coming around, his eyes more knowing.

"Give me some tea," he said abruptly.

She poured a cup half full and handed it to him.

He eyed her with disdain. "I knew you'd come back to me," he said in English. "You couldn't make it on your own."

"Apparently not," she said.

"I want you to apologize to me," he said.

"I could apologize to you a thousand times and you would still demand another one," she said with a tolerant smile. "And I am truly sorry about your willow boy."

"He'll come back. Nobody was ever better to him than I was. He will realize his mistake." He took a firm grip on the side of the bed. "I have to get up," he said. "I have work to do." But as he started to raise his head the nausea and the pain hit him. His head sank back against the pillow. "I'm dizzy," he said. "I think I'm drunk."

"You're better," she said. "You managed to tear up some of your collection downstairs, but fortunately you have good people working for you who have a great affection for you and who will put things back together."

"I'll never forgive either of you for leaving," he said with a moan. "You had no right to leave."

"We stayed too long by years," she said. "You have a great talent and you should have been forced to use it."

"Give me more tea."

She filled his cup half full again. This time when he drank his hand was steadier. "If you had not come, I would have called you," he said. "Just to talk."

"In your own way, you did call me," she said.

"I was one of the pioneers in Paris," he said, staring at the ceiling. "I came here when they were still ridiculing all things Japanese. I was one of the first."

"You should be very proud of that," Yuki said.

He was quite a long time. "I'm dying," he said. "I won't last another year. So all my darling willow boys have deserted me in turn, because they're afraid of death. You're the only person I know who is not afraid of death."

"Because I've seen so much of it." She touched his face. "You have become a very foolish man," she said purposefully. "You are trapped by your own self-pity. You're determined to defeat yourself to show the world what great injustices you've suffered, yet you have a wealth of talent in your own house. Given a year, Myoko will become a fine designer. And she's always been devoted to you. You can't be so blind that you can't see that."

"She has the talent of a stone," he said. "And I won't lie here and be insulted. And don't think you have been forgiven. I almost ruined you."

And she looked directly into his eyes. "You and Kanao wanted to put me out of business but your little willow boy ruined your plans for you, didn't he?"

"Who told you that?"

"It doesn't matter. What matters is that my collection will be ready. But you better see to yours if you want to save anything."

He looked away.

She poured more tea for herself. "I've instructed Myoko to work on your collection. I think you were a bit too generous in the shoulders and around the hips and I pinned up one of the gowns. So when you have strength enough to go downstairs again, don't take that out on her. It was my doing."

He scowled at her. "If you think you can ingratiate yourself . . ."

She smiled. "I won't worry about you any longer," she said. "You're healthiest when you're at your most abusive. I have to leave. Shall I call one of your girls to help you?"

"I don't need any help," he said bitterly. "Yours especially. And whatever you've done in the fitting room, I'll have Myoko undo."

"Of course," she said. She stood up. "If you really work at it, Itsugi-san, you can make everything impossible. But I want you to know that despite what you've done, I wish you well. You will have to work very hard and very long to get that statement out of your mind." She leaned over and kissed his forehead. His large eyes, uncovered by sunglasses, blinked at her.

She moved back and gave him a formal bow, her palms flat against the front of her thighs, the ultimate respect. "Sayonara, O-Itsugi-sama," she said, "And much luck." Her debt was paid.

She worked at the Opera House until past midnight. They were less than twenty-four hours away from the opening and tempers were growing short. Sakura was threatening to quit for perhaps the tenth time since noon, and Yuki went to her dressing room to listen to her complain that the director was working her far too hard, but Yuki had seen too many models not to know that something else was bothering the divine Sakura.

Yuki sat down across from her. "What's *really* wrong?" she said.

"I would like any tickets issued to Armand to be canceled."

"And why's that?" Yuki said.

Sakura studied her face in the mirror. Her eyes were troubled. "I didn't mean to make life miserable for him," she said. "At first it was just a joke because he's so old and then I was very flattered because he gave me expensive gifts, but finally he carried it too far. He wanted to divorce his wife and marry me. Can you imagine?"

"Easily," Yuki said. "He's an old man who remembers what it was like to be young, and you are one of the most glamorous beauties in the world."

"He *cried* when he talked to me last night. I told him I didn't want to see him again and he actually *cried*."

There was no cruelty in her voice, only a shame that she had caused pain and was too young to know how to deal with the guilt. She sat in a black body stocking, legs crossed, long tapering fingers shaping an eyebrow. "Are you afraid he'll make a scene if he comes tomorrow night?" Yuki said.

"Yes, madame. I don't want that. It frightens me just thinking about it. So he must not be allowed to come."

"I'll take care of it," Yuki said. "You needn't worry about it anymore."

"And the director?"

"You know how to handle the director," Yuki said. "You will give him your attention because tomorrow night is very important to his career, and then you will take the best of his advice and combine it with your instincts. The audience will love you and he will too."

"Thank you, madame," Sakura said. "From now on, if I have difficulties, I will discuss them with you. You are the only person who understands."

Yuki slept little that night, awakening in the small hours of the morning unable to go back to sleep. She clicked on the light and called down to the kitchen to have the night cook send up a pot of tea. To her surprise, Segawa brought it to her, red-eyed from lack of sleep, a worried expression on his face.

"I was in the kitchen when you called down, Nakamura-san," he said. "I need to talk to you."

"Of course," she said. "Have some tea with me."

He sat down. "I have a dozen calls a day, sometimes more, asking if the House of Dawn line is going to be manufactured."

"And what do you tell these callers?"

"That of course it will."

"There is something for you to think about," Yuki said thoughtfully. "I am making a new and dangerous gamble. And I will be showing my daughter's talent to the world. Even if I lose, she will always have a place in this business." She paused a moment. "If you decide to quit now, I won't hold it against you. And later a great many people might think you very wise."

"This gamble of yours," he said. "What are the odds?"

"I have a chance of winning and I'm willing to risk everything for that. I may be defeated, but I won't quit."

"I'll stay, if that's all right," he said, admiration in his voice.

"I'm grateful, because I need you," she said. "And I ask you to keep this conversation between us. I don't want to distract Dawn from the showing."

When Segawa had gone she thought about Sam. He would see his daughter at the party tonight. What would come of it?

She put the cup of tea aside, folded the pillow, lay down again, and dozed fitfully for the rest of the night.

By Friday afternoon, with just six hours left before the show, Dawn was close to exhaustion and Yuki knew there was still much left to be done. She made a final check of the racks of garments backstage to see that each was numbered and each in proper order. She heard somebody crying and found Cecile, one of Dawn's better English models, collapsed in a chair, a wet cloth on her forehead and a worried *midinette* trying to get her to drink some tea.

"I'll throw it up," Cecile said miserably, and when she spotted

Yuki she started crying again. "I'm so sorry. It was just a minor fever this morning. I'll be all right in an hour or so. You'll see."

"You just rest," Yuki said, but she called for a doctor. Even before he arrived to discover that Cecile had a virus and would be unable to work, Yuki had let Dawn know what was happening and had already started on plans for another model to take her place.

At four o'clock Yuki left the Opera House and found a pay telephone on the street. She put in a call to Chyka at his hotel in Lyon. He answered with an impersonal "Yes?"

Her mouth was suddenly dry. "I want you to go ahead now," she said.

"All right."

"Call me at exactly eleven o'clock tonight. You have the number."

"Oui, madame." He severed the connection.

At five o'clock Segawa intercepted Yuki backstage. "I just got news that Itsugi-san's show was a success. Not a smash, but he's going to have moderate sales."

I hope you appreciate your Myoko, Itsugi-san, Yuki thought.

The English director came fuming up to Dawn. "The bloody revolving stage has just frozen," he said through clenched teeth. "Now you have a choice. You can strike either the country set or the Edo set, but there's no way we can work them side by side."

"We're paying for an electrical engineer," Dawn said. She stalked through the elaborate stage, found an aging Frenchman in a pit full of gears on the circumference of the revolving stage. *"Écoutez,"* she said to him. "You have two hours to fix this marvel on the finest stage in the world and get it working again."

"It may take days," the man said in that deadpan Gallic hopelessness that set her nerves on edge.

"If it takes days, you won't be around to see it," Dawn said, steel in her voice. "I will kill you myself, personally."

The stage was working perfectly by six o'clock.

Lyon . . .

CHYKA HAD SCOUTED the mill for two days, checking the times when the employees left, and now, on this rainy Friday evening, he watched the managers in their tailored suits and expensive raincoats dashing across the parking lot to their flashy cars. Once they were gone, he started his truck and lit a cigarette, making a last examination of a false bill of lading. Success would depend on how well he had come to understand Valouch, the dock foreman. Chyka had met him at a beer hall a couple of nights ago, bought him drinks, led him into complaints against the managers, who always had the best of things and left the underlings to work late in the evenings on starvation wages.

But a man's actions did not always follow his words. And when he handed Valouch the fake bill of lading and the fifty thousand francs, Valouch could always yell for security and have him arrested, or Valouch could squint at the forged paper, accept it as real, pocket the fifty thousand, and much later, when confronted, erupt with injured innocence.

Chyka checked his watch. Within six hours he could be putting the bolts of fabric on a jet in Geneva or he could be sitting in a damp, cold cell in a local prison. *This is the reason I am paid so well,* he told himself. *Because I am willing to take chances.*

He shifted the truck into gear and drove toward the factory loading dock.

The twenty-two hundred seats of the Opera House began to fill by seven-thirty and Yuki had to force her mind away from Lyon. The gamble had either been won or lost by now and either Chyka had been arrested or he was on his way to Geneva. But if he had lost, she could trust Chyka to keep his word to protect her until after the showing.

She gave instructions to the security guards that when Trish Devane showed her invitation, she would be asked to join Yuki for a moment while her escort was conducted to his seat. Trish arrived at seven thirty-five and she was openly curious as she entered the reception hall.

"Has the situation changed?" she asked.

"I won't know for a while," Yuki said.

"Good luck," Trish said, concerned. She hugged her briefly. "I'll see you at the party afterward."

Yuki was about to go backstage when a security guard approached her and handed her a business card. "This gentleman insists on seeing you a moment, madame."

The fear flashed through her that things had gone awry in Lyon and the police were already here. But the card read ARMAND MEYER and so great was her relief that she agreed to see him. He came into the reception room and she was startled by his appearance. He looked as if he had been deflated, his hairpiece abandoned, his vanity a thing of the past.

"I want you to know, madame, that I told my wife everything," he said unhappily. "I told her the truth, that I had compromised my honor, and I asked her forgiveness now that the affair is over."

"Did she grant it?"

"Yes," he said. "I want to believe that I am an honorable man who suffered a temporary aberration and stared death and old age in the face and for a moment, a painful, costly moment, believed I could be made young again." There were tears in his eyes. "I ask for your forgiveness once again, madame."

She shook her head slowly. "I may understand how you feel, but your vanity has been too costly to me."

She brushed past him and made her way backstage. Even in the distraction of the activity in the darkened wings, watching her daughter work with the models, the director prowling the stage making certain that everything was ready, the orchestra tuning up in the pit, she was aware that before the night was over she would be facing Kanao in a battle for survival.

By five minutes to eight the auditorium was packed to standing room only, and Yuki scouted the crowd, feeling the electricity of the moment. They were all here, the critics and the press, the buyers and the celebrities. She went back to help Dawn, who was studying the schedule one last time.

At eight o'clock the house lights dimmed, and the first exotic notes of the samisens were sounded—the plaintive music of a Japan that no longer existed. And Dawn, standing by the curtains where she could inspect each of her models as they went onto the stage, closed her eyes and murmured prayers that belonged to her mother.

Lord Jesus and Lord Buddha, I pray to both of you to grant us good fortune.

The lights rose slowly on a rural scene in Japan. There was a suggestion of rice paddies gleaming in the moonlight, and in the far distance snow on the symmetrical cone of the sacred mountain. Spotlights picked up the first of the models. They were wearing dresses based on the layered look of Yuki's childhood.

Sam Cummings sat enthralled by the pageantry that formed the backdrop to the show. It was as though the House of Dawn was rolling back the years for him. As the lights shifted the scene changed to the old Yoshiwara, the old pleasure houses of Tokyo, the exotic fronts of buildings, with girls dressed in traditional kimonos forming a tableau against which the models moved in their colorful modern summer dresses. Then the scene shifted to Shanghai, the backdrop of the buildings along the Bund silhouetted against the evening sky, and Sam felt a special pleasure. This would always be his city. When Sakura appeared his breath caught in his throat because the young model reminded him of the Yuki he had first met at the consulate.

His mind drifted to the Chinese restaurant, the look of her—the grace she had, the sparkle in her eyes. Was there a future for them?

he asked himself. Or was the magic he felt between them an illusion, like the beauty of the world she had created on the stage?

Trish was fascinated by the way the designs that Dawn had created so brilliantly were set against their origins: the Japan of the early thirties, Shanghai, Manchuria and its Russian influence, and, finally, modern Japan.

Yuki, my dear, you and Dawn have achieved the impossible. Within hours all of Paris will be at your feet. But she was aware, even in the midst of this triumph, of Yuki's desperation. *I heard the fear in your voice.*

She used her opera glasses to locate Kanao and his wife. He was leaning back in his chair, a strange expression on his face, and she had an uncanny feeling that he was a predator, patiently waiting for a prey that could not escape him.

Kanao knew his wife was excited by what she was seeing on the stage. She leaned forward slightly in her chair, eyes bright. But when Kanao looked at the stage he imagined a fire burning across it like a wall of flames.

He imagined the fire, but he knew the world on the stage stood intact. He would bring it down by other means.

His wife's fingers dug into his arm. Her excitement had carried over, become sexual. But tonight she would have to wait.

His one great virtue, according to his astrologer, was patience.

The last gown of the evening was the wedding dress, traditional Japanese yet eminently modern, the round hat and veil enhancing Sakura's features. Yuki heard the collective gasp from the audience as she watched Sakura make her way onto a stage that was dark except for the spotlight that followed her and the faint glow of Fujiyama in the background. Then the bedlam broke loose, the rush of flashbulbs, the showering of flowers onto the stage. Applause and shouts of "Bravo" filled the Opera House. Dawn went onto the stage, filled with the excitement of the moment, and the triumph.

But as Dawn came offstage she approached her mother with a worried expression on her face. "Is everything all right?" she asked.

"Of course," Yuki said. "You have achieved a triumph. Enjoy it."

Dawn hugged her and moved on while Yuki began immediately to organize the models for the reception room. The buyers would soon have a chance to examine the creations close up. They would not write the line tonight, but they would pick up the spec sheets and get slightly drunk on champagne before they went to the party.

Yuki stood to one side of the room, watching the excited crowds. Segawa materialized at her elbow. "This is the moment of truth, Nakamura-san," he said. "I've never seen a more excited group of buyers. They're setting up appointments for tomorrow to write the line." He was quiet a moment. "Can we fill the orders?"

"I don't know," she said. "But write the orders anyway."

"That's good enough for me." He started to move away. She put a hand on his arm. "I want a check from you tonight for three hundred ninety-three thousand dollars," she said.

"Made out to whom?"

"I'll fill in the name if I need it," she said.

I will prepare for victory even if I expect defeat, she thought. *I will not give up.*

When Yuki and her party entered the hotel ballroom, there was an immediate burst of applause. The orchestra, midway through a waltz, switched to a traditional Japanese melody, and Dawn was swallowed up by an adoring public.

Sam came up to Yuki, took her arm. "I've been waiting for you," he said. "You two have just brought off the triumph of the season. And now I need to talk to you in private."

She looked at his face and guessed that he had heard the rumors that had been floating around. She followed him into a hospitality suite off the ballroom and waited until he had closed the door behind them.

"Now," she said, "before you say anything, dear Sam, please listen to me. You must let me handle my own problems."

"If what I've heard is true . . ."

"You must trust me despite whatever you've heard."

He sat down across from her, took her hands in his. "I do trust you," he said. "I have power and I have an almost unlimited supply of money. And if you can use either, they're available."

"I thank you with all my heart," she said. "And there is one thing you can do for me."

"Name it."

"I'm expecting a call in twenty minutes. I would like to stay here to receive it."

"Fine, I'll see that you're not disturbed."

"Thank you, Sam."

He paused at the door. "Remember what I said."

"I will," she said.

He went into the ballroom and closed the door behind him.

When the telephone rang she steeled herself for bad news and sat down before she answered it. The connection was not a good one.

"This is Nakamura-san," she said.

"It was touch and go," Chyka said. "But it worked." His voice was drowned out by a roar and it took her a moment to realize that the sound was that of a jet aircraft taking off. "I'm in Geneva. The goods are on the way to Hong Kong."

She found it difficult to breathe.

"Are you there?" Chyka said.

"Yes," she said finally. "It's really true, then?"

"The plane to Hong Kong just took off. And there will be no trouble, madame."

She thanked him and then put the telephone back on the cradle, savoring the moment, catching her breath, and then she stood up and examined herself in an ornate mirror to make certain that no remnant of shock remained in her eyes.

She went out into the ballroom and found Segawa engaged in earnest conversation with a party of American buyers who insisted on drinking to her success before she could draw Segawa aside.

"Do you have the check?" she said softly.

He passed it to her with great care, as if it might shatter if he dropped it. "There's no name on it," he said.

"It will be all right."

She did not have to seek Kanao out. He was waiting for her near the door to the hospitality suite. *I am grateful, Ito-san, that I see nothing of you in your son. He resembles his mother.* "I wonder if I might speak to you briefly," she said.

"Yes, indeed," he said, filled with confidence. He stopped a waiter, exchanged his empty champagne glass for a full one. He preceded her into the suite. She closed the double doors behind them and then sat down on a velvet love seat.

He leaned on a bronze bust of Napoleon. "I'm delighted that you had such a success tonight," he said. "It will make your fall an even harder one. I think the *kami* have a sense of irony after all." He looked around the opulent room. "My father never had the opportunity to live a rich life and he was a baron, wealthy beyond measure. You kept him from it."

"You're wrong. Your father lived a truly rich and meaningful life. And he would never approve of what you tried to do to me," she said.

He sipped the champagne. "My mother would approve," he said. "And so this brings us to it. I want you to hold a press conference in the morning. You will announce that the House of Dawn is going into bankruptcy."

"Why should I consent to that?" she said.

"Because I want you to be publicly humiliated," he said. "I've waited a long time for this."

She watched him as he moved to a desk, picking up a cut-crystal inkwell, which sparkled in the light. *There is something of you in him after all, Ito-san, a confidence in himself. And I will give him one chance to spare himself the indignity that he is about to suffer. I will do it for your sake.* "I ask you to do nothing more against me," she said. "Your vengeance has already cost you a fortune and it will exact an even greater price if you let it."

"I have all the power, not you."

"Then you leave me no choice," she said. "How do you intend to pay the balance on the mill?"

"That's none of your concern," he said. "My buying it was enough to ruin you and make a profit over the long term. It's a sound business."

"Then I think it's time for you to show your first profit," she said. She took Segawa's check from her purse and uncapped a pen, writing his name on the appropriate line before she handed the check to him.

He looked at it blankly. "What's this?" he said.

"I had an agreement with the mill," she said. "When I received my fabrics I would make payment in full. You now have that payment."

"You're bluffing," he said. "There's no way you could have your fabrics."

"My agents picked up my shipment tonight. I made certain you wouldn't be available in case the mill tried to call you for your approval. Why else would you suddenly have an invitation to this collection?"

She had startled him. She could see the terrible doubt in his eyes.

"Don't take my word for it," she said. "See for yourself. Check it out. Call the mill."

He reached for the telephone, stopped himself. "It makes no difference," he said. "There's no way you could have done it legally. So now I will have the pleasure of sending you to prison as well as putting you out of business."

"I doubt that will happen," she said. "They were my goods after all, and you have been paid in full for them. And the same thing that worked against me before is now against you. By the time the case gets to court, you'll be out of money."

"Impossible."

"The mill should be enough to drag you under," she said. "You will pay six million dollars for a business that is worth nothing. You saw my triumph tonight, enough not only to make me rich but to give me a great influence in the fashion business. And what will the other fashion houses do when they hear that you deliberately held back an order in an attempt to ruin me?"

"You won't tell them," he said.

"Oh?" And quite suddenly she knew that Kanao had weapons that he had not yet shown. "And how will you stop me?"

"I have some papers my father left behind," Kanao said evenly. "All the documents concerning his life. Some of them have to do with you and your daughter."

"You have nothing that can hurt me."

He removed some papers from his jacket pocket. They were yellowed with age. "You might like to see this," he said. He handed her an official form in Japanese, and she realized it was her entry visa into Manchukuo. Across the front of it, stamped in a brilliant red that had faded little over the years, was the character for WHORE.

"You hope to ruin me with a document that says I was a whore in my youth?" she asked with a smile. "Do you know how much marvelous publicity that would generate for me, a woman with a scarlet past who is such a success?" She put the paper down on the love seat. "This won't hurt me, but consider what it will do to the spirit of your mother. She will never give you any peace. Your father's name is on that visa as my sponsor. If I was a whore, I was your father's whore. You will never live that down."

"I have something else that you can't explain away," he said. He thrust at her a copy of the cable Sam had sent to the State Department so many years ago claiming Dawn's paternity. "Do you want your ex-lover to start his ambassadorship this way? And shall I be the one to tell your daughter of her father?"

"I'm willing to run that risk if you are," she said.

"It's no risk for me."

"Isn't it?" she said. "You will be attacking the American Ambassador to Japan and that means you will be attacking the United States. How do you think the Japanese government is going to feel about that, or perhaps you have enough influence to escape their wrath."

"I will do anything to see you defeated," he said.

There was a light rapping on the door. It opened to reveal Sam standing there with the Japanese Ambassador, a smiling little man in black tie. "I'm sorry to interrupt," Sam said pleasantly. "But this party is in your honor and we're ready for the toasts."

"Have you met General Ito's son, Ambassador?" Yuki said. "Kanao Ito, Ambassador Samuel Cummings."

"Your father and I were great friends," Sam said to Kanao.

"You came at just the right moment," Yuki said. "Kanao was about to come out to speak to you and the Japanese Ambassador."

"What can I do for you?" Sam asked.

And in that moment she knew that the battle was over, for Kanao had become stiffly formal, retreating into himself. He could not attack, knowing that he would simply destroy himself. He bowed to Sam and to the Japanese Ambassador. "It is a pleasure to meet a friend of my father's," Kanao said stiffly. "I appreciate your inviting me here tonight."

"My pleasure."

"I have been enjoying a conversation with your wife," the Japanese Ambassador said, and now Kanao left the room with him while Yuki gathered up the yellowed papers and put them in her purse. Sam looked at her, waiting.

"Winning is a pleasure," she said, smiling with triumph.

"Then you must be absolutely ecstatic. The word has been passed out there that you've had no ordinary success tonight. You've succeeded far beyond your wildest dreams."

"I had two very good teachers," she said. "Two men with very different backgrounds but with the same fine qualities. One was a Japanese general and the other an American diplomat. And they both taught me the same lesson, for which I will ever be grateful, that it is no sin to lose if you have done your very best, but that the only chance of winning lies in a refusal to surrender."

"God rest Ito," Sam said.

"I'm sure God has." She led him back into the ballroom, where Dawn was having a glass of champagne. She took Dawn's hand and looked at Sam with warmth. "Do you remember where you have seen the Ambassador before?" she said.

"Have we met?" Dawn said, embarrassed, mystified.

"He took you out for an afternoon in Shanghai," Yuki said.

"The limousine with the flags," Dawn said, delighted. "One of the most wonderful afternoons of my whole life."

The Count was at Dawn's side. "I believe this is our dance," he said.

"Yes." But before she moved away she smiled at Sam. "Do you remember the ox and the ice cream and the fakir's snake that was too cold to move? We'll have to have a drink and talk."

"Yes, we will," he said. He looked at Yuki as Dawn swept across the floor with the Count. "Thank you," he said.

"You're welcome," she said. *I am ready to face the future now,* she thought. "Something occurs to me. In all the time we've known each other, we've never danced together."

"That's easily remedied," he said. He took her into his arms and swept her onto the floor, and she loved the way he held her, tender, strong. She looked at his face, the smile of youth she had loved so much, a smile that had never changed.

There will be time for dancing in Japan, she thought.

AUTHOR'S NOTE

THIS NOVEL WAS begun over four decades ago, in 1946, when
I was assigned by the United States Army to serve as assistant manager in the Meiji Hotel in Tokyo, where we housed athletic teams,
USO units, and officers who needed a discreet place for romantic
liaisons.

The country was still in the early stages of the Occupation. The
major cities were still burned out, the people destitute. Desperate
for work, most Japanese took any jobs they could get, and so the
Meiji Hotel had a fascinating staff including a former Japanese ambassador to a Southeast Asian country; a distinguished university
professor; an ex-kamikaze pilot who had defaulted at the last moment and was working through his shame; and a number of delightful Japanese women who ran the offices, worked as translators and
interpreters, and who provided me with stories of Shanghai in the
thirties, of life in Manchukuo, of the Russian invasion and repatria-
tion to Japan.

Even then I realized that one day I would write this book, and
toward that end I recorded the stories. I collected pictures and
articles and early Japanese war propaganda. I attended the War

Crimes Trials, examined the Emperor and his automobile at close range, regularly stood outside the Dai Ichi Building to watch General MacArthur leave for the day, a cigar clenched in his teeth instead of the famous pipe. I made notes of everything.

Over the years I have lost track of the people I knew during that magical time, and even in trips back to the Orient I have been unable to locate them, but I thank them now for their many kindnesses toward a young *gaijin* eager to understand them. I have interviewed many people in the course of writing this book, and although this novel is true to the spirit of the times, it is in no way a history.

Special thanks are due to Henry and Betty Liu of Kuala Lumpur for their firsthand descriptions of growing up in Shanghai in the thirties and to Mrs. Nancy Cheng, one of the directors of the Chinese Writers Association in Shanghai, and her current project in chronicling the modern history of that city. Mrs. Susan Mathes, born in Singapore, was kind enough to lend me the unpublished memoirs of her grandfather, Dr. C. T. Wang, the Chinese foreign minister under Sun Yat-sen.

Spelling of the place names in the Far East conform to the gazetteers and newspaper reports of the period, but in some instances, when the name of a place was changed by a new regime, a single spelling has been retained for the sake of simplicity. The romanization of Chinese and Japanese phrases has been standardized by using those that appear most consistently in current usage.

The fashion sections of the book come from many sources, all of whom are acknowledged here with gratitude: Denis Hilger of the Otis Art Institute and Parsons School of Design in Los Angeles for his accurate overview of the fashion world; Leslie Ross of Bob Mackie's Design Studio for her tour of that esteemed designer's atelier and interviews with all the disparate people involved in producing a line; to Harriet Weintraub of New York City for her discussion of Japanese fashion in a Los Angeles boutique during a showing by her celebrated client, Kenzo; to Marjorie Taylor, textile designer with Holland and Sherry in London, for sharing her expertise; to M. J. Deventer, one of the better reporters to cover the Paris fashion scene, for her insights and anecdotes; and to Leo "Buddy" Rodgers, whose experiences as a buyer in Paris for his landmark store, Balliets, were invaluable.

This book is a collaborative effort with my wife, Wanda, and we

ROBERT L. DUNCAN

have been aided by a fine agent, John Hawkins, of John Hawkins and Associates in New York, and by Mike Kozlowski of that organization; by our friend, Charles E. Spicer, who worked hard on the early stages of this book. We are also grateful to Jackie Farber, Editor in Chief of Delacorte, for her belief in the project, and finally, to Jeanne Bernkopf, who demonstrated her invaluable skills most ably in the editing of this book.